EVER
AFTER

LENORA WORTH

LOIS RICHER

JANET TRONSTAD

Published by Steeple Hill Books™

STEEPLE HILL BOOKS

Steeple
Hill®

ISBN 0-373-78522-4

EVER AFTER

Copyright © 2003 by Steeple Hill Books, Fribourg, Switzerland

The publisher acknowledges the copyright holders
of the individual works as follows:

THE WEDDING QUILT
Copyright © 1997 by Lenora H. Nazworth

A WILL AND A WEDDING
Copyright © 1997 by Lois Richer

A BRIDE FOR DRY CREEK
Copyright © 2001 by Janet Tronstad

Visit us at www.steeplehill.com

Printed in U.S.A.

CONTENTS

Books by Lenora Worth

Love Inspired

The Wedding Quilt #12
Logan's Child #26
I'll Be Home for Christmas #44
Wedding at Wildwood #53
His Brother's Wife #82
Ben's Bundle of Joy #99
The Reluctant Hero #108
One Golden Christmas #122

*When Love Came to Town #142
*Something Beautiful #169
*Lacey's Retreat #184
**The Carpenter's Wife #211
**Heart of Stone #227

*In the Garden
**Sunset Island

LENORA WORTH

grew up in a small Georgia town and decided in the fourth grade that she wanted to be a writer. But first she married her high school sweetheart, then moved to Atlanta, Georgia. Taking care of their baby daughter at home while her husband worked at night, Lenora discovered the world of romance novels and knew that's what she wanted to write. And so she began.

A few years later, the family settled in Shreveport, Louisiana, where Lenora continued to write while working as a marketing assistant. After the birth of her second child, a boy, she decided to pursue her dream full-time. In 1993 Lenora's hard work and determination finally paid off with that first sale.

"I never gave up, and I believe my faith in God helped get me through the rough times when I doubted myself," Lenora says. "Each time I start a new book, I say a prayer, asking God to give me the strength and direction to put the words to paper. That's why I'm so thrilled to be a part of Steeple Hill's Love Inspired line, where I can combine my faith in God with my love of romance. It's the best combination."

THE WEDDING QUILT
Lenora Worth

To my sister, Glenda, who died from a wreck involving a drunk driver in 1991. We all miss you still.

To Suzannah, a friend who believed in the good in me and taught me so much about courage and dignity.

And especially…to my niece Crystal Howell Smith. Hope this helps to ease your pain.

Chapter One

"To everything there is a season, a time for every purpose under heaven."

Rosemary Brinson read the familiar words of Ecclesiastes and took comfort in the sure knowledge that God was watching over her, and that a new season was on its way.

Today would be different. Today was a new beginning, Rosemary decided as she gazed out her kitchen window, toward the tall spire of the First United Methodist Church of Alba Mountain, Georgia.

Today the steeplejack was coming.

Everyone was talking about Kirk Lawrence, the man Rosemary had personally hired, sight unseen, to come to the little mountain town of Alba to restore the fifty-foot-tall steeple of the one-hundred-and-fifty-year-old church, as well as renovate the church building itself. The small-town gossip mill had cast Kirk Lawrence to heroic proportions. From what Rosemary had found while doing phone interviews and research on-line, the man could leap tall buildings with a single bound, provided he had a good pulley and a strong rope and cable, of course.

In spite of her pragmatic, levelheaded approach to hiring the steeplejack, Rosemary couldn't help feeling the same excitement as the townspeople. She'd last spoken to Kirk Lawrence two days ago, and she still remembered the way his lyrical accent had sent goose bumps up and down her spine.

"I'll be arriving sometime, probably late afternoon, on Monday, Ms. Brinson. I've studied the plans and the photographs you sent me, and I do believe I can have your church looking brand-new in a few weeks. I look forward to taking on the task.''

"Please, call me Rosemary," she'd stammered, in spite of trying to sound professional and all-business. "And you're sure you don't need a place to stay?"

"No, I have my trailer. I'll be comfortable there." A slight pause, then, "It's home, after all."

Home. A travel trailer with another trailer full of equipment attached to it. What kind of home was that?

"The kind a wandering soul likes to hang out in," she reminded herself now as she finished her toast and mayhaw jelly. "Apparently, our steeplejack likes to travel light."

She was still amazed that the church board had agreed to let her use such an unusual, yet highly traditional, means of doing the work on the steeple. The old-timers had balked at first, but once Rosemary had convinced them that a steeplejack would be much more thorough and less expensive than cranes and scaffolding, they'd reconsidered and voted to back her.

"We have you to thank, Rosemary," the Reverend Clancy had told her yesterday as she'd closed down the church day care attached to the educational building across from the main sanctuary. "We'da never raised all that money without you in charge of the committee. You sure know how to get things done."

"Only because I wanted this so much, Preacher," she'd replied. "This church means a lot to this town, and to me. We have to preserve it."

This morning, as she stood sipping the last of her coffee before heading off to her job as director of education for the church school, she had to wonder why she'd poured her heart into renovating the old Gothic-designed church.

Maybe it was because she'd been christened there as a baby, as had her older brother, Danny. Maybe it was because Danny had married his high-school sweetheart there, and Reverend Clancy had christened Danny's new daughter, Emily, within the peaceful confines of the spacious sanctuary, illuminated all around by beautiful stained-glass windows. They'd been members of the church all of their lives, after all.

Maybe it was because Rosemary had sat there, through her mother's funeral last year, and somehow, she'd survived a grief so brutal, so consuming, that she wanted the church that had held her in its arms to survive, too.

Or maybe she'd taken on the task of renovating the old church because she needed to stay busy at something tangible, something worth fighting for, something that would bring about hope and rebirth, instead of despair and death.

Pushing away thoughts of the past year's unhappiness, Rosemary turned around to find her father staring at her with the dull, vacant look she'd come to recognize and dread.

"Coffee, Dad?" she asked as she automatically headed for the cabinet by the sink to get a cup. "Your toast is on the stove. Would you like a scrambled egg with it?"

Clayton Brinson stood just inside the kitchen door, his blood-shot gray eyes wandering over the bright, sunny kitchen as if in search of something, someone. He wore old, worn khaki work pants, left over from his thirty years as a line supervisor at the local manufacturing company, and a once-white ribbed undershirt that stretched across the noticeable paunch hanging over his empty belt loops. His sparse salt-and-pepper hair stood out in stubborn tufts on his receding hairline, its determined stance as stoic and firm as the man who refused to comb it— the man who refused to accept that his wife was dead and gone, the man who refused to even get dressed most mornings, who blamed God and his daughter for the death of his beloved wife, Eunice.

"Toast and coffee, girl," he said in a gruff, early-morning voice. "How many times do I have to tell you, that's all I ever want for breakfast?"

Rosemary didn't reply. She was used to her father's cold nature and curt remarks. It was, after all, part of the punishment, part of the penance she must endure. That she must endure was an unspoken agreement between the shell of the man to whom she'd once been so close and the shell of the woman she'd become.

Clayton had always been a hard, distant man. Strong, hard-working, a good father and husband, he'd never fully understood her mother's devotion to the church. But because he loved

Eunice, because she made him smile and laugh, he'd indulged her by dutifully attending services and giving money to the church. The pretense had ended with her death, though. Clayton existed these days on bitterness and loneliness, but Rosemary refused to give in or give up on Clayton. God would lead him home. She knew this in her heart. This morning, she'd asked for patience to see her father through, and guidance for herself. And she remembered how things once were.

Once, not so very long ago, her father would have bounded into the kitchen with a cheerful smile plastered on his face, to demand his eggs and grits. Once, her mother would have been standing at this window, admiring the spire of her church down the street, thanking God for the new day.

Eunice would have turned to lift a dark eyebrow at her husband. "Hungry this morning, Clayton?"

"Yep, and in a hurry. Got things to do down at the mill. A man's work never ends."

"Nor does a woman's."

Once, Rosemary would have come up on this scene, and she would have smiled at the good-natured bantering between her parents, before she'd gone off to school, or later, after work. Even after she'd moved out of the house to attend college, and then later to live in her own garage apartment just down the street, she could always count on finding her mother in the kitchen with a fresh-baked pie and her father humming and nuzzling her mother's slender neck before he headed off to work.

Once, her father would have greeted her with a smile and a kiss, and a teasing, "Found a fellow yet?"

Once.

As she searched the refrigerator for the raspberry jam her father liked on his toast, she thought about the fellow she'd found and lost, and thought about the life she'd planned with that same fellow, and lost.

"Here's your toast, Dad," she said as she set the plate in front of him. "I'll see you at lunch."

"And don't be late today," he called without looking up. "Twelve noon, girl."

"I won't. I'll be here at five till."

She escaped the house, her breath coming deep and long to take in the fresh air of the coming spring. The nearby foothills were near bursting with it, their greens as fresh as mint, their white dogwood blossoms as delicate as fine lace. A new beginning. A new season.

This morning, this fine new spring morning, Rosemary Brinson looked to God to show her what her purpose was, and asked Him to help her find a new season. She needed a time to heal.

Then she looked up at the towering, ornamental spire of her church and reminded herself—today would be different.

Today, the steeplejack was coming.

In spite of herself, she couldn't wait to meet him.

Kirk Lawrence turned his rig off Highway 441 to follow the Welcome sign to Alba Mountain, Georgia, population ten thousand. He couldn't wait to get started on the renovations for the First United Methodist Church of Alba Mountain. As always, he felt the hum of a challenge, felt the rush of adrenaline a new job always brought, felt the nudge of a new town, with new faces, calling to him.

Alba had called him just as he was finishing work on a two-hundred-year-old church in Maryland. Alba, or Alba Mountain, depending on whom you were talking to, was a small town on the southern edge of the Blue Ridge Mountains, just about seventy-five miles north of Atlanta. Alba, homesite to some of his own Scotch-Irish ancestors, the highlanders of north Georgia, who'd come from Europe centuries ago to find a new beginning on these rugged foothills and mountains. This would be interesting, to say the least.

Kirk loved to wander around almost as much as he loved his work. The work he could trace back to his great-grandfather, Ian Dempsey, on his mother's side, in his native Ireland. The wanderlust…well, he supposed he'd gotten that from some nomadic ancestor, or from his American father who'd come to Ireland for a vacation more than twenty-five years ago, and stayed to marry a local lass. Or maybe the need to keep moving was all Kirk's alone, since he'd grown up in a small village in county Cork. It really didn't matter. He liked his life and he liked his work, and all was right with his world.

A voice echoed in his head as he searched the street names for Crape Myrtle Avenue.

"And you're sure you don't need a place to stay?"

Rosemary Brinson. Rosemary. Pretty name. It meant unspoiled in Latin, but it could mean several different things in modern society. This particular Rosemary had a slow, soft southern accent that flowed through the telephone like a warm summer rain. Kirk was anxious to put a face to that voice, anxious to meet the woman who'd fought a whole congregation to get him here, because she believed in doing things the right way.

"Well, Rosemary, me darlin', so do I."

That much they had in common. And that would be all, as far as Kirk was concerned. No, Rosemary, he didn't need a place to stay, because no one ever really expected him *to stay*. Kirk had just enough single-minded intent to know that he'd come here with one purpose, and one purpose only. He was a steeplejack. He repaired steeples, working quickly, accurately and artistically, to make something lasting and beautiful out of wood and mortar and stained glass and stone.

God had given him the talent, and his grandfather had given him the technique, or so his mother still reminded him. He didn't take either for granted.

And he had one very important rule. Never get involved with the townspeople, or their problems or their plans. He wasn't a healer, after all. Just a fixer. He simply liked to restore things to their proper beauty.

To Kirk, that made all the difference.

But then, Kirk had never heard a voice quite like Rosemary Brinson's.

And, he'd never ventured this far south before.

In spite of himself, he couldn't wait to meet her.

Rosemary's voice grew lower with each beat of the favorite children's story she read to the preschoolers. All around the darkened room, small bodies stretched out on colorful mats, their little stockinged feet resting after a morning of running at full throttle on nursery rhymes and building blocks. As Rosemary finished the story, a collective sigh seemed to waft out over the long, cool, colorful nursery.

"I think you've sent them off to dreamland," her aide, Melissa Roberts, whispered softly as she sat down to take over so Rosemary could take a much-needed lunch hour.

Rosemary's own sigh followed that of the steadily breathing children. "Whew, I'm tired! They were in rare form this morning. Must be spring, giving them so much energy."

"Or maybe they've picked up on all the talk," Melissa said, her eyes wide and sincere. "You know...about the steeplejack."

"Could be," Rosemary said, rising quietly to tiptoe to the door. "I've tried to explain exactly what a steeplejack is, but they can't seem to grasp it."

"Just tell them he's a superhero who climbs church steeples," Melissa suggested, laughing as she waved Rosemary out the door. "Go on home and try to rest."

Rosemary wished she could rest, but home wasn't the place for that precious commodity. Bracing herself for her father's cold reception, she started out the door of the educational building, only to be waylaid by the church secretary, Faye Lewis.

"He's here," Faye, a petite, gray-haired woman with big brown eyes, hissed as she hurried toward Rosemary as fast as her sneakers could carry her. "You've got to come and see to him, Rosemary. Reverend Clancy's already gone home for his nap."

"See to who?" Rosemary asked, then her heart stopped. "The steeplejack? Is he here already?"

"Oh, yes," Faye said, her smile slicing through her wrinkled face. "And quite a handsome...devil...excuse the expression."

Rosemary groaned, then looked down the street toward the rambling white house she shared with her father. "Why'd he have to show up just at lunchtime? Dad will be furious if I'm late."

Faye gave Rosemary an exasperated look. "Well, just tell Clayton that you had something important to tend to. Surely the man can fix himself a sandwich this once."

"Yes, but you know he expects me to be there right at noon," Rosemary replied, already headed toward the main office, which, along with the educational building, was set apart from the original old church.

"Do you want me to call your father and explain?" Faye asked, a look of understanding moving across her features.

"Would you?" Rosemary hated having someone run interference with her father, but Faye was one of the few people Clayton respected and treated with a fair amount of decency. "Tell him I'll be a few minutes late, but I'll be there as soon as I can."

Faye nodded, then shoved Rosemary into the plush office reception room where a tall, blue-jeans-clad man stood looking out the wide arched window that faced the church.

Taking a quiet, calming breath, Rosemary said, "Mr. Lawrence?"

Kirk Lawrence turned around to find the source of that soft whispery voice and was at once hit with a current so strong, he wondered if there was a kinetic energy moving through the room. He didn't need to know her name to know this was Rosemary Brinson.

Long swirls of chestnut-hued hair, curly to the point of being unruly, caught up with twin pearl-encrusted clips in a sensible yet attractive style, off a face that was oval in shape. Her face was youthful, yet aged, touched by the sun, yet fresh and newblooming, with eyes that darkened to a deep blue underneath arched eyebrows the exact color of her hair. Her smile was demure, while her expression was...hopeful and hesitant all at the same time.

She was lovely.

"You must be Rosemary," he managed to say as he held out a hand to take the one she offered him.

She wore a bright pink cotton top with a long, flowing floral skirt that swirled around her legs as she stepped forward. A cloud of perfume as delicate as the scent of honeysuckle preceded her touch on his hand.

"That's me," she managed to say through a shy smile. "It's good to finally meet you, Mr. Lawrence."

Rosemary gave him a direct look, all the while thinking that Faye had been right. He was handsome, all right. Dark swirling hair, as close to black as she'd ever seen. When he smiled, his thick eyebrows jutted up like wings, giving him that certain appeal Faye had mentioned. But his eyes, they held Rosemary, causing her to stare at him. Their bright, clear color sharply contrasted with his tanned skin. She couldn't decide if they were green or blue, but whatever color they might be called, his eyes were deep and luminous and…knowing. He had the eyes of an old soul, as her mother used to say.

Realizing that she was staring, Rosemary let go of the warm hand holding hers. "Did you have any trouble finding us?"

"No, none at all," he said, wrapping his arms across his chest in a defensive manner. "I just followed the steeple."

That brought her attention back to the task he'd come here for. "Yes, it's hard to miss, isn't it?"

Together, they both looked out the window, up at the stark brown and gray stone of the rising bell tower that heralded the church from miles around.

"It's beautiful," Kirk said, meaning it. "I can see where you'd want to preserve it—those stones need a bit of cleaning and scrubbing, now, don't they?"

"Yes," she said, glad he understood the job ahead. "They came all the way from Dahlonega—granite with a little fool's gold mixed in."

"A sound combination, no doubt." He grinned over at her. "I've never been to Dahlonega. Hope to see it while I'm here, and I want to climb Alba Mountain, too. I hear Georgia is a lovely state."

She looked away from that intense set of eyes. "Not as pretty as Ireland, though, I'll bet."

"Ireland is a land all its own," he admitted, "but I haven't been there in a long, long time. My parents moved back to the States when I was in high school, and I came with them, thinking to get my college education in America. But I was a bit rebellious, I'm afraid." He looked sheepish, at least. "I went back to Europe, and I wound up in Sheffield, England, at Whirlow College. I got my degree there, mainly because they offered the courses I needed to be a steeplejack. I worked with my grandfather until his death, then I came back to America. I haven't been back to Ireland or England since."

She wanted to ask why, but manners kept her from doing so. "You've traveled all over the place, from what I saw on your résumé."

"I've seen the world." He turned away from the window. "And now, I've come to see Alba. If you'd just show me where to park my trailer—"

"I'm sorry," she said, snapping to attention. "The preacher is at lunch and I was just on my way home for a quick bite. Are you hungry?"

"Are you offering?"

Liking the way he lifted those dark eyebrows with each statement or question, she nodded. "I think I can manage a sandwich, at least. Of course, I need to warn you to save room for supper tonight."

"Oh, are you inviting me then?"

Mmm, that accent was so pleasing to her ears. "Yes, but we won't be alone. The entire town's turning out for a supper on the grounds, to honor you and to officially begin the renovations on the church, sort of a celebration."

He followed her out the door, then up the sidewalk. "I've heard about southern hospitality. Now I suppose I get to see it firsthand."

"You won't forget it. You'll go to bed with a full stomach, that's for sure."

Noticing his trailer and attached rig, she pointed to a clump of trees at the back of the church grounds. "You can park there. There are a couple of camper hookups we use for visitors— campers coming through to hike the mountain trails."

"How generous."

"Reverend Clancy figures if we treat them right, they'll stay for one of his sermons."

"Ah, tricky, but effective."

"Yes." She nodded. "Sometimes they stay, sometimes they leave. But they're always welcome."

Kirk eyed the little copse of trees settled at the foot of a rounded upward-sloping hillside. Tall swaying pines and fat, mushrooming oaks made a canopy over the area. It was an inviting spot, complete with a rustic picnic table and just-budding daylilies. It would do nicely for his stay here.

Rosemary watched his expression as he took in his surroundings. Then she touched his arm. "That's my house, over there. C'mon, I'll fix you that sandwich I promised."

Kirk looked up at the whitewashed wooden house standing down the street from the church. He studied the house as they approached. It had that certain charm he associated with the South—long wraparound porches, a swing hanging from rusty chains, two cane-back rocking chairs, lush ferns sprouting from aged clay pots, geraniums in twin white planters—and shuttered, closed windows.

"It's a beautiful place, Rosemary."

"Yes, it is," she had to agree. "Or at least, it once was."

She saw him eyeing the shuttered, dark windows, and she knew exactly what he was thinking.

Why would such a lovely, sunny, open home be closed up and so sad-looking?

She wasn't ready to tell him why.

She didn't have to. As they stepped up onto the porch, the front door burst open, and her father's angry voice told Kirk Lawrence everything he needed to know.

"Where have you been? It's almost twelve-thirty. A man could starve to death waiting on you, Rosemary. How many times have I told you—I like to eat my lunch at twelve o'clock! Your mother always had it ready right at twelve noon. Now get in here and get me some food."

Shocked at the harsh tone the man had used, Kirk stood with one foot on a step and one on the stone walkway. Maybe now wasn't the time to get to know his new employer.

Humiliated, Rosemary turned to Kirk. "I'm sorry."

"You go on. I can wait," he said, not wanting to intrude. "I'm really not that hungry."

"No, no," she said on a firm but quiet voice. "I promised you a sandwich, and I intend to deliver on that promise. Just let me take care of my father first."

Kirk stepped up onto the porch, his gaze on the woman moving hurriedly before him. He had the feeling that Rosemary Brinson always delivered on her promises, whether she wanted to or not.

Why else would she go into that house and face her father's wrath with such profound determination?

Chapter Two

Kirk watched as Rosemary made ham sandwiches with the efficiency of someone who took care of things with automatic precision. She went about her job with quiet dignity, slicing tomatoes to fall into a pretty pattern on an oval platter, then adding lettuce and pickles to finish off her creation. Then she lifted fat, white slices of bread out of a nearby bin and arranged them on another plate, along with the pink country-cured ham she'd already neatly sliced.

"It's ready," she announced to her father who sat across from Kirk nursing a tall glass of iced tea. "Do you want anything else with your sandwich—chips or some sliced cucumbers maybe?"

The man she had introduced as Clayton Brinson didn't immediately answer his waiting daughter. Instead, he frowned while he pieced together a sandwich on his plate. Then he looked up with harsh, deep-set eyes. "Your mother never slapped a sandwich together. She always had fresh *cooked* vegetables on the table."

"Mother didn't work outside the home either, Daddy," she reminded him patiently. "I do what I can, but you're right. Tonight at supper, I'll make sure you have your vegetables."

Clayton's look softened to a slight scowl. "Well, some dessert would be nice, too. A peach pie, maybe."

Rosemary sat down with an abrupt swirl of her skirt, then handed Kirk the fixings for his own sandwich. "I'm sorry, Daddy, but I haven't had time to do anything with those canned peaches Joe Mason brought us yesterday. I'll try to get to it later this evening.''

"They'll rot before you get to 'em," Clayton proclaimed before clamping his teeth down on his sandwich.

Rosemary looked down at her plate, then in a surprising move, clasped her hands together and said a quick blessing.

Kirk saw the look of disgust on her father's stern face, and said his own silent prayer. He didn't want to slap this man he'd just met, but it was very tempting.

But Rosemary didn't seem to need his help in defending herself. She fixed her own meal, then looked over at her father with compassionate, if not somewhat impatient, eyes. "I'll make you a pie, Daddy. I promise. You know I wouldn't let those peaches go to waste. I love peaches." Turning to Kirk, she gave him a quick smile. "Georgia peaches, just like Georgia tomatoes, are the best in the world, Kirk."

"Then I'll look forward to that pie myself," he replied, glad that she'd smoothed over the awkward rudeness her father didn't try to hide. Kirk chewed a big hunk of sandwich, then nodded. "The tomatoes are very good."

Out of the blue, Clayton spoke directly to Kirk for the first time. "Seems a waste to me—bringing you in special to fix that old steeple. Let the thing crumble, is what I say. A waste of time and money."

Rosemary shot Kirk an apologetic look. "Actually, Dad was on the board that voted to renovate the church, but that was a couple of years ago. Now…Dad doesn't support any of our church activities, especially the ones I'm involved in."

Clayton threw his sandwich down. "And we both know why, don't we, girl?"

Rosemary's hiss of breath was the only indication that her father's sharp words had gotten to her. She remained perfectly calm, keeping her attention on her plate as she toyed with a slice of tomato to hide the apparent shame her father seemed determined to heap upon her.

Wanting to shield her from any further tirades, Kirk looked across at her father. "Mr. Brinson, your church is one of the finest historic buildings I've seen, and I've seen a lot of churches and cathedrals both here in America and all across

Europe. The people who built your sanctuary did it the right way, it's as solid now as it was the day it was finished. You don't see that kind of craftsmanship much anymore. I've studied the layout from the pictures your daughter sent me, and I'm amazed…each joint and bent is intricately crafted with mortise and tenon joined together without the benefit of nails.'' He paused, then looked thoughtful. ''It's almost as if the church was built on spirit and determination alone. And I intend to make sure that spirit is sound and intact.''

Clayton glared across at the stranger sitting at his table, then huffed a snort. ''Foolishness, pure foolishness, to waste over forty thousand dollars on a face-lift for the church. If it was built to last, then leave it alone!''

''Daddy!'' Embarrassed, Rosemary touched her father on the arm in warning. ''Can we talk about something else?''

''I'm through talking,'' Clayton replied, then standing, he yanked up his plate and drink. ''I'm going to watch television.'' With that, he stomped out of the room, leaving an awkward silence in his wake.

Kirk realized two things, sitting there at that round little oak table in Rosemary's clean kitchen. One, he was more determined than ever to get his job done and done right, just to prove her father wrong. He was like that; he'd always risen to a challenge, and winning this man over would be a big one. And two, he did not like this man's hateful, hostile attitude toward his lovely, angel-faced daughter. In fact, with just a little encouragement, he would gladly be willing to do something about changing it.

Right now, however, the only thing he could do was try to make Rosemary's beautiful smile return to her pale, drawn face. ''Was it something I said?''

She did smile, but it was a self-deprecating tug instead of a real smile, and he didn't miss the raw pain hidden beneath the effort.

''No, it was something *I did*.'' Sending him a pleading look, she added, ''He wasn't always this bad. It's just…we lost my mother over a year ago, and he's still not over her death. I do apologize for the way he's treated you.''

''I'm sorry…about your mother, and I understand,'' he said,

but really, he didn't understand. Losing a loved one was always painful as he well remembered when he'd lost his grandfather a few years ago, but this anguish seemed to run much deeper than normal grief. Most families turned to each other in times of grief and loss. Rosemary's father obviously hadn't come to terms with losing his wife, but why was he taking it out on his daughter? Kirk had to wonder what had happened between these two to make one so sad and noble, and the other so bitter and harsh.

But, Kirk reminded himself too late, *you can't get involved in whatever is brewing between them. Just do your work, man, then leave.*

When he looked up, Rosemary was watching him with those beautiful blue eyes, her gaze searching for both retribution and condemnation. He gave her neither—her father was doing enough of that. Because Kirk didn't know what was going on, he smiled at her in an effort to comfort her. And somehow he knew, this time it was going to be different. This time, he just might have to get involved.

"Why didn't you simply explain things to him?" Melissa asked Rosemary later after she'd told her friend about the whole episode with her father.

They were sitting on a wooden bench out on the playground, watching the children as they scooted and swayed over the various climbing gyms and swings. Nearby, a tulip tree heralded spring with its bright orange and green flowers. The afternoon lifted out before them with a crisp, welcoming breeze that belied the turmoil boiling in Rosemary's heart.

"I can't get him involved in all that," Rosemary said, shaking her head. "He came here to work on the church, not its floundering members."

"Except your father hasn't set foot in this place in over a year," Melissa reminded her in a sympathetic voice. "How can you stand it, Rosemary?"

"Living with him, you mean?" Rosemary sat back on the hand-carved bench, then sighed long and hard. "I still love him. And I know he's still grieving. I keep thinking one day I'll

wake up and he'll be the father I always knew and loved...
before all of this happened. One day..."

Her voice trailed off as she looked up at the towering steeple
a few yards away. Amazed, she grabbed Melissa's arm, then
held her breath. "Look!"

A lone figure moved up the steep side of the church's wide
sloping shingled roofline, loping toward the center of the building.

"The steeplejack," Melissa said on her own breathless whisper. "He sure didn't waste any time."

"No, he didn't," Rosemary replied, her eyes taking in the
lean lines of Kirk Lawrence's broad shoulders and athletic
body. Not an ounce of fat anywhere on the man. And no wonder. He hopped and jumped over the roof like the superhero
Melissa had called him, his long, muscular arms swinging from
the rafters, so to speak, as he took his first close-up look at the
thing he'd come to wrestle with.

The steeple was a mixture of several different levels and
several different foundations. Set at the front of the broad, rectangular, Gothic church building, it started out with an open
square belfry, made from the stone they'd discussed earlier,
intertwined with sturdy, arched timber-framed beams that shot
up to form a tier, like the bottom layer of a wedding cake, over
which sat a smaller section with louvered openings surrounded
by stained-glass partitions and a smaller version of the same
arched wood pattern. That section lifted toward and supported
a spire made of thick iron beams that formed the tall shingle-
covered cone. This tier was followed by an ornamental rusty
iron cross that extended three feet across and four feet up.

The long front of the church was made of the same stone
facing as the belfry tower, mixed with the timber framing that
the original congregation had made with heavy columns and
beams, the arched pattern of the wood crisscrossing throughout
the stones, following the same pattern of the tower's beams.
The church was intact and sturdy; now it mostly needed scraping, painting, restaining and rustproofing. Which was why
Rosemary had hired the steeplejack. He'd do most of it from
his boatswain chair, inches at a time if necessary.

Kirk hauled himself up over one of the stone belfry walls,

clinging precariously for a moment before lifting over into the open belfry room where an aged brass bell hung from a sturdy iron frame. From his vantage point, he looked out over the town, then down at the playground where Rosemary and Melissa, and now the children, watched him in fascinated wonder.

"Hello there," he called good-naturedly, waving toward them, then holding out both arms as if to say he'd just claimed this spot as his very own. "What a view!"

Rosemary didn't doubt that the view of the surrounding hills and mountains was impressive. She'd never been up in the belfry, but her brother, Danny, had climbed up there many times, and he'd told her he could see the whole town—indeed, the whole county—from there.

"It's Spiderman," a little boy called, jumping up and down in glee. "Miss Ruzmary, Miss Ruzmary, see Spiderman!"

"I see," Rosemary said, smiling up at Kirk before returning his wave. Why hadn't he simply taken the narrow stone steps just inside the church narthex that led to the bell tower? "That makes me dizzy," she whispered to Melissa. "I've never been one for heights."

"I wouldn't mind getting up there with him," Melissa said, laughing.

"Melissa Roberts, you have a new boyfriend."

"Yes, but we're just good friends—really. And, your steeplejack is sure easy on the eyes. Not at all what we expected."

Rosemary had to agree with her. Kirk Lawrence was intriguing, good-looking and likable. And discreet. They'd talked at length for most of the afternoon, about his purpose here, about their mutual faith in God, about what the congregation expected from him, and he hadn't questioned her once about why her father had treated her in such an ugly way during lunch. For that alone, she appreciated him.

She'd expected a middle-aged, leathery, bowlegged monkey of a man to come and do this job. Instead, she'd gotten Tarzan himself, a man who was at once dangerous because of the profession he'd chosen, and noble for the very reasons he'd chosen this time-honored way of doing things. Knowing he didn't take shortcuts and that he was willing to risk everything for a dying art made her respect him even more.

"He's not *my* steeplejack," she said rather too defensively. "He'll be gone before we know it and all the excitement will die down."

"Then we'd better make the most of his visit," Melissa said, rising to check on a whining toddler.

Rosemary grinned at her blond-haired friend, then looked back up to where Kirk stood surveying the tower and steeple. He was stretched over the short belfry wall, perched with one arm wrapped around a fat stone-and-wood column as he viewed the perilous height of the spire above him. Rosemary wrapped her arms around her chest, fighting the goose bumps that had risen on her skin.

He turned to stare down at her for a long moment, then quickly got back to work, measuring and calculating.

As she just as quickly got back to her own work of watching the children she loved. Only she couldn't help but do some measuring and calculating of her own, from the corner of her eye—but her assessments had little to do with the wood and stone of the old steeple.

A few hours later, Rosemary walked into the living room of her home to find her father sitting in his usual spot in front of the television. Dan Rather was delivering an update of world events, and Clayton Brinson had the volume at full blast, as if he couldn't afford to miss a word of what the broadcaster was saying.

"I'm going to the church dinner now, Dad," she said as loudly as she could. "I left your supper on the stove—plenty of fresh-cooked vegetables to go with your fried ham. And—" she purposely came to stand in front of him now "—I made two peach pies. I'm taking one with me, and I left the other one for you. There's coffee on the stove."

Clayton's only response was a deep-throated grunt. He still wore his khakis and undershirt. He'd barely left this room all day.

Rosemary leaned down to place a small kiss on her father's forehead. "I'll be home early."

Clayton didn't move a muscle. He just sat with his gaze fixed on the talking head on the television screen. His daughter walked out of the room and gathered her trays from the kitchen, then left.

Not until he'd heard the back door slam did Clayton turn, and then it was only to lower his head and close his eyes tightly shut. When he raised his head seconds later, his eyes were calm and cold again. He sat silent for a minute, then lifted a hand to touch the spot where his daughter had kissed him so tenderly.

"So you couldn't get the old rascal to come on over?" Faye Lewis asked Rosemary much later.

"No, of course not." Rosemary shook out the white cotton tablecloth to cover one of the many portable tables they'd brought out underneath the oaks and pines for a good, old-fashioned dinner on the grounds. "He can hear us from his vantage point—that is, if he turns down that television long enough to listen."

"I'll bet he'll listen," Faye said as she grasped the other end of the cloth to smooth it out. "He's been listening all along, he just can't hear in the same way."

"He's lost all hope, Faye," Rosemary said, her eyes scanning the growing crowd of church members and townspeople who'd turned out to meet the mysterious steeplejack. "And I'm about at the end of my rope."

"Steadfast, Rosemary," Faye reminded her. "Remember, 'for as much as ye know that your labor is not in vain in the Lord.' You're doing the right thing, the only thing you can for your daddy. You're standing firm in your faith. Clayton will see that in time, and he'll come around."

Rosemary appreciated Faye's gentle reminder. "I certainly hope so."

Faye patted the cloth into place then began placing covered casserole dishes full of hot food on top of it. "Your father is a proud, stubborn man. He can't deal with his grief, but I must say I'm shocked that he'd fight against it this long, and in such an extreme way. Clayton and I were always so close—Eunice was my best friend, after all. I miss her, but my grief is different from your father's."

Rosemary glanced toward her house, then quickly began pulling disposable plates out of a large plastic bag. "No, you didn't turn away from God—or me—when it happened. Poor Dad, he used to be here every time the doors were open. He did it only to please Mother, though. He and Mom, with Danny and me trailing along.''

A commotion toward the edge of the crowd caused her to put away painful thoughts of her now-shattered family. She looked up to see Kirk emerging from his little trailer. He wore a clean white button-down shirt, fresh jeans and brown suede laced boots. His dark hair looked damp from a shower. His smile was fresh and enticing. He was working the crowd.

She lifted an eyebrow when the older woman poked her in the ribs and whispered, "Cute, ain't he?"

"Yes. And charming. I've always heard Irishmen are very charming, and probably dangerous."

"Well, the insurance adjuster would agree with you there. I hear the hazards of his work make him expensive to underwrite. The steeplejack's occupation alone makes him dangerous, as far as having to pay out if he falls off that thing."

"He won't fall," Rosemary said, knowing it to be true.

Kirk Lawrence seemed as sure of himself as anyone she'd ever met. He had the grace of an acrobat, and the concentration of a neurosurgeon. She'd watched him working this afternoon, taking measurements, touching the ancient stones and splintered wood, almost cooing to the towering steeple in his efforts to get a handle on his task.

"He might not fall," Faye cautioned, "but I sure hope he doesn't fail. We've got a lot of donations invested in this renovation."

Rosemary playfully slapped her friend on the arm. "Ye of little faith! Just look at the man. He's shaking hands and kissing babies like a politician. Why, he's even got old Mrs. Fitzpatrick's undivided attention."

Faye squinted toward the spot where Kirk had stopped to bend over an aged woman sitting in a wheelchair, her tiny body covered from the waist down in an even more aged quilt. "Sure does. Let's go see what he's saying to her."

"More, what's she saying to him." Unable to stop her curiosity, Rosemary followed Faye across the grounds to where Kirk had stopped in front of the old woman. She watched as white-haired Mrs. Fitzpatrick lifted a bony, wrinkled hand to clasp Kirk's lean, tanned fingers.

"I knowed you was coming when I woke this morning," she said, her wise eyes appraising him with sharp precision. "It was such a strong morning, all bright and crisp. The Lord saves special days like this one for special happenings. I knowed something was a'brewin', but I jist thought it wuz something in the air."

"I got here a little early," he explained.

She wheezed a crusty chuckle. "Yep, and so did spring."

Kirk grinned at that, then waited patiently for her to continue talking.

"I'm the oldest member of the church," the woman told him in a whispery, leathery voice as she held up her tiny bun-crowned head with pride. "Eighty-nine. Emma Fitzpatrick's my name, but they call me Aunt Fitz. You can call me that if you'd like."

"I'd like, indeed," Kirk replied, a twinkle in his eyes. "And I just might need your expert advice on how to go about working on this magnificent church and steeple. I'm sure you have lots of fond memories of this church."

The old woman lifted her chin. "Was christened here, got hitched here, bore seven children, all christened and raised in the Lord's good name here, buried my husband and now two of those children in the cemetery up yonder on that hill. Got twenty-two grandchildren, most of them running around somewhere here tonight." She patted his hand. "Ask me anything you might want to know, son."

"I might need your opinion on the stained glass," Kirk replied. "But not tonight. We'll work on it later."

"Boy, he's good," Faye whispered. "Buttering up old Miss Fitz right off the bat."

Rosemary whispered back, "Well, she did give a thousand-dollar check to the cause."

"Does he know that?"

"Of course not. He's just being kind to an elderly woman. I told you how polite he is."

"Oh, I see," Faye replied, tongue in cheek.

Ignoring her, Rosemary listened to the rest of the conversation. Mrs. Fitzpatrick seemed intent on telling him something.

"You've the look of a hunter," the old woman said, her rheumy eyes washing over Kirk's features in a bold squint. "Are you searching for something, child?"

Surprised, Kirk laughed. "Not that I know of."

Aunt Fitz moved her head in a shaking nod. "Sometimes we wander around looking, even though we don't realize we've been searching until we've found something to hold on to."

"Oh, here she goes, talking her riddles," Rosemary said beneath her breath. "Kirk will probably get a kick out of that."

Kirk's next words surprised Rosemary. "You might be right, Aunt Fitz. I was born in Ireland, but I know some of my ancestors and kinsmen came to the Appalachians to settle the new land long ago. Maybe I'll find a connection here. I've already fallen in love with the beauty of this place."

His eyes touched on Rosemary then moved back to the old woman still holding his hand. Aunt Fitz, her vision weakened by age and cataracts, still didn't miss the slight shifting of his gaze. She looked hard at Rosemary, then lifted her head back to Kirk.

"The mountains will touch your heart, boy," she said solemnly. "You might leave, but you'll be back here again."

Kirk looked uncomfortable at her prediction, but he quickly covered it by laughing down at her. "Thank you for speaking with me. Are you ready to eat?"

Apparently taking that as a sign that she'd best let go of his hand, Aunt Fitz dropped her hand to her lap to gather her tattered, brightly patterned quilt over her little legs.

"Starving," she said, motioning for her granddaughter to push her to a nearby table. Waving a hand at Kirk, she said, "I'll be seeing you, I 'magine." As she passed Rosemary, she smiled then winked. "A fine choice, Rosemary. Your steeplejack will do us proud."

"Wow," Faye said, glancing over at Rosemary's surprised face. "Praise from Aunt Fitz is like a blessing from above, Rosemary. Quite a coup, your steeplejack."

Rosemary gritted her teeth. "Thanks, but he's not *my* steeplejack."

Kirk came up to her then, his smile soft and shadowed by the coming dusk. "Well, I've heard tales of the folklore in these mountains, and I guess I just encountered some of it firsthand with Mrs. Fitzpatrick."

"She can tell the weather better than any forecaster with fancy computers," Rosemary said by way of explanation.

"And she knows every herb and bush on these hills. We all go to her for advice on everything from making jelly to easing arthritis. She's a dear and we all love her as well as fear her at times."

He looked out over the setting sun clinging to a nearby western hillside like a golden blossom. "She's a real intriguing woman, isn't she? She seems very wise," he observed.

Wanting to make him feel more comfortable, Rosemary shook her head and laughed. "Well, don't pay too much attention to her ramblings. All that nonsense about you coming back—she just wants every tourist and traveler to fall in love with this place the way she has."

Taking her by surprise, he bent low so that his breath tickled the curling hairs along her neck, and his eyes danced and shone like pure water cascading over rocks. "You mean, the mountain isn't going to swallow me up and touch my heart?"

Unable to breathe, she backed away, but didn't back down. She hadn't been out of circulation so long that she didn't know when a man was deliberately flirting with her. Shooting him a challenging look, she said, "Don't be silly—that's just folklore."

He reached out a finger to capture a wayward curl lying across her cheekbone. "It might be," he whispered, his words as gentle as the coo of a dove. "But some say there's always a thread of truth to be found in the old stories, Rosemary Brinson."

Slipping around him and taking her hair with her, Rosemary managed to get her breath back. "Right now I think would be a good time to sample some of Faye Lewis's fried chicken. We can talk folklore and riddles another time."

He ran a hand through his wavy locks and followed her, his eyes moving over the flowing lines of her floral-print sundress.

"Another time," he repeated, more to himself than to her. "But not nearly enough time to figure you out, Rosemary."

She heard him, but she kept walking. And reminded herself he'd keep moving too, once he was finished with this job, while she...she was as settled and grounded as the steeple he'd come to mend. She acknowledged the attraction, but knew there was no need to get attached to the man.

No need at all, and...certainly, no hope.

Chapter Three

"Why did you invite him to our family dinner?" Danny asked Rosemary the next night. "You know this is our special time together."

Rosemary stopped buttering bread long enough to give her older brother a stern look. At thirty, Danny was a younger version of her father in looks. Tall, brown-headed with deep brown eyes, he'd taken after the Brinson side of the family, while Rosemary looked exactly like her mother with her light chestnut locks and dark blue eyes.

Those blue eyes were now flashing fire at her stubborn brother. "Oh, please, Danny! The man is living in a trailer just down the street. When I saw him this afternoon, he said he was going home to eat a sandwich. I had to invite him, for manners' sake if nothing else."

Danny leaned back on the polished surface of an ancient cabinet, then picked up a fresh cucumber to nibble while he studied his sister. "You know how Dad feels about him."

Rosemary wiped her hands on a blue dish towel, the echo of those very same words coming from her father not so long ago, ringing in her ears. "Oh, yes, we all know how Daddy feels about the steeplejack, about the church, about me. He tells me often enough."

"Shh!" Danny rolled his eyes and held a finger to her mouth. "Want him to hear you?"

Loud sounds of baby chatter came from the den just off the kitchen. Rosemary had to smile. "I doubt he can hear anything over the shrills of your daughter. Emily takes after her mother—quite a chatterbox.''

"Who're you calling a chatterbox?" Nancy Brinson said from the doorway, a mock-stern look on her pretty, round face.

"You, sweetheart," Danny admitted readily, his own dark eyes twinkling. "Did you keep Dad occupied enough so that Rosemary could finish dinner?"

"I didn't have to say a word," Nancy said, tossing her ponytail over her shoulder. "Emily has him on the move."

"She's the only bright spot in his life these days," Rosemary said, quelling the envy she felt for her precious little niece. Clayton had taken to the child from the very first, maybe because in her innocence, Emily couldn't feel the tremendous pain they'd all endured since Eunice's death. Clayton didn't have to put up a front with her.

Nancy was pregnant when Rosemary's mother died. The baby was born two months later.

"I sure wish Mom could see her," Rosemary said to her brother.

"She does," Danny reminded her, his expression darkening with sadness. "I'm sure she's watching Emily from heaven, like a guardian angel."

The room went silent, as if out of respect for their mother's spirit. Nancy came to stand by her husband, one hand automatically going to his shoulder for a gentle, soothing pat. Rosemary turned away to busy herself with finishing dinner, the sight of the love and understanding between her brother and his wife too much to bear. She ached for that kind of bond; she wished for someone to pat her on the shoulder when she was feeling down. Oh, she had the love of all her friends and the congregation, but somehow, something was missing. That something was a husband and her own home. She wanted all the things Danny had—a home to call his own, a spouse who adored him, and a child. She'd come so very close to having her dreams. But, on a cold March night, that illusion had been shattered.

Maybe it wasn't her time yet. Right now, her job was to take care of Clayton, and to try to help him through this rough time. She owed him that much at least, after what had happened.

Meanwhile, she'd trust that God would guide her when the time was right for her to find a soul mate.

Nancy took the tray of bread away from Rosemary, startling her out of her frantic motions and punishing musings. "I'll stick this in the oven," her sister-in-law said, her hazel eyes compassionate. "How's the roast coming along?"

Rosemary managed a convincing smile. "Ready. I'm going to slice it in just a minute." Glancing at the clock, she added, "I told Kirk seven. He should be here any minute."

Nancy looked out the back door, toward the church. "Does your father know you invited him?"

"No," Rosemary said in a deliberate tone. "Dad isn't speaking to me very much these days, not that that's so unusual. But he's even more angry with me for bringing the steeplejack here. Thinks it's frivolous and unnecessary."

Nancy's smile was indulgent. "Well, you have to admit it's a bit unusual. I mean, I'd never heard of a steeplejack until you called me all excited about something you'd seen on the Internet, of all places."

Remembering how she'd sat in Reverend Clancy's office, fascinated with his state-of-the-art computer system, Rosemary had to laugh out loud. "I got kinda carried away on-line, but hey, I found what I wanted. Which was, someone to do the job right."

Nancy threw up her hands. "Whatever you say. You know more about this stuff than I ever will. And I don't care to know. I have enough to occupy me."

Meaning, little Emily. Rosemary again felt that pang of regret and remorse. Would she ever have children? Or would she have to be content with taking care of other people's?

"Hey," Danny said from his perch near the open back door, "your steeplejack is crossing the street. Better let Dad know he's coming, or he'll make another scene."

"He's not *my* steeplejack," Rosemary said. Even so, her heart started racing and her palms grew damp. Danny was right. Why had she invited Kirk to supper?

Kirk strolled along wondering why he'd agreed to go to dinner at Rosemary Brinson's house. After that fun lunch he'd shared with her father, he'd made a solemn vow to steer clear of Clayton Brinson. Yet here he was, wildflowers in hand, heading for the very spot where he'd been ridiculed and prodded just yesterday.

Had he only been here two days?

This place was so timeless, so quaint and eccentric, that it seemed as if he'd been here forever. Or maybe he'd dreamed about a place like this forever. Quite charming, this Alba Mountain and its eclectic group of inhabitants. Especially one blue-eyed inhabitant.

And that, he told himself with a shrug, was why he was willing to face down Clayton Brinson again. Kirk wanted badly to see Rosemary. Had to see her, in fact. Had to see her up close.

He'd certainly watched her from a distance all day today. Oh, he'd gone about his preliminary work and taken care of what needed to be done. He'd surveyed and measured and analyzed. He'd discussed hiring a local crew with Reverend Clancy—the good reverend was working on that right now. And he'd carefully considered how best to go about renovating and restoring the aging church and its beautiful, inspiring steeple.

All the while, he'd watched the day-care center across the way, hoping to get a glimpse of the angel who'd brought him here. Rosemary. Rosemary with the sweet-smelling, fire-tinged hair. Rosemary with the eyes so blue, they looked like midnight velvet. Rosemary with the guarded looks and the cloak of sorrow. Rosemary with the floral, flowing dresses and the tinkling, musical laughter.

He'd watched her with the children, laughing, singing and smiling. He'd watched her with the townspeople, talking, explaining and sharing. And he'd watched her with her father, hurting, obeying and hoping.

He was intrigued by her. Maybe Aunt Fitz was right. Maybe these mountains did make people long for things they'd never needed to think about before.

And maybe, just maybe, Kirk, old boy, you're getting caught up in something you have no business being involved in.

He didn't usually accept invitations so readily. Ordinarily, he worked from dawn to dusk, then slumped back to his trailer to grill a hamburger or a steak before falling into bed. Usually. Ordinarily. But then, there was nothing usual or ordinary about Rosemary Brinson. She was like an angel with a broken wing.

And he wanted to heal her.

Bad decision. Bad. Don't do it, man. Turn around and go eat that sandwich you lied to her about. Turn around and forget that you saw her heading out the door, and you purposely made it a point that she see you. Turn around and forget how she smiled up at you and lifted those luminous eyes to you and said, "Come over tonight and meet my brother. You can stay for supper."

Turn around, Kirk.

He knocked on the open door and waited, the sounds of domestication echoing through his wayfarer's logic. A child's laughter. Warm, home-cooked food. Fellowship. Rosemary.

He knocked, and waited, and wondered how he'd ever be able to distance himself from her so he could do his job and move on.

Then he looked up and saw Clayton Brinson's furious expression, and decided it might not be too hard, after all. Not if her overbearing father had anything to do with it.

In order to protect Rosemary from her father's wrath, Kirk decided he would have to force himself to stay away from her.

Somehow.

"Kirk, come on in," Rosemary said, moving in front of Clayton in an almost protective stance to open the screen door. "Supper is just about ready. In fact, I was just telling Daddy that I'd invited you."

Clayton's scowl deepened. By way of greeting, he grunted then turned to head toward the formal dining room. "Hurry it up, girl. I'm hungry."

Kirk followed Rosemary through the house to the kitchen. He looked around the small room, his gaze falling across the little group of people staring at him. "Hello," he said to Nancy a moment before shoving the wildflowers into Rosemary's hand.

She rewarded him with that little smile, then turned away, clearly flustered in a most becoming way, to put them in water.

"Hi, I'm Nancy Brinson, Rosemary's sister-in-law," Nancy said, taking matters into her own hands. "And this is my husband, Rosemary's brother, Danny. Sorry we missed you at the celebration last night." She patted little Emily on the head. "This one was teething and wasn't up to socializing, so we stayed home to take turns walking the floor with her."

Rosemary regained her composure enough to take one of Emily's fat hands into her own so she could kiss it and squeeze it softly. "This is our Emily, ten months old and full of energy."

Kirk nodded to Nancy, then shook Danny's hand while the other man sized him up. "Nice to meet all of you." He grinned and cooed at Emily.

Spellbound, the baby batted her long lashes and let out a squeal of delight.

"She never meets a stranger," Danny said proudly. "Hey, want a glass of tea?"

"Sure," Kirk said. "I'm learning to like it with ice. You know, my mother taught me to drink it hot."

"Not me," Danny said, grimacing. "I know it's a tradition over where you come from, and up North. But, man, once I was on a business trip in Detroit and ordered tea, and they brought it to me hot and in a cup—"

Nancy interrupted, a teasing smile on her face, "And he was so embarrassed, instead of ordering iced tea, he sat right there and sipped it hot, as if he were at a tea party or something."

Kirk laughed. "I bet you looked extremely dainty."

"I tried," Danny said, guiding Kirk into the dining room. "Have a seat."

Nancy put the baby down in her nearby crib and helped Rosemary carry in the food and drink. Clayton sat stone-silent at the head of the table.

Kirk looked around the long room. It was a lovely setting for a meal, complete with lacy white curtains at the tall windows and a matching lace tablecloth on the spacious mahogany table. Everything gleamed in the rays of the overhanging light fixture, while the scent of something fresh-baked set out on a matching buffet lifted out on the gentle breeze teasing through the open windows.

Noticing the formal settings at the table, he said, "I hope you didn't go to any extra trouble for me."

Before Rosemary could answer, Danny said, "Oh, no. It's a tradition in our house—having all the family together for a meal at least once a week. We usually do it on Sunday nights, but this week Emily was sick, so we put it off a couple of days."

"And used to, your mother would be here," Clayton said in a quiet voice, his stern look intact.

For just a minute, Kirk saw the raw pain and grief in the older man's eyes, and regretted his bad feelings regarding Rosemary's father. He didn't really have any right to judge the man. He'd known grief when he'd lost his beloved grandfather. Still, losing a wife had to be different. And maybe he would never know that kind of loss.

Because you never stay in one spot long enough to get that close to someone.

He glanced up at Rosemary, who stood just inside the wide archway, her gaze searching her father's face, her stance hesitant and unsure. The same pain he'd seen in Clayton's eyes was now reflected in her own.

Danny looked over at his father, then back to Kirk, his expression going soft with memories. "Yeah, Mom went to a lot of trouble. Cooked all afternoon. We'd come back around for leftovers during the week..." His voice trailed off, then he shrugged.

Kirk watched Clayton for signs of eruption, and seeing none, said, "I'm sure you all miss her."

"We do," Rosemary said, sitting down across from Kirk, her gaze still on her father. Clayton stared firmly at his plate.

Kirk watched as she reached for both her father's hand on one side and Danny's on the other. "Let's say grace."

Danny automatically took his sister's hand, then reached for his wife's. Nancy in turn held out a hand to Kirk so they would form a circle. Not knowing what else to do, Kirk followed suit and held out a hand to Clayton. On her side of the table, Rosemary waited for her father to grasp both her hand and Kirk's.

When Clayton refused to take either of their hands, Rosemary didn't bat an eye. She closed her eyes, holding tight to Danny's hand, and said a quick blessing, then let go of her brother's hand to start passing food.

But Kirk didn't miss the hurt, confused look haunting her eyes. She was trying very hard to stay steadfast in the storm of her father's rejection. How could a man do that to his daughter? How could he treat her that way and not know he was being cruel?

Maybe Clayton did know exactly what he was doing, Kirk decided. Maybe he was being deliberate. But why?

"If you don't mind me asking," he began carefully, "how did your mother die?"

Rosemary looked over at her father, then to Danny, panic in her eyes.

Wishing he could take the question back, Kirk added, "If you'd rather not talk about it—"

"She died in a car accident," Danny said quietly. "And, actually, we'd rather not talk about it."

"I'm sorry," Kirk replied, very aware of the undercurrent circling the table with the same fierce intensity with which Rosemary had just graced the meal.

"How'd work go today?" Rosemary said, her smile tight, her eyes shining.

Relieved that she'd given him an opportunity to take his foot out of his mouth, Kirk nodded. "Great. I talked to Reverend Clancy about hiring some of the locals to help with the sanctuary and the outside walls of the church. I'll need an assistant to help hoist me up and to help me from time to time up on the steeple. But for the most part I do all the steeple work myself."

"How did you ever become a steeplejack?" Danny asked between bites of biscuit with rice and gravy.

Kirk grinned. "I get that question a lot. Most people think I'm crazy, but actually, I'm a fourth-generation steeplejack. My mother's grandfather back in Ireland was a steeplejack and he taught my grandfather and my uncle. When I came along, I tagged around behind my grandfather so much, he had no choice but to put me to work, much to my mother's dismay. We traveled all over Ireland and England, repairing and renovating steeples and cathedrals, some of them stretching up a hundred and twenty-five feet.''

Rosemary went pale. "I can't imagine being that high up. I can barely make it up Alba Mountain without getting dizzy.''

Kirk gave her a warm look. "Afraid of heights, huh?''

"She sure is,'' Danny said. "I used to climb up to the belfry at the church all the time when we were little. But she'd get halfway up those old stone steps and turn around and crawl back down.''

"I never made it to the top,'' Rosemary said, "and I don't care who called me chicken.'' She glared at her brother. "The view from the mountain's good enough for me. I don't need to be on top of that narrow tower to see what I need to see.''

Kirk laughed at her stubborn tone, then gave her a hopeful, challenging look. "We might have to change all of that. The view from up there is something else. It's a shame you've never seen it.''

Danny patted his sister on the shoulder. "Hey, man, if you can get her up there, you really will be the miracle worker Reverend Clancy says you are.''

Everyone laughed at that remark. Everyone except Clayton. He ate his food in silence, motioning to Rosemary when he wanted refills or seconds.

Kirk, determined to win the man over in some form, turned to him at last. "Mr. Brinson, since you've been a member of the church most of your life, I could use your advice. Would you be willing to supervise some of the men on the ground level?''

Clayton's head came up and his eyes fixed on Kirk with a sharp intensity. "No, I would not. I'm not interested in the least. Absolutely not.''

Kirk glanced at Rosemary. She looked uncomfortable, but he thought maybe if he could get Clayton involved, it would take some of the heat off her. "I just thought, since you're retired now—''

"You thought wrong,'' Clayton said, scraping his chair back with a clatter. "Rosemary, bring my cobbler and coffee to the den.''

"All right.'' She rose to do her father's bidding, her eyes

centered on Kirk. "I'm sorry," she whispered as she rushed by.

She sure did apologize a lot, when it really wasn't necessary.

"Me, too." He looked over at Danny. "I didn't mean to upset him."

"It's okay," Danny said. "But you have to understand something about my dad. He hasn't been back to church since the day of Mom's funeral. He's turned his back on the world and on God. He can't understand why God would do this to him, after he tried to be faithful and loyal to the church all his life."

Kirk leaned forward, his voice low. "I don't mean to sound insensitive, but hasn't your father missed the point entirely?"

Nancy sighed and leaned in, too. "Yes, he has. But Reverend Clancy says it takes longer for some people than others. We're supposed to be patient and go about loving him no matter how he treats us."

Kirk ran a hand through his tousled locks. "I feel for all of you, but especially for Rosemary. And I think it'd be best if I go on back to my little trailer."

"Don't," Rosemary said from the kitchen door. "I mean, you haven't had your dessert yet." On a shaky voice, she added, "Now, my blackberry cobbler isn't as good as my mother's was, and granted, these aren't fresh blackberries, but Aunt Fitz herself helped me can them last year and, well…" Her voice trailed off as she brought a hand to her mouth. "Excuse me."

She turned and rushed back out of the room, out of the house. The kitchen door banged after her.

Danny rose out of his chair. "Maybe I should go see about her."

Nancy put a hand on his arm. "No, honey. Let's you and I get these dishes cleaned up." She looked at Kirk.

He was already standing. "I'll go to her," he said, meeting Nancy's gaze head-on. "I enjoyed the meal. Sorry if I dampened the evening."

Danny shook his head, his eyes dull with resignation. "Don't worry, buddy. This isn't the first time something like this has happened."

Well, it would be the last for him, Kirk decided as he stepped out into the cool spring night. The scent of a thousand budding blossoms hit him full force, the tranquillity of the peaceful evening clashing with the turmoil he'd just set off inside that house. Searching the darkness, he spotted Rosemary on the bench inside the church grounds, sitting where she sat every day watching the children.

He wanted to rush to her, but instead, he took his time, wondering what he'd say once he got there. Kirk wasn't used to offering words of wisdom or comfort. He usually dealt in small talk, or technical discussions. Every now and then, he'd get in a heavy philosophical discussion with someone he met, usually involving religion. But for the most part, he steered clear of offering up his opinion on a continuous basis. People didn't like to have their values questioned, and he wasn't one for questioning God's ways.

His mother had taught him simply to accept the daily miracles of life. Kirk firmly believed in God's grace, but he wore his own faith in an unobtrusive fashion, preferring to live and let live. Because he did move around so much, he'd learned to mind his own business.

Yet, his mother, Edana, a wise woman with strong religious convictions, had warned him many times about his nonchalant attitude. "One day, my fine son, you'll come across a situation that will demand more than you're willing to give. You'll learn all about being tested. Then, my lad, you'll start taking life much more seriously. And maybe then, pray God, you'll stop roaming the earth and settle down."

Was this his test then? If he got involved with Rosemary, he would be going against his own rather loosely woven convictions. How could he comfort this woman? Better yet, should he even try?

She looked up as he approached. He heard her loud sniff, saw her hurriedly wiping at her eyes. Oh, that he'd caused her any further pain—it tore at his heart, exposing him to something deep within himself, some strange sensation that tingled to life and pulsed right along with his heartbeat. He'd not let this happen again.

"Rosemary," he said, sitting down beside her to take her hand in his. "I'm so very sorry."

She didn't pull away, but she looked away, and then up, at the steeple looming in the darkness. "We both seem to be doing a lot of apologizing."

"You don't owe me an apology," he said, meaning it. "You've been through a terrible tragedy, and apparently, I've come in the middle of it and made it worse."

She let out a sob, then gripped her fist to her mouth. "People tell you it'll get better," she stated on a tear-drenched voice. "They pat you on the arm and say, 'She's at peace now, dear,' and they keep going. They don't want to see your grief. It makes them uncomfortable, you see.

"During the funeral, everyone was so compassionate and understanding. It was such a shock—it happened so fast. One minute she was there, standing in the kitchen, laughing, talking, making plans for my wedding. Then, the next, she was simply...gone."

She didn't speak for a minute, and he heard her swallow hard. "But then, life goes on, as they say. After a while, you become this robot. You go through the motions, you behave as if everything is back to normal, but you know that something is terribly, terribly wrong. When you see people on the street, you smile and you accept—dread—the sympathy in their eyes, but they don't want you to speak of it."

She stopped, taking a gulp of air, another sob escaping. "But inside, inside you have this silent scream that never, ever goes away, never stops. And you just keep on moving through each minute, each hour, each day. And that scream keeps following you until you think you'll go stark raving mad from hearing it. It...it never ends."

Unable to bear any more, Kirk gathered her into his arms, rocking her gently, whispering soothing words into her ear. Remembering the days when his own mother would try to comfort him, he said something in Gaelic to her, unaware that he'd even done it. He held her close, letting her sob quietly into the night, letting her purge herself against his strength.

How long had she carried this pain? How long had she been the one to be strong while her brother and her father depended on her to become a surrogate for her mother? How long had she struggled to become that perfect replacement, knowing she could never be the one they all longed for, the one she longed to have back in that little kitchen?

And, what had happened to those wedding plans she said her mother had been working on?

He had so many questions, but he didn't ask for any answers tonight. Tonight, he held her, and with a silent prayer, he asked God to give His strength over to her, and her suffering family. He asked God to give her the comfort he wasn't sure he could bring.

And in the asking, Kirk offered up the only thing he did have to give. He offered up his heart.

"Kirk," she said at last, her voice raw, her words muffled. "What did that mean, what you said to me in that beautiful language?"

He pulled her tight against him. "It means, 'I am here, little one.'" He swallowed the lump in his throat. "I am here."

She leaned her head against his chest, her cheek touching on the steady beat of his heart. "For a little while at least," she whispered.

Chapter Four

Kirk lifted her away so he could see her face in the moonlight. "What's that supposed to mean?"

She sat up, wiping the last of her tears, purposely distancing herself from the warmth of his embrace. "It means... well...you'll be gone in a few weeks. I can't start depending on you. I won't start depending on you. I shouldn't even be talking to you now. I mean, you came here to repair the steeple. You don't need me or my troubles getting in your way."

He turned on the bench to stare at her, wondering if the woman could read his thoughts since that was precisely what he'd been telling himself earlier. "I don't mind hearing your troubles. I just don't know if I can help."

"No, you can't help," she said as she got up to walk to a nearby fence. "And I don't normally go around feeling sorry for myself. According to the Bible, I'm supposed to rejoice, knowing my mother has gone on to a better place. And sometimes, I can do that. Then other times, I can't. I'm selfish because I miss her, but I've accepted my mother's death."

"Have you?" he had to ask. He got the impression she hadn't really come to grips with any of this. When she didn't answer immediately, he asked, "And have you accepted the way your father treats you?"

She whirled to glare at him. "I don't have much choice there. He's my father and he needs me."

"Why does he talk to you like that? Why do you let him?"

Rosemary swallowed back the urge to spill her guts to this man. She couldn't let him know; she couldn't let him see the pain, the open, festering wound that would never heal, no matter how hard she prayed, no matter how much she tried to forgive herself each and every day. "I...I don't want to talk about this anymore," she said into the wind. "After all, it's really none of your concern."

He lifted off the bench to come and stand beside her. "You're right. It's none of my business, but I think I've provoked this whole situation. Maybe if I knew what happened, I could understand better."

"There's really nothing to understand," she tried to explain. "My father is still grieving, he's still angry because my mother's death was so senseless. I have to hold fast and hope that he'll realize he can't change any of it."

Kirk knew she wasn't telling him the whole story. So her mother was killed in a car accident. That was a tragedy, no doubt. But why would Clayton take out his anger on his daughter? Suddenly, a sad, sickening thought crossed his mind. Well, he'd wondered it since he'd seen Rosemary and her father together that first day, sparring; he had to ask it.

"Does your father blame you somehow—for your mother's death?"

She turned away, her staunch silence shouting at him.

"Rosemary?" He urged her around, then lifted her chin with the pad of his thumb. "Is that what this is all about?"

She faced him squarely, her eyes full of shame and disgust. "Yes," she whispered. "He blames me. And you will, too, if I tell you the truth."

With that, she whirled and ran back toward her house, toward the torture her father would surely inflict on her once she slammed that screen door behind her.

Kirk heard the door slamming shut. It was as if she'd just shut him out of her life.

Over the next few days, Kirk managed to avoid Rosemary as much as possible, considering that she worked at the church, considering that he worked outside, mostly with a bird's-eye view of the comings and goings across the street, considering that he longed to see her again, that he yearned to hold her again, considering that he couldn't get her out of his mind.

He had to remind himself that he didn't want to get involved. He told himself, this way, neither of them would get hurt—especially Rosemary. She didn't need the complication of a short-term relationship added to her already stress-filled life. And short-term it would have to be. He never stayed long enough for anything else. That he was even considering having a relationship with her was enough to make him antsy and restless, and distracted.

Today, frustrated and tired from a day of scraping rust and paint from the gables of the church roof, he decided he'd take a late-afternoon hike up onto Alba Mountain. The trails behind his tiny trailer led straight to the top of the peak, according to Reverend Clancy.

Tomorrow, he'd interview people for the complete crew, then he'd get started on the steeple. That task would occupy his mind enough to keep him in line and away from Rosemary Brinson. Right now, he just needed to escape into nature, to let his mind wander. He needed time to think and regroup. The mountain peak would be the perfect spot.

It should have been.

Except that halfway up the steep, winding path that lifted to the rocky peak, he spotted Rosemary sitting in a field of wildflowers, in what looked like a cemetery.

Aunt Fitz had said she'd buried her husband up on the hill. Was that where Rosemary's mother was buried, too?

He stopped, catching his breath more from the sight of the woman sitting there than from the exercise.

She was wearing one of those soft, flowing dresses she seemed to favor, its colors rivaling the wild yellow roses and delicate pink-and-yellow-tipped lady's slippers bursting to life all around her. Her hair moved in the breeze, lifting away from her face in chaotic shades of deep red and burnished brown. As he watched, she reached one hand out to touch the headstone in front of her, closing her eyes in a silence that only the angels could hear.

He should have kept moving. He was intruding on a private moment, between Rosemary and her mother. Yet he couldn't seem to find the strength to put one hiking boot in front of the other. He couldn't move. He could only stand there, watching her, wanting to go to her.

Like a doe sensing danger, she opened her eyes and looked up, right into his eyes. For a brief time, she didn't move; she just sat there staring up at him, her expression a mixture of surprise and knowing. Then she waved to him and sent him that bittersweet smile he was beginning to need to see.

He forgot about scaling the mountain.

Rosemary saw him through the trees and felt the lurch of her heart against her chest. She'd sensed someone was near, she'd *felt* someone's eyes on her.

And somehow, she'd known it would be Kirk. She'd avoided him since their gut-wrenching encounter the other night. She was embarrassed by her tears, by her confessions, and by her need to have someone hold her. She disliked weakness in anyone else, but especially in herself. She'd avoided him, and she'd thought about him.

She'd thought about him enough in the past few days to conjure him up at any given moment, during work, during prayer, during play with the children. She'd thought about him, and wished she could just get the man out of her mind. She wanted to forget the way he'd held her; she wanted to remember the feeling forever.

Rosemary reminded herself that he was a drifter, a wanderer. His work was important to him, and because of that work, he couldn't stay in one spot for long. In spite of their closeness, she sensed an aloofness in him. Kirk held himself away from people, like a casual observer, watching and analyzing. He had to keep moving. And she had to stay here. Besides, if Kirk knew the real reason Clayton treated her so coldly, he'd turn away from her, too. And she couldn't bear to have him do that.

She told herself these things as he approached her now, looking like an ancient warrior from long ago. He wore hiking boots and jeans, and a torn T-shirt. His unruly hair was having a high old time playing in the wind off the hillside. His eyes, though, oh, his eyes. They held her, making her forget her pragmatic logic, making her forget her own self-disgust and guilt-laden remorse, making her long for something intangible and un-reachable.

Automatically, Rosemary gripped the sun-warm gray stone of her mother's headstone, as if asking for counsel. The silence answered her, as it always did when she came up here to visit her mother's grave. Only the wind and the chipmunks and the swallows gave her any conversation. Now, even nature's comforting forces seemed to go silent.

There was an intruder in the woods.

"I didn't mean to intrude," Kirk said as he came up the hillside to the level incline where Alba had buried its dead for two centuries. "I can leave if you'd like."

"No, don't," she said in a rush. As she lifted up, he reached out a hand to help her, causing her to feel the same disruption in her equilibrium as she usually felt when she reached the top of the mountain.

Kirk took her hand in his, then shifted his gaze from her face to the gravestone in front of them. "Your mother?"

She nodded, her gaze falling across the etched roses centered on the stone.

Kirk read the inscription: Eunice Grace Brinson. Born 1942. Died 1996. Beloved Wife and Mother. "And in heaven, the angels are smiling down on her, watching her sleep."

"That's beautiful, Rosemary," he said, still holding her hand.

"She used to tell us that," she explained, her gaze settling on the inscription. "She'd read to us from the Bible, then she'd say, 'Time for bed. The angels will be smiling down on you now, watching you sleep.'"

Not knowing what to say, Kirk just held her hand. Finally, he asked, "Do you come up here alone a lot?"

"At least once a week," she replied. "When I need to talk, when I need to get away." She looked around at the mountain laurel spreading like a pink-and-white-patterned quilt across the distant hills. "It's always so hushed, so peaceful."

"Would you like me to go?"

"No, I was just about to head back down. I've got to get supper fixed."

Not wanting her to leave just yet, he said, "I was planning on hiking the mountain. Want to come?"

She recoiled instantly, like a blossom settling in for the night. "No. I...I get so dizzy. I'd better go on back home."

"Come with me, Rosemary," he said, his hand tight against hers, his body pulling her toward the peak. "I won't let anything happen to you."

"I know that," she said, believing it to be true. "I'm afraid, is all."

"Afraid of the mountain, or me?"

"Both," she admitted, laughing shakily to hide her discomfort. "I feel so foolish after the way I acted the other night."

"Don't," he said. "You have no reason to feel uncomfortable with me. I don't judge people."

She gave a little huff of a laugh. "You'd be the first not to judge me, then."

That remark caught him off guard. "I can't believe anyone in this town would hold ill thoughts about you. You seem to keep the whole church together."

She laughed again. "I have a hard enough time holding myself together. But you're right. People here are good and strong, supportive. They've helped me through some rough spots, and...they've forgiven me."

"For what? What did they need to forgive?"

She pulled away. "That's private. I...I need to go."

"You tell me the whole town's forgiven you, yet you can't tell me why?"

"I don't want to discuss it," she said, hoping he wouldn't push her. Giving him a pleading look, she said, "It's too painful, Kirk. Please try and understand."

He was trying. And failing. Kirk had made mistakes himself, a lot of them, but he couldn't imagine something so horrible that a whole town would need to send out forgiveness for it. Maybe because he had no life beyond his work. Maybe because he'd been so indifferent to life, never taking it too seriously, that he'd never really experienced the type of pain she obviously had known.

"Come with me up the mountain," he said, taking her hand

back in his. "I won't force you to tell me your deep, dark secrets. I just want to walk with you."

She looked up the winding dirt trail, her heart pounding with a new fear that had nothing to do with conquering her vertigo. She couldn't lose her heart to this man. That frightened her more than any mountain ever had.

"Come with me, Rosemary," he said again, his captivating eyes willing her to trust him.

She wanted to trust him, wanted to go with him up the mountain, wanted to talk to him and question him, and get to know the man behind those aged, intense eyes. But, Rosemary reminded herself, she was supposed to be avoiding him.

She thought about what was waiting for her at home, then she thought about the fine spring wind and the smell of new-blooming honeysuckle, and the freedom to just go.

"All right," she said at last. "But we'll have to hurry to make it before sunset."

"We will," he assured her. "There's plenty of light yet."

She moved away for a minute, to stand in front of her mother's grave once again. "Bye, Mom. I'll be back soon."

A gentle breeze kissed her face with a soothing coolness, washing over her to leave her breathless and wondering. Then silence fell back on the hushed hillside.

Rosemary took Kirk's hand, and followed him up the path to the top of Alba Mountain.

Along the way, after getting her breath and calming herself, she stopped to show him the local flora and fauna.

"That's a sourwood tree," she said, pointing off to a jutting hill where a white-tasseled tree shot toward the sky. "Makes good honey."

He watched her expression, thinking her lips would probably taste like honey.

"And over there, growing along that bluff, that's ginseng. Some of the locals still gather it to send to the Orient—they're licensed by the state, though. You've probably heard how potent it is." She blushed, then shot him that endearing smile again.

He decided nothing could be as potent as her charm.

"Look," she said, taking his hand to pull him into the woods. "A rabbit."

Kirk had seen lots of rabbits. "It's lovely," he said, never taking his eyes off her face.

She looked up at him, his gaze warming her like summer rain. "Are you even listening to me?"

"Uh-huh," he said, his gaze moving over her face. "It's all very fascinating."

"Don't look at me like that," she said, moving to pull away.

He gently yanked her right back. "Why? I can't help it if I enjoy looking at you. You're a very attractive woman."

Rosemary's body buzzed with a fine current of electricity. This. This was why she couldn't stay away from him; this was why she should stay away from him. "I've heard about your Blarney stone over in Ireland, Kirk Lawrence. Stop flirting with me."

"I like flirting with you, Rosemary Brinson," he said, grinning when she managed to dart away. "I like watching your skin turn from pale to bright. I like seeing your hair lifting out, curling around your face—"

She interrupted him to put her hair in perspective for him. "Naturally curly and hard to deal with—that's my hair."

"Naturally curly and soft to the touch," he said as he drew near again. Standing apart from her, he reached out a hand to grab a few unruly strands, curling them around his fingers until his hand touched her temple. "There it is again—that becoming blush."

She didn't pull away this time. His hand on her skin felt too good. "You're mighty tempting," she admitted, her eyes moving over his face. "Handsome, single and apparently carefree. Tell me, Kirk, how many broken hearts have you left behind with each of your newly polished church steeples?"

He had to laugh. "I see, in spite of that innocent blush, you have quite a sting."

"Just being realistic," she replied, her cheek still touching his hand. "Tell me—the truth."

He pulled her into his arms, taking her breath and her resolve away. "There's only one broken heart in my past," he said near her ear. "And it's mine. Caused by a high-school sweetheart who didn't take to my chosen profession. She had her sights set on someone with a little more staying power."

Surprised, Rosemary looked him over to make sure he wasn't making it up. "Really? Did you love her a lot?"

He laughed again. "I thought I did. More like puppy love. She's married now, to a lawyer, I believe. Lives in a fancy house somewhere near New York City."

Fascinated, she asked, "Do you have any regrets?"

"No," he said automatically. "I couldn't give her what she wanted. I decided after that episode, though, I'd better be very sure before I let go of my heart again." Turning the tables, he asked, "What about you, Rosemary? What happened to break your heart?"

She went still in his arms. "We were talking about you, not me."

"And why can't we talk about you? What happened to your wedding plans?"

She wiggled away, then turned to head up the path. "Come on. It's getting late."

"Rosemary," he called. "You can trust me."

She whirled to stare down at him. "Oh, I don't doubt that. I know I can trust you, but I can't depend on you. You said it yourself, Kirk. You've chosen your path. And I...I have to live with mine, right here. There's no point in telling you all the details. It's over, in the past, and I don't want to talk about it with you when soon, you'll be a part of the past, too. I'd rather you didn't remember me that way."

Frustrated, he hiked up to meet her. "Why can't we just enjoy the time we have? I want to understand you, and...I want to remember all of you, good and bad. I could help you, comfort you."

"You already have," she said, taking his hand again. "More than you'll ever know."

He supposed he'd have to settle for that, for now. "Can I at least be your friend, while I'm here?"

"Of course," she said, smiling again. "I could use a friend."

It was a step forward, although why he should feel so gratified and elated was beyond him. They both knew it couldn't last. But then again, friendship wasn't something to be taken lightly.

They rounded the path, hand in hand, each lost in thoughts about the commitment they'd just made. Kirk looked up to find an old log cabin set in the middle of a clearing off the path to the left, its walls shaped and hunched by the various additions and lean-tos that must have been added throughout the years. Several brightly painted gourds in different shapes and patterns hung from its posted porch, while colorful quilts covering rough-hewn benches invited travelers to sit a spell.

"Who lives there?"

"Aunt Fitz," Rosemary replied, glad they'd dropped the subject of their relationship.

"How does she get up and down the mountain in that wheelchair?"

Rosemary had to smile at his joking attitude. "There's a road behind the cabin that leads down to the main road through town. Her children usually drive here to pick her up. She stays in the village with one of her daughters sometimes, but she might be home today. Want to stop in for a quick visit?"

"Why not—or are you stalling to keep from reaching the top of the mountain?"

She shot him a meaningful grin. "You know we need to hurry. Maybe I just feel the need for a chaperon."

"So you don't trust me, after all?"

Rushing on ahead, she called over her shoulder, "No, I think maybe I don't trust myself when I'm around you."

He followed her through the woods. "That's a good sign...I think."

Aunt Fitz was delighted to see them and immediately got them both a Mason jar full of dark, sun-brewed, heavily sweetened iced tea.

Kirk took a long swallow, then licked his lips. "I taste herbs in there. Mint, maybe."

"Scotch mint," Aunt Fitz stated proudly. "And a few other cure-alls."

"Such as?" Kirk asked in a tone full of suspicion.

Aunt Fitz laughed long and hard from her perch on an old bentwood chair on the porch. "A little sang never hurt, son."

Kirk squinted, then looked at his brew. "Sang?"

"Ginseng," Rosemary said, her eyes lifting to his.

"Shaped like a human figure, so the Chinese say it's good for all over," Aunt Fitz explained. "They believe in plants shaped like organs and such, and since sang looks like a human body, they believe it will cure whatever ails a body."

"How interesting," Kirk said, surprised at her obvious knowledge of the human anatomy.

Rosemary grinned at him from her spot on the porch railing. "Maybe it will give you a boost, Kirk."

Thinking the last thing he needed was a stimulant, he lifted an eyebrow to her. "We might not ever make it back down the mountain."

She laughed good-naturedly at that, but quickly caught herself when she felt the all-knowing intensity of Aunt Fitz's beady eyes on her.

"It's good to see you laughing, gal," the old woman said in a raspy voice. "I knowed one would come along one of these days, to make you laugh again. I seen the signs."

That sobered Rosemary. "Maybe we'd better get going, Kirk."

"In a minute," Kirk said, interested in what else Aunt Fitz had seen. Noticing the basket of bright material by the old woman's chair, he said, "What's this?"

"Quilt remnants," Aunt Fitz explained, her bony fingers grasping a piece of the material to hold it up to the light. "A wedding quilt, maybe." Her smile was serene, while her eyes fell on Rosemary. "A girl needs at least a dozen quilts in her hope chest, you know."

"Time to go," Rosemary said, hopping up to take Kirk's glass out of his hand, her eyes downcast and evasive.

Kirk immediately noticed her agitation, but decided all this talk of weddings was making her nervous, maybe since her own apparently hadn't worked out. "I'm not finished," he protested, enjoying the way Aunt Fitz stared with such all-seeing eyes at Rosemary.

"It will be dark soon," Rosemary said sharply. "Daddy will be furious."

"How is Clayton?" Aunt Fitz asked, rising on wobbly legs to see them down the steps. Finding her cane, she finally managed to stand to her full height of five feet four inches. She refused to use that dadgum wheelchair around the house.

"The same," Rosemary replied. "And he'll be fit to be tied if I'm late for supper."

"He'll survive, I 'magine," the old woman said with a wave of her skinny hand. "'The Lord hear thee in the day of trouble.'"

Rosemary appreciated the quote from Psalms, but wondered if Aunt Fitz's gentle reminder would help her father. "Daddy isn't listening right now, Aunt Fitz. He's forgotten how to ask for God's mercy and help."

"Have you forgotten, too, child?"

"No, I haven't forgotten," Rosemary answered softly.

"Then know He is with you, Rosemary, and He'll see to Clayton in His own good way. Go to the top of the mountain, girl. Enjoy the view. It's might pretty at sunset."

"And dark quickly afterward," Rosemary said on a warning tone.

"Your hunter there, he'll protect you," Aunt Fitz stated, laughing merrily.

"I don't need protecting." Rosemary was already moving up the path. "Hurry, Kirk."

Kirk had been standing in amazement at the old woman's serene but secure convictions. Aunt Fitz was content to live her days out on this mountain, her roots firmly embedded in the life she had made here. For a brief moment, he wanted to feel that same contentment, that same anchoring of faith. For just an instant, he wanted to stop roaming, searching, traveling.

Aunt Fitz looked at Kirk. "Better chase after her, boy. And let her catch you."

Kirk laughed at her simple solution to a very complex situation. Was that it then? Did he want to be caught? Was that why he was beginning to question his own outlook on life? Unsettled and unsure, he said, "Goodbye, Aunt Fitz."

"I'll be seeing you again, I 'magine."

He imagined she was probably right. That old woman knew too much, he thought as he hurried after Rosemary.

Chapter Five

They made it to the top of the mountain just as the sun was slipping through the Fraser firs covering a distant rock formation. The whole valley below them and the surrounding woods held a blue-green smoky fog that reminded Kirk of some of the faded squares of Aunt Fitz's quilting materials, while the bald where they stood was smooth and almost devoid of trees.

"So this is why they call them the Blue Ridge Mountains," he said, his hand holding tight to Rosemary's.

She stood back, too deathly afraid to come forward on the jutting rocky ridge. "That's it—the fir and spruce trees make the woods seem blue. Beautiful, isn't it?"

He heard the shakiness in her voice. "Are you okay?"

"Oh, I'm great," she said. "Just let go of me so I can sit down, please."

He did, watching as she backed up against a smooth stone that looked like a nature-made bench. "Is that your particular spot?"

"This is as far as I go," she replied, laughing nervously as she sat back on the rock, gripping the warm gray stone with both hands. "Guess the good Lord put this rock right here to hold me up."

"Maybe He did, at that," Kirk said, his gaze moving over her. She looked radiant in the red-gold light, her hair awash with all the colors of the earth and sun, her face expectant and hesitant, and glowing with the flush of their climb. "But you know, you're missing the best view."

"Maybe, but I can see enough from right here, thank you."

"Come to the edge, Rosemary," he coaxed. "I'll hold on to you."

"No," she said in an emphatic voice. "You take a few minutes to enjoy yourself and I'll take a few to get my breath back." She glanced at her watch, then moaned. "I am so very late."

"We won't linger long." He took a deep breath himself, his eyes moving over the town and countryside below. "I can see the steeple off to the left. Your trail obviously winds all around the mountain."

"It takes a few twists and turns," she said, silently noting that her mundane life was suddenly doing the same thing.

Kirk studied the houses and storefronts below, thinking how picturesque the whole place looked, then strolled over to sit beside her on the rock. Giving her a scrutinizing look, he grew concerned at the pale shade of her skin and the panicked look in her eyes. It just seemed natural to put an arm around her in a protective gesture. "Stop worrying. Surely your father allows you some free time. You are an adult."

She tossed her hair away and tried to smile. "Yes, I'm an adult. I actually used to live on my own, in an apartment down the street from my house. But that changed after Mama died."

"You moved back in with your father then?"

"Yes. I felt…it was the right thing to do at the time. It was supposed to be temporary, but one thing led to another and, well…I'm still there."

"Why can't your brother help out now and then?"

"He does. Or at least, he tries. He offers to take Dad to the doctor, or fishing, stuff like that."

"And?"

She looked out over the valleys and hills that were already filling with the first white dogwood buds, her breath calming down, her pulse almost back to normal again. "And…I usually wind up doing it all, because Danny has a demanding job— logging—and he has a wife and a new baby, and I—"

"And you've given up your life because you feel guilty and obligated."

She lifted her chin, then turned to stare at him. "I didn't give up anything, because…I had nothing to give up. Nothing."

"You mean, because your wedding was called off after your mother's death? Why?"

She would have stood, except that the only way to go was toward the ledge. "I thought you promised not to try and find out my secrets."

"That I did," he said, frustrated that she was so close to telling him about her life, yet still so very afraid to let go. Deciding he'd better make the most of this time with her, he took her hand in his and smiled. "No more talk. Let's just enjoy the sunset, then I'll take you home."

"Isn't it amazing," she said, her tone hushed and reverent, "that something so beautiful can exist? While we whine and moan and continue to feel sorry for ourselves, this mountain stays intact and solid."

"God put it here for just that reason," Kirk replied. "I think I'm beginning to understand what Aunt Fitz meant when she told me the mountain would touch my heart. It certainly has renewed my faith in God's handiwork."

Rosemary relaxed a little, very much aware of his arm around her, his fingers touching her bare shoulder on one side, and his other hand in hers, settled on the rough fabric of his worn jeans. His nearness made her head spin and she concentrated on the view instead. "It's good to share it with someone who understands."

He concentrated on her. "It's good to be here with someone so centered. And pretty to look at, I might add."

She smiled at that, liking the word *centered* as much as she liked being called pretty. She was centered. In spite of all her worries and fears, she knew that her faith would see her through.

"This land is so old," she said, her words whispered and awe-filled. "Millions and millions of years, at least, and created simply from weather and erosion. The Cherokee lived here before the settlers ever came. Most of what Aunt Fitz knows about cures was passed down from the Cherokee."

He couldn't help it. He had to press his cheek against her hair. "Yep, Aunt Fitz is a very clever woman."

Rosemary felt the tickle of his breath fluttering her hair, but she didn't stop him. She swallowed, lifting her head toward him, letting him bury his nose in the thickness of her wild curls. That little voice in the back of her mind told her that she should not be here, letting him do this. She ignored it for once. Later, when she was alone and lonely, she'd remember this and smile. That wasn't so much to ask for—just a sweet memory, a few stolen moments with a man she found intriguing and unique.

"That's nice," he said, letting go of her hand to pull her around with both arms. "Rosemary?"

"Hmm?"

"May I kiss you?"

Shocked, she drew back, her eyes locking with his as a heated flush moved up her neck. "I...I don't think—"

"Let's not think about it," he said as he lowered his head to hers. Using the only philosophy on life he'd followed up until now, he added, "Let's just enjoy the time we have."

She should have protested, but his mouth falling across hers ended any complaints she might have had. The kiss was gentle and sweet, demanding and dangerous, as untamed as the mountain they'd climbed, and just as beautiful.

Kirk pulled away, his dark eyes filled with a gleam of pure contentment, then pressed his forehead against hers. "I've wanted to do that since I first saw you."

"Oh, really?" she said on a shaky whisper. "I'm afraid Reverend Clancy would have been a little surprised if you had."

"No more than I," he admitted. "You taste so good."

"And that surprises you?"

He grinned. "No, I knew you'd be sweet. What surprises me is the impact—of seeing you, of wanting to get to know you, of wanting to be with you. I've never been jolted quite so hard before."

She drew back again, her eyes wide and playful. "I bet you say that to all the church girls."

He let her go, but not too far since she refused to move from the stone bench. Tracing a finger down the contours of her jawline, he said, "I've never taken the time to flirt with a church girl before."

"Kirk Lawrence, you expect me to believe that? Why, you're, you're—"

He grinned. "What?"

"You know what you are—good-looking—"

He lifted a dark eyebrow. "Do go on."

"Charming, interesting, mysterious, confident—"

"All of that, huh?"

"And you know it. I can't believe you haven't left a girl with every steeple."

He shook his head, laughing. "That's a new one."

"Well, I'm sure it's true."

"You're sure? You think you've got me figured out, right?"

She lowered her eyes. "Well, no. I'm trying very hard *to* figure you out." Then she lifted her gaze to meet his, her eyes widening with sincerity. "I don't want to be hurt again, Kirk. I...once was enough."

"Tell me who hurt you."

She reached up a hand to touch his cheek. "I can't. Maybe later, but not now. What did you say? Let's just enjoy the time we have."

Funny, he'd always followed that code before. Now he wasn't so sure it was the best solution for Rosemary and him. He wanted to linger; he wanted more time. But it wasn't fair to let her think they had that luxury. "So you're okay with the fact that even though I'm highly attracted to you, I can't stay here forever?"

"I never expected you to stay, and I really never expected you to be...highly attracted to me." She stood, and clinging to the stone, turned to start back down the mountain. Then, safe away from the ledge, she said, "And I certainly never expected you to kiss me."

He followed her, taking one last long look at the sprawling vista before them. "Neither did I."

It was late when they got back down to the foot of Alba Mountain. Dusk was long gone, and a new night greeted them, complete with singing crickets and hungry mosquitoes.

Kirk walked her to her porch, where a light was burning brightly. "Should I go in with you?"

"I don't think that's too smart," she said, her eyes darting to the screen door. "I'm used to handling my father. I won't have him browbeating you, too."

"I can take care of myself," he said, moving to go inside with her. Then, belatedly, he remembered he had made a vow to stay away from her, to save her any further grief with her father. "But you're probably right, I'd only make it worse for you."

"Thank you," she said, whirling to head up the steps.

Kirk grabbed her hand, pulling her back down close so he could give her a quick kiss. He wasn't quite ready to relinquish her yet. "I enjoyed the hike."

"Me, too," she said, flustered and thoroughly confused. "Does this mean we're still friends?"

"Always," he said, letting her go with regret because he wanted to keep her near, and with relief because he knew he shouldn't want that. "See you tomorrow."

Kirk watched her go in the house, then turned and strolled to his trailer. It looked sad and forlorn, sitting there underneath the great oak. He'd always adored his little traveling home. Now it seemed lonely. He dreaded going back in there.

He opted to sit outside and enjoy the nice cool evening. He told himself he simply needed to unwind after that long hike. Actually, he needed to think—about Rosemary, about what was happening here, about the devastating kiss they'd shared on the mountain. And he needed to listen. He didn't want to hear any shouting coming from the big white house across the street.

The shouting started almost the minute Rosemary entered the back door.

"Where on earth have you been?"

Not surprised, but saddened all the same, she simply looked at her father, then turned to find Faye Lewis standing in the doorway of the formal dining room.

"Hello, Rosemary," Faye said on a calm voice. "Come on in, honey, and eat. When Clayton called me looking for you, I offered to bring him supper. Stuffed peppers and corn bread, with string beans on the side."

"And a good thing she did." Clayton stomped past Rosemary, headed for his chair in the den. "Or else I'd be sitting here still waiting on you to get home."

Giving Faye a grateful look, Rosemary called to her father. "I went...I went for a walk and ran into Kirk. He asked me to take him up the mountain."

Faye shot her a warning look, but Rosemary refused to sneak around like a coward. After all, she'd done nothing wrong. And she knew from firsthand experience how gossip moved in a small town, with all the accuracy of a homing pigeon. Might as well confess here and now and get it over with, in case someone else had seen them together.

That got Clayton's attention. "I might have known it. You've done took up with that no-account carpenter. You don't even know the man, Rosemary."

The look he gave her only reminded her of her past indiscretions, but this time she wouldn't make the same mistake. "Kirk is a very reputable carpenter, as well as a licensed steeplejack, and I know him well enough to take a walk with him."

"Jesus was a carpenter," Faye said to Clayton, causing both him and Rosemary to stare at her in shock. "Oh, I'm not comparing, or saying Kirk is anything like the Lord. But carpentry and the kind of work Kirk Lawrence does isn't easy. You have to admire the man for taking on the hard jobs. He's been working day and night since he arrived, so I wouldn't exactly classify him as 'no-account.'"

"Well, I don't admire him, not one bit," Clayton said stubbornly, if not somewhat sheepishly. "Not if it means he'll be dragging her out to all hours every night." Glaring hard at his daughter, he held a finger in the air. "We went through this once, girl. Or have you forgotten already?"

Shocked, Rosemary stepped forward, her own eyes flashing fire. "No, Daddy, I haven't forgotten. And I never will, because you'll make sure I'm always reminded, won't you?" Pushing back bitter tears, she said, "Well, this time it's different. Kirk is different. He's a good man and he's just a friend—someone to talk to—someone who's traveled and has interesting stories to tell. And," she added before turning back into the kitchen, "he won't be here forever. So that makes it rather convenient for everybody."

Clayton wasn't through. Stomping after her, he said in a loud, condemning voice, "No, that just makes you even more crazy this time than before. Nothing can come of this, and you know it."

She whirled, the tears falling in spite of all her efforts to stop them. "Yes, I know it. Nothing will come of it. And that should make you very happy."

With that, she turned to go into the kitchen to finish the dishes Faye had obviously started. The silence that followed her was even more hurtful than the shouting that had preceded it.

Faye joined her after a bit. "He's watching television."

"That's what he loves best," Rosemary said, her tears replaced with cold resignation. "I'm sorry, Faye. I should have been here. I appreciate you coming over to be with him, though."

"I didn't mind at all," Faye said, taking up a dishcloth to dry the pots that wouldn't fit in the dishwasher. "In fact, we managed to have a pleasant evening. He actually opened up a little and really talked to me. You know, your daddy puts on this big front, but deep down inside, he's still a good man."

Rosemary stared at her friend. "You're kidding? He talked to you, in a civil manner?"

"He sure did." Faye smiled, then winked. "I can still turn on the charm, when I need to. Clayton and I had a good long talk."

Surprised, Rosemary couldn't help but laugh. "Oh, Faye, you're priceless. You always make me feel better. I guess I shouldn't have spoken to him like that, but lately, we stay at each other's throats."

"You don't owe me any explanations," Faye said. "He needs someone to be firm with him, especially you. Why, he's got you jumping through hoops, as it is. I know you love him, honey, and I know you respect him as the Bible tells you you should, but sometimes love has to be tough. You stand firm and remember that you've done nothing to deserve the way he's treating you."

"But I have," Rosemary said as she turned on the dishwasher. "And I suppose I'll pay for it the rest of my life."

"You don't need to. God has forgiven you, Rosemary. Maybe it's time for you to forgive yourself."

"I don't think I can," Rosemary admitted. "I didn't tell Daddy, but I went to Mama's grave this afternoon. That's where Kirk found me. I guess I should have come on home, but it was so nice...walking up the mountain with him. He's easy to talk to, and he's been all over the world. Kirk's a fascinating person, and I enjoy his company. But I doubt anything will come of it."

Faye patted her on the shoulder. "I think it's fine, you two becoming friends. You're right about him, he seems to be a good man. Reverend Clancy is real impressed with his knowledge of the Bible, and all the places he's been. They've had some lively discussions, let me tell you. And Clayton and I even talked about Kirk earlier, with not a harsh word mentioned. Clayton just grunted and said he wasn't impressed, but I think he is."

"Oh, really?"

"Yes, really. He told me Kirk had asked him to help with the renovations. Of course, he was all bluster, telling me he had refused in no uncertain terms. But I think he was flattered by Kirk's offer. You remember how Clayton used to be? All bluff, when underneath he was a big, old pushover."

Rosemary looked at Faye, seeing her in a new light, wondering why she'd really come over here tonight. A new hope sparking like a flame in her mind, she said, "Faye, do you...have feelings for my father?"

"Of course I care about him," the other woman said hastily. "He's been a friend for years."

"You know what I mean," Rosemary said, her eyes bright. "Do you care about him, maybe as more than a friend?"

"What if I do? How would you feel about that?"

Rosemary hugged the other woman close, a new happier set of tears misting in her eyes. "I'd feel as if...a prayer has been answered. I think that's wonderful."

Faye patted her on the back, then said, "Now if we can just get the stubborn old dog to realize that I even exist."

"I think that can be arranged," Rosemary said. "But we'll have to be very careful. He's still not over Mom."

"You let me work on it," Faye suggested, smiling. "I don't intend to replace Eunice, but I'm alone and so is he. I think we could make good company for each other. And, he's still got a lot of good in him. I want to help him find it again."

"You have my blessing," Rosemary replied, a warm feeling settling over her in spite of her earlier fight with her father. "I've certainly been praying for him to turn his life back over to God, and you could be a positive influence in that area."

"Keep saying those prayers," Faye reminded her. "If it's meant to happen, it will."

Rosemary wondered if she should use that same logic when dealing with her own growing relationship with Kirk. Alone in the kitchen after Faye left, she lifted a hand to her lips, remembering the way he'd kissed her. She'd been kissed before, of course, but somehow, she didn't remember any of the kisses moving her with such force.

She'd climbed that mountain a hundred times, so many times she couldn't count them. And yes, she'd been afraid to step to the ledge every time. But this afternoon, this time, she'd felt something besides the usual vertigo sitting there on top of that mountain. When Kirk had kissed her, something long dead had stirred inside her, lifting out like a delicate blossom shooting between a jagged crevice in a rock.

She tried to put a name to this new, unfamiliar feeling. Should she dare hope?

And then she knew, that was it. That was the feeling she'd experienced, a feeling she'd hushed and buried for so long now, she'd almost forgotten what it was like. Hope.

Hope. That was the difference, and now that she had accepted it for what it was, she felt renewed and almost at peace. Almost.

Rosemary read from her Bible, as she did each night before going to bed. And there in the aged book she'd received from the church in fourth-grade Sunday school, she read in Psalm 16 the message she had been longing for. "Therefore my heart is glad, and my glory rejoiceth: my flesh also shall rest in hope."

Hope. For a little while at least. Hope. For some cherished moments with a special person. Hope. To enjoy this time she'd been given with Kirk. She'd settle for that, and she'd accept that Clayton's prediction was true.

It couldn't last. But she could make the most of it while she had the chance. Right now, *that* was her only hope.

Later, as she lay in bed, she smiled and remembered that in heaven, the angels would be watching her while she was sleeping.

Then, the next morning all her hope was vanquished as her past came back to remind her she shouldn't hope for things she could never have.

Chapter Six

"**Y**our steeplejack has gone and done it now," Danny said to Rosemary after stomping into her office the next morning, his eyes blazing, his expression grim.

"What?" she asked, surprised to see him here, and even more surprised by the suppressed anger coloring his face. "What's going on, Danny?"

"Come here and I'll show you what's going on," he said, urging her to the window with a firm grip on her arm. "Look over there, Rosemary."

She craned her neck to see where he was pointing and her heart literally stopped beating. "Oh no. It can't be."

"It is," Danny replied in a dangerous tone. He clamped a fist against the windowpane so hard, the glass rattled. "It's him. I didn't think he'd ever have the nerve to show his face at this church again."

"Does Dad know?" she asked, sick to her stomach as she watched Kirk giving instructions to another man.

"He was sitting on the front porch, watching the renovations, until he saw him! Did you know anything about this?"

"No," she said, a hand coming to her dry throat. "Kirk said he was going to hire some locals, but I never dreamed...I can't believe this is happening."

"Well, it is, and Dad's in a fit. He called me a few minutes ago—caught me heading out the door."

Her mind filling with dread and worry, she asked, "What did he say?"

Danny snorted, then turned away from the view of the two men across the lot. "Oh, he had plenty to say. Such as, you were out to all hours with Kirk last night, and that you probably knew all about this, had probably suggested it. He's furious, almost as furious as he was the night he found out about the cause of Mom's wreck."

Rosemary sank into a nearby chair, all her energy draining away with each beat of her heart. "I can't believe he thinks I'd have anything to do with this. He must still think the worst of me, after all." This was like a nightmare, a nightmare she'd tried so very hard to forget. "Maybe if I talk to Kirk—"

"Do you think that would help?" Danny said, his tone calmer now. "I mean, maybe he didn't realize who he was dealing with."

"I'm sure that's it," she said, feeling slightly more balanced. "I'll just explain to him and then he can find someone else to help him."

"Well, first you'd better run home and explain to Dad. He's threatening all sorts of things."

Her gaze flew to her brother. "Such as?"

"Oh, you know—taking care of this once and for all, since the law didn't do its job."

"But they said two years," she reminded him. "They said two years in prison for vehicular homicide. The judge pushed for a speedy trial. He didn't even get out on bond after the accident. How did he get out of prison so soon?"

"That crafty lawyer, probably. You know how he made him look like a choirboy at the trial. He probably got out early for good behavior and the time he'd already served," Danny explained. "There was talk going around at work a while back, about him getting an early release based on letters and pleas from his old college buddies and coaches at his first parole hearing. You know how all the football coaches loved him. But I...I didn't have the heart to warn you, and besides, I didn't think he'd ever come back here again."

Melissa came rushing into the office, her eyes wide with excitement. "Rosemary, have you heard?"

"Yes," Danny said, guessing what Rosemary's assistant was about to tell them. "I just told her."

"Are you all right?" Melissa asked, falling onto her knees in front of Rosemary, her expression full of worry.

"I'll be okay," Rosemary said. "Can you cover for me for a few minutes? I need to go talk to Dad about this."

Melissa bobbed her head. "Sure. Take as long as you need."

Rosemary followed her brother out of the building, hoping against hope that Kirk wouldn't see her crossing the parking lot. After convincing Danny to go on to work, then telling him goodbye, she took a deep breath and steeled herself against her father's sure wrath. Then, with slow, deliberate steps, she headed across the church yard, her head down, her steps choppy and hurried.

She was halfway home when she heard Kirk's voice behind her. "Well, good morning to you, too."

She pretended she didn't hear him. Things would be much easier that way.

"Rosemary?"

She kept walking, willing herself to face forward. If she turned to him now, she'd crumble, and she had to face her father first.

She felt a hand on her arm, but she tugged away and kept walking. "I can't talk right now, Kirk. Something's come up."

"What?" he said, jogging to catch up with her. When she managed to scoot around him, he started walking backward just in front of her, so she couldn't get away.

Kirk took one look at her face and knew this was serious. She was as pale as the gray stone on the steeple facing.

"Rosemary, what is it?" Guessing, he said, "Did you and your father argue…about last night? I'll explain to him. I'll tell him it was my fault. I knew I needed to stay away from you, but I wanted to see you again."

She had been looking down, but now she lifted her head to face him, no longer able to control the turmoil bubbling inside her. They stopped in the driveway of her yard.

"It's not about last night, Kirk," she said, running a shaking hand through her hair to calm her jittery nerves.

"Tell me," he said, reaching out to touch her arm. "Tell me, Rosemary."

The door of the house slammed then, and Clayton came barreling down the steps toward them, his face flushed, his eyes watery and red-rimmed. "Well, don't just stand there, girl. Go ahead, tell the man why you're in such a hurry to cover your steps."

Kirk turned around, his own fury evident in his stance and expression. "This is between Rosemary and me, Mr. Brinson."

"Oh no, son," Clayton said, pointing a finger in Kirk's face. "This ain't just between the two of you. You done went and put your finger into my business now."

"Look," Kirk began, "Rosemary and I did nothing wrong last night. We simply took a walk. I promise it won't happen again, though, if it's going to cause her any more arguments and reprimands from you."

Clayton's hostile glare only deepened. "This ain't about that. This is about you coming here and stirring up trouble—trouble we don't need right now."

"What do you mean?" Kirk asked, holding his hands out palm up. "What could I have possibly done to upset you this way?" He turned to Rosemary, "And what did I do to make you afraid to even speak to me?"

Clayton didn't wait for her to answer. He stepped closer, his finger still jutting out in the air. "I'll tell you what you did. You went and hired on the man who killed my wife!"

Realization warred with shock on Kirk's face. He turned to Rosemary for validation, and saw it clearly in her troubled eyes. "Is that true?" he said, knowing it sounded redundant.

"Oh, yes, it's true," Clayton said, moving closer, his eyes blazing. Then he turned to his daughter. "Satisfied?"

"Daddy, please," Rosemary said, stepping between the two of them. "Kirk had no way of knowing about…about Eric, and neither did I."

"Eric?" Kirk looked from Clayton to Rosemary. "Eric Thomas?"

Rosemary lowered her head, the pain coursing throughout her body almost too much to bear. She glanced up at Kirk, then over to her father. "Daddy, I didn't know. You have to believe that. I didn't know anything about this, and if you'll just go back in the house, I'll explain to Kirk."

Clayton peered at both of them in disgust. "Oh, you'd better explain. And you'd better keep Eric Thomas away from my yard. I'll kill him with my bare hands if he tries to set foot anywhere near my property.'' Shoving away from Kirk, he whirled. ''And that goes for this one, too. I'm warning you, Rosemary! Keep them both away from me—I don't want you bringing this one home for any more suppers—not at my table, and I don't want to catch you going off to the mountain with him again!''

Rosemary watched her father as he headed back inside, then she looked at Kirk. He appeared to be as angry as Clayton.

''I should have never brought you here,'' she said on a weak whisper. ''I've made another terrible mistake.''

He stared at her, seeing the pain in her eyes, seeing the worry marking her face, and wondered what had happened to all the goodness he thought he'd seen in this town. ''No, I'm the one who made a mistake. I got involved, too involved, and I broke my own rule.'' Shaking his head, he added, ''But now that I *am* involved, don't you think I have a right to know what's going on?''

''Yes, you do,'' she said, moving her head in agreement, even while his regret became her own. ''But not here.''

He grabbed her by the arm. ''Then where, Rosemary? Where and when will you tell me the truth? *Did* Eric have something to do with your mother's accident?''

She nodded, then looked around. ''Yes. And I...I can't face him—not yet.''

''Come with me then.'' Kirk tugged her to his trailer, pulling her up the steps so he could shut the door firmly behind them.

Rosemary blinked, to adjust her eyes to the dim interior, and to stop the inevitable tears that she refused to shed. Later, she would remember her surroundings—books and CDs, a laptop computer, a cellular phone, economical and minimal—the trailer was consistent with the man who traveled in it.

Right now, however, she could only stare up at Kirk, hoping he could understand what a terrible mistake she had made in bringing him here.

''Talk, Rosemary.''

She did. She just blurted the ugly truth right out. ''Eric Thomas killed my mother. He was driving drunk and he crossed the centerline and ran her car off the road into a ravine. She died instantly.'' She looked up, her features twisting in an anguished frown. "He walked away with a few scratches.''

Kirk slumped onto the bench that made up his dining area, his elbows coming to rest on the small table where he usually ate his solitary meals. He released a heavy sigh.

They sat silent for a minute, then he asked, "Did he serve any time?''

"He got two years, but apparently he's out after only a year, on probation. That's why we're all so shocked—we didn't expect to see him here.''

"And I just hired him as my assistant.'' He ran a hand through his hair, then looked over at her. "I didn't know, Rosemary. Reverend Clancy told me he'd done some jail time, but didn't say why. I had no way of knowing.''

"Of course you didn't,'' she said, reaching out a hand to him, needing the physical contact to steady her own doubts. "I've caused you so much trouble.''

He took her hand, then scoffed at her statement. "I think that's the other way around, sweetheart. I've caused you trouble since I pulled into town.''

"No,'' she said, her eyes holding his. "Last night, for the first time in a very long time, I had a little glimmer of hope, Kirk. And you gave me that.'' At his confused expression, she held up her other hand. "I don't expect anything more. But I sure did cling to that little bit of...happiness.''

He knew what she was telling him. He'd felt it, too. They'd both been so practical, so upfront, telling themselves this couldn't last, couldn't go past friendship. But they'd kissed each other and something had shifted, something had bound them together there on that mountaintop. Kirk knew that no matter where he traveled or who he met after this, he'd never forget Rosemary. And he'd decided that he was fooling himself to even think he could actually leave her without feeling more than a little regret.

Well, he was feeling regret now. He'd hurt her again. "Reverend Clancy came to me,'' he explained. "He said he had a man who really needed a job, said he'd fallen on hard times and needed a second chance. He had some experience with carpentry, so I told the reverend I'd give him a shot. Eric isn't afraid of heights, like most of the others I've interviewed.''

Rosemary shook her head. ''No, Eric never was afraid of anything. He always was a daredevil. And a star quarterback in high school and college.''

''You knew him...before your mother's accident?''

She lowered her head, unable to meet his gaze. ''Yes. He lives in the next town, but we met in college.''

Kirk strummed his fingers on the table, impatient to know the whole story. ''Reverend Clancy said he wasn't a member of the church, but that he had attended in the past. He really pushed me to consider Eric, he said he could vouch for him.''

Rosemary lifted her head in surprise. ''How could Reverend Clancy do that, knowing about Eric? He knows how we all feel about what Eric did. My family is shattered, my life is shattered, because of what happened. I don't understand how my own minister could do this.''

Kirk reached over to stroke her trembling hand. Her fingers were cold, so he rubbed them between his palms. ''Maybe he believes Eric needs a second chance, here in the place where he made a mistake.''

She yanked her hand away, then jumped up to glare at him. ''A mistake? Is that what you think this is? Just a bad mistake? He took another human being's life, Kirk. And that human being happened to be my mother. It wasn't just a mistake. It was murder!''

Unable to deal with her rage, he stood to take her in his arms. ''What do you want me to do?''

She didn't mince words. ''I want you to tell him to get lost, to get away from me and my family. My father...well, he might do something we'd all regret if you don't fire Eric.''

''I promised the man at least a month's work, Rosemary.''

''And I've lost my mother forever! I can't bear to watch him working on that church every day, Kirk. It isn't right!''

Kirk stared down at her, wanting to understand her tremendous pain. Now, at least, he understood the rage behind the pain. No wonder Clayton walked around like a zombie, no wonder Danny's laughter was brittle with false cheer, and no wonder Rosemary was trying so very hard to hold them all together.

This wasn't just the loss of a loved one. This was much, much more, something so senseless, so wasteful, that none of them could deal with it or accept it. And he'd just brought them all face-to-face with their worst nightmare.

"No, it isn't right," he said at last. "This was a senseless act of a very irresponsible person. And two years—no, make that one year serving time—will never be enough to bring your mother back. Maybe that's why Reverend Clancy brought Eric here. Eric can learn a greater lesson having to see you each day. Maybe your minister wants to help all of you accept this, Rosemary."

She shook her head, her eyes burning with a dark fire. "I can never accept what happened. And Daddy certainly never will. But we were doing okay, until this."

"Were you really?" he asked. "Or weren't you just going through the motions? I've seen how your father treats you. I've seen how sad you look sometimes. You haven't even begun to heal, Rosemary."

"But we had a chance," she said, her hands clinging to his shirt. "We had a chance until Eric came back. Don't take that away from us, Kirk. Don't let this man back into our lives."

Her plea tore through his system. How could he deny her that one simple request. Yet, how could he tell that broken man out there that he didn't deserve a chance, either? Kirk had never faced such a dilemma before. Caught in the middle, he tried to understand both sides. But he did not want to cause Rosemary any more pain.

Tugging her close, he said, "I'll see what can be done. Maybe Reverend Clancy can find him work somewhere else."

"Thank you," she said, her body slumping against his in relief.

Just then a knock shook the small trailer, causing Rosemary to pull away. "I've got to get going," she said. "The children will be asking all sorts of questions."

She moved past him to open the door.

Eric Thomas stood at the bottom of the steps, his gaze meeting hers first in shock, then in shame, then finally in a firm resolve that sickened her all over again.

Rosemary stared down at the man who'd changed her life so

dramatically. Eric was slender and good-looking, with thick sandy-blond hair and hazel eyes. Apparently, prison life had changed him somewhat. He was still muscular and had the build of a born athlete, but he seemed calmer, older and more mature. He'd always been so restless and unsettled before. Or maybe, he was just too surprised to move, seeing her in Kirk's trailer.

"Rosemary," he said, moving to let her pass. "I didn't know you were here. I can come back later."

"I was just leaving," she said, her head down as she stepped past him.

"Before you go," Eric said, his hand on her arm, "there are a few things I need to say to you."

She jerked her arm away, recoiling from his touch with a look of disgust and loathing. "We have *nothing* to say to each other, Eric. You have to know how hard this is on my family. I'd appreciate it if you'd have the decency to just leave."

Kirk stepped outside, between them. "Eric, Rosemary told me what happened."

Eric looked from Rosemary to Kirk. "So you're going to fire me before I even get started, aren't you?"

Rosemary glanced over at Kirk. She could see the confusion in his eyes. She knew it wasn't fair to ask this of him, but what else could she do? What else could he do?

Eric shifted his feet, then placed both hands on his hips. "Reverend Clancy promised me a job, and I need the money."

"He had no right to do that," Rosemary said at last. "The money for the renovations came from church members."

"Oh, so I'm not good enough to make an honest living from it?" Eric asked, his tone sarcastic. "I thought you were a Christian, Rosemary. I thought you were supposed to forgive and forget."

"Forgive?" she shouted, throwing a hand in the air. "Forget? Forgive that you killed my mother, forget that you lied to me and everyone else? I don't think so, Eric. You see, I can't forget. I have to live with what you did each and every day of my life."

"So do I, Rosemary," he said on a soft voice, his eyes bright. "So do I."

Kirk pulled Rosemary away from Eric, afraid she'd pounce on him with both fists if he didn't do something.

"Look, Rosemary," he said, his eyes willing her to focus on him, "I've finished the preliminary groundwork. I have to get started on the steeple and Eric is the only one who qualifies for the work we'll be doing. Do you want me to delay the whole operation while I try to find someone else?"

She stared at him, wondering why he couldn't see this the way she did. "I want you to understand how I feel, Kirk. I can't let this happen. You can't let him work here."

"I don't have much choice," he said. "I promised the reverend, and I promised Eric. I'm sure his probation officer will check to see if he's got a job."

"Do you think I care about that?" she asked, pushing him away to glare at Eric. "I can't tolerate seeing him again, Kirk. And especially not here, rebuilding the church. This was my project, my restoration of the church I love. Please, help me."

"I'm not giving up this job," Eric said, his own stance stubborn and determined. "I've served my time and I'm trying to get my life together. Why would you deny me that chance?"

Rosemary whirled on him with all the fury she'd held in check for the past year. "Because you denied me everything, Eric. Everything. You took away my mother, and you...you broke my heart. My whole world has changed because you had to have one more drink for the road. So don't expect me to feel sorry for you, or to welcome you back here with open arms. I can't." She looked back at Kirk, a dark defiance coloring her eyes. "I won't. I'll go to the church board and demand that Kirk fire you."

"Rosemary," Kirk began, trying to reason with her, "listen to me. Let Eric help me until I can find someone else, or the church board will probably call off the restoration altogether. I won't waste my time or the congregation's on this. I've already stalled long enough, as it is."

Her head pounded and her heart wasn't far behind. Why? Why did it have to be Eric of all people? Should she try to be fair and let him stay? No. She couldn't face him, maybe because it meant facing up to her own guilt.

But did she have the right to judge him, in spite of what he'd done? Remembering her own part in the whole thing, in all the events that had led up to her mother's death, she closed her eyes and willed the bitter memories away. Maybe this was part of her punishment, after all. In her heart, she knew it didn't matter how she felt about Eric. They would both have their day of reckoning soon enough. And in the meantime, she could only pray—for both Eric and herself.

"Okay," she said at last. "Do what you have to do. But don't expect me to cheer you on." Then she turned to Eric. "Stay away from my father and my brother. I won't be held responsible for what they might do or say about this."

Then she faced Kirk. "You were right. We…we both made a mistake. Just get your work done and…leave me out of it, please."

Kirk's own heart beat out a frustrated cadence. He couldn't let her go away angry and upset. Yet he couldn't send Eric away, either. But he could keep him busy and out of sight for a while.

"Eric, for now you're still working for me. Right now, I need you to start unloading the equipment from that trailer parked over by the back of the church. You'll need to check the machinery and the cable ropes. Make sure they're all secure and up to standard."

"All right," Eric said, his eyes on Rosemary. He turned to walk away, then looked back at her. "I am sorry, Rosemary," he said. "I know that doesn't mean much to you, or your family. But I am truly sorry about everything."

Rosemary focused on the buds of a fire azalea growing underneath the oak tree. She didn't respond to his apology.

But Eric wasn't through pleading his case. "That's all I wanted to say to you, really. I know there's no chance for us, ever again, but I do want another chance to get my life in order. I only ask that you allow me that chance."

She put her arms across her chest, and kept her head down, her memories acting like a shield against his pleas, against the tender mercy the Bible told her she must issue as a means of forgiveness. She wasn't ready to forgive Eric Thomas. She might not ever be.

After Eric walked away, Kirk forced her head up with a hand

on her cheek, his eyes meeting hers. "There's more to this story, isn't there?"

"Yes," she said, thinking it didn't really matter if he knew the truth now. Whatever they'd shared yesterday was gone; vanished, like that spectacular sunset they'd witnessed together. She might as well push the wedge farther between them, and end it once and for all.

"Tell me," he said, his eyes dark with longing.

"I was engaged to Eric," she said simply, softly. At his gasp of surprise, she nodded. "That's right, my fiancé killed my mother." She shot him a wry, bitter smile. "That's why there was no wedding, Kirk. And that's why my father can't stand the sight of me today. Maybe now you can understand why I didn't want Eric here. Seeing him reminds me that my mother's death was all my fault."

Chapter Seven

Rosemary immediately went to find Reverend Clancy. He was in his study preparing to make the rounds of visiting the shut-ins and the church members in the hospital.

"Rosemary," he said as she marched into the cool, paneled room, "I've been expecting you, dear."

"Then you know how I feel about what you've done," she responded, standing over his desk. She couldn't be disrespectful to him. She loved him like a second father and he'd been a source of strength to her in the last few years. But she had to know why. Slumping down in a comfortable wing chair, she said, "Didn't you know what this would cause?"

The reverend placed his plump hands together over his heavily marked calendar pad, his gentle brown eyes never leaving her face. "I knew, Rosemary. I knew this wouldn't be easy, but I've been counseling young Eric in prison for some time now. He is an unofficial member of my flock, and the boy needs a guiding hand. Should I deny him the nurturing I'd gladly give to any other member of this congregation?"

Rosemary looked down at her hands clutched tightly together in her lap. "No, Preacher, of course not. That's between you and Eric. But to bring him back here and allow him to work on the restoration, of all things! I can't bear to see that."

"It's not for you to bear, Rosemary," the minister replied softly. "Turn it over to the Lord. Let the Lord bear this burden for you. You cannot judge Eric. He's already been judged and

condemned, and now he's asking for our prayers and our forgiveness.''

She brought her hands to her face. "I don't think I can do
that. I don't think I can find it in my heart."

"You have to." Reverend Clancy got up and shuffled around
the massive oak desk, then leaned back on it, his gaze never
leaving Rosemary's face. "Think about what you're doing,
child. Think about what the Bible tells us. We don't condone
what Eric did, but we have to forgive him and give him a
chance to prove himself. He's struggling, Rosemary. He's not
had a drop of liquor since he went to prison. Now that he's out,
the struggle gets even harder. I had to bring him here, because
he called me to ask for help. He needs someone to turn to when
he feels weak and wants to turn back to the bottle. You know
about his family life. He doesn't have any support there, with
both parents dead and a brother and sister who've turned their
backs on him. Should I really do the same?"

She looked up at him at last. "No. You wouldn't be doing
your job if you turned him away."

Reverend Clancy nodded and pointed a finger. "It's not just
my job, Rosemary. It's the entire congregation's. Following
God's word sometimes puts us in difficult and uncomfortable
situations."

Reaching out a hand to him, she said, "Oh, Preacher, this is
so hard. Almost as hard as seeing my mother being buried. Will
this never end?"

"Only when you let it," Reverend Clancy said, patting her
hand with both of his. "You have to remember that at one time
you cared deeply for Eric, wanted to make a life with him. And
while that can never be the same, you can learn to find that
love in your heart again, that Christian love that gives all of us
grace. And in that grace, you will find forgiveness. It's the only
way to get past all of the pain. Let's pray about it, Rosemary.
I'm here to help you, and Eric, too. And I haven't abandoned
you. Nor has your Lord. 'I will not leave you comfortless.' He
said it and now you must remember it."

"What about…what about my father?" she asked, her voice
cracking. "This isn't going to make matters any better for
him."

"Then all the more reason to pray," the minister said, closing his eyes as he gripped her hand.

Rosemary bowed her head, her silent tears falling even as she lifted her sorrow to God. She'd pray for Eric, but she would have a hard time forgiving him.

Kirk did something that morning he hadn't done in a while. He called his mother. "I'm having a hard time dealing with this," he explained as the wires carried his voice thousands of miles away to the Wisconsin hideaway where his parents now lived.

"Kirk, Kirk," Edana said, her voice soothing and still very much Irish. "My poor boy. Are you sure this is more than just a conflict with the people who hired you?"

She always did see right through him. He'd only told her of the problem with Eric. Just the facts. But as usual, Edana didn't deal in just the facts. His mother would have made a great Irish cop. She had an instinct for getting to the bottom of a situation.

He sighed long and hard. "I don't know, Mother. I came here with the usual intent. I was really looking forward to working on this particular church. It's so beautiful, you see. So old and intriguing. And the people here, they're unique and interesting. Now I've gone and caused a ruckus and I don't know how to fix it."

"Fix it same as you fix your steeples, lad," Edana said. "Slow and steady, with a care for each and every detail."

"But these are human beings, Mother. That's a little harder—I can't just slap a new coat of primer on them."

"Might help the lot of them," she replied, sending him a throaty laugh. Then turning serious, she said, "Tell me some more about this Rosemary—sounds like a nice girl."

"One of the best," he admitted, being cautious so his mother wouldn't read too much into his budding relationship with Rosemary. "She's lovely and so hurt by all of this. She tries so hard to do what's best for everyone, except herself maybe."

"And you, you encourage her to take care of herself, I suppose?"

"I've talked to her about that very thing, yes."

"I know the kind of talking you do, boyo. Have you gone and taken that girl's heart away?"

"No, oh no. I'm not after sweeping her off her feet. But I...I do care about her—a lot."

"I see."

Oh boy. Whenever his mother said that, he knew he was in trouble. "Don't go putting too much into this, Mother. Rosemary has been a friend to me, and a champion of my way of doing things. She fought to get me here, you know."

"How impressive."

"And she's still fighting, for her father's love and approval, for forgiveness, which I personally don't think she needs, and...she's sacrificed everything simply because she's that way. She does what's right, what needs to be done. She's amazing, really."

"Quite."

Kirk smiled, then tilted the phone away from his ear. He could just see his mother, her short clipped hair a mixture of salt and pepper, her cup of tea perched at arm's length, her feet up on her favorite stool, her flashing eyes bright with wisdom and a mother's knowing. Ah, he loved his mother, missed her, longed to tell her how he really felt. But he knew he didn't have to. She already knew. As she always did.

"I'll be all right," he finally said. "I just wanted to check on you and Da. How's the fishing?"

"Same as ever. The fish are in the lake and your da is waiting for them to jump on the end of his line."

"Mother, do you ever miss Ireland?"

"What ever kind of question is that? Of course I miss Ireland. Every day. But I'd miss your father more. That's the difference, lad. Why? Are you missing Ireland?"

"Some. But, lately, I guess I'm missing Grandpapa more. I know how Rosemary feels, but at least Papa died in his sleep at a ripe old age. I hope I go that way."

"Ah, Kirk, you're just feeling something you've not yet experienced till now," Edana explained, her voice going soft.

"Oh, and what might that be?"

"Well, you've never had to go through what that young lass has had to bear. But the fact that you're having some sympathy pains for her tells me a great deal—about Rosemary and about my traveling son.''

"Oh, all right, what do you mean?''

"I mean, you're maturing into a caring young man. And high time, I'd say. You've always given your best, son. Always done a good, solid job, worked hard with your body and your hands. Only this time you've put your heart into it. And once you put your heart to something, you get so much more back. But you find pain in the giving, and in the getting. And that's something you've avoided in your carefree, free-spirited gypsy life.''

"Well, you do make me sound rather shallow, Mother dear.''

"Well, you did have this nonchalant attitude about some things, son of mine.''

"Not now,'' he admitted quietly. "Not with Rosemary.''

"Will you miss her when you're gone?''

"Aye, I'll miss her a great deal.''

"That's the difference, then. You'll have to decide if you'll miss her more than you'll miss the traveling life.''

"But it doesn't really matter how I feel—I can't stay here, and I won't hurt her by causing her any more grief with her father. I have to do what I've always done. I have to walk away.''

"Without so much as a good fight?''

Kirk closed his eyes and remembered the feel of Rosemary's soft lips nestled close to his own. He remembered the curl of her hair under his palm. He remembered the bright hope in her eyes when she told him that he'd given her that, for a while at least. Rosemary was a fighter; she was willing to fight off her despair with only a glimmer of hope. She was willing to put her faith into God's promise, sight unseen. Should he do the same?

"Your silence speaks volumes, son,'' Edana said. "Do your work, Kirk. The rest will follow.''

He gripped the phone, then looked out the tiny side window of his trailer. "I...don't want to lose my heart, Mum.''

"That, my dear boy, is something you have no say over.''

Kirk finished his conversation then went back outside to start his day all over again. He stood there, looking up at the strong tower and the rising steeple of the church, wishing desperately he could fix Rosemary's hurts in the same way he knew he could fix the aging spires of Alba's antique church.

Then he remembered his mother's words.

Slow and steady, with great care for details.

Should he handle Rosemary in just that way?

He lifted up a silent prayer for guidance and for strength. And if he had to lose his heart, he decided, he wanted Rosemary to be the one to find it.

"This time, Mother, I think I'm willing to stay and fight." He just hoped he had the courage to see it through.

While Rosemary and Kirk both sought counsel on their mutual problems, Faye Lewis searched out Clayton Brinson to see how he was faring with this new development.

"Don't blame Rosemary," Faye said now as she handed him a cup of freshly brewed coffee to go along with the apple bread she'd baked him the night before. "The girl honestly did not know anything about this, Clayton."

Clayton looked over at the woman who'd been a friend to his wife and him for most of their lives. Faye wasn't a pretty woman, but she wasn't unattractive, either. She was petite and slender where Eunice had been tall and voluptuous. Faye's graying hair was styled in a neat, clipped cut that framed her face with spiky curls. Eunice had worn her dark hair neatly piled on top of her head most of the time. Why was he comparing, anyway? he wondered. No one would ever compare to Eunice.

Faye was determined, to say the least. "Clayton, stop staring at me like that and listen."

"I am listening," he said on a snarl. "The bread's good, by the way."

"Thank you. Now, will you please try to be civil to your daughter when she comes home?"

He dropped his fork with a clatter. "How can I be civil to her when she's heading for sure disaster, just like before. That steeplejack ain't much better than that murderer she took up with, and look how that turned out. We're all suffering because of her selfishness."

"Clayton Brinson, you are one stubborn man," Faye said,

her eyes blazing. "Rosemary had no control over what happened, no more than you did."

"If she had listened to me, none of this would have taken place. Eunice would still be alive."

Faye glared at him. "You're so sure of that, huh?"

"Very sure."

"And you're so very sure that God decided to pick on you by taking your wife away from you?"

"Yep. God musta had it in for me, and now I've got it in for Him."

"And what do you plan on doing to God—to get even?"

"I plan on sitting right here in this house."

"Oh, your grand boycott of the church? Who do you think that's hurting—God or maybe yourself?"

"I'm not hurting any."

"Baloney." Faye got up to clean away their dessert dishes. "I've watched you this past year, Clayton. We've all been very patient with you, hoping you'd come around, praying you'd stop this nonsense and get back to church. But you just sit in this house, like you're asleep, like you're waiting for Eunice to walk back in that door." Touching him on the arm, she said, "You've got to get on with your life, man. You've got a lovely, caring daughter who's trying very hard to seek your forgiveness, and you've got a son who buries his troubles behind a sad laugh and a hard day's work. And what about that grandbaby? Do you want little Emily to grow up without knowing the love and the faith that sustained you all these years? What kind of example are you setting for that child?"

Clayton slammed both hands down on the table, then stood to tower over her. "I don't recall asking your advice on this, Faye."

"No, you haven't asked my help on anything," she replied tartly. "And you haven't asked me how much I miss my friend, or how much the church misses Eunice, or how much your daughter is hurting. You haven't asked anything of anyone because you're too busy wallowing in your own pity to see that others are hurting, too."

"Nobody can be hurting the way I am," he said in a voice

soft with emotion and hard with bitterness. "You don't know a thing about how I feel."

She placed a hand on her chest and sighed. "Maybe you're right there. But I do know that when my Alton died, I lost my heart. But because I had the strength of this church and God's assurance that we'd be together again one day, I managed to dig myself out of my gloom. Death isn't easy for any of us, Clayton. And blaming others only makes it harder. Isn't it time you stop blaming and start back to praying and thanking God for your blessings?"

"I think you'd better go now," he said, turning away to head into the sheltered darkness of the den. "I don't want to miss 'The Price Is Right.'"

Mad, Faye shouted after him. "Oh, the price is right, all right. And you'll wind up paying a high one if you don't change." When he didn't respond, she mumbled, "Stubborn old man," then left by the back door.

Clayton plopped down in his easy chair, but his mind wasn't on the bright new car the game-show host was trying to give away. For the first time in a long time, Clayton was thinking about something other than his own sorrow. For the first time in over a year, he picked up the worn, dog-eared Bible that had belonged to his wife. He didn't read it, but just held it, his eyes centered blankly on the television.

Rosemary met Faye in the church yard as she was on her way back from making some copies in the office. "Faye, what's going on?"

"Nothing for you to worry about," Faye said. "I just had a nice visit with your father. He's better now."

Rosemary saw the high color in Faye's flushed cheeks. "You don't have to pretend with me. He's furious and he blames me again."

"Don't worry about it," Faye said, taking her by the arm to walk with her back to the educational building. "I gave him a good talking-to, but I don't know if I helped or hindered you. I do know he wants you to stay away from Kirk, though."

"That won't be a problem," Rosemary remarked, her eyes scanning the church. Glad to see that Kirk and Eric had knocked off for lunch, she turned to Faye. "I won't be overtly friendly with the steeplejack anymore. How can I, when he's gone and hired Eric right under my nose?"

Faye craned her neck, then frowned. "Rosemary, you sounded a lot like your daddy just then. It would be a shame to stay mad at Kirk for something he had no control over."

"He could have sent Eric packing once he found out the truth."

"He needed someone to help him, and since he had nothing to do with what happened, I guess he chose Eric based on the facts of his work record and a plea from the reverend."

Rosemary pushed a bouncing curl off her face. "Oh, I know, and Eric fit the bill. This is so complicated. Sometimes I wish I'd never found out about such a thing as a steeplejack."

"The church needed a restoration," Faye reminded her. Then, turning to pat her on the cheek, she added, "And maybe, sweet lady, so did you."

Over the next few days, Rosemary thought about what Faye had said to her as she attended church and listened to Reverend Clancy's sermon on grace, then started her week watching Kirk going about his work. He was a presence in her life now, good or bad, and she couldn't get him out of her mind or out of her sight.

Oh, but watching him was like watching a ballet in motion, or a song lifting out on the wind. He moved with such grace and such confidence, extended in his tiny chair from heavy cable lines draped over the sturdy steeple columns. He washed and scoured the granite facings, polishing the stones until they shone like precious gems. He lifted away rust spots and fixed leaking corners. He climbed ever higher to nail down loose shingles and replace broken ones. He lovingly washed the stained glass, and good on his word, he walked up the mountain to consult with Aunt Fitz since she had pictures of the church from way back.

Rosemary had heard this last bit of information from Melissa, who'd heard it from Eric. Rosemary didn't want to think about Eric, so she pretended he didn't exist and avoided watching the work when he was involved.

But she couldn't avoid her feelings for Kirk.

Rosemary marveled in the lines of his body, with its sculptured muscles and tanned skin. She appreciated the artistic nature of his work, and the way he took such pains with each detail of his job. He was a beautiful man, a gentle man, who'd been thrust into something beyond his control.

Maybe Faye was right. Maybe she shouldn't blame Kirk for something she had started. Tonight, as she sat reading her Bible, she prayed as Reverend Clancy had advised her to do. But when she got to the part about asking forgiveness for Eric, her stomach knotted and her head began to pound. She couldn't bring herself to form the words.

Hopping up, she went to the open window of her bedroom to take in the scent of the honeysuckle growing near the back fence. Bugs hissed at the screen, seeking the light from her tiny bedside lamp. The night was sweet and crisp, fresh and enticing. A soft flow of light shone from the tiny trailer parked across the way.

What was he doing in there? Was he reading one of the many books she'd seen stacked here and there in the small space he called home? Was he lying there on that narrow cot, wondering how he'd ever gotten caught up in such a twisted mess? Was he regretting that he'd gotten to know her?

He was lying there, and he was regretting that he couldn't see her, talk to her, kiss her. They'd established a quiet truce since the first of the week, when he'd looked down to find her in the play yard with the children. Each of them went about their work, methodically doing what had to be done, but they no longer laughed or waved or talked between chores. There were no more invitations to lunch, or supper, and no more hikes up the mountain.

Rosemary was punishing him for working with the man who'd killed her mother. Or maybe, she was punishing herself by denying her feelings.

Kirk rose from the cot to throw on a T-shirt and a pair of jeans. He needed some fresh air. He needed to talk to Rosemary. Slamming the trailer door behind him, he walked out underneath the great oak and automatically set his sights on the house across the street.

The image he saw in the window at the rear of the house took his breath away.

Rosemary. Rosemary silhouetted by the light of a single, muted lamp. Rosemary in a white cotton gown that fluffed out over her shoulders with demure ruffles and fell around her curves in pristine folds. She was standing there, bracing her hands on the frame, her head tossed back as she sniffed the night.

Kirk stood staring, his heart pounding a beat that scared him with its intensity. He couldn't move; didn't want to move. He simply waited.

Instinctively, Rosemary brought her head down. Someone was watching her. She knew it. Felt it as a fine chill moved up her spine. She looked over at the trailer and saw him standing there, one hand braced on the pole of his awning-covered side porch.

Kirk.

At first, she started to turn away. After all, she was standing here in her gown and even though it was made of a thick white cotton, it was still her nightgown. And also, she didn't want to see him—that would make her ache even more, longing for something she had no business wanting.

But she didn't turn away. She just stood there, her eyes moving over him, memorizing him, her soul reaching for him, calling to him, until finally he started walking toward her.

"Oh no," she said, turning quickly to grab a floral robe to throw over her gown. Quickly, she tied it tightly around her waist, making sure she was decent. But she didn't put the window down, nor did she run away.

She simply waited.

And he came.

"Rosemary?"

"Hello." Kirk stood eye-level with the window. She couldn't see his face in the shadows, but she could smell the spicy soap-clean scent of him.

"Are you all right?" He couldn't see her face, and that irritated him to no end since he wanted to reach out and touch her sweet-smelling hair.

"I'm okay. How about you?"

"I couldn't sleep."

"Me neither. I was reading the Bible, and trying to pray."

He smiled at the innocent admission. "Did you?"

"Did I what?"

"Did you...were you able to say your prayers?"

Rosemary leaned down, then fell to her knees so her face would be level with his. It was her undoing. Kirk's intense eyes centered on her face, burning her with such a sharp, heated appraisal that she blushed all the way to her feet. "I...I had to give up. I'm just having a hard time with all of this."

"Me, too. I'm so sorry if I caused you any pain."

"I told you—no more apologizing."

"You've been avoiding me."

"Yes. It's for the best, Kirk."

"Why, Rosemary? Why is it for the best? We...we were just getting to know each other."

"You don't need to know me. You don't want to know me," she said on a shaky whisper. "It's for the best."

"Stop saying that," he hissed, his face close to the screen, his eyes flashing fire. "You have nothing to be ashamed of, and I really *want* to know you. I don't care about your past, except to understand it. We shouldn't let this thing with Eric come between us."

"But it has," she said, placing her hands underneath her chin as she gazed at him. "I'm almost glad, too. Seeing Eric reminded me of all I've done, of how I've hurt my daddy and my brother. I can't do that again, Kirk."

"So you'll just forget how we feel, because your father doesn't approve of me."

"No, I'll remember how I felt when my mother died, and know that it's because of me—my own father doesn't love me anymore because of what I did."

Frustrated, Kirk stomped a foot on the ground. "How can you blame yourself—simply because you were engaged to Eric? You had no way of knowing he'd have a wreck with your mother."

She lowered her head for a minute, ashamed to look him in the eye. "But I knew he had a problem. Kirk, I knew Eric had a drinking problem and I did nothing about it."

Kirk's heart went out to her. "What could you have done?"

"I should have broken things off with him, but I thought…I thought I could change him."

"Why would you want to marry him in the first place?" From what Kirk had seen of her ex, the man had major problems to begin with, problems he was only now coming to grips with. "You can do better than that."

She looked up, laughing bitterly. "That's exactly what my daddy used to tell me. But I didn't want to listen to him because I thought I loved Eric. I was so sure, so secure in that love, that I was blinded by the truth."

Suddenly, Kirk realized what he was up against. She wouldn't make the same mistake twice, no matter how attracted she was to him. Because she would deny her feelings, thinking she didn't deserve them, thinking she was wrong to even feel anything for him. Thinking she'd finally win her father's approval and forgiveness if she showed him how strong she could be.

"Don't do this, Rosemary," he said. "Don't punish yourself or me this way. Forget Eric, forget your father. Think about us, think about the mountain. Think about this."

He reached up a hand, touching it to the screen, his eyes touching on her. "Put your hand on mine, Rosemary."

"No," she said, a plea in the one word. "I can't."

"Rosemary," he said, "touch me. God doesn't want you to be alone. He's not cruel that way. Together, with His guidance, we can figure this out."

"No," she said again, her heart breaking. "Let's just leave it the way it is."

"I can't do that," he admitted, slamming his hand against the screen hard enough to rattle it.

"Go," she whispered, glancing back over her shoulder. "Before we wake Daddy."

"I'll wake him," Kirk replied, angry now. "I'll wake this whole town and tell all of them that I care about you and I want to be with you and there's nothing wrong with that."

Hearing him say that made her realize she felt the same way, but she was still afraid to make good on her feelings. She didn't have his nerve, after all.

So she sat there, looking down at the man who'd come into her life and started her heart beating again.

Was this wrong? She didn't have the answers, but she knew who did. And she knew that Kirk was right. She'd asked God to forgive her, to give her a second chance. Maybe this was that chance.

Slowly, she reached out a hand, stretching her fingers over the thin mesh that separated her from Kirk, touching her palm across the wiry screen.

Kirk placed his hand against hers, and felt the warmth of her skin through the brittle barrier dividing them.

"Tell me you'll pray about this, Rosemary. Promise me you'll ask God to guide us."

"I will," she said, meaning it. "I'm asking Him right this very minute. Please, Lord, show us the way."

"And so will I." He looked up, toward the velvety sky. "We only ask that You show us the right way, the way that was meant to be." Not used to making such appeals, he added, "Whatever happens, we place our lives in Your hands."

"That was beautiful, Kirk," Rosemary said. "Thank you."

Kirk pressed his hand there, near hers, his eyes searching her face in the moonlight, while the heavens watched and the angels listened.

And he prayed someone up there had heard their plea.

Chapter Eight

Things changed between Kirk and Rosemary after that night. They were in a soft truce, both treading lightly toward what they hoped would be a lasting relationship.

Yet the realities of everyday life seemed to get in their way, in spite of their prayers for guidance. Rosemary would find herself watching Kirk work, only to see Eric down on the ground gathering supplies, or worse, climbing the steeple to assist Kirk as the work became more intense and dangerous. At these times, Kirk would look around, his gaze searching her out as if to reassure her.

She tried very hard not to resent Eric, but the pain was still too great. And the bitterness—she wondered if that particular emotion would ever go away entirely.

Today, she was heading up the mountain to a quilting session at Aunt Fitz's cabin, hesitant to get back into quilting since her ill-fated wedding. But Aunt Fitz had asked and Rosemary couldn't say no to the old woman, so now Faye and Melissa joined her just outside the church grounds. It was Saturday, a cloudy, rain-threatening Saturday, but a good day to start the quilt Aunt Fitz was making for one of her granddaughters.

"Why she insisted we come and help, I'll never understand," Melissa said as they started up the winding path. "She knows I failed sewing class."

"You know Aunt Fitz," Faye replied, holding on to Rosemary so she could make a particular curve in the path. "She likes to mix in lessons on life with her quilting. She's probably heard all the latest news and wants to set us straight on how to deal with it.''

"Meaning me," Rosemary said, her gaze moving back down the path.

She hadn't seen Kirk this morning. Usually on Saturdays, he went hiking or visiting the shops in the village. Sometimes, though, he just kept on working. Which meant only a couple more weeks and he'd be through. They were aiming for Easter Sunday as the dedication for the restoration.

Thinking of Sundays, Rosemary suddenly realized she'd never seen Kirk in church on Sunday. Where did he go when everyone else was singing hymns and praising God? She'd be sure to invite him to tomorrow's service if she saw him before then.

"Maybe you, since you seem to be struggling with so much these days. This will do you good. Aunt Fitz's advice is usually as sage as her spices and herbs.''

"And just as full-strength." Melissa laughed, then tossed her head. "Well, I can tell her I just got rid of that new boyfriend. Things didn't work out. He wanted to play the field, so to speak.''

"Melissa, child," Faye exclaimed. "You have the worst luck with men.''

"Yes," Melissa agreed. "And I intend to tread lightly from now on.''

Rosemary was only half listening to the conversation. Following this path brought back memories of being here with Kirk. True, they'd agreed to slow down and let God guide them in this growing relationship, but she couldn't help being impatient. She felt time slipping away; Kirk would be leaving soon. Then what?

"Frowning causes wrinkles," Melissa teased. "Thinking about your steeplejack?''

"No. Yes." Rosemary had given up on correcting people when they called Kirk "her" steeplejack. Maybe because she was beginning to consider him that herself. "I haven't had a chance to talk to him much this week.''

"She's trying to avoid upsetting her father," Faye explained as they reached the cove where the cemetery stood. "I think it's a shame you can't just be with the man. He's so nice, and handsome, to boot. What's the harm in dating him?''

"The same harm as when I dated Eric, I reckon," Rosemary replied. "My father doesn't trust my choices in men, and with good reason."

"So you intend to spend your life as an old maid?" Faye nudged her on the arm. "That would be a shame. You have a lot of love to give and Kirk seems to be willing and able."

Melissa glanced over at Rosemary, then looked up at the darkening sky. "He's different from Eric, isn't he?"

Rosemary had to agree with that. "Yes, he certainly is. He's mature and quiet-natured and rarely ever loses his cool. I believe he has a strong faith."

"Eric—was he a Christian, Rosemary?"

Rosemary looked at Melissa, surprised by the question. "He pretended to be, I think just to impress me, or to fool me maybe. And I fell for it."

"You believed in him," Faye said as they stood to take a breath. "There's a difference."

"Is there?" Rosemary automatically started walking toward her mother's grave. "I believed I could change him. I believed I could make a difference in his life, the same way my mother made a difference with my father. But somehow, I failed."

"Is that what you think?" Faye followed her up the moss-covered stone steps built into the hillside. "You know, Eunice's influence on Clayton was strong, strong enough to get him to church every Sunday. But look at him now. His own faith wasn't firm enough to sustain him. Once your mother passed on, so did Clayton's attempts at being a true Christian. Rosemary, you didn't fail. Eric just didn't have the strength to overcome his obstacles."

Rosemary stood there soaking up what her friend had just said. "You're right. Daddy gave up the pretense once Mama died. But at least he tried, for her sake."

"Eric tried, too, didn't he?" Melissa asked softly.

Rosemary gave her young friend a thoughtful look. "Yes, I guess he did." They were now standing at the foot of Eunice's grave. Rosemary looked down on the clean, pristine stone, then back up out over the mountainside. "I really miss her, especially now. I lie in bed wondering what advice she'd give me about Kirk, about everything. She always knew exactly what to say.''

Faye patted Rosemary on the back, while Melissa stood apart, her own expression grim and thoughtful. The silence was a tribute to the woman they all missed. Rosemary missed having a mother. Faye missed her friend. And Melissa remembered Eunice teaching her in Sunday school, directing the Christmas play each year and baking cookies for Vacation Bible School.

"Your mom was always involved in the church, wasn't she?'' Melissa said at last.

"Always. I took that for granted until the day of her funeral. Reverend Clancy read passages from her Bible, passages she'd marked and studied over and over again. I never knew just how devout she really was, because she didn't preach to us. She taught us by her example.''

Faye gave a soft chuckle. "That was Eunice. She used to say, 'Teach, don't preach.' And she lived by that code.'' Placing an arm around Rosemary's shoulders, she said, "Her example will help you through all of this, Rosemary. I do believe she would have approved of Kirk.''

Rosemary dropped her head to stare down on her mother's grave, then said, "She tried to approve of Eric. She wasn't sure about him, but she wanted me to be happy. And she didn't want to interfere. She offered her guidance and her opinion, when I asked for her advice. I guess that's one of the things I miss the most.''

Unlike her father, Rosemary reflected, who'd disliked Eric on sight and was always insisting she break off the relationship. Then, when the tragedy struck, her father felt proven right—and never missed a chance to remind her.

After a few minutes of silence, Rosemary turned, ready to continue their journey. "Looks like rain, after all. We might have to wait it out at the cabin.''

As they moved back up the path, Melissa said, "Is it hard, seeing Eric again?''

Rosemary didn't look back. "Very. I've had to do a lot of praying to get through these last couple of weeks.''

"He seems like a likable person," Melissa stated almost too nonchalantly. "And…he is cute."

Faye shot Rosemary a meaningful look, then they both stared at the young girl.

"So you've talked to him some?" Faye asked, her tone controlled and casual.

"A little, just in passing. He likes to tease me about chasing after the children."

"Eric used to be a big tease," Rosemary said, a sick feeling rolling through her stomach. "And a big talker. Don't let him talk you into anything, Melissa."

Melissa looked shocked. "I won't. I hardly know him. But he does seem nice. And he is trying to change."

They reached the cabin in silence. Rosemary got the distinct feeling that her young friend had been seeking her permission to get to know Eric better. Poor Melissa. Eric was an attractive man, and he didn't mind flirting with a pretty girl. Rosemary certainly knew that firsthand. She hoped he didn't influence Melissa in the same way he'd influenced her. Maybe Melissa would be wiser, knowing about his past. Maybe Melissa wouldn't be taken in by his persuasive promises. She hoped not.

Aunt Fitz was ready with the quilting rack extended and her supplies piled on a nearby chair.

"Come on in, ladies. It's kinda dark in here, what with that rain cloud overhead. Melissa, light that kerosene lantern and bring it close, child."

"Aunt Fitz, you have electricity," Melissa said, her eyes wide. "Want to turn on the overhead light?"

"Yeah, I suppose we could do that, too, though I don't think it will provide much to see by. I still forget that I've got the blasted thing."

They smiled at that. Aunt Fitz's children had insisted she get electricity and a phone after their father died. But that didn't mean she had to like either or use the modern amenities, as she told them often enough.

Rosemary settled down on her patch of the quilt, gathering her threads and needles to get started. Refusing to dwell on the dark memories creeping near in the muted light of the cabin, she said, "Mmm, do I smell bread baking?"

"Of course. We'll have some mint tea and honey and jam with it. And I got a jar of pickled peaches."

"I knew there was a good reason to come," Melissa joked. "Except I'll gain five pounds."

"You could use it," Aunt Fitz told her as she pointed her needle through a colorful piece of paisley fabric. "So, how's life treating the three of you?"

"Good."

"Fine."

"Okay."

Aunt Fitz dropped her needle to stare through her bifocals at the three women sitting in her cabin. "Sounds like we need to talk. I like enthusiasm in my quilting circles."

Outside, a clap of thunder applauded her efforts to cheer up her friends.

"It's been a busy week," Rosemary began. "I needed to get away. Thanks for inviting me, Aunt Fitz."

"How's your father, child?"

"He got upset when he found out Eric Thomas would be helping Kirk with the church restoration."

"So did his daughter," Faye reminded her.

"Yes, I was upset," Rosemary admitted. "But Reverend Clancy talked to me and told me to pray about it."

Aunt Fitz scanned Rosemary's face. "And have you?"

"I've put forth the effort, but it's not easy. Especially when Daddy still blames me for my part in all of this."

"No doubt. He still has bitter feelings toward Eric, I'm sure, so he takes that out on you."

"Very bitter feelings. And...he's even more aggravated with me...because he disapproves of my talking the church into hiring Kirk."

Faye huffed a breath. "The man actually accused her of bringing Eric back here to work with Kirk!"

Melissa sat up, her eyes wide. "But you didn't, right?"

Shocked, Rosemary stared across at the blonde. "Of course not. I never wanted to see Eric again. But Daddy thinks I still care about him."

Aunt Fitz yanked a strong cord of thread through her square. "Now, that's downright unreasonable. You broke off your wedding with the man. That Clayton always was a stubborn, proud man. Your ma, she knew how to calm him down and make him see things in a better light."

"I don't seem to have that capability," Rosemary replied, her eyes centered on the floral square she was tacking across the heavy quilt backing. The design was part of a favorite quilt pattern, the variable star. She couldn't help but remember other designs, other patterns from her own wedding quilt—packed away now, but not forgotten.

Aunt Fitz listened, all the while watching her helpers closely to make sure they did their assigned task correctly. "Remember, Rosemary, ten stitches to the inch." Then, "You have your mother in you, girl. 'Haps that's why Clayton finds it hard to look upon you. Keep trusting in the Lord, and fight the good fight, Rosemary. And in the meantime, redo that stitch right yonder on the end, child. It's puckering."

Rosemary smiled, a genuine full-faced smile. Aunt Fitz had seen her discomfort, and as usual, had forced her mind back to the task at hand. "I love you, Aunt Fitz."

"I love you, too, honey."

The rain came, drenching the green woods in a clean shower that perked up the lush ferns sprouting at random from the coves and balds. A fresh-smelling mist settled over the mountain as Aunt Fitz declared it break time because her old eyes were starting to "draw up" and because the bread was officially ready to cut.

"Better be careful going back down, children. Don't anybody slip up and break a bone."

"We'll hold on to each other," Faye said before biting into a fluffy slice of white bread dripping with honey and butter. "That was a quick shower, but we sure needed it."

Melissa came to sit on a stool by Rosemary, her blue eyes bright and eager. "So...how do you feel about Eric now?"

Rosemary thought the girl didn't possess very much tact, but she answered the question anyway. "Honestly, Melissa, I feel nothing for Eric Thomas. Absolutely nothing." Placing her cup of tea down carefully, she gazed across at her friend. "Be careful with him. I hope, I really, truly hope that he has turned his life around. But I'd hate to see you get hurt in the same way I did."

"We're just friends," Melissa said on a defensive rush. "I didn't want you to think—"

"It doesn't matter what I think," Rosemary interrupted. "I care about you, though. I can't interfere, but I can offer you my opinion."

"I appreciate your concern," Melissa said, her smile tight and controlled. Then she touched Rosemary on the arm. "You are a lot like your mother, you know. And I understand why it's hard for you to see Eric in a different way."

No, you don't, Rosemary thought, touched by Melissa's comparison of her to her mother, yet worried by the girl's impressionable nature. Melissa was young, several years younger than Rosemary. And Eric was clever and manipulative, and very convincing. She'd said she wouldn't interfere, but she wouldn't stand by and let him get away with it again, that was for sure.

A knock rattled the screen door of the cabin, then a deep voice called out, "Hello, Aunt Fitz. Got a cup of hot tea for a wet and chilled soul lost on the mountain?"

"Kirk?" Aunt Fitz lifted up with a spurt of energy, her old eyes twinkling with the sure knowledge that things were about to perk up around here. "Come on in, boy. You look like a drowned rat."

Actually, Rosemary thought as her heart hit the pit of her stomach, he looked wonderful. His dark hair was drenched, but he had tugged it back, slicking it down across his head to reveal the broad lines of his forehead. He wore a flannel shirt and torn jeans, and his hiking boots.

When he looked up to find the room full of women, his eyes stopped on Rosemary as if she were the only occupant of the suddenly tiny room. Without blinking or taking his eyes away, he said, "Good afternoon, ladies. Did I interrupt some secret meeting?"

Aunt Fitz went along with his assumption. "Oh, yes. A highly clandestine meeting of the minds. No men allowed."

Kirk laughed nervously. "Maybe I'd be better off out in the rain."

Aunt Fitz chuckled, then urged him into the room. "Sit yourself down, son. We're jest stitching a quilt for my granddaughter's wedding."

At the reference to a wedding, Rosemary lowered her head. Kirk didn't miss the gentle action.

Faye handed him a dish towel to dry his face. "What brings you up the mountain?"

"I took a hike," he said, his gaze holding Rosemary's when she looked back his way. "There's this one particular spot I've fallen in love with."

Aunt Fitz nodded her understanding. "Sit a spell with us, then. We're taking a little break from our work."

Kirk did sit, his eyes shifting to the colorful quilt across the room. "A wedding on the mountain, then? That will be a blessed event."

Aunt Fitz gave him a direct look. "Weddings are always blessed events. How come you ain't never hitched yourself up with a good woman, Kirk?"

"Never found the right one, I suppose," he replied as he took a long sip of the strong tea Aunt Fitz had slid in front of him, his eyes still on Rosemary.

The direct intensity of his eyes heated her, making her shift uncomfortably on her stool. Faye and Melissa both sat mesmerized by the silent courting ritual going on between the two of them, but Aunt Fitz worked the room like a pro.

"A good partner is sure hard to find," she said as she placed a hunk of buttered bread before him. "I sure had me a good match. My Samuel, now that was a fine man. Came up the mountain a'courting, went down the hill to his own wedding. Never knew what hit him."

Kirk finally tore his gaze away from Rosemary. "I guess you set him straight right away, Aunt Fitz."

She chuckled again, the movement causing the wide ruffle on her rickrack-edged apron to shake. "I laid down the law first thing. I told him I was a God-fearing, Christian woman and I wouldn't cotton to no drinking, smoking or cussing in my home. Then I told him I wanted lots of children and enough land to plant a good garden.''

Kirk chewed his bread, then sat back to give her a broad grin. ''Obviously he agreed to your stipulations.''

''Oh, he agreed all right. Stuck around for over fifty years, until the good Lord called him home.''

''Fifty years.'' Kirk looked over at Rosemary again. ''I've never stayed in one place longer than a few months.''

''You had a home once, didn't you, though?'' Melissa asked, surprising everyone.

''Aye, county Cork in Ireland was my home growing up. But once we moved back to the States, I got the wandering spirit. I never could get settled here for some reason.''

''Maybe you didn't want to leave Ireland,'' Faye said quietly.

''I never bothered to give it much thought,'' he admitted. ''I was young though, and resented having to leave my friends, even though I'd heard so much about America. I think that's why I took off—I wanted to see what everyone was talking about.''

''And have you seen enough yet?'' Aunt Fitz asked.

''I'm beginning to think it's time to slow down a bit,'' he said, his gaze once again seeking out Rosemary. ''My mother would be thrilled to hear that. She wants me to give her grandchildren before they cart her off to the old folks' home.''

Aunt Fitz clapped her wrinkled hands in approval. ''Children are a blessing. Best handled with great care.''

Rosemary jumped up off her stool. She was warm, too warm, in the close confines of the room, with all this talk of weddings and babies and with Kirk's eyes watching her every move. ''I...I think I'll step out onto the porch. I do love to watch the rain.'' Smiling at Aunt Fitz, she added, ''Don't worry. I won't shirk my quilting duties. I've just about got that star stitched.''

''It's a lovely star, too,'' Aunt Fitz said after her retreating back. ''A corner star—solid and tightly stitched.''

''Why, thank you,'' Rosemary said over her shoulder.

Faye and Melissa watched Kirk as he watched Rosemary. Aunt Fitz winked over at them from her spot by the stove.

It took all of two seconds for Kirk to stand up to follow

Rosemary. "I enjoyed the tea and bread, Aunt Fitz. I think I'll go out and look over your gourd collection before I leave."

"Suit yourself," the old woman replied, bowing her head to him. "My gourds are mighty pretty."

"Yes, she is—I mean, yes, they are." Embarrassed, Kirk made a beeline for the door.

The remaining women grinned silently as they went back to their stitching.

"He's got it bad," Aunt Fitz whispered.

He did have it bad. Nervous and unsure, Kirk pulled up to the railing beside Rosemary, needing to talk to her, wanting to be with her, and all the while thinking fifty years was a long time to stay with one person. Then she looked up at him with that endearing, innocent, hesitant smile and he realized fifty years might not be nearly long enough to spend with her.

As if sensing his doubts, Rosemary tried to smooth things over. "Aunt Fitz prides herself on her matchmaking skills. No wonder she's always making a new quilt for yet another wedding."

Kirk relaxed a little at her pragmatic observation. "Poor Samuel. The man probably stayed on a very tight leash."

Frowning, Rosemary replied, "Not a leash, Kirk. More like a tight bond, a connection that joined them together. He wanted to be with her. And he was so attached to her, so very caring and solicitous of her feelings. They were a special couple."

He sighed, then stepped closer. "I meant no disrespect. Actually, I'm in awe of the whole thing. And it's made me take a good, hard look at my own philosophy on life."

Taking this opportunity to find out more and get her mind off her own failure as a bride, Rosemary asked, "And just what is your philosophy on life?"

He snorted. "Just that. Just a philosophy, never applied. Up until now, my whole attitude was one of shallowness and a definite stance against any form of commitment other than my work, at least according to my dear mother."

Intrigued, she said, "And…was your mother right?"

"I'm afraid so." His gaze moved over her features. "But

I'm working hard on changing all of that. You talked about
how I'd given you hope, remember?''

She remembered. Nodding, she matched his gaze with one
of her own, her breath holding against her ribs as she waited
for his next words.

''Well, Rosemary, you've given me something I'd neglected
to nurture in my solitary existence.''

''Oh, and what's that?''

''You've given me back my faith, and my ability to trust in
God's plan for my life.''

Surprised, she frowned. ''But your faith seems so solid to
me.''

He touched a hand to her hair. ''Oh, it's solid. But it was
much like your precious church building. Built on a firm base,
built to last, but it needed rejuvenating.''

Touching her nose with a finger, he added, ''I guess I needed
to see that life isn't an easy road. Before, I could simply pack
up and move on. Now I'm starting to realize that in order to
be strong in our faith, sometimes we have to face tough obstacles. I teased you about being afraid of heights. Well, I'm just
as afraid, but it's a different kind of fear.''

''So even though you're able to leap tall buildings, you're
unable to take a leap of faith?''

''Exactly. Or I was before. That's changed now, though. Because of Reverend Clancy, and Aunt Fitz, but mostly because
of you, I'm beginning to see that in order to win what we want,
in order to achieve our goals, we have to depend on a source
beyond our control.''

Rosemary swallowed back the dryness in her throat. As his
finger drifted down the line of her cheek, she ignored the little
tingling sensations cresting in the pit of her stomach, to ask,
''And what exactly has changed, as far as your goals in life?''

''Only one thing,'' he said honestly, his eyes meeting hers.
''Now I want to share my journey with someone else, that spe-
cial someone who makes it all worthwhile and complete. I think
I want to stick it out, for fifty years or longer at least.''

She closed her eyes as he lowered his head to kiss her, then
quickly opened them again to glance sideways, concerned about
being seen.

"Don't worry," he whispered. "We have three very capable chaperons and—don't look now—but they're all watching us through the kitchen window. I won't do anything to embarrass you."

Glad to know he was aware of her feelings and their audience, she concentrated on the question burning a hole in her brain. She had to ask, had to hear him say it. "Who is this special someone, Kirk?"

He kissed her then, a quick, feathery touch that left her breathless and wanting.

Then he nudged her chin so she could see into his eyes. "You," he whispered. "Only you."

Rosemary forgot all about the three women watching them from inside. She let him kiss her again, and she kissed him back, meaning it with all of her heart, wanting it with all of her being.

Inside, Aunt Fitz shooed away the nosy observers, her smile gentle, her eyes watery as she ordered her charges to get back to stitching. "Soon as we're finished here, I think it's time to pull out that quilt we made for Rosemary." She motioned toward the couple out on her porch. "And I do so hope this time, she gets to use it."

Unaware of her friend's hopeful words, Rosemary rested against Kirk's broad chest, watching as the rain began to fall again in a gentle rendering, its water washing over the hills to clean away the residue of winter, bringing with it the sure promise of spring.

Chapter Nine

"Those two are certainly becoming mighty friendly," Faye said a few days later as she stood at the window watching Melissa and Eric laughing and talking out in the prayer garden.

"Yes," Rosemary agreed, keeping her eyes purposely averted. "And I can't stomach it."

Faye turned back to helping Rosemary divvy out cookies and fruit juice for the children's morning snack. "Have you tried talking to her?"

"I warned her straight off," Rosemary said. She counted the cookies to make sure each child had the same amount. "But it's not my place to tell her how to live her life. She'd only think I was doing it because of my resentment toward Eric."

"That's probably true." Faye finished pouring the juice, then placed the container back in the large refrigerator located in the church social hall. "Maybe I should talk to her. Poor girl. Her parents don't come to church with her. I wonder if they even know she flutters from one boy to the next."

Putting away the cookie container, Rosemary shook her head. "I doubt it. I don't think they've given her a very solid foundation. From what she tells me, they fight all the time and generally make her own life miserable. She took this job to pay for her night courses at college because they don't have the money to finance her education, or the inclination to encourage her."

"That's a shame. She's a sweet girl."

"Which Eric will take full advantage of."

Faye leaned into the counter to study Rosemary's frowning expression. "Is that what happened with you?"

Rosemary looked off into the long, dark hall filled with tables and chairs for the Wednesday-night supper meeting. "No. I mean, maybe. But I take responsibility for my failures with Eric. I knew he had problems, I just didn't want to admit it."

"And now that's why you're being so cautious with Kirk?"

"Yes. Although there is no comparison between the two."

Faye lifted the tray full of juice cups. "No, not at all. So don't be unfair to Kirk. Honey, the way that man looks at you— you'd be an idiot to let him get away."

After Faye left with the juice, Rosemary stayed behind to make a fresh batch for the afternoon break. Naturally, her thoughts shifted to Kirk. In spite of her growing feelings for him, she still didn't have the answers to their particular problems.

First, there was her father, of course. She'd managed to keep him calm and consistent in his indifference by avoiding any mention of Kirk or the work on the church and steeple. And she didn't dare stop and talk to Kirk outside the church, where her father might see them together.

In fact, the only time she managed with Kirk was during one of their chance meetings, such as up at Aunt Fitz's cabin the other day. That particular meeting still lingered like a sweet dream in her consciousness, making her hum with joy and happiness. Chance meetings were one thing, but despite Kirk's sweet admission, a lasting relationship still seemed impossible. In order to have that with any man, she had to win back her father's approval and love.

And mostly, his blessings.

Then of course, she knew Kirk would be moving on soon. And he knew it, too, even though neither of them had talked about it the last time they'd been together. Yet it was there between them, and needed to be discussed. Would Kirk pledge his heart to her, then simply pack up and leave?

Would he ask her to go with him?

In her heart, she wanted to go. But in her mind, she knew it would be impossible. She had to stay here for now, near her father. She had made a pledge to see him through this horrible time, to help him find his faith again.

She wouldn't abandon him, even for the man she...loved.

A small gasp escaped from Rosemary's parted lips as the realization hit her full force. Shocked and embarrassed, she glanced around the empty hall to make sure no one was watching her, as if her true feelings had just been teletyped across her forehead.

She loved Kirk. Maybe she'd loved him from the first time she'd heard his voice, or seen him standing there with the church in the background. It didn't matter; what did matter was the new responsibilities that came with that love. She'd have to be very sure this time. She'd gone against her father's wishes once before, and it had only brought her family tragedy.

She turned to take the second tray out to the room across the catwalk where the children were finishing up their alphabet lessons, only to find Eric standing there staring at her.

"Oh, you startled me," she said, anxious to get away from him, and afraid he'd be able to read her thoughts.

But when she tried to move past, he reached out a hand to stop her. "You could be civil, at least, Rosemary."

Gripping the heavy plastic tray so tightly her knuckles turned white, she lifted her chin in defiance. "I don't have to be civil to you, Eric. Now let me by. I have work to do."

"Ah yes. Taking care of the children, such a sweet and noble profession. But then, you always were sweet and noble. And so sanctimonious. Does it even matter to you that I'm trying very hard to make a new beginning?"

"Yes, it matters," she said in a tight, controlled tone. "I'm glad you're making a fresh start, but I can't be a part of it."

He folded his arms over his chest, then leaned back against the doorjamb. "That's because you think you're so much better than me. You always did, didn't you? You went on and on about the church and your beliefs, hoping some of that holier-than-thou junk would rub off on me, didn't you?"

"Yes," she said, angry that he'd make fun of her convictions. "But obviously I failed at trying to save you, Eric. And it looks like you still haven't learned anything from what you've done."

"Oh, I've learned," he said, coming close so his face was near hers. "I've learned that I never want to go back to prison. I've learned how it feels to know I've killed another human being. And...I've learned what it's like to be turned away from the very people who wanted to turn me into a decent Christian man. I've learned I can't trust any of you, because you all spout out one thing when you really mean another."

Shaking now, Rosemary tried to move past him. "Eric, I don't want to discuss this with you. I'm trying so hard, so very hard, to find it in my heart to forgive you."

"Don't do me any favors," he said, the words ringing loudly in the empty hall. "I don't want your forgiveness. I only wanted your love—that's all I ever wanted."

"And you know I can't give that anymore," she said, tears brimming in her eyes. "Now, let me go."

He stepped forward, but a strong arm from behind stopped him from touching Rosemary. Shocked, Eric turned to find Kirk glaring at him from the open entry doors.

"You heard the woman," Kirk said, his eyes almost black with rage. "Now, if you want to keep working for me, you'd better get back out there and finish putting that weatherproofer on the roof beams."

Eric rolled his eyes, then lifted a hand. "Fine. I just came in to get a drink of water. I didn't mean any harm."

"I'll keep that in mind," Kirk replied, his gaze moving to Rosemary. "From now on, I'll set a watercooler outside so you won't have any reason to venture inside the educational building."

"That's very thoughtful," Eric said in a sarcastic tone.

Kirk watched Eric walk past, then said, "This will be your final warning, Thomas. I hired you in good faith. I expect you to do your job and stay away from Rosemary."

Eric snorted. "Right, so you can have her? I've heard all about you two—pretty hot and heavy, huh?"

In a blur of motion, Kirk pounced on the smaller man and sent him crashing back up against a concrete wall. Rosemary screamed and dropped the tray of cookies, her heart pumping with fear, humiliation coloring her face.

Kirk pressed Eric close to the wall, one hand firmly gripping his throat. "I'm not going to waste my energy on hitting you, Eric. And out of respect for Rosemary and this church, I'm not going to cause a scene. Now, get back to work, or you will be out of a job come nightfall." Lifting Eric away from the wall, he added, "Oh, and before you go, I think you owe Rosemary an apology."

Eric immediately looked sheepish. After a long, controlled sigh, he turned to Rosemary. "I'm sorry. I really am. And I am trying, Rosemary. You have to believe me. It's just hard being back here. Almost worse than being in prison, but I can't lose this job."

"Then stop losing your cool," Kirk suggested, his own temper simmering. "Now go."

He watched to make sure Eric went back out to the yard, then turned to find Rosemary on her knees picking up broken butter cookies. He didn't need to see her trembling body to know that she was shaking uncontrollably.

"Come here," he said, dropping onto the floor beside her.

She pushed him away. "I...I have to pick the cookies up and get more. The children are waiting."

"Rosemary, let them wait." He took both her hands in his, stopping her frantic efforts. "Rosemary, look at me."

She faced him then, her eyes red-rimmed and wet, her hair falling in soft waves around her damp, flushed face.

"Oh, Kirk." She fell into his arms like a drowning woman seeking a lifesaver. "Oh, Kirk."

"Shh," he said, kissing her hair as he sat on the floor and held her close to rock her gently against him. "It's okay. It's okay. Don't think about him. Think about us, instead."

About that time, Faye came in. "All right. The natives are getting restless—" Seeing Kirk and Rosemary huddled together on the floor, she stopped. "What happened?"

"I'll explain later," Kirk said. "Will you take the cookies to the children. Rosemary is too upset right now to face them."

"Of course." Faye hurriedly grabbed the white plastic container from the refrigerator, then, skirting around them, headed out of the building again.

"Thank you," Rosemary managed to murmur against his chest. "I'm sorry I lost it like that."

"Silly," he said, running a hand over her wet face. "You had every right to lose control. Eric has a long way to go in the grace department."

"He's as bitter as my father, and he has no right to feel bitter. He's the one who messed up."

"Yes, and he's just feeling his own guilt. Believe me, I've had quite a few talks with him and he's fighting this every step of the way. He thinks he can justify his actions by making excuses, but there is no excuse for what he did. If it weren't for my promise to Reverend Clancy, I'd fire him today."

Rosemary lifted her head to stare up at him with open, luminous eyes. "How can you do that?"

"Do what?"

"How can *you* be so gracious to him, after what just happened? I wish I could be more like that."

Kirk adjusted her to a more comfortable position in his arms. "I can afford to be gracious. He didn't kill my mother. You, on the other hand, have a lot to work through before you can extend your hand to him in forgiveness."

"I don't think I can do it."

"I'm willing to help," he said as he lifted her onto her feet. "Can we go somewhere and talk?"

She shook her head. "I have to get back to the children."

"When, then? I want you to tell me everything. I want to help you through this, Rosemary."

She wanted that, too. She wanted to unload this tremendous burden once and for all. And if she really was going to have a strong relationship with Kirk, she needed to be honest with him from the very beginning.

Straightening her mussed hair, she thought for a minute, then said, "We could…we could go up the mountain after work this afternoon."

Amazed that she'd agreed to open up to him, Kirk smiled. "I'd like that. I'd like that very much."

"Me, too," she said. "But right now, I've got to go back to work." She wiped her eyes. "Do…do I look together enough?"

He kissed her quickly, then held her away for a careful inspection. With the tail of his cotton shirt, he wiped the rest of the moisture off her face, then smiled. "You look lovely."

She started to leave, then saw the broken cookies all over the floor. "Oh, I've got to clean this up."

Kirk stilled her. "I'll do it. You go, take care of your children. I'll see you this afternoon."

Rosemary hurried away, wanting to cry all over again. But not because she was upset. This time, the tears were for Kirk's kindness. It had been a long time since any man besides Reverend Clancy had offered her any form of kindness, no less such tender concern. She accepted it and wore it like a shield as she went on with her day.

From his work station, Eric watched her walk by. Rosemary glanced up in time to see the regret in his eyes. That regret didn't soothe her one bit. It only made her more determined to get past all of this, no matter how much it hurt.

The Wednesday-night suppers were a tradition at the church. Different groups took turns cooking or furnishing the meal, and the rest of the congregation paid a small fee to help cover the expense. After the meal, everyone went inside the church to listen to a short sermon and sing a few hymns. Reverend Clancy said these services and the fellowship made the middle of the week go by better.

Rosemary usually attended, but she'd missed the last couple of weeks. Tonight, she planned on inviting Kirk to go with her after their hike up the mountain.

Looking at her watch, she decided she'd better hurry. It was four o'clock. Melissa would see that the rest of the remaining children at the church school got home all right. She usually stayed late, along with another aide, so that the teachers could go home to their own families.

Rosemary buzzed out of her office, intent on getting home to fix her father's meal—a meat loaf she'd already cooked at lunch, and some potatoes and corn—before taking her walk to meet Kirk. That would give Kirk and her at least two good hours before the church supper and service.

Faye met her as she was leaving. "Feeling better, honey?"

Rosemary smiled at the older woman. "Much better. I'm

going to check on Daddy and get his dinner, then I'm going for a walk up the trail."

"With Kirk?"

"Yes." Stopping to grab Faye's arm, she asked, "Is it wrong of me to go without telling Daddy?"

Faye put a finger to her cheek. "Hmm. You said you were going for a walk. You can't help it if Kirk's planning on doing the same thing."

"I don't like being deceptive, though."

Faye took her by the arm and started walking down the cat-walk with her. "I can't blame you there, but you're not exactly being deceptive. Clayton told you to keep Kirk out of his yard. And you've done that."

"But he also told me to stop meeting Kirk on the mountain."

Faye lifted her gaze, then shrugged. "Like I said, if you both happen to be going the same way…"

"I like your logic," Rosemary said. "I just need to talk to Kirk, to explain all of this once and for all. Then I'll talk to Daddy when I get back."

"I think that's a good idea after that stunt Eric tried this morning," Faye said. "And don't worry about Clayton. I was planning on going by to see him anyway, to ask if he'd walk over to the supper with me."

"Good luck," Rosemary replied, waving a hand.

"You, too."

Faye turned to find Melissa standing in the gated door of the toddler room. She walked over to the girl. "How's it going?"

"You tell me," Melissa said in a hushed voice. "Something happened between Rosemary and Eric today, but he won't tell me anything about it. Are those two getting close again?"

"I hardly think so," Faye said, keeping a cheerful smile on her face for the benefit of the children. "They had an argument, I believe. But Rosemary's okay now."

Melissa tossed back her hair. "Well, if you ask me, she's not being fair to Eric. He only wants her to give him a chance."

"Was it fair of him to fill himself with liquor then get behind the wheel of a car and cause her mother's death?" Faye countered, her tone firm and full of fire.

"Of course not. That was a tragedy, but we're all supposed

to be Christians," Melissa said. "Shouldn't we treat Eric a little better now that he's turned his life around?"

Faye thought about that, then said, "We're giving Eric all the support we can, under the circumstances. And you're right. We owe him the benefit of the doubt."

"Including Rosemary?"

"I wouldn't worry about Rosemary," Faye told the young girl. "She's happy, for the first time in a long time, and Eric would do best to just let her be." With that, Faye waved and started toward her own office. "See you tonight at supper."

"Yeah, see you."

Bored, Melissa looked toward Kirk's trailer. Kirk emerged and started walking up the trail that led to the top of the mountain. About thirty minutes later, she saw Rosemary come down her back porch and hurry in the same direction.

"Now, that's interesting," Melissa said to herself.

Rosemary fluffed the flowing denim skirt she was wearing, then put her hands in her pockets as she approached the halfway point up the mountain. Right above her stood the cemetery. Deciding to visit her mother's grave while she waited for Kirk, she lifted her skirt to climb the stone steps. When she reached her mother's grave, she found a bundle of colorful fresh-cut flowers lying there.

Looking around, she wondered if Kirk had placed them on the grave. When she heard footsteps from a nearby ledge, she whirled to find him climbing down.

"Oh, there you are." She motioned to the flowers. "Did you do this?"

Kirk hopped over the last of the rocks, then looked down at the flowers. "No, it wasn't me. I was up on the ledge watching for you." He sent her a compassionate look. "Your father left those, Rosemary."

She looked around, afraid Clayton might still be near. "That explains why he wasn't home when I got there. I couldn't imagine where he might be since he rarely leaves the house, except to drive into town for household supplies when I remind him. But his truck was still in the shed."

"He walked up here, kneeled down for a few minutes, then left the flowers," Kirk explained. "Does he do that often?"

Tears pricked at Rosemary's eyes as she looked down on the black-eyed Susans mixed with pink phlox, white daisies and fresh red clover. "He's...he's never done this before. I've tried to get him to come up here with me, but it's always been too much for him." She reached down to touch a velvety soft cluster of phlox. "Why now?"

Kirk bent down beside her. "Maybe all of this with Eric has made him miss her even more."

Rosemary lifted her head. "Yes, that could be it. Or it might have something to do with Faye. She cares for him, but she's been holding back out of respect for my mother. Lately, though, she has been spending more time with him."

Kirk sat back to study her, thinking how gorgeous and natural she looked in her white cotton blouse, thinking no one wore their feelings more beautifully than Rosemary. Or more openly. "Does it bother you, to think your father might find happiness with another woman, maybe get married again?"

She waved a hand. "Oh no. Especially not when it might be Faye. She's a good friend, and she'd take care of Dad. She and my mother were close, so she knows how my father is—she can deal with him, I think."

"Then why the frown?"

She lifted her mouth in a smile then. "I was just thinking how I wish I could have been here with Daddy. Did he look... okay?"

Kirk hesitated a minute, then decided to be truthful with her. "He was crying, Rosemary." When she gasped, he added, "But...that might be a good sign. That might be the first step toward acceptance."

Rosemary sank onto her knees to begin automatically pulling away weeds. "You're right. I just can't stand to see him in so much pain."

Kirk stopped her weeding with a steady hand. "Wouldn't you rather see him in this kind of pain, rather than so cold and distant that no one can reach him? I mean, that has to be the worst kind of suffering."

She looked over at him, amazed that he'd managed to calm

her worries and assure her that her father was on the mend. Taking his hand in hers, she said, "Mama, I'd like you to meet Kirk. He's a good man. Very compassionate and understanding. And patient, real patient with the likes of your daughter."

Kirk laughed softly. "I could say the same about your daughter, Mrs. Brinson."

"Say a prayer with me," Rosemary told him. "For my father, and for my mother."

"And for us," he replied, his gaze holding hers.

"And for us," she agreed. "For all of us."

A little while later, they reached the peak of Alba Mountain. Rosemary found her rock and sat down to get her breath, her eyes scanning the distant peaks and valleys while Kirk strolled around to get a closer look. Off in the distance, a white spark of lightning flashed through the sky.

"Oh, looks like rain again," Rosemary said, trying hard to still the spinning in her head. If she just sat here long enough, she'd be able to enjoy this without too much vertigo. "We'd better hurry."

Kirk walked up to take a seat beside her. "Oh no. Not so fast. You promised me you'd tell me everything. Do I have to hold you up here against your will to make you do that?"

"No," she said, shaking her head. "I want to tell you the whole story, Kirk. I'm just afraid—"

He touched a hand to her hair, something he'd wanted to do since he'd spotted her coming up the trail. "Afraid that I'll turn away, like your father did?"

"You might be disgusted with me."

"I can't imagine that. Rosemary, why don't we apply some of the teachings of Jesus to this situation. One, you don't have to carry your burden alone. Jesus carried all of our burdens when He carried the cross. And two, there is no sin so great that it can't be forgiven. That's why He died for us."

Awestruck, she stared up at him, seeing the sincerity in his face, hearing the conviction in his words, fascinated by the simple truth he'd just spoken. "You really know your stuff, don't you?"

He grinned then. "Aye. My mother certainly raised me in

the best Christian tradition. I'd just forgotten my stuff until I met you.''

She leaned against him, thankful that he felt the same as she did. ''You don't know how much that means to me, that you believe in the same way as I do. That's important to me, you know.''

''I do know. And I also know that you need to talk to someone, get this off your chest. I want to listen, I'm willing to listen, and I won't condemn you, or judge you. Indeed, I have not the right to do either.''

''Okay, then,'' she said, taking a deep breath to brace herself. ''You know most of it—the worst of it. But it's important that you know the rest, so that you'll know me better, and my father, and so that you'll understand why I need to see him through this—no matter how long it takes.''

Kirk didn't like the tone of that, but he pushed the uneasy thoughts to the back of his mind. For now, she was here in his arms and they didn't have to hurry. They had a little time to be together. That alone was a blessing.

In spite of the threatening rain clouds hovering off in the distance.

Chapter Ten

"I met Eric in college," Rosemary began, her gaze moving over the blue-green, flower-sprigged hills and valleys before them. "I was so in awe of him. I guess I fell for him right off. He was funny and carefree, a star football player, and I was shy and awkward, the studious straight-A student. He captivated me."

Kirk could imagine only too well how Eric might be capable of doing just that. And, knowing Rosemary the way he did now, he could see her being demure and endearing, and completely vulnerable. "He swept you off your feet?"

"Yes, he did. And I let him," she continued, her fingers laced with Kirk's. "When I came home and told my folks, at first they were happy for me. Then when Eric started coming for visits, my daddy noticed something right away—Eric seemed too animated at times, too wound up. Daddy suspected he was drinking, but at first he didn't say anything."

"Did you know?"

"No, not at first. I was so naive, I didn't have a clue. And Eric was very careful, very secretive about what he was doing. He didn't want me to find out because he knew how I felt about such things. I told him from the first that I was a Christian. I'm not ashamed of my beliefs. My only mistake was in thinking Eric was the same. He did pretend, for my sake." She shook her head, causing her fiery hair to spill all around her face. "And to his credit, I think he wanted to be like me, wanted to change for me. But...he was already in too deep with the drinking. All of his friends did it, so it was hard for him to just give it up.''

Kirk nodded his understanding. "It's hard to resist when you're hanging around with the wrong crowd.'' At her questioning look, he said, "I went through a partying phase myself, until my grandpapa got a hold of me and set me straight. He said, 'Lad, how can ye be dangling off one-hundred-foot buildings if your head's not on straight. Liquor and steeplejacking don't mix, and your poor mother will kill me if I let anything happen to you.' He gave me an ultimatum that probably saved my life.''

"You were wise enough to listen,'' she said. "Eric wasn't listening to anything or anybody. He thought he could lead a double existence, I suppose.''

"Only it caught up with him?''

"Yes.'' She jumped as another fierce streak of lightning flashed in the distance. After a moment, she relaxed again. "People started dropping hints to me about Eric being seen drunk at places without me. At first, I passed it off, telling myself he was entitled to some time with his friends, that surely if he did take a drink, it was in moderation. Then when my brother came home telling me some people he worked with had seen Eric very drunk at a local bar, I had to listen. Of course, Danny wasted little time telling our parents. He thought he was doing what was best for me, but things got pretty ugly after that.''

"He wanted to protect his baby sister,'' Kirk reasoned. "Understandable.''

"Yes, but not to me at the time. I got so mad at him. Then when Dad tried to reason with me, I told him I loved Eric and that I would talk to him and try to make him give up the drinking.''

"How did that go?''

"Not very well. We fought and broke up, mainly because Eric said he was hurt that I couldn't trust him.'' Her voice became still for a minute as she remembered. "I was so heartbroken. I'd been sheltered and protected and Eric was my first love, and my first rejection. I thought I'd never get over him.''

Kirk gave her a grim look. "Well, obviously, you got back together."

"Yes, we did. Eric promised me he'd change. And for a while, he did try. He started coming to church with me. We had meals with my family. He gained my trust, but he also charmed my parents just enough to convince them he had dropped the drinking. Then he asked me to marry him."

"And you agreed."

"Oh, yes. I loved him, or so I thought. Mom was happy for me, but hesitant. Yet she didn't try to interfere, except to offer advice here and there. Daddy, though, did not want me to marry Eric. It caused a rift between us, the first we'd ever had. When I stood up to him and told him there was nothing he could do to stop me, I think I broke his heart. But I was young and so caught up in wanting to have a marriage and a family, I didn't see what my actions were doing to my parents."

Seeing the pain in her eyes, Kirk urged her on. "What happened next?"

Rosemary swallowed, then took a deep breath. Kirk felt the tightening of her fingers around his and waited for her to find the right words to finish her story.

"It happened a few nights after my shower—an engagement party and combined shower at the home of one of Aunt Fitz's daughters in the next town. Eric and I had attended the shower together. Daddy stayed home, angry and hurt. Danny didn't come, either—he had to work late—but his wife, Nancy, did. She was seven months pregnant with Emily, but she wanted to be there with me on my big night. The party was great—a buffet with all the trimmings, a beautiful cake, and so many gifts, so many lovely, homey things to get Eric and me off to the right start in our marriage. Aunt Fitz had made a beautiful wedding quilt for us. She presented it to me at the party, but needed to add a few finishing touches. So, a few days later, my mother went back to Aunt Fitz's daughter's house to pick it up."

She stopped, her breath leaving her body with a great trembling sigh. "Sometimes I think back on that night and wonder if I dreamed the whole thing. I can still see Mama standing there in our dining room surrounded by shower gifts, her eyes misty with tears, happy for me in spite of her misgivings, loving and caring. Her faith sustained her—she prayed for Eric and me to be happy, and then she turned it over to the Lord."

Rosemary's voice caught, but she went on in a rush. "I can still remember waving goodbye to her. We'd had supper with them, Eric and me, and he was giving me a ride back to my apartment. She said, 'You two go on, honey. You spend some time with your intended.' She kissed me, and she smiled and said, 'I'm gonna run over to Linda's house to get your wedding quilt so we can display it with the rest of your things.' Mom and Aunt Fitz and several other women from the church had worked on it together. It had a creamy-white background, with flowers and ribbons embroidered on it in mint green and rose colors. It was so beautiful. I can still remember Mom's smile, so peaceful, so serene."

Kirk wrapped an arm around her as she hung her head. "Go on, Rosemary," he coaxed.

"That was the last time I saw her. She never reached Linda's house," she said, the anguish in her broken words echoing over the still mountaintop. "Eric took me back to my apartment. We talked for a while, but he…he seemed restless. I thought he was just nervous about the wedding, so I kissed him goodnight…and he left."

Kirk's own heart began to beat a swift tempo. He knew what she was about to tell him, yet he didn't want to hear it. He also knew how very much it was costing her to tell this tragic tale. Taking her face in his hands, he held her, touching his fingers across her moist cheeks, his eyes centered on hers. "Tell me, Rosemary."

Rosemary gulped back the tears, then steadied herself, leaning into his hands, his touch, clinging to the solid strength he offered. "About an hour later, I got a call from Danny." She stopped, her own hands gripping Kirk's shoulders. "Oh, Kirk. I don't think I can—"

"Hold on tight and tell me," he said, his eyes watering up in spite of his tightly clenched jaws. "I'm here, right here."

She moaned, much like a hurt animal, then looked up at him, her eyes pleading and pain-filled. "Danny was crying. I'd never heard him cry like that. He told me to come home right then.

Something…something had happened to Mama." Her eyes held a faraway look then, as the horrible memories rushed through her. "I ran all the way down the street to Daddy's house. I could hear him screaming, screaming. He kept saying, 'No, no. Oh, God, please, no.' When I was finally able to get to him, I tried to take him in my arms. I kept asking what had happened. Danny looked at me, this strange kind of look on his face. Nancy took me by the shoulders and pulled me away from my father."

She shuddered, a lone sob racking her entire body. "Then my daddy…he looked up at me. I can't get that look out of my mind—I'd never seen him like that before. I'll never forget what he said.

"He lifted a finger to me and he…he said, 'Your mother is dead. Dead, Rosemary.'

"I remember crumbling, I remember Danny and Nancy catching me, holding me. Then I whispered, 'How?'

"Daddy jumped up, coming at me…and Danny held me away. Daddy said, 'It was him, the one you had to have. It was Eric Thomas. He was driving drunk and he ran her car off the road. He killed your mother.'"

She quieted then, her eyes brimming with tears, her hands so tight on Kirk's shoulders he could feel her fingers digging into his shoulder blades. And still, he held her, kept her steady, murmured softly against her skin.

Finally, she spoke again, her voice weak, hoarse. "I think I must have fainted then. Danny and Nancy led me to the couch, but Daddy…he just stood there staring at me with this awful vacant look in his eyes. Danny told me that…that Eric had apparently met my mother on one of the winding roads, at the spot we call the S-curve. He veered his truck over the centerline and…ran my mother's car off the road. It crashed into a ravine. They told us she died instantly."

Kirk moaned, then pulled her into his arms, rocking her much in the same way he'd done earlier that day. He felt drained, washed away, numb. Now he understood completely. Now he knew why Clayton held such denial and resentment. Now he saw how Rosemary had survived, had been sustained only by the threads of her faith. How else could anybody endure this kind of pain? No wonder she'd held it all inside for so long. It was much too unbearable to talk about.

But now that the floodgates had been opened, she did talk, softly and huskily and in a quiet, calm tone. "They took us to the scene and...I thought I would die. I wanted to die right there with my mother. It was awful, Kirk. The black night, the woods, the mountain on one side of us and that dark, deep hole on the other. And we saw, knew that was where they'd found her car, shattered and burned, broken.

"It was so awful to imagine her trapped down there, all alone in the dark. They wouldn't let us see her, not then. They wouldn't let *me* see her."

Kirk hushed her then, unable to picture the grim scene she must be reliving. After a minute, he asked, "So...there was no hope?"

She moved her head against his chest, frantically, hurriedly. "No hope. No hope. Dead on impact." Then she moaned again and wrapped herself against the shelter of his arms. "Eric had called the authorities from a nearby house. He walked away! Walked away after his truck skidded to a stop a few feet from a pull-off—a place where people stop to enjoy the view."

Without realizing it, she lifted away from Kirk, then started beating her fists against his chest. "I hate that view. I get sick to my stomach if I even have to drive that way. I hate that view because each time I go there I can still see the shape of the car down in that ravine. I can see them handcuffing Eric and I can hear him calling to me, telling me how sorry he was, telling me he didn't know it was her. He didn't know he'd killed my mother until we arrived at the scene.

"And my father—I remember him trying to...to climb down the side of the mountain to get to her, and Danny holding him back, both of them crying. Oh, Kirk, my father kept calling her name over and over."

The raw pain in her eyes sliced through Kirk. Stopping her almost hysterical movements, he took both her hands in his, stilling her. "Hush, hush. Rosemary, look at me, love. I'm here and I do not blame you. Do you understand what I'm saying to you? Do you?"

Rosemary stared up at him, her gaze searching his face for

condemnation. She saw none. Instead, she saw compassion, sorrow, pain and...absolution. "How can you touch me?" she asked, disgusted with herself. "How can you forgive me, when...when I can't forget what I caused, when I can't look at myself in the mirror without wanting to be sick."

"I don't need to forgive you," he said. "God already has. And for you to turn away from that forgiveness, that unconditional love, is a sin in itself."

Her features sharpened in surprise. "How can I expect God to forgive me, Kirk? My father can't. My brother pretends to, but I know, I know that deep down he resents me because of what happened. I was so intent on getting married I became selfish. I ignored all the warnings. I knew Eric wasn't so sure about the marriage, but I was determined to make it work. He couldn't deal with the pressure so he drank even more. I pushed him to this, Kirk. It's all my fault, so you see I don't deserve your forgiveness. I don't deserve their forgiveness or their love. I don't deserve yours, either."

"No," he shouted, the echo of the one word crashing against the distant mountains and vibrating back to them. "No, Rosemary, I won't let you continue to do this. I won't let you go on punishing yourself for something you had no control over. It was Eric's responsibility to stop drinking, not yours."

The lightning clashed, closer now, threatening them with its white-hot intensity. A clap of thunder followed a few seconds later.

"We need to go," she said, pulling away from him, suddenly unable to face him after her full and complete confession.

"No, not yet. You have to see—you can't go on living this way." He held her even as the first drops of rain splattered across their skin. "Rosemary, you have to forgive yourself or...or everything you believe will only be a sham."

"Let me go," she said, gripping the rock to find her footing. "I didn't tell you all of this to ask for forgiveness. I don't know why I told you. I'm...I'm so ashamed, so ashamed. I want to go home now."

But Kirk refused to let her run away. "No, Rosemary," he said. "We're not finished yet."

The rain started pouring harder now. She looked up at him,

letting the rain wash over her, hoping that God's glorious power would wash all her sins and doubts and fears away. But she knew it wouldn't be easy. As strong as her faith had always been, she'd fought against using it to heal herself. Because she didn't believe she deserved to be healed. Better to bear the scars as a reminder of her mistakes.

Indeed, she'd been fighting against absolution since the moment she'd seen the twisted wreckage of her mother's car. Afraid now, she said, "We need to go, Kirk."

Kirk lifted his face to the cool rain. The fresh wetness hit his fevered skin, sending a refreshing, awakening chill over his body. Then he looked back down at Rosemary, and knew in his heart that he wanted, needed, to be here with her, rain or shine, good or bad.

Pulling her into his arms, he shouted over the rain's increasing fury. "Rosemary, I...I can't let you go. I love you. Do you understand me? I love you."

She heard his words coming through the storm. Her heart lurched, bumped against her being, moved beyond a mere beating. It pumped with new life, new joy, through her battered system. "How can you say that?" she asked, amazed that he could even stand to be near her.

Kirk reached out a hand to touch her wet face. "Because it's true. It's true. I love you and I don't care how much you fight me. I can't change it, and neither can you."

They stood there, inches separating them, the only contact his fingers touching her face. Then he wrapped his hand through her hair and urged her to him, kissing her hungrily as the wind and rain moved over them and washed them and purged them.

Fighting for breath, fighting for control, Rosemary lifted her body away from his, her eyes wide with wonder and fear. She wanted to tell him that she loved him, too. But she was so afraid of saying it, afraid that she'd be struck down. She didn't deserve his love. And she wasn't sure she could give him the kind of love he needed. So she stood there, her screams still silent, her secret pain still safe.

Kirk saw the need in her eyes, saw the love she wasn't yet ready to give him, and realized she'd fight against it with all her being.

Well, he intended to fight, too. To win her over.

He kissed her again, wordlessly telegraphing an affirmation of his commitment, his awakening, his ability to love and be loved. But when he lifted his mouth from hers, her next words stopped him cold.

"Don't waste your love on me," she said, shouting into the wind, "because there's nothing you can do about it. There's no hope for us, Kirk. No hope. And you might as well accept that now, before we go any further."

"I don't think we can make it down," Kirk said minutes later as the rain ran in rivers and rivulets around them to form a muddy, treacherous path down the mountain.

Worried, Rosemary gripped his hand as he guided her along, the blinding rain and heavy wind making their descent almost impossible. "Aunt Fitz's cabin," she called. "It's just ahead. We can wait it out there."

She'd be in trouble. They were already late and Faye was the only person who knew where she was. Clayton would be so angry, and she deserved that anger, she decided. She'd deliberately gone off to meet a man her father had told her to stay away from. It was as if the nightmare of being with Eric was happening all over again.

Except this time, the man she'd fallen in love with was a good, decent human being. And this love, ah, this love was twice as powerful as anything she'd ever thought she'd felt for Eric. This was real, and abiding, and secure. And unconditional.

But she couldn't acknowledge this love; she couldn't follow her heart with Kirk without destroying what little love her father had left for her. This was her punishment for being so determined to find happiness.

And from the looks of this storm, even the heavens weren't pleased with her tonight.

"Come on," Kirk said, leading her to the slippery plank steps of the cabin. The porch looked dark and gloomy in spite of Aunt Fitz's cheerful, colorful gourds. "I don't think she's here," he said to Rosemary as they trailed water up onto the porch.

"Oh, she's probably down at the church dinner," Rosemary

explained. "I know where she keeps the key. She won't mind if we go in to get out of the storm."

She lifted a nondescript gourd, then fished inside. "It's not there," she said, stretching to make sure she hadn't missed the heavy key to the planked front door. Sinking back onto her wet loafers, she looked at Kirk, worry evident in her words. "Guess we'll have to stay out here on the porch."

Kirk took matters into his own hands when he saw her shivering. Grabbing several dry quilts from a large wooden rack on the wall, he urged Rosemary to the bench settled back well away from the driving rain. "Here. Sit down and I'll wrap us in this. We can wait for the storm to pass and then decide what to do."

"She has a phone," Rosemary said, thinking the statement was redundant. "Only it's locked inside. They'll be worried."

"Meaning, your father?" Kirk arranged her against his chest, then pulled a bright comforter over them. "Speaking of your father, we didn't get to finish our conversation, did we?"

Rosemary purposely avoided looking at him. Instead, she watched the rain as it fell in sheets across the heavy mountain foliage. They'd said a lot of things up on the mountain. But reality would be back soon enough. Especially when she had to face her father.

"Rosemary, we need to talk," Kirk whispered against her wet hair. "I meant what I said, love."

She shifted her head then, to see his face. "So did I, Kirk. You have to understand, no matter how strong my feelings for you are, I can't act on those feelings."

"Because of your father?"

"Yes. I made a vow to stay by him until he's over this. However long it takes."

"So you won't be able to just pack up and leave with me?"

"No. Not that I ever expected you to take me with you. I…I was willing to settle for what little time we have while you're here."

"Well, I'm not willing to settle," Kirk replied tersely. "Oh, I was at first, I'll admit that. But it's just not that simple anymore. I want more. I want you with me. I don't think I can leave you here, Rosemary."

She held on to him, willing him to understand. "I can't go, Kirk. I abandoned my father once, turned away from him, and you just heard the horrible consequences of what I did. I won't do it again."

"Aye, and you're setting yourself up as some sort of martyr. Do you think your dear mother would want you to waste away like that, out of some sort of obligation?"

Rosemary knew the answer to that. "No, she'd want me to be happy. But she'd expect me to do what was right, too. And that means helping my father, staying near him, until he's better."

Frustrated, Kirk turned her in his arms. "Or until he forgives you, right?"

She buried her face against Kirk's chest. "I need his forgiveness, Kirk. I have to have it before I can go on with my life."

"And what about love, what about how we feel for each other?"

She sat up, her features going soft with yearning. "I...I don't have an answer for that."

He had a question for her, though. "Do you compare your feelings for me with the way you felt about Eric? Are you thinking you'll be making the same mistake again?"

"No," she said simply. "No mistakes this time. What I feel for you is completely different from the infatuation I felt for Eric. But I do have to be sure. I can't take any more regrets."

With fierce determination, he kissed her again, then held back, his eyes searching hers. "You love me. I can see it in your eyes, but you think you might regret loving me, don't you, Rosemary? Is that the way of it, then?" His Irish accent became more pronounced with each question, a sure sign he was as frazzled and frustrated as she felt.

Wanting, needing to soothe him, Rosemary leaned forward to place her hands on his face. "I could never regret loving you, Kirk. You've saved me, helped me to heal and to realize that I need love, I need forgiveness."

"But you think you don't need me in your life?" Trying to make her see reason, he pulled her close. "Don't turn your back on us, Rosemary. Don't turn away from something God wants for you.''

"Does He want this?'' she had to ask. "I was so sure with Eric, so sure I was doing the right thing. I intended to make him a good wife, and I intended to change him into a better human being. What went wrong?''

Kirk pushed heavy strands of wet hair away from her face. "I surely don't have all the answers you need, but I think I can tell you what went wrong between Eric and you. You had the best of intentions, but you forgot one important element in your relationship with Eric.''

"What's that?''

"You forgot to turn the changing and the intending over to God. You should know, Rosemary, my love, that you can't change another human being. That has to come from above. And in Eric's case, the changing had to come from within. It didn't happen, through no fault of yours, but because Eric wasn't willing to open his heart and *receive* the change willingly. God gave us free will. It's certainly up to us to use it for its best purpose.''

Sitting there, all wet and shivering, and listening to his lyrical, inspiring voice, Rosemary felt a strange sense of peace settling over her soul. Was Kirk right? If she had left the changing up to the Lord and Eric, between the two of them, would things have been different?

She didn't have any answers, true. But she felt immensely better, after hearing Kirk's compelling reasoning.

"You're right,'' she said at last. "I've certainly learned that lesson well. I won't meddle with the Lord's work anymore, or more specifically, I will learn to accept the things I can't change, and pray about the rest. But where does that leave us, Kirk?''

"Together, I hope,'' he said. Then he tugged her into his arms and kissed her with all the love and warmth flowing through his heart. "But only if you use the same logic with your father. You can't change him, Rosemary. Oh, you can stand by him, pray for him, show him your example by loving him in spite of how he treats you—that's exactly what your mother did, isn't it? But any change in your da will have to come from his own heart. It will have to come from within. Please, keep that in mind before you shut me out of your life.''

''I will,'' she promised. ''Starting tomorrow. I'm going to be completely honest with Daddy. I think it's time my father and I had a long talk.''

The rain gentled, slowing to a soft tinkling. The night darkened around them, and in spite of the wet and the cold and the worry, they fell asleep, huddled there together underneath Aunt Fitz's warm quilt.

It was the best sleep Rosemary had had in a good while.

It would also probably be the last she'd have for some time to come.

Because with the morning came the sun—and the hour of reckoning with her father. Somehow, in spite of his sure wrath, Rosemary had to convince him that this time, things would turn out differently. And she had to ask him to forgive her so she could go on with her life.

Until then, she couldn't make any promises to Kirk.

Chapter Eleven

A search party met them about halfway up the mountain, with Rosemary's brother Danny at the head of the pack.

"Rosemary," he called, waving to her as he rushed to greet them. Giving Kirk a level look, he asked, "Are you all right?"

Rosemary nodded to her brother, then lifted wild curls away from her face. "I'm fine, Danny." She and Kirk waved to the other men with him. "We got caught in the storm and couldn't make it back down. We stayed on Aunt Fitz's porch all night."

Danny looked skeptical, but didn't question her in front of the others. "Daddy is fit to be tied, I might as well tell you."

"I'm sure he is," Kirk interjected. "And I take full responsibility. I'll explain things to him."

Danny shook his head. "I don't think that'd be too wise, buddy. My father doesn't want you around Rosemary, and this didn't exactly endear you to him."

Rosemary touched Danny's arm. "We don't need to go into that right now. I'll talk to Daddy. He and I need to talk. We've been avoiding it for too long."

Danny called to the other four men. "Go on back down, fellows. They're okay. Thanks for your help."

After Rosemary shouted her own thanks to the departing men, Danny turned back to her. "Oh, he's ready to talk, all right," he said, turning to lead them down the still-slippery path. "In fact, if Faye hadn't been there with him last night, I think he would have tore off up here to find you."

"Faye stayed with him?" Rosemary asked, glad to hear her friend had been there to spend time with her father.

"Yeah, till around midnight," Danny said, shooting her a questioning look. "What's that all about anyway? I've noticed she's been coming around a lot more lately."

Rosemary glanced over at Kirk, then back to her brother. She'd wanted to approach Danny about this, but had purposely put it off. She didn't think he'd accept Faye as readily as she had. "She cares about Dad, Danny. She's a good friend."

Danny didn't miss the evasiveness in her words. "I don't think I like the tone of this, sister. Are you telling me our father has...a girlfriend?"

"A friend," Rosemary corrected. "Someone to share time with, a companion. It's a healthy sign, if you ask me."

"I didn't ask you," Danny snapped. "But I bet you had something to do with this. Rosemary, how could you condone something like this so soon after Mama's death?"

Hurt that he didn't seem to be thinking of her father's best interest, and that he immediately wanted to blame her, Rosemary stopped walking to stare across at him. "Mama's been dead over a year now, Danny. And I think Daddy needs to get on with his life. I can't stand to see him so lonely and cooped up in that house. If Faye can make him smile again, yes, I am all for it."

"That figures," her brother said on a hushed whisper, so the men farther down the path ahead of them wouldn't hear. "I guess you think if you can keep Daddy distracted with Faye, you'll have more time to pull stunts like this one. Rosemary, haven't you learned anything?"

Kirk saw the humiliation on Rosemary's face, and wanting to shield her from any further unjustified attacks, moved toward Danny, his face inches from Rosemary's brother's. "You've got it all wrong, Danny. Rosemary cares about her father, and Faye is a good woman. And your sister didn't try to distract your father. I asked her to walk up the mountain with me. I needed some answers, and Rosemary poured out her heart to me. I know all about what happened, everything. And I think it's time both you and your father stopped blaming Rosemary for your mother's death."

Temper flared in Danny's eyes. "Man, you don't know a thing about me or my family. And I suggest you just stay out of it before you do any more damage. I'm telling you, my daddy is furious."

"Why?" Kirk asked, his own temper matching anything Danny could throw at him. "Because Rosemary wasn't at her appointed spot in the kitchen when he got home? Because people will talk? Is he angry because he was worried about his daughter, or because his daughter didn't check with him first before she took a walk? Does he even care that she's hurting as much as any of you?"

Danny stepped close, but Kirk refused to back down. "I don't want a fight with you, Danny. But someone has to make both you and Clayton see that Rosemary has suffered enough."

Danny scowled. "Oh, and I suppose you're the one who's going to set all of us straight. Thinking you can fix us, patch us up like you're doing to that old church? Well, pal, this family will be a lot harder to work with than rocks and wood, let me tell you."

"I don't want to fix anything," Kirk replied. "I just want to have a chance to get to know your sister. And she deserves that same chance. You're happily married, with a child. Doesn't your sister deserve some happiness, too?"

That question stopped Danny in his tracks. Confusion warring with pride and anger in his eyes, he turned to Rosemary as if looking at her for the first time. Kirk watched as Rosemary stared up at her brother, her eyes brimming with hope and pain.

Rosemary lifted her chin, daring her brother to say anything more. She certainly wasn't ashamed of being with Kirk. They'd done nothing wrong, and now he was defending her honor like a knight of the realm. She'd never had anyone do that for her before. It only reinforced her feelings for him, and her determination to face her father with the same courage she was showing her overprotective brother.

Danny spoke at last. "I'm sorry, sister. I guess I've been so caught up in my own bitterness I never stopped to think what all of this has cost you. Rosemary, you know I don't blame you, don't you?"

Rosemary swallowed the lump in her throat, then said,

"We've never really talked about how you feel, Danny. Oh, I know you've never said a harsh word to me, but sometimes I see you looking at me with that strange expression and I wonder if you're remembering that night, too. And I have to believe you do blame me. You've been a good brother, but I miss the closeness we had before...before Mom died. I love you, Danny."

Danny tugged her into his arms. "I love you, too. You have to know that. And I don't blame you." When she lifted her head, he added, "Okay, at first I was upset and resentful, but that passed. Nancy helped me work through all that. And I've prayed, and talked to Reverend Clancy about it. I hope I haven't made you feel that way, Rosemary."

"You just always seem to take Dad's side," she tried to explain. "And when I ask you for help with him, you always have a ready excuse, something to do. I can't do it alone, Danny. He needs both of us."

Danny looked down at the muddy path. "I know, I know. It's just...it's hard for me to be around him. I can't sit there and take it the way you do. I can't stand to see him like this...like he's half-dead or something. It's hard, Rosemary."

"Tell me about it," she retorted, but with a gentle smile. "Danny, you don't have a clue how hard it is to face him each day, or how hard it is to live in that house with him. You've got Nancy and Emily and your friends at work. Me, I have a good, satisfying job and my friends from church, but I always have to go home to face him each and every day. Until Kirk came along, I didn't have any hope of ever finding my own happiness again."

Danny looked at Kirk then, a sheepish expression falling across his face. "I'm sorry, Kirk. I guess Rosemary turned to you for help because I didn't offer her any." Extending a hand, he shook the one Kirk offered him. "Thank you, for listening to her, for helping her, for making her happy again." Then he gave Kirk a mock punch on the arm. "But did you have to take her off in a storm?"

Kirk shrugged. "Sorry. I can't predict nature. But I'm glad you didn't belt me one when you saw me."

Danny ran a hand through his short, thick hair. "I was just

worried. In spite of my acting like a stubborn mule, I do love my sister.''

Rosemary smiled at her brother. ''Do you mean that, Danny?''

He grinned. ''Yes, even though I haven't slept all night from worrying about you, I do mean it. I want you to be happy. And from now on, I'll sure try to be more open and sensitive, as my pretty wife would suggest—if that's possible for someone as bullheaded as I am—and I'll try to come around and spend more time with Dad.''

''Thank you,'' Rosemary said, reaching up to give him a kiss on the cheek. ''And thank you for coming to look for us.''

Danny frowned then. ''I had to, to keep Dad from charging up here.'' Then he took his sister's hand. ''Come on. You've got to face him sometime. Might as well get it over with.''

''You'll go with me?'' she asked, surprised.

''I'll go with you,'' he said. ''And this time, I'll stand up to him. I don't like taking sides, but I'm willing to try and make him listen.'' Then he halted. ''Only if you promise you won't sneak off like this again.''

''I won't,'' she said, glancing over at Kirk. ''From now on, I'm going to be up front with Daddy. It can't make things any worse than they already are.''

''Might make them better,'' Kirk said, wishing that for this family with all his heart. Of course, he had his own selfish reasons for wanting peace in the Brinson household. He wanted Rosemary to love him, completely, and without any regrets.

''I sure hope so,'' Danny replied. ''I hate missing a good night's sleep.''

A crowd of curious townspeople greeted them at the foot of the mountain, everyone whispering and speculating about what had happened.

Faye waved, tearing away from the crowd to come forward. ''Oh, you're all right. We were so worried. That was some storm and we had a bit of flash flooding during the night.''

''I know,'' Rosemary said, patting her friend's hand. ''That's why we couldn't make it back down the mountain. The path was a river of water.'' Looking down at her rumpled clothes, she added, "And I'm a mess. The rain caught us on top of the mountain and we had to sit it out on Aunt Fitz's front porch. I'm really sorry I had everybody in such a state."

Faye glanced at Kirk, then back to Rosemary. "Aunt Fitz spent the night with one of her daughters. She said she hoped you'd try to stop at her place, but she worried because she forgot to put the key in the gourd."

"We found that out quick enough," Rosemary said, glancing around. "Where's Daddy?"

"Where do you think?" Faye said on a snort. "In that house, pouting and fuming." Touching Rosemary on the arm, she added, "Be careful, honey. He's not too happy and he hasn't slept at all."

"Did he eat supper at the church?" Rosemary asked on a hopeful note.

Faye lifted her eyes. "I had him just about talked into it, but he wanted to wait for you. When the storm hit and you didn't come back, he told me to forget it."

Rosemary moaned. "Oh, why didn't I just tell him where I was going!"

"Too late to worry about that now," Faye said. "And I encouraged you, so it's partly my fault."

"I've got to go talk to him," Rosemary said. Turning to where Kirk stood making polite conversation with several people about the storm, she told him, "Danny and I are going to see Daddy. Then I'm going to get cleaned up and get to work."

"That'd be good, if you feel up to it," Faye called. "Melissa isn't here yet."

"Neither is my help," Kirk said, his eyes searching the grounds for Eric. Then he said to Rosemary, "I'll see you later—unless you want me to go with you now."

She shook her head, very aware that the crowd gathered around to make sure they were safe was also making sure they hadn't done anything scandalous while up on that mountain. "No. There'll be talk enough without you and my father having a fistfight."

"I'm not afraid to face him," Kirk said, his gaze holding hers. "And I'm not worried about what people say. Remember what I told you, Rosemary."

Several people nearby leaned in to see if they could hear exactly what he had told her.

Rosemary shot him a meaningful look, then turned to leave. Gossip. Just one more thing for her to worry about.

Deciding she'd deal with that later, she hurried to confront her father.

Clayton sat in the dark kitchen, nursing a lukewarm cup of coffee, his eyes bloodshot from lack of sleep, his mind numbed by the fear that he'd lost his daughter for good.

Rosemary. His lovely little girl, so afraid to face him that she'd run off up the mountain into a storm. How had they come to this? he wondered as he glanced around the clean, empty kitchen. If it hadn't been for Faye, encouraging him, comforting him, telling him Rosemary was a sensible, smart girl, he'd have gone crazy. Again.

He'd been up on that mountain mere minutes before his daughter, he reckoned. They must have just missed each other. His first time to go there, and now this.

He'd gone because of the dream. Eunice. He'd dreamed about Eunice. And in the dream, she had spoken to him in that soft, quiet voice. "Clayton, be kind to her. Clayton, show her how much you love her. Clayton, remember God's promise. We will be together again."

So he took flowers up to her grave, for the first time since her funeral. Having survived that painful experience, he decided he'd have a talk with Rosemary. Just a few civil words, just an opening, a beginning. He couldn't promise anything beyond that, even to Eunice.

Only, Rosemary hadn't come home. Faye came and told him Rosemary had gone for a walk with the steeplejack, told him not to worry.

But he had worried. He'd had all night to think about how he'd treated his daughter this past year. A long night, an angry, storm-tossed night that only reminded him of another horrible night. Had he really slept any since then? Had he really lived at all in the past year?

No. He'd been too busy punishing his daughter, too busy blaming God for taking his wife away from him.

And now he had Faye to contend with. That woman didn't mince words, or beat around the bush. But a lot of what she said made sense.

"You need to get out of this bleak house, Clayton. Come on over to the church supper. I fried some of my famous buttermilk chicken."

"I'd rather stay here, if you don't mind."

"Well, I do mind. You can't go on like this. Why, you're wasting away, and you're hurting Rosemary. Don't you care about her? Don't you see what you've done? Is it really your place to sit in judgment of your own daughter?"

He'd come so close to making it across the street to that lovable old church. So close.

Then the storm had hit, and Faye, worried enough herself about Rosemary, had told him where his daughter had gone.

Lost in the storm. Lost and alone and frightened and searching. Lost with a man he didn't want to like, didn't want to respect, didn't want to admire. Lost with Kirk Lawrence.

Clayton told himself he wouldn't be angry, if she'd just come home safely. He told himself he wouldn't shout or nag, or condemn her. He only wanted another chance.

He told himself these things as he sat there, afraid someone would come in and tell him it was too late, afraid that once again God would take away someone he loved.

But when the back door opened and both his children walked in, safe and sound, all he could do was glare up at his daughter. He didn't have the courage to face her, or to ask for her forgiveness, so he just sat there, staring, the echo of his dead wife's words still fresh in his mind, along with Faye's warning.

"Good morning, Daddy," Rosemary said, coming to sit down in the chair across from him, her nostrils flaring at the scent of fresh-brewed coffee. "You made coffee?"

"Had to, now, didn't I?" Clayton retorted hotly, all graciousness gone now and hidden away like her mother's pictures. "Do you know what a bother you caused everybody, girl?"

Rosemary slumped her shoulders for a second, then sat up straight. "Yes, I do, Daddy. And from now on, I'm going to tell you exactly what I'm doing and who I'm doing it with, whether you like hearing it or not."

"Defiant as always." He glared up at Danny, waiting for his son to confirm what he'd just said.

Danny, however, didn't react as his father had expected. Instead, he went to the cupboard and got two cups, then he poured coffee for Rosemary and himself.

Coming to stand between them, he told Clayton, "She's had a long night, Daddy, and she's tired. But she's also right. Rosemary and Kirk didn't do anything wrong last night. They just got caught in the storm. With the flash flooding, they had no choice but to sit it out on Aunt Fitz's porch."

"That's where you were all night?" Clayton asked, thankful in his heart, but firm in his anger.

"Yes," Rosemary replied, nodding her head. "And I don't mean to sound defiant." She paused, hoping she wouldn't lose her courage. "But...I'm a grown woman, and I won't do anything to disgrace you any, Daddy. I've purposely avoided even dating anybody since Mom's death, but I...I like Kirk. And I think it's time we get everything out in the open, between you and me. I can't keep going on, hoping you'll change, hoping you'll...start loving me again."

Clayton started, his hand reaching out in the air, but then he let it drop on the table before he touched her. "Then why do you continue to do things that only cause all of us pain, Rosemary? Why did you go off with Kirk Lawrence?"

Steeling herself against his rejection, she said, "Because Kirk needed to hear the truth, from me. I told him the whole ugly story, Daddy. I had to tell him before I could let things go any further between us."

Regaining some of his righteous anger, Clayton slammed his hand down on the table. "And just how far did things go last night, daughter?"

Rosemary gasped and jumped up as if he'd slapped her. "How can you even ask me that? You and Mama taught me to have principles and morals, and to do what is right. I'm asking you to please trust me, and all you can do is accuse me of something immoral and shameful?" Shame surfaced, old and worn and waiting, but this time, this time, she refused to wear it. "Kirk and I sat and talked on Aunt Fitz's porch, then we fell asleep, sitting straight up, with all of our wet clothes on, with a pile of quilts on us to keep us warm until morning. That's all that happened.''

Clayton looked down at the dregs of his coffee.

Danny shot Rosemary an encouraging look, then touched a hand to his father's shirtsleeve. ''Daddy, are you more concerned about appearances than about what's really going on in this family?''

Clayton snorted and pushed his son's hand away. ''Oh, I see she's got you convinced now, huh? I guess you've decided to condone her wild ways.''

Danny stomped to the sink to pour out the remains of his coffee. ''Rosemary has never been wild, and I'm not condoning anything, except her right to have a life of her own and her right to some happiness.'' Pivoting to face his shocked father, he added, ''There's been too little happiness around here in the last year.''

Then he lifted a finger to point to the church across the way. ''We've attended church all our lives, we've read the Bible, we've heard the Lord's teachings, yet somehow, we've conveniently forgotten to apply those very teachings to ourselves and our own situation. So do we turn away from everything we've held dear just because God decided it was time to call Mama home? Do we, Dad? And will that bring her back? Will that really make anything any better?''

''You're out of line, boy,'' Clayton said as he rose. ''I don't need to sit here and listen to this kind of talk.''

Danny was right by his father's side. ''Oh, yes, Daddy, you do need to sit here and listen. We need to talk, really talk about how we feel—we've hardly talked about Mama's death at all because you refused to let us even mention her name.''

Proud of her brother, Rosemary said, ''He's right. Mother was a wonderful, warm person, but she's gone. Instead of shutting that out, we need to accept it and...celebrate her life, instead of being bitter over her death.''

''There is nothing to celebrate,'' Clayton said, his jaw clenched, his face white with rage. ''I will not listen to any more of this.'' Waving a hand at Rosemary, he added, ''You go where you want, do what you need to do. You find that happiness you want so much, girl. But don't expect me to be happy along with you. I lost my happiness the night I saw your mother lying dead in that ravine."

Crushed, Rosemary reached out to him. "Daddy, please, can't you just try to...to start over? Can't you try to forgive me?"

Clayton heard the pain in her voice, saw the anguish in her eyes, but pride held him back from taking her in his arms to comfort her. Pride born of his own pain, stubborn, hateful pride that wouldn't let him give in or give up. After all, his pride was the only thing holding him together. If he let go of that, he'd crumble completely. So he used that pride as a shield, and he used his anger as a sword. And with that sword, he slashed at his daughter's defenses.

"There's nothing to forgive, Rosemary. You only did what you wanted to do. Same as now. Well, go ahead and be with Kirk Lawrence. Go ahead and shame me again. Go ahead and live your life. Just leave me alone."

Before he could push past her, Faye came through the screen door, her face white, her hands trembling. "There's been an accident," she said on a breathless, worried voice. "Eric—"

At the mention of that name, all heads came up. Clayton halted his tirade, stilling as he waited for Faye to continue. Rosemary sank into her chair, too weak, too afraid of the horrible images playing in her head, to ask Faye what had happened. Danny clutched the counter, his eyes darting from Rosemary to his father, then back to Faye.

"Eric had another wreck," Faye explained. "And, Rosemary...well, Melissa was in the car with him."

Chapter Twelve

The county hospital buzzed and hummed with all the efficiency of a well-honed machine, its doctors and nurses hurrying by with purposeful steps and set gazes while the four occupants of the tiny waiting room lifted their own faces each time a swinging door flapped open.

"Why won't they tell us something?" Rosemary said, worry evident in her question. Faye sat beside her on a blue vinyl divan, while Reverend Clancy and Kirk sat across from them on an identical one.

"They're busy, Rosemary," the reverend said gently. "When they have all the details, we'll be the first to know."

"I'm glad we all came," Faye said. "Especially since we couldn't get in touch with Melissa's parents."

"And poor Eric," Reverend Clancy added. "His brother didn't even seem concerned when I finally got him on the phone. At least I got a chance to speak with Eric myself for a few minutes."

Rosemary stayed silent, her gaze locking with Kirk's. He'd insisted on coming, not only for her sake, but because Eric worked for him. And she was glad to have him here. She was having an extremely hard time feeling sorry for "poor Eric."

After they heard the news, Danny had gone on to work, asking for an update later. And Clayton, well, he'd gone back into the dark den to watch a talk show, his cold shroud firmly intact.

Before Faye interrupted them, Rosemary had sensed a change in her father though. She couldn't put her finger on it, but somehow he had seemed different this morning. Not as cold, not as condemning. And the way he'd looked at her—had she seen a flash of compassion and concern in her father's eyes?

No. She was probably only hoping to see something that could never be there. His clenched jaw and tight fists told her how he felt about hearing Eric was involved in another accident, and whatever he'd been about to say ended when Faye came with this latest news. Now Rosemary felt the same as she had the day Eric had come back—sick to her stomach and so afraid. How many tragedies would it take before Eric reached inside himself to make a change?

Kirk got up to come and kneel in front of her. "Want something to drink?"

"No. I'm fine."

"You need to eat. You didn't have breakfast."

She smiled at the sweet concern in his eyes, savoring the surge of joy his attention brought, in spite of their reason for being here. "I'll eat later. I'm too keyed up now."

"And probably exhausted," he said. "We didn't get much sleep."

While Faye talked quietly to Reverend Clancy, Rosemary looked down at Kirk, studying his face with bliss-filled intensity.

"What?" he asked, clearly intrigued by her direct look.

"I was just remembering how we talked last night. I haven't stayed up late to talk to anyone like that in years. I feel as if we've known each other for a very long time."

He grinned, then touched his forehead to hers. "That's the way it's supposed to be between two people who love and care about each other."

Rosemary closed her eyes for a moment to soak up his words. "I haven't had anyone to love and care about for some time now. And this time, I don't intend to take it for granted."

He gave her a hopeful look. "Is that your way of admitting you're madly in love with me?"

She wanted to say yes to that question, but fear still held her in a solid grip. "That's my way of saying thank you for helping me through this."

Kirk lifted her face with a finger underneath her chin.

"You've grown up a lot since Eric, Rosemary. And I'm not the same as him. We'll work through all of this, together."

She looked around as a doctor came out of the room where they had taken Melissa. Kirk stood, taking her by the arm as she lifted up off the couch to hear what the doctor had to say.

"Hello, folks," the young, redheaded Dr. Harris began, shaking hands as he prepared to give them the news. "Sorry you had to wait, but we wanted to be sure. Melissa will be all right."

After the collective sigh that came from the group, he paused then continued. "She's badly bruised, though. Her head hit the windshield, so she has a slight concussion. I'm afraid she's going to be sore for a while, but things could have been much worse. She was wearing her seat belt, so that prevented her from getting hurt more seriously. We'll keep her overnight just to make sure we've covered everything."

"And what about Eric?" Reverend Clancy asked.

"A couple of cracked ribs," the doctor said. "And a cut to his left cheek. We stitched that up, but his eye will be black-and-blue for some time to come. He can go home today, though."

"I'll call his brother to come and pick him up," the reverend said, shaking the doctor's hand again. "Thank you, Doctor."

Rosemary turned to Faye. "So, he walks away again while Melissa has to stay here. Honestly, I don't think I can face him."

"Why don't we go in to see Melissa?" Kirk suggested. "That way you won't have to deal with Eric."

But it was too late to avoid him. He walked out into the hall just as they were making their way to Melissa's room. Rosemary had to admit, he looked scared and worried. As well he should, under the circumstances.

His gaze searching Rosemary's face, Eric asked, "Is Melissa all right? They won't tell me anything."

Rosemary wanted to lash out at him, but Kirk's firm grip on her arm helped her to quell that particular desire. "She's going to be okay. But they're keeping her overnight. She has a concussion."

Eric closed his eyes in relief. "It was the storm. I couldn't see, the car swerved.'' When he opened his eyes, he focused on Rosemary's skeptical expression. ''Why are you looking at me like that?''

Rosemary couldn't speak. The anger, the resentment, boiling up inside her was too raw, too strong.

Eric leaned back against the wall, his face going pale. ''You think…you think I was drinking, don't you?''

Kirk put a protective arm around Rosemary, then turned to Eric. ''Were you?''

Eric threw his hands in the air. ''Why do I even bother? Why should I have to answer that question? You've all already decided, haven't you? You've already judged me and condemned me and now you're wondering how I managed to survive one more time, right?'' When neither Rosemary nor Kirk responded, he shouted, ''Right, Rosemary?''

The nurses looked up from their work at a nearby station, then Dr. Harris finished signing Eric's release forms at the desk and turned on his heel to stomp toward them, his stern look centered on Eric.

''What's the problem, Mr. Thomas?''

''Tell them, Doc,'' Eric said, his eyes wide, his face red with rage. ''Tell them I wasn't drinking when I had that wreck last night. The police checked me out, they can tell you.''

The doctor stared long and hard at Eric, then pivoted to face Rosemary and Kirk. ''I don't know what's going on here, but there was no sign of alcohol in Mr. Thomas's bloodstream, folks. The police did a routine check because of his being on probation, but he had not been drinking. Just a case of bad weather and slippery roads.''

''You see,'' Eric said, his gaze moving over Rosemary's face. ''Bad weather—same as you and him.'' He pointed a finger to Kirk. ''You got stuck in the weather—Reverend Clancy told me all about it—and nobody jumped to conclusions about what you were doing. I had an *accident,* Rosemary. But it's different with me, isn't it? I've been condemned for life.''

Rosemary couldn't speak. Her breath seemed to be stuck in her throat. All she could do was cling to Kirk and watch Eric's face, her emotions churning from fear and frustration to guilt and remorse.

"I want to see Melissa," Eric said. Then he turned to head toward the room to which a nurse pointed.

Reverend Clancy came back, shaking his head. "Eric's brother refuses to come and get the boy. I'll take him back to the parsonage and see that he gets a good breakfast."

For the first time since her mother's death, Rosemary felt a spark of sympathy for Eric. But it was short-lived and weak, and gone as soon as she reminded herself that because of Eric, she'd been condemned, too.

Still, on the way back home, she was quiet and contemplative. She had been quick to judge Eric this morning. Maybe, just maybe, he really was trying to make a change this time. She hadn't questioned Melissa about Eric, or why she'd been with him in the car. Melissa had been too weak to do anything more than whisper, yet Rosemary had glimpsed the defiance in the girl's eyes. Then Melissa's parents had shown up before Rosemary could ask her too many questions, so she couldn't say much about her concerns for the girl.

Kirk sensed her withdrawal and reached across the seat of her car to touch a hand to her arm. "Are you all right?"

"Just worried," she admitted as she steered her economy car around the looping mountain roads. "Melissa seemed so quiet, I know she's in a lot of pain."

"She'll be okay," he reminded her. "She's very lucky, that's for sure."

"But why was she with Eric in the first place?"

Kirk studied her face for a minute, then sighed. "Rosemary, they both have a right to see each other. In spite of how you and I feel about Eric, Melissa is a very headstrong young lady. I have a feeling she's attracted to the danger she senses in Eric."

Shocked, Rosemary glanced over at him for a split second before returning her focus to the road. "That's silly. Why would any woman be attracted to a man who's committed vehicular homicide—murder? And especially when she knows all about what he did?"

"That doesn't matter to some people," he tried to explain. "Melissa is sorry for what happened to your mother, but she's interested in Eric anyway. From everything you've told me about the girl, and from watching her each day, I'd say she's looking for love in all the wrong places.''

Rosemary shook her head. ''Then the song's true, huh?''

''In some cases, yes,'' he replied, nodding. ''Think about her home life, Rosemary. No guidance, no good examples to follow. No wonder the girl is attracted to Eric. He represents the type of freedom she craves, the excitement she can't find at home.''

Putting his theory to the test, she said, ''Then explain why *I* was attracted to him? I had a good home life, and I didn't crave excitement.'' She grew quiet then, remembering how in awe she'd been of Eric. And how exciting it had been to be noticed by someone she didn't know everything about, someone who was a bit mysterious. That realization brought her current motives into sharp focus. Was that why she was attracted to Kirk, too?

Kirk shrugged, but didn't miss the added anxiety her thoughts had brought. ''I don't know. Maybe because you were so sheltered, so structured in your upbringing, you turned to Eric because *he* showed an interest in you?''

She scoffed. ''You make it sound as if I was needy or something, Kirk. I had boyfriends before Eric.''

He had to smile at that. He could only imagine Rosemary as a beautiful teenager, tempting all boys, both good and bad. ''But did you feel the same about any of them?''

''No.'' She watched the road, a frown marring her face. ''He was like a breath of fresh air, so different from anybody else I'd ever known.'' She shrugged. ''Okay, maybe I was attracted to him for all the wrong reasons myself.''

''And that's how it is with Melissa, except the difference is, you didn't know about his dark side, and she does.''

Starting to understand, she glanced back at him. ''So, I was interested in Eric's good side, while Melissa is attracted to his dark side?''

''Exactly. Because you have strong moral fiber, based on your upbringing, you could only see his good, and try to change the part of him that you didn't like. Melissa, on the other hand, hasn't had the same solid upbringing as you, so she's tempted by a man who should be forbidden. She doesn't necessarily want to change him.''

"And I sure did. Melissa won't do that, will she?''

"Not at first. But the newness will wear off soon enough. Only, we can't make her see that now. I have a feeling if we try, she'll just run right into his arms.'' Then, taking a different stance, he added, "Of course, because she doesn't judge him the same way you did, Melissa could be the one to help Eric turn around. And in doing so, she just might settle down herself.''

Rosemary didn't like the tone of that. Had she been too judgmental of Eric? She had demanded perfection from him, but only because she'd cared about him. "So you're telling me to stay out of their relationship?''

Kirk waited until she had stopped the car in her driveway, his own dark thoughts swirling like the leftover rain clouds passing by in the sky. "I'm not telling you anything. I'm asking you to concentrate on *us,* and let Melissa and Eric work this out between them. Unless, of course—''

"What?'' she interrupted, not liking the serious look on his face.

He had to voice the one fear he'd held since Rosemary had told him the whole story about her mother's death and her own sudden breakup with Eric. "Unless you're still attracted to Eric.''

Amazed that he'd even dare to voice that, she stared at him, her hands tightly gripping the steering wheel. "How can you think that, Kirk?'' Her voice softened, while her eyes held his. "Especially after last night?''

Kirk lowered his head, then glanced out at the tall pines swaying in the morning breeze. "I had to ask, Rosemary. You seem so defensive whenever we talk about Eric. And you're sure set against Melissa seeing him.''

Angry now, she opened the car door. "I'm defensive because the man ruined my life. And I'm trying to protect Melissa—I won't let the same thing happen to her.''

Kirk got out, too, then came around the car to stand in front of her. "Are you sure that's all it is? Or do you have unresolved feelings for him? I have to know, Rosemary.''

Hurt, she wondered how she could make Kirk see that she was so in love with him, no other man could ever compare in her mind. Of course, Kirk himself had just alerted her to the danger of falling for someone she didn't know very well. Her first instinct was to lash out at him, but then she stopped to remind herself that she'd learned something from her talks with Kirk. She'd tried to change Eric, and that had backfired. Was she still trying to change him in her own roundabout way? And would she wind up trying to do the same with Kirk?

"Maybe you're right," she said at last. "But not about how I feel about Eric. I do not feel anything for Eric anymore. And that's the truth. I care about you, I care about what happens between us now, Kirk." Wanting to be honest, she told him, "But...I still have a lot to work through. I can't make any promises, but I do know that what I feel for you is very real."

He reached out a hand to touch her cheek. "I want to believe that, but we both know if I were to leave tomorrow, you wouldn't be going with me, now, would you?"

She took a minute to let that soak in. "No, but not because of Eric. Because of my father. I can't leave him yet, Kirk." *And if I try to make you stay, I'll be repeating the same pattern.*

"I know that's what you're telling yourself, but...Rosemary, you can't change your father any more than you can change Eric. All you can do at this point is pray for both of them."

"I am, I have," she said, her temper flaring again. "I've prayed for my father every day and night since my mother died."

"And what about Eric?"

"I'm trying, Kirk. Really, I am."

He dropped his hand away, then stood watching her. "How can you pray for someone you say you have no feelings for?"

"It's not easy," she admitted. What she couldn't admit was that her prayers hadn't been nearly sincere enough to be heard. They were feeble at best, but that was because she still had so much anger and bitterness inside.

Kirk brushed his hair off his forehead with one hand, then looked down at her, his eyes full of longing and compassion. "Rosemary, until you find it in your heart to forgive Eric, we won't be able to make a full commitment to each other. You have to resolve your feelings for him before you can move on with your life.''

''That's crazy,'' she said, turning to stalk away. ''I don't have any unresolved feelings for Eric. I told you, I don't have any feelings for him, period.''

''My point exactly,'' he called after her.

She kept walking toward the church.

''Rosemary, you loved the man once and…that love ended so suddenly. Have you even stopped to think about it?''

''No,'' she called back. ''I don't want to think about Eric Thomas. Ever again.''

Kirk watched her hurry to the educational building. She'd pour herself into her work with the children to keep from thinking about what he'd said. But she would have to face it sooner or later. And until she did, things would be at a standstill between them. He wouldn't allow her to pretend she was okay, when she was still hurting over Eric.

And, he told himself as he headed to his own work, he wouldn't let her settle for loving him to replace what she had lost with Eric. She'd said she wanted to be sure this time.

Well, so did he. Kirk knew he was in deep, so deep that he wouldn't be able to walk away so easily. He was willing to fight for Rosemary, but only if she was willing to fight for herself. She wouldn't be completely free until she resolved everything with her father and with Eric. And that meant letting go.

That also meant forgiving.

Rosemary wasn't sure how she made it through the rest of the day. Tired and restless, she went home after making sure all the children were safely on their way, only to find a mess waiting for her in the kitchen.

Digging in with all her might, she began putting dirty dishes into the dishwasher with absentminded concentration. Maybe Kirk was right. Maybe deep down inside, she was denying her true feelings.

Did she still feel something for Eric?

Thinking about how much she had loved him once, she recalled their good times, and couldn't help comparing them to her few precious minutes with Kirk.

There was no comparison. True, she'd loved Eric once. But that love had stopped suddenly, swiftly, the night her mother died. In fact, she had only spoken to Eric briefly that night, to say they would talk later.

Only, later never came.

Her family was so distraught, she couldn't bring herself to see Eric again. So there were never any final goodbyes, no spoken words, between them in the following weeks. Eric was in jail, unable to make bail. Then his trial came up a few weeks later, and she'd attended, determined to make sure he got what he deserved.

His pleading looks, his sorrowful words, had gone unheard. Out of respect for her grieving father, and because of her own raw pain, Rosemary had refused to listen to him.

Stopping now, she looked out over the yard, her eyes automatically searching for the church steeple across the way. "Was I wrong, Lord, to refuse to talk to Eric? Was I wrong to turn away from him so suddenly?"

He killed her mother. What else could she do?

The echo of Kirk's words came back to her, loud and clear. "How can you pray for someone you have no feelings for?"

"How can I, Lord?" she asked out loud.

As she gazed at the steeple, she saw Kirk scaling one side of the tall tower. So, he was working late to make up for lost time. Or maybe like her, he needed to stay busy to keep his mind off everything else. Maybe he was wishing he'd never fallen in love with such a mixed-up person.

"But I'm not mixed-up," she told herself. "I know where I can find my strength. And I know God will show me the way."

She watched, fascinated, as Kirk went about his work. He hung suspended by a cable wire, his body held inside his little wooden chair, his tools dangling from his belt. Kirk worked with meticulous care. Today, he was washing the stained-glass windows that sparkled with such brilliance each time the sun hit them.

The windows were beautiful. Kirk would clean them, nurture

them, make them shine all the more for God's glory. Because of his care, they would be better. But he wouldn't change them.

He wouldn't change them.

The brilliance from the windows shot through Rosemary at about the same time realization flowed through her, sharp and clear, and sure.

She couldn't change Eric, or her father, by simply praying for them to turn their lives around. She could only change others by changing herself, and by changing *how* she prayed.

"I've been doing it all wrong," she said, a rush of joy sweeping over her. "I've been asking for the wrong things."

About that time, Clayton came into the room. "Talking to yourself, girl?"

Rosemary turned, a fresh smile on her face. Why, she never really smiled at her father anymore. She was always pious and quiet, trying so hard to respect his grief. Today, though, she really smiled at him, the kind of smile she used to give to him whenever she'd see him walk into a room.

"No, Daddy," she said as she approached him with a purposeful intent. "I was talking to God."

"Hmmph." Then, "How's Melissa?"

"She's going to be all right." She waited, then looked up at her father. "And...we found out Eric wasn't drinking. The weather was bad, he lost control of the car."

Clayton stood there, so silent, so still, she wished she hadn't mentioned the accident. He started to turn away, but Rosemary reached out to touch him, startling both of them. They rarely touched each other anymore.

"Daddy?"

"What?"

She saw the hesitation in his eyes, but she couldn't stop herself. Rosemary hugged her father. Hugged him hard, hugged him tightly to her. Patted him on the back. "I love you, Daddy."

Clayton stood rigid for a minute, then to her amazement, he awkwardly patted her on the back before pulling away. He didn't say a word, just stared down at her for a long time.

Then he whirled and shifted away. But he didn't head for the dark den as she had expected. Instead, he went out onto the porch to sit in one of the rocking chairs. Then he said, "Call me when supper's done. I'm going to watch your steeplejack."

Rosemary could have squealed with joy. This, *this* sounded like the father she had always remembered.

She took him a glass of tea, then stood there to stare down at him. Finally, she asked, "Daddy, why did you go to Mama's grave yesterday?"

Clearly surprised that she knew, Clayton refused to look at her. "A man has a right to visit his wife's grave, doesn't he?"

It wasn't the answer she needed or wanted, but it would do for now. "Yes, a man has every right," she said quietly.

Then she went back into the house to fix his supper.

That night, Rosemary didn't ask God to make Eric a better person, or to make her father love her again.

That night, Rosemary asked God to help her instead.

"Help me to forgive," she prayed. "Help me to heal. Help me to feel something for Eric, so that I can learn to forgive him."

When she finished her prayers, she automatically went to the window to see if Kirk was still up. She saw him standing there in the moonlight, watching and waiting.

And she knew she loved him completely. This was a different kind of love from what she'd felt for Eric. Kirk was a different man from Eric. Mysterious, yes. But willing to tell her all his secrets. Refreshing, very. But not in a dangerous way. Changeable? Maybe, but not to the point that he'd resent her trying to mold or shape him, and she didn't feel the strong need to mold or shape him the way she had with Eric. Kirk was willing to compromise and to commit in order to have a life with her. Just when and where that life would be was a question they had yet to answer.

But, unlike with Eric, Rosemary wouldn't have to make all the decisions alone this time. There would be no ultimatums, no one-sided set of values, no showdown. This time, she and Kirk would decide their future together, through open and honest communication, and through prayer.

She loved him completely. She loved him for all the *right* reasons. She'd prove that love, somehow.

And one day soon, she'd be able to tell him exactly how much she loved him.

Chapter Thirteen

Melissa came back to work a few days later, but she was sullen and withdrawn. Worried about the girl's state of mind as well as her physical health, Rosemary tried to talk to her. They were having lunch in the prayer garden while another aide watched over the children who were napping inside.

"Isn't it a beautiful day?" Rosemary said, her eyes centered on her friend, her smile full of contentment.

"Great," Melissa said, purposely avoiding glancing up at Rosemary. Instead, she pulled little bits of wheat bread from her ham sandwich to toss to the squirrels roaming in the nearby oak trees.

"Melissa, aren't you hungry?"

"Not really."

Rosemary stayed silent for a while, then tried again. "How have you been feeling?"

"I'm well, completely well," Melissa snapped, her head still down.

Concerned, Rosemary leaned forward on the stone picnic table. "Have I done something to upset you?"

Melissa looked up then. Rosemary recoiled from the malice in the girl's blue eyes.

"Obviously I have upset you," she said. "Talk to me, Melissa. Tell me what's bothering you."

"As if you didn't know," Melissa said, her gaze sweeping the church yard. "You had Eric fired, didn't you?"

"What?" Shocked, Rosemary glanced around. "I haven't

seen Eric since the accident. As far as I know, he's still working for Kirk.''

"Then why hasn't he been back?"

"I honestly don't know," Rosemary replied, hoping the girl would believe her. "I assumed he was still recovering from his injuries. Have you heard from him?"

"No, and I doubt I ever will again," Melissa said, throwing down the remains of her half-eaten sandwich. "Why did you have to interfere, Rosemary?"

Angry now, Rosemary took a deep breath to hold her temper. "Melissa, I haven't interfered. I don't know what you're implying, but I'm telling you—I don't know where Eric has been for the last few days. As I told you, I haven't seen him since the hospital."

Thinking back, she realized he hadn't shown up for work Friday. She'd chalked that up to his cracked ribs.

But why was Melissa treating her like an enemy? "So you think I've driven Eric away? Is that it?"

Melissa shot her a hostile look. "Well, you did accuse him of drinking the other night. And he wasn't!"

"I know that now," Rosemary said. "And I'm sorry I jumped to the wrong assumption. But I was only concerned— for both of you."

"I don't need you mothering me, Rosemary," Melissa retorted, her eyes flashing. "I have enough nagging from my parents, when they even notice I'm around."

Taking that into consideration, Rosemary cooled her own anger at the girl. "Okay, I won't mother you. But you do work for me, and I'm entitled to worry about you because we used to be friends. Are we still friends, Melissa?"

The girl looked away then, but when she finally faced Rosemary again, her eyes held a cloudburst of emotion. "I'm in love with Eric, but he's still pining over you, Rosemary. Why do you lead him on when you know you don't want him?"

"Lead him on?" Surprised, Rosemary could only stare at Melissa with an open mouth. "I haven't done that. Just the opposite. I've tried to avoid Eric since he came to work here."

"He claims you flirt with him to make Kirk notice you,"

Melissa admitted, a despondent sob leaving her body. "Is that true?"

Her own appetite gone, Rosemary put down the shiny red plum she'd been about to bite into. "No, that's not true. Not at all." Wording her explanation carefully, she said, "I talked to Eric a few days ago, in the fellowship hall. We had an argument—"

"I know," Melissa interrupted. "He wouldn't tell me everything, but he did say you were angry with him for talking to me."

"That's not exactly what happened," Rosemary replied, her lips set in a grim line. "We didn't talk about you at all, Melissa. Eric…was bitter and defensive, and he accused me of being holier-than-thou."

"Well, aren't you?" the girl questioned, her eyes bright. "You can't seem to forgive him."

"No, I can't. I'm having a really hard time dealing with his being released so early, but I'm trying to cope. I only asked him to stay away from me, and Kirk backed me up on that."

"So you did provoke him to get Kirk's attention?"

"No! Kirk came in and found us arguing. Look, Melissa, Eric and I will always have trouble being around each other. I'm not out to make anyone jealous, or get anyone's attention. And…I no longer have the same feelings for Eric that I once did." Frustrated and hurt that Melissa would even think such things of her, she stood up to go back inside her office. "And as far as you and Eric go, I promise I will not interfere. I can pray for both of you, though. And I certainly intend to do just that."

"How very gracious of you," Melissa said, her voice cracking. "Well, go ahead and pretend you're so good. The whole town's talking about what went on between you and Kirk up on that mountain."

That stopped Rosemary in her tracks. Whirling, she stared across the breezeway at the mixed-up girl sitting there watching her. "Kirk and I have nothing to be ashamed of, Melissa. And I believe you realize that. Eric is the one trying to cause trouble here, but I guess I'll have to let you find that out for yourself. Just be careful."

"You really hurt him, you know," Melissa called after her. "You let him go to jail without ever hearing his side of the story. How can you live with yourself?"

Rosemary had to grip a steel pole supporting the catwalk, to keep from lashing out at Melissa. What did the girl know about *her* suffering, anyway? Calming herself, she turned one last time. "I have to live every day with the knowledge that my fiancé was driving drunk and killed my mother," she said through a clenched jaw. "Isn't that enough?"

Melissa looked embarrassed and, thankfully, remained silent. Rosemary went into her office and collapsed into her chair, her hands shaking.

Kirk found her there, the cluster of wildflowers he'd picked for her forgotten. "I can see I missed lunch. What's the matter?"

She lifted her head, glad to see a friendly face, glad it was his face, and glad for the fresh-smelling honeysuckles and Cherokee roses he'd picked for her. "Melissa and I just had a nasty confrontation. Eric has her thinking I'm some sort of evil person." Shaking her head, she said, "How did things get so twisted?"

"He's just grasping at straws, Rosemary," Kirk said as he came around the desk to drop on his knees beside her chair. Handing her the bundle of fragrant flowers, he told her, "Eric is so confused, so full of guilt, he has to say things like that in order to live with himself."

"But hasn't he caused us enough suffering? Haven't we all suffered enough?" She reached out a hand to touch his face. "I just want to get on with my life. I want to be happy again, Kirk."

He took her hand then kissed it, his lips warm and firm on her clammy skin. "I want to make you happy again. As far as Eric—you haven't seen him around here because he's too banged up to be much good to me, and the toughest part of my work's finished anyway, so I told him...I told him I no longer needed him."

Relieved that Eric wouldn't be hanging around anymore, Rosemary was also worried about Melissa's warped accusations. "Well, Melissa thinks I had him fired."

He shook his head. "If Eric hadn't gotten hurt, he'd still be working here. But I didn't see any point in letting him come back. In fact, his injury was a perfect excuse to get rid of him. We've only got a week or so to go, anyway."

That brought her head up. "You'll be leaving soon."

"Yes," he said, the one word soft-spoken and hesitant, his dark eyes full of questions. "And we need to talk about that, but first, I want you to do something for me."

She laid the flowers on her desk, the tone in his voice alerting her, warning her. "What's that?"

"I want you to go see Eric."

"What? I…I can't."

"Yes, you can. You have to face him, Rosemary. Really face him and get it all out of your system. That's the only way to stop these rumors he and Melissa are spreading, and that's the only way to really get on with your life."

She lifted her eyebrows, her expression skeptical. "You're not making this easy."

"This isn't supposed to be easy," he said. "I should know that better than anyone. I'm still fighting—as much as I want to be with you—I'm still terrified of making that final commitment. But I'm willing to try. I wouldn't ask this of you if I didn't believe it's really important."

"You didn't come to church Sunday," she said, glad to turn the tables for a while. "You've never attended a service, Kirk? Why not?"

Kirk lifted up to lean on her desk. "That goes back to my carefree philosophy, I suppose. I always had this unspoken rule—work on the church but don't become a part of the congregation. It was just less messy that way."

"And now? Have I made your life too messy?"

He grinned, then crossed his arms over his chest, giving her a good view of his large biceps and muscular shoulders. "Let's just say you've messed up my *way of life.*"

"But you still aren't ready to be a part of the church?"

"I can't be a part of the church," he admitted. "To do so would mean I've taken that final step."

"Which means—you're not really as committed to me as I thought?"

"No, I'm committed to *you,* but if I give in and become a part of the congregation, it will be like I'm putting down roots. And I can't afford to do that. My job requires that I travel—a lot."

"Then we're right back at an impasse," she said. "I can't go with you, you can't stay here with me."

"I'm hoping after you talk with Eric, you'll be ready to move on," he said, his gaze gentle and coaxing.

"And what about my father?"

"He's a grown man, with friends who care about him. I think he'll be all right."

"I can't leave him, Kirk."

Kirk moved away from the desk and headed for the door. "Just go and talk to Eric. It's a start. We'll worry about your father after you sort through all your feelings for Eric."

She rose, both hands pressed on her desk pad. "I told you, I have no feelings for Eric."

"Talk to him, Rosemary." With that, he turned to leave. Then before she could form a retort, he stomped back into the room to pull her into his arms. After giving her a thorough kiss that left her longing and aching for more, he stood back with a hand on each of her arms. "I won't settle for being a replacement for something you lost, Rosemary. I'm willing to bend, I'm willing to meet you halfway, but I won't be second-best."

"Is that what you think?" she asked, her breath leaving her body in a soft whisper. "That I'm trying to…to get back what I lost, by falling for you?"

"I have to be sure," he said. Unable to stop himself, he reached up a hand to pull his fingers through her curly hair, then held her head against the weight of his hand. His gaze moved over her lips, then across her face, his eyes filled with longing. "I'm treading new waters here. When I look at you, when I touch you, I know I want to be around you for a very long time. It's when I'm away from you that I start doubting. So, just like you, I have to be very sure."

Shocked, she asked, "Do you think I love you for all the wrong reasons, Kirk?"

"Oh, I hope not," he whispered, his fingers pulling through her hair. "Not when it feels so right between us."

With him looking at her with such intensity, with him touching her, holding her like this, as if he could never let her go, it certainly felt right. But was it wrong? Well, she'd wondered the same thing herself, and she'd been working hard to convince herself that this time, *this love,* was good and right. She wouldn't blame him for wondering the same thing. She was embarrassed that he could read her so well, though.

Kirk pulled her close to kiss her temple, then her forehead, his touch soft and confident, gentle and disturbing. "I want you to love me for all the right reasons, truly I do. I pray that you can see it in your heart to do so without any doubts or fears."

"How can you *doubt* me?" she asked on a breathless whisper, her eyes closing as his lips skimmed over her jawline.

He reluctantly lifted his mouth away from her creamy-sweet skin. "Because I know that you doubt yourself. I can see it in your eyes, Rosemary." At her guilty look, he let out a deep sigh. "Your fear of loving me is just as strong as your fear of heights. I want to conquer both, but it's not up to me. You have to conquer your own fears, if we are to have a true and abiding relationship."

Rosemary fell against him, holding him to her, clinging to his strength, his wisdom, his spirituality. "I hate it when you make sense."

"Aye, and I hate to see that doubt and pain in your lovely eyes."

She lifted her gaze to his. "Tell me again, Kirk. Tell me in that beautiful Gaelic language what you told me the first night you held me."

Touched, and even more determined to make her his own, he crushed her close, then pressed his mouth to her ear and spoke the timeless language of his ancestors. Then he repeated the phrase in her language. "I am here, little one. I am here."

Kirk held her for a few minutes longer, then he backed away, his parting words coming on a low, hopeful growl. "Go and see Eric, Rosemary. Then please...come back to me."

Rosemary took comfort in Kirk's words and touch even after he was no longer there in the room with her.

How would she survive when he was no longer there at all?

Praying for strength, she decided she would begin the process

Kirk had suggested. She would try to conquer her fears; she would prove her love for him was strong, and right, and good.

And so, with that thought in mind, that afternoon after work, she got in her car and drove to Eric's house.

She would begin by conquering her bitterness and her anger. It was time she said some things to Eric that needed to be said. She couldn't change him, but she could shift her own attitude.

It was time she faced the her past.

Eric lived in a garage apartment on his brother's property a few miles from the next town. Rosemary hadn't been there too many times, and now she wondered if she'd been wise to come today. The place had been shut down while Eric was in prison. Now it looked forlorn and unkempt, lonely.

She parked and climbed the rickety steps leading to his front door, then took a deep breath and knocked twice. At first, no one answered. She was about to turn and leave, when the door slowly swung open.

Eric stood there in a pair of faded sweatpants and an unbuttoned cotton plaid shirt, the bandages from his bruised ribs clearly visible across the flat expanse of his midsection. He was a handsome man, in spite of the stubble on his jawline and the red-rimmed, sleep-laden darkness in his eyes. It was no wonder Melissa found him attractive.

"Rosemary," he said in a grainy voice. "What are you doing here?"

She hated the hope in his question, hated having to do this, hated herself for being here. Remembering the warmth of Kirk's lips on her skin, the tenderness of his endearments, and her own need to show him she did indeed love him, she squared her shoulders and tried to smile at Eric. "I...I wanted to see how you're doing, and...we need to talk."

Eric stood back, then swept a hand out. "Come in."

Rosemary entered the tiny, cluttered apartment and felt the assault of a thousand memories. It was amazing how scent could bring back a multitude of feelings, how seeing a particular photograph could set her mind to reeling. The smell of his favorite aftershave warred with the smell of the musky, closed room. Sitting on a plastic shelf, along with his CDs and record collection, was a picture of them together back in college—a dance they had attended during football season.

"I...I never could bring myself to get rid of that picture," he stated bluntly, as if daring her to say something about it being there.

Rosemary didn't comment. Suddenly, she saw with clarity everything Melissa and Kirk had already seen. Eric still cared about her, maybe even still loved her. Looking around, she wondered how much he had suffered, sitting here in this dump of an apartment, and worse, sitting in a prison cell.

Well, whatever he'd suffered wasn't nearly enough to bring back her mother, she reminded herself. They should have given him ten years, but then, he'd had a crafty lawyer who'd tried to make it look as if her mother's driving had contributed to the accident. Not wanting to dwell on that particular memory, Rosemary lifted her head to face him. "Could I sit down?"

"Sure." He hobbled over to the gold plaid couch to shift magazines and newspapers off onto the ratty carpet. "Best seat in the house. You want something to drink? Strictly nonalcoholic, of course."

Not missing the sarcasm, she shot him a stern look, then quickly softened her features. "No, I'm fine."

Eric leaned back against the tiny dining table filled with dirty dishes, a grimace of pain twisting his features. "Okay, Rosemary, cut to the chase. Did you come here to see if I'd been on a drinking binge or were you hoping you'd find me dead from too much booze?"

"Why do you do that?" she asked, heat rising across her face. "Why do you assume that I'm here to condemn you?"

"Haven't you already done that?"

"Yes," she admitted with too much ease. "Yes, Eric, I did condemn you the night my mother died, and that's why I'm here. But not to do it again."

"Oh," he snorted, throwing up a hand, only to wince when his sore ribs protested. "You've decided I need a little pep talk, or maybe your sympathy." He pointed to the door. "Well, too little, too late, Rosemary. Get out."

"No," she replied, her throat dry, her hands clammy. "I

want to talk to you and I'm not leaving until I say it all—everything that's on my mind.''

"This oughta be fun.'' He rubbed a hand over his face, then looked down at her, temper lighting his eyes. "What do you want from me?''

Frustrated and beyond aggravation, she snapped, "I want you to feel some remorse. I want you to act like you care, Eric. I want you to show me that you truly are sorry for what you did to me, to my family. Do you even care that you destroyed all my hopes, my dreams, my life? Do you even care that my father detests me because of you? Don't you want to have a better life, a life free of alcohol, a life free of this guilt?''

"Are you finished?'' he asked, his eyes blazing, his face red.

"Not nearly,'' she said simply, her breath hissing out in a rush. "You've come back into my life, unwanted and unwelcome, and everyone tells me I'm supposed to forgive you! I'm supposed to turn the other cheek and forget that you…you killed my mother! Well, I can't do that. I want to, I've prayed to be able to forgive you, but it just won't come. I can't get beyond what you did—''

"What I did,'' he shouted at her, pointing a finger in the air. "What I did, Rosemary,'' he said on a low growl, "was despicable, was beyond any of the low-life things I'd ever done before in my lousy life. What I did was unforgivable!'' At her surprised look, he shouted again. "Yes, unforgivable. Lady, you talk about your need to forgive me—well, don't bother. I can't be forgiven. I'm beyond your worth, Rosemary. Can't you see that? Can't any of you see that I'm just not worth the effort?''

Rosemary started to speak, but he held out a hand to stop her. "I mean, I've been told that all my life. First by my old man before he drank himself to death, then by my brother before he booted me out of the house. Then by the law, by my teachers, by the bosses who couldn't tolerate me, then…then I got a scholarship to go to college. The only thing I had going for me was my ability to throw a football. I thought I had a chance, but…I liked to party too much. I was having such a high old time.

"Until…I met you.'' He stared down at her, his red-rimmed

eyes widening in awe, his harsh expression changing to one of tenderness. "You, Rosemary. Such a sweet, *good* girl. You were like this beautiful flower that I wanted to touch, so fragile, so pretty. I had to be with you."

Rosemary caught a fist to her mouth, the tears rolling down her cheeks as she listened to him. Oh, how she had loved him once. She knew exactly how he'd felt back then. She'd felt the same way. And now, for the first time since her mother's death, she could actually acknowledge that feeling, and the anger that came each time she thought of his betrayal. Although she no longer loved Eric, she'd denied what she'd once felt for him, because of her own guilt. She hated him now because of what he'd done to her mother, but mostly because of what he'd done to her. It was a bitter realization.

Eric let out a long breath, then held his arms to his chest. "I could always get what I wanted, so I got you, through charm, through guts, through sheer determination. And from the beginning, I lied to you, but worse, I lied to myself." He shook his head, his eyes bright. "I actually thought I could pull it off. I tried, heaven knows, I tried so hard. But it was too late for me."

He looked down at her then, and Rosemary saw the torment in his eyes. She couldn't speak, couldn't move.

"It was just too late for us, Rosemary. The drinking took over...because I was so scared, you see. I was so afraid of losing you, so afraid I wouldn't meet your high standards, so afraid you'd see through my act."

She stood up, her worst fears hitting her full force in the face. She had to get out of here. She didn't want to cave in; she didn't want to *feel*, to feel anything for this man. But the feelings came, rushing at her, clawing at her with a vengeance, taking her breath away. Had she driven Eric to this?

Eric pushed her back down. "Oh no. You wanted to talk, so I'm talking. I was so scared the night of our party, Rosemary. After seeing all those people, all those good, Christian people, bringing gifts to...to me. Wishing me a wonderful life, wishing us a great future, and me knowing I didn't deserve it, I didn't deserve you. Then, a few nights later at your folks' house, it was the same thing all over again. Only maybe worse, with your mom so sweet, treating me like another son. And your father—well, we both know what he thought of me.'' He shook his head. ''I just got so scared.''

He whirled, turning away from her, turning away from the scene in both their minds. ''So, yes, after I dropped you off that night, I stopped and got a fifth of whiskey. And I drank it, a lot of it. I was too drunk to be driving. I even pulled over a couple of times, but that just gave me a chance to think about us getting married, and what you and all those people expected of me. So I drank some more.''

Rosemary moaned, then buried her face in her hands.

Eric pivoted back to give her a direct look now. ''And then I took off down that winding road and…yes, Rosemary, I…'' His voice cracked and the tears began to roll down his face. ''I killed your mother.'' He gulped, trying to hold back his emotions. ''I was so drunk, at first I just sat there in the truck, wondering what had happened. Then I saw the fire, heard the crackling…and I got out and I ran and ran—''

''Stop!'' she cried, rising from the couch to skirt around him, her stomach heaving, her throat filled with bile. ''Stop, Eric. I can't listen to this.''

''You wanted to know,'' he said, his voice weak. ''You wanted me to show some remorse, well…'' He slumped over, the tears racking his body. ''I've paid, Rosemary. I've paid dearly for what I did. And you've never, ever known how much I regret it, because you never took the time to let me tell you.''

Rosemary leaned her head into the door, her body so weak she thought she'd faint, the rush of emotions tearing through her too strong to fight. Then she heard a crashing sound, and turned to find the picture of her and Eric lying on the floor, its glass shattered, broken, mangled, over their smiles.

''Your life wasn't the only one that was splintered into a million pieces, Rosemary,'' he said. ''I lost everything. I lost you.''

His admission tore through her, making her realize what they'd both lost. She had loved him. Maybe part of her still did, but the main part, the good part of what they'd had, was gone forever. She'd never really accepted that, had never mourned that loss properly. Kirk had seen it, had warned her about it. But how, how did she go about healing this terrible, horrible rift?

She turned then, slowly, and with a hesitation that told of her own bitter pain and the revulsion she still felt, she reached out a hand to him. "Eric—"

"Don't," he said, backing away. "Just don't. I waited so long for you to do that, but now it's too late. I know that. I'm working toward accepting it." When she stepped forward, her hand still extended, he told her, "Go, Rosemary. Go back to him. He loves you, and...he'll be good to you. He's the kind of man you deserve."

Rosemary stood there, wishing a million different wishes, seeing the broken person Eric had always been, the person she had never really understood at all. Maybe she didn't deserve any absolution or happiness. Maybe she didn't deserve Kirk.

"I could have helped you," she said at last. "I didn't know, Eric. I didn't know about your life."

"I didn't want you to know. I was ashamed."

Rosemary turned to leave. He wouldn't let her help him now, not when she'd turned away from him just as everyone he'd ever cared about had turned away from him. What kind of Christian was she, to do that to a person?

She was about to tell him she was sorry, when the door burst open and Melissa rushed into the room.

"I saw your car," she said, her eyes focused on Rosemary's tear-streaked face. Then she glanced over at Eric, her own expression condemning and demanding. "You couldn't stay away, could you, Rosemary?"

Rosemary wiped her face. "Melissa, it's not what you think."

"You don't have to explain," the girl said. "I'm not stupid, you know. You rushed right over here after I poured my heart out to you." She went to Eric, her eyes bright, her words harsh. "She'll hurt you again. Can't you see that?"

"Melissa, stay out of this," Eric warned, his own face streaked and flushed. "Go on back home. Both of you, go on back and leave me alone." On a softer note, he told Rosemary, "I'll be okay. Really. I haven't had a drink for over a year, and right now, I want one bad. But I won't take it, I swear. I won't take it, Rosemary.''

Rosemary looked at him, proud of him for the first time in a very long time, then turned to face Melissa. "You're right. I did hurt him. And I'm sorry for that. I'm leaving, but…I think you should stay, Melissa. He needs you.''

Relief washed over Melissa's features, but Eric's expression changed as rage colored his face. "Always the do-gooder, huh, Rosemary. Even now, you're still trying to make things so much better by giving Melissa and me your blessings.''

Melissa sent Rosemary an understanding look. "We don't need her approval, Eric, but I do appreciate her giving it.'' Then she turned back to Eric. "We've got each other. We can forget about all the rest.''

Unable to bear being there any longer, Rosemary rushed out the door and down to her car. But it was a long time before she could crank the automobile and actually drive away.

"Oh, Kirk,'' she whispered, her heart breaking with grief, "you were right. There's so much more to this, so much more to be resolved.''

On the way home, Rosemary stopped her car at the lookout where the wreck had happened. The confrontation with Eric had been necessary, as painful as it had been. She could now accept what they'd had and lost. She could accept Eric as a human being with weaknesses and problems just like any other human being. She couldn't give him her love, but she could show him some compassion. At last.

As the sun set in the distance, a bloodred ball of fire, Rosemary stood there, shaken and broken, looking down on the spot where her mother had lost her life. And she asked God to help her to find her own again. She wanted peace; she wanted joy. She wanted to know love again. With Kirk. Only Kirk. Somehow she had to find the courage to acknowledge that love.

She still didn't know if she deserved it, though.

As she stood there, back from the edge of the ridge, her heart pounding with a new hope in spite of her ever-present vertigo, Rosemary also asked God to help Eric find his own peace.

After all, they had all suffered enough.

Chapter Fourteen

When Rosemary got home, she found Danny waiting on the front steps for her. He immediately jumped up, the dark frown on his face mirroring his black mood.

"What in the world is going on around here?" he barked, his hands on his hips, his eyes snapping open.

"Nothing that I'm aware of," Rosemary said, not ready to deal with her brother's questions after all the revelations she'd had today. "Why aren't you inside with Dad, anyway?"

Danny placed his hands on his hips, then rolled his eyes. "Because he's *not* inside. I found a note on the front door. He's gone to eat supper with Faye Lewis."

"What?" Rosemary was as stunned as her brother, but not nearly as upset as Danny by this bit of news. "Well, good. I'm too tired to cook, anyway."

"Can you believe that woman?" Danny said, following her up to the door. While Rosemary struggled with the key in the lock, Danny struggled with the image of his father with another woman other than his mother. "I mean, she's going after him with all the energy of a she-bear after honey. This is embarrassing, Rosemary. We've got to talk to him."

Rosemary threw her purse on the couch and went around turning on lights. "Danny, slow down. I've had a full day and I don't need this right now."

"Oh, fine," her brother said, folding his arms across his chest. "I make good on my promise to come by more often, and now I find Dad gone and you informing me you don't need this right now. I'm telling you, Rosemary, ever since your stee-plejack came to town, things have been getting wackier and wackier around here.''

Rosemary turned from pouring a glass of water from the tap, to stare at her confused brother. "So you want to blame this on Kirk! I can't believe you. Kirk has nothing to do with Faye and Daddy becoming close.''

Danny threw his hands in the air. "You didn't start encour-aging this until he came here. You're too busy chasing him around to even care about Dad.''

"You're wrong there, brother,'' Rosemary said, her temper flaring, her patience shot. "You, of all people, should know, I care about our father. But I'm not going to discuss this with you right now. Now, do you want something to eat, or did you just come by to fuss at the rest of us?''

Danny looked humbled for a minute, then asked, "What do you have? I did get kind of hungry, waiting out there.''

"Pound cake?'' She turned to get him a slice, knowing it was his favorite. "But you can take it home with you. I'm just too tired to fight, Danny.''

"What about Dad?''

"What about him? He's getting out more. He's found some-one to spend time with. I'd say that's a good, healthy sign that he's coming to grips with Mama's death.''

"You would say that.'' Danny took the large chunk of cake she'd wrapped in foil, then stood there with his head down. "I don't know. Somehow, it just doesn't seem right. I can't picture him with anyone else but Mom.''

"He visited Mama's grave the other day, Danny,'' she said softly. "I think he's finally healing.''

Danny stood silent for a minute, then braced a hand on the counter. "Wow. I never expected him to do that.''

Rosemary patted her brother on the arm. "He'll be with Mama again one day. In the meantime, he needs a friend, if nothing else.''

"Well, I don't have to like it,'' Danny replied before he sniffed the cake. "Did you bake this?''

"Afraid you might eat some of Faye's cooking by mistake?'' Rosemary teased. At his guilty look, she added, "Yes, I baked it." Then, just to pester him further, she said, "How does Nancy feel about Dad dating Faye?"

"Don't call it dating," he warned. "And my sweet wife told me to mind my own business."

"A wise woman, that Nancy."

Danny held his cake in one hand, and raked his other hand through his thick hair. "How can I mind my own business when the whole town's talking about my sister and the steeple-jack camping out together on the mountain, and now, my father flying off to be with another woman?"

Slapping him on the arm, Rosemary said, "I would hope you'd tell everyone else to *mind their own business.* Kirk and I got caught in a storm. And our father has a right to some happiness. Are you going to defend our honor, or whine about your good name being run through the mud?"

Danny frowned, then stood up straight. "I'll sock the first person who says anything nasty about either of you, but that doesn't mean I don't have concerns myself."

"Well, stop worrying," Rosemary said, so drained she just wanted to curl up and sleep. As she pushed her brother out the door, she told him, "Danny, I went to see Eric today."

Danny groaned, then stared at her as if she'd gone daft. "One more thing for the rumor mill. You need to stay away from him, Rosemary."

Rosemary looked out into the gathering dusk, quiet for a minute. "I will from now on, but I'm glad I went today. We got some things off our minds, got things settled between us. Eric has had a hard life, harder than I ever realized—"

"Oh, don't tell me you're feeling sorry for the man!"

"No, I'm still struggling with what he did, but now, now I can at least accept that he's suffered, too. And I do believe that he's going to turn his life around."

Danny snorted. "How can you be so sure?"

Rosemary looked up at the first star of the evening. "I've prayed for it," she replied softly.

Danny didn't have a retort for that, except to say, "Then I guess I better go home and try to do the same thing, since I'm not accomplishing very much by trying to reason with you."

Rosemary followed him out onto the back porch. At Danny's soft hiss, she looked up.

"Now I know why you're in such a hurry to get rid of me," he said.

Kirk was coming across the street, carrying what looked like a picnic basket.

"Didn't you say you were tired?" Danny whispered.

"I am," she said, even as her heart soared and tripped into a faster beat. Then to her brother, "Danny, go home and kiss your wife and your daughter."

"Good advice." With that, her brother got in his truck and drove away.

Kirk grinned as he waved to Danny. "Hope he didn't leave on my account."

Rosemary shook her head. "Danny's just confused. Things are changing, and he's never dealt with change too well."

Kirk set the basket down, then pulled her into his arms, his eyes searching her face. "And how about his lovely sister? Do you deal with changes better than your brother?"

She looked up at him, her eyes touching on his in the scented dusk, her pulse beating a warning tune against her throat. "I'm learning to."

Kirk rubbed a hand down her spine, then enjoyed the little moan of pleasure that escaped through her parted lips.

He tilted his head toward the basket. "I brought you dinner. I was restless, so I grilled burgers and I'm afraid I got carried away. I made too many." Then, "Did you see Eric?"

"I did." She stretched, leaning into the swirling massage of his fingers on her back, her whole body coming alive at his touch. For just a minute, she forgot all her troubles and her tired state of being.

"And?"

She didn't miss the hint of vulnerability in the one word. "And I think I've purged myself of him." Placing her arms around Kirk's neck, she told him the truth. "You were right. I did have feelings for Eric, strong, hidden feelings. I think I wanted to love him still, but the shame, the pain, was too great. I was so angry at him, not just because of the wreck, but because...he hurt me and betrayed me. But I didn't want to admit to it. So I simply buried everything away.''

''What happened today?''

She stood silent for a minute, seeing the coiled tension in the tightening of Kirk's jaw. Then she told him the whole story, detailing the scene between Eric and her. ''It all came rushing out. My anger...and his. Eric is really hurting.''

At his questioning look, she raised a hand to his chest. ''I can't feel any sympathy for Eric, but I do feel compassion. You know, the Bible tells us to pray for our enemies, and that's what I've tried to do. But until today, until I actually heard him telling me how sorry he was, how much he regretted what happened, I'd never felt any compassion when I prayed for him. Now I can.''

Kirk stepped back, his expression guarded. ''And do you feel anything else for him?''

Rosemary lifted her hands through his hair, wanting, needing, to touch him. ''No. Only compassion, and a new understanding. I feel so sad, so empty. The bitterness is gone. All that's left is the acceptance, and this great sadness. But I can deal with that now.''

''Are you sure?''

''Very. And I owe you a big thanks.'' To prove it, she lifted up to kiss him.

It would have been a chaste kiss, except that Kirk needed more. All afternoon he'd waited, wondering what would happen when Rosemary finally confronted Eric. Would she cave in and tell Eric she still loved him? Would she run away, and become unable to really love anyone again? Or, would she find a certain peace and...come back.

''You came back to me,'' he said just before her lips grazed his. ''You came back.''

With that, he hauled her close and took her mouth against his, punishing her and rewarding her at the same time. This, this was more than a kiss. This was a dance, a ritual of timeless need, a meshing, a merging, of two souls that had paid the price for the love they couldn't deny.

Kirk burned with the fire of new hope, of renewed promises. He'd asked her to go to another man, neither of them knowing what the outcome would be. It had been a risk, but now it might pay off. He wouldn't let her get away again.

Rosemary sensed the change in him, in the way his mouth moved over her own, in the way he held her to him. She became lost, lost in the need to be with him, lost in the way he showed her his love, lost inside the sweet fantasy of a life with this man.

When he lifted his mouth from hers, his breath labored and hard, she took a minute to regain her own equilibrium. Then she stood back to stare up at Kirk, her love for him undeniable. ''You sent me to him, not knowing what would happen, didn't you?'' Amazed, she saw the answer in his tense expression, in the dark depths of his eyes. ''You actually thought I might...I might go back to Eric, didn't you?''

Kirk closed his eyes in relief, letting his guard down at last. ''Aye, that thought had crossed my mind.''

''Why would you think that?''

''Because you loved the good in him once, and you're a nurturing soul, Rosemary.''

She understood, and was touched and humbled by his unselfish gesture. ''So you figured I might remember that good, since he's working toward dealing with his alcoholism, and you thought I might be tempted to try again with him. That's why you insisted I go to him. You wanted me to make a final choice.''

He opened his eyes. ''Yes.''

Rosemary brought her hands up to cup his face. ''I don't love Eric.'' Her heart thumped and thudded; her pulse raced. She had to take a deep, calming breath, and on that breath, she told Kirk her one last secret. ''I love you. And...I love you in a different way from the way I once loved him.''

Kirk's world shifted, broadened, expanded to include her and a future that would change everything. ''Oh, and how is that?''

She brought her mouth close to his. ''This is stronger, deeper. Kirk, I've never felt this way before. I feel so safe with you, so secure. I never felt that way with Eric. I was always nervous and cautious with him, trying to rationalize all of our problems away. I don't have to rationalize with you.'' She hushed to a soft whisper. "I've never loved anyone the way I love you. But…I was so afraid to tell you that."

Groaning, Kirk pushed her back against the porch wall, his lips meeting hers again and again. "And I…Rosemary, sweet Rosemary, I've never loved at all—until you. I want you with me, forever."

"Oh, Kirk, I wish, I pray for that, too. But I don't see how—"

"Come away with me," he said, his eyes holding hers. "Marry me."

She looked up at him, awestruck and still afraid. "What?"

"We can travel together," he said, giving her a tight hug. "I'll show you all the ancient cathedrals in Europe. I'll take you to Ireland to meet my relatives. We'll sleep under the stars, dance in the rain." He stopped, looking down at her with a clear, confident hope in his eyes. "I want you with me, wherever I go. I want to fall asleep with you in my arms every night, and wake up with you there beside me, no matter where I am. I want to take you to the edge, Rosemary."

Rosemary's heart pumped a fast-paced beat throughout her entire system. This was her dream. This was what she'd thought about over the last few weeks. She wanted to be with Kirk, to know his world, to love him, to have him. But…

"I can't, Kirk," she said at last, the finality of her statement ringing out over the still, settled night.

He lifted away to stare down at her, the hazy porch light illuminating his confused expression. "Why not?"

"You know why not," she said, already feeling the distance between them. "I can't leave Daddy yet. Not until I'm sure he's going to be okay."

Kirk tilted his head back, then faced her again. "He has Faye. And Danny's been more cooperative lately. You have to let go sometime, Rosemary."

Rosemary leaned back against the wall, fanning mosquitoes away as she tried to form her words. "Yes, but I have to be certain that he's going to be all right. I can't abandon him, not now, not yet."

Kirk backed up to the porch railing, slumping against the white spindles as he stared over at her. "So all of your talk about loving me and feeling secure with me—what was that, Rosemary?''

"I do love you," she said. "And I want a life with you. I know that now, more than ever."

"So why are you denying what we both want?"

She swallowed, then lifted her head. "I guess I didn't expect things to happen so fast. I…I thought you'd come back for me, one day."

Kirk pulled a hand through his hair, then shook his head. "One day? And how long will one day be, Rosemary?" Pushing away from the railing, he stalked the confines of the small porch. "You know, you're running out of excuses. You're coming to terms with your mother's death, you've finally faced Eric, and your father is beginning to accept Faye as someone he can turn to—what's left for you to fix, anyway?"

His words hit a nerve, but he had a point. She was running out of excuses. But she wouldn't leave her father, not yet. "I have to know that he…I have to know that my father can forgive me, Kirk. I'd be heartbroken if I had to leave without his blessings."

Kirk nodded his head slowly, steadily. "So you're willing to throw away what we feel for each other, the happiness we can have, simply because you've been through this once before with your father?"

"Yes," she said, craning her head forward to glare at him. "Yes, I have been through this once before. I acted too hastily, I was too rash and it caused my entire family too much pain. I won't do that again."

Kirk stopped pacing to stare down at her. "I thought you were sure, after today, after talking to Eric."

"I'm sure that I love you," she replied. "But I'm just not so sure about taking off on this new life." Wanting him to understand, she touched a hand to his arm. "You said you want to take me to the edge. Well, maybe that's the last excuse I have. Maybe that's the real reason I can't just pick up and go with you. Can't you see, if I do that, if I leave behind my life here, and everything and everyone I hold dear, it will be like stepping to the edge of a cliff. I don't know what's waiting for me out there. I don't have a net, or a rock to cling to. I'll be out there, free-falling. That's too risky, especially after what I've been through.''

Kirk jerked away from her touch, but she came to him, both hands on his arms. "I'm only asking you to give me some time. You can go on to your next job and…we'll see how we feel then.''

He frowned, then lowered his head to within an inch of hers, his eyes flashing fire. "I don't need to wait to know how I feel. Rosemary, I've bared my soul to you, I've changed my whole outlook on life because of how I feel, because of how you *make* me feel. That's all I need to know.''

Taking her hands in his, he held her away, his expression dark and dangerous. "Can't you see, we didn't have a choice in this matter? From the moment I saw you, I knew. I *knew* that I wanted you, that I belonged with you. I didn't want to accept that, but I had no control over it. I won't let you walk away from something so good, so right—just so you can be a martyr.''

"I'm not trying to be a martyr,'' she retorted, pulling away. "I just want to win back my father's love and respect.''

"Aye, and what if he never changes? What if he continues to punish you by holding you here forever. Do you honestly believe that's the right way to do something—to sacrifice yourself, your own needs, to live out your life swallowed up by sorrow, because you happened to fall in love with the wrong man once?''

"I don't know,'' she said, her heart breaking with the weight of wanting to be with him. "Please, Kirk, don't give up on us. Let me work through this, and…when you're finished with your next job, we'll find each other again.''

"No, Rosemary,'' he said, turning to place a hand on each of her shoulders. "Listen to yourself. Listen to what you're asking. I'll be far away, and I'll call for you. And you'll have another excuse, another reason to keep you tied here. Your father, your brother, your job at the church.

"Maybe you're right. Maybe you do love me, but we come from different worlds. You're not willing to risk being a part of mine. And that, dear Rosemary, is the heart of the matter. For all your talk of a strong faith in God, you're not willing to turn things over to Him. You're not willing to take a leap of faith with me. All of this other, well, that's just a facade."

Hurt, dazed, desperate, she said, "And what about you, Kirk? Are you willing to settle down here in Alba with me?"

At his silence, she continued. "No, of course not. We've both known that all along, and I've told you all along that I wasn't ready to take off into the wild blue yonder. But you've never once offered to stay."

"Did you expect me to?" he asked, temper flaring like lightning in his eyes. "Is that what this is all about? You thought maybe I'd just hang around until you found the courage to let go and love me?"

Lifting her head, she faced him squarely. "I told you I never expected anything from you, remember? I told you I'd settle for what little happiness I could find, and I guess that's exactly what I got."

Kirk heard the finality in her words. "So you're willing to end things right here, with just a few sweet memories between us? What about our prayers, Rosemary? What about our hopes, and our struggles? I fought against your father, I stood up to your brother, and I've had to deal with Eric. I threw all my so-called principles to the wind—just to be near you. And now you expect me to walk away—just walk away—because we can't seem to compromise?"

"You told me you never settle for second best," she reminded him, her voice shaking.

"And I also told you I was willing to meet you halfway."

"Then do it. Give me some time."

How could he explain to her? How could he make her see that he wasn't willing to let her slip away? "I can't do that, Rosemary," he said flatly. "If I leave, I won't be back. I won't give you time enough to start doubting all over again."

"So it's now or never?"

He nodded, then turned to go down the steps. "Aye, that's the way of it."

Rosemary watched him go, her heart crying out in a loud, silent scream. She could go after him, tell him she'd follow him anywhere, but she stood there, frozen, numb, cold with grief.

Then she wondered why it hurt so much, when all along, she'd known this time would come.

She couldn't go.

He couldn't stay.

That had been between them all along, only she had hoped, had prayed, that she could make him see they could have a long-distance relationship until they were sure.

Aren't you sure right now, this very minute? she asked herself.

Oh, how she wanted to be completely sure, how she wanted to trust in her faith, in her love. But she felt as if she were standing on top of Alba Mountain, looking down into the jagged rocks and dark, deep crevices. She was so afraid of taking that final step. So very afraid.

Needing to hide away, she turned to head into the house, then almost tripped over something by the door. Looking down, she saw the spilled contents of Kirk's forgotten picnic basket. She reached out then fell to her knees to gather the things back together. Then she saw the wrapped food he'd fixed for them, and a small handful of sweet-smelling lilies he'd taken from the garden by his trailer. And a small box.

Unable to stop herself, Rosemary lifted the square white box out of the basket and opened it.

Inside, lying against the soft, padded cotton was a ring. An unusual ring made from what looked like silver, knotted in an intricate weave that formed the wide band and came to a knotted crest that coiled and looped to form the ring's center.

"Three knots," Rosemary whispered. She turned the ring over and over in her hand. Then she saw by the yellow porch light that there was an inscription engraved across the smooth silver backing of the ring's center.

Without thinking, Rosemary held the ring close to the light, squinting to make out the inscription.

It read: A Union of Three, My Lord, My Love and Me.

Touched beyond words, and torn beyond grief, Rosemary carefully placed the ring back into its white box, tears blurring her vision. Kirk loved her, wanted to marry her, wanted theirs to be a union of love with God guiding them. Why couldn't she let go and follow her heart? Why was she holding back, when her heart was breaking by doing so? Was she waiting for forgiveness from her father? Or would she be forever unable to forgive herself?

Rising, she wiped her eyes and looked over to Kirk's small trailer. The faint light from inside flickered, then went out.

Rosemary felt as if that same light had just gone out inside her soul.

Chapter Fifteen

Easter morning.

Kirk stood underneath the oak tree he'd started thinking of as his own, sniffing the scent of the white Easter lilies lining the church steps in celebration of this sacred Christian day.

Easter. A new dawn lifted out from the east, its yellow sun plump and ready, set to shine on this brilliant Sunday morning. Set to shine on the steeple he was now through restoring.

He was leaving today.

He would go; but he'd be leaving behind so much this time. He'd be leaving his heart here in this rustic mountain village. Aunt Fitz had predicted it and she'd been so very right.

The mountain had captured Kirk. Because he'd been to the mountain with Rosemary. And he'd given her his heart. But not without a struggle; not without a fight to the finish.

Well, he'd lost. She wouldn't be coming with him.

Kirk had watched his Rosemary over the last few days. They'd avoided each other, but it was impossible to avoid the multitude of feelings that surfaced each time she was near. Love had warred heavily with regret. Pride had won out over humility.

She'd left his picnic basket by the door of his trailer, along with the ring he had planned on giving her.

Was that her final answer?

Kirk sat there in his lawn chair, sipping the strong coffee Reverend Clancy had introduced him to. He watched as the churchgoers slowly started coming to their house of worship.

And he wondered how a day could dawn so incredibly beautiful, how these people could show up here all decked out and smiling, when so many of them were hurting and hoping, still broken inside, still punishing themselves each and every day for simply being human.

Maybe that was why they entered those great open doors. Maybe that was why they couldn't stay away. They found their sanction, their solitude, their peace, inside the womb of their church. And today, some of them would enter that church for the first time in a year, hoping to find the resurrection within themselves through the timeless story of the Resurrection of Jesus Christ.

Today, they would hold a dedication ceremony in celebration of the renovations. Reverend Clancy invited him to stay and celebrate, but he wouldn't, couldn't do that. He didn't belong here, after all.

Earlier, much earlier, just before daylight, Kirk had gone inside the hushed sanctuary to study the stained-glass window depicting Christ. He'd stood in front of the altar, lifting his eyes and his heart to God, wondering and questioning, asking for some sort of miracle to bring Rosemary back to him.

Now, as he saw the sun cresting on this new day, he wished he had the courage and the right to go to her and ask her to be his. Courage, he could muster. But he didn't figure he had the right to ask something of her that she wasn't capable of giving.

So he sat there, the dweller by the church, and watched the fresh-faced children running around in their Easter finery, their mothers in spring hats and floral-print dresses chasing after them to straighten mussed clothes and bruised feelings.

And he wished. He wished he had a child to straighten out. He wished he had an Easter suit to don. He wished he had someone special to escort into that sanctuary.

Then he glanced up and saw her coming across the yard. Rosemary. His Rosemary, wearing a flowing creamy dress with a lacy collar and a hip-hugging sash. Rosemary, in her straw Easter bonnet, her chestnut curls as wild as ever, her eyes lifting up, her head turning until she saw what she was searching for.

Him.

She centered her gaze on him, stopping, her hand touching

on the tousled hair of a child who'd come up to hug her, her chin lifted in pride, her eyes bright with regret.

The sun washed over her, illuminating her in a pale, ethereal morning light that took the breath straight out of his tired, aching body. Oh, he'd remember her just like this; he'd remember her as spring, and laughter, and sunshine and fire. His Rosemary.

Kirk told himself to get up and go to her. But his body wouldn't move. The weakness of his love held him down, the gravity of his own pride pulled him back. So he just sat there, watching as she moved toward the church, her eyes darting over the crowd, and always, back to him.

He'd be gone when she came out of there.

He'd be gone soon. Rosemary tried to accept this as she took one last look at the man who'd come to Alba to restore a church steeple, and had managed to change her life in the process, the man she loved with all her heart.

Kirk. Her steeplejack. Sitting there in his jeans and his button-down shirt. Sitting there in his foldable chair, by his mobile home, ready to move on. Ready, if not willing, to go.

Rosemary stood on the wide stone steps, listening to the comments about the newly renovated church.

"Why, it looks better than ever. See how that stained glass shines. And the steeple looks taller, somehow. Straighter. He really fixed it up right."

"Brand-new. I wish my great-granddaddy could be here to see this. You know, he had a part in the original building of this church."

"It's so beautiful. Kirk Lawrence has the touch. He has a way about him. I'd a never thought he could make it any prettier, but he sure did a mighty fine job."

"He poured his heart into it. That's his secret. He believes in his work. And he ain't afraid of climbing up there to get the job done."

"Someone told me he's leaving today. Is he coming to the dedication before he goes?"

"Let's ask Rosemary."

Somehow, Rosemary was swept along into the flow of finery and festivity. Somehow, she was inside the church before she could turn and run back out, before she could run to him and ask him not to go.

"Rosemary, is Kirk staying for the dedication after the service?"

Rosemary looked down to find Aunt Fitz watching her with those keen, clear eyes.

"No," she managed to say. "He has...another commitment."

"Are you sure about that, child?" the old woman asked quietly, patiently leaning her head to the side while a granddaughter adjusted the pink carnations and fuchsia orchids of her Easter corsage.

"Very sure," Rosemary said, taking the wrinkled hand Aunt Fitz offered. "Kirk has to move on."

"That's a shame. I liked that boy."

"I...I did too. So very much."

Aunt Fitz had to have noticed the tears glistening in her eyes, but thankfully, the old woman didn't push the issue. Instead, she said, "Come on in and sit down, Rosemary. The sermon today is all about forgiveness."

Kirk waited until a Sunday-morning hush fell over the church grounds and gardens, then he got up to put his chair away and gather the rest of his things. He wanted to be gone before those doors swung open and the whole town flowed out to honor him.

He didn't deserve their honor, nor did he want it. He'd come here to do a job, and having done it, he'd be moving on. Same as always.

As he turned to go back inside the trailer, he saw Rosemary's father standing out on the back porch, staring up at the church steeple, his stern features set as firmly in place as the stones of the building he watched.

Something snapped inside Kirk. Without thinking, without hesitation, he slammed the trailer door shut and stalked toward Clayton. There was one last thing he had to do before he left Alba Mountain.

*   *   *

Rosemary sat toward the back of the overflowing church, her nostrils flaring at the scent of Easter lilies wafting out from the hundreds of potted arrangements sitting on the altar in honor of loved ones, both dead and gone, and living.

One of those lilies was in honor of her mother.

Remembering the lilies Kirk had picked for her, Rosemary pushed back the sudden burst of tears she knew was coming. She wouldn't cry anymore.

Crying wouldn't bring back her mother. Crying wouldn't change how her father felt about her. Crying wouldn't keep Kirk from leaving her. No, she wouldn't cry anymore. She was done crying; done feeling sorry for herself.

Kirk told her she couldn't change those around her, and he was right. So she intended to change herself. She intended to rededicate herself to this church, to this town, to the children she loved to take care of, to God. Thanks to Kirk, the church had been restored, and…so had she.

She owed him for that. He'd shown her how to face her past and fight for her peace of mind. Although the latter might be a long time in coming, she intended to find it again, somehow.

It would be hard, so very hard, without him.

The choir sang the ''Hallelujah Chorus,'' their voices lifting in praise and joy.

Rosemary looked around to see her brother there with Nancy and Emily. Mother and daughter wore matching chambray dresses and white straw hats. Emily giggled and pulled her hat off, her eyes full of mischief and delight.

A few rows over, Rosemary saw Eric sitting with Melissa. They held hands and whispered, but Eric's eyes touched on Rosemary briefly.

She should be angry that he was here. He didn't have any right showing up here as if nothing had happened. How could he smile and act normal, anyway? Rosemary searched deep to find the compassion she had stored up for him, but maybe because she knew her own happiness was about to take off down the road, she resented Eric's happiness with Melissa.

As the joys and concerns were announced, Rosemary thought about her father, still so firm in his refusal to come back to church. Was he changing? Or would he always be bitter and full of sadness? Would he even care if he knew she was giving up her dreams with Kirk, just to stay here and be near him? Would he ever forgive her?

Kirk stepped up onto the porch, a squeaking floorboard groaning in protest, a lazy lizard sunning on a nearby azalea bush scurrying off at the intrusion. Clayton stood with his hands in his belt loops. His hair was combed and he was wearing a clean blue cotton button-down shirt.

"You did a nice job," he said to Kirk by way of greeting.

Kirk took that as an invitation to come on up onto the porch. "So you approve, after all?"

Clayton kept right on looking at the shining steeple. "I still say it was a waste, but the thing does look better."

"I didn't change it," Kirk responded, his own gaze sweeping over his handiwork. "I simply improved on its existing beauty."

"Is that what you're trying to do with my daughter?"

The question, as well as the glint in Clayton's eyes, took Kirk by surprise, but gave him the opportunity to fight for his lady.

"Rosemary needs no improvement, sir. I'm leaving today, but before I go, I just wanted you to know—I've fallen in love with your daughter. I asked her to marry me and come with me, but she reluctantly refused."

Clayton seemed dazed by Kirk's directness, but quickly recovered to glare down at him. "Did you do something to hurt my daughter?"

Kirk shook his head, one hand on his hip, the other braced on a porch column. "No, sir. My only mistake was in the loving of your daughter. You, sir, you've done the hurting. Rosemary loves me, and wants to be with me, but she refuses to do so, because she feels she has to stay here with you."

Clayton snorted to hide the sorrow cresting in his eyes. "I don't need her hovering over me."

"She hovers because she loves you and she wants you to love her in return. She's waiting for your forgiveness."

That got Clayton's attention. "You mean to tell me, she won't go with you because...because she thinks I need to forgive her first?"

"That's the way of it," Kirk said, his gaze level with Rosemary's father's. "And I'm here to tell you—I don't like it one bit. I'm here to ask you to please release your daughter from this punishment you've put upon her. Rosemary has been punished enough. It's time you let her go."

"With you?"

"I'd like that, but I'm leaving in a few minutes. I can't force her to come. Whether or not she decides to come with me doesn't matter as much as whether or not you can find it in your heart to forgive her. If I can't have her, if I can't love her, then I'm asking you to give her back her worth, so she can find someone to share her life with."

Clayton looked toward the church. "I've never held my daughter back."

"Ah, but you have, sir," Kirk retorted, his Irish temper flaring. "She waits for a kind word from you, a gesture to tell her that you don't blame her for her mother's death. Can you give her that?"

Clayton's expression softened then and for the first time he looked Kirk in the eye. "I loved my wife, son," he said, his voice so low Kirk had to strain to hear. "It's been a hard year, getting over what happened."

"But you need to get over it," Kirk said gently. "Bitterness won't bring your wife back."

"No," Clayton agreed, his eyes growing misty. "If that were true, she'd certainly be standing right here."

"Your daughter *has* been right here, all along," Kirk reminded him. "And she's been patiently waiting for your forgiveness. Please offer it to her. My coming here to ask you— it's the only gift I can extend to Rosemary, as proof of my love. But I don't ask this for myself. I ask it for her."

With that, he turned on his heel before he started begging, and headed to his waiting trailer. He couldn't stop. He couldn't look back. He'd done enough restoring on this old church. His work was finished.

The choir and congregation finished singing "On the Wings of a Snow-White Dove," and everyone settled in to listen to Reverend Clancy's sermon. Rosemary tried to focus on his words, tried to snap to attention when he lifted his voice during a strong declaration, but her mind kept going back to Kirk. Was he gone already?

She heard Reverend Clancy say something about forgiveness, then she looked over at Eric. She didn't think she'd ever be able to forgive him completely, but she would try very hard to accept things now.

Then the minister talked about how Jesus had died for our sins.

"You don't have to worry," he said. "You don't have to ask for others to forgive your transgressions. This is what Easter is all about. This is why we are here this morning. Not to mourn death. But to celebrate life. We celebrate the life of Jesus Christ, who died for us, and was resurrected for us, therefore giving us eternal grace in heaven.

"'We walk by faith, not by sight,'" the reverend quoted. "And by faith, we must learn to forgive. 'For the things which are seen are temporary, but the things which are not seen are eternal.'"

Rosemary wanted to celebrate life, wanted to see eternity, but she didn't think she had that right. Maybe she didn't deserve to celebrate. Maybe her faith wasn't strong enough, after all. She was afraid to follow something she couldn't see, she was afraid to let herself heal.

The reverend went on, talking still about forgiving offenders. "'...on the contrary, you ought rather to forgive and comfort him, lest perhaps such a one be swallowed up with too much sorrow.' This is what Paul told the Corinthians," the minister said, one hand lifted high, "and this is what I say to you today. Don't be swallowed up by sorrow on this Easter Day, don't be consumed by grief. Rejoice. Christ is risen. And He lives in each and every one of us, and it is by His grace that we can rejoice. It is by His grace that we are reborn."

The morning light shifted through the stained-glass windows of the sanctuary, casting out a pale net of warmth, a beacon of brilliance that shimmered across the altar and glistened off the stark white blossoms of the Easter lilies. Rosemary saw that light, felt its warmth from her spot in the back of the church.

And in that bright, comforting light, she at last saw her own redemption.

The minister preached on, his voice gentle now as he retold the story of Jesus dying on the cross. Her heart pumping, her palms sweating, Rosemary heard him loud and clear, as if a church bell had just tolled for her only. She remembered Kirk telling her she would spend her life swallowed in sorrow. Swallowed in sorrow. Drowning in pain. Sinking in a pit of gloom and despair. Letting her only chance for happiness drift away when she should be rejoicing in a second chance.

She looked over at Eric, tears streaming down her face. Eric stared at her, a soft pleading light in his eyes. She saw Danny, concern coloring his features as he watched her. Aunt Fitz's sweet face became a blur as Rosemary rose out of the pew to push her way into the aisle. She had to get out of here. She had to find Kirk before it was too late for her second chance.

She ran down the aisle toward the exit, her breath cutting through her body. She didn't want to be swallowed by sorrow. She wanted to be healed. She wanted to rejoice in her love for Kirk.

And now she knew, now she saw with a crystal, shimmering clarity, what she had to do. *She* had to forgive in order to be healed. She'd been waiting for her father to offer her redemption, when she wasn't willing to offer it to herself. She'd held her own forgiveness away from Eric, sitting in judgment of both him and herself when it wasn't her place to judge at all.

She stumbled out into the narthex, then lifted her head to the tiny stone steps leading to the belfry. Suddenly, she wanted to go up there where Kirk had worked and sweated. She wanted to see her world from his viewpoint, to be near all the places he'd touched and transformed; she wanted to be closer to God. She wanted to find her redemption, not from her father, not because she could at last forgive Eric, but because she had been given redemption all along, from God.

Absolution was there. All she had to do was climb the steps to find it. She'd been searching, asking, praying for answers, and God had sent Kirk to her.

Yet she'd turned him away.

Forcing herself to a slow calm, Rosemary started up the steps to the tower, her heart pounding, her tears fresh and cleansing, her mind clear for the first time in a very long time. Gripping the heavy wooden railing, she took one slow step after another until she was past the point she'd always stopped at before, until she was past returning down the winding stairs. Slightly dizzy, but determined to make the climb, she lifted her sandaled feet one step at a time.

At last, winded and deathly afraid, but adamant and resigned, she reached the opening to the belfry. A ray of white-hot sunlight streamed down to touch her clammy skin, its warmth like a signal from the hand of God. She felt Him there, knew He was guiding her. She took the last few steps on faith alone and found herself standing inside the belfry, the morning wind rushing over her damp face, the birds singing a song of joy that lifted out on the breeze. And then, she looked out over the world she'd always known, and felt the healing power of God's love.

The view was incredible. The same houses, the same trees and gardens, the same mountains—but different now. She could see it all so much more clearly.

Then her heart shattered as she saw a trailer-truck hauling another trailer, moving slowly down the street, moving away from the church, moving toward the interstate.

"Kirk!" she said, wanting with all her heart to bring him back. She needed to tell him she wasn't afraid anymore. She needed to tell him that she'd been wrong, so wrong.

All this time she'd been waiting to be *given* forgiveness, but she hadn't been willing to *accept* forgiveness. Yet it had been hers for the asking.

Just as it was Eric's for the asking. Melissa was right. He didn't need her permission or her acceptance to start a new life. He had God's love and grace. And because Reverend Clancy had known that, Eric had, for the first time in his life, someone who believed he could be forgiven.

It all made such perfect sense now.

But too late. Kirk was gone. Rosemary watched as his rig rounded the corner. How could she stop him, when she'd sent him away?

Then she heard another truck cranking up, and fascinated,

watched as her father backed his vehicle out of the driveway and headed in the same direction as Kirk. Unaware that she was even doing so, Rosemary leaned toward the edge of the sturdy stone belfry wall to watch the two most important men in her life, both of them driving away.

Her father pulled his truck up behind Kirk's, then honked the horn to get Kirk's attention. Then he hopped out of the truck, leaving the door wide-open.

"What's going on?" she whispered, afraid her father had finally snapped.

But as she watched, horrified and fascinated at the same time, something amazing, something special happened between the two men.

Kirk got out of the truck to confront her father. They exchanged words, then to her amazement, Kirk grinned and clasped her father's hand. But even more amazing, Clayton returned the handshake, and...he actually smiled. Then he got in his truck, turned it around and headed home.

Kirk, too, turned his rig around and drove back, back toward the church. Back, Rosemary realized with a soaring heart, to her.

At about the same time Kirk switched off the engine and climbed down out of his rig, the church doors came open as the congregation poured out, laughing and chattering, happy.

Rosemary watched, and waited as Kirk lifted his face up to find her standing there in the tower, underneath the steeple he'd repaired. Without hesitation, she lifted a hand to wave down at him. Kirk smiled up at her, then took off running, pushing through the amazed crowd, past the startled, curious faces, to step inside the church, then take the steps two at a time until he'd reached her side.

"Rosemary?" he called, his breath coming hard and heavy as he took the last step up beside her.

"You came back," she said much with the same awe he'd held when she'd chosen him over Eric.

"Aye, I was just about to turn around and come drag you out of the church, when your father literally hauled me out of me truck and told me to get myself home to you right away."

"My father said that? Whatever made him have such a change of heart?"

Kirk shrugged and tugged her into his arms. "Only the good Lord can answer that." He kissed her, then said, "I'm back, that's a fact, Rosemary, my love. And I'm willing to stay—"

"You don't have to," she interrupted, her eyes shining with a new joy. "I'm willing to go with you. I want to be with you, Kirk. I...I want to take that leap of faith."

His dark eyes grew misty. "Are you sure?"

"Very sure," she said, one hand roaming through his tousled hair. "I realized something today. I was waiting for everyone else to forgive me, waiting for everyone involved in this to change, when I was the one needing to make a change, I only had to forgive myself. You tried to tell me, but...I'm stubborn about some things."

"I like that in my women," he said, relief washing over his features. "I do so love you, though."

"Enough to carry me away?"

"Aye, enough to marry you right here in this church." He gazed down at her, then said, "We'll build us a house on the mountain."

Amazed, she asked, "But what about your work?"

"I'll work, and...you can come with me when the mood strikes you. I could use a good office manager. I want you with me, but...I know how important your home is to you." He lifted her chin, his eyes shining and sincere. "I promise you this, Rosemary. I will always come home to you. And that's not a compromise. It's what I want. It's my life."

"Sounds more like a commitment," she said, grateful that he was willing to make one, thankful that it wasn't too late for them.

"A firm, grounded commitment."

She kissed him, then laughed when a round of applause exploded from the captivated audience below.

Then Danny shouted, "Well, go ahead and ring the bells. This is a celebration, remember?"

Rosemary laughed, her heart soaring as she saw Clayton standing in the crowd, with Faye by his side.

Kirk let her go to reach for the bell rope. Then he took her hand in his free one. "Are you ready to step to the edge, then?"

Rosemary looked down at her father, her one last hope shining clearly in her eyes. Clayton lifted a hand in greeting, his eyes telling her what his heart had felt all along. She had his blessings, and his love, always.

She was forgiven. She was healed.

Rosemary looked at Kirk and nodded. "I'm ready."

Kirk grinned, then held her steady as he rang the bell several times. The chimes lifted out in a sweet melody, heralding a new beginning, for the church, for Eric and Melissa, for Clayton and Faye, and…for Rosemary and Kirk.

Epilogue

A few weeks later, a wedding was held on Alba Mountain. Clayton gave his daughter away, without remorse or regret, without any bitterness left between them, in the church that they both loved. Then the entire town headed for the top of the mountain, and Rosemary then stood on the edge of the cliff, stating the rest of her vows to the man she loved.

When the ceremony was over, Aunt Fitz handed Rosemary her wedding quilt which had been lovingly stored. "I knowed you'd be needing this. Knowed it the day I set eyes on your steeplejack. I saw the signs."

"I saw them, too, Aunt Fitz," Rosemary replied as she gazed up with loving eyes at her handsome husband. "It took me a while, but I finally saw all of the signs, too."

"Thank goodness," Kirk said, bending to kiss his wife, his finger touching on the meshed ring he'd inherited from an artistic Celtic ancestor, the ring he'd placed on his bride's finger to forever seal his love.

"Thank God above," Kirk's mother replied, lifting her hands toward the sky. "The boy was pining away something fierce."

Aunt Fitz, who'd taken an instant liking to Edana, laughed heartily. "Ain't love grand?"

A new season had begun. Rosemary's time to heal had come. Now, with Kirk, she would have her time to love. Kirk hadn't changed Rosemary; he'd only added to her existing beauty.

After all, that was his job.

And in heaven, one special soul watched over Rosemary and

her new husband with eternal care and immeasurable pride, sending out blessings of hope as her daughter started a new life with the man who'd restored Rosemary's faith, in herself, and in love.

*   *   *   *   *

Dear Reader,

This book is based on the death of my sister, Glenda. She and her husband were coming home from a shopping trip when another car pulled out in front of them. They both received extensive injuries, but after a complicated surgery, my sister went into cardiac arrest and died. The person driving the other vehicle was drunk.

This wasn't the driver's first offense, nor would it be her last. Since then, I've become very active in MADD (Mothers Against Drunk Driving) as a means of coping with this horrible tragedy.

While this story is fiction, the emotions I and my entire family went through are mirrored within these pages. This was one of the hardest books I've ever written because I felt drained with each scene. But it was also very cathartic, because in spite of all of Rosemary's very real pain, she found her happy ending through her faith and through Kirk's unconditional love. These two things have sustained my family, too.

On a lighter note, I decided to write about a steeplejack after reading an article in my local paper. A friend called right after I'd read the article, and I told her I'd just found an idea for another book. That was a few years ago. I never gave up on that story, and I'm thrilled that my steeplejack has become a character. I loved him from the minute he popped into my head. I truly hope we can all learn from his work.

Restoration is an important thing, for both steeples and souls that need repair. We all need time to heal. Writing this book has helped, and I hope it helps you, too.

Until next time, may the angels watch over you while you sleep.

Lenora Worth

Books by Lois Richer

Love Inspired

†Faith, Hope & Charity
*Brides of the Seasons
‡If Wishes Were Weddings

LOIS RICHER

Sneaking a flashlight under the blankets, hiding in a thicket of caragana bushes where no one could see, pushing books into socks to take to camp—those are just some of the things Lois Richer freely admits to in her pursuit of the written word. "I'm a book-a-holic. I can't do without stories," she confesses. "It's always been that way."

Her love of language evolved into writing her own stories. Today her passion is to create tales of personal struggles that lead to triumph over life's rocky road. For Lois, a happy ending is essential.

"In my stories, as in my own life, God has a way of making all things beautiful. Writing a love story is my way of reinforcing my faith in His ultimate goodness toward us—His precious children."

A WILL AND A WEDDING
Lois Richer

Chapter One

Jefferson William Haddon III wanted a son.

Badly.

The problem, as Jefferson defined it, was that at age thirty-five, he had yet to find the type of woman with whom he would consider raising a child. And the very last thing he had expected was that someone would find such a woman for him.

"Would you say that again, please?"

Jefferson turned to stare at the woman across from him once more, unable to believe that his Aunt Judith had considered her suitable for marriage.

Not to him.

She wasn't the type to be his wife.

If he had wanted one.

Which he did not! Not like this.

"Miss McNaughton will continue her sponsorship of you in your endeavor, Miss Newton, provided that you and her nephew, Jefferson Haddon, marry within the next two months. Until that time, you may both reside in her home, Oak Bluff, all expenses paid." Judith's old family lawyer cleared his throat.

"Mr. Haddon, when you marry you will receive Miss McNaughton's fortune less Miss Newton's yearly allowance of one hundred thousand dollars. You will both receive the deeds to the house and its entailments, free and clear. Miss Newton will, as your wife, continue to live in the house as long as she wishes." The snowy haired gentleman paused to glance up at the couple seated before him. His light blue eyes darkened as he continued.

"If you should choose to ignore her wishes, Miss McNaughton has directed that neither of you shall benefit. Miss Newton will be forced to make other arrangements for her work and Mr. Haddon will have no further claim on her estate. The property will be sold and the money will go to an animal shelter she has so named."

Even as he wondered what the woman's 'work' was, Jefferson's mouth fell open.

"But surely we can contest the terms of this will, Mr. Jones. You were her friend for years, surely you realize what a terrible position this places us in." He stopped, conscious of the glowering countenance of the old lawyer.

"Your aunt was of perfectly sound mind when she made out this document." The wrinkled old hand shook Judith's will in front of them both. "Should the opportunity arise, and you decide to contest, young man, I will be happy to testify to her sanity. In court. Under oath." The old man's tone was frosty with contempt.

Jefferson was furious. He raked a hand through his perfectly groomed dark head in agitation. Yes, he wanted a child, but he had no desire to get married for money. And he certainly would not be forced into it by a busybody old aunt with nothing better to do than play matchmaker.

Blast, what a mess.

That woman, what was her name? Cassie, he remembered suddenly, Cassie…something. Anyway, she sat staring at him in horror. As if she could do worse than marry into one of the oldest families in Toronto!

"I'll move out immediately." He heard her words through a fog and turned to stare.

"What?"

"Are you hard of hearing, Mr. Haddon? I said, I will move out of the house immediately." Her voice was sharp with scorn. "I have no intention of marrying you or anyone else to provide a roof over my head."

She surged to her feet with all the pomp and ceremony of a miniature warship, sailing off to battle. She stood in front of

him, hands on her shapely hips. Grim determination turned
down the edges of her mouth. Jefferson laughed at the absurdity
of it, and then watched fascinated as her body went rigid with
fury.

"Your aunt was a gracious woman who treated everyone
with dignity and respect. It's too bad you didn't turn out the
same."

He studied the wide green eyes, huge and full of turmoil in
a face white with strain. Her black hair curved around her oval
face in a riot of curls that bounced merrily with each move she
made.

She was not like any woman he had seen before, Jefferson
decided. This Cassie person's appearance fell somewhere between comfortable unconcern and brilliant chic. She wore a
bulky red sweater that hung well below her hips. A flaring skirt
in a wild pattern of reds and oranges dropped to her ankles.
She had on some type of granny boot that should have looked
ridiculous and instead suited her crazy outfit. The gypsy look
was further embellished by gold hoops that hung from her small
earlobes.

Jefferson found those turbulent eyes fixed on himself.

Coldly.

"Look, Mr. Haddon. I'm not a charity case. I lived with your
aunt because she asked me to. She was lonely, I think, and
gradually she developed a fondness for some of my charges. I
think they provided some amusement for her when she couldn't
get out anymore." Her glittering eyes reminded him of a cat's
when it was hissing with fury, ready to strike. "But I am not,
I repeat not, going to live with you in that house, let alone
marry you, just so I can get my hands on a hundred grand."

She stared down her pert little nose at him, which would
have been effective if she hadn't had to tip her head back so
far to meet his eyes. He wondered where she had learned the
slang terms for money even as he appreciated the fact that she
also had no intention of going along with Judith's machinations.

Grinning, he held up one hand.

"No offense, Miss, er, uh—" Jefferson looked toward the
lawyer to fill in the gap.

"Newton, Cassandra Newton," she repeated, her voice seething with unspoken emotions.

Jefferson watched as she rolled her eyes upward and then closed them. She was whispering. Some kind of a prayer. He recognized the same habit his aunt had employed during his own rebellious youth. He listened unashamedly to her softly spoken words, a half smile on his mouth.

"God, I need some help here. I know you're leading me and I'm trying to remember that this is Judith's nephew, so for her sake I'll try to be polite." She sighed deeply, her shoulders rising. "But, Lord. You know I don't tolerate egotistical, arrogant, spoiled brats very well."

That said, she wheeled away toward the door, ignoring Jefferson as she spoke directly to Mr. Jones.

"Thank you for inviting me to hear the will, Mr. Jones. I appreciated Miss McNaughton's help when she was alive, but I just can't marry someone because she wanted me to." She cast a disparaging look over Jefferson.

Especially not him, her turbulent sea green gaze seemed to say.

Mr. Jones thoughtfully stroked the snowy white beard that made him look like a jovial Santa Claus. He held on to the tiny hand she had offered, while silently contemplating her determined stance. Finally he spoke.

"You have two more months to live in the house before the will dictates that you must move out, Miss Newton. May I suggest that you stay there and use that time to sort out your plans for the future? In the meantime, Miss McNaughton has provided some funds for your living expenses."

Jefferson watched as the woman accepted an envelope, which he assumed contained a cheque, from Jones. They spoke quietly together for a few moments before she left. Jefferson smiled as she deliberately ignored his presence.

Good! He had no desire to deal with some moneygrubbing female just now.

The next few hours were fraught with tension as he and the older man went over the legal documents several times. Finally Jefferson was forced to give up in defeat. There was little hope of breaking this will. And he wasn't sure he wanted to, not really.

Aunt Judith had been the one person to whom he'd been able to run when life got rough during those difficult childhood years. She had always been ready to offer a shoulder, a handkerchief and a cookie when he desperately needed all three. She had been the calm mothering influence he had never found at home. She had also been tough and uncompromising when her mind settled on something. If Judith McNaughton wanted it, she invariably got it. Apparently she wanted to see him married.

"Mr. Jones, I have to tell you that this doesn't fit in with my plans at all. Not at all."

He fingered his mustache and considered the older man. There was nothing but courtesy and consideration in that lined face and Jefferson decided to explain his blueprint for the future.

"I have invested a substantial amount of money and a large of amount of time researching the possibilities of obtaining a surrogate mother and defining exactly what her rights in such an arrangement would be."

"You want a child badly, Mr. Haddon."

Jefferson nodded.

"I want a son. I've interviewed couples who have gone through the process and inspected the children produced from such a union. I'm satisfied that they seem normal healthy children with a parent who truly wants them."

Mr. Jones coughed discreetly behind his hand, hiding his thoughts behind a large white handkerchief.

"And after this research you feel you have an idea of what you want?"

"I know exactly what I want in the mother of my son, Mr. Jones." He enumerated the qualities for the lawyer. "Calm, rational, levelheaded, to name a few traits. Unemotional. A woman who won't expect to be involved in my life other than in matters to do with my child in the first few months of his life."

There was a gleam in the older man's eyes that was extremely disconcerting.

"This hypothetical woman, then. You believe she will just

calmly hand over her child and disappear? That the two of you would live happily ever after?''

Jefferson nodded.

''Yes, that's exactly what I want from the contract. A calm, rational agreement between two adults.'' He barely heard the mumbled aside.

''Seems to me a woman would have to be very calm to agree to such a thing. Dead, in fact.'' Mr. Jones shook his head slowly.

''I would make it worth her while,'' Jefferson rushed in and then stopped, appalled at how the words sounded when you said them out loud.

His face flushed a deep red at the intensity of Jones's scrutiny. Jefferson had always known he came from a family of wealth and prestige; tact and diplomacy were the rule. Never once had he been tempted to misuse his assets. But suddenly he wished he could spend a portion of his father's overblown bank account to buy back those words, unsay them.

Lawyer Jones evidently felt the same way for he frowned, his wise blue eyes accusing in their scrutiny.

''But what about this woman? How long will you need her? What happens to her once the first few months of the baby's life have passed and you no longer need her? Do you expect she will have no feelings for the child...that she'll just disappear with cash in hand?''

When stated in those terms, Jefferson's plan sounded arrogant; even slightly odious.

The older man snorted in disbelief.

''And what if the child is a girl?''

Jefferson hadn't thought about that.

''And what do you tell the child about his mother in ten or fifteen years?'' the old man asked in a no-nonsense voice.

It was too much information overload, especially on a day when everything seemed out of sync.

''I don't know. But I'm confident that I can handle whatever needs to be done.'' Even now, Jefferson's mind whirled with plans.

He had chosen a name for the boy. Breaking with eons of family tradition, Jefferson had decided his son would be named

Robert, Bobby for short. It was all planned out, everything was in place. His lawyers had the financial details organized into a formal agreement.

"Mr. Jones, I merely require the right woman for my purpose. It will mean that my business plans for expansion will have to be shelved for the moment, but I feel it's worth it." Jefferson hoped the man understood that he would not be swayed by these trivial problems.

Willard T. Jones sat polishing his round spectacles, staring at them for a long solemn moment. When he finally glanced up, Jefferson caught a sparkle of amusement in the old man's eyes.

"Well, Mr. Haddon. I'm sure you've thought about this long and hard. If I may, I'd like to offer a suggestion."

Jefferson nodded.

"My advice is this. Put everything on hold. The issue of Miss McNaughton's estate has yet to be settled and if you recall—" he smiled dryly "—your marital status may well change."

"Oh, I don't..."

"In six months' time, the entire picture will look very different. I suggest you take the time necessary to think everything through. You might start with the estate." Jones tipped back in his chair and gazed at the ceiling while speaking. "Judith Evelyn McNaughton was a cagey, stubborn old woman who went to the grave with a last-ditch effort to manipulate you into marriage. She specially chose Cassie Newton."

Privately, Jefferson thought Judith's latest bid for control of his future made all her other matchmaking attempts picayune by comparison.

"She knew how hard you've worked to make a success of your company. Just last month she was telling me of your need to expand your business. And of your need for more cash."

Jefferson was startled by the words.

"I didn't realize she had kept such close track of me while I've been out of the country," he murmured, staring at his hands.

"She wanted you to have the means to expand."

Jefferson grinned. "But only if I got it on her terms. Good old Judith."

"The way I see it," the older man continued, "she gave you two months' grace. Think long and hard before you decide, my boy. Make very sure you won't regret giving up the very things Judith wanted you to have."

As he walked down the street, Jefferson Haddon shook his head at the ridiculous situation he found himself in. Memories, sharp and clear, tumbled around in his mind. He could still visualize Judith's thin, severe face with that prim mouth pressed into a firm line as she bawled him out.

"One must always consider the other person, Jefferson. For in one way or another, whatever you do will affect him."

That had been the time Freddie Hancock has socked Jefferson in the nose for saying Freddie's mother was fat. Well, Jefferson grinned fondly, it was true. All the Hancocks had been fat. But Mrs. Hancock was enormous and when her arms wrapped around him in a hug, his eight-year-old body had been suffocated against her overflowing abundance.

He'd also been embarrassed. Aunt Judith had remonstrated with him on the social niceties before patting his hand gently.

"That's the way many people show their affection for you, dear," she had said. Her golden eyes had been sad. "I wish you would open up more. Most people just want to be friends. If you give them a chance, you will enjoy them."

Needless to say, that had not been Jefferson's experience. There were few opportunities for boyhood friends in the austere home his father maintained and very little free time to pursue such interests. There were even fewer people in Jefferson's young life who had ever hugged him.

Aunt Judith had understood that. She had also been one of the few to whom he had granted that particular privilege. And as she gathered his gangly body against her thin, frail frame, he'd felt warm and cared for inside.

His mouth curved in remembrance.

Of course, Melisande Gustendorf had tried to hug him a number of times in those days. Usually when he was with the guys. Mel would sneak up behind them and wrap her arms around him. She was weird that way. And at twelve, what boy wants to be hugged in public by a girl?

Jefferson smiled fondly as he remembered the lesson about

birds and bees that Aunt Judith had related when she heard about Melisande. Aunt Judith had never married; never had children. Explaining the details must have been embarrassing, but she had persevered until Jefferson's every question had been answered. And then he had made darned good and sure Melisande never got within six feet of him!

His memories of Aunt Judith made him chuckle as he drove back to his penthouse apartment on the waterfront. Most of the time he was satisfied with the place. But today he felt hemmed in, constricted by his aloof tower.

"Dinky little rooms stuck way up in the sky," Judith had scolded him constantly about his chosen lifestyle. "You live out of reach of people. Why, you can't even touch God's wonderful creation, the earth, without driving for twenty minutes."

In a way, Judith was right. From his panoramic living room windows, he could see the city clothed in her glorious fall colors. By late October the leaves had all turned to vibrant oranges, brilliant reds and sunny yellows. Many had fallen, but there were still enough to create a picturesque view.

But it would take a while to drive to one of the reserves, park his car, and walk among the beauty.

"You should be out in the fresh air, chop a few logs when the weather gets crisp. A fire feels good in that stone fireplace when winter sets in."

"But Aunt Judith, I have to be near my work."

She had glared at him then and his eyes had dropped first.

"You know blessed well that your work could be conducted from anywhere. Why, these days some folks use a computer for everything. Don't have to leave home to talk to people, shop or even go to the library."

She had tapped her walking stick against the bricks of the patio, almost knocking over one of the pots of rusty orange chrysanthemums she always set out in the fall.

"Don't hold with it myself. People need people. A body should have a time to work and a time to play. Too many folks taking their work wherever they go. And those danged cell phones."

Jefferson grinned in remembrance.

"The blamed things always ring at the wrong time." She

had glared at him angrily as his own pealed out. "A body can't have a decent conversation nowadays."

At Judith's estate, Jefferson knew there would be crunchy crisp leaves underfoot when you first stepped out the door. They would float down on the fall breeze, covering the vast expanse of lawns. A few pumpkins and some of the hardier vegetables would sit outside in the garden, and he could almost taste the ripe red crab apples weighing down slender trees in the orchard.

The decision was made without thinking and moments later, Jefferson found himself ensconced in his luxury sedan, hurrying toward Judith's huge estate, aptly named Oak Bluff. Suddenly, he had a longing to see the old, sturdy brick house with its huge oak and maple trees standing guard around the circular driveway; to walk in the naturally wild terrain at the back of the grounds and feel the fresh air wash over him.

It was exactly as he remembered. Stately majestic and yet welcoming. The house stood firm against the elements, its pottery red brick and spotless white trim gleaming in the bright fall sunshine. Bennet had cleaned the debris off the walkway and the front lawns, but Jefferson knew there would be a thick carpet of crackling, wrinkled red and gold leaves just outside the back door.

He let himself into the house with the key Lawyer Jones had given him and dropped his overcoat on a hall table before glancing around. Richly polished oak paneling led the way into the library, his favorite room in the entire house.

Aunt Judith had a vast number of books, both old and new, crowded onto the shelves, carefully catalogued and indexed by subject, then author. Nestled into a nook on the far side, Jefferson knew there was a computer, printer and fax machine that Judith had frequently used. In one corner, under a window, stood the old desk her father had given as a birthday gift many years before. Its rolltop cover was closed now that the owner was gone. He brushed his hand over it fondly.

"Hello? Anyone home? Bennet?"

There was no answer. He wandered through to the patio.

The deck was littered here and there with golden yellow poplar leaves that whirled and wafted down on the delicate breeze. The redwood patio furniture was still out and since the afternoon was warm, Jefferson decided to sit outside until Mrs. Bennet returned. In his mind he could hear Judith's voice as she fondly reminisced.

"No one can ever deny the power a home has on a family. It's like an old friend. It wraps its arms around you and shields you from life's problems while it draws people closer together."

This was exactly like coming home, he thought, staring at the beauty around him. And it was nothing like the house he'd grown up in. This house was made for laughing children, a family, love. Suddenly, Jefferson wished he might raise his son here. When he had one, he reminded himself.

Obviously, Aunt Judith had wanted him to have that experience. But at what a price—married to someone he didn't even know!

Voices from the garden area penetrated his musings and he got up to investigate. Down past the patio, a shortcut through the maze and Jefferson was almost across the lawns when he identified the happy laughing shouts of children.

"Chicken! I let you roll me."

"No, you didn't. I made you."

"Ow! David! He pulled my braid."

What were they doing here, he wondered? The estate was fenced but there were no nearby neighbours with children. At least none that he could recall. From the sounds quite a few people were present now. And they were having a riot on his aunt's property.

"Can't catch me."

When he finally rounded what Judith had called the summerhouse, Jefferson Haddon III stopped dead in his tracks. There were at least ten of them, he decided. The oldest was no more than fifteen or sixteen. They were carrying the cornstalks from the side of the garden to the center, forming a huge cornstalk teepee while one person stood at the edge, arms outstretched to the sky.

"Autumn leeeves begin to faaall…"

At least the shrill voice had good volume, he decided, wincing at the wobbling pitch.

They all had jeans on, from the toddler holding another

child's hand, to the eldest who seemed intent on adding a few more stalks to the already monstrous heap. All except for one boy, the tallest of the group. He wore tight black pants that looked painted on, and a red checked shirt that hung way down his lean body.

Startled, Jefferson watched as the skinny one lit the teepee. In seconds there was a huge crackling bonfire in the center of his great aunt's garden, and a pack of kids were dancing round and round, laughing happily.

"Ring around the rosy!"

Disgust and anger coursed through his veins as Jefferson watched the scene unfold. They had no right to intrude, he fumed. No right at all. This was private property. For some reason the Bennets were not here, so these children were trespassing. They certainly didn't have permission to light a fire.

Breaking into a run, Jefferson jogged across the lawn and through the black tilled soil of the garden to grab what he thought was the ringleader by his jacket.

"Exactly what do you think you're doing?" he demanded through clenched teeth and then sucked in a lungful of air as shimmering green eyes glittered out from a tousled mop of black hair.

"Having a wiener roast, Mr. Haddon. Want to join us?"

Cassie Newton stood grinning up at him as the children ran circles around them happily. She looked like a child herself in the bulky old coat and decrepit jeans. Her face was smudged with dirt and her blunt fingernails were filthy.

"Who are all these children?" he asked, ignoring the grin. "And what are they doing here?"

"They're mine," Cassie told him proudly. "And I already told you. We are going to roast wieners." Her voice dropped to a whisper as she hissed a warning up at him, green eyes flashing. "For the short time they have left here, this is their home and their party. And you will not spoil it, do you hear me?"

Sensing the tension surrounding them, most of the children had stopped their wild play and stood staring at the two adults facing each other.

Jefferson watched as the tall, skinny boy sporting the tight pants moved forward to stand protectively next to Cassie. He topped her by a good ten inches and it was clear from his stance that he would take on anyone who challenged her.

Jefferson was flabbergasted.

"All of these children are yours?" His voice squeaked with surprise and he heard one of the kids snicker. He strove for control. His eyes moved over her assessingly. "How old are you, anyway?"

But she ignored him.

"David," she addressed the young soldier at her side. "Would you please tell Mrs. Bennet that we're ready. Then you could help her carry out the hot dogs and the hot chocolate."

A sweet smile accompanied her words and Jefferson was surprised to see the sour-faced lad grin back good-naturedly before loping off to do her bidding.

She directed the rest of the children to arranging a picnic table that stood off under the trees, and finding wiener sticks. Satisfied that everyone was occupied, Cassie turned back to face him.

"I'm a foster mother," she told him matter-of-factly. "The kids stay with me until the agency is able to find them families." Her green eyes glimmered with mirth as she spied his Gucci shoes filling rapidly with rich black garden soil.

"You're not really dressed for this," she observed, eyeing his pure wool slacks, black vest and once pristine white shirt. "Perhaps you should wait inside until I am finished if you wish to speak to me."

Jefferson seethed at the dismissing tone of this—this interloper. So she thought she could reject him so easily? He grabbed her arm as she turned away. His eyes opened wide as she turned on him like a fiery virago, ramrod stiff in the filthy garments.

"Mr. Haddon, you will let go of me. You will not create a scene to spoil our day. You will return to the house and wait there."

Her voice was as crisp as a fresh fall apple and he found himself turning to obey her militarylike orders before he realized what he was doing and turned back.

"Just a minute here," he protested, angry that she had him dancing to her tune. He pointed to the fire.

"You cannot let that thing rage away. What if it got out of control? The city has bylaws, you know."

The urchin before him drew herself to her full height, which Jefferson figured was maybe a hair over five feet, before deigning to speak. When she did, her resentment was clear.

"I am in charge here, Mr. Haddon. If I need help I can call on Bennet. But I won't." Her hands clasped her hips and he couldn't help but notice the way her hair tossed itself into silky disarray around her face. "And for your information, I have a permit to burn."

Jefferson shook his head. He refused to be deterred. Someone had to protect Judith's wonderful old estate.

"Bennet's nowhere to be seen. Fat lot of help he'd be."

She refused to answer him, her full lips pursed tightly. Instead, one grubby fist pointed toward the shed in the corner of the garden. Jefferson saw a man leaning against the side, watching them.

"We'll manage, Mr. Haddon. You'd better go before you ruin those designer duds completely."

Jefferson almost choked. The stately old butler Aunt Judith had insisted wear a black pinstripe suit coat and spotless white shirt stood clad in a red flannel shirt and tattered overalls with a filthy felt hat on his silver hair.

Jefferson whirled around to speak to Cassie but she ignored him as she dealt with one of the children's requests. When the little girl had toddled away, he tried a more conciliatory approach.

"My name is Jefferson," he told her softly, intrigued by a woman who would don such unsightly clothes to stand in the center of a dirty garden with a pack of homeless kids for a wiener roast in late autumn.

She whirled to face him, having obviously forgotten his presence.

"What?" Her voice was far away, lost in some never land.

"My name is Jefferson." He told her again, more clearly this time.

That sent her big green eyes searching his for something. He didn't know exactly what, but evidently she was satisfied. Moments later she moved forward to help Mrs. Bennet set out the food. He thought he heard her clear tones whisper softly through the crisp air.

"Goodbye, Jeff."

As he watched her walk away with that energetic bounce to her step he was coming to recognize, Jefferson tossed the sound through his mind several times.

Jeff. Jeff, he said to himself. He'd never had a nickname before, not with his father's strict adherence to family traditions. At boarding school he'd always been Jefferson or Jefferson William.

Jeff.

He liked it. A smile flickered across his sober face. He had never been to a wiener roast, either. Perhaps it was time he broadened his horizons. So that he could teach Bobby, he told himself.

He strode back to Judith's house with anticipation as his companion. The boy, David, was just coming out and looked suspiciously at him before moving aside at the door. He avoided Jeff's eyes, striding quickly past, obviously eager to join the group in the garden.

"David," Jefferson called after him. The boy stopped, unsure. Finally he turned around, angling a questioning black eyebrow up at the older man.

"What?" His voice was sullen.

"I need to change clothes. Do you know where there are some old things I can borrow?" Jeff ignored his petulant expression.

They stood facing each other for long moments, searching brown eyes scrutinizing him steadily, before David nodded. Moving into the house, he stopped to let Jeff remove his dirty shoes.

"Mrs. Bennet will skin you 'live if you track that dirt through the house," he ordered, his tone smugly superior.

As they marched the length of the upstairs hallway, Jeff noticed that every room seemed to be occupied. It was odd. He'd been here hundreds of times before and no one had ever occupied the second floor.

Other than Judith.

They finally stopped at the linen closet at the far end of the hall. The boy tugged out a cardboard box and began pulling things out.

"Here, you can wear these," the kid offered, measuring Jefferson's body mentally before choosing his attire.

Jefferson winced at the ragged denim shirt and much patched jeans that were proffered from a box that had undoubtedly come from the Goodwill center. There was very little to commend the shabby articles except that they would save his own clothes from stains the black garden soil would inflict.

"You can change in my room if you want," David suggested hesitantly.

"Thank you very much." Jefferson kept his tone properly appreciative, considering this was half his house. David stood staring out the window while he slipped out of his pants and into the rags.

"Why do you have your own room?" Jefferson asked curiously, having already noticed two beds in each of the other bedrooms.

The boy's head swung round, his grin wide.

"Cassie says a guy who's sixteen should have some privacy. So I get to have my own room. I never had that before." His serious brown eyes stared at Jefferson. "In most of the foster places we don't have half the fun we have here." His solemn face brightened.

"Cassie says this is a fun stop on the highway of life. While we're here we get to do lots of neat things. Like the bonfire." His eager eyes inspected Jefferson from head to stockinged feet. "There's some old boots in the back porch," he said softly. His dark head tipped to one side, anxiously waiting.

"Are you just about ready? They're gonna be cooking the hot dogs soon an' I'm starved."

Jefferson nodded and they went down the stairs together. Well, sort of together. The boy bounded down happily in front, eager to rejoin the fray.

Jefferson slipped on the boots slowly, mulling over the child's explanation. If he understood correctly, this boy was in limbo. Waiting. And while he was here, that woman, Cassie

Newton, made the time seem like a holiday. It was a curious occupation; one he didn't understand. What did she get out of it?

They walked toward the others, David half running until he stopped suddenly. Wheeling around, he asked, "Are you going to live here, too?"

Jefferson paused, head tilted, wondering how to answer.

"I'm not sure yet," he hedged finally. "Why?"

"Just wondering what we're s'posed to call you," David mumbled, turning away.

Jefferson reached out impulsively, pulling at the boy's sleeve.

"My name is Jeff..." The rest died away as the teenager bounded toward the others, yelling as he went.

"This is my friend Jeff," he bellowed to the assembled throng. That settled, he got to the matters at hand. "I'm having four hot dogs."

They crowded around Cassie eagerly as she handed out wieners and sticks to the younger ones first, then the older children. To his credit, David waited until the last for his portion, Jeff noticed. He took his own place behind the patient boy and only belatedly wondered if there would be enough of everything for the adults to share in the feast.

He would have backed away then, but Cassie thrust a stick and a wiener at him.

"Slumming, Jeff?" she asked, one eyebrow quirked upward expressively. There it was again, he mused, that shortened form of his name. To his amazement, he found that he enjoyed hearing it on her lips. He was even starting to think of himself as Jeff, he decided.

He ignored the hint of sarcasm and threaded the wiener on the stick crossways. It didn't look very secure and he wondered how long it would stay on.

Evidently, Cassie Newton was mentally posing the same question for she reluctantly took the items from his clumsy hands and patiently demonstrated the fine art of roasting hot dogs.

"You have to do it like this," she instructed, pushing the

meat on lengthwise. "Otherwise it will fall off when it begins to cook."

Her eyes took in his curious outfit then, widening in surprise as she focused on the sizable tear above his left knee. She forwent the obvious comment and, with a grin, turned to skewer a hotdog for herself before moving toward the fire.

Jeff followed her, wishing he'd had this experience before. Feeling totally inept and out of place, he watched carefully, noticing the way she turned and twisted the stick to get each part of the meat cooked. He tried to follow suit but after several minutes, Cassie's wiener looked golden brown and plumply delicious while his was shriveled and covered with black spots. Even the youngest child in the group had done better than he.

"Good for you, Missy. That looks great!" She praised the littlest imp with a glowing smile.

Jeff decided he liked the way her face lit up when one of the children teased her. A softening washed over her clear skin as she spoke to each. She didn't talk down to them, he noted, and she didn't boss. Cassie Newton treated each child as an adult person, entitled to her full attention. And as she listened to their little stories and jokes, Jefferson sensed her pleasure in them.

"We're very happy to have you here, sir." It was Bennet, grinning like a Cheshire cat as he bit into his own food. "Miss Judith used to say that sweet dill relish was what made the difference between a really good hot dog and a great one."

Jeff smiled while his brain screeched to a halt. Aunt Judith had done this? Joined in a wiener roast in the garden? Stiff and stern Aunt Judith who wouldn't tolerate a speck of dirt under seven-year-old fingernails?

He could hardly imagine such a thing. His curious eyes moved over the assembled throng.

It was like watching a huge family, he mused. Something like Norman Rockwell would have painted and totally unreal. He munched on the liberally ketchuped, but still charred, hot dog and thought about the curiously vibrant woman laughing down at seven wildly active children.

That Cassie managed all this with children who weren't her own was wonder enough. But when you considered that they were children who were here for a short duration only, the bond she managed to create was amazing.

He wondered how she had achieved such a rapport with them even as a tinge of jealousy wove through his mind. He wanted, no, he dreamed, of having such a relationship with his own children.

Just then the real-life Norman Rockwell portrait happened right before his eyes. A little boy, no more than five, tucked his hand into Cassie's and proceeded to tug her behind him to the lush green grass beyond the garden. On one end, it was covered with a pile of red and gold leaves in various stages of drying. As Jeff watched, they took turns tossing handfuls of the vibrantly colored foliage over each other, giggling merrily as the leaves stuck to their hair and their clothes. The picture stayed in his mind, clear and bright long after the game ended.

A whole new plan began to form in his mind.

One that involved the son he had longed for.

One that involved the petite dark-haired woman, industriously swiping at the mustard stain on the mouth of one of her charges.

One that involved Judith's extensive estate and the money she'd wanted him to have.

Jefferson William Haddon III sipped his hot chocolate and thought about that idea.

A lot.

Yes, he decided at last. It might just be workable. As long as he kept his mind focused on the long term plan: A business that stretched around the globe and a son to leave it to.

Chapter Two

"Oh, Lord," she prayed, "why me and why now?" Cassie wasn't nearly as nonchalant about the sudden appearance of Jeff Haddon as she would have liked him to believe. In fact, the sight of those broad muscular shoulders and lean, tapered legs had quickened her heart rate substantially in the lawyer's office. And again when he appeared in the garden. But he need not know that.

Neither did he need to know the way her heart sped up when she looked into those rich chocolate eyes. Maybe it was because he sometimes looked like a lost little boy himself.

She laughed at the thought. Boy, indeed.

Don't be a fool, she scolded herself. *Jefferson Haddon certainly doesn't require your mothering skills.*

So she continued her ministrations with the children, hoping they would enjoy the wonderful fall weather while it lasted. And if ever there was a place for them to run and yell, free of the constant strictures of their everyday life, it was on the grounds of Judith McNaughton's estate. The place was like a bit of heaven God had sent specially for their use. It seemed that now He was changing the rules.

When the afternoon sun lost its warmth, she scooted them all inside.

"Come on, guys, let's go in and watch that new video Mrs. Bennet rented." They trooped into the TV room with barely a complaint and settled down while she took the opportunity to relax for a moment in the sunroom.

Cassie glanced out the window longingly, thinking wistfully of what she would lose when she moved out in two months. Not that she wanted to; the place was made for hoards of children and Judith had been the best surrogate grandmother Cassie could have ever asked for.

She remembered the day she had filled out the first forms to become a foster mother. It seemed like yesterday and yet there had been a variety of children since then. And nothing had ever been as wonderful as Judith's invitation to stay at Oak Bluff. That will had come as a surprise. Fondly, Cassie recalled the old lady's words about the children.

"They need stability and order, my dear," she had said. "And I think you are the one to give it to them."

Cassie's lips tightened as she remembered Judith's comments on her nephew.

"He's a stubborn one, is Jefferson, but underneath he's a good lad. Honest and kind. Maybe a bit reserved."

Judith had been fond of rambling on about her family and Cassie hadn't paid as much attention as she should have.

Obviously.

She was still amazed that the 'boy' Judith had talked about was over thirty years old, tall, dark and handsome and from one of the city's oldest families.

That he was here now seemed unbelievable. After all, he had not made an effort to see the old woman during the last few months of her life.

"It's a wonderful old house, isn't it?"

Cassie whirled around to find the object of her thoughts standing languidly behind her. His deep voice sounded friendly, without the arrogant tones she had heard at the lawyer's. She decided to give him the benefit of her many doubts and listened as he continued speaking.

"I used to come here quite a lot as a child. Aunt Judith had a way of making me feel better at Oak Bluff when things at home weren't going very well."

She cocked her dark curly head to one side, appraising him with quizzical jade eyes.

"You haven't been around for quite a while," she accused.

"I've been living here for six months and in all that time Judith never saw you once."

Jeff shook his dark head. "No, she didn't."

He refused to justify himself to her, Cassie noted. He might as well have told her to mind her own business. Still, she had needed to ask.

"Where will you live when they sell the house?" she asked curiously. The way he kept watching her made Cassie nervous.

"The same place I've been living for years," he commented sarcastically. Jeff's dark eyes stared down at her unperturbed.

Cassie bristled at the condescending note that filled his low voice. Her temper was one of the things she constantly tried to rein in, but inevitably she forgot all about control and let loose when she should have kept cool. This was one of those times.

"Look, *Mr. Haddon,*" the emphasis was unmistakable. "Perhaps I don't have the obvious resources you have and your aunt had, but I am not some subhuman hussy trying to swindle you. I am interested in what happens to this house because it involves my family and my employment. When I move, I will lose these children because I don't have the housing resources to meet government standards. Pardon me if I seem concerned!"

She would have angrily spun out of the room, but Jefferson Haddon grasped her arm and forcibly tugged her back. When she looked up, his rugged face was stretched in a self-mocking grin. His long fingers plucked the ragged denim away from his lean form.

"I'm sorry," he proffered humbly. "I'm dressed like a bum and now I'm acting like one. Can we at least try to be friends?" When she didn't answer, he pressed her hand. "For Aunt Judith's sake? I'm sure she thought a lot of you to ask you to live here."

Cassie eyed him suspiciously through her narrowed eyes. Regardless of what attire Jefferson Haddon III donned, she doubted if anyone would ever question his status as the lord of the manor. And that mildly beseeching tone didn't suit him at all.

Expertly cut black hair lay close against his well-shaped head, the back just grazing the collar of his shirt. Broad forehead, long aristocratic nose and a wide mouth seemed chiseled into classically perfect proportions which screamed blueblood.

Jeff Haddon had the lanky, whipcord-strong type of body Cassie had always assumed belonged to cowboys, not playboys. His shoulders looked muscular and wide beneath the torn flannel, his hips narrow with long, long legs. He looked what he was, a rich business tycoon dressed in let's-pretend-we're-slumming clothes.

Right now his dark eyes beseeched her to understand. Grudgingly she accepted his apology even as she tugged her smaller hand from his. She hated having to tip her head so far back just to look at him and vowed to buy some four-inch heels to wear when he was around.

"I don't think friendship is exactly what your aunt had in mind when she made up that will," Cassie quipped, curious about the red stain that covered his pronounced cheekbones.

"Then I guess we'll just have to pretend," he retorted.

"Fine. Truce." Cassie turned to leave.

"Where are you going?" His voice was an exact replica of two-year-old Mark's and Cassie smiled at the sound of petulance.

"I thought perhaps you would prefer to be alone. This house is big enough to get lost in and failing that, I can go help in the kitchen," she replied, moving toward the door.

His rumbly voice stopped her.

"Why don't you have coffee with me instead?" he asked, holding out a slim hand toward the huge armchair that had always been Cassie's favorite. "Mrs. Bennet just brought a fresh pot in," he cajoled.

Cassie studied him for a few minutes, assessing his intent with all her senses on alert. Finally, she allowed herself to be guided to her seat. Her fingers closed around the mug of steaming coffee with pleasure. She sipped the rich dark brew slowly, closing her eyes in satisfaction.

"Don't you just love coffee?" she murmured, inhaling the aroma that steamed off her cup. "I can never get enough."

"I limit myself to three cups a day," Jeff told her. "Too much caffeine is unhealthy."

Cassie ignored him, rolling the hot liquid around on her

tongue. "Nothing that tastes this good could be that un-healthy," she countered, curling herself comfortably into the chair.

She watched him sit stiffly erect in the straight-backed chair. His silent appraisal unnerved her.

She could feel the tension building as electric currents snapped in the air between them. She had felt it before, that nervous awareness whenever he watched her.

Suddenly, she felt extremely conscious of that same, powerful attraction she had felt earlier today. It made her jittery. Cassie had plenty of contact with men in the course of her work, but they were colleagues, older than her, often balding with paunches.

And none had sent her pulse soaring or her heart thudding the way this man did. It was disconcerting. She tried to bury feelings she didn't understand under a bluster of bravado.

"Coffee's not a risk. It's a necessity." Her gaze fixed on his. The silence in the room yawned between them. Cassie searched her mind for trivial conversation that would break the current of magnetism drawing her into the dark depths of his eyes.

"Are you married?" she blurted out and then chided herself for her stupidity. When would she learn to control her tongue?

Jeff stared at her through narrow-slitted eyes, his mouth tight. "Obviously not, if my aunt is trying to marry the two of us off." His answer was short and did not welcome further comments.

Cassie ignored that. "I just wondered what you would do with all this room if you did live here," she pondered, glancing around the beautiful space. "It's a home meant for a family."

"What would you do?" His tone was razor sharp but Cassie ignored that, preferring to lose herself in a world of dreams. "Cassie?" His voice had softened and she dragged open her eyes to find his dark gaze resting on her in an assessing manner.

"I'd fill it with children," she told him simply.

"Ah, you're planning on getting married, then?" he asked shortly, dark eyes glittering.

Cassie sat up straight at that, untangling her feet from under her.

"Good grief, no." She laughed. "I meant with foster kids."

She was pretty sure her face gave away her thoughts. She'd never been much good at pretence and there was no point in trying to hide her plans for this house.

Not that it mattered now.

"There are so many kids who could really benefit from a few months here. Away from the pain and confusion that have left them wondering about their future. This is a place where they could feel safe and carefree." She grinned up at him. "Sorry. When I get on my soapbox, I tend to start preaching."

Jeff's eyes raked over her curiously.

"But don't you want your own children? I can't imagine that you would waste all your efforts on someone else's offspring. Don't most women want to get married and have children?"

He was watching her again. His eyes were bright with what she privately termed his banker's look, as if he were assessing her net occupational worth.

"Oh, but these are my children," she exclaimed. "Every child that comes under my care has a special place in my heart."

"You can't possibly love them all," he snorted derisively. "There's no way anyone could have enough love for all the needy children of the world. Obviously even their parents can't provide them with what they need."

Cassie smiled sadly, her eyes glistening.

"I didn't say all of them, just the ones I come into contact with." Her small hands stretched out toward him in explanation. "And if I never have my own children, at least I will have the experience of loving these. But you know—" her green eyes twinkled across the room "—love isn't something that you run out of. The more you give, the more it grows."

It was a strange statement, he decided. And it proved that Cassandra Newton had no real grasp on reality. He sat quietly in the flickering firelight, lost in his own thoughts.

"It's been my experience that there is never enough to go around," he murmured finally, staring down at his toes. He let the silence stretch starkly between them uncomfortably before speaking again.

"What will you do now?" he asked, curious about her plans now that her access to the house would be denied. "How will you be able to look after all your children when you have to move?''

Jeff watched Cassie closely, noting the white lines of strain that etched themselves around her eyes and the thin line of her mouth as she considered his question.

''I don't know. The younger ones won't have as much difficulty finding a place. It's David and Marie I'm really worried about. And all the other kids like them.''

''Why will it be so hard for them?'' Jeff asked curiously. ''Are they in trouble with the law or something?''

''That's usually what everyone thinks.'' Cassie smiled sadly. ''They'll take the younger ones because they're cute and cuddly. But the teenagers always have a more difficult time.'' She grinned at him, tongue in cheek.

''After all, how many adolescents do you know that are easy to get along with?'' she queried. ''Usually they're already struggling to find out who they are. Fitting in to a strange home is just another problem added to an already staggering load.''

Jefferson thought about his own teenage years. They had been difficult, all right. And he'd had the advantage of knowing that there would be food and the same place for him to sleep every night.

As he sat watching her slender form, slim legs tucked beneath her, Jeff could see the enthusiasm and concern Cassie brought to her job. He considered his own idea once more. Somehow he doubted that the small spitfire in front of him would welcome his idea just yet. He decided to hold off for a while. Perhaps once they got to know each other, Cassie Newton would be more amenable to the plan that was floating half-formed in Jefferson's busy mind.

Jeff made it his business to go out to Aunt Judith's a number of times during the next weeks. He made more than two dozen trips over the next three weeks to the stately old home, and not all of them were to do with settling Judith's estate.

He was drawn to the family atmosphere that prevailed but his curiosity was piqued by the small, green-eyed sprite who played board games sprawled on the floor, drank coffee incessantly and squealed in delight when the children tickled her.

Oak Bluff was as comfortable for him now as it had been when Judith was alive. More so. Now he felt an insatiable interest in the inhabitants that he had never experienced with his aunt.

With a little ingenuity and a few well-framed questions, Jeff managed to inveigle himself into the household routine without much fuss. Before long Bennet was relaying bits and pieces of information that were very enlightening when one was trying to understand Cassie Newton. He also learned more about her charges.

Friday afternoon he found Cassie alone in the library. He wandered over to the armchair and stood peering down at her, noticing the tearstains on her pale cheeks. She glared back at him impolitely.

"Do you ever work?" she demanded rudely.

"You forget," he teased. "I have my own company. I'm the boss." Jeff smiled. He had her rattled. That should help.

She raised her eyebrows as if to say, so what? Jeff grinned.

"It so happens that I just finished the graphics for a new computer system and I'm taking a break. How's it going with you?"

She sat cross-legged on the floor. Some tight black material clung to her shapely legs and stretched all the way to her hips where a big bulky sweater covered the rest of her obvious assets. Her hair was mussed and tousled in disarray around her tearstained face.

"It's not going, not at all," she muttered, staring at her hands.

"I thought some of the kids had moved." Jeff flopped into a big leather chair and propped his elbows on his knees.

"They have. Only David, Marie and Tara are left now. Tara has a place to go on the first of the month, but the other two..." Her voice died away as huge tears plopped onto her cheeks. "I just can't seem to find anywhere for them to live. If nothing comes up, they'll have to go into temporary care, or worse, the juvenile home. They'll hate that."

She slapped her hand against the newspapers spread out on the floor around her. Jeff felt the energy she projected buzzing in the air around him as she jumped to her feet.

"Why did Judith have to make those stupid rules?" she demanded, standing in front of him. "I could have tried to purchase the place outright if she had put it up for sale, but this way, even when I move out, there's no opportunity to get it." Her tone was disparaging. "A cat home, for Pete's sake!"

Jeff grinned. He'd seen this side of her quick temper before and he knew there was at least one way to calm her down. He grasped her slim arm and tugged.

"Come on," he urged. "Let's go for a walk."

Seconds later they were striding through the dense, musky woods. Cassie might be short, but she set a fast pace and Jeff was forced to move quickly to keep up.

She strode along the path muttering to herself, clad in a brilliant red wool anorak that left her long, slim legs exposed in their black tights. Cassie's raven curls glistened like a seal's coat in the autumn sunshine as they swirled around her taut face.

"Absolutely ridiculous," he heard her mutter as she stomped on a rotted tree, splintering it in the crisp air. "People shouldn't be allowed to waste valuable resources just because she wants her nephew married."

Jeff picked up the pace, anxious to hear this.

"Can't he find himself a wife?" she mumbled angrily.

"I haven't really looked," he told her and watched, satisfied, as her skin flushed a deep rose. "Are you volunteering?"

"I don't want to get married," she told him as she looked down her pointed little nose. "I just want the kids and the house."

Jeff pursed his lips to stop the chuckle from escaping. "Isn't that putting the horse before the carriage, so to speak?" he queried, teasing her. "You should probably marry me first before we start discussing children."

Cassie stopped in her tracks at his heckling tone, which sent him colliding into her from behind. Jeff struggled to regain his balance, but they both went crashing to the ground anyway with Cassie's firm little body landing squarely in his lap. He sat there winded while she scrambled off him, and wondered at the reaction her tiny presence always created.

Her giggles of sporadic laughter sent his head tipping back to scrutinize her laughing face.

"You look like you've landed in something particularly nasty," she told him, chortling at his discomfort.

"It sure felt like it," he muttered, dusting the pine needles from the seat of his pants. Her laughing green eyes stared down at him curiously.

"What did you mean?" Her soft voice was hesitant, as if afraid to hear the answer.

Jeff thought for a moment, rehashing their conversation.

"Aren't you at all interested in volunteering for the position of my wife?" he asked, his voice teasingly serious.

But Cassie didn't laugh as he had expected. Her haunting green eyes stared at him, assessing his meaning.

"Why would you need to hunt for a wife?" she inquired, walking slowly beside him, her earlier ill humor dissipated like a morning mist now that curiosity had taken over. "I'm sure there are droves of women who would eagerly offer themselves on the marriage block to the infamous Jefferson Haddon the fourth." Her tone was softly disparaging but her companion seemed not to hear it.

"It's the third. And there are hardly droves," he drawled. "Anyway, that's not the kind of woman I want for the mother of my son," he mused, his thoughts turned inward.

Cassie stopped dead in her tracks as she stared at him in shock.

"What did you say?" Cassie squeaked, sure she had misunderstood. "What son?" She wrinkled her brow in thought. Surely there must be something she had missed. When he didn't answer, Cassie shook the muscled arm hanging loosely at his side. "Do you have a child, Jeff?"

"Not yet," he told her, black eyes snapping fiercely. "But I plan to."

His pronouncement left her speechless, mouth gaping in wonder. Jefferson William Haddon the third was going to get himself a child? How, she asked herself dryly. By mail order and stork delivery? She stared unblinkingly at the grim determination turning up his wide mouth. When she heard his next question, Cassie's jaw dropped a little further.

"Want to help?" As a come-on it lacked finesse. As a proposal, it left something to be desired. It also left her gasping, as if someone had ploughed their fist into her midsection. She moved weakly down the dusky trail, totally ignoring the illustrious Mr. Haddon, flummoxed by his ridiculous statement.

In fact, the whole conversation was preposterous, she told herself. Totally ridiculous. The inane concept of marrying him and helping him provide an heir to the family fortune was...

The answer to her prayer, a small voice whispered. She tried to brush it away, but the flow of words refused to stop. For years, it reminded Cassie, she had dreamed of raising her own children. Now, at twenty-eight, she had almost lost hope that the right man would ever come along.

Maybe he had finally shown up.

What are you holding out for? Prince Charming? her subconscious chided her. *There are all kinds of love. Some of them are learned, like your love for the children. Forget the fairy tale—take reality.*

Cassie replayed the lawyer's voice as it read Judith's will. Marry him, it said, and she could live in this house, have her foster family, continue with her work and have a large amount of money as well.

Flickering images of her own family's needs slipped through her mind. Samantha desperately needed cash with the second baby on the way and her husband's death just last month. Ken was struggling, too, with two stepchildren who needed some professional help.

And Mom and Dad. Cassie pictured the couple's dilapidated old farmstead. Neither of her parents were in good health and the place had become worn and rundown. One hundred thousand dollars would make an immense difference all around.

But one thought kept surfacing. She would be a kept woman, Cassie reminded herself. She would be marrying Jeff for the money.

And for a child.

Strangely, that thought didn't bother her as much as Cassie expected it would. Instead, darling little cherub babies floated across her mind, kicking their chubby legs and gurgling in happy voices. The agency never brought her the babies. Her arms ached with the need to hold and cuddle one of those baby-lotion scented bodies.

And there was David. If anyone needed a father, he did. Could Jefferson Haddon possibly be the man God had sent to ease David's path into adulthood? It seemed impossible; it didn't jibe with the dream she'd held for so long.

A godly man, proud to be a follower of God, happy to share her work in the church and take his place as the head of their family—Jeff Haddon? A man who would share the same pain she felt when broken, unhappy children were brought to their home; a loving husband who would stand next to her and help in the healing process? Would marriage and children with Jeff give her that Christian family she'd planned for so long?

God, is this really from you?

Cassie heard a voice and turned to find Jeff's long lean body directly behind her. He was speaking in a low tone that riveted her attention.

"We could both benefit, Cassie. Obviously that's what Aunt Judith intended."

She stared at him, transfixed by the dark conviction glinting from his stern face.

"But you're not in love with me," she objected, softly. "And I consider that a prerequisite to marriage."

His gleaming dark head came up at that, his eyes boring into hers.

"No, I'm not," he agreed dryly. "But then, neither, I think, are you in love with me." He peered at her as if assessing her ability to understand what he was about to say. Cassie felt an anxious quiver spring up inside. "I'm thirty-five years old. I am fully capable of deciding what it is I want out of life. I want a son."

Cassie marveled that his voice was so strong and steady. She felt like a quivering mass of jelly herself.

"I've been noticing your relationship with these children over the past few weeks," he told her, his long stride adapting to match her shorter one. "You have the kind of rapport a child needs during its formative years. I think you would make a splendid mother." His voice added reflectively, "and wife."

He was serious, Cassie realized. Prince Jefferson actually expected her to agree to marry him and provide the heir to his kingdom.

"Is it so important, this successor for the Haddon family," she demanded disparagingly, "that you would marry someone you don't love, someone you barely know, just to continue the family line?"

"No," he smiled at her sadly, tiny lines radiating around his sardonic mouth. "It's not important at all, for that reason. But it is important for me to have my own child." He straightened his shoulders then and grasped her elbow briskly as if getting down to business. "Think about it, Cassie. You would be able to do those things you're always talking about for kids who need your help." His voice lowered provocatively. "And you would be able to continue your writing without the kind of interruptions that any other place would afford."

Cassie whirled to face him, amazed that he knew of her secret life as a children's author. Then she realized that a man like Jefferson Haddon would have had her thoroughly investigated before considering the possibility of proposing.

The air went out of her suddenly.

"So it would be a business proposition," she intoned softly, glaring up at him in the silence of the woods. "I get money and the run of the house to continue my work and you get your child. I do have some scruples, you know," she told him, furious at his extended silence.

"I can't just coldly and callously go to bed with you because you want a child. Lovemaking is a part of marriage and that's a serious step that two people take because they want to commit themselves to the future together. If you think that I could treat such a commitment so lightly, then you really don't know me at all."

She wasn't prepared for his strong arms as they wrapped around her. Jeff tugged her against his muscular frame, a tiny smile turning up the edges of his lips. His head tipped down, his mouth meeting hers in a kiss that rocked her to her boot-clad feet.

Cassie felt a longing stretch deep inside. It surprised her with its strength. As she felt his lips touch hers, Cassie curled her arms round Jeff's strong neck and twined her fingers through his dark, immaculate hair.

She knew that time passed, that one kiss had become many. But each gentle touch of his lips created a need for more.

When he finally drew away from her, Cassie felt bereft. He pressed her head against his chest while they each drew deep calming breaths of crisp fall air.

His voice, when it rumbled against her cheek, was softly mocking as his hand stroked over her windblown hair.

"I don't think anything that happened between us could be cold or calculated," he told her, a smile of satisfaction curving his tight mouth.

Jeff tipped her chin up, forcing her turbulent gaze to meet his melting dark chocolate one.

"We both know there's something smoldering between us," he rasped. "And I think it's only a matter of time until it bursts into flame." He held her gaze steadily. "But I'll guarantee you this. I'm not going to force or coerce you into anything. Whatever we do, it will be after a mutual decision."

Cassie felt as if the ground were falling away and she wrapped her fingers around his arm.

How could this be happening to plain, ordinary Cassie Newton? She seldom dated. Goodness, she didn't even know many men who weren't involved with the children's agency or her church.

"If you'd prefer, we can go the route of artificial insemination." His mouth tipped up wryly. "Although, personally, I don't think it would be nearly as, er, interesting."

Cassie felt her cheeks burn with the implication behind his words. How could he say these things? It wasn't, well, decent somehow.

"The direction of our relationship will depend on you, Cassie."

She knew her mouth was open; that she was gaping at him like some starstruck teenager. She couldn't help it. The world had tilted in a crazy angle and she couldn't get her bearings.

"Come on. If we don't walk, we'll freeze."

He tugged her along beside him then, continuing their walk as if nothing unusual had occurred. Except that he kept her hand enfolded in his.

Cassie let the whirl of emotions pirouette through her mind

in fast forward. Marry him? She hardly knew him, although he had somehow become an intricate part of their lives over the past weeks.

And always, Jeff watched her with David. Dark head cocked to one side, he would listen intently as she spoke with the boy. Subject matter wasn't important. Jeff seemed to focus more on the child's acceptance of Cassie as the authority on the matter. At least marriage to Jefferson Haddon would ensure a home for David and Marie, she thought ruefully.

Nasty suspicions crowded into her confused brain and Cassie stopped dead in the pathway to cast a curious glance at the tall man beside her.

"What's really behind this proposal?" she demanded, hands on her hips. "Why do you suddenly need *me* for your plan?"

He looked sheepish. And not a little embarrassed.

"The truth this time," she ordered. "All of it."

"I do want a son," he said firmly.

"And?"

"Well, the fact is that most of my funds are tied up in the family trust. Oh, I make a good living," he offered quickly as she frowned. "My company is doing very well. But I want to expand and that takes a lot of capital. It's a private company and I'd like to keep it that way."

He studied her face as if deciding whether she understood what he was saying.

"You mean you don't want to offer stock or something to raise money?" Cassie asked him doubtfully.

"Yes, and I don't want to take on private investors unless I have to. Computers are a risky business right now. The markets are changing so rapidly and new advances occur daily. I'd rather not risk anyone else's hard-earned money."

Cassie sank onto the iron bench nearby, thinking about what he'd said.

"Judith once told me that your father has money. Maybe he could…"

"No!"

It was a vehement denial that brought two red circles to his cheeks. He flopped down beside her, hands shoved into his pockets. Cassie couldn't see his face, he was turned away from her. But she could hear the cold hard tones and the anger under them.

"My father would never agree," he told her. "He wants me in the family business and would be just as happy to see Bytes Incorporated go down the tubes." He watched her speculatively for a moment. "If he knew about the son idea, he would have a fit. He's had my wife picked out for twenty years now. He won't take it lightly when he finds out I've married someone else."

"Oh, but I don't want to create more problems. Family is very important." Cassie stared out in front of her, barely registering the beauty of the fall landscape.

"Mine isn't," she heard him mutter sotto voce.

"This marriage, if it happens, will already be starting out with a lot of obstacles," she protested. "If only Judith hadn't tied everything up." She swung her head around to stare at him. "Does your father know about the will?"

He shook his head, then bent to pull an oak leaf from her hair.

"He knows she died, of course. And that she left a will. But beyond that, nothing. I specifically asked Jones to keep things quiet until it was all settled."

Cassie pulled herself to her feet and wandered farther into the woods. It was all so confusing. And she had no one to confide in. On the one hand, it would be ridiculous to turn down such a wonderful opportunity. On the other...well, it certainly wouldn't be a love match.

You always said you'd only marry for love. This is business. Her conscience pricked her once more.

Yes, but if you marry him, you get to keep the house for the kids. Lots of kids. You could continue the work God called you to. It could become a sort of sanctuary.

It was an internal argument that went on for the duration of their walk. Jeff spoke no more about the issue, leaving Cassie time to sort through in her own mind all the ifs and buts that flew like quicksilver through her muddled thoughts.

How could she deny David and Marie the opportunity that Oak Bluff with all its wonderful prospects presented to the two homeless teenagers? They could have a stable life without worrying about the future. They could blossom and develop into capable, responsible adults without worrying whether or not they would be able to continue their activities tomorrow or next week, or whenever they moved on.

And what about the other children who came into her hands? Cassie asked herself. Could she deny them all the things Judith's money would buy just because she was holding out for love? Was this windfall really from heaven, or did she just think so because she'd benefit?

It wasn't an easy question. And it was one Cassie decided to think on long and hard. But after all, she reminded herself, it wasn't as if she had ten other offers sitting on the table.

And there *were* definite sparks when Jeff had kissed her back there. More than sparks!

"Help me," she prayed silently. "You gave me the job. Now show me how to make the right decision. Direct me away from the biggest mistake of my life."

Chapter Three

"Chocolate cake! Thanks, Mrs. Bennet. It's my favorite." David's pubescent voice was squeaky but full of happiness.

Jeff and Cassie ate dinner with the children, feasting on a succulent stew and featherlight homemade biscuits that Mrs. Bennet had prepared.

The older woman stroked her hand over the boy's perpetually tousled head and winked at Cassie.

"I know it's your favorite, dearie. Yours and someone else's." Her gleaming eyes settled on Jeff's loaded plate. "That's why I baked it."

Cassie watched David inhale the generous slice and marveled at his appetite. Of course, teenage boys did grow by leaps and bounds, and devoured everything edible along the way. David was shooting up by inches and Cassie had taken him shopping several times to accommodate feet that expanded in direct proportion to the seemingly endless stretch of his legs.

"Are you finished your homework, Marie?" Cassie watched the girl shift restlessly in her seat.

"Almost. I'll be done before Nate phones later."

"Well, don't stay up all night talking to him. You will see him at school tomorrow, you know." She smiled at the happy little grin that appeared on Marie's face.

"I'll try not to be too long, Cassie."

The flush of pink in the girl's cheeks gave her a glow of beauty. It was too bad people couldn't see how kind and loving these two were, Cassie fumed. David and Marie had been subdued during the meal, barely speaking unless they were addressed first. It bothered Cassie.

They were afraid of a future over which they had no control, she realized. Worried that they would be separated after having spent so much time depending on each other. A permanent home, one they could rely on, would make such a difference in their young lives. And with so few people interested in raising teenagers, Cassie doubted anyone would create much fuss if she asked to keep the two on a permanent basis.

She studied Jeff as she ate, watching him speak to the teens. He was especially good with David, drawing the quiet boy out with each comment. He had a knack of treating David as if he were an equal. He listened to what he had to say with interest most people would only offer an adult. It was a manner Cassie had found sadly lacking in many of the homes that housed foster children.

"How about a Monopoly tournament after dinner?" she asked brightly.

David grinned at her, eyes shiny with mischief.

"You must be feeling lucky," he teased. "Watch out, Jeff. She owned everybody last time. I'm lucky I'm not still paying back what I borrowed."

They played for an hour before Marie's soft voice broke into the silent concentration.

"You'd better get started on that science project," she reminded David in a sisterly tone. "The proposal is due in a week and you haven't done any research."

"And you'd better go phone Nate before he dies from not hearing your voice."

It was typical sibling banter and Cassie smiled as she heard it. David and Marie were not related at all but from their teasing demeanor no one would have guessed.

Marie left the room quietly, her long blond hair flowing behind like a cape, but not before she tapped David on the shoulder.

"Jealous?" she asked pertly.

Groaning, David stretched to his full five-foot-ten-inch height.

"You wish!" He carefully replaced the game pieces in the

box and snapped it shut. "I hate science," he muttered, before glancing shamefaced at Cassie. "Sorry, Cassie, but it's so boring."

"What kind of a project are you supposed to do?" It was Jeff's deep voice. Cassie stared at him in surprise.

"We can choose," David replied, kicking his toe in the carpet. "That's worse," he confessed, "because I haven't got a clue what he expects us to do."

"I know a little about science," Jeff murmured softly. "Could I look at your text? Maybe together we could come up with an idea that would get you started."

"Cool" was all David could manage to answer.

Cassie smiled as they left the room, talking and gesticulating. She hadn't expected Jeff to take such an interest in the boy. In fact, she recalled, he had spent several evenings doing things with both children this past week.

Well, since he had taken over the science problem, it left her free to start a project that had made her fingers itch for weeks. Cassie buried herself in the library for the next three hours, refusing to allow her mind to dwell on the marriage proposal she had just received. She'd always found her work the best panacea for solving personal problems.

Cassie was knee-deep in sketches of Bored Boris, the magical dragon, when she startled at the soft touch on her shoulder.

"Don't do that," she squeaked, holding a hand over her heart. "People my age have been known to keel over from a shock-induced heart attack."

"That's okay." Jeff grinned. "I know both CPR and mouth-to-mouth. Want a demonstration?"

Cassie frowned at him reprovingly. "No! Thanks, anyway." She studied him closely. The immaculate shirt was unbuttoned allowing her glimpses of dark curling hairs that covered Jeff's broad chest. His tie hung haphazardly out of one of his jacket pockets and his made-to-order jacket was slung carelessly over one shoulder.

The perfectly creased black trousers he'd sported earlier in the day were dusty and wrinkled. And that impeccably trimmed hair was tousled and disorderly, one black lock hanging over his left eye.

He looked smug, Cassie thought. As if he had swallowed a whole bowl of canaries. She stood in an attempt to bolster her bravado which was a little shaky after this afternoon.

"Well, did you come up with something?" she demanded, her low voice sharper than she had intended.

But Jeff merely stared at her curiously before answering.

"Depends," he replied cryptically, head tipped to one side as he studied Boris. His dark eyes met hers. "Can we use that big empty room downstairs for a lab?"

"A lab," she repeated, wondering what on earth they had concocted between them. "Why do you need a lab? It's just a simple science project."

Jeff stepped backward and pushed the door closed with his foot before speaking.

"That kid is very bright," he told her seriously. "And mighty ambitious. But he hasn't had much encouragement and he doesn't know where or how to begin." The muscled shoulders shrugged.

"I would have thought the teacher could have done a bit more explaining, but at any rate, I want to get him interested in some preliminary physics so that later on he won't be overwhelmed by everything. He's got a natural curiosity about things that hasn't been stifled."

Jeff studied her quizzically through those melting chocolate eyes. Cassie rushed into speech before he could say anything more.

"But what about when the house is sold and he can't have his lab anymore?" She stood straight and tall in front of him, prepared to do battle for her child. "What about when you get tired of teaching him and want to go back to the playboy scene? What does David do then?"

Cassie could see the brown sheen change to black in Jeff's darkening gaze. His eyes were like a sheet of the notorious black ice that covered Toronto highways in winter. You could sail along with no problems until you needed to put on the brakes. Then you were in big trouble.

When his hands tightened around her upper arms, Cassie was pretty sure this qualified as big trouble.

"Will you please get it through your head that I am not, nor have I ever been, a playboy."

The words snarled out between lips so tightly pursed, Cassie wondered if they had ever been as softly caressing as she remembered.

"And this house only has to be vacated if you refuse to marry me." His mouth was a straight line of disapproval. "I like the kid and I want to help him with this." He stared down at her furiously.

"Or maybe you're jealous because you wanted to do it?" he demanded suddenly.

Cassie tipped her head back and laughed. She fixed him with her own gaze.

"I'll have you know that I hate anything to do with grade ten science projects." She laughed again. "It's a great relief not to have to help him with his homework." She pushed his hands away before stepping backward. "I am concerned only for David and his welfare. I have to be sure that this will be a positive experience for him and not one where he'll feel abandoned when it's no longer convenient for you to help him out."

The air crackled with tension as they stared each other down. Jeff was the first to move by thrusting out his hand toward her.

"Okay, truce," he mumbled. "I know your primary duty is always to protect the kids' interests. I promise I won't leave him in the lurch regardless of what happens between us." His black eyes sparkled down at her.

"Although, if you hate science that much and you're going to opt for the artificial route to children of your own, I suppose someone will have to do some remedial work with you, too." He grinned at her, obviously delighted with the flush of color that stained her cheeks.

"Close your mouth, Cassie," he teased. One finger brushed down her tip-tilted nose. "It's a part of life…grade eight health, in fact. Certainly nothing to be embarrassed about. And it's something we do have to think about. I still want that son."

Cassie was embarrassed. It was nice to know that he had given some thought to their future situation, she supposed. It was good that he was considering all the pros and cons. But how could he say such things out loud with absolutely no warning? And how could one touch of those long fingers make her all quivery and shaky inside. Could this be from God?

"You are a very lovely woman, Cassandra."

And then she forgot everything. His arms surrounded her and hugged her against his muscular form. She could feel the silky brush of his mustache against her cheek, the smell of wood smoke on his clothes.

But most of all, she could feel his heart thudding just as quickly as hers. And she knew that Jefferson Haddon was no more immune to her than she was to him. Which should have been reassuring.

Shouldn't it?

Moments later, when all Cassie wanted was more of his touch, Jeff pressed her gently away from himself, easing her arms down from his neck. She couldn't even remember how they'd gotten there.

"Think about what I said," he whispered in her ear.

Then, leaving her bemused and befuddled, he walked out of the room. Moments later Cassie heard the powerful roar of his car. But it was virtually impossible to think coherently as she carefully put Boris and his friends away. And if she listened, Cassie was sure she could hear Judith's hearty laughter resounding through the room.

"Go for it," she seemed to say and Cassie smiled as she fingered the portrait on the old desk of her benefactor.

"Perhaps I will, Judith," she murmured. "Perhaps I will. But not before I get a second opinion."

She picked up the phone and dialed, a faint smile tipping the corners of her lips.

"It said what?" Robyn's voice squeaked with surprise. "You mean to say that if you marry the guy, you get to keep the house and a pile of dough besides, and you can't decide what to do?" She snapped her fingers in Cassie's face. "Earth to Cassie. Hello?"

"I know it sounds simple," Cassie admitted. "Take the house and the money and go with it. It would solve a lot of problems." She thrust away the thought of her own family. "But this is serious. I have to *marry* Jeff, as in forever. And that's serious business. I can't just go into it with a way out already prepared. I don't believe in divorce any more than you do.''

"Yeah, that's heavy stuff all right," Robyn agreed. "But I wonder if you're looking at this right." She frowned, her blond head tipped to one side as she considered her friend.

"What do you mean?" Cassie frowned. "I've thought about nothing else for ages. I just can't see a way through."

"Think, Cass. Think about the book of Genesis. In those days there were arranged marriages all the time. In fact, that's how they got started. Isaac needed a wife and Rebekah was the one that was chosen by God. They didn't even know each other until after she'd already promised to marry the guy!"

"That was thousands of years ago," Cassie protested. "We do things differently nowadays."

Robyn laughed sourly.

"Yeah, we do," she agreed. "And does the world seem any better for it? There are kids all across this country growing up in homes where the adults have separated because they've lost that love that seemed so wonderful when it first grabbed hold of them."

Cassie nodded.

"I know, Rob. I know. But this is my future I'm deciding here. It's not at all what I had planned...." Her voice died away as she let her mind roam.

"Cassie," Robyn said, drawing her attention back to the present. "Wasn't it you who told our entire grade nine class that you wanted to look after kids who needed help?"

"Yes, but..."

"And wasn't it you, just last week," Robyn continued unfazed, "who said that even though Judith had died, you still believed God would provide a way for you to do this work?" She waited for Cassie's dark head to nod agreement. "Well, then. Maybe this is God's way of providing for you."

Cassie studied her friend as she thought about her work. She had always felt a connection with children; but she was especially drawn to the needy ones. They lacked so much that mere human kindness and a stable home could provide.

"I know you said Jeff's not religious. I know he's got a

problem with his family. And I know you said he loved Judith." Robyn's face screwed up in thought. "Maybe that's the key," she muttered.

"What key? What are you talking about?"

"Yes, it makes sense. Don't you see, Cass? Jeff likes what he sees in you."

"Which is?" Cassie frowned.

"You're resemblance to Judith, your faith in God and His power in your life. Maybe it's what he craves for himself. You can be His light, Cass. Maybe your job is to show him the way to the source of that light, to help him understand that God loves *him*."

"It sounds like an awfully convenient excuse for me." Cassie shook her head dubiously.

"I think this is the only way there is for you to keep the kids. At least right now. And while you're doing that, you can help influence Jeff's life in the right way." Robyn studied her. "Have you got enough courage to take a leap of faith and trust God to work it all out for the good?"

Cassie stared at the ceiling, her mind whirling with problems. It was a lifelong commitment, she knew. Marriage was a solemn promise to another person. It was not to be entered into on whim, or discarded when things got tough.

"I'm praying for you, pal." Robyn patted her on the shoulder. "Whatever decision you make, I'll still be here."

"Thanks," Cassie muttered, picking up her handbag and moving to the door. "I think."

"Are you telling me that you *will* or that you *won't* marry me?" Jeff queried, his eyes darkening to a deep sherry brown.

Cassie focused her own gaze on his left shoulder and said the words that needed saying.

"I'm saying that if we can come to some agreement on the conditions of this marriage, I will agree to it. The first thing is the children. I want us to adopt David and Marie. Legally," she added when he continued staring at her.

"And?"

"And I want to continue to accept foster children whenever I'm asked, for whatever time. If the arrangements become too unwieldly, we can discuss it then.'' She said it in a puff of energy, as if she were afraid to stop.

He stood there, tall and silent, staring at her. Cassie could feel his eyes pressing into her, but she stood firm.

"Fine. I agree."

It was as if someone had punched her in the tummy. Just like that he was agreeing?

"So, what date shall we set?"

Cassie sucked in a lungful of air. "There is one other thing."

He frowned.

"I think we should wait out the two months' grace period that Judith gave us. We'll be engaged but free to break off the arrangement if either one of us changes our minds.'' Her heart lost its regular beat for a moment and then resumed a breakneck speed as she met his dark eyes.

"Why?"

"We have to be sure, Jeff. Both of us. I don't believe in divorce and I'm not going into this marriage with a way out already prepared. If I'm going to be married, it will be whole-heartedly. For life."

"But waiting means another five weeks," he complained. "That puts us right before Christmas."

"I know. It's enough time to really think things through, don't you think?'' Why did her voice sound so uncertain, Cassie wondered. She'd gone over this a thousand times and this was the way it had to be.

Those liquid chocolate eyes were fixed on her, staring deep into the doubts and fears that filled her tortured mind.

"I don't need to think about it," he murmured, never breaking the stare. "I feel quite sure we can both achieve satisfaction from this arrangement, but if you need the extra time, I'll go along with it.'' He tugged a small leather-bound booklet out of his jacket pocket and consulted it for several moments.

Cassie wanted to say something—anything. They weren't having an *arrangement,* for heaven's sake. They were getting *married!*

"Saturday, December 10th," he muttered. "That would give us time to prepare for the Christmas celebrations afterward." One long lean finger tapped the book thoughtfully as Jeff glanced up, eyes gleaming. "How is December 10th for a wedding day, Miss Newton?"

Cassie blinked. That was it? He agreed to everything and then checked his calendar? Somehow she had expected a fuss or an argument. Anything but this calm acceptance.

"Cassie? The tenth?"

She stared up at him, bewildered and confused.

"Uh, yes, okay. I think so."

"Good." He brushed his lips across her cheek before rechecking his book. "Now. About the ring. I think if we were to go now it would be best. I know a jeweler who will meet with us privately and design exactly what you want. Maybe he can do everything right now, while we wait. Then we can announce it to the children and the staff. I assume you'll want the Bennets to stay on?"

He was holding her red wool coat out, ready for her to shrug into. Cassie didn't move. She couldn't. She could only stand there staring at him. He was moving way too fast.

"Ring? What ring?"

"Your engagement ring, of course." His tone was soft and gentle. Teasing even. "We are talking about a marriage, you know. A real marriage. And like you, I'm fully prepared to make it work."

"Yes, but..."

He had her bundled into the coat and moving out the door before Cassie could even think. She stopped on the step, stubbornly refusing to be moved.

"Wait a minute!"

Jeff stopped politely, tugging his collar up around his ears as the cold north wind whipped down from the roof and tugged at their clothes. His eyes were mildly inquiring and he didn't move his hand from under her elbow.

"Is there a problem?"

"Yes! I don't need a ring." She said it fast so she couldn't retract it. "And there won't be any big wedding. This is an agreement between us two. That's all."

"I don't think so." He grinned boyishly.

Cassie felt the strong warm arm around her shoulders as he hugged her against his side. If he had ordered or hollered she wouldn't have listened. But this soft cajoling was something entirely different.

"I asked you to marry me. You agreed. That means we're going to be man and wife. And I'm going to give you a pledge of my commitment."

"Yes, but..."

He cut her off, blithely ignoring her objections.

"We will now move to the next stage of this courtship which entails finding an appropriate ring for this finger." He rubbed her ring finger with his hand.

"Yes, but..." Cassie stopped as his lips brushed across hers softly.

"I am not finished, Cassandra." His deep voice whispered in the still silent evening, effectively stifling her protests. "Maybe we're not the traditional love match, but we can still go into this as friends. And totally committed to making this marriage work. I don't want anyone thinking anything else. The ring will solidify our position."

He sounded so loverlike one moment and businesslike and coldly calculating the next that a shiver of apprehension rippled down her spine to dissipate like the morning dew at his next softly spoken words.

"Besides, I don't think any bride should miss out on the old traditions. Especially not one as lovely as you."

Cassie swallowed her nostalgia. A diamond ring didn't have to mean love, she told herself. It was just a stone. It could signify friendship as well as love; or commitment to making something work. Why not relax and enjoy it?

She curtsied.

"Thank you, kind sir. I would be pleased to accept your ring."

It began as a fun evening which came as a surprise to Cassie. She hadn't expected that someone like Jefferson Haddon would be able to unbend so easily. They laughed and joked about the strange customs of marriage as they visited Jeff's favorite jeweler but neither could agree on just what type of ring Cassie should wear.

"I work with kids, Jeff. I don't want some big, gaudy showpiece. Something small and practical will be just fine."

"This isn't overly large." He held up an opal close to the size of a golf ball with glittering diamonds surrounding it.

"It's both ostentatious and pretentious. Besides that, it's ugly."

He frowned at her. "All right. You pick one."

"This is lovely." Cassie chose a small diamond perched on a thin band of gold.

"Hah! I can't even see where the diamond is—if there is one. How about this?" He held up a dinner ring that nearly blinded her.

"I don't like clusters," she told him, grimacing. The thing would take arm supports just to carry it around.

"And this?" It was a rock the size of a cherry.

She shook her head in dismay. "Jeff, that thing would cost a fortune to buy let alone insure." She glanced at the display cases once more. "I do like this." She fingered the tiny sparkling stones imbedded in the thin gold band.

He snorted with disapproval.

"So do I, for two kids in high school maybe."

She watched as Jeff buttoned up his coat. Then, thanking the jeweler for his assistance, he ushered her out the door without a word. Cassie found herself being led toward a dark and rather intimate-looking restaurant moments later.

"I thought we were supposed to go shopping," she protested, casting worried glances at his annoyed face. "Are you giving up on our marriage already?" It was supposed to be teasing, but Cassie held her breath until he answered.

"We'll discuss this over dinner" was all he replied in an exasperated tone.

She watched speechless as the maître d' greeted him by name.

"Mr. Haddon! Good evening, sir. I didn't realize we had a reservation for you tonight," he added nervously.

Jeff smiled that broad grin that made him look like a mischievous boy and laughed.

"Your memory's not slipping, George. You don't. Is there anything available?" Cassie watched him slip the man a twenty-dollar bill.

"We're very busy, sir. I'll just check." It took George less than three minutes to return smiling. "We have a small table in the corner, Mr. Haddon. Right by the fireplace. Will that suit?"

Apparently it did as Cassie found herself being seated mere seconds later.

"Cassie," Jeff said, "George here is a good friend of mine." He slipped his hand on top of hers and squeezed gently. "George, this is Miss Newton, my fiancée."

The older man beamed down at them both.

"My congratulations, Mr. Haddon. That's wonderful news!" His voice dropped. "Miss McNaughton would have been so pleased."

Cassie watched the smile tug at Jefferson's wide mobile mouth.

"Yes," he drawled. "Aunt Judith would be very happy."

When they were alone, Cassie leaned forward.

"I'm really not dressed for such an expensive restaurant, Jeff. And I'm not very hungry, either." She heard the whine in her own voice and endeavored to get rid of it. "Why are we here?"

Brisk and to the point, that was better.

He leaned back in his chair, smiling benevolently at her across the candlelight. A waiter arrived with champagne in a silver bucket, forestalling any further conversation.

Jeff picked up the glass and held it aloft.

"A toast to us, Cassandra."

She frowned at him and he laughed.

"Don't worry," he told her. "It's nonalcoholic. I guess that's another detail you should know. I don't drink. Ever."

His voice was cool, almost hard and Cassie wondered if she should ask why. The dark look on his face was not encouraging, however, and she decided discretion was the better part of valor. Slowly she picked up the slim, fluted crystal and tinkled it against his.

"What are we toasting to?" she murmured.

"To us and the solutions we're going to find to our disagreements. All of them."

As she sipped the bubbly concoction, Cassie looked around curiously. The restaurant glowed warmly in the flickering light cast off smoothly polished oak walls. It was a gracefully elegant room with brass fixtures, potted flowers and tall willowy plants strategically placed here and there to provide privacy for its diners. The sound of softly soothing classical guitar played in the background as the tinkle of good china, silver and crystal rang out occasionally.

"I'm having a steak," Jeff declared, laying down the huge menu. "What would you like?"

"I've heard about this place," Cassie mused, staring at the preponderance of items listed. "A friend of mine said the veal is excellent. I'll try that."

Somehow, Cassie felt Jefferson Haddon wouldn't understand that her friend Moira had only been able to enjoy the veal on her twenty-fifth anniversary because her children had surprised their parents. He probably had no idea that not everyone frequented Vicenzo's on the spur of the moment.

The waiter bustled away to return seconds later with their soup, a delicious mushroom blend that teased and tantalized her tongue.

"I don't recognize all of these greens," Cassie admitted when her salad arrived. "But the dressing is fantastic." She licked her lips at the flavor of it only realizing how childish her action was when Jeff's laugh rang out.

"It's nice to see someone enjoy their food," he assured her. "And you don't have to worry about dieting, thank goodness."

Cassie grinned.

"Are you kidding? With kids around all the time, I'm lucky if I get to eat." She peered up at him through her lashes. "Why are we here, Jeff?"

She watched as a tiny flush of pink colored his cheeks.

"I, um, well, you see I was hoping that, well," he stopped, obviously at a loss.

Cassie smiled. For once it was nice to see the elegant, assured Jefferson Haddon stumble for the correct phrasing.

"Just say it," she advised. "Don't worry about how it sounds."

"Very well. I was hoping to show you, by coming here tonight, that your choice of a ring is important in more ways than one."

Cassie frowned. "It is. Why?"

He placed his fingertips together, tent-style and studied them for several minutes.

"Perhaps I'm not being very clear. I don't want to offend you."

"You won't," she assured him as she frowned again. "Just let's get the truth out between us. Then we'll deal with it. What seems to be the problem?"

"Cassie, do realize how big a company Bytes Incorporated is?"

She frowned. He wanted to talk about his computer company?

Now?

"No, I've never really thought about it. Why?"

His brown-black eyes met hers almost apologetically.

"It's a worldwide enterprise. Which is why it will take so much money to expand. I travel quite frequently to Europe, Asia and Australia."

She wasn't getting any of this, Cassie decided. It was nice that he was successful, but so what?

"Would you please just say whatever it is clearly," she demanded.

"Cassandra, your ring is important because more people than you and I will see it. And misinterpret it." The last part was muttered under his breath.

"I want something that represents me, my status, if that doesn't sound too arrogant." Jeff frowned at her, but kept speaking. "I'm not exactly a pauper, you know. I have a certain status, an image, I guess you'd say. I want people to recognize you as my wife and the ring should symbolize how highly I esteem you as my wife."

A light dawned. Cassie glared angrily across the table.

"Oh, I get it. You mean that people will think you're cheap if I have just a small ring."

"Well, no, not exactly. I mean that people will think it's only a temporary liaison, without duration. A sort of affair. That's not the impression I want to give."

He looked angry, Cassie decided, noting the tightening around his mouth. She should have realized sooner that she was marrying into an elitist group. Judith had never been flashy about her wealth but she certainly had not denied herself anything, either.

Cassie called herself a fool. She couldn't care less about his money and hadn't given it a thought. Which was obviously a mistake. Clearly the money and the image it could create were very important to Jefferson Haddon.

"I'm sorry." Jeff's dark eyes were frowning down at her. "I didn't express that very well."

"No, it's all right," she murmured softly. "If you want a larger stone, then, of course, that's what we'll get. After all, as you've just pointed out, you are the one who's paying for it."

It was a mean and nasty remark and Cassie wished she had never said it, but it was too late now. So she bent her head over her meal and tasted the famous dish.

"You are determined to misunderstand me. I merely meant that if I could afford it and you liked it, why shouldn't you have the nicest ring we can find."

They ate in silence after that with Jeff glancing up at her from time to time. He tried to initiate some small talk, but Cassie couldn't carry the conversational ball. Her mind was on other things. Like how a farm girl from the sticks was going to carry off this charade.

She ordered coffee and sipped the dark fragrant brew.

"This is excellent." She smiled up at the waiter. "Colombian Supremo with just a hint of mocha, isn't it?"

The solemn face creased into a smile.

"Madam knows her blends," he affirmed. He held out the pot toward Jefferson. "And you, sir?"

Cassie watched the dark head shake.

"Never at this time of night," he replied. "I'll have herbal tea. Mint."

She shuddered and sipped another mouthful of coffee for courage.

"Mint tea? Now? I always have a good strong cup of coffee before bed. Helps me sleep."

He stared at her as if she'd just told him his ears were green. Then he shrugged, obviously forgiving her that flaw.

"That sounds like something Aunt Judith would have said," he told her softly.

"But not what you'd advise, I gather?" she asked with a knowing grin.

"I think you already know the answer to that, Cassie. But in reply I think I'll just quote part of a poem by Ogden Nash that I found in one of Judith's books."

His eyes glittered with anticipation as he met her curious ones across the table.

"Whenever you're wrong, admit it. Whenever you're right, shut up."

"Is that an inscription you want on the wedding cake?" She giggled and laughed out loud at his facial expression.

"I was thinking it might be more fitting inside that ring we're not going to get tonight."

This time she couldn't help it. The laughter burst out and she was embarrassed to see several gray heads nod benignly in their direction.

"My mother always told me to marry a man that makes you laugh. She's going to love you."

"Better than what?" he demanded. He cocked one eyebrow, joining in on the friendly banter.

"Oh, better than marrying some handsome ne'er-do-well, I suppose."

"I think I'll enjoy your mother. Great minds think alike," he told her smugly.

Cassie giggled, shaking her head. "I find that tiny minds think alike, too."

Their waiter showed up just then.

"Anything else, sir?"

Jeff's dark eyes glowed across the table at her in the dim light of the restaurant.

"No," he stated. "I think I've had just about enough."

Cassie hid the smile that tugged at her mouth.

"Tell me about your parents," he prompted, tugging her arm through his as they walked along the brightly lit street.

There wasn't any point in prevaricating. He would know soon enough, if he didn't already.

"They're farmers. They live about an hour away but they

don't get to the city very often. Money's pretty tight right now.''

He shook his head. ''No, I mean, tell me the important stuff. Are they happy together?''

Cassie smiled.

''They've been married almost forty years so I think so,'' she told him. ''I once asked Mom how she and Dad had stayed married so long. She told me that she followed Erma Bombeck's prescription for a happy marriage.''

''Erma Bombeck? The humorist?''

Cassie smiled at the surprise in his voice.

''Yep. Mom said if Erma could forgive her husband for not being Paul Newman, she couldn't do any less for Dad.''

He chuckled. ''I guess that's good enough advice.''

''She also told me that she leaves five or six things unsaid each day. According to her, there isn't so much to be sorry for.''

''You have three siblings, I understand.''

Cassie was about to ask him how he knew when she remembered the security check. Apparently nothing had slipped by and she was probably only regurgitating what he already knew.

''Yes, although one sister is overseas right now. I haven't seen her for two years.''

''She works for UNICEF, I believe.''

Cassie nodded.

''The pay is very low for such an undertaking,'' he murmured. ''Why would she sign up for a second term?''

Cassie bristled. ''Not everything in life is about money,'' she declared, yanking her arm free of his. ''Giselle loves her work and there are other advantages.'' She glared up at him. ''In my family money came way down on the list of our priorities.''

''You were lucky,'' he said gruffly. ''In mine it was everything.'' He slipped her arm through his once more and nudged her onward. ''I apologize. I didn't mean to be condescending.''

Cassie peered up at him and then decided it was best to get things out in the open now, before this went any further.

''Just exactly how wealthy is your family, Jeff?'' she asked, frowning.

''I never took you for the mercenary type.'' His dark eyes

glittered with sparks of anger. His head whipped around to stare at her.

Cassie giggled.

"I'm not mercenary about it." She laughed. "I just need to know what I'm getting into. Are you going to be jetting off to Timbuktu every other afternoon? Will I have to make an appointment with your secretary to speak to you about something?" She stopped laughing when his silence stretched out between them.

"Jeff? Did I say something wrong?"

His face was white and strained when he glanced down. Cassie held her breath as he spoke.

"No," he muttered, "nothing wrong. You just reminded me of something that happened once."

Cassie said nothing, holding her breath lest she break the spell between them. For the first time Jefferson Haddon was going to tell her something about himself. She wasn't going to spoil it.

"My father hated to be disturbed. When I was four, I made the mistake of entering his office at home one time and forgot to knock first. I'd cut my wrist, you see, and it was bleeding. Rory and I were playing, and Mother was away and I forgot all about asking his secretary if it was okay to go in.

"He hated having me burst in like that. Hated that his eldest son was standing there bawling in front of his business associates. I was weak…unworthy of the family name. He sent me to my room." A hard bitter smile tipped the corners of his lips.

"Yes, but your arm? What about the cut?" Cassie could hardly imagine anyone so cruelly abandoning a child in need. Anger surged through her at the callous treatment.

"Mother took me to the emergency ward after the dinner party was over and they stitched me up. It's fine." He smiled lopsidedly and bared his wrist as if to prove it had been a fuss for nothing.

Gently, softly, Cassie pressed her finger to the faint white scar. Four years old? It was obscene. Tears welled in her eyes at the cruelty he'd suffered and the ugly memory he carried.

"I'm sorry, Jeff. So sorry that you had to be hurt like that."

"It really wasn't that bad. I suppose I was being rather a

baby about it.'' His eyes were wide and full of surprise as he stared at her.

"It was terrible," Cassie disagreed, angry all of a sudden. "Children are supposed to have parents who are strong for them, not the other way around.''

"Thank you." It was softly spoken. So softly, Cassie almost didn't hear it.

He helped her into the car and then slid in beside her, letting the motor idle as he turned to face her.

"You're very good with children. Natural and caring. Why don't you have your own?''

Cassie smiled.

"It's rather embarrassing," she told him. "I've always had this dream that I'd marry someone who thought I was the most special person in the world, a prince charming in fact. We would live in a big house and have a huge family.'' She grinned up at him. "Somehow, here I am at twenty-eight with lots of kids and no house or man.''

"Until now," he murmured.

Her eyes flew to his in startled surprise.

"Well, yes. Until now, I guess." She shook her head at him. "Are you sure you know what you're getting into?'' she asked, head tilted to one side as she watched the gold flecks in his eyes glitter brightly.

"Um-hm," he half whispered. "Pretty sure. I'm getting a woman who doesn't mind when someone interrupts her sketches of Bored Boris to get a cookie or kiss a boo-boo better. I'm getting a wife who barely reaches five feet but fights like a heavyweight for the kids she believes in.''

His fingers slipped across her hair, twirling several glossy curls round his fingers. The words were whispered in her ear as he leaned over.

"I'm getting a woman who is as beautiful inside as she is out. I think it's a pretty good deal.''

His mouth settled on hers and Cassie kissed him back. It was a gentle kiss, a promise. And it was full of possibilities. Maybe that's what had her so flustered.

For as she sat there with Jeff's hands cupped around her face, his own mere inches away, all intelligent thought left her mind. She blurted out the first thing she could think of.

"Don't forget you're also getting a house full of kids."

"More and more like your fantasy, isn't it? Good. They'll get me into practise for when our own come along." He grinned that dangerous playboy grin that did odd things to her tummy.

That flustered her.

"Jeff, I don't really know much about men. I mean, I have a brother, but it's not the same thing."

His finger chucked her chin. "I should hope not."

"Well, no, I mean I'm not very good with the social niceties or dating, or, well, anything." She swallowed. It wasn't easy to tell him all her faults at one go. "I've never been outside Canada while you've probably traveled around the world. Those business associates of yours might be impressed with my ring, but I don't think we'll have much in common otherwise. And I have a terrible temper. I try to control it but…"

She couldn't look at him. Her face felt as if it were on fire and she nervously twisted her hands in her lap.

"Cassie?" His voice was full of rich, smooth laughter, but he held it in check. A gentle smile tipped his mouth up at the corners. "Look at me."

She did.

"You've got this playboy image of me that I can't seem to shake. I'm not. Haven't had time even if I were the type." His eyes stared into her, willing her to listen to what hidden meaning lay under his words. "I'm glad Aunt Judith left the old place to both of us. It needs a big family to make it come to life again. David and Marie make a fine start."

His voice was like a thick chocolate covering, rolling over her, keeping her snug and safe.

"You don't know much about me and I don't know much about you. Or children. There are bound to be problems. But we're in this together and we can help each other through the tough times as long as we keep talking and trust each other to do what's right. That's what I want from this marriage. Okay?"

Cassie nodded slowly. "Okay."

But as she lay in bed later that evening, staring up at the ceiling, Cassie wondered why his touch haunted her. She had never ached to feel a man's arms close around her; never felt bereft when they left. Why now? And why did the touch of those soft, cool lips send her heart rate into overdrive?

This was going to be a marriage of convenience.

Wasn't it?

Chapter Four

Here comes the bride.

Jeff stared at the arched doorway, waiting for his bride to walk down the aisle of the tiny country church. Cassie, once she had given in, had insisted on a church wedding with her family there to see it. First Marie, and then Cassie's sister had sauntered down the aisle and now it was his bride's turn.

He grinned at the thought. Jefferson Haddon was getting married he told himself giddily. Who would believe it? Well, David for one. He'd insisted on being in the wedding party.

"I can be Marie's partner," he told Jeff importantly. And Jeff had accepted that. He knew the boy wanted to fit into their new family. Hmm, he liked the sound of that. Family. He grinned again just as Rory nudged him in the ribs.

"You're supposed to watch your bride come in."

Trust his oh so prim and proper brother to know the appropriate moment for the groom to glance toward the back. Jeff turned his head and then sucked in his breath at the sight of his wife-to-be.

Cassandra Newton looked like a fairy princess. She wore an ankle-length suit made of a gossamer white silk fabric. The top was a fitted filmy jacket that gave Jeff provocative glimpses of her glowing peach-tinted skin underneath. The jacket ended at her waist where a slim skirt flowed straight down to touch her satin-covered toes. Around the hem a delicate embroidery pattern was woven in silvery silken thread. A tiny white hat perched on her dark curls with just a fluff of veiling at the back.

Her only jewelry was the diamond stud earrings he'd given her last night and the pear-shaped diamond solitaire that sparkled on her ring finger.

He felt good about that ring. He'd chosen it himself after Cassie had refused to be drawn into a second trip.

"If it's supposed to be a gift, then I don't want to see it beforehand."

And she hadn't. He'd surprised her with it one afternoon when the kids had disbursed and left them with five minutes of peace.

"From me. To you." He'd held out the ring for her to see and breathed a sigh of relief at the look of delight on her exquisite face.

"Oh, Jeff. It's perfect."

He'd slipped it on her hand and then tugged her into his arms. That was happening a lot lately.

So were those kisses.

His pulse raced as he remembered how she had kissed him back and then flushed bright red when Marie had come upon them.

"Pay attention, Jefferson." That was Rory nudging him in the side. "This is *your* wedding, man."

Jeff came back to earth with a thud.

One slim arm wound through her father's as Cassie walked slowly down the aisle, carrying the deep indigo blue irises she favored over roses. Her fathomless green eyes fixed on him and never wavered until her father placed her hand in Jeff's. Then she glanced at her dad one last time as if to say goodbye.

Jeff squeezed her hand reassuringly before facing the preacher. As he promised to honor and cherish Cassandra Emily Newton, he made a vow to himself. He would do his best to make their marriage as happy as possible. Perhaps they didn't love one another, but if they worked at it, there shouldn't be any problem they couldn't overcome.

As he glanced down at the diminutive beauty beside him, Jeff thanked heaven they had agreed to take a short holiday together after the wedding.

"I don't want my parents to know all the reasons for our

marriage," Cassie had told him. So she didn't have a leg to stand on when he suggested a honeymoon.

"Everyone will expect it," he'd cajoled. "And anyway, it will give us time to get used to each other before we live with the kids. You know teenagers, always on the watch for anything unusual. Then they'll bribe us with it."

Cassie had given in. Finally. But not without some stipulations of her own.

"We are going to take our time getting to know one another. You are not to force me into anything. I want to make very sure we're on firm and solid footing in this marriage, headed in the same direction. We are not going to be the kind of parents who tear each other apart."

The thought of a baby with her bright inquisitive eyes had Jeff's blood sizzling through his veins, but he forced himself to concentrate on reassuring her with some casual response.

Not that he wasn't sincere. He was. But he also wanted his wife to be just that, his wife.

It was funny. In the last two months he'd done a complete turnabout. Suddenly, he wanted a home and a family and all the other normal everyday things men his age had. A relationship between two adults who were friends, who could share things, who cared about one another. A relationship that would benefit both members. A relationship that was nothing like the one between his parents. Which shouldn't be too hard. After all, he wasn't anything like his father.

Was he?

Jeff shook off the ugly thought. Smiling, he slid the wide gold band onto Cassie's slim finger as he repeated the words.

"With this ring, I thee wed. With my body, I thee endow."

He smiled even more when Cassandra Emily slid her own gold band on his finger. It had been one of her requirements.

"If I wear one, so do you."

Not that he'd argued. It was the reasoning behind her logic that made him smile.

"If women are branded as some man's property, then in this day of equality, men should be branded, too."

"Does that mean you consider yourself my branded property?'' he had quipped, knowing she would have a ready response.

"Guess again, pal." Cassie's wide mouth mocked him. "*You* know very well what *I* meant."

He merely laughed at her red face.

Her look had been the severe one he'd seen used on a recalcitrant child. "You'd better clean up your act."

Perhaps it had been a good idea to get married here, Jeff reflected. The well-used church held the perfect atmosphere and the old-fashioned words said precisely what he meant, he told himself as bending, he kissed his new wife. Exactly the sentiments he felt right now, he reiterated, staring at the beauty of her oval face.

As Cassie felt her husband's lips move away, she felt a return of the shakes. She'd had them before. Numerous times over the past few weeks.

What had she done?

Grimly she pasted her smile on and moved through the old church decorated in its Christmas finery of red and green. It was impossible to ignore the terror that gripped her soul.

You have just married a man for money, she told herself. A very handsome, very desirable man, yes. A man who can ignite your senses faster than any man had ever done, it was true.

But still, it was all happening because of Judith's ridiculous will. The shock of it made her hands tremble. Please, dear God, don't let me regret it.

"It went okay, didn't it?" she whispered as they stood in the receiving line at the back of the church.

"It went perfectly, just as you planned."

Cassie watched Jeff surreptitiously. When anyone congratulated him, he accepted their good wishes with a smile but his fingers stayed firmly wrapped around hers during the next few hours, coaxing his strength into her.

And Cassie needed strength. She was so nervous, she felt sick. There was no going back now.

She was married!

Her family had gone all out; to such an extent that their reception housed most of the small town where she had grown up. The tables were beautifully decorated in crimson red and kelly green. A tiny favor wrapped in tulle sat at each place setting. And everywhere there were flowers, fragrant and full of life.

The rent on the hall alone would make a huge dent in her parents' savings account, Cassie acknowledged sadly. She vowed to see about a house in town for them as soon as she and Jeff returned from their holiday.

She refused to call it a honeymoon just as she refused to think about everything else right now. She would manage. Somehow.

Cassie took a deep breath as the tinkling of forks on glassware began.

Not again! Jeff teased her with his kisses at every opportunity. Cassie wondered how long this game of torture would continue.

''Pucker up,'' he whispered just before his mouth closed on hers.

It was a teasing sort of kiss, featherlight with just enough enthusiasm to whet her appetite. Cassie frowned when he pulled back, chastising herself for wanting more. How could she possibly feel desire for a man she had known such a short time?

The fact was, she knew nothing about Jefferson Haddon.

Oh, she knew he was good with the kids; kind but firm when he needed to be. And he had more than demonstrated his generosity with all of them, acquiescing with alacrity to the many changes she wanted to make at Oak Bluff. He'd agreed to David and Marie's adoption without a qualm.

And when it came to the wedding, Jeff had simply told her what he would like, listened to her views and then helped her make the decisions with compromise on both their parts.

He was fair, she knew that. But she knew only the barest of details about him personally. It was a strange thing to admit about one's husband, she acknowledged.

He had taken her to meet his parents several times but the last occasion was not particularly happy. On that visit, Mrs. Haddon had been generously kind about their plans but it was evident that she, too, felt the atmosphere grow more strained when Jeff and his father disappeared into the library.

Cassie wondered how Jeff's parents felt, seeing their firstborn

son marry a small-town nobody. To their credit, they had politely welcomed her into the family, although without warmth
or enthusiasm. Mrs. Haddon had graciously accepted her
mother's refusal to hold the event in Toronto.

"This is your special day, my dear," she said smiling.
"Yours and Jefferson's. You must do whatever you wish. Mr.
Haddon and I will help in any way you would like."

"I'm sure there are certain people you'd like to invite. If
you'll give me their names and addresses, I'd be happy to send
an invitation." Cassie tried to ignore the Ming vase at her elbow and the white kid leather sofa she sat on. If she was to do
this, she would have to fit into Jeff's world and learn to relax.

Mrs. Haddon stared at her in surprise before recovering that
veneer of composure.

"Jefferson will tell you whom he wishes to invite. We will
abide by his decision. As usual."

Since that was settled, Cassie endured a short discussion on
the best catering service in the city. Everything had gone
smoothly until father and son emerged from the study a scant
ten minutes later.

"We're leaving now." Grim faced, Jeff had announced their
departure moments later without even bothering to glance his
father's way. Jefferson Senior never spoke directly to Jefferson
Junior which left Rory to act as buffer between the two men.
Mrs. Haddon offered no comments of her own on their short
visit.

Jeff had been terse and uncommunicative until they'd arrived
back at Judith's home. Cassie had questioned him then.

"What is this family tradition he's talking about uphold-
ing?" she demanded, hands on her trim hips. And when he
hadn't spoken, she had grasped his shoulder. "Jeff?"

He'd kissed her then, she remembered. With a tenderness that
made her heart ache. Made her believe for an instant he truly
cherished her as his wife. But that was impossible—wasn't it?

Long moments later she had stared up at his face through
eyes glazed with emotion. It was ridiculous to find herself so
drawn to a man she had known such a short time, but Cassie
made no effort to deny the joy she always found in his embrace.

Her legs wobbled with the effort of standing and she had

been glad when he'd whipped her up into his arms to settle into a nearby armchair. Cassie rested comfortably in his arms, bonelessly pliant as he hugged her small body against his.

"What is it?" A tiny frisson of fear coursed through her veins. Jeff had held her gently then, his chin nestled on her head as he muttered an apology.

"It's always bad when I go there," he told her. "But I apologize for taking it out on you. It's not your fault."

His long fingers played with her hair, curling the glossy strands about his fingers as he sat silent and foreboding.

"Why?" She shouldn't have asked it, but Cassie's tender heart ached at the pain she saw on his handsome face. She wanted to bring back that darkly sardonic grin.

"What's the tradition?" Her tone was quietly insistent and eventually Jeff answered her.

"The firstborn male in the Haddon family is always called Jefferson with the appropriate numeral behind. It's a tradition my grandfather began and my father insists on having it upheld."

Cassie was dumbfounded into blurting out, "How can it be upheld? You don't have any children." A horrid thought crossed her dazed mind. "Do you?" Cassie fixed him with her gaze, her face severe.

He'd laughed at that.

"No, of course not. The old man is just planning for the future."

"Well, I hope you told him he's just the slightest bit premature."

His darkly handsome face had grown stiff then.

"You don't tell him anything," he had muttered, staring down at her hands in his. "No one ever could. It's his way or not at all." He straightened in the chair, the tenseness obvious in his rigidly held backbone. "But I have my own plans. My son is going to be called Robert, Bobby for short."

She heard it, she just didn't believe it.

"Uh, Jeff, don't you think I might want some say about that?"

He had stared right through her for several long moments before a devilish glint lit his dark eyes.

"Well, when the time comes, I guarantee to let you have your say," he'd promised, grinning at her.

It had been a ridiculous conversation, Cassie admitted. Particularly when she didn't even know how this marriage would be played out. She liked his kisses, enjoyed their walks and discussions and they had settled more than one argument with reason. But Cassie also recognized that so much remained unsettled between them. Jeff had agreed that she could take as long as she wished before their marriage would become a real one. Cassie wasn't sure just how long that would be.

"Cassandra?"

She turned to stare into the sparkling pools of dark chocolate and remembered that he was her husband now; she was married.

"Yes," she blinked, staring at him.

"It's time to go," Jeff whispered in her ear, his hand wrapping round hers. "We have a plane to catch."

How could she have forgotten the honeymoon?

Jeff stood then, tall and handsome as he pulled her up beside him and spoke to the assembled group of grinning faces.

"My wife," there was a firm emphasis on the second word, she noticed. A sort of proud stress on the syllable. "My wife and I have to be on our way," he told them, smiling at the various catcalls. "We'll miss our plane if we don't hurry."

Jeff turned to her parents and thanked them again for his bride. The words were a tribute to her and Cassie surreptitiously wiped away a tear from the corner of her eye as she watched the glow of pride on her mother's face.

They moved around the room distributing wedding cake to their guests and thanking each one personally before edging toward the doorway.

"Throw your bouquet, Cassie," she heard her sister call and so she did. Turning her back on the assembled group, she tossed the beautiful flowers over one shoulder and then turned to identify the recipient.

"Good luck." She grinned at Robyn. "It's fitting," she whispered in her friend's ear. "If God planned this, He probably has something up His sleeve for you, too." And then they were out the door and into the car as showers of confetti cascaded around them.

She heard the happy goodbyes from a distance as her glance focused on Jeff. He was watching her, his dark eyes intent on her face.

"Hello, Mrs. Haddon," he murmured before his lips closed over hers.

"Hello, Mr. Haddon," she replied, but it was in her mind. Her mouth was too busy returning his eager caress.

When he finally pulled away from her lips, her new husband buried his face in her neck, drawing in deep breaths of air before his head lifted, dark eyes shining into hers.

"I think we had better drive away." Cassie blushed, embarrassed by her overwhelming response to him.

He nodded and drove off without a word.

It was only after the first five or ten miles that Cassie realized she was still wearing her wedding dress.

"I don't want to show up at an airport wearing this," she exclaimed, suddenly aware of her predicament.

"And I don't have my suitcase. We should go back to Mom and Dad's. We could change there." She tossed a glance at his formal suit and raised an eyebrow. "I expect you would like to get out of that, too."

He grinned that boyish smile that always sent a tiny shaft to the center of her heart.

"Well, I would," he admitted. "But there is no way we are going back to your parents'."

"Why? I thought…"

"Cassie, they think that's where we're going and your brother has a big party lined up. If we go, we'll never catch the plane."

"Well, where then?" She faced him, shifting in her seat uncomfortably.

Jeff stared into the darkness falling around them before pointing to a grove of trees just off to the side.

"I think we can make do there." He smiled easily. "And I put our bags in the trunk this morning before anyone could tamper with them."

It wasn't easy, wiggling out of her wedding finery behind a

bush in the chilly middle of nowhere, but it was infinitely preferable to arriving at the airport in it.

Jeff made fun of her shyness when Cassie shielded herself carefully from his interested glance before removing her dress.

"We're married, Cassie. It's perfectly all right. After all, you can't hide from me forever," he mocked, laughingly.

"True," Cassie muttered to herself. "But I can until I pick the time and place."

Jeff helped her fold his suit and her dress into the garment bags Mrs. Newton had thoughtfully provided.

"That should keep them till our fiftieth anniversary," he teased, revving the motor before they drove off down the highway. "That's when we'll take them out and try them on once more."

Cassie marveled at his calm assurance. He seemed so confident of their future together, while millions of doubts swirled around in her own head like sharks ready for a feeding frenzy. She hummed along with the Christmas carols on the radio and ignored them all.

They arrived in Banff several hours later. Cassie unfolded herself from the plane and tried to peer around at the mountains but it was so dark, little could be seen.

"We were lucky," Jeff said, leading her to the waiting car. "If it had been stormy we wouldn't have had nearly such a soft landing." The small cabin he drove them to was several miles away, up a winding treacherous road.

"We'll admire the view tomorrow," he teased her as she stood gazing up at the giant cliffs overhead. "For now, let's get inside and get warm."

It was a charming cottage and she admired the soft glow of wood that lent the inside such a rustic air.

"It was very kind of Rory to lend us his cabin," she acknowledged, watching as Jeff lit the fire in the big stone fireplace.

"Does he come here often?"

"I'm not sure he can get away from Father's demands that easily," Jeff replied. His dark eyes were watching her flit here and there, touching the soft leather of the sofa and the smooth sheen of the log walls.

"Would you like something to eat or drink?" he asked at last.

"Yes! I'd love some coffee."

He frowned. "Rory doesn't drink stimulants. I'm not sure if there is any," he admitted.

"I'll look," she volunteered. Anything to get away from that yawning silence. "I found it. Want some?"

She was surprised to find Jeff standing immediately behind her in the little kitchen.

"I don't usually... Yes, why not? Just not too strong."

Cassie busied herself with the pot and grounds and wondered how she was going to get through the next three days.

And nights.

In fact, it wasn't really difficult at all. They sat by the fire, sipping at their coffee as they discussed their wedding day in minute detail.

"I'd say everything went perfectly," Jeff said with a yawn. "But it was a long day and I for one need some sleep." He nodded to the larger bedroom on the left. "I've put your suitcases in there. Water heater's lit."

Cassie stood awkwardly, feeling strangely out of place. As if something were not quite right.

"Oh. Okay. Well, good night, Jeff." As she turned to leave, his hand closed around her upper arm. She glanced up at him curiously, face flushed. "Yes?"

"Good night Cassandra Emily Newton Haddon. Sweet dreams." His arms closed around her as his mouth slanted down to cover hers. "See you in the morning," he whispered at last.

"Yes," she whispered. "In the morning."

As she lay in the big soft bed listening to Jeff moving slowly through the cabin, banking the fire and locking the door she thought about her wedding day.

"I'll really try," she promised, eyes squeezed tightly closed. "I'll do my best to be the kind of wife you expect. But please, just keep showing me the way, would you? I'm so afraid I'll take a wrong turn."

"You've taken a wrong turn." Cassie giggled across at Jeff. "This is the third time we've circled in front of the Banff

Springs Hotel and even though it is a wonderful old structure, I think I've seen enough for today.''

"Smarty-pants," he chided, peering through the windshield at the snowy landscape. "I'm trying to get to the Upper Hot Springs. I am not lost."

"You should have turned right when I told you to," Cassie said with a chuckle. "How amazing—a man who won't admit he's lost."

His dark brows lowered forbiddingly as he stared across the confines of the small car. "I know exactly where I am. You see, there are the Bow Falls." He said it triumphantly, as if they hadn't driven past them several times already this morning.

"I really believe you'd handle this better if you would just stop for a good strong cup of coffee," Cassie muttered, holding her hand over her mouth. "Coffee has wonderfully restorative powers."

"Says who?" Jeff demanded sourly. His eyes glowered at her. "That stuff you made last night kept me up all night. I didn't sleep a wink."

"You're kidding! I slept like a baby. It was wonderful." Cassie stretched her arms over her head and almost purred in the warmth of the bright sunlight flooding through the windows. "I would have had a cup at the cabin but I couldn't find the coffeepot." She watched his face flush a dull red and wondered at the strange tone in his voice.

"I, uh, er, had a, sort of accident with it."

Curiouser and curiouser, Cassie thought, peering across at him as he wheeled the car into a parking spot in front of the town's only McDonald's. The place was buzzing with activity but she made no move to leave the car.

"It was all right last night. What happened?"

Jeff's dark eyes didn't meet hers as he zipped up his jacket and stared through the windshield.

"I, um, thought you might want some coffee when you woke up, so I put the pot on." His face was very red now, she noticed interestedly.

"Yes?" She tried to sound encouraging.

"Um, er, apparently I forgot to...that is, the top wasn't on.

Not properly and uh…'' His voice was muffled in the fur collar and Cassie leaned forward.

"Pardon?"

"It perked all over the ceiling and the counter and the floor. I spent ages cleaning up the grounds and by then the pot had boiled dry. I think it's burned out now. All right?'' He was glaring at her belligerently, daring her to speak but Cassie couldn't have spoken then. She was too busy laughing.

"Well, thank you for the thought anyway.'' She giggled. "I know you don't like the stuff yourself. It was kind of you to think of me. Perhaps tomorrow you'll have better luck.''

But Jeff was vehemently shaking his head from side to side.

"Don't look at me,'' he denied, holding up his hands. "I'm totally useless in the kitchen. This proves it. I think we should just eat and drink out. No dishes.''

Cassie smiled at the shudder that crossed his shoulders. Evidently he wasn't a great success in the kitchen. Well, she could manage. Just barely.

"I'm no great shakes myself,'' she told him. "At home we have the Bennets so that's no problem. But I think I could rustle up a small meal if we wanted to eat in some night.''

Jeff was standing outside, holding her door. As she stepped from the car, Cassie couldn't help the flutter of awareness that rippled through her at the brilliance of his smile.

"That's why there's takeout,'' he whispered conspiratorially. "For klutzes and newlyweds.'' She couldn't stop the flood of red to her cheeks either as she fingered her shining new rings.

They spent the next few days relaxing, sightseeing and skiing. They also discussed everything under the sun. Cassie learned of Jeff's affinity for Toronto's SkyDome and the city's beloved baseball team. As they relaxed in the hotel's spa after a day on the slopes, he found out her wish to be taller and her love of football.

He frowned. "You don't look like the football type,'' he muttered, staring at her size.

"I know.'' Cassie giggled. "That's why I usually managed to score. Underestimated.'' She nodded sagely. "Nobody thought I'd carry the ball the whole nine yards.'' She caught the amused smile that flew across his face.

"What kind of music do you like?" she asked hesitantly, wondering if she should mention her dislike of country.

"Easy listening stuff. Upbeat rhythms that cheer you up. Some jazz." His head tipped backward in the pool as he allowed the warm mineral water to relax the knots of tension in his neck. He turned his head. His eyes opened and fixed on hers. "And you?"

"The same, I guess. Do you like country music?" She waited, praying that he would say he hated it.

"I like some country music," he said, staring off through the wisps of mist that floated from the pool out across the snow-covered valley. "Not the whiny stuff and not the 'dog bit me and wife left me' kind of stuff." They compared favorite musicians for a while and then discussed the view.

"God really knew what he was doing when he created this beautiful place, didn't he?" she mused, staring at the jagged peaks glistening in the bright sunlight.

"Actually, I think most geologists give that credit to the glaciers." He chuckled.

"Well, someone had to create the glaciers," she asserted reasonably. "They didn't just appear from a big bang. I think He made the Rockies specially for folks to sit back and relax. Take a look at the way their lives are going."

"And," Jeff asked curiously, "is your life going the way you wanted?"

Cassie tipped her head to one side as she studied him seriously.

"Just lately it's taken some very odd twists and turns," she confessed. "I didn't even have a husband, much less a home and two children last month. Suddenly I have all three."

He stared down at her. "I thought that's what you wanted."

"I did," she murmured. Her wide eyes studied his muscular form, deciding immediately that Jeff was the best-looking man in the crowded pool.

"Are you having second thoughts?" Jeff's voice was low and serious and full of reservation as his hands closed over her shoulders.

"And third and fourth thoughts." She grinned at him. "But don't worry. I'm not changing my mind." Cassie's eyes remained locked with his in a stare that seemed to search her heart for answers. That intense scrutiny made her nervous.

"Why does that Moraine Lake seem so familiar?" she asked finally, anxious to break the extended silence between them.

"Probably because it's on the back of that wad of twenty-dollar bills you handed over at the Christmas store," he teased. "How, exactly, are you going to get that oak rocking horse home?"

"I didn't spend too much, did I?" she queried anxiously. "It's just that I thought it would be so perfect for the wee ones to play on. And it hasn't a sharp edge on it."

Jeff felt his blood begin to simmer as he stared into her bright green eyes. He had a similar feeling two hours later when he saw that she had the same soft, doe-eyed look in her eyes as she tried to talk to a young girl they'd met panhandling in the park. Cassie tried to convince her to go home.

"I'm sure your parents love you very much," Cassie assured her, smoothing her hand over the girl's thin shoulder as she spoke. He'd felt uncomfortable watching but there was no way he was leaving his wife alone at night in the park with that young hoodlum. "They're probably wondering where you are right now, hoping you'll be coming home for Christmas."

"Naw, they won't," the teen declared as she sat down on a bench. "They don't care about anybody or anything but their stupid old rules. They have a rule for everything," she added bitterly.

"Oh, honey, in real life there are rules for everything," he heard Cassie murmur. "And if you break them, you always have to pay. Sometimes the cost is pretty high." He noticed his wife's quick summation of the girl's thin jacket and lack of boots.

"For instance, society's rules say you have to work to eat. I bet you've been panhandling for a while, haven't you. Trying to get people to give you something for nothing."

The girl had started to nod at Cassie's words and then objected strenuously. "It's not for nothing. I sing and Jack plays. Or he did. He's gone off with another girl now."

"And you're getting pretty hungry, right?" Both Cassie and

Jeff watched the straggly blond head nod. "Will you make me a deal?"

"Cassie, I don't think..." Jeff had swallowed his objections when Cassie fixed those glittering emerald eyes on him.

"What's the deal?" the waif demanded, obviously afraid Jeff would talk Cassie out of her offer.

"I'll buy you anything you want to eat if you'll promise to phone your parents first." Cassie met the glare from his eyes evenly, daring him to contradict her offer. "Anything at any place. You name it."

They both watched as the almost-woman struggled with her offer. At last she shook her head.

"No can do," she said in forced gaiety. "No cash for the call." She stood as if to leave. "See ya."

"Wait a minute." Cassie walked beside her, leaving Jeff to trail behind. She deliberately stopped in front of a pizzeria and stared at the youngster. "If they won't accept a collect call, I'll pay for that, too. Deal?"

It couldn't have been easy, Jeff decided, to ignore the delicious smells of tomato sauce and garlic and fresh yeasty bread wafting on the night air. His own stomach growled in response. At last he saw the blond head nod.

"You have to try, Shelley," Jeff heard Cassie tell her as they hurried to the bank of public phones across the way. "You have to take the first step. After all, you walked out on them. Give them a chance."

As he wondered how she had found out the girl's name, he saw Cassie's hand slip into the younger girl's. She held on the entire time and moved away only when the conversation became emotional. Then his wife slipped her tiny hand into his and held on tight. He heard her breathing a prayer for the troubled child and her family.

They looked up together as Shelley quietly hung up the phone. The girl looked dazed, lost in a haze.

"Are you okay, honey?" Cassie asked, tugging him forward with her. "Is everything okay?" Jeff felt her fingers tighten around his.

"Not yet," Shelley muttered. "But I think it might be. My mom said they've been looking all over for me. They want me to go home. She said we need to work out the rule thing together.'' Her blue eyes were full of tears. "She said she loves me."

"Of course she does.'' Cassie hugged the thin shoulders with a laugh. "You're her daughter. She wants the best things she can give to you. It hurt her to have you leave home and live on the streets. She knows how dangerous life can be. That's why she made the rules."

"I guess.'' Shelley looked around. "Can we go eat? I feel like I'm going to faint."

They had eaten a huge meal at a spaghetti house. Their young charge socked away two large helpings of lasagna, three glasses of milk and a huge slice of chocolate brownies.

"I've never been so full in my life,'' Shelley groaned at last, her hand fluttering across her mouth. "It feels wonderful.'' She bent to pick up the scruffy backpack she carried. "But it's late and I'll bet they want to close."

Jeff cast an eye on the short, rotund man who sat sipping something at the counter. Indeed, the place was deserted. They were the last customers in the place. He felt Cassie press against him as she moved, obviously expecting him to vacate the booth and let her out. He decided he liked the feel of her slim shape against him and stayed put.

"Where will you sleep tonight?'' he asked curiously.

"I dunno. The park, I guess. It's only for one more night anyhow.'' Jeff barely caught the shaft of ice-cold fear in her eyes.

"Oh, Shelley, that's not safe! Why, you could be attacked. Anything could happen there.'' Cassie glanced sideways at him as she spoke, obviously expecting Jeff to add his voice to her objections.

"It's okay. Really.'' Shelley stared down at her scuffed runners. "If you stay near the others nobody bothers you much.'' She stared down at Cassie's concerned face. "Thanks a lot, Cassie. Really. I don't know what would have happened to me if you hadn't made me phone my mom."

"It won't be easy, you know,'' Cassie warned. Her face was serious. "There will be times when you will think that running away will solve everything. You've just got to stick it out and find a solution with your mom."

"I have an idea," Jeff interrupted quietly. He had his doubts about this young girl's sincerity but there was no question that Cassie was trying to help. He offered the words for her sake. "There's a small place about two blocks over. The lady there offers bed and breakfast. Would you stay there as my treat, Shelley?"

Jeff didn't know why he offered. There was no reason. The girl was nothing to him. But something about Cassie's concern for a young girl alone and scared was getting to him.

"No!" Shelley's head shook vehemently. "You guys have done more than enough. I'm not a charity case. Honestly! I'll be fine." She grinned at Jeff impudently. "It'll probably break your budget just to pay the bill."

Jeff stood up, silent, staring at her.

"No," he murmured at last. "I insist. Cassie and I couldn't possibly just leave you alone now. Not when things are about to change for the better. Come on, it's not far to walk. We'll go together."

To his complete amazement, the girl burst into tears. Loud sobs that sent the manager's curious stare to the lone group standing by the door. Jeff stood there, totally nonplussed.

"Why?" she demanded, gulping back her tears. "Why would you want to do this? You don't even know me. Why are you so concerned about me?"

As he watched, Cassie wrapped her arms around the thin pathetic shoulders and squeezed.

"Oh, Shelley," she whispered, a catch in her voice. "You're a human being...a wonderful girl who's in a little trouble right now. Why shouldn't we help you out? Wouldn't you do the same if you found someone in trouble?"

Shelley's troubled eyes studied the smaller woman for many moments. "I will," she promised. "If I ever get the chance, I'll help out some other girl just like you helped me."

They left her moments later, under the gentle ministrations of a round, sunny-faced woman named Mrs. Beedle who was obviously just aching for someone to fuss over.

"Now don't you folks worry about her one little bit," she

clucked, hugging the thin body against her own ample chest. "I haven't had a young thing like Shelley to worry about for years. I'm going to enjoy this. Would you like a nice hot bath, dearie? I have some bubble bath my grandchildren sent me."

Jeff and Cassie tiptoed out the back door as the two new friends walked upstairs, chattering madly to each other. They were half a block away when they heard Shelley's shrill voice.

"Cassie! Wait up." She came rushing up and hugged her friend tightly. "Thank you. For everything. And you, too," she added, wrapping her thin arms around Jeff's waist. "I'll write you as soon as I get home." And then she was gone, dashing away in a flurry of white fluffy snow.

"Fresh powder," Jeff murmured, holding Cassie's hand in his own. "Someone's going to be enjoying a good run on Sunshine tomorrow."

"Uh-huh." Cassie peered up into the plethora of stars overhead. "Isn't it a perfect night?" she exclaimed, grinning up at him.

"Mmm," Jeff agreed, pausing a moment to brush her lips with his. "Absolutely perfect."

He stared down at her.

"Why did you do that?" he asked quietly, watching as her face flushed a dull red.

"You, er, kissed me first," she reminded him.

He grinned. "Not that. Why did you go to all that trouble for someone you didn't even know?"

Cassie shrugged.

"Because she was in trouble and I was there. Because I could, I guess." Her green eyes peered up at him. "What would you have done?"

Three days later he still couldn't answer the question as Cassie sank into the airplane seat and whooshed a sigh of contentment.

"It was a pretty good holiday, wasn't it?" Jeff smiled, noticing how quickly she slipped out of her fashionable heels.

"Very good," she agreed. Her eyes studied him. "How do you think the kids have made out?"

"I'm sure that between your parents and the Bennets, they're probably spoiled rotten." He waited, knowing she wouldn't let it go without an argument. It was just a small bit of the knowledge he'd gathered in regard to Cassie.

"Our kids are too perfect," she teased him, grinning with happy abandon. "They could never be spoiled. Just like me. Although you've made a darn good stab at it these last few days."

It was true, Jeff decided. She couldn't be spoiled. Cassie Haddon was as clear and true as Banff's new snow. He wondered how he'd come to acquire such a perfect wife. And then he wondered how long it would take her to discover all his flaws. And his fears.

Chapter Five

Two weeks later, Cassie wished sadly that she had relaxed more on her honeymoon. There certainly wasn't any time now.

"There will be four of them, Cassie. They could become very important clients and I want to have them in for dinner. Nothing special...just a nice quiet family meal. Okay?"

"Uh, well actually, Jeff, we have..."

"Look, the other phone is going. I've got to go. Talk to you later."

"But Jeff..." Cassie frowned at the hum in her ear and glared at the receiver with malevolence. "Apparently he doesn't want to hear about you guys," she muttered, staring down at the two children at her feet and the gurgling baby in her arms.

"Mrs. Bennet," she called out and then remembered she'd given the woman the day off. "Of course," Cassie muttered slapping her forehead. "Murphy's Law." She glared down at the little boy who'd come into her care several previous times.

"That's your law, Jonathan Murphy. If anything can go wrong, it will go wrong." The two newest arrivals stared up at her curiously.

"Cookie?" The dark-headed one seemed confused.

"Sure," Cassie replied resignedly. "Cookies and coffee, that's what we need more of in this house."

The table sparkled with good china, delicate crystal and glittering silver. Cassie had set it early, while the kids were napping and unable to touch the delicate things. But what to do for dinner?

"Hi, Cass. What're you doing?" Marie's words came out garbled as she stuffed a granola bar into her mouth.

"I'm trying to decide on dinner. Jeff's bringing home clients and I want to do something special. Trouble is," she mused, one finger twisting her hair in a spiral, "I don't know any meals that don't include burgers, hot dogs and pizza. Kid's stuff!"

"Hey, don't knock it!" Marie was openly laughing at her. "I'll give you a hand if you want. We've been doing some cooking in Home Ec and Mrs. Edmonds gave us this recipe for gazpacho. It's great!"

Cassie tipped her head to one side as she considered.

"That sounds pretty elegant," she agreed. "What will we do for the main course?"

"Well," Marie said as she lifted four chocolate-covered fingers out of the cookie jar and set it back on the counter. "For one meal we fried pork chops and then put them in a casserole in the oven with mushroom soup on top. They stayed there while we made quick rice with peas and carrots in it. It was good. And you can always have a salad."

Cassie grinned, fluffing the girl's long straight hair.

"Marie, you are a lifesaver. Can you watch the kids while I run to the store?"

Marie eyed Jonathan with disfavor.

"That's the Murphy kid again, isn't it?" She frowned at Cassie's nod. "You'd better make it quick then. He's a terror to watch out for." She scribbled out a list and handed it over. "I've written down cheesecake on the bottom. Try and get one of the frozen kind with swirls. It looks fancier."

Cassie kissed the soft cheek with fervor.

"I love you, do you know that?"

"You only love me for my cooking," Marie quipped with a grin. "Fair-weather friend, that's what you are." Her eyes narrowed slyly. "Otherwise you'd up my allowance."

Cassie left, shaking her head. Children!

"Pssst! Cassie?"

Cassie turned from her discussion with the abrasive woman

she assumed was once Jeff's girlfriend. Melisande Gustendorf had her arm wrapped firmly through his and the mere presence of a wife seemed to bother her not a whit.

"Jefferson and I have always been so close," she gushed in a babyish voice that grated on Cassie's nerves. "Why, we were practically raised together!"

"Cassie!"

"Please, excuse me," Cassie murmured and eased away from the gaily chattering group gratefully. It wasn't hard. No one even seemed to notice her absence. "What is it, Marie?"

The kitchen was a disaster area. There were pots and pans all over the floor as two small children amused themselves clanging assorted spoons and lids to produce a piercing clang that defied conversation in a normal tone of voice. Cassie swept across the floor, laundry basket in hand, as she picked up the pans and swiftly replaced them with plastic containers and lids that were much easier on the ears.

"Now that I can actually hear you, what is the problem, Marie?"

Pale and nervously biting her lip, Marie stood in the middle of the kitchen with tears coursing down her cheeks.

"I forgot to turn the oven down," she burst out bawling. "The meat is all dried out and hard. We can't eat that."

Cassie stared at the shrivelled-up darkened mass in the silver container and shuddered. It did look bad.

"You haven't put the mushrooms on yet," she murmured. "Perhaps if we added a little liquid to the soup it would soften them up." She nudged one solid little piece of meat with her finger. "Do you think?"

"I think we should phone for pizza," David offered helpfully. "Jeff's gonna die when he sees that lot."

Cassie scooped the baby's fingers away from the cheesecake on the counter and smoothed the faint indentation they had left on top with the tips of her finger. A huge strawberry helped cover the mark.

"That isn't going to help, David. It's too late to get anything here in time. We'll just have to hope for the best." She watched Marie spread the thick mushroom mixture over the meat and pop it into the oven. "How about your special soup? Do you think it will be okay?"

"Oh, the gazpacho's great," Marie smiled happily. "I changed the recipe a little but if we serve it with those fresh rolls you bought, everyone will be gasping for the recipe."

Gasping wasn't the word, Cassie decided half an hour later. One mouthful of the potent red concoction in her soup bowl had set her mouth on fire. She whipped the babies' soup bowls deftly away and gave them a roll to chew on.

"This is a very different style of gazpacho," the lovely Melisande wheezed, swallowing a huge mouthful of ice water. "It tastes rather like salsa."

"That's our Marie," Cassie gushed, smiling at the blushing girl who sat near the end of the table, right next to two older gentlemen Jeff had referred to as the Remus brothers. They, too, were sipping their water. "Marie learned this recipe at school. Isn't it delicious, Jeff?"

Jeff's eyes bulged in his face as he swallowed a mouthful of stingingly hot spicy liquid. He wheezed for breath several times before gulping down his water. Apparently "Mmm," was the best he could manage. Cassie decided it was better than nothing.

"Just how did you make this stuff?" Melisande asked scornfully, flicking her spoon through her soup as if searching for some hidden poison.

"Well," Marie began softly, "our teacher, Mrs. Edmonds, showed us that if you take hot salsa and add jalapeño peppers, you can achieve an unusual flavor." She frowned, noticing that no one was touching the remainder of their soup. "It's not too hot, is it?"

"It's just delicious, Marie," Cassie reassured her, filling in the gaping silence. "But you know, I imagine these folks all had a large and probably late lunch." She glanced round the table, forcing a smile to her parched mouth. "We eat early in our home because of the babies. We love to have a family meal. Perhaps you'd rather have some salad?"

The Remus brothers and Melisande were nodding eagerly as Cassie removed their soup dishes to the kitchen while Marie served each a small tossed salad. Jeff wasn't saying anything, she noticed, but then that could be because he hadn't known about Marie's cooking lessons.

"This little guy is sure a cutie," Mr. Weatherby cooed, leaning nearer Jonathan's hovering fingers. In a flash, the little boy had fastened his hands on the ends of the man's curling mustache and refused to let go.

"I'm so sorry," Cassie apologized as she pried open the fat grubby fingers. "He's always been curious."

"Children should be seen and not heard," Cassie heard Melisande say under her breath.

"Oh, I'm sorry you don't enjoy children, Miss Gustendorf. I'm afraid that we always have several running around, don't we Jeff? We just love children, you see." The Remus brothers were nodding benignly at her. Cassie looked to Jeff for reassurance and found him staring in horror at the platter of hardened brownish objects which his fork could not pierce. "Allow me to serve you," she offered and whisked two of the pork chops onto his plate.

Cassie moved round the table swiftly, dispensing food generously until the platters were clean. Then she refilled the water glasses before sitting down. The two babies began to fuss then, tired of their ridiculously inedible meal. Actually so was she. Rice was scattered all over the high chair tray tops and some had fallen into her shoes. Since David was merely stabbing at his food, Cassie decided to free him.

"David, dear, would you mind taking the babies upstairs? I think they're tired." She helped him remove the children from their high chairs. As he moved away, she breathed a sigh of relief. At least further disaster from that corner was removed. Now for the meal.

She sawed doggedly at the dried meat, dragging a hunk away to chew on. When it became evident that her teeth would no longer survive the effort, she lay down her fork and knife and stared round the table.

"That is a really excellent meal, Marie. What a lot of work you've gone to. You just keep practising. Some day you'll make a wonderful chef."

A deadening silence greeted this profound lie until Cassie's glare seemed to penetrate even Jeff's blank stare and he also praised her efforts. Gradually, one by one, the others joined in until only Melisande said nothing. At last her words emerged. Cassie cringed in expectation.

"Well, your cooking is certainly the most unusual meal I've ever tasted. Is there coffee?"

"Oh, I'm sure Cassie has coffee," Jeff commented sourly. "She never goes without that."

"Actually, Jeff, Marie also planned dessert. It's strawberry cheesecake." Cassie watched as the young girl proudly served her dessert. Each slice had been artfully decorated with several fresh strawberries and a drizzle of chocolate.

She watched as first one then the next of their guests carefully pressed a gleaming fork through the soft creamy mixture and tasted the smallest bit.

"It's delicious," they exclaimed, their voices a cry of surprise.

"It's really quite tasty," Melisande offered. "May I have another slice?"

Flushed with pride, Marie cut her a huge slice and carefully set it on her plate. "Please excuse me," she whispered softly. "I have homework."

"Certainly, dear. And thank you so much for all your work. We really appreciate your efforts." The others chimed in cheerfully, relieved that there seemed nothing wrong with this course.

Cassie was about to serve coffee when she noticed Jeff's breathing alter. She glanced down and inhaled sharply as her eyes lit on the round rubber ring of the baby's soother where it protruded from under one fat strawberry.

"I...I..." Jeff stuttered his dismay, drawing all attention their way. Quickly as she could, Cassie plunked the coffeepot down in front of him and slapped him on the shoulder.

"Yes, yes, dear. I'm serving coffee right away." She smiled serenely at the assembled group and picked up the silver server as her other hand whisked the foreign object into the napkin on his lap. "Jeff just loves his coffee," she crowed.

Five pairs of eyes stared at her in stunned disbelief. It was obvious they knew better and thought she was nuts.

"But I thought you only drank two cups a day and never

after noon," Melisande croaked, peering at him as if he'd grown two heads. "It's after seven."

"Oh, but this is decaf," Cassie murmured, realizing she'd been caught in her lie. "He loves that. Come on, let's take our coffee into the library everyone. Go ahead, dear," she smiled sweetly at him. "I'll be along in a minute."

They trooped out eagerly, anxious to escape the remains of their inedible meal. Well, not totally inedible. The rice was almost gone, the salad bowls were clean and Marie's cheese-cake had been a hit. With everyone except Jeff. His slice sat abandoned, an indentation in the center of it testifying to the soother's presence there just moments ago.

"You can't fool us, you know." Melisande's condescending voice cut through her reveries and she glanced over her shoulder to find the older woman glaring at her through narrowed eyes.

"I'm sorry," Cassie began politely. "I don't know what you mean." She squeezed the damning napkin in her fingers and prayed for strength. "Is something wrong, Miss Gustendorf?"

"Yes!" The low seductive tones were tight with frustration. "There is definitely something wrong. You're trying to pretend that you're all one happy family here when everyone knows that you only married Jefferson for his money. What I want to know is what he got out of the deal?" Her eyes narrowed disparagingly. "What in the world would someone like you have to offer someone of Jefferson's status and means?"

Cassie was furious. What right did this condescending person have to come into her home and criticize her marriage? She was about to launch into the attack when she felt an arm curve around her waist warningly. Her nose twitched at the faint hint of woodsmoke on his jacket as she remembered Jeff had called the woman a possible client.

"Jefferson! I was just saying how ridiculous it is to have those children running through this mansion. Why the house simply isn't made to be treated so shabbily." Melisande waved a hand toward the pair of high chairs nestled at the end of the elegant rosewood dining suite. "Your great aunt would turn over in her grave."

"On the contrary," Cassie answered, smiling. "Judith loved

to hear the children in the house. She said it came alive with the sound of their laughter.'' She frowned as she watched Jeff's friend cast a disparaging look at the litter of dishes still covering the table. "Don't worry about this. I'll clean it all up before Mrs. Bennet gets back.''

"You see! That's exactly what I mean,'' Melisande crowed. "She doesn't even know how to handle the servants. Clean up before they come home indeed! They should have been here to serve the meal. Surely they could have managed better than that distasteful display that ragamuffin girl served us.''

Cassie bristled at the disparaging tone.

"Now just a minute,'' she began, tugging her arm away from Jeff's tightening hold. "Marie offered, of her own free will, to help me out on our housekeeper's day off. And she did the best job she possibly could while baby-sitting three small children. So what if the chops were a little overdone. We won't starve. The important thing is that her heart was in the right place.''

"What's important is that Jefferson's business associates were treated to the most abominable meal on this earth! I don't understand your necessity to house these societal strays, my dear. It's simply not appropriate for someone in Jefferson's position.''

"Societal strays!'' Cassie stared. "They're just little children who need love and a place to stay that's safe and warm. We've got lots of that. What's the big deal?''

"It's not fitting,'' the woman continued, staring as David and Marie walked into the dining room, each carrying a crying baby.

"It's perfectly appropriate.'' Cassie cuddled the sweet little bodies to her and buried her face in their softness. "I had a great childhood. I'd like to share that experience with other kids. Is that wrong?''

"Jefferson, speak to her. Surely you understand that this fiasco tonight was...''

"I understand that Marie pitched in when she was needed and I'm proud of her for that,'' Jeff interrupted. "It takes a pretty big heart to cancel your date so you can baby-sit,'' he murmured, looking straight at Marie. "Cassie and I want to thank you for that.''

The young girl flushed with pleasure.

"Oh, that's all right. I'm just sorry that…"

"You have nothing to be sorry about, Marie. It was a lovely meal. And Mel, in regards to money—" he smiled down at his old friend calmly but with a hint of sympathy "—Cassie has lots of her own money. She doesn't need mine."

Cassie stared at him in amazement. He cared—he really cared that Marie's feelings weren't hurt by this cold, selfish woman. She would have hugged him but one of the babies started wiggling and she handed one over instead.

"Actually, I just came in to tell Cassie that Mrs. Butterworth and some other ladies from the church are here for a meeting?" Marie raised her eyebrow at Cassie who had completely forgotten the event. "Should I put the coffeepot on again?"

"Yes, please, dear." Cassie sighed. "And if there's any of that cheesecake left, we'll have that, too." She felt Jeff's body move abruptly behind her and turned her head to stare at his suddenly impassive face.

"Yes," he murmured. "If you'll cover mine so nothing falls into it, I'll eat it after I put the babies to bed." He plucked Corky out of his wife's arms and bent to press a kiss against her cheek in front of them all. "You go ahead, dear. Have your meeting. David and I will look after these two. Right, son?"

"Uh, right. I guess."

David followed the happy group, stopping abruptly at the door when Jeff turned to ask, "Coming, Mel?"

A look of extreme distaste marred the beautifully made-up face of Jeff's dinner guest. She glanced around the room once and then straightened her spine with determination.

"Actually no," she told them shortly. "I've just realized that I also have plans for tonight. I have to leave. I'll drop the Remuses off when I go." She cast a second deprecating look around the room before glancing perfunctorily at Cassie. "Thank you for the, er, dinner. It was interesting."

"Oh, you're welcome." Cassie grinned cheerfully. She slung an arm around Marie's shoulders in friendly companionship. "Feel free to come again. Anytime."

They waited until they heard Jeff at the front door bidding his clients good-night before looking at each other and bursting into gales of laughter. And they didn't stop until Amanda Butterworth came marching through the door.

"Cassie Haddon! You know blessed well that we can't start our meeting until the secretary arrives. What is the problem?"

It wasn't easy but Cassie forced her mouth into a prim line and walked along obediently behind the older woman's plump figure.

"Yes, Amanda. Sorry. I've just had a rather full day. What is it we have on the agenda for tonight? Oh, yes, the Christmas hampers. Well then, let's get down to work." She sailed through the door, prepared to battle through the next challenge. With His help, she determined, she would handle them all. "Good evening, ladies," she called out cheerfully. "Anyone care for coffee and leftover cheesecake?"

Chapter Six

"**W**hat in the world possessed you to offer to bake sixty pumpkin pies for those Christmas hampers?" Robyn demanded, lugging another bag of groceries into the kitchen. "Haven't you got enough to do with a new husband, two adoptions in the works, a four-almost-five year old boy, a toddler and a baby?"

Cassie grimaced ruefully. "Amanda talked me into it," she admitted. "I felt so guilty for spouting off to that Gustendorf woman that I didn't have the heart to turn her down."

"Cassie—" Robyn's eyes were wide open "—you don't bake. Trust me, I know this from personal experience."

"Oh, how hard can it be? You buy those frozen pastry shells and the pumpkin stuff in the can and you mix it up and bake it. Hello," she added, snatching up the ringing phone.

"Cassie, I was just checking the balance on our bank account and I noticed a major withdrawal. It's for cash." Jeff's voice sounded oddly uneven as he named the amount.

"Yes, that's right. I wrote it yesterday." She stuffed the foil pie plates into a cupboard and closed it quickly. "Didn't my money come through yet?"

"Yes, of course." She could almost see him scratching his head. "That's a very large amount of money, Cassie. Are you sure…?"

"It's too near Christmas to be asking those kind of questions, Jeff. Besides," she frowned at Robyn's leather-covered back.

"It is my money to spend, isn't it? Wasn't that part of Judith's will?"

There was a long pause.

"Never mind. We can talk about it later. When I get home." His voice lightened. "What are you doing?"

"Baking pies. Sixty pumpkin ones for the church Christmas hampers."

"Cassie, you don't bake. Not at all." He snorted with amusement. "Trust me—I know this for a fact."

She glared at the receiver.

"I've already heard that," she muttered. "It seems that everyone's a comedian in this house."

"The comedy was that unusual dessert we, er, enjoyed last night." He chuckled. "It's the first time I've had pineapple upside-down cake that was turned inside out." His voice came softly teasing across the line. "Did I get the part that fell on the floor?"

"If you've quite finished," she mumbled, a flush of red covering her cheeks, "I do have a few things planned for the rest of the day. Unlike some office personnel with their computer toys."

It slid off his back.

"Don't bake," he ordered. When she didn't reply he added, "Please." He chuckled again when Cassie refused to answer. "See you later," he said finally before a click cut their connection.

"Vengeance is mine, saith the Lord. I will repay." She recited the verse with her eyes closed, trying to forget all the nasty things she wanted to do to Jefferson Haddon.

"Cassie, what are you muttering about over there?" Robyn's query cut through her visions of just recompense for the slander on her culinary skills.

"I'm planning my Christmas list," she retorted. "And don't bother looking because you're not on it. Nor is that sneaky Jefferson Ungrateful Haddon." She flicked the grocery bags into a neat pile and pressed them into the drawer. "But there might be a way you could get back into my good graces, Robyn," Cassie suggested, smiling meaningfully at her friend. "Somehow."

"I know that look," Robyn protested. "You're going to finagle your way around and I'll end up saying yes to whatever you ask." There was a tilt of amusement to the corners of her mouth.

"Not at all," Cassie gestured airily. "I merely thought that as my nearest and dearest friend, you would want to help me plan a day out with my new husband. In the interest of joy, peace and goodwill toward men. You know," she cajoled, "the Christmas spirit."

Cassie watched Robyn from the corner of her eye as she packed the groceries into the fridge and freezer. Her friend's big blue eyes were wide open as she stared back at her, azure depths sparkling with mischief.

"Do I look like Santa Claus?" Robyn squeaked helplessly. Cassie knew Robyn was going to give in. "What exactly do you and hubby have planned?"

"Oh, Jeff doesn't know about this yet," Cassie explained with a giggle. "But I thought it might be fun to go Christmas shopping for the kids. You know, get something special for each of them—something they really want."

Robyn watched with amusement as her friend's eyes glazed over. It was just like Cassie to go all out at Christmas. She was like a little kid herself reveling in everything from candy canes and Christmas oranges to the carols and decorations.

"Poor Jefferson." Robyn shook her head sadly. "He has no idea of what will hit him on Saturday morning."

"Then you'll do it," Cassie crowed, flinging her arms around Robyn's shoulders. "You'll baby-sit the kids for us?"

"Oh, baby-sitting." Robyn's head sunk onto her chest. "That's what you want. And you've got that Murphy kid here, haven't you?" She peered down at Cassie. "I'll be dead by the end of the day." She sighed mournfully.

"Thank you, thank you, thank you. A thousand times thank you." Cassie danced around the room excitedly, listing the items she wanted to get on her fingers. "There's the cutest little pedal car in Sage's..."

"Cassie? Cassie!" Robyn snapped her fingers in front of her friend's glassy green-eyed stare.

"Yes?" Cassie answered, but Robyn had a feeling she was drifting off into never-never land.

"How many kids am I baby-sitting?"

"Mmm? Oh, six, I think. The Tyler boys are supposed to be here for the day."

"Not the Tyler twins?" Robyn groaned in defeat. "No wonder you tried to con me. Those two are the worst little brats...."

Her voice died mournfully away. "You owe me, kiddo. Majorly big-time!"

"You left her with those two juvenile delinquents?" Jeff stared at his wife, openmouthed. "And you call yourself a friend?" He smoothed his ruffled hair and disentangled the yellow sucker from his mohair sweater with resigned disdain. "No wonder you had to write such a large check!"

"Are we back to that again?" Cassie grumbled, trying to slip on her jacket and sip her coffee at the same time. "I told you— it's for a Christmas gift."

"Twenty-five thousand dollars for a Christmas gift?" Jeff stood transfixed as he stared at Cassie's blue-jeaned figure. "Isn't that a little extreme?"

It wasn't any of his business, of course, but he couldn't imagine what she'd spent the money on. And it seemed his wife wasn't talking. Apparently she was more interested in her coffee.

"Well, aren't you going to tell me?" he persisted. A new idea occurred to him. "Wasn't it you who said we should share more, work as a team? Team members tell each other the plan, you know."

Cassie sighed. It was one of those long-suffering sighs that Jeff was learning meant she would give in but she didn't like it. He waited calmly, watching as she sank into the nearest chair.

"You know I don't do well at conversation in the morning," she hedged, staring into the bottom of her now empty cup. "Especially on one measly cup of coffee." Her drooping jade eyes stared up at him tiredly.

"You've had three cups and quit stalling. What is this mysterious Christmas present?'' He fixed his eyes on her and watched her squirm. ''Cassie?''

''Three? Really?'' She stared at the cup with a blank look.

''Cassie!'' He roared it out of frustration.

''What?'' Her eyes studied his angry face. ''Oh, the money.'' He nodded. ''It was supposed to be a surprise and now you're ruining it,'' she lamented. Jeff refused to look away and she finally relented.

''Oh, all right,'' she huffed in frustration. ''I put a down payment on a house.''

He was shocked.

''What!'' He eyed her with pity. ''My dear woman, you live in a house with eight bedrooms, six bathrooms, a suite over the garages, a television room, a library, more sitting rooms than we need and a huge amount of land.'' He shook his head dazedly. ''What in the world do we need another house for?''

''I knew I should have brought a thermos,'' she muttered tiredly. ''The traffic will be deadly.'' Cassie picked up her cup and headed for the kitchen. ''I'm getting another cup before we go.''

Jeff trailed behind her helplessly. She was insane, that was it, he decided. With all these children coming and going, she had finally flipped. It wasn't any wonder really. He'd felt the strain himself when that social worker, Gwen Somebody, had dropped off two more boys on Thursday. And he wasn't home all day with them.

He'd take her away for the day, just as she'd planned. He hadn't been too hot on the idea when she'd first mentioned Christmas shopping, but now he understood. Cassie needed a day away from this nuthouse.

''Sit down, honey.'' Jeff pressed her gently down onto a kitchen stool and poured her mug full of black strong coffee as compassion took over.

''Take a big long drink and then we'll talk about this.'' He watched her sip the brew as his fingers gently massaged her shoulders. ''You need a break. I can see that. But we can arrange something here...get some extra help for you or send some of those hoodlums back. You don't have to move out, Cassie.''

Her eyes opened wide then—very wide. She stared at him stupidly. As if it were he who had put a deposit on a home they didn't need, Jeff grimaced sourly. He tried more reassurance and ignored the throb of panic that the thought of her moving out brought to his brain.

"It's okay, just relax," he directed. "I'll look after things. I know you wanted Oak Bluff for your kids but it's getting to be too much. I understand, believe me. We don't have to keep taking them, you know." He slid his hand over her black glossy curls as he spoke, hoping his touch would soothe her.

"Just stay. We can work this out together. Isn't that the way we said we'd handle our marriage—by talking out the problems?"

She couldn't move out, Jeff told himself. Not now. Not when he'd just begun to get used to having someone to touch and talk to—even hug sometimes. He didn't want to lose the closeness they were just beginning to build.

"We can change things, if you want," he murmured. "My old apartment is still up for rent. I could..." His voice died away as he thought of those lonely rooms so far from the hustle and bustle of Oak Bluff. And Cassie.

"Uh, Jeff?" She was staring up at him strangely. As if he were the one who was ill. "It's not for me."

"Pardon?" His hand stopped its caress midway as he peered down at her.

"I bought the house for my parents. I got a buyer for the farm and they're going to move into the city sometime in January. It's supposed to be a surprise." Her green eyes studied him as if she were afraid he would faint.

In fact, Jeff felt poleaxed. His knees were wobbly with relief that Cassie wasn't going anywhere.

"Are you sure?" he asked softly. "Things around here aren't getting to you?" He watched the big smile light up her face as she glanced out the window. He could see half a dozen assorted bodies playing in the snow and Robyn's long arm chucking snowballs at everyone.

"Everything around here is perfectly wonderful." She grinned up at him. "A little crazy, but wonderful. Thank you for asking."

Jeff couldn't help himself. She looked so happy sitting there, her eyes glistening with joy as she gazed up at him. He slipped his arms round her waist, leaned down and kissed her. A soft wonderful kiss that lasted for ages and sent his heart rate through the roof.

And Cassandra Emily Newton Haddon kissed him back!

"Ahem! Excuse me, I just need to get a glass of milk." Marie's face was wreathed in smiles as she padded across the room in her stocking feet. "Go ahead with what you were doing," she added and then flushed bright red.

Jeff cleared his throat.

"Uh, thanks, Marie but we can't right now. We've got some Christmas shopping to do. Right, Mrs. Claus?" He held out one arm and felt Cassie's smaller one curve through it immediately.

"Right you are, Mr. Claus. Bye!" She winked at Marie saucily before they sailed through the door together, grinning like children.

Later, as Jeff watched Cassie pour over possible gifts, he began to appreciate the amount of thought she put into each one. It had taken an hour to choose a silly little purple plastic pedal car which Jeff had insisted she have delivered.

"I cannot possibly lug that thing back to the car," he told her seriously.

"I'm warning you. They'll give us one in a box and you'll have to assemble it." The dimples in her cheeks grinned up at him.

"I don't care. I'll pay extra to have it assembled. Anything so that I don't have to walk through this crowd carrying that!"

He'd paid extra. Then they'd tramped from one end of the mall to the other searching for another hour for a telescope for David.

"Nothing too elaborate," she'd insisted. "But something he can study the heavens with." When Jeff had commented she'd turned on him. "It's either that or more rocks for his collection. You want to handle the excavations for that?"

He'd chosen the black medium-range telescope without further discussion. But this two-hour marathon for a metal construction truck was wearing him down.

"Can't we just get the yellow one for Jonathan?" he asked at last, tired of trailing through the Eaton Centre. "He's only four. I doubt he'll notice."

"Of course he'll notice," Cassie snorted. "Didn't you notice when Santa didn't bring you exactly what you asked for?" Her eyes sparkled up at him. "No, don't tell me. You came from one of those families that didn't have Santa, right?"

"Well, actually," Jeff began mildly, somewhat amused by her vehemence, "we did. But we got oranges and nuts and stuff in our stockings. The gifts came from our parents."

"I hate that," she declared loudly, blocking traffic in the middle of the busy mall. "People get so hung up on Santa Claus. As if it were a bad thing for children to believe that there is actually one man in the world who actually gives gifts just because he wants to!"

"Cassie, I don't think…" His voice died away as she poked him in the chest.

"Well, let me tell you, Jefferson Haddon the third, my kids are having Christmas. All of the things and traditions that make it the most wonderful time of the year."

She glared up at him furiously. As if he'd objected.

"They'll know Christmas is about Christ's birth in Bethlehem. But they'll also know that it's okay to do something nice just because it will make someone else feel good."

"Yes, dear. Whatever you say, dear," he agreed softly. His amused eyes met her surprised look. "But we're not doing a lot for the spirit of goodwill by parking ourselves right here in the middle of traffic. Let's have lunch."

He watched her glance around, as if she were only just then aware of the people jostling them and their packages.

"What put the bee in your bonnet about Santa?" he asked carefully as they sat indulging in burgers and fries. Jeff smiled as that rosy color flushed over her face once more. She got flustered so easily, it was almost fun to egg her on.

"We had the most wonderful Christmases when I was a kid. I used to start planning months ahead of time. When I got older, I managed to get an odd job here or there to raise money, but when I was little I had to save every dime. Everybody had to have a gift, you see. And it had to be something really special."

She grimaced. "And it had to come from me—not from my parents or with money that I hadn't earned. From me."

Jeff studied her earnest face as he remembered his mother handing him money and a list of items to purchase for each person.

"Just get what I've written on the list, Jefferson. And have the store wrap them. That will save a lot of fuss and bother." She had even chosen her own gift, he recalled.

Cassie seemed to consider nothing was too much bother and he was carrying the huge rolls of gift wrap to prove it.

"My parents believed that it was important for us to learn to give selflessly." She smiled. "I remember one year there was a scarf I really wanted from the catalog. But I couldn't buy both it and the sewing kit I'd picked out for Sam. It was really hard to buy that kit and leave the scarf, but oh, the look on her face Christmas morning!" Her smooth round face glowed with happiness. "It was probably the same look I had when I found a brand new pair of figure skates beside my stocking."

She studied him seriously.

"Every child has the right to believe in wonderful possibilities. There's a magic about childhood that makes kids so fragile. And yet they can learn from those dreams that they can do anything they set their minds to. That giving has its own rewards."

"But what's that got to do with Santa?" Jeff asked, munching on another fry and wondering why he hadn't ordered adult food when he'd had the opportunity.

Cassie grinned impudently up at him.

"Do you know any adults that still believe there is a Santa Claus?" she demanded. "Well, do you?"

"Not sane ones, anyway." Jeff grinned.

"And that's my point. We all come to realize that Santa Claus is basically the spirit of giving. Some decry it as consumerism and say it's a 'getting' philosophy and they're the ones who can't wait to scurry out there and shatter every little kid's belief in Santa. I think they do that because their own parents handled it wrong. The whole philosophy of Santa Claus is one of giving and I think it reflects the Christmas message perfectly."

"What's the Christmas message?" Jeff asked doubtfully. "Peace on earth and all that stuff?"

"That *stuff* and more," she nodded. "Do unto others...to give is better than to receive...but most of all, God sent his son; his only child. Not because he should have, or had to, or because we deserved it. But because he loved us and *wanted* to." She frowned up at him.

"So you think giving is the important part of Christmas?" he asked curiously. "The gifts and all that?"

"Not just the gifts," Cassie denied, shaking her dark head. "Giving the love. That's the key. It doesn't matter if it's a thing or not. The love will far outlast any *thing*."

Jeff grinned. Gotcha, he crowed mentally.

"Then why don't you just send all the kids a card that says 'I love you,'" he joked.

Cassie studied him seriously, her beautiful face staring into his.

"I will," she told him. "And I'll hug them and squeeze them and thank God for them. But that red truck is the tangible evidence that I care. And we haven't got it yet." Her eyes sparkled back at him, daring him to deny it.

He groaned, standing slowly.

"I knew it would come back to shopping," he moaned. "And you're like a missile on a search-and-destroy mission. I can barely keep up."

"Must be your age," she teased, piling up their assorted parcels.

"Hey, I'm not *that* much older than you!" Jeff felt about a hundred just then and the mere thought of dragging these parcels about sent his head reeling.

"I'm talking about mindset, not years," Cassie chuckled, grabbing his hand. "Stick with me, buster. I'll show you the way to stay young in spirit forever."

"Or kill me in the process," he grumbled, following meekly behind. He managed to get her to promise to stay in the jewelry store while he carried their parcels out to the car. "Don't leave here," he ordered. "I'll never find you in this crowd."

Cassie was peering through the glass excitedly and seemed not to hear him. He called her name once but her eyes merely passed over him fleetingly before returning to the window. Jeff grinned. There was only one way to get her attention. Using his shoulder to block them from passersby, he bent down and pressed his lips against hers in a soft caress. This was getting to be a habit he could enjoy, he told himself.

"What was that for?" she demanded, but her gaze was fixed entirely on him and him alone, Jeff noticed with satisfaction.

"Just trying to get your attention," he said smugly. "I'll be back in a minute. Don't move."

She stood staring bemusedly at him, her forefinger pressed against her full bottom lip.

"Yes, all right," she agreed bemusedly. "I'll be right here."

He'd learned an awful lot about her today, Jeff mused as he strode through the mall to the parking lot. Cassie was one of the true-blue people who followed her principles with practice. He envied that happy childhood that had given her such a strong foundation. And he understood her desire to pass it on, sort of.

He tucked the boxes and bags away, remembering how she'd hesitated over each purchase except the sweater for Marie.

"She's been coveting this for ages," Cassie had informed him, a smile of pure pleasure tilting those full lips up. "But she's never asked for it for herself. Not once."

He fingered the soft silky fabric from the coolest, hippest or whatever the word was now, place in the mall. That wide-eyed look of delight in Cassie's big green eyes stuck in his mind, tucked away for future reference. Jeff wondered what he could give to her that would make her face glow like that for him. He had a feeling a sweater wouldn't do it.

He stalked as quickly as he could back through the crowds, hesitating near the door of one store where a tall, slim Santa collected for charity in a large black kettle. The unlikely looking Santa jingled his bell, reminding people that there were others less fortunate than they.

Finally Jeff tugged a five-dollar bill from his pocket and tucked it into the slot. As he did so a familiar voice chirped back at him.

"Thank you very much, sir. And Merry Christmas."

"David?" Jeff's voice was a squeak of surprise and he strove to modulate it. "What are you doing here?"

David grinned, motioning to the big swinging bucket.

"Just what it looks like. Ringing the bells. The money goes toward Christmas presents for poor families in the community. Thank you, ma'am," he called to the tiny frail woman who had carefully put her money into the plastic ball. "God Bless You."

"But David, isn't today the day of that game at school? You're going to miss it." Jeff couldn't believe the teenager had willingly abandoned his friends to stand in a crowded mall and do this.

"Naw, I'll see the last half. We only take three-hour shifts. Besides, there will be other games. The charity only does this at Christmas—to pay for the stuff for needy families, ya know. Thank you, sir." A tall distinguished man pushed a fifty through the slot.

"Oh." Jeff didn't know what else to say. "Do you need a ride home?"

"One of the guys is gonna pick me up at three. He's at the other end of the mall. Thanks anyway. See ya later." David jingled the bells a little harder and smiled at the group of kids pushing and shoving their way past. "Merry Christmas," he called.

Jeff moved away, to continue down the strip. His mind whirled with what he had just seen. David was a foster kid. He'd been taken in by Cassie and, if she got her way, he would soon be adopted into their fairly wealthy family. What on earth possessed him to stand in the mall ringing bells for charity?

"Jeff? Where are you going? Jeff?"

He stopped at the sound of Cassie's voice and turned to find her rushing up behind him.

"I've been waiting for ages and then you walk right past. Trying to get rid of me?" she teased. Her eyes darkened as she noticed his expression. "What's the matter?"

"Nothing, really. It's just that I saw David back there." He jerked a thumb over his shoulder. "Took me by surprise."

"David?" Cassie frowned. "What's he doing here?"

Jeff studied her face. She seemed innocent enough—as if she had no idea. His theory that Cassie had put him up to it evaporated.

"He's ringing the bells on one of those charity kettles."

"Oh, how nice. What a kid! And today's his basketball game, too."

"I asked him about that," Jeff murmured. "He said he'd be off in time to see the second half." He searched her face. "Why would he suddenly decide to do this?" Jeff asked. "It's not normal behavior for a teenage kid."

"Well, it should be," Cassie announced firmly, tugging his arm with her own. "There are a lot of people who benefit from that program, and teenagers can help as well as anyone."

When he didn't move, she pulled a little harder.

"Come on, Jeff. We haven't got anything for the Bennets yet. I know just what Mrs. Bennet wants."

As he let himself be led through the throngs of shoppers, Jeff resolved to have a little talk with David later. His mind pricked his conscience.

So what have you given back to anyone lately, Jefferson, my boy? Anything of value?

Chapter Seven

Cassie pushed the tendril of hair off her face and puffed out a sigh as she swished the bubbles over Jonathan's wiggling little body.

"How do the beautiful people stay that way, Johnny Boy?" she asked, catching a glimpse of herself in the mirror. Jonathan gurgled with laughter as she stuck her tongue out at the urchin reflected back. He smacked the water with one hand, sending a tidal wave of water over the edge of the tub and onto her sweatpants.

"Thank you, darling." She smiled. "I needed that dose of reality."

"The beautiful people often aren't very beautiful where it really counts," Jeff's sardonic voice muttered. She whirled around to find him leaning nonchalantly against the door frame.

"Daddy," Jonathan crowed and thrust himself up from the water. Cassie just missed catching his arm at he launched himself at Jeff. The boy's soaking body soon drenched her husband's elegant white shirt and pressed navy slacks.

Jonathan snuggled himself against the expansive chest and pressed his soft little lips against Jeff's neck.

"I wuv you, Daddy."

Cassie watched in suspended animation as Jeff's stern features froze into a mask. He recovered himself moments later to grasp a towel from one of the rods and wrap it around the little boy.

"Well, thank you, Jonathan. I appreciate that."

"I'll take him," Cassie offered. "He's getting you soaked."

But Jeff shook his head. "No, he'll just get you wet, too."

"As if I'm not already." She chuckled. Her eyes glinted with good humor as she pulled the plug and swished the suds down the drain. "Come on, kiddo. Into your pj's."

"Daddy do," he squealed, hanging on to Jeff's hair with his fingers.

"Ah, I think I'd better comply," Jeff murmured, wincing at the tight grip. "I'm too young to be bald." His head cocked to one side as the sound of a baby's cry penetrated the steamy room. "Which one is that?"

Cassie pointed to the Batman pajamas lying folded on the tile counter before moving toward the door.

"We've only got one baby now, remember. Corky went home this afternoon." She moved down the hall, his mumbled response following. "Make sure he gets into bed right away," she told him. "It's way past his bedtime."

She spent a few moments quieting the fussy baby before moving back down the hall to check on Jonathan. When she heard low-pitched whispers coming from his room, she stayed outside the door to listen, allowing only her eyes to peek around the corner.

What she saw startled her. Jefferson Haddon, Esquire, sat on the edge of the bed talking to the little boy who was snuggled under the covers.

"Can I stay here forever and ever Amen, Daddy?" Jonathan's big brown eyes peered up curiously.

"Well..." Jeff began haltingly. "I think this is sort of like a holiday. Your mom and dad might want you to come back to your own house after the holiday is over."

"Will my other daddy take care of me like you and Cassie do?" he queried, tugging at the button on Jeff's pocket. "He doesn't smell nice and pretty like Cassie does. I like that smell." He snuggled down in his little bed. "I like Christmas, too. Are we gonna have a Christmas tree with lights 'n' everything?"

"I don't know," she heard Jeff answer hesitantly. "What did Cassie say?"

"I never asked her." The little boy yawned. "But she really

likes Christmas. She was singing songs about Baby Jesus all day today. And she letted me have two gingerbread boys.'' He yawned once more. ''Don'tcha got no more little boys here, Daddy?'' he whined, glaring at Jeff accusingly. ''I like to play with the other kids, ya know.''

''No,'' Jeff murmured so softly Cassie had to strain to hear him. ''I guess you're the only little boy we have here right now.''

Jonathan stared at him for a few moments before he shrugged and let his heavy eyelids fall shut. ''Kiss me g'night, Daddy,'' he mumbled and held up his cheek.

Cassie watched, her heart in her throat as Jeff leaned down to press his lips against the soft smooth skin.

''Good night, son. Have a good sleep.''

The chubby arms wrapped tightly around Jeff's neck as Jonathan gave his famous bear hug.

''I love you this much, Daddy,'' Jonathan crowed, squeezing his eyes tightly shut and grunting with the effort. Cassie thought she saw tears on Jeff's face as he hugged the little boy back and then tucked him in once more.

''Good night.''

She realized suddenly that Jeff would be coming out of the room at any moment to find her standing there, eavesdropping on his conversation. Cassie scurried down the hall and downstairs to the big family room. She was ensconced on the plush overstuffed sofa when he ambled in several moments later.

''Everything okay?'' she asked as he sank down in the cushions beside her.

''Well, he's in bed,'' Jeff offered. ''That's the best I could do. He's quite a touching little guy, isn't he? What's his background?''

She stifled the gasp of joy that threatened to overwhelm her. At last! Jeff was finally asking to know more about the children who came to stay in their home. It was a good sign. It had to be, she told herself.

''His mother leaves him here periodically when she goes in for treatment. She's a crack addict.''

Jeff stared at her. ''And she chose Christmas to get herself cleaned up?''

"Not exactly," Cassie shook her head. Her voice lowered conspiratorially. "They can't find her. She left Jonathan with some neighbors and never came back."

Jeff shook his head sadly.

"And his father?"

"He doesn't have one. At least not one he knows about."

She picked up the cross-stitch bookmark she was working on and bent over it until she felt his hand on her arm. His face was a puzzle.

"But he must have. He talks about his other daddy all the time. He even said he didn't smell good." Jeff's eyes were dark pools of curiosity, but Cassie was more intent on his arm which had flung companionably around her shoulders.

"I know," she murmured, trying to repress the delicious shiver of excitement that coursed through her at his touch. "It's a sort of game he plays. I suspect Jonathan is confused by the different men his mother brings home. To simplify things he just calls them all daddy."

"It's sad," he reflected, fingering the cotton fluff on her sweater. "He seems such a cute kid." Jeff leaned his head back against the sofa. "He even asked me if we were going to have a Christmas tree."

"And are we?" Cassie asked softly, keeping her head bent over her work.

"Cassie," he chided, laughing down at her. His forefinger moved to press her chin up, forcing her to meet his gaze. "You know very well that you'll go hog-wild and insist on the biggest tree there is and then load it down with all sorts of baubles."

She grinned back irrepressibly.

"Oh, I'm so glad you agree. I asked Bennet to find one. I said you'd help get it into its stand." With her eyes, she dared him to back out now. "Think of it as something you'll do for the kids," she advised laughing.

Seconds later, her laughter caught in her throat as he cupped her cheeks between his hands. His eyes were darker now and searching her face intently.

"Okay," he agreed. "I'll set up the tree and help you decorate it for the kids. But this—" his thumb slid across her bottom lip "—this is just for us."

He waited. Long, aching moments until he was sure her attention was fixed on him and him alone.

And then he kissed her.

To Cassie it was exactly right. A tender, but promising kiss that said everything she needed him to say without the words. He cared about her, just the tiniest bit. And he was beginning to realize how much he cared about the children.

She kissed him back, trying to put all the longing that she'd hidden in her heart into her caresses. But she hadn't begun to say half of what she needed to when his head lifted from hers. His eyes were only half aware as he cocked his ear to one side and listened.

She was expecting him to say something romantic, some confession of the heart. What she heard was, "Is that the smoke detector?"

"The child's a pyromaniac!" Jeff's angry voice rose above her explanations loudly.

"He is not. He's just a little five-year-old boy who misses his mommy." Cassie tried to wipe the black soot from her face with one sleeve of her good sweater. At least, it had been her good sweater once.

"An arsonist at the very least! He could have killed all of us in our beds, not to mention destroying this house you love so much." Jeff glared around the master bedroom as if he suspected he would find Jonathan hiding somewhere behind the massive furniture.

"You shouldn't have left those matches lying around," she remonstrated firmly. Her toe kicked uselessly at the huge burn in the rug. "Not when there are children around."

He strode across the room to stand in front of her, his face tightly drawn.

"So now it's my fault? The *children* are supposed to be in *my* room, now are they?" He stared down at her, breathing heavily with the force of his anger. "Maybe if we had a set of stricter controls in place, they wouldn't have this problem."

"Oh, thank you! Now I'm not strict enough?" Cassie grit her teeth. "Maybe you should start seeing them as children who need help and love," she growled. "Instead of little robots who are supposed to do your bidding no matter what!"

"Oh, give it up," he muttered disgustedly. "You're a bigger child than all of them." He surveyed the damage and shook his head. "Who's going to pay for all of this?"

"Ah," Cassie squealed. "Now we come to the crux of the matter. Money. That's always your main concern, isn't it? Money, money, money. Well," she said, dashing the sopping curls out of her eyes as she marched to the door, "don't worry about it anymore, *Jefferson*. I'll pay for it out of my own money."

She cast a scathing glance at the heavy dark wood and thick velvet draperies.

"Believe me, this place could use a face-lift. It's so dark and dingy it looks like a cave." She turned to fix him with her best angry stare. "A cave for a bear."

As she flounced down the stairs, Cassie stopped suddenly as she realized exactly what she'd said. And how foolish it had been. Her allowance had dwindled down to a paltry amount once she'd paid for the house, helped Sam out and found the best psychiatrist for her brother's step kids.

"Ooof!" She hung on to the balustrade with an effort as someone knocked into her from behind. "Can't you look where you're going?" she snapped angrily.

Jeff's eyes peered out at her from above the stack of blankets and pillows he carried.

"No, I can't," he growled. "I can't see a thing. Anyway, you shouldn't be standing on the stairs. You could fall and hurt yourself." He brushed past her, bumping her aside with the soft blankets.

"Especially if I'm pushed," she muttered and then hurried after him. "What are you doing?"

"Finding a nice *quiet* place to sleep," he almost bellowed. "The bedrooms next to mine and across the hall are filled with leftover smoke. I can't sleep there. That leaves here." He fluffed the blankets and quilt out on the maroon leather sofa and dropped two pillows on top. "You might as well have them cleaned and redone while you're redoing mine."

"I can't." She hadn't meant to say it. It just sort of slipped out when she was thinking about ways to come up with more cash.

"Can't what?" Goodness, he did sound like a grouchy bear, Cassie decided. She avoided meeting his black gaze.

"I, er, can't pay for the, uh, repairs," she half whispered and then peeked up. His face was dark and foreboding.

"And why not, might I ask?" His hands hung on his hips in a question mark, ready to castigate her for her frivolities.

"I haven't got enough left. My money's almost gone," she told him softly. She turned away at the hiss of disgust.

"It can't be," he said incredulously, the blankets suddenly forgotten. "What on earth did you buy? Another house?"

"No, I didn't," she replied angrily. "I made a small loan to my sister and brother, that's all. They'll pay me back. When they can." Cassie didn't even flinch as she told the white lie. She no more expected repayment than to fly to the moon. "Anyway, I'll do what I can. You don't have to worry about it. It's my fault it happened, anyway. I should have warned you."

He sighed heavily, raking his hand through his dark hair with reluctance.

"It's nobody's fault, Cassie. And don't worry about the rooms. Insurance will cover all that." He peered down at her through the gloom. "Why didn't you tell me about Jonathan's *little* problem with matches?"

"I don't know." She shrugged, avoiding his eyes as her toe scuffed the beautiful Persian rug. "I guess I thought you'd make him leave and I want Jonathan to spend this Christmas here with us, in Judith's house."

It bubbled out in a torrent of words that brought a rueful grin to his craggy face.

"What is it about this house?" he muttered. "It's as if you're totally captivated with it."

Cassie stared up at him.

"Oh, it's not the house," she assured him. "It's what I want to happen in it." She watched him frown.

"What exactly do you want to happen here?"

"Love. And joy. And peace and goodwill." She enumerated

them for him with arms outstretched. "I want it to fill every corner and every person."

"For Christmas, you mean?" he asked, obviously trying to understand.

Cassie smiled softly as she walked from the room.

"That would be a good start," she acknowledged. She retraced her steps to poke her head back into the study. "By the way," she informed him. "The Christmas tree decorating is scheduled for tomorrow after church. You are going to help, aren't you? After all, you're the boss!" She ducked when he threw the pillow at her and ran racing up the stairs.

"Now, if You could just get him to go with us to the service tomorrow morning," she prayed softly. "That would be the best possible start to the day."

And the good Lord seemed to hear for when Jeff came into the kitchen for breakfast the next morning he was telling Jonathan that he could sit on his knee during the service.

"But only if you promise to behave," Jeff said sternly. "We can't have any more fires or Cassie and baby Steve and all the rest of us will have to move out. It's too dangerous. Is it a deal?"

"Thank you, Daddy," Jonathan chirped happily and promptly spilled the baby's cereal all over the floor.

As they sat together in the solemnity of the church later that morning, a child in each lap, Cassie let herself join in the singing wholeheartedly. After all, she had the best of all possible worlds, didn't she?

Not quite, her conscience reminded. She had the house and the children and she was married to Jeff. At least in name. She stuffed away the rest of the silly notions that filled her head at inappropriate times. Unlikely things like his sweet kisses, his arm slung around her waist as he told her how much he loved her.

She felt a hand tugging on her skirt and glanced down to note that Jeff was seated. So was everyone else. She sank onto the hard wooden pew hastily and tried to hide her face in the baby's neck. Which was impossible given the stench emanating from that small being. Jonathan picked that particular moment to kick up a fuss, too, and Cassie prayed for strength as she reached for the diaper bag.

"Trade you," muttered a frustrated Jeff. He picked up the baby and the bag with one motion and left the bench and Jonathan as everyone bowed to pray. Cassie was pretty sure that's when the odor hit him because he turned to frown fiercely down at her before heading reluctantly for the nursery.

"Wanna go wif Daddy," Jonathan squeaked. She hushed him, mentioning the words *Junior Church* which always worked magic on the little boy's demeanor. He sank onto the seat as quiet as a church mouse and closed his eyes reverently.

"And bless us Lord as we enter the season celebrating your birth. May we feel that peace and goodwill toward men flood our hearts with joy. Amen."

"Ahhhmen," Jonathan repeated loudly. His big eyes opened wide as he glanced around and noticed the other children stirring. "Church time," he crowed, earning a laugh from the small congregation.

"Kids are frighteningly straightforward, aren't they?" Pastor Jake remarked, watching as the children filed out haphazardly. "That's why we love them so much."

Jeff slipped in beside her again. Cassie noticed that his lovely navy tie seemed damp. And there were spots on his jacket and shirt, too.

"What happened?" she asked, leaning over to whisper in his ear.

"This kid is a little too accurate with his aim." When she still looked puzzled he continued. "Especially without a diaper to hamper him."

She couldn't help the small giggle that escaped her at his disgusted look. "Just keep repeating 'I love kids' to yourself over and over," she whispered.

She thought she heard him mutter, "I'll get Cassie," but the offertory ended just then and she didn't want to ask him to repeat it.

Jeff had just gotten comfortable in his seat when the minister launched into his sermon.

"I've chosen the topic of love for a pre-Christmas series," the smooth eloquent voice began. "As we read in first Corinthians, there are many faces to love. Let's read that passage together.''

Love. He was sick and tired of hearing about it. But the way the man spoke, his attitude that nothing mattered if love wasn't involved, twigged some bit of curiosity in his mind.

"If I gave away everything I have, but didn't love others, what good would it do?''

Harrumph, he felt like saying. That must be the law Cassie operated on. It seemed to him that she was determined to give away every last cent she owned.

"Love is not selfish or rude. It doesn't demand its own way.'' The minister continued his discussion, enumerating the qualities of love. "You see folks, when we were children we acted and reacted like children. But now that we're adults we need to stretch our thoughts far beyond childhood and embrace the world around us.''

The words chewed at Jeff's mind, repeating themselves over and over. Put away childish hurts and move on. But how? How could he forget the deep-seated pain and anguish of those days—just let them roll off his back?

"No,'' he told himself firmly. He wasn't going to just forget about all the heartache and anguish he'd carried for so long. He would remember it so that he never allowed it to happen to him again.

Pastor Jake was winding things up now. Jeff's ears perked as he listened to the closing remarks.

"When everything else is gone, folks, there are only three things that will remain. Faith, hope and love. And the Bible tells us that the greatest of these is love. Let's spread a little around this Christmas, shall we?''

Jeff rose with everyone else and sang the old familiar hymn from memory while his mind worked overtime. He wasn't a heathen. He could be as charitable as the next guy. His wife wanted a big happy Christmas; fine. He'd see that she got one. And in the process he'd make darned good and sure that no child under his roof ever had cause to complain about his treatment.

But love?

That was something he couldn't afford. It cost too much.

Chapter Eight

"It's a little lopsided." Cassie giggled as Jeff wired down the pine's sticky trunk. "No, the other way. That's better." She picked the pine needles out of his hair with a laugh. "You're really getting into this Christmas business, Jefferson," she teased.

Jeff grinned. She always called him that when she was up to something. Usually something sneaky.

"Well, that looks steady," he joked heartily, smacking his hands together. "Now the rest of you can take over while I relax and watch." His rear end had barely touched the sofa's cushion when he found her standing over him.

"Great! You can watch Stevie." She dumped the burbling baby on his lap and moved to free the lights from the new kid's fingers. Jeff could never remember the little girl's name.

"After the indignities he subjected me to in church? I don't think so." Jeff placed the baby on a nearby blanket on the floor and handed him a ring of plastic keys.

"I've been meaning to ask you about that," Cassie murmured faintly. Jeff could see the twitch at the corner of her mouth. "The janitor said you asked him for rubber gloves? And when I changed him just now, his diaper was on backward." She gazed across at him innocently. "Well?"

"It seemed the best solution to the problem of getting wet again," he told her. "I just put him on his stomach and put the diaper on. I forgot the little animals would be marching across his backside.'' He made a face. ''I would have asked the guy for a face mask if I thought he'd have one. That's disgusting!''

He heard that full-bodied laugh burst out and ring through the room. The children stopped what they were doing to stare at her as she doubled over in hysterics.

''Aren't you the guy that wanted his own son?'' she chortled. ''How were you planning on handling the diaper business?''

Jeff glared at her, feeling like an idiot. Trust the old codger to go blabbering his business, or rather Stevie's, to the whole church!

''My kid isn't going to descend to that disgusting level,'' he told her shortly. When she burst into renewed hysterics he bristled with frustration. ''Are you going to decorate that tree or not?''

''Come on, guys,'' she called, still chuckling as she called in the children. ''It's tree-trimming time.''

It was more like a day at the loony bin, Jeff grinned, surveying the mess in the family room later. There were bits of packaging and torn pieces of paper littering the carpet, and empty red tumblers sat here and there about the room, evidence that everyone had enjoyed Mrs. Bennet's egg nog.

''Doesn't it look magnificent?'' Cassie exclaimed behind him, her eyes as wide as the baby's. ''They did a fantastic job.''

He glanced at the heavily laden tree with its twinkling white fairy lights and combination homemade and store-bought decorations. It was a family tree. Not fancy. Not overdone. Just decorated with something from everybody.

Everybody except him. Apparently Cassie had noticed that, too.

''I popped the popcorn for the ropes. Marie made the angel. David did those clove spice ball things. Jonathan glued the paper chains and Stevie—'' she paused, thinking ''—Stevie licked most of the candy canes. The ones hanging toward the bottom, anyway,'' she cried triumphantly. Her big green eyes studied him seriously.

''What are you going to add to our family's Christmas tree, Jeff?''

He stared at her.

''Me? Why…nothing. I told you, I'm not really good at

Christmas.'' He felt an irrational anger at her for pointing out that he didn't fit in here, either. ''What?'' he barked, noticing her shaking head.

''That's a cop-out you don't get to use here,'' she told him, sinking down onto the fluffy cushions. ''I'll just wait here until you think of something. Go ahead.''

He glared down at her and wondered anew how less than one hundred pounds of femininity could be so aggravating. He crossed his arms stubbornly.

''Jeff, we agreed that we'd share things in this family. You have to do your part.'' She frowned at him. ''You're not even trying. Come on.''

''All right,'' he muttered, giving in to her bossiness. ''What do you suggest I do? Pick cranberries in the woods and string them up? Or cut boughs off another tree and decorate the mantel?''

She had that glint in her eye again!

''Hey, that mantel idea is a good one. I wonder...''

''Kidding,'' he hollered, frustrated by her intransigence. ''I was kidding.'' He crossed his arms once more and smiled down on his petite nemesis smugly as a new idea occurred to him. ''Anyway, I've already contributed.''

Her eyes flew to the tree and he watched them flick swiftly over the baubles and lights.

''I don't see anything.''

''Of course you don't.'' He laughed, pleased at his little joke. ''Can't see the forest for the trees, can you?''

''I don't get it. What are you talking about?'' His wife stood there in her stockinged feet, glaring at him balefully. ''I was here the whole time. You just sat there and watched us put all this stuff on.''

''Which you wouldn't have been able to do if I hadn't set the thing up in the first place.'' He smirked. ''So my part in this, er, decoration, was completed first.''

She laughed good-naturedly.

''Sneaky,'' she grumbled. ''Very sneaky.''

''You haven't seen the half of it,'' he drawled, slipping the mistletoe from his pocket and holding it over her head. ''You're so big on Christmas—do you know what this tradition is?''

He watched delighted as that pretty rose flush suffused her neck and face, forming bright circles of color on her cheeks.

"Jeff, there are children present in this house."

"I know," he murmured. "So what? We're married. It's allowed." She didn't even try to move as he tipped her face up toward his, Jeff noticed. Matter of fact, she even leaned in a little, in anticipation.

He'd barely even touched her saucy little mouth when the phone rang.

"Oh, for Pete's sake! This place is like Grand Central Station at rush hour. Hello," he barked into the phone and then modulated his voice as Pastor Jake's friendly tones intruded. He kept his arm wrapped around Cassie anyway, just in case it wasn't another minor emergency.

"She's right here. Just a moment please." He handed her the phone with resignation, allowing one finger to wrap around a fat glossy curl that fell forward onto her cheek. "Pastor Jake. Something about angel costumes."

"Oh, good grief." She sounded as frustrated as he felt, Jeff decided. He kept his arm right where it was, wrapped around her waist as she spoke, and let his other hand brush over her shining head.

"I'll be there right away," he heard her say before she hung up the phone. Her head tipped forward on his chest as she leaned against him tiredly. "I have to go to the church. Apparently Sue Ellen Withers forgot to finish the costumes for the Sunday School's Christmas pageant tomorrow evening." She sighed as his hands massaged the knot in her shoulders.

"Not that you can blame her."

Jeff couldn't have cared less about Sue Ellen Withers or the angel costumes or anything else just then, but he felt compelled to ask.

"Why?"

Cassie's big emerald eyes sparkled up at him.

"She went into labor last night and just gave birth to a ten-pound baby boy. I think she's entitled." Her voice sounded misty, full of daydreams.

Jeff bent and pressed a kiss against her glossy head.

"Go ahead," he mumbled. "I'll look after the kids."

"Are you sure?" She frowned at him assessingly. "Marie's out baby-sitting and David's working in his lab. There will be just you, Jonathan, Alyssa and Stevie."

When that soft, caressing look fixed on him, Jeff felt a new energy surge through his veins. He could do this, he told his quivering insides. He could manage.

"I'm sure we'll be fine," he answered. "You'd better get going."

All the screaming denials his subconscious was pushing forward died an instant death when Cassie smiled her special smile and stood on her very tiptoes to press her lips against his cheek.

"You're a sweetheart," she whispered. "Thank you." And then she scurried from the room just before his fingers tightened to hold her back.

Jeff heard a gurgle of sound and glanced down to see Stevie sucking on some tinsel.

"Okay kid, it's just you and me. And you're not eating any more of that stuff. Strictly dairy products from now on."

All of a sudden, Jonathan left the toy train he'd been vrooming round the track and ran over to cling to his leg.

"I want a story, Daddy. The one about the baby who came to bring love."

As he stared down at the two innocent faces, Jeff felt the same old pangs of loneliness strike once more. Was this how a father felt, he wondered, when his children asked for something? Did all men get this mushy feeling inside their gut when a little kid snuggled against them? Had his father ever felt this strange feeling when he smelled the soft dewy skin of his own freshly bathed baby?

A short time later, Jeff pushed the traitorous thought away as he snuggled Stevie against his shoulder and burped him. He concentrated on the baby's sweetly powdered skin as he laid him in his crib and turned out the light.

Kids were so forgiving he noted as he scrubbed down the bathroom before starting Jonathan's bath. They didn't care where the love came from, as long as somebody took the time and effort to listen and care for them. And if a parent wasn't prepared to put in that time and effort, why should they be entitled to care for that little life?

Jeff refused to dwell on the things his father had missed out on. Things that he was sharing now with Jonathan. Things like bath time with a zoo of plastic animals that had specific names. Things like toothbrushing—Jeff had never known how truly complicated that simple operation could become. And other things like bedtime stories and prayers.

"But how does God get to hear everybody's prayin'?" the little boy demanded. "Does he have lots and lots of ears or something?"

"Something like that," Jeff answered, hoping he wasn't agreeing to something sacrilegious.

"Oh." The eyes scrunched closed once more as Jonathan started on the God blesses. They popped open seconds later. "Did God bless you, Daddy?" his little voice chirped.

Jeff thought about that. The truth was he was very blessed, Jeff decided. He had a wife and a wonderful sort of hodgepodge family around him that he'd done nothing to deserve. And he had this little boy. For a while anyway. A tiny bundle of curiosity and innocence that made him long for his own son more and more.

"Daddy?"

Jeff stared down at the angelic little face and thought about his current life.

"Yes, Jonathan. I think he really did bless me. Good night now."

"You have to kiss me." The little imp grinned. "Cassie always kisses me good-night."

Jeff leaned down and pressed his lips against the downy soft skin. "Is that right?" he asked. "I don't know very much about bedtimes."

Jonathan nodded thoughtfully.

"It was pretty good," he decided. "But you have to hug, too. Like this." He wrapped his eager little arms around Jeff's neck and held him in a stranglehold.

And Jefferson Haddon the third reveled in the discomfort as he hugged the little waif back again.

He thought about that hug long after Cassie returned from the church and questioned him intently about each child. He thought about it as she kissed his cheek and bade him good-night. And he thought about it many minutes after he'd retired to his charred lonely room.

How could any man reject what was so freely offered? How could a father reject his own son?

Cassie fidgeted with the bright red velour suit she had chosen to wear to the children's Christmas pageant, tugging the tunic down as she admired its clean straight lines. She peered at herself in the floor-length mirror and wondered if it wasn't a little too showy, a bit too bright.

After all, the children were the feature attraction this evening she told herself severely, as she brushed her glossy curls into some semblance of order. And just because she wanted to attract one man's attention in particular didn't mean she had to spoil the evening for them.

"Well, he can hardly miss me in this outfit." She chuckled and turned away to put on the shiny gold star earrings and matching star brooch. "And red is my favorite color."

She cast one more doubtful look at her image and shrugged. For better or for worse, she had promised. Well, tonight was definitely going to be for the better. She was adamant on that.

"Wow!" Marie flashed her huge shy grin as she stood in the doorway. "You look great."

"Thank you, my dear." Cassie curtsied, taking care not to overbalance on her new black patent heels—three-and-a-half-inch heels. She would have worn higher ones, but she had enough trouble staying upright on these. "You look pretty hot yourself."

Marie's straight blond hair gleamed brightly against the black velvet jacket and lace-edged white blouse. In her matching slim-cut pants, she looked exactly what she was. A beautiful young teenage girl.

"It's not too much is it, Cassie? I'm supposed to meet Nate after the service. We're going to exchange gifts and I wanted to look special."

Cassie hugged the tall slim girl against her and brushed a kiss against her head.

"You are special, Marie. You're a very beautiful daughter."

Marie flushed with pleasure, her eyes downcast.

"Not quite yet," she whispered hopefully, her tone eagerly wishful.

"The papers don't say it," Cassie agreed, tipping the girl's chin up to stare straight into her eyes. "But I do. And no judge in any court could make it more official than it feels right here." She tapped a finger against her heart. "Okay?"

Marie nodded, grinning from ear to ear. "Okay."

"Don't spend too long saying goodbye to Nate. He'll be back in a week, remember." Cassie fluffed her black locks once more and then picked up her small beaded bag. "And we have carolers coming around afterward."

"I know," Marie agreed softly. "I'll be here to help."

Cassie frowned. "I don't want you to be there to help, Marie. I want you to be here as part of our family as we welcome people into our home." She grinned. "You've done more than enough helping lately."

Marie smiled back, taking no offense at the words. "Well, you have to admit that I'm better at baby-sitting than I am at wrapping oddly shaped gifts."

Cassie rolled her eyes in agreement. "I'll say."

They walked down the staircase giggling like young girls as they joked back and forth. Jeff stood waiting at the bottom, little Stevie cradled happily in his arms and Jonathan standing beside him. To Cassie's surprise the little boy was dressed in a tiny black-and-white tuxedo that exactly matched Jeff's.

"Wow," she whistled. "Don't you guys look great!"

Jonathan grinned and puffed his chest out proudly.

"Daddy buyed me a new suit for Christmas," he told her smugly. "That's 'cause we're the men in the family."

Cassie swallowed the lump in her throat as her misty eyes met Jeff's. "Well, good for you, Daddy," she whispered softly, placing her hand on the soft smooth wool of his white sweater. "You look pretty good, too. For an older man." She couldn't help the little joke, praying that it would take away some of the tension that had suddenly fallen in the room.

"Ha-ha!" Jonathan chortled with glee, pointing upward to the sprig of mistletoe hanging in the archway above their heads. "Now you have to kiss Daddy, Cassie."

"Do I?" she whispered softly, staring into the dark chocolate depths of Jeff's clear eyes. She could no more look away than remove herself from the circle of his arm as it curved around her waist.

"Yes, you do," Jeff murmured, dipping his head down.

"Well," she breathed on a silky sigh of delight. "If I have to, I have to."

Jeff kissed her. Thoroughly, completely and to her great satisfaction. And she kissed him back until the chuckles of several assorted children brought them back to reality.

"We do have to get to the church," David mumbled, red faced with embarrassment as he tugged at the brown housecoat that enveloped his spare form and rearranged the white dishtowel held on his head by a thick cord. "This shepherd outfit is the pits," he muttered finally. "I'll probably die of heatstroke."

"No one in this family is dying tonight," Jeff declared, squeezing Cassie's waist in a gentle caress. "Let's go everybody." He handed Stevie to Marie and held out Cassie's white lamb's wool jacket with a flourish. "Madame?"

Cassie tried to curtsey and nearly toppled over on her brandnew spiky heels. She reached out to press against his chest for support. And promptly lost her breath as his dark, amused eyes sparkled down at her.

"It's not necessary to throw yourself at me," he murmured so quietly no one else could hear. "I'll be available later tonight, in front of the fire. Care to join me?"

She got lost in those smooth, liquid chocolate depths and forgot to answer until his fingers closed around her upper arms, setting her back on her own two feet. His fingers slid upward to brush through her hair.

"Cassandra?"

"Hmm? Oh, later. Yes, later," she chirped brightly and slipped her arms into the coat.

As he lifted it around her shoulders, Cassie thought she heard him whisper, "Just the two of us. Alone."

That promising thought stayed with her on the short drive to the church where they met and greeted their friends. It haunted her as she stood beside him, singing the same Christmas carols she'd sung for years and hearing Jeff's low voice join in. And it nagged at her subconscious while she watched the children's presentation of the age-old Christmas story.

"Doesn't Alyssa look sweet?" she leaned over to whisper, her shoulder rubbing companionably against Jeff's.

"Who?" He stared at the stage with a frown on his face, trying to figure out who she was talking about.

"Alyssa, the littlest angel." She nodded toward the stage and watched his eyes search out their newest addition. The little girl stood silent in her gleaming white robe and crown of tinsel, the frills at the top of her little socks bobbing as her feet tapped rhythmically against the floor.

"Oh, her. Yeah, she looks cute. I forgot her name." He grinned back at her with that smile that tugged at her heart and made her want to hug him. It was almost as good to feel his fingers thread through hers as he held her hand.

"Here comes Joseph," he whispered. "I sure hope Stevie behaves." He smirked, lips twitching at he watched Mary place the squirming child in his makeshift manger. "I wonder if he knows he has the most important role in the whole play."

"I doubt it. He only knows when it's feeding time and that's getting pretty close now." Cassie inclined her head to the diaper bag at her feet and smothered a smile. "He's a true male—his brain is connected directly to his stomach."

Jeff's arm curved around her shoulders, drawing her more tightly against his side. She could smell the fresh clean scent of the soap he used as his head bent close to hers. "Look—Jonathan's about to sing," he whispered excitedly, his breath stirring the strand of hair over her ear.

Cassie smiled at the gleam of pride in his eyes, but before she could reply, the soft, clear tones of Jonathan's childish voice as he sang "One Small Child" filled the air. The pure treble notes rang to the rafters with joy, bringing a tear to many eyes in the small, cozy church. For a moment, Cassie felt suspended in the wonder that God had cared enough to send his only son to earth as a small defenceless child who, at one time, might have looked much as Jonathan did.

Then there was much clapping and laughter and Jeff removed his arm. But the joy and pleasure stayed, hidden snugly under her heart as she thought eagerly of the evening ahead.

An hour later, Judith's old brick house was full to the brim with excited squealing children, embarrassed teenagers and adults of all ages. They gathered around Judith's baby grand in the brightly lit conservatory and blended their voices together in songs of worship, celebration and joy. Then the children were bundled up for a sleigh ride through the softly falling snow in an old-fashioned sleigh drawn by two fine horses that Bennet had borrowed for the evening. And through it all, Mrs. Bennet scurried around, replenishing glasses, offering pastries and beaming with happiness.

"Isn't it wonderful to see the old house alive again, Mr. Jeff?" The housekeeper glowed, refilling his glass with her special raspberry punch for yet another toast. "Your aunt would have loved this sight. She always wanted people to enjoy her home."

Cassie's tinkling laughter rang through the room just then and, if possible, Mrs. Bennet smiled even wider.

"That's a rare young woman, Mr. Jeff," she whispered. "Knows exactly what she's about bringing happiness back into people's lives. Miss Judith did right to try to keep her here."

Jeff grinned. "I think so, too, Mrs. Bennet." He leaned over and kissed her wrinkled cheek. "And I think Aunt Judith found a real treasure when she found you, too. Merry Christmas, Mrs. Bennet."

"Now what are you doing kissing the likes of an old lady like myself?" Mrs. Bennet gushed, her white skin tinged a faint pink. "'Tis your wife you should be kissing tonight, Mr. Jeff." She winked and scurried away after directing a pointed glance at the mistletoe hanging just above them.

"Isn't it a wonderful night?" Cassie exclaimed, threading her arm through his. "The happiest night of the year."

"Mmm-hmm, wonderful," she heard him murmur and looked up to find his gaze locked on her lips. "I've just received some wonderful advice from Mrs. Bennet. Older people are sometimes very wise."

Cassie stood transfixed as he bent his head and kissed her soundly in front of a houseful of people. Her face flushed as red as her suit when their guests began clapping merrily.

"I think that's our signal to leave you newlyweds alone."

Pastor Jake grinned. He tugged his wife's hand. "Come along, Sara. Let's get home to our own mistletoe."

"Jake!" His wife protested, but it was a weak one and her face glowed with happiness. "Merry Christmas, Cassie. And you too, Jeff."

One by one the families drifted out the door until no one was left but the two of them, Marie and David. Jonathan lay curled up near the fire, sound asleep in his brand-new suit. Maryann Craven had handed a sleepy Stevie to Cassie before she, too, went out the door.

"Good night," they called out into the brisk night air. And heard the resounding "'night" echoing back.

"Come on, big guy." David grunted, lifting Jonathan's slack body. "It's time to go to bed."

"But I hafta get my stocking ready for Santa," Jonathan mumbled, barely awake.

"We did it before church. Remember?" David laughed down at the little boy. "Everything's all ready for Santa."

"But I wanted to change socks," Jonathan protested wearily. "I was...gonna use—" he yawned hugely and settled into David's arms with a sigh "—a bigger one," he finished as his eyelids drifted down.

"Good night everyone," David said, smiling as he moved toward the stairs. "I'll put him in bed, Cassie. Don't worry."

Cassie walked over and brushed her hand over his dark head.

"Thank you, David. Merry Christmas, dear." She brushed a featherlight kiss over his cheek. She watched tenderly as the boy moved up the stairs with his precious bundle.

"Mom! Look!" It was the first time that Marie had ever called her Mom and Cassie felt a pang clench and unclench in her breast. She turned toward the girl, misty eyed as she cradled the sleeping baby. "It's a promise ring. From Nate."

"Honey, that's lovely. Really lovely." With a worried smile she fingered the thin gold band that held Marie's aquamarine birthstone. "But, Marie, don't you think you're a bit young to be promising anything to Nate?"

"Here, give me the baby," Jeff said. "I'll put him to bed while you two talk." He glanced down at Cassie with a glint in his eyes. "I'll share some punch with you in front of the fire. Later."

Cassie couldn't say anything around the lump in her throat. But she smiled in what she hoped was an encouraging way and agreed. "Later."

"Love can't be wrong, Cassie." Marie's voice broke through her musings. "You always say God wants us to love people. Well, I love Nate. And someday I'm going to marry him."

It was the first time Cassie had heard defiance in the young girl's voice and she realized suddenly that Marie had chosen Christmas Eve to challenge her authority.

"Come and sit down, sweetie. Let's talk about this." She guided Marie to the sofa in front of the crackling fire and sank down onto it with relief. "I've got to get these shoes off. I don't know how anybody wears the things for more than five minutes."

"That's because you're not used to them." Marie giggled. "They're new and cool, but they're not your usual style."

Cassie wiggled her toes and groaned. "You're not kidding, kid," she agreed with heartfelt enthusiasm. Her face softened as she looked at the girl who would soon legally be her daughter.

"I know you're excited that Nate gave you such a lovely gift, Marie. But please try to hear me out," Cassie began softly. "Nate's a wonderful boy. And I can see why you're attracted to him. He's kind and considerate and a wonderful friend." She watched Marie nod and then continued, choosing her words with care.

"Sweetheart, you're just starting out on your journey of life. You are getting to know and understand boys in a new and different way than you did before and that's perfectly normal. But just because you meet someone you like right now doesn't mean that you can plan your whole life around that person."

"But Nate loves me," Marie broke in angrily.

"Of course he does! You're a very lovable girl." Cassie smiled as she searched for the right words. "But there are all kinds of love and you and Nate have years and years ahead to plan for. You told me you want to travel, to visit France where your grandmother came from. Does Nate want to go there? And what work will you choose while you are there? What will you do?''

She smoothed the blond hair with a shaking hand and prayed for guidance as she searched for the words to help Marie see the possibilities ahead.

''You and Nate are changing every day. You're finding out new things about one another and the world all the time. Enjoy that. Go places and do things with all your friends. See the kinds of things that make people happy and then set out a plan for yourself.''

Cassie sighed softly, staring into the fire as she wondered if she was being hypocritical in her advice.

''You and Nate have a whole future lifetime to be friends. Don't rush anything. Enjoy being young and carefree. Make it a time to remember.''

Marie stared down at her ring, twirling it round and round on her finger. At last her head tipped back, eyes meeting Cassie's concerned ones.

''Okay,'' she agreed. ''I'll tell Nate that this is our friendship ring and that no matter what, we'll always be best friends.'' Her forehead furrowed as she searched Cassie's face. ''But I am going to marry Nate,'' she insisted. ''Sometime.''

''Maybe,'' Cassie temporized. ''Sometime in the future. When you've both decided to make a commitment that will last the rest of your lives. That's a pretty serious thing to decide at fifteen, Marie.''

''Like the commitment you and Jeff made so you could keep the house and adopt David and me?'' Marie queried.

Cassie stared, unaware that the girl knew so much about their private affairs.

''Well, yes,'' she admitted. ''Although, everyone makes their own decisions about what they want out of life. I wanted you and David to live with us for as long as you want,'' Cassie said softly.

Marie nodded. ''Just like Jeff wants his own son,'' she murmured.

Cassie gaped, her mouth hanging open in surprise. ''H-how do you know about that?'' she asked.

''He talks about it all the time,'' Marie informed her. ''But only when he's with Jonathan.'' Her forehead puzzled in thought. ''That's what the meeting in front of the fire's about, isn't it?'' she asked, smiling.

''Sort of,'' Cassie admitted, flushing an embarrassed pink.

''Well, go get fixed up then,'' Marie chided, glancing around. ''I'll clean up this place while you're gone.''

Cassie stood, smoothing her slacks and picking up the heels with one finger. Her mouth stretched in a wide smile.

''Thank you, Cupid,'' she quipped, tongue in cheek.

Marie merely winked and set about picking up glasses and discarded napkins. It was clear that she was all in favor of a romantic evening for Cassie and Jeff.

The very thought of it made Cassie's knees shake.

Chapter Nine

"Mmm, this coffee is delicious," Cassie murmured, sipping from the porcelain cup once more. She wiggled her toes and basked in the warmth from the crackling fireplace. "We did fill all the stockings, didn't we?"

She glanced around the dimly lit room and smiled at the bulging felt stockings she'd sewn so carefully. Her grin grew as she realized Marie's idea of romance was to light a zillion candles and turn off the lights. An assortment of stringed instruments softly played Christmas carols in the background. She had to admit, Cassie decided, it was a darn good idea.

"We filled the stockings, we wrapped the gifts, we put out Santa's lunch, which I hope you didn't make," he teased, brown eyes glinting. "The Bennets and all of the kids have gone to bed and it's just you and me." He handed her a huge sheaf of crimson red roses. "Merry Christmas, Cassie."

"They're beautiful," Cassie gasped, burying her face in the fragrant petals. "Thank you!" He was staring at her in a way that made her feel strangely uncomfortable. Cassie contemplated the wisdom of escape. "I'll just get a vase." His hand on her arm prevented her from moving.

"Already done." He handed her a crystal vase half filled with water. "Courtesy of Marie."

"Oh. Well. Thank you again."

"You're welcome again." He grinned. "You've done a great job with the house," he added, glancing around at the surfeit of decorations on every window and wall. "And the kids are certainly looking forward to tomorrow. Or today, rather.'' He held up his watch. ''It's after one.''

''Mmm,'' Cassie answered, sipping her coffee slowly. ''I hope tomorrow or today, whichever it is, goes as well.'' She tipped her head up to glance at him. ''Are you sure your parents wouldn't come for dinner? There will be lots of food that I didn't cook and you know I'd like to have both our families present.''

He removed the cup from her hands and set it on a nearby table before clasping his big palms around hers.

''Cassie. You have this idealized version of my parents that is nothing like the reality. They don't like children. They like perfection, order, neatness. Watching Jonathan slop around with his mashed potatoes and gravy would drive my father nuts.''

''He can be well behaved,'' Cassie protested. ''Sometimes.''

''That's not the point. My parents aren't like yours. They don't think in terms of sing-alongs and board games and popcorn. Father's more like Melisande in his view on children. They're tolerable if they are kept at a safe distance from him.'' He peered down at her, a set smile on his lips. ''You can't fix this Cassie, so leave it alone. We'll manage.''

Cassie heard the note of pain in his voice as he laughed dryly. ''Maybe they would loosen up if they saw other people relaxing and having fun,'' she offered quietly.

He moved a little closer to her on the soft, plushy cushions and put his arm around her shoulder.

''I do not want to talk about my parents tonight,'' he whispered quietly, pressing his mouth against her ear. ''Surely we can think of a more interesting topic?''

Cassie sat motionless as his hand threaded through her hair.

''Like how beautiful you look tonight.'' His eyes slid over the red velour. ''Red is definitely your color. I remember you were wearing it the first time I saw you. I thought it suited you then.''

Cassie's eyes widened. ''You did not think any such thing,'' she protested, laughingly. ''You thought I was some money hungry woman who had latched onto your aunt for all the freebies I could get.'' Silently, she dared him to deny it.

''Okay, maybe I didn't see it right away,'' he allowed as one fingertip slid down the pert tip of her nose. "But I can see it now. And I like what I see." His hands came together around her neck, cupping her face. "You're a very beautiful and giving woman, Cassandra Haddon." His lips nibbled on her earlobe. "I'm very glad I married you."

She couldn't say anything then because his mouth moved to cover hers as he told her without words exactly how much he thought of her. Of their own volition, Cassie's arms lifted and wound themselves around his neck as she shifted a little closer, returning his caresses with gentle touches of her own.

"I'm glad I married you, too," she whispered when his mouth finally moved away. His hands smoothed over her back slowly, cradling her closer. "Did you hear something?" she asked a second later, dark headed tilted to one side.

Jeff's mouth was buried in the curve of her shoulder, his lips nuzzling the delicate white skin there.

"Mmm-hmm," he agreed. "Bells."

"No, it's more of a whirring," Cassie whispered and then forgot about it as his lips moved to her ear. She heard his words with an acute ache in her heart even as she thanked heaven for them.

"I think you'll make the most wonderful mother," he confided softly. "You've got so much warmth and love to give. Give a little bit of it to me," he begged in a muffled voice just before his mouth moved over hers.

And Cassie did. She poured out as much of her love as she could, only realizing then that she loved him more than she'd ever thought possible. Her love was overwhelming, powerful. And it demanded expression.

With a light delicate touch she fingered the collar of his shirt, slipping her fingers upward through the soft, silken strands of his hair. One finger traced the smooth dark eyebrows and thick full eyelashes around his eye. It moved down his aquiline nose and traced the sensuous outline of his lips before lowering to press against the dent in his chin.

Her lips followed a natural progression down to where her fingers had left off. As she kissed him on the mouth, and felt his immediate response, Cassie wondered how she could tell him of her love.

"Cassie, honey, I want…" There was a definite whirring sound now and they both glanced up at the same time, staring into each other's eyes. "What was that?" he demanded quietly.

"I don't know." Cassie studied her hands. "One of the kids maybe?"

"I don't think so." Jeff set her gently away from him and stood. The sound penetrated the silence of the room clearly. "It seems to be coming from behind the Christmas tree," he muttered, striding across the room.

Cassie watched as he peered through the branches and jumped nervously at the loud curse. "What is it?" she asked curiously, standing just in time to see him remove a video camera fastened on a tripod from the corner.

"Now, how in the world…?" her voice trailed away in stupefaction at the recording device that had obviously been set up to record them both.

"I'll tell you how it got there," Jeff stormed. "It was planted there. To film us. And I know exactly who did it."

Cassie frowned. "You do?" She thought for a moment and then gave in to curiosity. "Who?"

"Your soon-to-be daughter, that's who. Of all the prying, sneaky, underhanded…" She let him spout off for a few minutes while she tried to sort things out.

"You think Marie set this up to record us?" she asked at last.

"That's exactly what I think. No wonder she was so accommodating," he griped, snatching the cassette out of the camera. "She wanted to set things up exactly right so she could tape us."

"Marie would never do that." Cassie shook her head. "She's much too thoughtful to intrude on us like this."

"I know you think they're all perfect," Jeff muttered, shoving the camera and tripod into a closet. "But somebody set us up and then recorded it. I'm going to find out who."

Cassie trailed up the stairs behind him, recognizing deep inside that it had to be Marie. Everyone else had long since gone to sleep. Only the young girl was awake, sitting cross-legged on her bed with her headphones on, humming quietly to the music playing in her ears.

"Marie!" Jeff barked her name only to be shushed by Cassie. Marie stopped the player and slipped the earphones off her head in surprise when she saw them.

"You'll wake the whole house, Jeff," Cassie admonished, pushing the heavy fall of hair off her forehead. "And frankly I'm not up to that." She stared down at the young girl. "You and I and Jeff need to have a serious talk, Marie. Now." She saw the trace of fear threading through the girl's troubled gaze before she nodded and headed for the stairs.

Marie was sobbing by the time they reached the family room, great gulping sobs that shook her thin body.

"I'm sorry," she wept, twisting her robe between her fingers. "I didn't mean to hurt anyone."

"How could you not mean to hurt anyone," Jeff demanded, towering over her. "You deliberately invaded our privacy and set up a camera to record it. What were you planning to do— sell copies?"

Cassie heard the frustration and embarrassment in Jeff's tone. And she felt exactly the same way. But right now they had to put their own feelings on hold and deal with a mixed-up young girl who had her first crush and didn't know how to handle it.

"Why, Marie?" She asked it softly, letting her disappointment show. "Why would you do such a thing?"

"I wasn't going to show anyone," Marie promised tearfully. "I never meant for you to find out."

"But honey," Cassie said with a sigh. "It was still wrong."

"And underhanded, too," Jeff added. "How would you like it if we spied on you and Rick?"

"Nate!" Cassie and Marie said the name together.

"Whatever! How would you like it if we videotaped the two of you out on a date and then sat here and watched your private conversations?" Jeff looked as if the very idea of watching young love at work made him cringe.

"I wouldn't. But I didn't mean any harm. Honestly."

"Okay, sweetheart. I believe you." Cassie patted the wringing hands. "But I want to know why you thought you had to do such a thing."

"I had to know about love," Marie whispered.

Cassie swiveled her head up to stare at Jeff. He shrugged, obviously without the answers she wanted.

"What about love did you need to know that you thought you'd find on a videotape?" His voice was soft with steel edges as he stared down at the girl. His eyes glittered with anger.

"You remember I told you Nate gave me a ring?" She looked to Cassie for confirmation. At Cassie's nod she continued. "And you said that there were all different kinds of love. Well, I want to know what they are." She stared up at Jeff, dashing the tears from her eyes as she spoke.

"I want to know about the love between you and Cassie so that I'll know it's the real thing when it comes to me."

Cassie sat on the cushions with her mouth hanging open. She couldn't say a word. Well, really, what could she say? Jeff doesn't love me, Marie, but I married him because I needed this house to continue with my work? Not likely.

She started in surprise when Jeff sat down beside her and curved his arm around her shoulders. She felt the squeeze of his hand as his words came out slowly, as if he were feeling his way.

"Marie, people all experience what you're calling love differently. You can watch someone else and admire what that emotion has done for them, or you can appreciate the difference someone's caring makes in another person's life. Do you know what I mean?"

"You mean like the difference Cassie's love made in David's and my life when we got to live here permanently?" Marie asked as she nodded slowly.

"Yes," he agreed softly. "Exactly like that. But you can't just spy on other people and then try to take what you think works for them and apply it to you. I think love probably means something different to you than it does to either Cassie or me."

Cassie didn't utter a word. She was too amazed to hear Jeff's interpretation of love. Up until now, he'd refused to even use the word.

"You see, I think when you meet someone and you think that you have fallen in love with them," he continued softly, "you'll know if that's the person you want to spend the rest of your life with. You might think you know it right away or it might take you a while to sort it all out.''

"Sort of like you two," the girl snickered mockingly. "It's taken you forever to sort things out."

Cassie stared, amazed that this soft-spoken, quiet girl had seen through their pretence. She felt Jeff's hand tighten on her shoulder once more and decided to let him finish the job.

"We haven't sorted everything out *yet,*" he told her honestly, staring down into Cassie's bright eyes. "I think our marriage is going to be about continually sorting things out." He grinned a self-deprecating smile. "But that doesn't mean yours will be."

"What I'm really saying," he advised, "is that you can't use someone else as the yardstick for your life. You have to decide what it is you want out of life and hold out until you get it. You're not me and you're not Cassie. You're you—Marie. And your experiences are going to be totally different from ours."

"And Marie?" Cassie couldn't help but add the last word. She remembered those turbulent teenage years too well not to tell the whole story. "There will be all kinds of love along the way. A gentle, tender first love. A friendly kind of love for the date at your prom." She smiled and brushed her fingers over Marie's bent head.

"A stronger love for someone you meet in college who seems like the answer to your prayers and makes you cry instead. And the one man who makes you feel special and beautiful and a whole lot of other miraculous things. Only you can decide which one will last a lifetime. But don't sell yourself short by grabbing the first one that comes along or by trying to make your life into someone else's. Okay?"

Marie nodded, standing straight and tall before them.

"I owe you both an apology," she said softly. "I know you'd respect my privacy. I'm only sorry I didn't respect yours. I hope you'll forgive me?"

Cassie hugged her close. "Of course we do," she whispered. "Now go to bed. It's almost Christmas."

"Good night," she murmured, heading for the stairs.

"Good night," they answered in unison.

When the door to her room closed with a soft thud, Cassie met Jeff's bright gaze with a shrug.

"Well, that was interesting." It was not the right thing to say.

"It could have been," he muttered, moving to place the fire screen before the fire. "I was hoping we might get some time to ourselves for once."

Cassie felt the same disappointment. Right to the end of her toes. She had been on the verge of discovering something wonderful; anticipation of some understanding or personal communion had hovered for a moment and then flown away. Now she just felt tired and drained.

"We'll manage it," she promised weakly. "One of these days."

His head tipped to one side as he studied her. Carefully, without touching her anywhere else, he leaned over and placed a soft kiss on her lips.

"Promises, promises," he drawled. But when she studied the dark expressive eyes, she could find no clue to his meaning. "Who is it that makes you feel special and wonderful and all those other things, Cassie?"

But he didn't wait for her answer. He merely snuffed out the candles and walked her to her door. "Good night," he murmured, staring down at her.

"Good night, Jeff. Merry Christmas."

"Yeah. Thanks."

From the corner of her eye, Cassie caught just a glimpse of the gold foil box he slipped surreptitiously into his pants pocket. It had been a gift, she was sure. Something personal he'd chosen especially for her.

Then why hadn't he given it to her? she asked herself sadly.

Chapter Ten

"I'm telling you, Rory, it's positively hair-raising. To think that a kid would do something like that." Jeff smacked his hand against the counter and glared at his brother. "It could have been very embarrassing, you know."

Rory grinned back at him, obviously pleased at the sight of his uptight elder brother. "But nothing happened, did it?"

"No!" Jeff glared across the room, wishing he didn't feel so stupid.

"Well, then," Rory asked reasonably, "what's the problem?"

"She's my wife and I'm getting tired of never having a moment alone with her." Jeff barely contained his anger. He forcibly restrained himself from kicking the solid wood table leg as he explained.

"There's always another child to cuddle or some emergency job that needs handling. It's like she's constantly running away from me." He glared at his chuckling sibling. "It seems like the only one who wants me around is Jonathan."

"Well, there's a consolation for you." Rory smiled. "Why don't you take that ball and run with it?"

"I don't just want a child. I want my wife!" Jeff heard himself bellow the words. His eyes opened wide as he realized what he had just said. Rory wasn't slow on the draw, either.

"Now there's a switch." His brother grinned. "It was always 'my son' this and 'my son' that. Are you saying you're giving up that lifelong dream of the perfect son in favor of a new dream named Cassie Haddon?'' He shook his head. ''Hard to believe, big bro. Hard to believe.''

''I'm not giving it up. Not completely,'' Jeff protested. ''It's just that I'm married now, and I would like to make a go of that before I introduce any more children into this madhouse.''

He whined plaintively about the past week's activities and added the fact that he'd been awakened today at five-thirty a.m. by a small child jumping on his midsection.

''It's pretty hard to get romantic after that,'' he muttered.

''Are you in love with Cassie, Jefferson?'' Rory peered at him seriously, his glasses dipping low on the end of his nose as he stared over the top of them.

''You know very well that I don't believe in love.'' Jeff dismissed the question with a wave of his hand. ''I'm attracted to her, yes. Who wouldn't be? We share some of the same interests and values. I feel a fondness for her and of course, I want her to be happy. But love?'' He shook his head. ''It doesn't exist. Except in the movies and fairy tales.''

Rory rearranged the test tubes littering the basement workshop as he considered his brother's words. His eyes were intent when they focused on Jeff's.

''Yeah,'' he muttered to himself. ''Love exists. Especially in this house.''

''What?'' Jeff demanded, straightening the bottles back in a neat row. He frowned at the strange look covering Rory's handsome face.

''Never mind.'' Rory shoved his hands into his pockets. ''So, what do you want from me?''

''I thought, maybe, just once, the great Rory Haddon might have the answers.'' Jeff infused his voice with biting sarcasm as he glared at the smiling face.

''I probably do. What's the question?''

It was a terrible thought, this being Christmas day and all, but Jeff decided he'd really like to plant his fist on that smugly grinning countenance.

''How can I get Cassie to spend more time with me? Alone.'' Jeff bit the words out from between his gritting teeth. If his brother had set out to annoy him purposely, he couldn't have burrowed under his skin more.

Reginald Thomas Haddon, Rory for short, smirked at his elder brother in delight.

"Perhaps a date? A little fun and frolic. A carefree night of pleasure? You remember dating, don't you, Jefferson? That couples pairing thing all the other people did in college?"

Jeff frowned. "A date?" He tossed the idea around in his mind before glancing up at Rory. "Doing what?" he queried.

"How do I know what old married people do for fun? I'm the youngest brother. Dinner and a movie, maybe. Bowling? I don't know." His eyes widened as a new thought occurred to him.

"Maybe you could get her interested in your work. If you slaved together over the computer, who knows what could happen?" He grinned with delight.

"Work together?" Jeff frowned. "I was thinking of something a little more...imaginative."

"Hey, don't knock it till you've tried it." Rory laughed. "And speaking of knocking..." He motioned his thumb upstairs.

"Not another hour of one-sided chitchat while the parents sit there glowering," Jeff groaned at the series of thumps on the stout basement door. "Cassie's so big on this family thing, you'd think she'd notice that they're not into it."

Rory frowned. "I think you're misjudging them, bro. Dad held the baby for ages earlier on."

"Yeah." Jeff grinned sardonically. "About six inches off his knee in case anything got on his cashmere pants."

Rory was shaking his head.

"No, I meant after that. Later on, once he got used to him. He was dangling the kid on his knee and babbling away like a regular grandfather. It was amazing."

Jeff climbed the steps wearily. He laughed harshly at the tender picture his brother painted of the hard-nosed, acrimonious man he'd spoken with earlier.

"In your dreams," he muttered.

In fact, he'd actually been surprised when his parents had accepted Cassie's invitation for brunch. They'd shown up with a carload of gifts and a giant bouquet of flowers for his wife.

Cassie had been almost as excited about that as she had been about his roses, he grumbled silently.

"Oh, Jeff. Good." Cassie slipped her hand into his arm and dragged him over to where Stevie sat in a brand-new walker. "Did you know your father picked this out himself?" she asked softly.

"Really?" He tried to infuse a modicum of warmth into his voice while keeping his eyes averted from that familiar white head.

"And your mother says he searched all over to find that crane to match Jonathan's truck." He winced at the nudge she directed to his ribs.

"They're very nice," he muttered dutifully, feeling less than grateful. "Thank you both."

Jeff watched as his stiff, austere mother, whom he had known as a cold, unapproachable woman for the entirety of his life, leaned over and pressed a kiss on little Stevie's head.

"Nonsense, Jefferson," she murmured softly, staring at the babbling baby. "It's our right as grandparents, isn't it, Jeffie?" She looked to her husband for confirmation.

"Yes, dear," he said staunchly, obviously daring his son to contradict him as he jiggled Jonathan on his knee.

Jeff looked from one to the other of them with astonishment.

"They're not your grandchildren, Mother," he said clearly. "They're not even our children. They're just here for a short while."

"But that doesn't mean we can't love them," Cassie countered from her place at his side. "It doesn't mean they can't have a grandma and grandpa whenever they come here, does it, Jeff?"

As he stared down into her lovely face, Jeff couldn't stop the words from coming. Who could deny her anything when she looked like that?

"No," he agreed, his voice strangling as it came out. "I suppose it wouldn't hurt for them to pretend for a little while." He glared over at his father who was slowly getting to his feet. "Better a little affection than none at all, I suppose."

He heard Cassie gasp and winced at the pointed elbow she embedded between his ribs.

"That was mean," she hissed angrily. "They're trying to be nice. Maybe you could try, too?"

"Cassandra, my dear, thank you for a lovely afternoon." Jeff watched his mother regain her composure. Her face was white with strain and she didn't look at him, but kept her eyes fixed firmly on his wife. "I enjoyed meeting the children again. Perhaps you could bring them over one afternoon."

"I'd like that," he heard Cassie agree. "How about next week sometime?"

He left them discussing dates and walked Rory to the door.

"Can you believe it? They want *kids* running around that mausoleum? A little late isn't it?" he mused bitterly.

"Jefferson." Rory's voice was soft and hesitant. "Maybe you haven't realized it, but Mother hasn't been well. She's..."

"Probably worn out from the old man ordering her around," Jeff finished angrily.

"Oh, shut up for once, will you," Rory snapped, shrugging into his jacket. "Can't you just once let go of all that anger and accept that our parents are human beings? Maybe they did make mistakes. Get over it. They're not going to be around forever, you know." He stamped his feet into his boots and glared at his brother angrily.

"Find a little forgiveness, would you? You might need it yourself some day when kids like Jonathan or David come back to you with complaints."

Jeff stared after him as Rory strode down the driveway and then raced away with a grinding of the gears in his fast sports car. He had never seen his brother stand up for his father like that. Not once in thirty years. As he stood in the cold, brisk air, staring down the road, he heard a voice clearing behind him.

"You and your wife seem very happy here, Jefferson," his father observed. "I'm sure Judith would have enjoyed knowing you've put her home to such good use." Jefferson Haddon, the second, thrust out his hand.

"Merry Christmas, son."

Jeff stared at him bitterly. He thought he could just wash it all away, did he? Years of pain and heartache, self-doubt and recriminations? Not very likely.

"Yeah," he muttered angrily, refusing to take that outstretched hand. "Merry Christmas." His voice was full of bitter recriminations.

"Why did you have to do that to them?" Cassie asked softly, when everyone had left the room. "They really tried and you slapped them in the face." Her eyes studied him sadly.

"Is it worth it to hang on to all that bitterness and anger?" she demanded. "Does it make your life better to know that regardless of how hard they try, you're never going to let your parents off the hook? Will that even the score?"

It should have ruined the day, Jeff decided hours later. But somehow, with the advent of Cassie's excited parents, her sister and brother and all of their children, the rest of the day had passed happily. The new house had obviously been a fantastic idea since her parents couldn't stop talking about it.

"If that isn't just like our Cassie," her father announced happily, throwing his arm around his daughter's shoulder. "Always planning some wonderful surprise."

Jeff had watched their interaction carefully after that, curious about the obvious rapport between the two. In fact, he noticed that the whole family giggled and laughed and teased one another. He could learn from them, Jeff decided. For the benefit of his own son.

He had just decided to question Frank Newton when Mrs. Bennet announced dinner and the family gathered around the table, still jostling one another until her father had called a halt to say grace.

"Father, we thank you for this day, the day you sent love to this earth in the form of your only son. And we thank you for Cassie and Jeff and their family. Help us to share together now with full hearts for the peace and goodwill you've brought to us this day. Amen."

"Ahhhmen," Jonathan repeated happily.

It was a noisy evening, bordering on riotous as the mob of laughing children clustered round, trying every toy they'd been given. The adults spent their time playing board games and talking after the dishes had been cleared away.

Jeff found himself sitting next to Frank later on as they sipped Cassie's unusual Christmas punch.

"You've done a wonderful thing here, my boy," Frank congratulated him. "These kids couldn't have had a better experience than Christmas day filled with love."

"It's not so much my doing," Jeff denied. "Cassie's the one who insisted they stay here."

"Yep." Frank grinned. "She's got a big heart. I can see how much she loves you, too."

There wasn't much he could say to that so Jeff let it go.

"How'd you like her gift?" Frank's bright eyes gleamed with happiness. "I'll bet you were surprised. Cassie spent a long time on that."

"Actually, we haven't gotten around to exchanging gifts yet," Jeff told him, the gold foil box in his pocket burning a hole. "With the kids and everything, there just hasn't been time." His face flushed a dark red at the curious look in his father-in-law's eyes.

"I think it's time you did, my boy. Christmas is almost over. Edna," Frank called, hoisting himself from his comfortable chair. "It's time for us to go. These kids need some sparkin' time to relax." His eyes sparkled down at Jeff. "Alone."

They were all gone within a matter of twenty minutes, leaving the house quiet—or at least as quiet as it ever got, Jeff decided. Cassie disappeared to put the excited kids to bed with Marie's help.

"Jeff?" David stood before him, holding a small box in his outstretched hand. "I know I gave you that tie already. But this is your real Christmas gift. I made it for you."

A lump the size of a mandarin orange rose in Jeff's throat as he read the small burned-wood plaque nestled inside.

A Father is someone who is there when you need him.
Someone who doesn't need to be asked for his help.
A Father knows kids make lots of mistakes. He does too.
Fathers forgive and forget about them and move on.
Fathers include their kids in the important things.
Real fathers are hard to find.

"It's wonderful David," he managed to say. The tears in his eyes were embarrassing and he tried to blink them away as he stared at the young boy who had come to depend on him. How could he let him down?

"It's oak from the front yard. See, I routered the edges and sanded it myself," David told him proudly. "Since you're going to be my official dad, I thought you wouldn't mind hearing my views."

"I don't mind at all," Jeff whispered. He stared at the tall gangly boy and felt the weight of his responsibilities land heavily on his shoulders. It was an awesome obligation. And he had no practise. "I just hope I can live up to all this," he uttered.

"I'll help you," David offered. "And if it gets too bad, we can always get Cassie to be the tiebreaker." David grinned.

"Thank you, David. This is the best Christmas gift I've ever had." He hugged the boy and then quickly let go as David glanced around. "It's okay, son," he teased. "I think hugging between fathers and their kids is okay. Maybe even cool."

David's eyebrows rose at that but he grinned anyway.

"I guess so. G'night."

"Good night, David."

Jeff tucked the little board into his briefcase carefully. He'd post it on a wall at work, he decided. Where he would see it every day and remember his new job as a parent. As he left the study, Jeff glanced out the window, his eye caught by a movement outside.

It was Cassie. His fingers curved around the gift in his pocket. There were only a few more hours left. He'd give it to her out there, Jeff decided. Where no one could interrupt them.

He found her sitting in the garden on a weathered bench Judith had always favored. Her face was tilted toward the sky as she stared at the navy-blanketed heavens with pinpricks of rhinestone bright light flecks scattered here and there. Jeff sat down without making a sound, content to watch her.

"Isn't it beautiful?" she breathed, the warm air leaving her mouth in a cloud that was soon whisked away by the light wind.

"Beautiful," he agreed, staring at the pure clear outline of her face.

"Just think of the changes that occurred on this earth on this very night a little less than two thousand years ago," she whispered. "Can you imagine the love it must have taken to let your only son leave home and come to a place where you knew he would be mistreated? Even killed." Jeff saw the tears sparkling on her cheeks as she turned to look at him. "Sometimes I can hardly believe in so much love."

Jeff sat silent, contemplating her words solemnly as he, too, stared at the wondrously lit sky. There it was again. Love. It was like a mantra, chanting constantly in his mind.

"Oh, look," Cassie cried happily. Her outstretched arm pointed to the heavens. "The northern lights. Aren't they magnificent? So bright and yet they change constantly. It's kind of like our world," she mused quietly.

"Everything's always shifting, altering. And yet God remains constant in His heaven, directing our actions if we let Him." She smiled, a wide, delighted smile that stretched her mouth in its joy. "I love Christmas," she said, laughing.

In her happiness, she hugged him. A friendly, outgoing hug that begged him to share in her pleasure. And Jeff hugged her back because for once, he also liked Christmas.

"What's this?" she murmured, picking up the small gold package off the snow where it had slid from Jeff's hand. "Is it for me?" she asked wide-eyed, a smile tugging at the corners of her mouth.

He nodded.

"But you've already given me a silk blouse and a new jacket and those books I wanted."

"I know." Jeff picked up her hand and fingered the rings he had put on her hand short weeks ago. "This is for this Christmas and next Christmas and all the ones to come. Go ahead, open it. You'll see what I mean."

She did. And breathed a sigh of delight as she lifted the delicate gold links from their bed of cotton. Dangling from one gleaming circlet hung a tiny angel, its wings outstretched ready to fly.

"It's lovely," she breathed, studying him with her bright eyes.

Jeff fastened the tiny clasp around her wrist and fingered the angel with his thumb.

"It's sort of like Marie's promise ring, I guess," he said,

embarrassed that he'd even thought of getting something so personal for her. "The angel reminded me of you." He grinned, hoping to ease the tension. "Next year I'll get a star."

Cassie smiled, a radiant look of pure joy lighting her features as she leaned over and kissed his cheek.

"Thank you," she said softly. "It's the most lovely gift I've ever had."

Jeff twisted his head to brush his lips against hers, wanting to deepen the kiss and yet afraid to spoil the sweet sense of wonder between them. But he kissed her anyway, with all the pent-up longing he felt. When at last Cassie moved away, he noticed her hands trembling.

"I have something special for you, too," she murmured, eyes downcast. "It's still under the tree."

Together, arm in arm, they walked slowly back along the snow-covered path to the house and made their way silently through the dimly lit hall to the family room. And there, tucked away behind the tree, Jeff saw the large flat package. She handed it to him and he read the attached card curiously. "Judith helped make some of your dreams come true. My wish is that you realize the rest of them in the coming years. God bless you, Jeff. Love, Cassie."

He studied the second last word with interest. There it was again, he mused. Love. But then, coming from Cassie that was normal wasn't it? She was full of what even he had to admit was what he thought of as love. He wondered what she meant.

"Open it," she demanded, dancing from one foot to the other. "Quickly."

With a laugh, he tore the paper open. The mirth caught in his throat as Judith's smiling face stared up at him. Her tired blue eyes sparkled out through the acrylic daubs that Cassie had used to portray his aunt so accurately. Her mouth tilted at the corners in that old familiar way, chastising him for some long forgotten misdeed. Her image was so lifelike that he could almost hear Judith's voice chiding him for waiting too long to visit.

Tears squeezed out of his eyes and rolled down his face as he stared at the wonderful woman who had taken such good care of him all those years ago. The woman who had continued to keep her guiding hand on his life through the years.

And he had never said thank you. Not properly. Not in a way that expressed the thankfulness he felt for her care, concern and yes, maybe even love in his young life. A pain tightened in his chest. A pain that told him he would never have the opportunity again.

"Jeff," Cassie touched his shoulder gently. When she saw the tears in his eyes, she gathered his head gently against her and held him tightly. "Oh, Jeff."

"I never told her," he moaned sadly, wrapping his arms around her waist and leaning into that soothing touch. "I never said how much I loved her."

Cassie brushed the dark strands back off his forehead and kissed it tenderly. Her words gently soothed the gnawing ache in his chest.

"She knew, Jeff. Judith always knew."

Chapter Eleven

"I can look after three small children every bit as well as you can, Cassandra. I'm not totally incompetent." Jeff stared at her with the light of battle in his eyes. "After all, Marie and David will be nearby to lend a hand."

Cassie frowned.

"Yes, but you wanted me to help you with that new program you're working on and instead of helping you, I'm landing you with more work." She glanced around the kitchen once more. "I'll try not to be too long although his mother did tell the social worker that Greg's pretty sick." She hesitated. "Are you sure…"

"Just go will you," Jeff bellowed. "We'll be fine."

Cassie tugged on her jacket and strode to the door.

"All right, I'm going. I'm going." She yanked open the front door. "Come on, Robyn. I can tell when we're not wanted."

Robyn raised her eyebrows, staring behind her with curiosity. "What in the world's gotten into him?" she grumbled. "Has he been working in that lab for too long or what? First he can't stand kids and now he wants to be alone with them. Yikes!"

"I know," Cassie nodded. "He's been like this ever since Christmas. It's as if he's trying to make up for lost time or something. He, David and Jonathan are like the Three Musketeers. When Jonathan goes to bed, Jeff buries himself in the basement."

"What are they working on?" Robyn asked, steering confidently into a skid and then out again. "It must be something pretty big."

"Search me." Cassie shrugged. "It's something to do with David's science project that's due the first week of January. My guess is they're going to make some spectacular presentation that will, hopefully, impress the teacher."

"What is it for anyway?" Robyn demanded. "Physics, biology, chemistry?"

"Robyn, you know I hate all three of those terms," Cassie grumbled, shuddering. "Why are you asking me?"

Robyn laughed and gave her friend a sly sidelong look.

"I figured things must have changed if you're helping Jeff with his computer programs," she said dryly. "You never used to know a hard drive from an autoexec bat."

Cassie frowned. Robyn was teasing her, that was it. She could tell from the tone of her voice. But she had absolutely no idea what her friend was talking about. She decided to change the subject.

"How bad is Greg?" she asked instead. "Sondra didn't say much when I called the agency."

"Not much to say," Robyn frowned sadly. "He was beaten up pretty badly." She risked a glance across at Cassie, taking her eyes off the road for just a second. "It's those teenage gang thugs," she explained. "He made the mistake of saying no to them and they didn't like it."

Cassie's heart sank as she saw the twelve-year-old boy swathed in bandages in the intensive care ward at Sick Children's hospital. Greg's face was a mass of cuts and bruises but thankfully the doctor had said his eyes had not been damaged. He did have internal injuries that were causing problems and it would be touch and go for the next twenty-four hours.

Cassie folded the pale hand with its IV infusion tube gently into hers and sank onto a nearby chair. Silently, with her eyes staring at his poor battered face, she began to pray for Greg's recovery.

"Cassie?" She opened her eyes to find Greg's mother, Nina, standing nearby. There were tears on the woman's cheeks as she stared at her son.

"Hi, Nina." She hugged the frail woman gently, smoothing the tears from her thin, haggard face. "How are you?"

"He was a good boy, Cassie. He didn't get into drugs and he kept going to the youth group like you said." She stared down at the still figure. "Why didn't God keep my boy safe, Cassie?"

It was a tough question and Cassie didn't have a ready answer. She hugged Nina close and whispered a prayer for wisdom.

"Honey," she said softly, feeling her way along. "Maybe we're looking at this all wrong. God did keep Greg safe. He kept him out of the gang and off the drugs. I don't know for sure, but maybe he had to go through all this so the boys who did this to him could see his faith."

Nina still wept softly.

"God always has a purpose, Nina. Maybe we can't see it right now, but we can know that He didn't keep Greg out of the bad stuff just to abandon him. We can't stop trusting Him now."

"I know," Nina sniffed. "And I'll try to keep strong. He was so happy when he came back from your place in August. He was like a new kid." She grinned. "No, he was more like the old Greg."

"And he will be again." Cassie smiled. "You just wait and see."

They sat together until Robyn came in to take a turn. Cassie agreed to meet her later in the cafeteria and had just sat down with a cup of rank black coffee when Jeff's father walked in.

"Why Mr. Haddon," she greeted him, smiling happily, "what are you doing here?"

Jefferson Haddon looked bone weary, she decided. His eyes were sunken into his head and his whole body seemed to sag under the expensive suit.

"We were visiting a friend," he told her. "And Glenda fainted." His eyes were listless. "They don't want to move her until they know what's wrong."

Cassie drew in a deep breath and steadied herself. Not now, she prayed. Please God, don't take her now.

"Can I do anything for Mrs. Haddon, sir?" If there was

anything to be done, Cassie knew that Jeff's father would have spared no expense for his wife. Still she had to offer.

"No." He shook his head sadly. "I don't think…" His eyes brightened suddenly. "Well, maybe if you wanted to stop by for just a moment," he ventured. "I know she'd like to see you."

"Of course I will," she agreed. "What floor is she on?" Jeff's father agreed to take her himself after they had finished their coffee.

Cassie barely stifled the gasp that rose involuntarily when she found Jeff's mother lying on a narrow cot half an hour later. The woman was gaunt and gray, her ashen face drawn in haggard lines of pain.

"I'm so sorry you're not feeling well, Mrs. Haddon," she murmured, grasping the outstretched hand. "Do they know what the problem is yet?"

Glenda Haddon's white face turned toward the wall.

"I've known I was ill for some time now, dear," she whispered. "I was supposed to begin treatments last week but I wanted to wait until after Christmas." Her eyelids slipped closed with a sigh of weariness.

"That's why we've been so anxious to try to restore our relationship with our son," Mr. Haddon murmured. Tears pooled in his eyes. "I know we've had some problems, but I thought maybe the time had come to settle things. I'm afraid I was wrong." He stared at her sadly. "My son will never forgive me for not being the father I should have been to him."

Cassie wrapped her arms around the bowed shoulders and hugged him tightly.

"Don't you dare give up now," she ordered tightly. "Don't you dare. Jeff will come round. It's just going to take some time, some prayer and a lot of love. And I've got lots of all three."

Mr. Haddon smiled tiredly. "I think you do, Cassie. You're very good for my son. He's changed since he married you."

"So have I," Cassie managed to respond through the lump in her throat. "I've come to understand another side to God's love. With His help, I'm going to help Jeff to see it, too."

"Good for you." Jefferson Senior clamped his hand on her

shoulder. "Just promise me that you won't give up on him. No matter what. You're all he has left." His sad eyes dropped to his wife's sleeping form. "We spoiled our chances with him. And now it's too late."

"It's never too late," Cassie told him firmly. "God can work through the biggest mountains. Just keep praying for him."

"We will, dear. And thank you. I don't know how we would have gotten through these past few months without you."

Cassie stood in the elevator thinking about his words. In truth she felt like a fraud. What right had she to promise that sick woman that her son would find it in his heart to forgive her before it was too late? She saw Jeff every day. Ate her meals with him and raised children with him. She loved him more than any person on earth and yet even she couldn't force him to lay aside the old bitterness.

"Father, I need your strength now," she prayed. "Lead me in the right direction. And help me to follow your leading."

Robyn was waiting in the coffee shop, grinning from ear to ear.

"Greg woke up," she informed her cheerfully. "He said his whole body ached like a bad tooth." She grinned. "It was worth every misbehaving moment he spent in my Sunday School class just to hear those words."

They made a swift detour so Cassie could congratulate the boy on his firm stance before she directed Robyn to take her home.

"Missing hubby already, are we?" Robyn teased. Her eyes widened at the solemn look on Cassie's face. "What's the matter?"

As she related her chance meeting, Cassie dumped the whole burden on her friend. "He's just got to come round, Rob. I don't know how much longer Mrs. H. has."

Robyn patted her shoulder.

"She has as much time as God wills. You can't change that. Just keep on keeping on."

It was good advice, Cassie decided as they turned up the driveway to her home. It was a good feeling—home. She stepped out of the car and stopped abruptly as she spied the little crowd gathered on the front lawn. In the middle she could see the bright blue of Jeff's ski jacket. He seemed to be lying on the ground.

"What's going on?" she demanded, racing over to the huddled group and sinking to her knees beside Jeff's still body.

Jonathan wailed as he grasped the still hand. "I didn't mean to hurt him. Please God, make my daddy all better." His little mittened hands patted the dark head tenderly.

"What happened?" Cassie asked David, who stood nearby holding Stevie. As she talked, her hand smoothed the hair away from Jeff's forehead and brushed over the lump at his hairline.

"We were having a snowball fight. All of a sudden he just toppled over." David's eyes were weaving back and forth from hers to Jonathan's small crying figure. "This is what hit him."

Cassie peered down at the snow-encrusted ball of ice.

"But Jonathan couldn't have thrown this hard enough," she murmured, trying to piece events together.

"I threw it for him," David admitted, his face pasty white as he stared at the big man lying in the snow. "I didn't notice the ice."

"His pulse is strong," Robyn observed, kneeling beside Jeff's other side. "I think he's coming round."

Cassie cupped his cold cheeks in her hands.

"Jeff," she called softly. "Jeff!" His eyes blinked open slowly. "Oh, thank God!" she exclaimed, wrapping her arms around him and pressing little kisses all over his face. "Are you okay?"

"I'm getting better by the minute," he assured her, drawing her head down to his. "Just keep doing what you're doing. I'll be in heaven."

Jonathan started wailing again. "I don't want my daddy to go to heaven."

David shushed him with a grin. "I don't think he's going anywhere right now," he teased. "He's too busy kissing Cassie."

Cassie heard them all laughing and pressed Jeff's hands away as her cheeks flushed an embarrassed red.

"Come on, faker," she muttered. "Let's get you upright."

"Aghhh," he breathed, one hand fingering the skin on his brow. "What hit me, a Mack truck?"

"No, a snowball." David moved to support him with one arm under Jeff's broad shoulder. Cassie noted the care with which David helped him stand. "I'm afraid I threw one I shouldn't have."

"Yeah, he throwed this one, Daddy. He's a bad, bad boy." Jonathan frowned at David fiercely. "Don't hurt my daddy anymore," he ordered.

"Who gave David the snowball, Jonny?" Cassie eyed the child sternly, daring him to deny it.

"We were playing. I didn't mean to hurt him!" Jonathan's voice was full of indignation.

Cassie bent down and faced him squarely.

"I know you didn't. But we have to be careful. Some things that are hidden inside can hurt other people very badly." She risked a glance up at Jeff and found his dark eyes fixed on her. Cassie continued her reprimand, averting her face from that searching look.

"Covering that piece of ice up with snow just disguised it," she said softly. "But the ice was still there underneath and it still hurt Daddy. We don't throw ice at people, Jonathan."

"I'm sorry, Daddy. I didn't mean to hurt you."

Jeff nodded, patting the child's covered head. "I know you didn't Jonathan."

"Do I have to go to my room now?" Jonathan sobbed, tears pouring out of his eyes.

"Have you learned a lesson?" Cassie asked, brushing the tears away.

Jonathan tipped his head to one side, a mittened hand under his cheek as he thought about it. One foot tapped silently on the packed snow.

"Yes," he crowed at last. "Don't try to hide bad things."

"Good." Cassie smiled, patting his head. "I think you've all had enough snowballing for one day. Let's go have hot chocolate."

When everything had settled down once more and Robyn had gone her own way, Cassie cornered Jeff in the study.

"I still think you should have a doctor check out that lump," she said frowning.

"I've already told you," Jeff complained, holding the ice

pack to his aching head. "I'm not going to any emergency room for a dinky little bump on the head." His eyes glowed mysteriously. "If," he added teasingly, "you should feel the desire to continue what you started outside, however, that might help with my cure."

Cassie frowned. "What I started?"

He smiled, flicking his finger against her cheek. "Yeah. You were kissing me and calling my name like you really cared whether or not I was dead."

"Of course I care." She brushed his hands away and took a step backward, flushing a deep dark red. "But I certainly wasn't kissing you," she argued. "You must have been dreaming."

Jeff shook his head. "Liar," he whispered. "Come here—" he beckoned to her "—I'll show you what I saw in my dream."

"Jeff!" Cassie protested weakly, wishing she could just relax and snuggle into the circle of his arms, feel them support her. She needed that just now. But to what would it lead?

"I came to help you with the computer stuff. If you don't want my help, I have other things to do. David's youth group is coming over after their tobogganing party tonight, you know."

"Cassie, honey," he drawled, "you can help me anytime. And I mean that from the bottom of my heart." He kissed her lips with a laugh as she flushed a dark red for the second time.

"Sorry." He grinned unrepentently. "I couldn't help kissing you. You're so irresistible." He kept his arms around her waist. "And I do think it's quite normal for married couples to exchange these pleasantries from time to time." His lips touched her temples. "If fact," he whispered, "I think we should do it more often. Much more often."

Cassie pulled herself away with difficulty, moving slowly toward the door. "I guess you don't want my help."

"Yes, I do. Really." He had that little-boy look that Jonathan used so often. She couldn't help giving in.

"Fine. Then let's get to work."

He waved a hand at the chair behind his desk. "Be seated and I'll explain."

It seemed simple enough to Cassie. She just had to type in some funny little symbols in between those short abbreviated words. She'd never actually done it before, she reminded herself an hour later, but it really wasn't that hard. She studied her work with a proud smile and then glanced at Jeff who sat at his laptop, punching madly at the keys.

How would she tell him, she wondered sadly. How could she explain that it was time to forget the old hurts and get on with the future? A future that his mother might not have.

Her fingers punched in the key commands he had listed. Suddenly there was a squeal from the computer that hurt her ears. Then everything went black.

"What in the world was that?" Jeff demanded, frowning as he strode across the room. "Cassie," he inquired softly, a forbidding look on his face. "Where is the stuff you just inputted?"

Cassie punched several buttons on the computer but nothing happened. Not a thing. Everything stayed black, totally unresponsive to her panicked state.

"I don't know. I was just going along and suddenly everything went black. Did you hear that squeak it made before it died?"

"Don't punch in anything else," he ordered, turning her chair around. "Let me in, please. Don't touch that!" he yelled as she hit the reboot button once more.

Cassie scrambled out of the way, shrinking from his angry face.

"You don't have to holler," she huffed, watching him try a combination of different keystrokes. Finally the screen lit up in its usual bright blue. "You see, I didn't do anything wrong."

Jeff just kept muttering as he punched in a variety of access codes. The screen remained blank for ages while Cassie held her breath.

"Come on! Come on," he implored, fingers flying over the keys. Finally a bright white message flashed onto the monitor.

Bad file name. No such path exists.

"I don't believe this," he groaned. "Come on, baby. Where's the backup?"

No backup for that file. Do you want a search?

"Yes," he bellowed angrily. "I want you to search and find my program." He typed in another message.

No existing files. Do you wish to create a file?

Cassie stood helplessly by as he punched key after key, searching for the missing program. And as she did, she listened to his voice grow angrier by the minute.

"What did you do?" he growled finally, standing and towering over her. "Six months of work went into that program and in one fell swoop you've deleted every bit of it." His face was dark and menacing as he advanced on her retreating figure. "What did you do to my program?"

"I didn't do anything," she squeaked. "I just keyed in what you told me to type from those notes."

"The notes," he hollered, a light brightening his glowering face. He turned toward the desk and then stopped dead in his track. "My notes," she heard him whisper as he stared at the desolation in front of him.

Jonathan sat cross-legged on the floor with the small metal trash can in front of him. A plume of smoke rose from inside it as the child clapped his hands excitedly, dropping in the last bit of yellow lined paper she'd been working from.

"Look, Daddy. Garbage all gone."

"My notes," Jeff yelled, grabbing the can and blowing on the flames with gusto. Bits of ash and blackened paper fell on the carpet around them, but only one piece of the yellow paper remained. Unfortunately, Cassie saw, it was blank.

Quickly she snatched up Jonathan in case any of the ashes were still hot and held him on her hip. Jeff turned at the sudden movement, his eyes black with fury as he glared at her.

"Get that little pyromaniac out of my sight," he stormed, his teeth bared. "And do it before I warm his bottom so hot he'll never touch a match again. He's a danger to society."

"Oh, Jeff," Cassie protested hugging Jonathan close. "You don't mean that. He didn't mean…"

"Nobody seems to mean anything around here," her husband shrieked. "I get knocked out, but no one means it. My designs are ruined and you tell me you didn't mean to erase everything off my computer? Thanks a lot! For nothing!"

Cassie walked to the door and handed Jonathan to a gaping Mrs. Bennet. Then she quietly closed the door and turned to face the ranting man in front of her.

"Just calm down," she advised smoothly. "There's a way around this. There always is."

He glared at her, teeth gritting.

"Oh, really Miss Peace and Goodwill. Well, here," he thrust the rolling chair toward her. "Be my guest. Magically restore my software designs again." When she simply stared at him in amazement, he grasped her arm and led her to the desk. "Well, go ahead, lady. Wave your magic wand and make everything okay."

"Stop shouting," she ordered in her best no-nonsense voice. "There are children in this house and they deserve a calm, stable environment."

"This is my house and I'll yell all I want." He raked his hands through his hair in frustration. "There are always children around," he barked angrily. "From the moment you wake up and even after you go to bed, there are children. They squawk and bawl in the middle of the night, they muck up my clothes and they try to do me bodily injury. Yesterday I found a dog in my sock drawer."

His voice had risen proportionately with each complaint, Cassie noticed. She wondered about tossing a glass of ice water at him and then decided to tough it out. He obviously needed to blow off steam.

"Oh, that's not staying—it goes when Stevie does. I know it's been busy these past few weeks—" she began placatingly. She didn't get further.

"Busy? This place is worse than a zoo. I can't even wear my clothes anymore because they either smell of smoke or baby spit or worse." He scowled at her, eyes narrowing. "I've had three hours of sleep a night for the last three weeks and when I get up, you're prancing around dispensing peace and goodwill like some nauseatingly sweet fairy godmother. It's disgusting."

Cassie tried to swallow the smile but she just couldn't do it. Unfortunately Jeff saw it and turned on her.

"Don't you laugh," he ordered in savage tones. "Don't you dare! I've had it up to here with this nuthouse." He sank down onto the sofa and then jumped up again in agitation. "Do you know how ridiculous I felt at that parent-teacher interview? How many men do you know who are married one week and show up the next carrying a set of twins through the local high school?" He snorted. "Not to mention the mess they made!"

"They were only here overnight," Cassie reminded him. "It didn't hurt us to take them along. Anyway, I couldn't find a sitter for everyone."

"That's the problem," he shrieked, throwing his hands up. "There's never time for anybody but these kids. I thought we might spend some time together this afternoon and now look!"

Cassie sighed as her glance encompassed the messy desk, the bits of ash scattered across the floor and the look of defeat on Jeff's handsome face.

He stared at her from under his eyebrows.

"Why don't you spend a little of that boundless energy on me?" he whined sourly.

"I tried to," Cassie defended herself. "I'm not good with computers but I tried to help you out because you asked me to. I know it's been hectic and I thought that maybe if we were to work as a team on this then, well..." She nodded at the mess. "I guess it wasn't a very good idea."

"What do you mean you're not good with computers?" he asked softly, advancing to stand directly in front of her. "You do know how to type in a program, don't you, Cassandra?"

She hated it when he said her name like that—low and sort of threatening. Her chin tilted up defiantly.

"I just know how to put in exactly what you told me to. Sort of."

He gripped her elbows in his hands, forcing her to meet his flinty gaze. "Put what in where?"

"Put those squiggly things into whatever file it was in when I took over. How should I know? I'm not the computer genius. I thought it was all set up and ready to go."

Jeff let go of her and forcefully stepped backward two paces before speaking. His face was hard and set in rigid lines of fury.

"You deliberately sabotaged my program," he asserted clearly. "You sat there and tampered with something you knew nothing about purposely to ruin me."

Cassie was aghast.

"I did no such thing. Jeff, I didn't know..."

"And you have the nerve to talk about love," he snarled scathingly. "How could someone so full of *love*—" he spat the word out "—intentionally do that?"

She had held on for as long as she could; Cassie simmered furiously. There was no way she was taking this sitting down.

"If you would shut up long enough to listen to me, you'd know that I didn't do anything on purpose. I was trying to help."

"Gee," he muttered hatefully. "Don't help me anymore, okay? You'll kill me with all this kindness."

"Listen," she stressed, squeezing her fingers into tight fists. "If you weren't so self-involved you might be able to see that the people around you really do care about you. Believe it or not, we're trying to help you in spite of yourself."

"How?" he demanded silkily, leaning back on the desk. "By making my company go under?"

"I wasn't trying to do that," Cassie enunciated clearly. "I was trying to help. You know—assist, aid, support. But, you know what?" She brushed the tears from her eyes and turned toward the door. "Forget it, okay? Just forget it. You don't need anybody. You're doing just fine on your own." She pulled open the door and turned to face him.

"Tell me, Jeff," she asked softly, "if you're doing so well in this solitary world you've built for yourself, why do you need me or Rory or David or anybody? Why don't you just dump us like you dumped your parents? We're only gonna mess things up in your perfect world. You see," she swallowed the sob in her throat and spoke clearly. "That's what humans do—they make mistakes."

She stepped through the opening and pulled the door shut behind her. But not before she whispered the last words remaining on her tongue and in her heart.

"You don't need any of us, Jeff. You're much better off on your own."

Chapter Twelve

"There isn't a whole lot more that could go wrong, Robyn. We're not even speaking to each other at this point. I don't dare tell him about his mother." Cassie sighed as she took another swallow of the fresh coffee Mrs. Bennet had just made.

"Where is he now?" Robyn asked, trying to hide the smile on her lips.

"Downstairs with David. Tomorrow's the big day for their presentation, you know. They're trying a test run tonight." She made a face. "The rest of us have strict orders not to set foot in the basement. Hah! Who'd want to?"

"What, exactly, are they building?"

Cassie shrugged. "Who would know? Not me."

Robyn looked around the empty family room with curiosity. It looked sort of stark and bare without the Christmas decorations.

"Where is everyone?" she asked.

"Alyssa's gone back to her father for now. Stevie's with his grandparents. Jonathan is asleep and Marie's out with Nate." Cassie frowned. "I don't know exactly what to do about those two." She glared at her friend. "And don't say leave them alone. I'm worried about her."

"Why? Marie is a perfectly lovely girl. She loves living here with you and Jeff." Robyn grinned. "Separately," she added softly. "Anyway, she would never do anything to hurt either of you."

"It's not me I'm worried about," Cassie admitted. "It's her.

She's fifteen and she's convinced herself she is in love with Nate. She's talking about marriage, Rob. Marriage!''

"I thought you believed in marriage, Cassie.'' Robyn's tones were full of smug humor. "Doesn't look quite so rosy now, does it? Changed your mind, girl?'' She patted Cassie's knee with sympathy. "Tell Auntie Rob all about it,'' she whispered in commiseration as big fat tears rolled down Cassie's face.

"I do love him, Rob. More than I ever thought I could love anybody. And I want so much for us to be close, like a husband and wife should be.'' She sniffed, tucking her legs up under her.

"But...'' Robyn encouraged.

"But he won't let me in. He thinks love is just a silly emotion that wears thin after a while. Just when I think he might really be learning to love me, he throws a fit and shuts me out again.'' She sniffed sulkily.

"And then there's his family.'' She groaned. "I can't begin to talk to him about that. He won't even sit in the same room as me anymore let alone talk about his parents.'' Cassie blew her nose, staring into the fireplace.

"How is his mother?'' Robyn's face was sad. "Has she started the treatments, yet?''

"Uh-huh.'' Cassie nodded. "She's actually had several chemotherapies. The doctors seem quite hopeful about her chances if she can just get her spirits up. I talked to her on Monday, you know.'' Cassie swallowed another mouthful and then pushed her cup away. For some reason coffee didn't fill the same gap it once had, she decided ruefully.

"She desperately wants to settle things between Jeff and herself. And I said I'd help, but with this cold war on, what can I do?''

Robyn shook her head doubtfully. "I'm not sure it's a good idea for you to get involved, Cass. If what his father said is true, Jeff has good reason for his painful memories. You can't blame him for feeling hurt when his own father treated him like a visitor in a military academy. But he is going to have to confront it for himself. You can't do that for him.''

"I know.'' Cassie nodded. "I wish I could. And I don't have to tell you not to breathe a word of it, do I?'' A tremor of uncertainty ran through her. "If Jeff knew I had been seeing them, I think he'd be so angry he'd never forgive me. Not that he will anyway," she finished sadly.

They sat silent, staring into the fire together, each busy with their own thoughts.

"He watches you all the time, you know," Robyn told her, smiling at the sparkle that rose in her friend's eyes. "Whenever you come into the room, when he thinks you're not looking, his eyes are on you with this pathetic sort of wistful look. I think he loves you."

"I'm sure," Cassie mumbled.

"I mean it. I think he is genuinely attracted to you and wants to do something about it. He just doesn't know what yet." She patted Cassie's hand. "Give it some time, kiddo. Jefferson Haddon will come round eventually."

A sudden boom resounded through the house at that moment, shaking the pictures on the walls and rattling the dishes.

"What in the world…?" Robyn exclaimed, but she was talking to herself for Cassie was already running barefoot toward the basement door. Robyn caught up to her as she ripped the door open and bounded down the stairs.

Thick gray smoke hung in puffs in the brightly lit room. The assorted test tubes were all knocked over, gray powder spilling from some of them. Cassie, however, had eyes only for Jeff's blackened face.

"Jeff, what happened? Are you hurt? Is there a fire?" The words stopped suddenly. He grabbed her as she descended to the bottom step and swung her round and round.

"It worked," he gloated triumphantly, soot-covered face wreathed in smiles. "We actually did it. David's going to get a double A plus for this one." He grinned at her jubilantly before his lips closed over hers suddenly, drowning her response.

And Cassie did feel as if she were drowning as she exulted in his embrace. Without thinking, she wound her arms around his neck and gave herself to that kiss, wishing it could go on forever. Unfortunately, Jeff quickly came to his senses and swiftly set her down.

"Sorry," he murmured, averting his eyes. "I guess I was a

bit excited. Isn't it fantastic?'' He couldn't suppress the grin that stretched his mouth wide.

"Way to go, Dad!" David high-fived him in a complicated ritual of thumbs and fingers that gave Cassie time to regain her composure. She stared at the series of duct-taped loops, twists and turns that descended in an intricate pathway from the ceiling to the floor.

"What is this?" she asked, catching sight of several dominoes, pieces of Jonathan's plastic building set, six paper tubes and two pulley systems. There were also bits of racetrack, miles of string, marbles and a host of other articles she didn't recognize.

"It's a Rube Goldberg machine," David told her grinning. "We set it up so that once you let the marble go it takes twenty-two steps to light the firecracker that we manufactured at the other end. Each step illustrates an example of one of the principle laws of physics—like the law of gravity. Isn't it great!"

He looked so delighted with his invention that Cassie didn't have the heart to mention that his teachers surely wouldn't permit him to set off a firecracker in school. She would have never allowed him to do such a thing at home if she'd had any idea what they were up to down here.

"David, you're a genius," Robyn declared, studying the intricate machine as if she knew something about it. "How are you going to get it to school?"

As he explained his plan for transporting the fragile device, Cassie looked toward Jeff's still figure. He was staring straight at her and for once, Cassie did not avoid his eyes but held his gaze steadily, searching the dark brown depths for an answer.

"I should probably go get cleaned up," he muttered at last, glancing toward David. "We've got a lot of work to do to pack this thing up for the morning."

"Yes, I imagine so." Was this stilted conversation the way they would always converse? she wondered sadly. "David called you Dad," she remarked softly.

Jeff's face lit up with an inner glow that made him look boyish and carefree.

"I know," he admitted. His eyes held hers. "I like it."

"Well, good," she murmured, turning to move up the stairs

in order to hide the ache she was sure must be in her glance. "I'm going to make some tea if you want some. I need something hot to calm my nerves after that sonic boom."

She had only taken three steps when his hand on her arm stopped her.

"Tea, Cassandra?" he asked quizzically, his chocolate eyes melting as they moved slowly over her black leggings and long red sweater.

"Yes, tea," she breathed, loath to tear her gaze from him. "Peppermint, I think. Coffee just doesn't taste right tonight." She held her breath and asked the question uppermost in her mind. "Want to share some?"

Oblivious to the other interested spectators, Jeff lifted one hand and brushed his fingers over her smooth cheek with the lightest caress imaginable.

"Yes," he whispered. "I think I would." His eyes shone into hers. "Thank you."

"You're welcome," she answered automatically as she turned and walked up the stairs on a cloud of air. "You're very welcome."

What does it mean? Cassie wondered later that evening as she lay in bed thinking about the past hour the four of them had spent eating David's favorite chocolate cake and sipping peppermint tea in Mrs. Bennet's sparkling clean kitchen.

That strange, funny look—what does it mean? Could it be that Robyn is right for once? That my husband really is falling in love with me?

"Please, Father," she prayed softly. "If this is your will, let it happen. I love him so much."

The Bible verse she'd read this morning came back to mind just before she drifted off to sleep.

I will be with you in trouble and rescue you and honor you. I will satisfy you with a full life.

"He can't go," Jeff said in a low harsh voice. "Not now."

Cassie glanced from the young girl crouched nervously in their family room to the bulky form of Selma Bay, her social worker.

"Surely you knew that Jonathan was not intended to stay here forever, Mr. Haddon. His mother had to leave him but she is more than ready to care for him again. We have to give them every opportunity to be together, to renew their bond."

"What bond?" Cassie heard the anger in Jeff's voice. "She abandoned him to go make a hit!" His scornful eyes raked over the young girl. "She's a drug addict and heaven knows what else. How can you say she's fit to care for an innocent child like Jonathan?"

Cassie's heart ached for him. She knew how he felt. He had become Jonathan's daddy in every way but one. The months had passed so quickly. It was almost spring and now the little boy was being ripped away.

"There's no point arguing about it, Jeff," she soothed, tightening her hold on his hand in sympathy. "We only get them for a little while and during that time we try to do whatever we can for them. Then we have to let them go and let God take over."

"And where was He when she—" he jutted one finger at Jonathan's mom "—left him alone?" He turned to the social worker and glared. "How do you know she won't do it again?"

The girl burst into tears.

"I won't. You have to believe me, I won't. I've spent weeks now worrying and wondering about him while I've been in treatment." She swiped a hand across her eyes and met his angry gaze head-on. "I never even knew I'd left him alone," she admitted tearfully. "I needed a fix so bad I couldn't think of anything else."

Jeff's dark eyes raked over her scornfully. "So what's changed?" he demanded.

"If Lisa leaves him again, Mr. Haddon, the courts will consider taking Jonathan away on a permanent basis." Selma looked sternly at the rake thin form of the young mother. "This is your last chance, Lisa. Jonathan needs his mama but if you can't handle it, we have to find someone who can."

Lisa stood and walked over in front of Jeff. Her voice was soft but full of courage.

"I want to thank you and Cassie, Mr. Haddon. I know you've

taken good care of Jonathan for me.'' Her voice dropped. ''And I can see that you really care about him. But so do I.''

Cassie watched Jeff's eyes harden to pieces of black coal.

''Prove it,'' he said at last. ''Give him to me. I can take care of him, give him the things he needs.''

''Oh, Jeff, no,'' Cassie cried, but it was all in her mind. She knew there was nothing she could say to remove that look of misery from his hard, bitter features.

Jonathan came racing through the door then on his fat stubby legs. He stopped short at the sight of the thin, tear-faced girl on the sofa.

''Mama,'' he cried, holding out his arms and running toward her happily. ''Hi, Mama.''

Cassie watched as Lisa swung her son high up in the air and down into her arms. She hung on tearfully, kissing his cheeks and his hair as she slid her hands over his soft, pudgy body.

''Oh, baby! Mommy's so glad to see you. Are you all right? Did you miss me?'' Lisa's voice was filled with love as Cassie watched the young woman's eyes beam down on her son.

''I got a new truck, Mama. Daddy buyed it for me.'' Jonathan grinned at Jeff brightly, but when his 'daddy' didn't grin back, he climbed down from his mother's lap and scurried over to pull on Jeff's pantleg with one sticky hand. ''Daddy sick?'' he asked softly, pressing his head against the black wool pants.

Cassie rose and went over to Jeff, picking up Jonathan in one arm and then wrapping her other arm around her husband's waist as she spoke to the little boy.

''No, sweetie. Daddy's not sick. He's just a little bit sad that you're going home with Mommy. Remember we talked about that?'' Jonathan nodded. ''Daddy loves you very much, you know, and he's glad that your mommy's going to look after you.''

Jonathan nodded again, sinking his head onto Jeff's shoulder. Cassie felt his weight lift as Jeff took the little boy into his own arms.

''I wuv Daddy, and I wuv Mama, and I wuv Cassie.'' He beamed as he pressed a big smack against Jeff's cheek. ''Daddy doesn't like matches,'' he informed his mother. ''I sorry.''

He looked mournful and Cassie decided they'd had enough

sadness. A child returning to his family should be a happy event. At least for the child.

"I know you are, darling," she reassured him. "But I'm very happy you're going back to your own house with Mommy. She's all better now but she needs her little Jonny-boy to hug her at nighttime and read stories to her and kiss her good-night. Do you think you can do that?" she asked softly.

"But I want Daddy to come to my house," Jonathan sniffed on the verge of tears.

"I can't, Jonathan. I have to stay here and help Cassie with the other boys and girls that come for a visit." Jeff's voice came at last, low and gravelly, but he held on to his control. His eyes were huge pools of sadness as they gazed at Jonathan.

Cassie felt her own throat clog as she watched the two size each other up.

"Okay," Jonathan agreed at last. He scrambled down and went to sit on his mother's lap. "Will I come to visit again, Mama?"

Cassie broke in before anyone could say anything.

"You have to come and visit Jonathan. Every week. Daddy will need to make sure you're eating all your vegetables." Her eyes shone as she watched Jeff kneel down beside the little boy.

"And you remember, no playing with matches. They hurt people. And no ice, either." She noticed Jeff's hand shake.

"I know." Jonathan smiled his generous wide smile at them all. "Jonny's a good boy," he crowed.

Quickly, Lisa bundled him into his new winter jacket and pulled his tuque on his head. Cassie stopped her as Jeff carried the little boy to the car.

"Lisa, please bring Jonathan for a visit soon. We're going to miss him so much and we'd like to keep in touch. Please?"

"They really bonded, didn't they?" Lisa smiled as she watched her son kiss Jeff's rough cheek. "I can see your husband is a very loving man. Congratulations. We'll be around next week and every week after that until you're tired of us." She squeezed Cassie's hand. "Thank you," she whispered as the tears flowed down her cheeks. "Thank you for caring for my baby."

"You're welcome, but now it's your job," Cassie answered, watching Jeff stride back toward the house. "Don't let us down."

"I won't."

They stood together for a long time after the car rounded the bend, staring at the empty, barren landscape. Winter's end always seemed so lifeless, Cassie decided. Dead and dirty and worn as it waited for new life to spring. She felt Jeff move and turned to go inside the house with him.

"Don't ever do that again," Jeff ordered in a hard cold tone.

Cassie wheeled around in surprise. "Do what?"

"Don't bring another child into this house and expect me to look after it, care for it and then hand it over when the time is up." He moved jerkily toward the study.

"Jeff?"

He stopped but refused to face her. Cassie prayed for the right words to ease his turmoil.

"That's exactly what my work is all about. I only have the children for a short time—an interval in their lives. I know that. It's why I try to pour as much love and caring in their little hearts as I can. Hopefully it makes them stronger and better equipped to face the future."

The silence yawned between them starkly, full of pain and torment.

"He called me Daddy," she heard him whisper, heartbroken.

Cassie moved silently over behind him and placed her hand gently on his shoulder. Jeff flinched but did not move away.

"And to him that's who you are. So be there for Jonathan whenever he needs you. Let yourself be his refuge, his touchstone of stability in a mixed-up life."

He turned to face her and Cassie felt her heart shrink at the awful agony in his dark eyes.

"I can't," he groaned. "It hurts too much."

She reached up and cupped his cheek with her hand, smiling gently as she tried to ease his sorrow.

"Then focus on the happy times you had together. Fix your mind on the wonderful things you gave to Jonathan at a time when he most needed you." She smoothed his dark hair back, speaking gently as she caressed his face. "Remember the way he looked at you with that great big grin, and those funny little hugs he insisted upon. And know that you gave that security of trust to him, Jeff. Treasure those memories and be prepared to be there when he needs you again.''

Jeff straightened at that, drawing himself rigidly erect as he glared down at her.

''And he will need me again, won't he? He'll be abandoned again, left out in the cold or something worse.'' He scowled at her fiercely. ''Why, Cassie? You tell me why he should have to leave here and go back to that kind of a life with a woman like that. Tell me why?''

Cassie breathed a prayer even as the words slipped through her lips.

''Because Lisa is his mother, Jeff. She's his mother.''

His smoldering embittered eyes tore at her heart. Suddenly he wheeled away from her and strode out of the room. Cassie barely heard him speak.

''I thought he was mine,'' he whispered on an agonized sigh. ''He should be my son.''

''Yes! Yes! Yeees!'' Cassie thrust her arms toward the heavens in a yell that brought Mrs. Bennet running up the stairs at top speed.

''Is everything all right, Miss Cassie?'' The older woman's chest heaved with her sudden exertion as she stared at her mistress with a frown. She rubbed her apron over her glasses before settling them back on her nose.

''Everything is absolutely, positively, fantastically glorious.'' Cassie laughed, grasping her by the hands and dancing her around the room.

Jeff came striding into her bedroom moments later to find the two of them laughing hilariously as they flopped onto the side of the bed. His eyes widened in shocked disbelief as he gaped at the two of them.

''Uh, is there a problem here?'' he asked slowly.

Cassie burst into fresh paroxysms of laughter and bounced across the room, standing before him huffing and puffing.

''Today,'' she announced giggling, ''there will be no problems at Oak Bluff.''

"Oh?" He quirked one dark eyebrow curiously. "And that is because…"

"That is because…" Cassie dragged the moment out for all it was worth. "Because Bored Boris and I have just landed an interview with an editor who likes my work and wants to talk to me about a possible publishing date!" She let the rest of it flow out in a rush, too excited to hold back as she grinned up at him. "Isn't that fantastic?"

"Congratulations," he said, staring down at her. "You've worked hard for this."

"Yes, but it's such an opportunity," she babbled, not even noticing Mrs. Bennet had left until the door closed behind her. "Just listen to this, Jeff." Cassie sank onto the side of the bed and sighed.

"They had a children's book slated for publishing in October but the work hasn't yet been completed or they don't like it or something. Anyway—" she beamed "—mine is finished and the woman said they really want to use it."

"So what comes next?" Jeff asked, sitting on the velvet chair she kept in the corner. "Do you have to hire a lawyer or something?"

His face creased in a frown as he stared at the assortment of small pictures decorating the walls. Cassie saw his eyes rest on Jonathan's snapshot for several moments before he jerked his head away.

"Well, not quite yet." Cassie laughed, pretending she hadn't seen the slash of pain cross his face. "I'm supposed to go in Monday for a conference." She danced a little jig at the excitement of it, stopping suddenly as she noticed his clothing.

"Where in the world did you get those?" she gasped, staring at the same ragged jeans and tattered shirt he'd worn to the wiener roast so long ago. "Don't tell me you kept them all this time?"

His face flushed as he glanced down at himself.

"I didn't, Bennet did. He resurrected them when I started building the playhouse."

Cassie frowned. "You are building a playhouse," she repeated, unable to picture it. "Where?"

"By the creek, in the elbow of that big old oak tree. It's a fantastic setting.'' His face lit up with excitement as he spoke, Cassie noticed. ''Come on, I'll show you.''

He held out his hand companionably and there was no way she was going to refuse such an offer, Cassie decided happily. Wasn't this just what she'd been praying for—time to spend with her husband? An opportunity to open up the lines of communication once more? A chance to get closer?

They strolled through the lawns and gardens to the back of the property where a bubbling little creek roiled past. Everything looked fresh and green, sprouting with life in the warm spring sunshine.

''Isn't it wonderful how much difference a few weeks can make?'' Cassie sighed, breathing deeply of the fresh, fragrant air. ''It seems like only yesterday it was Christmas.''

''That's because you and Boris have been buried in the library,'' Jeff teased. He held out his hands. ''Ta-da!''

Cassie stared at the lopsided structure tilting forward crazily from the boughs of a sturdy oak. The tree seemed the most secure thing about Jeff's tree house as it swayed in the gentle breeze, but she wasn't going to admit that.

''It looks very nice,'' she offered generously, patting one new board suspended from the base. ''Did you do all this by yourself?'' she asked curiously.

''Well, Bennet helped me with the floor,'' he told her stamping on that part firmly. ''But the rest I did myself.'' He swung down and barely missed scraping his head on the jagged end of a protruding two-by-four.

''I see.'' Cassie peered intently at the firmly anchored floor. Bennet, she decided, must have a better grasp of construction methods.

''Look out,'' she heard him yell and then felt herself pulled sharply back from the tree. A board which moments ago had formed the top section of the window, toppled to the ground a mere six inches from their bodies.

Jeff lay on the ground facing her. ''Are you all right?'' he wheezed, breathless from their sudden tumble.

''I think so.'' Cassie giggled, brushing off her shirt and jeans.

He sat up, hugging his knees to his chest as he stared at his work. ''I just can't seem to get the nails to stay put,'' he told her seriously. "And just when I think I've got one part of the thing stable, something else comes loose." His dark head tipped to one side as he considered the problem.

"Can I help?" she offered, trying to hide her smile. It was obvious that tree house construction was not Jefferson Haddon's best hobby. In fact, the whole thing reminded her of a edifice built by preteenage boys in her hometown years ago.

He stared down at her for a moment and then shook his head.

"No, thanks. I want to do this myself, with my own hands. You see," he explained, his head averted from her, "I always wanted a tree house when I was a kid. I thought it would be so wonderful for Rory and I to have our own little place where we wouldn't bother anyone."

"And did you get it?" she inquired softly.

"We tried." He grimaced, standing to dust off his pants. His face was hard and bitter. "My father had it torn down and hauled away. He said it ruined the value of the property and the look of the trees."

"Well, it's certainly hidden away back here," Cassie observed, glancing through the dancing leaves overhead to the bright clear sky. "You have to really look to even find it."

"I know." His chest puffed with pride. "That's why I chose this place. It's kind of like—" he paused, thinking. "Oh, I don't know. The secret garden, maybe. A secluded little oasis for kids to come and think things over." His eyes were fixed on something far away in his imagination that no one else could see.

"What kids?" Cassie probed gently watching his stare swivel and focus on her. "Kids like Jonathan who come to us for a break?" she murmured softly.

His shadowy eyes searched hers as he stood beside her. Cassie felt the tension melt away between them as his mouth curved in a tiny mocking smile.

"Or our own kids," he amended speculatively, his eyes lighting up as she flushed a bright pink. "They might enjoy a picnic out here or a place to play their music as loud as they want. Hey!" His face brightened. "Maybe we could send David out here with his boom box."

Cassie let the moment stretch between them, waiting for him

to make the first move. Her heart thudded with love as she stared into his dear face. How she wanted him to love her! She ached for that special closeness that she knew could grow between them. If only he would let go and let love in.

As he made his way over to the pile of lumber stacked haphazardly nearby, she felt a pang of regret for what could be. And wasn't now. But she wasn't giving up, she told herself. God had sent her to Judith, given her a chance to stay in Oak Bluff and continue her work. Surely He hadn't done all that to leave her alone, aching for a love that would never be?

"Jeff," she said hesitantly. "Soon Marie and David will legally be our children. Are you ready for that?" He turned to examine her with a questioning look.

"It will be permanent, Jeff. For the rest of our lives. There won't be any going back. Are you ready to commit to that? Can you accept that they'll grow and change and move away from us whether we want it or not?" She hesitated. "Can you love them and let them go?"

He studied his boots as she spoke, giving them an intense scrutiny she knew they didn't merit. When at last he lifted his head, she studied his serious face.

"I don't know," he said. "David and I, we're very close and he means more to me than I ever thought he would. But love?" He pressed the drooping curls off her forehead and cupped her chin in his hand. "I don't know if I can do that."

It should have depressed her and yet Cassie found herself full of hope. For the first time Jeff hadn't openly denied love's existence. He'd merely said he didn't know if he could deal with it. That was all right because she had more than enough faith for both of them.

"That's okay," she said, holding his hand between two of hers. "Caring enough to give them a home and a future is a start. We'll take it one day at a time."

His lips joined hers in a seal of promise that left her heart fluttering madly. Thank you, thank you, thank you, her heart whispered fervently as she relaxed in the warm comforting circle of his arms. Just keep your spirit working in him.

"Can I help you build?" she asked when he finally moved

away to pick up his hammer once more. She flushed at the mocking grin on his face.

"Do you know any more about building tree houses than you do about baking?" he asked, tongue in cheek, his eyes flicking over her shining eyes.

"Well, no," she admitted. "I've never built anything before." An idea surfaced and she giggled with delight. "I am quite good at painting, though," she offered.

He sauntered over to her and flicked an amused finger across her cheek before bending to kiss her cheek.

"Especially dinosaurs and dragons." He grinned. "Okay, when I'm done this thing—" he jerked a thumb backward at the odd assortment of boards "—you can paint it. Anything but pink," he qualified. "Is it a deal?"

Cassie thrust out her hand. "Deal," she agreed happily.

Jeff worked all Friday evening at the tree house. Cassie ventured out several times but found very little progress in the construction, although his stock of nails and pristine lumber had seemed to diminish rapidly.

He came in three times on Saturday. The first time Cassie nearly lost her breakfast at the gash on his head.

"It's nothing," he muttered. "Just a little cut."

"But how on earth did you get it?" she demanded, dabbing the damp towel gently against his black hair as she tried to staunch the blood. He winced at the sting of the antiseptic, jaw tightly clenched.

"One of the boards didn't stay exactly where I put it," he told her. Cassie watched in the mirror as his eyes narrowed. "I think the nails they sold me are an inferior grade," he complained suspiciously. "They don't seem to hold at all."

She averted her face and mumbled a reply.

"By the way," he said, hesitating on his way out. "I think we should celebrate your success. Let's go out for dinner tonight, someplace fancy." He glanced around. "Are the kids away?"

Somewhat amazed, Cassie agreed.

"Yes, they're both on school trips for the weekend, remember." She stared at him. "What time were you thinking of?"

He thought for a moment, studying her relaxed figure in the slim blue jeans and matching shirt.

"We should leave around seven," he said matter-of-factly. "I thought we might go to that new play at the Pantages after dinner."

"Fine." She stared after his disappearing figure with shock widening her eyes. A date—they were going on a date. Just the two of them.

"Cassie, do you know where there are another pair of gloves I can use?" That was the second time; right after lunch.

She looked up from her watercolor sketch of the patio and stared at the single glove he wore on his left hand.

"I thought you had a brand-new pair on this morning," she frowned, trying to remember. For some reason his face grew red at that.

"They were new. But now I need another pair."

Bennet came through for them, digging out a shabby, threadbare pair of gardening gloves from the shed.

"May I help you, Mr. Jefferson, sir?" he offered hesitantly, his eyes widening at the grass stains and tears covering Jeff's already filthy garments. "Two often make the load lighter."

"No, no. Thanks, Bennet," Jeff waved airily. "But I want to do this myself. And please call me Jeff," he replied. Cassie grinned as she heard her stiff, formal husband casually use the nickname she'd given him last fall. It seemed a long time ago now.

The third time he came in, Jefferson Haddon was steaming mad.

"I'm going back to that ridiculous lumber yard and demand they replace this second-rate material with the premier grade I paid for," he stated angrily. His eyes blazed into hers. "Is it okay if I take your car? Bennet's cleaning mine for tonight."

"Of course," Cassie said, clearing her throat. "It's almost five, though."

"I know," he called over his shoulder. "I'll be quick."

Once he'd driven down the driveway, Cassie gave in to the urge and walked out to see the progress he'd made. As she stared at the mess of broken and multinailed boards, her mouth curved in amusement. It was obvious that Jeff had tried very hard to create something. She just wasn't sure what it was.

Oddly cut lengths of lumber hung here and there at strange angles forming a sort of peekaboo wall that wouldn't have stopped a flea. One white glove was nailed between two boards and that was the only solid nail Cassie found. She walked around the entire thing several times, without finding the entrance.

"Probably best if you don't go up, Miss Cassie," Bennet suggested from behind her, his face held in its usual stern facade. "I don't believe Mr. Jefferson has quite completed his work."

He pressed a hand on one wall which immediately dismantled before their eyes. Cassie could see the marks of nails which had been partially pounded in and then removed. There were innumerable amounts of the shiny green nails all over the ground, partially hidden in the grass. She picked several up. They were bent, most had their heads flattened. None could be used again.

"Begging your pardon, Miss Cassie, but I don't believe the children will be safe playing in such a thing unless some changes are made." Bennet cleared his throat as they stared at the short, rough-cut ends that were nailed fan style to the side of the oak tree.

Cassie grinned at the older man when he pointed to the pile of splintered and now totally unusable clean white spruce headers that had been hacked into a useless mass lying in a heap by the creek bank. On top Jeff had written, Firewood.

"It might not hurt to get Jonathan down for a visit," she agreed, laughing. "He could light the place on fire. But not now. I don't want Jeff to know we've been here. It was a good idea. Just leave it for now."

"As you wish," he agreed, walking back beside her. "But I do hope the next group of children that come to Oak Bluff don't find it until it's been, er, reinforced."

The smile left Cassie's lips.

"There won't be any more," she whispered sadly. "Jeff won't allow it."

"I'm sure he'll change his mind, my dear," he told her,

giving her a gentle pat of commiseration on the shoulder. "He'll begin to miss them as much as we do."

"Thank you, Bennet." Cassie smiled tearfully. "And may I say how much I've appreciated Mrs. Bennet's and your help these past months. I know it has been rather unusual for you to have so many children here."

"Mrs. Bennet and I have never enjoyed ourselves more." Bennet smiled widely. "It's the little ones, you see. We never had any of our own and Mrs. Bennet dearly loves children." He grinned. "Spoils them rotten, she does."

"So do you." Cassie grinned back. With a return of sadness, Cassie thrust away pangs of mourning for her loss. The children would come back. After all, it was only temporary. It had to be. Carefully she began preparations for the evening ahead. An evening with just the two of them.

Is this what you want, Lord? A time for Jeff and me to relax with each other? Alone. It was a scary thought for a woman who was as much in love as Cassandra Haddon was with her husband. Would she give herself away? Would he realize that she loved him and feel embarrassed by it?

Cassie tossed the thoughts out of her mind and concentrated on what to wear. She wanted to look her best after months of caring for small children without a moment to herself. Tonight she intended to make up for all that slovenliness and wow him with pizzazz.

She only wished she had been given more notice. Cassie grimaced as she stared at the clothes in her huge closet. If a wife only got one chance, she should make the most of it.

Chapter Thirteen

Cassie was curled up in the sunroom enjoying the last weak rays of the spring sun when her husband finally came through the door. He was covered from head to toe in mud, but his face wore a huge grin.

"Sorry," he apologized. "I got a flat tire and had to change it on Cordouvan Road. It hasn't dried up there yet and some kids splashed me." He swung around, his brown eyes opening into huge round 0s as he stared at her in her finery.

"Wow!"

She stood and curtsied, enjoying the look of admiration on his surprised face. She'd chosen a silk vest and matching pants in palest peach with an even paler chiffon blouse underneath. In her ears were the diamond studs he'd given to her and a thin gold chain hung around her neck. Her only other jewelry was the delicate gold bracelet Jeff had presented to her on Christmas night.

Cassie glowed as his eyes widened at the black hair she had piled on her head. It had grown longer over the past few months and she'd only managed the intricate style with Robyn's help.

"Ten minutes," he promised grinning and raced up the stairs like a boy to a baseball game.

Actually it was closer to twenty but Cassie didn't mind. It gave her time to practise in the spindly spikes Robyn had persuaded her to buy with the suit.

"They match perfectly and so does that bag. And they're on sale."

Cassie stumbled haphazardly over the thick plush carpet and prayed that wherever they were going she wouldn't land on her face. Or her rear.

"Are you sure you want to spend another night with those things on your feet?" Jeff stared at the strappy leather sandals suspiciously. "Aren't they a little, er, extreme?"

"On purpose," she told him glowering. "They give me height. And when you're this short you need all the height you can get."

"I think you look perfect, with or without stilts." He grinned. He held out one black-clad arm. "Shall we, Mrs. Haddon?"

Cassie drew in a breath of air for courage and linked her arm through his. "We shall, Mr. Haddon." She whispered a prayer as he escorted her into his gleaming car. *Lord, please…*

Jeff wanted it to be an evening of laughter and fun. The restaurant was very haute elegance and he hoped Cassie would enjoy it. It was certainly a change from the places they'd taken the children and he watched her eyes grow huge as she stared at the beautiful crystal and shimmering silverware. He suddenly realized that her lack of pretence and sophistication didn't matter anymore. He felt comfortable with this woman wherever they were.

A number of people stopped by their table to speak with him, obviously curious about Cassie. He introduced her proudly, pleased with the way she spoke to each. A surprised Melisande stopped dead in the middle of her grand entrance to stare at them openmouthed.

"Jefferson, my dear. Had I known you would be dining here tonight…" Her voice died away as Cassie spoke up.

"How wonderful to see you again, Miss Gustendorf. Jeff and I have been intending to have everyone over again one evening but things have been so hectic."

He felt like crowing with delight. At last, Cassie was assuming her position as his wife. He wondered how far this new bravery extended.

"May I join you?" Mel asked, motioning for a waiter.

Jeff choked on his ice water. No way, he decided. Not tonight. But Cassie was way ahead of him.

"Oh, I'm so sorry, Miss Gustendorf." She shook her head imperceptibly at the waiter. "But Jeff and I are celebrating a special occasion tonight. Just the two of us. Aren't we, dear?"

Her fingers closed lovingly around his and Jeff held on. It was the first time in ages she had touched him of her own accord and he savored the sensation.

"Yes, darling," he murmured. "A very special occasion." He kissed her fingers softly and folded them back into his own.

"Celebrating what?" Melisande demanded rudely. "Taking on yet another homeless child?" Her tone was spiteful and Jeff watched Cassie flinch.

"Well," he murmured softly, staring her down until her face reddened. "That would be something to celebrate but this is much more personal. You see…"

Cassie's voice cut across his.

"Jeff! Darling," she admonished, covering her surprise. "It's a secret." She smiled at the interloper. "We're not telling anyone just yet."

Melisande's spiteful blue eyes opened wide as she stared at Cassie in disgust.

"Don't tell me…" Her voice was full of disdain.

"Oh, we won't," Cassie replied. She smiled intimately at Jeff, who leaned back in his chair and let her do the work. "We'll share it for just a while more before we tell the world."

Jeff motioned to the waiter surreptitiously. In microseconds the black jacketed youngster was at Mel's elbow.

"Your table is ready, madame."

With one last malevolent dagger-piercing glare, Mel slinked off to her own table. Jeff watched as Cassie snapped her napkin into her lap and sipped her fruit punch mixture.

"Old nosey parker," she muttered angrily. Her eyes glared at Jeff as he sat there grinning.

He pretended to clap. "Bravo, Mrs. Haddon. You are a very good defense for a poor helpless male."

Cassie blushed and then burst out laughing.

"I'm sorry," she apologized. "I shouldn't have done that." Her eyes were downcast as she refused to meet his. "She'll probably go around telling the world that I'm pregnant, you know."

Jeff nodded calmly. "Probably," he agreed. He lowered his voice to ask the next question. "Would that bother you?"

He watched as she stared off into space, the lights of the lovely crystal chandelier reflecting in the emerald depths of her eyes. Her whole face softened tenderly as he watched.

"Cassandra," he murmured finally, and watched her eyes move back to him hazily. He didn't need to ask anymore, Jeff decided. From the look on her face, he knew exactly how she felt about having her own children to care for.

"Hmm," she whispered softly, still half involved in her daydream as she looked at him.

Jeff moved over to stand behind her.

"I asked if you wanted to dance," he drawled into the smooth shell of her ear.

As Jeff guided her around the tiny floor to the light, delicate notes on the piano, he wondered at the beauty of his wife. They had been married for, let's see. His eyes opened wide.

Four months! And in four months this was the first time he'd held her for any length of time. His hand pressed on her back, coaxing her a little nearer as he caught the faint hint of her perfume. It was a light, delicate scent that seemed to cling to her. The smell of flowers but with an underlying hint of spice.

"I like your perfume," he whispered, allowing his lips to move slowly down the curve of her neck. "What is it?"

"Soap," she murmured, smiling into his shirtfront.

"Oh." His fingers smoothed over the sheer sleeve of her blouse to the bracelet he'd given her. "Well, I like it anyway."

"Thank you." It was a whisper and he watched as she closed her black lashes and swayed against him to the music.

"You have beautiful hair," he told her, fingering the tendril that lay against her long smooth neck. "So soft and shiny. It looks like sable."

Cassie tilted her head back to peer at him with amusement. "You're comparing me to an animal." She chuckled. "That's original."

They moved several more steps together before he heard her whisper into his ear.

"It's all held up by hair spray. If you touch it, it will come down."

He grinned, tightening his hold on her narrow waist as he nestled her against himself.

"I'm not touching your hair," he avowed softly as his fingers curved round her waist. Her wide-eyed stare acknowledged the truth with a tiny shiver. Jeff felt it to his toes. And was blissfully happy.

At least she wasn't indifferent to him.

He heard her soft musical voice through a fog.

"Jeff?"

"Yes, my…" He caught himself in time, glancing down to peer into her face. "What is it, Cassie?"

"Could we sit down now?" she asked plaintively.

A wave of frustration hit him as he realized she wanted to get away from him, wanted to break this wonderful contact they had finally achieved.

"Certainly," he agreed harshly, drawing away as his arms fell to his sides.

She leaned over, wrapping her fingers in his as she whispered softly, "My feet are killing me."

Jeff grinned and slid his arm back around her waist.

"I did warn you." He smirked, suddenly thrilled with life. "Vanity, thy name is woman."

"Hah!" She glared at him, glee sparkling in those turbulent green depths. "And I suppose you wear that bow tie because you like being trussed up?"

They sparred laughingly all through the delicious meal of salmon steaks and fresh spring potatoes. Jeff noticed Cassie eyeing the dessert cart and looked at his watch with regret.

"We'll miss the opening curtain if we stay too much longer," he advised softly.

"Maybe later," Cassie agreed. "I'm satisfyingly satiated now anyway." As he drove to the theater she studied him oddly. "What is this show we're going to see?" she asked curiously.

Jeff grinned as he guided her inside the theater.

"Afraid of my taste," he teased.

"I think your taste is wonderful," she told him seriously. "You always seem to know exactly the right thing to say and do."

"Thank you, although I think you're flattering me just to get dessert." He chose to make it a joke rather than dwell on what, exactly, she meant. Besides, he might be way off base tonight. "It's a return of *The Phantom of the Opera*," he told her, watching her face for a response. "You've probably seen it before but…"

"No, I haven't, but only because I've never been able to get here when it was on," she cried, clasping his arm in delight. "How wonderful! Thank you."

She was an appreciative audience, Jeff decided later. She had laughed and cried and clutched his arm at intervals throughout the musical production. And as the end neared, she only snuggled a bit nearer when he dared to wrap his arm around her shoulders.

After the houselights came up, Jeff smiled as she pawed through her tiny leather bag for a tissue.

"I'm sorry," she sniffed. "I'm such a mess. It really was a great show."

"Come on." He smiled soothingly, folding her hand in his. "Let's go have dessert."

Her wide eyes more than made up for his efforts, Jeff decided later as they sat by a window at the top of the CN Tower watching the brightly lit Toronto skyline slowly revolve past.

"This is excellent," she proclaimed, closing her eyes to fully savor the texture and flavor of her cappuccino cheesecake.

Jeff grinned. He might have known she would choose a coffee-flavored dessert, he decided. Coffee was like a trademark with her. As if on cue, the waiter returned with her espresso cup once more.

"Are you sure you won't try this?" she cajoled, sipping the rich potent brew.

"Cassie, you know very well that coffee and I do not mix." He flicked his finger toward her empty plate. "And I daresay there was enough caffeine in that to put me on a high for a week. I don't know how you can pack away that much and not be up at least all night."

She tipped her head back and smiled. "I believe they do have decaf," she said, staring out at the sparkling night lights. "Thank you for a wonderful evening," she murmured, staring at him with a soft wide-open look. "It was a fantastic way to celebrate. Although, technically—" she giggled "—I'm not sure if I have anything to celebrate."

Jeff closed his hand around hers and squeezed. He felt a gentle protectiveness for this small delicate creature that urged him to shield her from the problems of the world. What would she say, he mused, if he kissed her. Later on. At home. In the dark?

"You'll do it," he assured her. "If anyone can do it, you can. And when you sign that contract, we'll celebrate again. Is it a deal?"

She stared at him silently for a moment.

"Yes," she whispered at last. "It's a deal."

It was a quiet drive home. Neither of them felt inclined to talk and Jeff was content to ride along in the smoothly purring car with her hand threaded in his. As they pulled into the driveway and he helped her out, Cassie stood staring at the starlit sky.

"It was wonderful way up there in the tower," she murmured, eyes huge as she gazed at him. "But I think we have the best view of God's heaven right here." Her hand lifted up and Jeff followed it, hugging her close in the cool air as they stared at the constellations.

"Maybe you're right," he replied finally, lowering his eyes to stare into hers. "But I think I've got the brightest new star right here."

Slowly, tenderly, he drew her close and wrapped both arms around her snugly.

"I'm going to kiss you," he whispered. "Any objections?"

Cassie shifted just a bit, sliding one arm around his waist and the other over his shoulder to touch his hair.

"Just one," she answered so softly he had to bend his head to hear. "What took you so long?"

Jeff stared, unable to believe he'd heard it. Cassie actually *wanted* him to kiss her? Had even been waiting? He laughed at the absurdity of it. Talk about mixed signals!

"What's so funny?" Cassie complained, tilting her head back to study him. She had to look way up because she had long since removed her heels in the car.

Jeff grinned.

"All you had to do was ask," he stated dryly. Her fingers nudged his head a little lower.

"I'm asking," she confided.

"I'm kissing," he whispered back. And proceeded to do just that.

"Oh what a beautiful mooorning. Oooh what a beautiful day!" Cassie slipped on her new silk stockings with a smug little curve to her lips. "I've got a wonderful husband—I wish he would make up his mind."

She smiled at the little poem. Very little, she decided wryly. Stick to kids' stories, Cassie, she told herself. Robert Louis Stevenson you will never be.

It felt good to know that Jeff had as much difficulty pulling away from her as she had from him Saturday night. And yesterday they had spent the entire day together; attending church, picnicking in the park with Robyn and her friend and later bicycling to the ice-cream store for a treat. All in all, the weekend had been a giant step forward in their, well, unusual relationship. Best of all, Jeff hadn't uttered one single protest when the social worker had dropped by unexpectedly last night with two preschool children. He'd merely helped her bathe and prepare them for bed, a funny little smile curving his lips.

And today, wonder of wonders, she was actually going to talk to someone about publication of her book. Publication! Her heart rate accelerated at the thought.

She slipped the silk blouse Jeff had given her for Christmas over her shoulders and buttoned it up with a gleam in her eyes. The man had taste, she decided.

"Cassie?" A rap of knuckles alerted her to Jeff's presence outside her door. Good heavens, she hoped he hadn't heard her singing. She cringed.

"Just a second," she answered, zipping up the creamy wool skirt of her suit. Yes, she told herself jubilantly. Smart, elegant, not too dressy.

"Good morning!" She tugged the door open and found him standing on her doorstep. Her eyes widened at the delicate purple blue irises he held out.

"For good luck," he told her. "With my best wishes."

"Thank you!" Cassie leaned over to press her lips against his cheek and found his mouth pressed against hers instead.

"Now that's how we say 'good morning' in this house," he teased, grinning at the flush of color in her cheeks.

"I'll have to remember that when I see Bennet," she retorted smartly. She twirled in front of him. "Do I look all right?"

"You're not wearing those, are you?" Jeff's dark eyes remained fixed dourly on her pale spiky high heels. "I thought you'd learned your lesson about those ridiculous shoes."

Cassie frowned.

"I need the height," she told him seriously. "I want to look professional and businesslike."

"You look great," he told her sincerely. "Knock 'em dead."

"Thanks." Cassie beamed up at him, willing her heart to slow down its ridiculous pace.

"Well, uh, I've got to get going." He turned to leave and then glanced over his shoulder. "Phone and tell me how it went," he said. "I'd like to know."

Cassie smiled softly. "I will," she promised.

Monday mornings were always the pits for traffic on the 401 into Toronto. It seemed that no one took public transportation on that particular day of the week.

"Including me," she muttered, grinning in spite of herself.

For the hundredth time, her glance moved over her portfolio as she checked to be sure her drawings were intact. They sat there, just as they had five minutes ago, waiting for her proud presentation.

Cassie thought once more of Jeff's thoughtful gift. Even now the flowers lay beside her on the seat, filling the car with their faint odor.

He'd remembered that irises were her favorite. She grinned to herself. After all this time, he'd still remembered. What a guy!

She pressed the accelerator to ease past a semi when the steering suddenly jerked to one side.

Not now, she prayed fiercely. Please not now.

But apparently the car didn't hear, for it veered drastically as she tried to stay in her own lane. Slowly, carefully, she signaled right and eased past the other vehicles into the caution lane. Her heart sank as she stared at the flattened tire on the driver's side.

"Why today?" She moaned. She knew a tow truck wouldn't make it through until well after the throng of cars had dissipated. There was nothing for it but to change the tire herself.

She wished desperately for the trench coat she'd left at home, even though the temperature was well above twenty degrees Celsius. It would at least have protected the cream-colored fabric of her suit.

"There is absolutely no point groaning about it, kid," she told herself, lifting out the jack. She might just as well spend her time working.

It took a little over fifteen minutes to work the tire free and the effort cost her four fingernails. Thankfully she had a spare pair of panty hose, Cassie thought glancing down and grimacing. The ones she had on were history. Sweat beaded her brow as she rolled the mulish tire to the rear of her car. She just knew her makeup would be a write-off.

Five more minutes lapsed while she strove to figure out just exactly how one undid the carpet covering the spare and lift it out of the trunk. With a grunt of satisfaction Cassie finally lugged the tire free and whooshed a sigh of relief as it thunked on the ground.

"Thank goodness," she groaned, rolling it along. That was when she noticed the huge grease mark across her skirt. Her heart sank as she realized there was no way she could disguise it. Her only hope lay in arriving early enough to make a quick purchase someplace near her appointment, she decided, glancing once more at her watch. She brushed her hand across her face and realized that she had just smeared the black sticky stuff from the hub all over herself.

"Oh, Lord, I need help," she prayed, shoving the wheel into place with a sudden burst of energy. She had almost finished fastening the last nut when she noticed the time. "I really need help," she thought again, whisking the tire iron round once more. There was mud all over her clothes and grease covering her hands, but Cassie ignored it as she rushed. Quick as a wink she had the jack down and out and was walking around the fender when she noticed the tire.

It was absolutely flat! How in the...

Like a movie camera, her mind rolled the film of Jeff arriving home on Saturday. "I had a flat," he'd said.

Anger, white-hot and steaming rose in her as she realized just what this meant to her future career. She would miss her appointment with the editor. She would lose the once-in-a-lifetime opportunity to have her book published. She would never have a chance to autograph Bored Boris or his friends.

Cassie snapped the car door open, uncaring that she lost another fingernail on the door handle. With one hand she grabbed the car phone and punched out Jeff's private office number.

"Jeff Haddon," he answered brightly.

A tide of red cast a film across Cassie's eyes as she heard his voice. That he would purposely do this to her was...

"Hello?"

"You wanted to hear how I did," she snarled, clenching the phone and gritting her teeth.

"Cassie, love. Yes, I did. Isn't it a little early—"

"No, *love*," she yelled, frustrated beyond endurance. "It's far too late."

"I don't understand...."

"I don't imagine you could," she snapped. "After all, you've got it all, haven't you, Jeff? The house, the money, me stupid enough to promise you a son. And I haven't got anything!"

It came out on a wail that started the rush of tears from her eyes.

"She didn't like it?" Jeff queried in a puzzled tone. "But I thought you said..."

"She hasn't even seen me yet," Cassie screamed. "I'm sitting on the 401 with a flat tire and no spare." She lowered her voice. "A spare that you used and deliberately didn't have repaired."

"I didn't..."

"You had the nerve to accuse me of sabotaging you," she accused in a cold, hard voice. "You tried to insinuate that I would deliberately spoil your designs." She sniffed and brushed the tears away with the back of her hand, noticing anew the scratches left from the sharp metal on the fender.

"Well, I would never deliberately do that to you, Jeff. I have never tried to hurt you and I can't believe that you would go to these extremes to ruin something that is so important to me. My suit is ruined, my nails are ripped, not to mention my stockings. I've got oil and grease and goodness knows what else covering me and my heels are broken." The tears started afresh.

"I trusted you," she sobbed. "I thought you were...I'll never forgive you for this. Never."

Disappointment overwhelmed her as she wept for the chance of a lifetime that was gone. She forgot she was even holding the phone until Jeff's voice bellowed across the airwaves from the general direction of her filthy skirt.

"Cassie, pick up that phone and talk to me," he ordered in a no-nonsense voice.

"I have to go," she muttered sadly. "I have to call a tow truck." She reached out to hang up and heard his voice once more.

"Cassie!" It was a loud, peremptory order.

"Yes," she whispered, staring mournfully at her portfolio.

"I can get a truck there faster than you can. Tell me exactly where you are."

She told him in dull, uncaring tones.

"Okay. Stay put and lock the doors. Cassie?"

"Yes, all right," she answered, returning the phone to its rest.

She didn't know how long she sat there until the red-and-white flashing lights in her mirror drew her attention. The tall handsome officer jumped out of his car and strode forward, obviously intent on checking for injuries.

"Are you all right, ma'am?" he inquired, peering into her car. "Need some help?"

"No thank you, officer. My husband is sending someone to..."

"I'm here, Cassandra."

Cassie twisted her head to see the man she was most angry with, Jefferson Haddon the third, standing behind the policeman, looking as pulled together as always in his gray pinstripe, perfectly pressed shirt and coordinated tie. His black hair lay perfectly groomed against his head. And his hands were clean, Cassie thought miserably.

"It's all right, Officer," she heard him say brightly. "I've called a tow truck. My wife will be coming with me."

Cassie unlocked the door and eased herself out of the car, her muscles aching in the process. There wasn't any point in arguing, she decided laconically. It simply didn't matter anymore.

She followed him woodenly as he led her to his car and climbed inside the plush, cool interior without a word.

"Stay put," he murmured. "I'll be right back." And he was; carrying her sketches of Bored Boris and the box with her wonderful, useless manuscript. Carefully he placed them on the back seat.

"It doesn't matter," she uttered listlessly. "You could have left them there. I don't need them." Tears welled as she thought of what she had lost. And why.

"Yes," he told her firmly, slamming the door as he climbed in beside her. "You do. In about one hour, to be precise."

Cassie frowned at him. "It's too late," she insisted bitterly. "I missed my appointment. And she's tied up in conference the rest of the day."

"Except for one little opening in exactly—" he twisted his wrist to look at his watch "—one hour and three minutes. Look at me."

Cassie turned toward him, wondering at the look of tender care on his face as he unscrewed a thermos and tipped hot water onto a snowy white towel. Gently he dabbed at the blotches of grease and oil and smeared makeup covering her face, wiping them carefully away with gentle strokes.

"And make no mistake," he continued, eyes flashing. "You will be there." His compassionate ministrations moved to her raw, battered hands and as he cleaned each finger he pressed a kiss to it.

"I would never hurt you, Cassie," he murmured. "Do you honestly believe I would ruin something that I know is so important to you? Do you really think I would do that to my own wife?"

"I d-d-don't know," she stammered, amazed at the strong but kind, considerate touch of his hands when he soothingly pulled a brush, oh so gently, through her tousled hair.

"Well, know this, then," he stated. "I wouldn't. It was simply a stupid oversight on my part. It should never have happened, but I accept all blame." He tipped her chin up.

"The important thing is that you can still make that appointment. If you want to. Do you?"

"Yes!" Cassie voice materialized from nowhere as she stared at him, new hope dawning. "But how, when...what will I wear?" she cried, staring at her ruined clothes.

"I, er, took the liberty of picking out something for you. I hope it's all right." She studied the red spots of color on his cheeks. "You can change at the first gas station," he continued briskly, heading into the traffic with ease. "Meanwhile—" he motioned toward the floor "—there's a thermos of coffee there if you want some."

Gratefully, Cassie poured a mug of the steaming dark brew and sipped it as her sore toes wiggled into the plush carpet of his car.

"Thank you," she said at last, at a loss to fathom it all out. "But how did you know where to phone? Or who?"

"It's whom," he corrected her absently.

"Pardon?" She frowned at him as she filed the now stubby fingernails.

"Whom—the object. Never mind. The answer is that I phoned Mrs. Bennet who had a number you left in case there was a problem with the children. I merely went from there." He pulled off on the access road, finally stopping before a dingy-looking gas station. "We don't have a lot of time," he said in an avuncular voice. "If you're going to change..."

Cassie was out of the car in seconds. He handed her a black plastic garment bag with the elegant gold lettering of La Place across the top left corner.

"There are some other things you might need in here," he added, handing her a paper sack. Cassie's eyes grew even larger. Love and Lingerie was imprinted on the plastic in huge red script. "You'd better hurry."

She scurried into the cubicle, mind whirling as she tried to imagine Jefferson Haddon III entering a shop called Love and

Lingerie. It was unthinkable. Gingerly she opened the bag. There were stockings in it. The sheerest black stockings she had ever seen with elastic tops to hold them up.

Cassie slid out of her tattered hose and the ruined suit. Her Christmas blouse wasn't a total write-off; it would clean up nicely. Slowly, with anticipation, she slid the zipper down and stared at the contents of the black bag as her fingers lifted the hanger free. Cassie gasped as she spied the tag, bearing the name of a famous designer. An *expensive* famous designer.

An elegant heavy silk jacket with a full lining swished across her skin like velvet. It was cut in a straight, severe style that emphasized her slim figure. One solid gold button was the only bit of color in the deep rich black. That button and a host of hidden hooks and eyes held the jacket closed around her ample bosom. The skirt was designed in a straight slim cut that smoothed over her hips and fell just above her knee. It was a perfect fit, Cassie decided and the stockings made her feel pulled together, ready to face the world. She fluffed her hair, checked her makeup and stepped out of the bathroom with a swirl.

"You look great," Jeff complimented. He offered her a pair of not quite so high black leather heels and a matching handbag. "The saleslady said these would go with it," he murmured, glancing at her pale broken-heeled shoe. "I think they're the right size. I know they're not as high as you usually wear, but I thought..."

"They're perfect," she whispered hoarsely as the tears formed in her eyes. "I don't know how you had time to do all this, but thank you." She smiled tremulously at him, fingering the rich kid leather. "Thank you very much."

He grinned. "You're welcome." His eyes moved over her with a gleam that warmed Cassie's heart and made her blood tingle. He waved one hand toward his car. "Your chariot, madam."

As they sped down the highway, Cassie transferred her belongings to her new purse with wonder. How had this happened? she asked herself. She wore a designer suit, elegant silk stockings and handmade leather shoes all courtesy of the tall handsome man beside her.

"How do you come to know so much about women's

clothes?'' she asked curiously, delighting in the flush of red under his skin.

''I don't know anything about them,'' he answered distractedly, steering smoothly in and out of traffic. ''I merely described you to the saleswoman, told her you were a very classy lady on a very important professional mission and asked her to give me something suitable.''

''And the stockings?'' she asked softly.

His face turned even redder, but he turned, just for a moment and looked directly into her eyes.

''I wanted something especially suitable to show off your legs,'' he admitted. His eyes fell to inspect her limbs. ''And they certainly do a fine job.'' His voice was a caressing whisper and this time it was she who was blushing.

In a matter of minutes after that, they were driving up beside a tall, glass office building.

''This is the right place, isn't it?'' he queried, staring at the bit of paper in his hand.

''Yes,'' Cassie replied, stepping from the car with a song of hope in her heart. She slid her work from the car and felt someone take it from her.

''I'm coming up with you,'' Jeff murmured in her ear. ''Just to make sure you actually get there, this time.''

''Oh. But you're double-parked,'' she observed, searching the depths of his darkly glowing eyes.

He shrugged. ''Who cares?,'' he murmured as they entered the elevator with a host of other business types. ''This is important.''

In fact, he walked her right through the door and into the office of Ms. Mary Gaspard, senior editor for Malton's Publishing. And in front of Ms. Gaspard, her secretary and anyone else who cared to see, he kissed her full on the lips.

''You don't need good luck,'' he whispered. ''Just go in there and show them who Cassandra Emily Haddon is. That oughta knock their socks off.''

As she listened to the introductions Ms. Gaspard made five minutes later, Cassie's mind slipped back to that kiss.

Who was that man? she asked herself dizzily.

Chapter Fourteen

Cassie got in the elevator and walked out onto the main floor. Somehow. She wasn't aware of anything but the fact that she had just been offered a nice, juicy contract for a series of children's books to be presented to a host of booksellers country-wide.

"Lord," she said in amazement, "when you answer, you really answer."

The feeling of stunned confusion stayed with her as she was driven home with Bennet behind the wheel of her car, now polished to a high gloss with new tires on every wheel. It was hard to believe this car and her old putter were the same one. Even harder to believe Jeff's words as she related the good news later.

"I knew you could do it," he said smugly. "Now we're going to celebrate—really celebrate."

Cassie hesitated, caught off guard as she stared at the phone. "Tonight?" she questioned. "But it's a Monday."

Jeff laughed uproariously at that.

"What's wrong with Monday?" His voice changed, lowering as he murmured into the phone. "I'd really like to Cassie. But the thing is, I have to fly to London tonight. There's a client interested in taking a very lucrative deal with Bytes Inc. I've been working toward this for months now and it looks like it might finally be in the bag." He paused, speaking hesitantly after a few moments. "Are you upset?"

Cassie smiled. "Of course not," she said matter-of-factly.

"After what you pulled off today, and the wonderful things you gave me, how could I be mad?"

"What about if we do something Saturday night?" he asked in coaxing undertones. "I should be back Friday and that will give us something to look forward to."

They agreed that it was a date and Cassie hung up, finally, with a grin. Life was getting pretty darn wonderful, she decided happily.

That evening David stopped by her room.

"Cassie you know that uh, tree house thing Jeff's building out back?"

Cassie nodded, wondering at the curious look on the boy's face. "Yes," she said uncertainly. "What about it?"

"It's a mess," he told her bluntly. "If a kid tries to play in that he's going to get really hurt. I went to look tonight and got caught on some of those nails he's so fond of." He showed her the six-inch tear in his sleeve and the red angry welt underneath. "I think we should tear it down."

Jeff's words came back to Cassie just then.

"He tore it down. Said it devalued the property."

"No, David, I don't think we can do that," she murmured. "He's very proud of his work."

"But Cassie..." David's voice died away at the odd look on her face. "You've got a plan, haven't you?"

"Sort of." She beamed up at him. David grinned as she patted his shoulder gently. "Don't worry, I'll look after it. Thanks for telling me."

The plan flew into her mind fully formed. She would have the thing rebuilt. Oh, not some grand edifice. If she could, she was going to have it redone exactly as he'd left it, only stronger. And when Jefferson Haddon the third returned from London he would celebrate with her there.

It was time, her whirling mind told her. A man who took such tender care of her, bought his wife a suit like that, and made sure she got to her appointment on time had to care a little bit. And, of course, there *was* that kiss.

As she considered Jeff's mixed reactions to her over the past few months, Cassie felt sure he was coming to love her. She prayed it was so. She wanted his love more than anything and since God had brought them together, she was pretty sure Jeff would come to see that light soon, too.

But who would rebuild the tree house as she wanted? She contacted several firms. None of them were interested.

"Ma'am, if our name was associated with that...thing—" one burly contractor growled, jerking his thumb at the sorely built conflagration of boards "—our customers would cancel their house contracts, for sure."

Another claimed it would take too much time to remove everything and then reconnect it solidly.

"Much easier to rip the whole thing down and start from scratch," the man with the wizened old face told her sadly. "That mess wouldn't stand a winter breeze."

Cassie was considering that advice when the Haddons senior arrived for a visit. Mrs. Haddon looked tired, but much better than she had in the hospital. As they sat sipping their tea, Bennet came in.

"Excuse me miss, but I wanted to warn you to stay away from the creek." Cassie knew exactly what he was referring to when he inclined his head sideways. "Whole wall has caved in."

"I was afraid of that. Thank you, Bennet."

Jeffie, as she had come to think of Mr. Haddon, Senior, frowned.

"What wall?" he demanded, searching the interior house walls for imminent structural damage. "I thought Judith had kept the place up."

Cassie took a deep breath and launched into the story, pausing only to take a breath now and then.

"So you see, the tree house is important to him. I just wanted to get it sort of—" she shrugged wearily "—I don't know. Shored up, I guess."

Jeffie hustled to his feet.

"And that's exactly what we're going to do, Missy."

Cassie stared at him, frowning at the elated look on his face.

"What I meant was that I'll have to hire some knowledgeable person..." she began. And never finished.

"I am the best architect this side of the Pacific," he told her, chest puffed out proudly. "And I've got the company to prove it. I can design and rebuild anything you want. Just point me to the place.''

Cassie's mouth formed a round, startled 0. ''Haddon and Son,'' she murmured at last. ''I'd forgotten all about that.'' She wondered how to explain this latest rejection of his help.

''I'm sorry, Jeffie, but I don't think that would be a good idea. You see, this was Jeff's baby...his scheme to make a place for the younger kids to come and be out of everybody's hair.'' She lowered her voice, keeping her gaze on his tanned face. ''Apparently it's something of a dream with him. From the time he was a small child.''

Jeff senior's face fell as he remembered. He nodded finally. ''Yes,'' he said regretfully. ''I remember that thing.'' Suddenly he grinned. ''Sounds like his ability hasn't improved much.'' He chuckled. His eyes widened with excitement. ''I could do it,'' he offered raggedly. ''I could redo it and he'd never have to know.''

''I don't think...''

''Don't think about it, Cassie. Just think about him out there with the kids, having a whale of a time. Oh, please,'' he begged. ''Let me do this one thing for my son. Something I should have done a long time ago.''

His face had such a wistful look about it as he told her how rudely he'd had Jeff's dream removed all those years ago. Cassie felt herself giving in long before she said the words.

''All right, all right.'' She held up her hands at last. ''I give up. If you can rebuild the thing so it will be safe and yet make it look like his work, I'll agree. But,'' she added softly, glancing from him to his wife. ''Jeff can never know. I don't think he would appreciate my meddling.''

''It'll be wonderful,'' Jeffie, Sr. crowed, waving his hands madly. ''It'll be our little secret.'' He bent over a piece of paper, drawing madly as he muttered to himself.

Later Cassie left him still muttering, in disbelief this time, as he stared at the mess.

''Hard to believe he comes from a long line of architectural designers,'' she heard him huff as he tugged away one board after the other, pausing only to write something in his little book.

He worked all day Tuesday and Wednesday, too. On Thursday she was invited to take a look at coffee time.

"It's fantastic," she told him, stomping and pushing for all she was worth. Nothing, not a single board moved. The general work site was just as Jeff had left it last weekend; as if nothing had been touched.

"I can't believe you did this," she told Jeffie, wide-eyed with amazement as she sat inside staring out. "It's perfect." She handed him some coffee in a foam cup.

"It's a long way from perfect." He grinned. "But you can't tell where his work ends and mine begins, I'll give you that." He sank down beside her, laying his hammer aside as he sipped thankfully at the cup. "This is really good coffee." He shook his head, grinning. "Jefferson never serves a decent cup. Always kind of watered down."

Cassie grinned right back at him as she thought about what she would paint on the outside. Considering her sudden success and his part in it, she decided that a dinosaur was indeed appropriate. On Friday she started the project, praying that the forecasted rains would hold off until long after she and Jeff had shared an evening to remember in the tree house.

She had it all planned out and thankfully, the household numbers were back to her, David and Marie by Saturday afternoon when Jeff finally arrived. This was one date she had no intention of sharing.

"I'm sorry," he told her ruefully, kissing her mouth quickly as he came in the door. "I got held up at the last minute and couldn't get free to phone. But it was worth it!" He grinned from ear to ear as he held up his briefcase. "I've got a contract signed, sealed and delivered that will keep Bytes Inc. in the black for a long time."

"Good." Cassie smiled. "Then we can celebrate that, too. Come on, get changed. We're going to have a picnic in the tree house. Just the two of us."

His eyebrows raised at that but only for a second before he frowned.

"Cassie, about that tree house," he began, pulling his tie free. "I'm not sure we should..."

"Oh, come on, Jeff," she encouraged. "Even big business

tycoons like you have to slow down once in a while. Besides—'' she smiled brightly ''—I want you to see what I've painted on it.'' And not see what your father has done, she added silently.

He was ready at last; wearing a brand-new pair of designer jeans, she noticed ruefully and a silk and linen blend shirt. Oh, well! Not even that was going to spoil tonight, she decided. This was the night she would tell Jefferson Haddon how much she loved him; how much she wanted him in her life.

The light was beginning to fade when they reached the tree house. Here and there through the canopy of newly leafed oak trees overhead, a bit of daylight poked through. It was exactly the right setting for a dinosaur.

''This is fantastic,'' he declared, touching the wall gingerly. When it stayed in place, his whole face lit up. ''It must have been the nails,'' he murmured to himself. His finger ran down the dips and peaks of the dinosaur's back until he was tracing the puff of smoke that led to the entrance.

''I'm not sure these steps...'' His voice died away as she bounded up inside.

''Come on in,'' she coaxed, pleased with his surprised expression, and watched eagerly as he took in all of her work. It had been a labor of love and Cassie had spared no effort.

Here and there wild animals could be seen. Her favorite was the perky little squirrel whose head rose above the crack between boards, making it appear that he had just popped out of the tree she'd sketched in. Huge vivid green leaves and vines covered the inside walls, a tree branch visible here and there. She heaved a sigh of relief at his words.

''This is wonderful, Cassie. A perfect retreat for kids.''

''Sit down,'' she urged, motioning to the disreputable old cushions she had retrieved from the house. She sank onto one herself. Cassie had nailed a piece of board onto a section of tree trunk he'd left behind and that was their table. Carefully she lit the assortment of candles she had arranged earlier and pointed to the covered trays.

''Your dinner, sir,'' she murmured softly and lifted the salver on six, plump juicy wieners nestled into buns. ''I tried to keep the meal appropriate to the setting,'' she told him, winking.

The usual condiments stood nearby as did two cans of pop and a bowl of chips. With a flick of her wrist she had poured the ginger ale into two stemmed glasses and held one out.

"To success," she cheered, tinkling her glass against his. "Yours and mine."

"To success," he agreed and sipped the "champagne" thoughtfully. They munched away contentedly and as they ate, Jeff told her about his trip. Cassie, in turn, told him about her week.

"And I'm hard at work to meet that deadline," she concluded. She stared up at him happily. "Isn't *deadline* a wonderful word?" She grinned.

Jeff eased the table away and placed a companionable arm around her shoulders as they sat leaning against the wall, sipping their drinks.

"It's a wonderful world," he concurred thoughtfully. His eyes cast around for one more look as the flickering candles created scary shadows on the wall. "And so is this." She felt his arm tighten around her meaningfully.

"Wouldn't it be wonderful to watch our own children playing here, telling scary stories and having high tea?" She felt his lips move smoothly across her neck. "They might even want to sleep out here. There's lots of room."

"Yes, lots," Cassie agreed, wrapping her arms around his neck and kissing him back with fervor. He kissed her hungrily, like a man who was starving and couldn't get enough of the delectable taste of her lips. His fingers massaged the tender flesh on her upper arms, smoothing over it with gentleness.

"I want you, Cassandra," he growled low in his throat, his lips playing with hers. "I want to make love to you…to create a child with you and watch it growing inside your body. I want to share with you all the things a man and a woman can share." His lips closed over her coaxingly. "Cassie?" His voice was a soft murmur.

"I want you, too, Jeff," she whispered in the stillness of their hideaway. "I want to stay with you forever."

"Thank heaven," he whispered fervently. "All I could think about this past week was how fantastic you looked in that outfit on Monday." He groaned into her mouth. "And those legs!"

Cassie shifted a bit, wanting his arms all the way around her now. And Jeff moved, too. Not much, just a little to stretch his long legs out.

"Ow," he yelped suddenly, sitting up to rub his leg.

"What's the matter?" Cassie asked while her body hummed "not now, not now!"

"There's something sharp here in the corner. I'll just move it. You might hurt…" His voice died away as he stared down at the silver-headed hammer in his hands. "How did this get here?" he demanded.

Cassie stared at it. "I don't know." She pointed to the JWH inscribed on the wooden handle. "It must be yours. It's got your initials." She slid a little nearer, brushing one hand over his chest. "Forget about it. Think of something else," she whispered in her best Mae West voice.

Jeff pushed her away roughly and stood to his feet, towering over her in the dim light.

"I can't forget it," he said harshly. "It's my father's. Rory and I gave it to him years ago." He stared down at her and when he spoke his voice was full of bitter recrimination.

"What was my father doing here, Cassie?"

Cassie swallowed the lump of fear in her throat and tried to ignore the panic that was rising. She stood slowly, grateful for his helping hand, unforgiving though it was.

"He wanted to help with the surprise," she told him softly.

"Help? How? By rebuilding this place?" His fist smashed against the wall in fury. "By redoing what his *useless* son couldn't? By building a tree house that would stay in one place?" He glared at her. "That's what he said, you know. I was useless because I couldn't draw a straight line let alone draft the plans for an apartment complex."

"Oh, Jeff, you're not useless." Cassie slid her arm through his. "You merely have different specialities. You're a master at what you do."

He knocked her hand away roughly.

"Don't ever patronize me, Cassandra. I warned you that I wanted nothing to do with my father. I've told you time and again and yet still you use him against me."

Cassie was aghast. Never had she dreamed he would be so hurt by her actions.

"I only wanted to make it a special place for you and me." She sighed sadly. "I wanted a place where we could be alone for once." She took her courage in both hands and stared up at him with her heart in her eyes.

"I wanted a chance to tell you that I love you," she whispered. "And since I wanted it to be private and David and Marie are up at the house, the only other place I could think to be alone was here." She threaded her hands together in confusion. "I do love you, Jeff. More and more each day. I love the way you're always there for me, cheering me on."

"Then couldn't you have thought to do the same for me, if you love me as you claim." His eyes were cold hard rocks that bit at her with indignation. "Don't you think you might have offered me the slightest courtesy in your so-called love and not have deliberately ignored my feelings about him?"

"Jeff," she pleaded, tears welling in her eyes. "He's your father. He loves you, as I do. He knows he made a mistake but he wants to get past that and try to make amends. That's the way families work." She dashed the tears from her eyes and continued.

"Families are at the root of our society because that's what holds people together, bonds them. Families love each other, no matter what. They don't bail out on one another and they don't quit."

He laughed harshly.

"Heaven spare me all this love claptrap," he snarled, gripping her arms. "I don't want it and I don't need it. What I do want is someone who will understand that I don't need anyone messing up my life with old history. Dead history." He whirled away to the steps but before he could descend them, Cassie stopped him.

"Yes, you do, Jeff. You need us all and if you keep turning your back on everyone who reaches out to you, it's going to be too late for both you and your mother." She covered her mouth as soon as the words escaped but it was too late. He had already heard.

His hands gripped her arms, propelling her backward until she was pressed up against the wall.

"What do you mean, too late for my mother?" he enunciated in a cold, hard voice. When she didn't answer his face dropped nearer hers. "How do you know anything about my mother?" he shouted angrily. Cassie made the decision in a split second.

"I've been visiting her since Christmas. Your mother is sick, Jeff. She's having chemotherapy treatments. The doctors are hopeful but her attitude isn't conducive to healing. She may not have too much longer."

Jeff's face hardened as she watched, into a bitter, angry inscrutable mask. He let her go and stepped away.

"I trusted you, Cassie," he whispered hoarsely. "I thought you were on my side—that we were a team. And now you go behind my back and become one of them. How could you?" he uttered through clenched teeth. "How could you go and let them come here, into my home? How could you betray me like that?"

With her heart aching inside Cassie stepped nearer and cupped his face in her hands, forcing him to meet her gaze.

"I could do it," she whispered softly, praying that he would hear the words. "I could do it because I love you more than anything and I want you to be whole. I want you to forgive and forget and move into the future with me. Help me build something we can share together, Jeff. Something beautiful, not something full of hate."

His dark eyes searched hers, blazing into their depths with a scrutiny that rocked her to her soul. They were full of pain and hurt and anger. And something else. Something that tugged at her heartstrings and ached to hold his head to her breast as she reassured him over and over. When at long last, he pulled away, his eyes were dull, lifeless.

"You can keep your so-called love, Cassandra," he said with a measured tone. "It can't fix things this time. I could have used it thirty years ago but it's too late now. I don't need it or you. I don't need anybody." With a lunge he slammed down the steps, dropping the hammer to the floor.

"Yes, you do, Jeff," she murmured sadly, long after he had

departed. "You need all of us. More than ever. You just don't know it yet."

And there in the tree house, she sank to her knees and cried out a prayer for him. For both of them.

Chapter Fifteen

Cassie stared morosely at the official document in front of her. Finally, at long last, the words penetrated her almost inactive state of consciousness.

"Oh, no," she whispered in disbelief. "Not now."

"What, not now?" Jeff frowned across the table at her, gulping down a quick cup of coffee as he did every morning now in order to avoid talking to her. When she didn't answer, his long fingers snatched the papers out of her hands. "The court hearing for David and Marie's adoptions."

"Are you still okay with that?" she questioned in a tight voice. Tears burned her eyes as he stared down at her with contempt.

"Unlike some people, Cassandra, I do keep my promises. You made it part of our agreement that I adopt them and I will honor that agreement." His eyes were chips of black onyx as he stared down at her. "Just remember what you promised," he warned finally. "Because I am holding you to it. I still want my own son."

Tears welled in her eyes as he left, closing the front door softly behind him. The pain in his eyes hurt her far more than anything he could say. And it was that pain that made her reconsider the future. A cold dark future without love. A future of fulfilling her rash agreement to give him a child.

Jeff complained all the way into Toronto, even though there was no one to hear him. And he was still fuming when his brother called just before noon.

"What did you do to Cassie?" Rory demanded belligerently. "I just tried to invite her for Dad's birthday dinner tonight and she started blubbering all over the place."

"Maybe she just doesn't like birthdays." Jeff grimaced, hating himself for the sniping response, but feeling fully justified.

"That's baloney and you know it. Cass loves people and she and Dad have been spending a lot of time talking recently...." His voice died away.

"I already know about it." Jeff smiled bitterly. "He would try to enlist her in his campaign," he muttered angrily.

"What campaign?" Rory demanded.

"The one that gets me to join in on this big happy family malarkey," Jeff said in a tight voice. "To pretend that the past never happened."

There was a long silence, then Rory came back on the line, his voice brisk.

"I have to go, Jefferson. I've got a big client on the other line. Seems the electrician goofed. I'll see you at one. At Taylors."

"Wait a minute, Rory," Jeff protested. But his little brother had hung up. "Taylors," he muttered angrily. "Like I need a six-course lunch today." But Jeff went anyway. Just to hear what Rory had to say. His brother was pretty blunt.

"Look, Jefferson, you're wasting your life with this stupid feud. And you're hurting a lot of people besides."

"I'm not trying to hurt anyone. And it's not a feud. I just choose not to get involved in this unrealistic pipe dream you and Cassie have that my father and I could ever be soul mates."

Rory studied him seriously.

"He doesn't believe that, either, Jefferson. He just wants a chance to apologize for the past. And to try to make amends."

Jeff couldn't believe what he had just heard.

"I don't expect Cassie to understand," he said in a tightly controlled voice, glaring at his brother. "She wasn't there. But you were. You know how he treated us—the ranting, the drinking, the misery. How can you sit there and pretend life was rosy when it was the furthest thing from that? How can he make amends for that hellish childhood?"

406 A Will and a Wedding

Jeff stared at Rory, unable to forgive his brother's betrayal. He had been there, for Pete's sake. He'd suffered the same things. How could he just let it all go without a word?

"Jeff." Rory was using the shortened version of his name. It sounded right, Jeff decided, because it made him seem a different person than that sad, needy little boy. "I know you're hurting. And I know that you think that Dad's neglect of us was unforgivable. But that's exactly what you have to do."

Jeff snorted. "Yeah, right. Like I can forgive him for publicly disowning me the day he said he didn't know who I was. And just wipe the slate clean for the time he left me behind because I wasn't in the car at the appointed hour." He glared bitterly at the silver place settings. "Was it so easy for you to forget about the toys Aunt Judith sent? He took them away, Rory. He took them and right in front of our noses, he gave them to his friends. Laughing as he said we didn't deserve them. No," he exploded. "I can't forget that. Don't ask me to."

"All right," Rory murmured at last, his face drawn and sad. "Hang on to it, then. Nurture it inside of you where it can fester and grow and eat away at the rest of your life. It will ruin your relationship with Cassie, though," he warned sadly. "Bitterness and hate have a way of penetrating through to everything we do. It's already ruining your chances to make amends with Mom before she dies."

Jeff glared at him. "I suppose that's my fault, too," he snapped.

Rory rose to his feet with disgust, tossing his linen napkin on the table.

"No, stupid. It's your opportunity."

"To do what?" Jeff demanded.

"To move ahead. To let the past go. Everybody makes mistakes, Jeff. Mom. Dad. Even you. We acknowledge them and then we try to do better. It's called life. Don't waste any more of it."

As he left the restaurant Jeff thought how alone he was. Even his own brother had turned on him. It was even more important now that he have his son.

He'd show them.

He'd show them all that he could be a far better father than the example he'd had.

Cassie sat in the solemn stillness of the courtroom holding her breath. It didn't seem right, somehow. She and Jeff were sitting here side by side, pretending that they were this happy couple, only too anxious to adopt these two children, when Cassie knew that Jeff had only agreed because of their marriage contract.

Just this morning she had given him an escape route once more.

"If you don't want David and Marie as your legal children," she had said quietly, "I won't hold you to that promise. I don't want you to adopt them because of some agreement. I want you to adopt them because you want to be their father."

Jeff had merely raised one mocking eyebrow. "It's a little late to change your mind, Cassandra," he had replied before leaving the room.

"Order in the court."

Cassie jerked to attention, noticing that their judge was a tall, stately woman with silver-gray hair. She smiled at everyone as she began to relate the purpose for the hearing.

"I know Mrs. Haddon's record with children very well," Judge Pender told them easily. "And I realize that Oak Bluff has been a sanctuary to a number of needy children. I commend those efforts." She nodded her head at Cassie, who felt even more like a fraud.

"What I want to hear this morning is the opinions of the minors in this case, Marie and David. I want to know why they want to make their home permanently with Mr. and Mrs. Haddon. Marie, will you come over here and tell me?"

Marie stood up slowly and walked over to the chair beside the judge. Her fingers twisted the edge of her sweater nervously as she sat down.

"Well," she began softly, her voice betraying an anxious tremble. "I want to stay and be part of their family because I'm a real person there." She glanced up at Judge Pender, who merely nodded her silver head. "You see, Cassie doesn't care about things, like if I mess up her dinner party. And Jeff ate those horrible pork chops anyway because he didn't want to hurt my feelings." The story was slightly convoluted in the telling, but the judge nodded understandingly.

Marie stared at her feet for a moment before continuing.

"It's like you can just be whoever you are there. You don't have to be perfect or pretend you're happy when you're not or agree with everything they say."

"You mean there are no rules?" the judge asked quietly, writing something in her book. Cassie held her breath as Marie continued, praying the young girl would explain clearly.

Marie grinned. "Oh, there are rules," she said laughing. "And if you break them, you are responsible. I should know." She giggled. "I tried them out enough times at first. But even if you do something wrong, Cassie doesn't think you are bad. You just made a mistake and she hopes you'll do better next time."

"Do you and the Haddons ever disagree over things?" Judge Pender questioned next.

Marie's brow furrowed. "Well, Cassie doesn't think I should get engaged to my boyfriend right away. She wants me to finish school and go to university and stuff so I'll see more of the world."

"And what do you think?"

"I think I'm going to marry him anyway eventually. But I guess it's a good idea to be sure." A big smile lit her young face.

"You keep talking about Mrs. Haddon. Is Mr. Haddon not around very much?"

"Oh, Jeff's there whenever we need him. He has this big company to run, of course. And that takes a lot of time."

Cassie felt Jeff shift uneasily beside her.

"So he's mostly pretty busy?" The judge was frowning now, noting another series of scribbles on her pad.

"Yeah, he's really busy. But when I was sick, I called him from school one day and he came right away and took me home. I think he was in a meeting or something, but when I asked him, he said it didn't matter. That I was more important and business could wait.''

Cassie frowned. How was it that she hadn't heard anything about this? she wondered.

''Nate, told me—'' Marie broke off and grinned at the judge. ''Nate's my boyfriend. Well, he told me that Jeff had a talk with him one time and sort of laid down the law. Nate was kinda ticked but I thought it was really nice of Jeff to worry about my boyfriend.''

''I see.'' Judge Pender looked up from her notepad to study the man in question. Cassie felt as if her heart had stopped suddenly. There was a huge pressure building in her chest that demanded release. It hurt to hear all these things about Jeff and know that he had only done them out of a sense of duty. How she wished it could have been different.

''David, I would like you to come here, too, please.'' David sauntered up, flopping down in his chair easily. ''What do you think about being adopted?'' the judge asked.

''It's okay,'' David muttered finally.

''You don't want to be adopted by the Haddons?'' The judge's tone was perplexed. ''Why not?''

''It's not that I don't want to be,'' David said blithely. ''But what difference would it make? Jeff's already my dad. At least—'' he grinned at Jeff ''—that's what I call him now.''

''I take it that you and Jeff get along pretty well?'' The judge had a funny look on her face that Cassie couldn't discern.

''Well, most of the time.'' David grimaced. ''He can be pretty stubborn but he listens to what I have to say.''

''And Mrs. Haddon?''

David beamed. ''Oh, she's great. Where I was before, the lady made me call her Mom. I hated that because she wasn't my mom. My mom died.'' His voice had faded away to a soft murmur. When he looked up, Cassie could see the hint of tears in his eyes.

''Cassie isn't like that,'' he said stoutly. ''It's like it doesn't matter as long as you're comfortable. You know,'' he leaned forward to face the judge. ''I think a person could do just about anything and they'd still love you.''

''It's a good place to live then?''

"The best," David agreed. "They really care about each other and about us. Like my dad," he said the words proudly. "He built this tree house for when the little kids come. Or something. Anyway—" David grinned saucily, shaking his head "—it was a real mess. I mean, he tried but the guy's lousy with a hammer. Sorry, Dad, but you are."

Cassie heard Jeff murmur, "That's okay. It was pretty bad."

"Yeah, well anyway, Cassie wanted that tree house to stay there but pieces of it kept hurting people. One day Bennet got hit by a board that fell on him. He made me promise not to tell anybody. Gosh, I hope I don't get him in trouble."

Just another little thing she'd missed. Cassie grimaced ruefully.

"Cassie phoned all over trying to get somebody to rebuild it but stronger, so when the little kids came again they could go there and not get hurt. But she wanted it to look like Jeff had made it, see, and nobody wanted to do that. Know what I mean?"

He looked at the judge to see if she had followed. When she nodded, he continued.

"Finally she got Jeff's dad to help her and he took it all apart and put it back just like she wanted. I even helped a bit. That's what I mean. It was just because she loved him that she did it. She didn't want him to find out, she just wanted him to use it with the little kids. Jeff really loves little kids; almost as much as he loves Cassie," David told Judge Pender softly.

"They really do love each other a lot," Marie added. "You can see it in their eyes when they look at each other. Jeff tries to pretend he's not watching her when Cassie's drawing and she stares at him all the time. And they are always touching each other. And they're like there for the other one when things get bad. I've seen Jeff get this look on his face sometimes that makes me feel kind of, I don't know, special. I think that's the kind of look I want Nate to have when he looks at me."

The room was silent as they all watched the solemn-faced woman write down a few more phrases.

"And do Jeff and Cassie love you two?" she asked.

Cassie flinched, wondering how the kids would answer. Everything was so important; each word they said would determine their future. Let them say the right things, she prayed softly, closing her eyes. They flew open when Jeff's hand wrapped comfortingly around hers and she felt the strength he was lending her.

"Yes," they answered in unison, with no hesitation.

"How do you know? Do they buy you lots of stuff or get you neat things or what?"

"Well, we did get some really nice things for Christmas," Marie offered. "But that's not what tells you if someone loves you and cares about you."

The judge smiled. "What does then, Marie?" she asked quietly.

"It's more the way they act around you," she replied hesitantly. "Like Cassie showing me how to use makeup even though I ruined her lipstick and eye shadow. And Jeff showing me how to use his new computer game that he designed for some big company. That was cool!" She grinned happily. "And he didn't have a fit when one of the kids knocked him out with a snowball, either. He just got up and went on with things."

"And like my driving lessons." David glanced at Cassie with a grin. "I got to drive his car a little bit each day after I got my learner's. Some of the guys can't do that, you know. They have to take lessons from the driver ed people."

"Don't you want lessons?" the judge asked curiously.

"Oh, yeah! But by then I won't be so uptight. I'll know a little bit to start with and the other kids won't make fun of me. I was pretty bad at first," he admitted, frowning.

Cassie wiped away the tears at the look of relief on the young boy's face. She hadn't known about that, either. What was the matter with her?

"And when all the other kids came to our house, Cassie let me have my own room. That felt really…I don't know. Kinda special. Like I was important enough to rate my own private place."

"Thank you very much, David and Marie," the judge said. "You've helped make this decision much easier. You can sit down."

When they had returned to their seats, Judge Pender snapped

her notes together and laid them flat on the desk. She stared out at them for a moment before speaking.

"In my work I have seen many families in all sorts of conditions," she told them thoughtfully. "And always, it is the families that have a care and regard for one another that survive the tough times. I see that here." She smiled.

"David and Marie want to be part of the Haddons' family because they can see and feel the love and regard that is present between Mr. and Mrs. Haddon. It's a love that includes rather than excludes. Mr. Haddon has shown a nurturance and care for these children that I hadn't expected given his unfamiliarity with children. Mrs. Haddon has continued the excellent care she has always shown to children under her roof. I commend them both for their careful handling in such a situation and find no reason why David and Marie should not be legally adopted by them after a period of not more than sixty days, making them and the Haddons a family."

The judge gathered her documents together before glancing down at the group of people gathered before her. Cassie felt like a fraud as she listened to the words.

"A strong, loving marriage is always the best basis for children to be nurtured in. Often, in our society, our children have less than optimum conditions during the most formative years of their lives. They emerge as bitter, hardened adults who cannot allow themselves to forget the past and care deeply for another human being, or to accept the love offered to them. You have opened your hearts and your home to David and Marie and others, without reservation. May God bless you for your efforts. We are better for it."

It was a moving tribute that was totally undeserved. As she left Jeff outside the courthouse and drove the children home, Cassie felt the sting of tears prick her eyelids. It would have been so wonderful if it had been true; if only Jeff loved her even half as much as she loved him.

Cassie wanted nothing so much as to lock herself in her room and give way to the misery that held her in its grip. She ignored the happy whispers coming from the back seat as she contemplated the future. Everything seemed so futile now. All her dreams of a happy family at Oak Bluff were just that—unrealistic dreams, illusions. It was time to face reality. She had agreed to a loveless marriage with a man she loved more deeply than her own life. She would soon be the mother of these two teenagers who had based their future plans on her hopes and dreams.

How would she endure it?

"Cassie?" It was Marie looking apologetic, except for the tiny sparkle at the corners of her eyes. "I forgot that my geometry set broke yesterday and I have to have another for class tomorrow. Could you possibly drop us off and then pick one up?"

"Why don't we all go," Cassie suggested. "We could have a drink or something to celebrate."

"Uh, no, thanks. I've got a chemistry test tomorrow and I have to memorize formulas." Marie's face flushed a bright red. "You know how much I hate chemistry. I've just got to study."

Actually, Cassie had always thought Marie found her subjects rather easy, but then she'd been missing a lot lately. This was just another thing to add to the list.

"Yeah," David said quickly. "Uh, me, too. I mean I have to work on my English paper. Again."

Cassie frowned. "Didn't you finish that last week?" she asked curiously.

"Um, no. That is, this is another one." He stumbled out the door without looking at her and then turned back. "Oh, by the way," he added. "Dad said he'll be a little late. And not to make anything for supper. He's ordered pizza, or something, I think. To celebrate."

"Fine." A celebration. Great, just great. In slow motion, Cassie put the car into gear. "See you later then," she muttered.

"Yeah. Later." David and Marie scurried into the house without a backward glance.

As she drove down the road watching the sun slowly sink behind the ridge of trees in the west, Cassie swallowed her tears.

There's no time to cry, she told herself sternly. You've gotten exactly what you wanted. Haven't you?

Chapter Sixteen

The entire house was lit up like a Christmas tree when Cassie finally arrived home after scouring the stores for a geometry set. This late in the season, no one seemed to carry much in the way of school supplies in the local drugstore.

Searching for some enthusiasm, she walked up the path to the front door, starting backward when it was flung open.

"Cassandra! Where have you been? Where are the kids?"

Jeff stared at her with a strange look on his face as Cassie moved past him to toss her jacket on a nearby chair. She pushed the heavy fall of hair back off her face and turned to look at him, emotions held in check. For the moment.

"They were here when I left," she told him, walking through the dining room and jerking to a halt. "What is this?"

There was a trio of three uniformed waiters standing behind an elegantly set table of Judith's best crystal, silver and china.

Jeff studied her with a thoughtful frown.

"I thought you'd ordered it. David said you had something special planned tonight and not to be late."

"He told me you were bringing pizza," she told him, smiling bitterly at the irony of the situation.

"What's so funny?" he asked pointedly.

"It's obviously an attempt to give us some privacy," she answered. "They're not here, are they?"

"No, but…"

"Dinner is served, sir. Whenever you are ready."

They both turned to gape at the tall white-gloved man who

stood behind them. Jeff searched Cassie's face with a questioning glance and she shrugged.

"Why not?" she murmured. "It saves me making dinner."

The big, brilliant chandelier was switched off. Instead, a huge silver candelabra with many candles gave off a golden glow in the room, faintly accenting the rose centerpiece.

"Marie," they said together.

Jeff grinned at her. "She alone could cause a rise in candle stocks!"

Soft stringed music played in the background sending out the smooth mellow tones of a romantic ballad. Cassie studied her food with bitterness. There was no love for her here. Not for her. It was just a pipe dream she'd had.

The food was elegantly served and should have been delicious. Cornish game hens in a mandarin cherry sauce with wild rice and tiny peas; it was a dish she'd enjoyed before. But tonight everything tasted like sawdust including her favorite key lime dessert.

When the last dish was finally removed and the coffee poured, Cassie breathed a sigh of relief. The tension was killing her. Jeff hadn't said two words in the last five minutes and she couldn't think of anything else to break the long silence between them.

"Is there anything we can get for you, sir? Madam?" Their waiter stood, smiling benignly at them as if he couldn't feel the stress tangible in the rose-scented room.

"No, that's everything. Thank you very much." Jeff handed the man a tip which was refused.

"Oh, no, sir. Everything's been taken care of."

Jeff frowned. "It has? How?"

"Everything was arranged by telephone and credit card. We appreciate it, sir. You've been very generous."

Jeff groaned. "*My* credit card, I'll bet," he muttered. "I gave it to David when he went on that trip. Just in case there was an emergency." He frowned. "I never got it back."

"Sorry," Cassie apologized bitterly. "Just another little side effect of raising children. My fault. Sorry."

Jeff frowned at her, hands thrust deep in his pockets as he watched the caterers move out through the front door.

"I didn't mean that," he said, inclining his head. "I was just..."

"I'm going to drink my coffee in the family room," she mumbled, cutting him off.

He followed along behind like a meek little puppy, Cassie thought grimly. As if he were afraid she didn't know where to go or something. The sofa closed around her tired body like an eiderdown and she laid her head back on the seat with relief.

"It was a tense day, wasn't it?" Jeff began, coming behind her to massage the tight cords on her neck. "But, in a way, I'm glad it's over. Finally settled." She felt his lips against her throat and jerked away.

"Cassie..." He paused, thoughtfully studying her face as he walked around the sofa and sank down beside her. "That judge gave me some things to think about today. I wanted to tell you..."

"Yeah," she snapped. "Me, too." The sadness of their situation overwhelmed her like a tidal wave swamping her with the futility of pretending any longer. She had everything: the home she'd always wanted, a husband whom she loved more than anyone could imagine and two wonderful children.

She had far less than she had ever dreamed, Cassie realized. Because without Jeff's love, the house, the kids...they were just dreams. Idle dreams.

"I can't do this anymore," she whispered, the tears coursing down her cheeks. "I love you more than anything, Jeff, but I can't adopt those children. I can't pretend to be your wife when you won't let me in...not really into your life."

She let all the pain and hurt flow out like a river bursting its banks. Nothing could stop it.

"I'm not your wife, Jeff. You want some glamorous society woman like that Melisande who can put on fancy dinners and dine at elegant restaurants and shoot the breeze with the best of them. And that's not me," she wailed.

"Cassie, if you'd just let me explain...."

She ignored him. "I'm not the wonder woman the kids think I am, either. I'm not strong. I need somebody to lean on—someone to talk over the hard parts with and help me deal with the kids who need so much help. I don't even know half of what's going on with Marie and David.'' She sobbed the words out. ''They've gone to you when I should have been there.''

Cassie stared at him through her tears and acknowledged her defeat.

''It isn't right,'' she admitted at last. ''We can't bring another child into all these problems. I can't ever be the mother of that son you want so desperately, Jeff. I can't, I won't do that to a child.'' The words were harsh and full of pain.

When she jumped up to race out of the room, Jeff caught her arm. He pulled her tightly against him, burying his face in her hair.

''Cassie,'' he groaned, holding her close. ''You already are the mother of my son. The judge said so today. And if David and Marie are the only children we ever have, we will be the luckiest parents in this world.''

She glared up at him tearfully, pushing away as she did so.

''No, we won't. Because those kids need love—all that they can get. They need parents who are committed to their family, close and extended. I want my children to grow up in a circle of love. I want them to hear the old family tales and feel the bonds of love that knit us all together.'' She stared down at her hands miserably. ''But you can't forget the pain in your past.''

Cassie didn't dare look at him. She knew the loathing that she'd find on his face as soon as she mentioned his father.

''I thought God led me here,'' she whispered. ''I thought I was following his will when Judith left the house to both of us. I thought that eventually you'd understand how much family means to me.'' She paused and then said it. ''Eventually, I thought, you'd come to love me, too.''

She did look at him then. A piercing scrutiny that told her more than any words could how wrong she had been.

''God didn't lead me here,'' she whispered sadly. ''I just wanted it so badly, I thought He did, too. But wishing and hoping can't make it so.''

She turned to leave the room as fresh tears cascaded down her cheeks.

''Sit down, Cassandra.'' Jeff's voice was soft but firm as he tugged on her arm. ''I have something I want to say.''

''You don't have to,'' she began, but he ignored her.

"I came here six months ago, after my aunt died, full of anger that she would dare to manipulate me. And then I got to know you. That was an eye-opener!" He grinned at her.

Cassie sank back onto the sofa, unnerved by the look on his face.

"You didn't take those kids into your heart and love them because you were supposed to. Or because someone said you had to. Or even because you would benefit from them. You took kids in and cared for them, loved them, and then sent them back home because it was the right thing for you to do. And you stuck to that, no matter what obstacles I put in your way.

"I admired that, Cassie. And I've seen the difference it makes, that love of yours. I've watched the children come and go and they never left here the same. Each one of them took away the knowledge that he held a special place in your heart. And gradually I came to realize that what you were so freely doling out to everyone else, was exactly what I had always wanted. To belong, to matter."

Jeff slipped to his knees and grasped her hands with his, staring straight into her eyes with a light of wonder in his face.

"I was so jealous of your childhood. You had all the things I wanted and never had. And here you were, transplanted to Judith's and you made your own little world again. The people at the church, the kids that came and went, the agency people. They were like one big happy family to you and I thought, 'At last! This will be my own special little corner of the world.' And I began to enjoy the kids. Then you started harping on my dad."

He stopped and swallowed, obviously organizing his thoughts.

"And every time his name would come up, so would the word *love*." He grimaced. "I began to hate the sound of that word. And yet, somehow, I knew it was exactly what I wanted—what I had to have."

Jeff smiled sadly, fingering the beautiful rings he had given her.

"I was head over heels in love with you at Christmas and more than anything I wanted to make our marriage a living and breathing partnership. But I just couldn't swallow the hate that

I felt for my parents. You, sitting there, laughing and joking with them made it worse. I felt like you had taken their side.''

''Oh, Jeff,'' Cassie murmured, tightening her fingers. ''They can never make up for the past, although they will spend the rest of their lives trying to get you to see that.''

''I went to see them today, Cassie. After the court hearing.'' He flushed a dull red as he stared at their entwined hands. ''Something the judge said got to me and I realized that the only reason I didn't have a family wasn't because God had given me a rotten one. It was because I had pushed them away.''

He kissed her lightly. ''I'm not doing that anymore, Cassie. I'm not pushing my parents or you away ever again. It will take awhile for my family to work out our differences, but we've made a start this afternoon.''

His eyes, huge and melting, met hers and searched their emerald depths for an answer.

''What I need to know now is whether you'll help me? I love you more than anything in the world. I don't care about Judith's money or the estate or anything but you. You're the most important thing in my life.''

''But, Jeff, I'm not at all the type of wife you need. I can't bake, I'm no good at society things. I certainly won't be an asset to your business. And I can't guarantee that I'll have that son you want.''

He kissed her then, full on the lips, with all the fervor she could ever have asked for. And when she was breathless and only wanting more, he cupped her face in his hands.

''Cassandra Emily Newton Haddon, you are the only person I will ever need and you're exactly the woman I need to teach me about love. I'm only beginning to understand the meaning of that word, but I know that you are a master at loving. You've proven it over and over. It doesn't matter about children. Not anymore. There are more than enough kids in the world to care for. Besides—'' he grinned happily ''—I'm already a parent to the two most wonderful kids in the world. David and Marie are the perfect additions to our family. If God sends us more, fine. But if not, can't we be happy with what we have?''

Cassie gazed at him with love shining out from her happy

face. God had promised and He had more than fulfilled her dreams. Her heart sang His praise.

"Cassie, why don't you say something?" Jeff was peering at her worriedly. "Didn't you mean what you said about loving me? Were you just saying it?" He swallowed and straightened his shoulders. "It doesn't matter, you know. We can still build something beautiful if you'll just say you care for me at least a little, that you'll stay with me."

Cassie placed a finger over his lips to silence him. As he kneeled there in front of her, she thanked God for his mighty mysterious works.

I will use this gift of love wisely, she promised. *And with Your help we will make it grow and spread out to encompass others who need it so badly.*

"Jefferson William Haddon the third," she began softly. "I love you more than life itself. I think I have since the day you tried to put out my campfire." She smiled. "And yes, I'll live with you. I'll love you and work with you to raise our children, with God's help."

She kissed him gently; a kiss full of promise and love. And Jeff kissed her back.

"I love you," he murmured. "And I will never tire of saying that to you."

He picked her up in his arms and carried her up the steps.

"And tomorrow," he promised softly, "after we visit Judith and tell her how much we appreciate her hand in everything, you and I are going away for a real honeymoon."

"We are?" Cassie breathed, as he closed the bedroom door and set her down to face him. "Where?"

"I really think it would be best if we went back to Banff," Jeff whispered in her ear, his hand curving down her back as he pulled her closer. "After all, we've already seen the scenery and I want to spend my time looking at my wife."

Cassie moved back just slightly as his lips drew near.

"What about Marie and David?" she asked.

"They're not coming." He chuckled intimately. His lips feathered the delicate skin at her neck. "We'll have lots of time together as a family, Cassie. But for a while, I want you all to myself, Mrs. Haddon.''

''Wonderful idea, Mr. Haddon,'' she agreed.

And then neither of them said anything for a very long time.

Chapter Seventeen

The stately old brick house resounded with the sound of families laughing together. Outside, on the vast leaf-covered lawns, David looked at Marie and grinned at the giggling children throwing the brilliant red oak leaves at one another.

"Doesn't seem that long ago, does it?" he asked. "Two years goes past pretty fast in this place."

"Just wait." She chuckled. "It will go even faster now that you're a senior."

Half an hour later everyone gathered in the conservatory for the christening of Robert—Bobby for short—Jefferson Haddon and Emily—Emmy—Judith Haddon who slept like angels in their parents' tender arms.

"Father, we thank You for Your great blessings to Cassie and Jeff. We ask that You keep Your hand on them. Guide them gently as they raise these babies and Marie and David and remind them often of the love that binds all families together— a picture of the love that You, Father God, have for us."

As the reverend pronounced the benediction, a gentle wind suddenly jingled the chimes, sending their light airy tinkling reverberating through the open window and into the house that was now a home.

Cassie glanced at her husband and smiled happily at the love she saw glowing in his eyes.

"She knows," she told him softly. "Judith knows."

* * * * *

Dear Reader,

Thank you for reading my first book in the Love Inspired series. I'm a strong believer in the benefit of a good laugh and I love a happy ending, so I particularly enjoy writing Christian romances full of hope for the future. If my readers come away from my books feeling as if they've escaped their own confusion for a little while, if they've laughed and cried along with my imaginary friends, I have done what I set out to do.

I grew up in a small prairie town where everyone knew everyone else. My parents had their own business and I was constantly in the company of their friends, neighbors and customers for miles around, which provided wonderful fodder for my imagination and world of pretend. I remember being Laura Ingalls hiding from the enemy in a "cave" of caraganas. I stalked an elderly town hermit in the best Nancy Drew fashion, and I was the Cinderella of more imaginary romances than you can imagine. But I was also Joan of Arc, a missionary to the Congo and Dr. Livingstone's special assistant. Much of what I now write stems from my memories of those happy, carefree days.

As a child I was always puzzled by the dour expressions of some Christians. I still am. The joy that comes from God is large enough to encompass all of our daily problems and carry us through even the worst of times. Sometimes it's difficult to see even the next step, let alone visualize a whole lifetime, but isn't it wonderful to know that there is someone who sees it all and will guide us perfectly if only we trust in Him?

I wish you joy and much love for each new day.

Books by Janet Tronstad

Love Inspired

*An Angel for Dry Creek #81
*A Gentleman for Dry Creek #110
*A Bride for Dry Creek #138
*A Rich Man for Dry Creek #176
*A Hero for Dry Creek #228

Silhouette Romance

Stranded with Santa #1626

*Dry Creek

JANET TRONSTAD

grew up on a small farm in central Montana. One of her favorite things to do was to visit her grandfather's bookshelves, where he had a large collection of Zane Grey novels. She's always loved a good story.

Today, Janet lives in Pasadena, California, where she works in the research department of a medical organization. In addition to writing novels, she researches and writes nonfiction magazine articles.

A BRIDE FOR DRY CREEK
Janet Tronstad

Dedicated with love
To my two brothers and their wives
Ralph and Karen Tronstad
Russell and Heidi Tronstad
May God be with all of you
Now and forevermore.

Chapter One

A single fly buzzed past Francis Elkton and swooped up to the bare lights that hung from the rafters of the old barn. Francis didn't notice the fly, but on most nights she would have even though her eyes were now half-closed as she slow danced to an old fifties tune.

Francis was an immaculate housekeeper. And a first-class manager. She often said, in her job with the City of Denver, that the two went hand in hand. You only needed to look in someone's top desk drawer, she'd say, to predict what kind of a city manager they would be. Whether it was paper clips or people or drainage pipes, everything needed an order.

She would never have tolerated an out-of-place fly if she hadn't been so distracted.

But tonight, the fly was only one more guest at the wedding reception, and Francis was too busy trying to keep her unwanted memories in their place to give any attention to the proper place of a mere insect. Every time she opened her eyes she realized that things were not turning out the way she had planned.

She'd taken a three-month leave from her job and come back to Dry Creek, Montana, because she thought she'd be able to stand up to her past—to look her memories of Flint L. Harris square in the eye—and be free of him once and for all. She was mentally cleaning out her files, she told herself. Throwing away outdated papers. Putting her life back in order even if it had taken her twenty years to face the task.

The only reason she'd decided to do it now was that Sam Goodman, her neighbor in Denver, had said he would not wait forever to marry her. She'd realized suddenly that she could not give her heart to Sam, or any other man, until she got it completely back from Flint.

It had been a sentimental decision to come back to Dry Creek to purge herself. She reasoned that the memories had started here in this ranching community, in the shadows of the Big Sheep Mountains. And they would surely end here if she just screwed up her mind and willed them to be gone. It was like reaching deep inside herself to pull out the roots of an unwanted weed that had refused to die over the years.

But, for the first time since she'd come back, she realized her heart wasn't bending to her will. The past had not grown dimmer because she'd stood up to it. No, the past was right here before her in living color whether she wanted to see it or not.

The pink crepe paper streamers coming down from the rafters were the same color her high school class had used twenty years ago for their prom. Back then her classmates had gone to Miles City to school and had decorated the gym there with their streamers.

Tonight, the dance was being held in the large old barn her brother Garth had built for loading cattle. He had not used the barn for his cattle for several years now, and the community of Dry Creek had scrubbed it clean for their annual Christmas pageant some months ago. On a cold winter night like tonight, the inside of the barn shone bright and the windows were covered with frost.

Dry Creek was fast making the barn into an informal center for all kinds of occasions. Like tonight's dance to celebrate the wedding of Glory Becker and Matthew Curtis. The dance wasn't a prom, but the music was the same. The same swaying music. The same soft laughter of other couples in the background.

Francis could close her eyes and almost imagine it was Flint who held her in his arms. Flint with his shy halting gladness to see her and the tall wiry length of his twenty-year-old body.

Even back then, she should have known that dancing with him would come to no good

"Francis?" A slightly alarmed man's voice growled in her right ear.

Francis blinked and then blushed. Jess, one of her brother's older ranch hands, had invited her to dance, and it was his face that now looked at her suspiciously. She hadn't realized until he spoke that her arms had crept up his back until she had him in an embrace that was more than friendly. She shook the memories from her eyes, cleared her throat and loosened her arms. "Sorry."

"That's okay." Jess ducked his head, apparently reassured once the sensible Francis was back. Then he added teasingly, "After all, your brother did tell me to stick close to you tonight."

"He's not still worried about that phone call?" Francis gladly diverted the conversation to her brother's needless caution. "Just because some guy calls up and says someone might be out to kidnap me—it's all nonsense anyway. Even if Garth did know something about the rustlers who have been hitting this area—which he doesn't—well, it doesn't make sense. Before they start making any threats, these rustlers should find out if Garth knows anything that's a danger to them. Any manager would tell them that's the first step. They might be criminals, but that's no excuse for sloppy planning. You need to identify your problem and then verify how big it is before you can even hope to solve it."

"Way I hear it, it wasn't just some guy that called."

Apparently Jess only heard the first part of what she'd said. Francis had noticed that the ranch hands who worked for her brother tended to let their eyes glaze over when she tried to teach them management techniques.

"The man never gave his name," Francis corrected stiffly.

"Didn't need to from the way I heard it," Jess mumbled. "Begging your pardon for mentioning him. Still—can't be too careful."

No wonder she was having so much trouble getting rid of her memories of Flint, Francis thought. He seemed to have more lives than a stray alley cat. She'd bury him one day and he'd be resurrected the next. Did everyone in Dry Creek know about that phone call?

"I don't believe it was Flint Harris on the other end of that phone call. For pity's sake—he probably doesn't even remember Dry Creek." *Lord knows he doesn't remember me,* Francis added silently. "He never had roots in Dry Creek. He only came here that one spring because his grandmother was ill. He hasn't been back since she died."

"Hasn't sold her place yet, though," Jess argued. "Even pays taxes on it. That's got to mean something."

"It means that it isn't worth selling. Who would buy it? The windows are all broken out and it's only got five acres with it. The only thing you could raise there is chickens and with the low price of eggs these days—"

Francis stopped herself. She didn't need to be her own worst enemy. She needed to forget chickens. That had been their adolescent dream—that they would live with his grandmother and make their living by selling eggs. A fool's dream. Even back then, it wouldn't have kept them in jeans and tennis shoes. She cleared her throat. "The point is that Flint Harris is nowhere near here."

"Like I said, I'm sorry to bring the louse up. If I'd have been here back then and met the boy, I'd have given him a good speaking to—treating a nice girl like you that way."

Francis stopped dancing and looked at Jess. He seemed to expect a response. "Well, thank you, but that wouldn't have been necessary. I could take care of myself even back then."

"If you say so."

Francis looked at him carefully. There it was. A steady gleam of pity in his eyes.

"Those rumors are not true." Francis bristled. The one thing she didn't miss in Denver was the gossip that flowed freely in a small community. "While it is true that he and I drove to Las Vegas after the prom and looked for a justice of the peace, it is not true that we were actually married."

"Mrs. Hargrove says—"

"Mrs. Hargrove wasn't there. I was. The man was not a justice of the peace. My father called down there and asked.

They had no justice of the peace by that name. It doesn't matter what words we said, those papers we signed were worthless.''

''You signed some papers?'' The pity left his eyes. It was replaced by astonishment. ''You still have them?''

''I didn't say I have papers,'' Francis said patiently. The last time she'd seen those papers, Flint had had them. She remembered the way he had carefully folded them and put them in his coat pocket. She hadn't realized at the time that any young bride with any sense asks to keep the papers herself—especially when the wedding takes place in Las Vegas. That should have been her first clue.

''Besides, that is long ago and done with,'' Francis said briskly. ''As Mrs. Hargrove probably told you, even if it had been a marriage, it would have been the shortest marriage ever on record in Dry Creek—probably the shortest in all of Montana. I don't even think it lasted forty hours. We had the trip back from Vegas and then he dropped me off at my dad's to pack. Said he was going to Miles City to buy me some roses—every bride needed roses, he said—those were the last words I ever heard from him. He never came back.''

Francis believed in slicing through her pain quickly and efficiently with a minimum of fuss. She'd held her breath when she recited the facts of those two days with Flint and now she let it out slowly. ''I'm sure it was one of the smoothest exit lines in the book and I fell for it. Five weeks later I made arrangements to graduate early from high school and I left for Denver. That's all there was to it.''

''But no one knew,'' Jess reproached her softly. ''That's the only reason the folks here still remember it. No one but your father knew and then you just left so suddenly. These were your neighbors and friends. They cared about you, they just didn't know what was happening. Even now Mrs. Hargrove keeps trying to think back to something she could have said to make it better in those days for you—blames herself for not taking a more motherly role in your life—what with just you and your dad out there alone when Garth was in the service—keeps having this notion that Flint did come back in around that time and stopped at her place to ask for you.''

''She's confused,'' Francis said flatly. People meant well, but it didn't help to sugarcoat the truth. "If he'd tried to find me, he'd have tried my father's place. He knew where it was. He'd been there enough times."

"I suppose you're right."

The dance ended and suddenly Francis felt foolish to be standing there arguing about whether or not a man had stopped to see her neighbor twenty years ago. "I think I'll sit the next one out if it's all the same to you. You can tell my brother I'll be fine. I'll just be taking a rest."

Jess looked relieved. "I could use a break myself. My arthritis is acting up some."

"Well, why didn't you say so? We could have sat the last two dances out—no need to be up and moving around on a cold night like this."

"It is a blistering one out tonight, isn't it?"

"All the more reason to forget about the kidnapping threat," Francis agreed. "No one but a fool would be out setting a trap tonight. It's too cold. No, I think the kids are right when they said it was that rival gang they have in Seattle calling to make mischief."

Francis's brother, Garth, had offered the use of his ranch to a woman who ran a youth center for gang kids in Seattle. At the moment, thirty of the kids were learning to be better citizens by spending a few weeks in Dry Creek, Montana. Garth had been in charge of teaching the boys how to be gentlemen, and Francis had been astonished at his patience. He'd had them out in the barn practicing how to dip and twirl their dance partners, and the boys had loved it.

A rich society woman from Seattle, Mrs. Buckwalter, was underwriting the cost of the trip to Montana, and Francis couldn't help but notice how excited the older woman was tonight. Mrs. Buckwalter couldn't have been prouder of the teens if she'd given birth to every one of them.

And Francis couldn't blame her. The teenagers sparkled at this dance, the boys in their rented tuxedos and the girls in the old fifties prom dresses they'd borrowed from the women of Dry Creek. It was hard to believe that they were members of various gangs in Seattle. A few dance lessons and a sprinkling of ties and taffeta had transformed them.

"That's really the logical explanation," Francis concluded. If the other gang could only see the youth center kids now. She couldn't help but think they'd be a little jealous of the good time these kids were having.

"Maybe." Jess didn't look convinced. "Just don't take any unnecessary risks—your brother will have my hide. He's worried, you know—"

"Even if Flint did kidnap me, he'd never hurt me—no matter what Garth worries about." As Francis listened to herself saying the words, she realized how naive she sounded. She didn't know what kind of a man Flint might be today. She'd often wondered.

Jess looked at her. "Still, things happen."

"What could happen?" Francis waved her arms around. She might not know about Flint, but she did know about the people of Dry Creek. At least a hundred people were in the barn, some sitting on folding chairs along the two sides, a few standing by the refreshment table and dozens of them on the floor poised ready to dance to the next tune. A lot of muscle rested beneath the suits that had been unearthed for this party. "One little scream and fifty men would come to my rescue. I'm surrounded by Dry Creek. There isn't a safer place in all the world for me."

Jess grunted. "I guess you're right. Maybe you should go visit with Mrs. Hargrove a bit. Talk to those two little boys that belong to Matthew Curtis. Find out how they like the idea of having a new mama."

Francis smiled. She was fond of the four-year-old twins and liked to see them so happy. "Everyone knows how they feel about that. She's their angel. If their dad wasn't going to marry Glory, I think they'd wait and marry her themselves."

Meanwhile, outside in the dark...

Flint watched a fly buzz up to the headlight of the old cattle truck. Now, what was a fly doing in the middle of a Montana winter night so cold a man's nose hairs were likely to freeze?

Flint slid into the niche between two cars and hunched down in his black leather jacket. The worthless jacket was nearly stiff.

That fly didn't belong here any more than Flint and his jacket did. He would bet the fly had made the mistake of crawling into that cattle truck when it'd been parked someplace a lot warmer. Say Seattle. Or San Francisco.

Even a rookie FBI agent would make the connection that the truck didn't belong to anyone local. And Flint had been with the Bureau for twenty years. No, the truck had to belong to the three men he'd identified as cattle thieves. He'd call in their location just as soon as he had something more concrete to tell the inspector than that he'd listened to them talk enough to know they were brothers.

The last time he'd made his daily check-in call, one of the guys had said the inspector was grumbling about him being out here on this assignment without a partner. Flint told him he had a partner—an ornery horse named Honey.

The fly made another pass close to Flint's face, seeking the warmth of his breath.

Flint half-cursed as he waved the fly away. He didn't need the fly to distract him from the mumbled conversation of the three men. They'd been standing in front of the cattle truck arguing for several minutes about some orders their boss had given to deliver a package.

Flint sure hoped they were talking about which cattle to steal next.

If not, that probably meant his tip was accurate and they were planning to kidnap Francis Elkton. He hoped Garth had taken the phone call he had made seriously and was keeping Francis inside, in some controlled area with no one but the good ladies of Dry Creek around her.

Flint envied all of the people of Dry Creek the heat inside the barn. The warmest he was likely to get anytime soon was when he went to feed Honey some oats.

It hadn't taken him more than a half hour on Honey's back to realize that her owner must have had a chuckle or two when he named her. She was more sour than sweet. Still, Flint rubbed his gloved hands over his arms and shivered. Honey might be a pain, but he missed her all the same. She was the only breathing thing he'd talked to since he came to Montana.

By now Honey would be wondering when they'd go home.

When he'd ridden her to town tonight, he'd tied her reins to a metal clothesline pole in a vacant lot behind Mr. Gossett's house. The pole was out of the wind, but Honey would still be anxious for warmer quarters. Last night, he'd bedded her down in an abandoned chicken coop that still stood on the farm he'd inherited from his grandmother when she died fifteen years ago. As far as he knew, no one but gophers ever visited the place anymore.

He was half-surprised the men hiding by that cattle truck didn't use horses. The terrain on the south slopes of the Big Sheep Mountain Range wasn't steep, but it also wasn't paved. There were more fences than roads. The long, winding strings of barbed wire and aging posts did little in winter except collect snowdrifts. Flint had followed a dozen of those fences to reacquaint himself with the area last night and didn't see anything more than a thick-coated coyote or two.

But then these men probably didn't know how to ride a horse. Which meant they weren't professionals. If they had been pros, they would have learned before heading out here on a job like this. A pro would realize a horse would be a good escape option if the roads were blocked. Yes, a pro would learn to ride. Even if he needed to learn on a bad-tempered horse like Honey.

Flint's observations of the men had already made him suspect that they were not career kidnappers. They were too careless and disorganized to have lived long if they made a habit of breaking the law. But Flint knew that the crime syndicates liked to use amateurs for some jobs—they made good fall guys when things went sour.

Granted, the Boss—and the Bureau didn't know who he was yet—had other reasons to use amateurs here. A pro would look so out of place in this rural community he might as well wear a red neon sticker that said Hired Killer—Arrest Me Now.

The fact that the men were too tender to ride horses made Flint hope that they would give it up for tonight and go home. The night was clear—there was enough moonlight so that Flint could see the low mountains that made up the Big Sheep Mountain Range. But it was ice-cracking cold and not getting any warmer.

The little town of Dry Creek stood a few miles off Interstate 94, which ran along the southern third of Montana from Billings on through Miles City. The town was nothing more than a few wood frame houses, an old square church, a café called Jazz and Pasta that was run by a young engaged couple, and a hardware store with a stovepipe sticking up through the roof. The pipe promised some kind of heat inside. Flint had not gone in to find out if the old Franklin stove he remembered was still being used. He hadn't even tried to find an opening in the frost so he could look in the window.

The memories Flint had of his days in Dry Creek were wrinkled by time, and he couldn't be sure if all the details like the Franklin stove were true or if he'd romanticized them over the years, mixing them up with some old-fashioned movie he'd seen or some nostalgic dream he'd had.

He realized he didn't want to know about the stove so he hadn't looked inside the hardware store.

Flint had only spent a few months in Dry Creek, but this little community—more than anywhere else on earth—was the place he thought of as home. His grandmother had lived her life here, and this is where he'd known Francis. The combination of the two would make this forever home to him.

None of the chrome-and-plastic-furnished apartments he'd rented over the years could even begin to compete. They were little more than closets to keep his clothes out of the rain. He couldn't remember the last time he'd cooked anything but coffee in any of them. No, none of them could compete with the homes around Dry Creek.

Even old man Gossett's place looked as though it had a garden of sorts—a few rhubarb stalks stuck up out of a snowdrift, and there was a crab apple tree just left of his back porch. There were no leaves on the tree, but Flint recognized the graceful swoop of the bare branches.

The trash barrel that the man kept in the vacant lot had a broken jelly jar inside. Flint suspected someone was making jelly from the apples that came off the tree. It might even be the old man.

Flint envied the old man his jelly and Flint didn't even like jelly. The jelly just symbolized home and community for him, and Flint felt more alone than he had for years. Maybe when he finished this business in Dry Creek, he should think about getting married.

That woman he'd started dating—Annette—he wondered if she could make apple jelly. He'd have to find out—maybe he should even send her a postcard. Women liked postcards. He hadn't seen any that featured Dry Creek, but maybe he'd stop in Billings when this was all over. Get her something with those mountains on it. In the daylight the Big Sheep Mountain Range was low and buff-colored with lots of dry sage in the foreground. Looked like a Zane Grey novel. Yes, a postcard was a good idea. That's what he'd do when this was all over.

From the sounds of the ruckus inside that old barn, the whole community of Dry Creek, Montana, was celebrating tonight. All eighty-five adults and the usual assortment of children.

Flint had checked the vital statistics before he headed down here. The place didn't have any more people now than it had had that spring he'd spent at his grandmother's place. The only new people that had come to the community were the busload of Seattle teenagers who were there for a month to see that all of life wasn't limited to the city streets. As long as Francis stayed with the people inside the barn, she would be safe.

That thought had no sooner crossed his mind than the side barn door opened. A woman stood silhouetted in the golden light from inside the barn. Flint felt all breath leave his body. It was Francis.

Francis let the winter air cool her. The ruby red material of her dress was thin, but it had still suddenly gotten much too hot inside the barn. The rumor that Flint had been the one who made the phone call to Garth this afternoon had opened up all of the speculation about her and Flint. She saw it in the eyes of her neighbors. They were asking themselves why she'd never married, why she'd moved away so quickly all those years ago, why she'd never come back to live in Dry Creek until now— why, why, why. The questions would be endless until they'd worried her heart to a bone.

She only wished the asking of the questions would help her find an answer, she thought ruefully. Because, even if no one else had been asking those questions, she would be asking them.

But not tonight, she decided. Tonight she would just breathe the crisp night air and look at the stars that were scattered across the sky like pieces of glitter sprinkled over velvet. She used to love to go out on a winter's night like this and find the Big Dipper.

Now where is it, she asked herself as she stepped through the open door and outside. The barn was hiding the constellation from her. But if she went over by that old cattle truck she could see it.

She suddenly realized she hadn't gone looking for the Big Dipper in many years.

Flint swore. No wonder being a hero had gone out of style. His leg still stung where Francis had kicked him in her glittery high-heeled shoes, and one of his toes could well be broken where she had stomped on it.

Next time, he'd let the kidnappers have her. She was more than a match for most of the hired toughs he'd seen in his time. She'd certainly hold her own with the men in the cattle truck.

And thinking of his toes, what was she doing with shoes like that, anyway? Women only wore shoes like that to please a man. That meant she must have a boyfriend inside that old barn. That was one statistic he hadn't thought to check before heading out here.

Flint's only consolation was that his horse seemed to know he needed her and was behaving for once.

"Now I know why they call you Honey," Flint murmured encouragingly as he nudged his horse down the dark road.

"Hargh." An angry growl came from the bundle behind him, but Flint didn't even look back. Except for being temporarily gagged, Francis was doing better than he was. He'd even tied his jacket around her. Not that she had thanked him for it.

"Yes, sir, you're a sweetie, all right," Flint continued quietly guiding his horse. Honey knew the way home even if it was only a humble abandoned shed. That horse could teach some people the meaning of gratitude.

Or, if not gratitude, at least cooperation, Flint fumed.

If it wasn't for his years of training as an agent, Flint would have turned around and told Francis a thing or two. What did she think?

There was no time for niceties when he knew those two hired thugs were waiting for Francis. He'd heard them repeat their instructions about kidnapping Garth's sister in her black jacket with the old high school emblem of a lion.

Early on in the evening, the two men made a decision to wait for her by the bus—parked right next to that old cattle truck they'd come in. They hoped Francis would tire of dancing and come to sit in the bus. Flint had winced when he heard the plan. The two men were clearly amateurs, unfamiliar with Montana. No one, no matter how tired, would come to rest in a cold bus when the engine wasn't running.

But he saw their dilemma. They couldn't face down the whole town of Dry Creek or even the busload of kids that would be going back to the Elkton ranch. That's why he wasn't surprised, after the men had waited a few hours and gotten thoroughly cold themselves, to hear them start talking about going home and waiting until the next day to kidnap Francis.

Flint was hoping they'd leave soon. And they would have, except who should come outside for a late night stroll but Francis. She wasn't wearing the black jacket, but Flint couldn't risk the thugs getting a close look at her and realizing who she was, even without the jacket.

There was no time for fancy plans. The only way to protect Francis was to grab her first and worry about the men later.

Flint knew the men might be a problem if they realized what he was doing, but he hadn't counted on Francis's resistance. He thought once she knew it was him she'd come quietly. Perhaps even gratefully. But the moment he saw recognition dawn, she fought him like he was her worst enemy. He hadn't planned on gagging her until she made it clear she was going to scream.

And all the while she was kicking and spitting, he'd been doing her a great service.

Yes, he sighed, he could see why being a hero had gone completely out of style. It wasn't easy being the knight on the shining white horse. Not with the women of today. Come to think of it, it wasn't even easy with the horses of today. Honey made it clear she'd rather be eating oats than rescuing a damsel in distress.

"Tired, that's what you are," Flint said softly as he leaned over the horse's neck. Honey sighed, and he gave the horse another encouraging nudge. "We're both tired, aren't we? But don't worry. We're almost there. Then I'll have something sweet for you."

The bundle behind him gave an indignant gasp and then another angry growl.

"I was talking to the horse." Flint smiled in spite of himself.

Chapter Two

Francis wished she had worn those ruby silk flowers in her hair like the teenagers had urged her to do. At least then, when the horse shook her, the petals would fall to the ground and leave a trail in the snow for someone to follow when they searched for her in the morning. Maybe if she were lucky, some of the sequins on her long evening dress would fall to the ground and leave a trail of reddish sparkles.

She still didn't understand what had happened.

One minute she'd been looking at the night sky, searching for the tail star of the Big Dipper. The next minute she'd felt someone put an arm around the small of her back. She hadn't even been able to turn around and see who it was before another arm went behind her knees and she was lifted up.

Suddenly, instead of seeing the night sky she was looking square into the face of Flint Harris. For a second, she couldn't breathe. Her mind went blank. Surely, it could not be Flint. Not her Flint. She blinked. He was still there.

She was speechless. He was older, it was true. Instead of the smooth-skinned boy she remembered, she saw the face of a man. Weather had etched a few fine lines around his eyes. A tiny scar crossed the left side of his chin. His face was fuller, stronger.

Oh, my Lord, she suddenly realized. *It's true. He's kidnapping me!*

Francis opened her mouth to scream. Nothing came out. She took a good breath to try again when Flint swore and hurriedly stuffed an old bandanna into her mouth. The wretched piece of cloth smelled of horse. She understood why it smelled when Flint slung her over his back like she was nothing to him but a sack of potatoes in a fancy bag. He then hauled her off to a horse tied behind Mr. Gossett's house.

Once Flint got to the horse, he stopped to slip some wool mittens from his hands and onto her hands. The mittens were warm inside from his body heat, and the minute he slid them onto her hands, her fingers felt like they were being tucked under a quilt.

But she didn't have time to enjoy it.

There was a light on in old man Gossett's house, and Francis struggled to scream through her gag. She knew the man was home since he never went to community gatherings. He was a sour old man and she wasn't sure he'd help her even if he knew she was in trouble. Through the thin curtains on his window, she saw him slowly walking around inside his kitchen. Unless he'd grown deaf in these past years, he must have heard her. If he did, he didn't come outside to investigate.

Flint didn't give her a second chance to scream. He threw her over the back of the horse, slapped his jacket on her shoulders and mounted up.

Ever since then she'd been bouncing along, facedown, behind his saddle.

Finally, the horse stopped.

They had entered a grove of pine trees. The night was dark, but the moon was out. Inside the grove, the trees cut off the light of the moon, as well. Only a few patches of snow were visible. From the sounds beneath the horse's hoofs, the rest of the ground was covered with dried pine needles.

The saddle creaked as Flint stood to dismount.

Francis braced herself. She'd been trained to cope with hostage situations in her job and knew a person was supposed to cooperate with the kidnapper. But surely that didn't apply to criminals one knew. She and this particular criminal had slow danced together. He couldn't shoot her.

She'd already decided to wait her chance and escape. She had a plan. Flint had made a mistake in putting the mittens on her. The wool of the mittens kept the cord from gripping her wrists tightly. When Flint stepped down on the ground, she would loosen the tie on her wrists, swing her body around and nudge that horse of his into as much of a gallop as the poor thing could handle.

Flint stepped down.

The horse whinnied in protest.

"What the—" Flint turned and started to swear.

Francis had her leg caught around the horn of the saddle. She'd almost made the turn. But almost wasn't enough. She was hanging, with one leg behind the back of the saddle and one hooked around the horn. She'd ripped the skirt of her ruby sheath dress and all she'd accomplished was a change of view. Her face was no longer looking at the ground. Instead, she was looking straight into the astonished eyes of Flint L. Harris.

Francis groaned into her gag. She'd also twisted a muscle in her leg.

And she'd spooked the horse. The poor thing was prancing like a boxer. Each move of the beast's hooves sent a new pain through Francis's leg.

"Easy, Honey," Flint said soothingly as he reached out to touch the horse.

Francis saw his hands in the dark. His rhythm was steady, and he stroked the animal until she had quieted.

"Atta girl." Flint gave the horse one last long stroke.

Flint almost swore again. They should outlaw high heels. How was a man supposed to keep his mind on excitable horses and bad guys when right there—just a half arm's length away— was a dainty ankle in a strappy red high heel? Not to mention a leg that showed all the way up to the thigh because of the tear in that red dress. He was glad it was dark. He hoped Francis couldn't see in his eyes the thoughts that his mind was thinking.

"She'll be quiet now." Flint continued speaking slow and calm for the horse's benefit. "But she spooks easy. Try to stay still."

Even in the darkness inside the pine grove he could see the delicate lines of Francis's face behind the gag. Her jaw was clenched tight. He hadn't realized—

"I know it's not easy," he added softly. "I didn't mean to frighten you."

A muffled protest came from behind the gag.

Francis had worn her dark hair loose, and it spilled into his hands when he reached up to untie the gag. Flint's hands were cold, and her hair whispered across them like a warm summer breeze. He couldn't resist lingering a moment longer than necessary inside the warmth of her hair.

"It's not how I meant to say hello again," Flint said as he untied the bandanna. And it was true. What he'd say when he met Francis again had gone from being a torture to a favorite game with him over the years. None of his fantasies of the moment had involved her looking at him with eyes wide with fear.

"Don't pretend you ever meant to see me again." Francis spit the words out when the gag was finally gone. Her voice was rusty and bitter even to her own ears. "Not that it matters," she quickly lied. "I—"

Francis stopped. She almost wished she had the gag in her mouth.

"That was a long time ago," Francis finally managed.

"Yes, it was," Flint agreed as he finished unraveling the cord he'd used to tie Francis's hands behind her. It might seem like a long time ago to her. To him it was yesterday.

"Cold night out," Flint added conversationally as he stuffed the cord into his pocket. He needed to move their words to neutral territory. Her wrists had been as smooth as marble. "Is it always this cold around here in February?"

"It used to be," Francis answered. She'd felt Flint's fingertips on the skin of her wrists just at the top of her mittens. His fingers were ice cold. For the first time, she realized the mittens on her hands must have been the only ones he had. "Folks say, though, that the winters lately have been mild."

"That's right, you don't live here anymore, do you?" Flint asked as he put his hand on Francis's lower leg. He felt her stiffen. "Easy. Just going to try and unravel you here without scaring Honey."

Flint let his hand stay on Francis's leg until both his hand and that section of her leg were warm. He let his hand massage that little bit of leg ever so slightly so it wouldn't stiffen up.

"Don't want to make you pull the muscle in that leg any more than it looks like you've already done."

Flint had to stop his hand before it betrayed him. Francis was wearing real nylon stockings. The ones like they used to make. A man's hands slid over them like they were cream. If Flint were a betting man, he would bet nylon like this didn't come from panty hose, either. No, she was wearing the old-fashioned kind of nylons with a garter belt.

This knowledge turned him first hot then cold. A woman only wore those kind of stockings for one reason.

"You won't be dancing any time soon," he offered with deceptive mildness as he pressed his hands against his thighs to warm them enough to continue. "So I suppose that boyfriend of yours will just have to be patient."

"He has been," Francis said confidently. "Thank you for reminding me."

Francis thought of Sam Goodman. He might not make her blood race, but he didn't make it turn to ice, either. He was a good, steady man. A man she'd be proud to call her boyfriend. Maybe even her husband. She almost wished she'd encouraged him more when he'd called last week and offered to come for a visit.

Flint pressed his lips together. He should have thought about the boyfriend before he took off with Francis like he had. It had already occurred to him that he could have simply returned her to the good people of Dry Creek. Instead of heading for the horse, he could have headed for the light streaming out the open barn door and simply placed her inside. If it had been anyone but Francis, he would have.

But Francis addled his brain. All he could think of was keeping her safe, and he didn't trust anyone else—not even some fancy boyfriend who made her want to dress in garters and sequins—to get her far enough away from the rustlers. He had to make sure she was safe or to take a bullet for her if something happened and those two kidnappers got spooked.

Still, a boyfriend could pose problems. "I suppose he'll be wondering where you are," Flint worried aloud as he slowly turned the saddle to allow Francis's leg to tip toward him.

Francis stared in dismay. Flint was helping her untangle herself, but he was obviously positioning her so that she would slide off the back of the horse and into his arms.

"I can walk," Francis said abruptly.

"You'd have better luck flying at the moment," Flint said as he put a hand on each of her hips and braced himself. "Put your arms around my neck and I'll swing you around."

"I don't think—" Francis began. Flint's hands swept past her hips and wrapped themselves around her waist. She took a quick, involuntary breath. Surely he could feel her heart pounding inside her body. The material on this wretched dress the girls had talked her into wearing was not at all good for this sort of thing. It was much too thin. She could feel the heat from Flint's hands as he cradled her waist.

"You don't need to think—just move with me," Flint directed. He couldn't take much more of this.

It must be the cold that made his hands even more sensitive than usual. He not only felt every ridge of beaded sequin on the dress, he felt every move of her muscles beneath the palm of his hands. He knew she was trying to pull herself away from him. That she was struggling to move her leg without his help. The knowledge didn't do much for a man's confidence. He remembered the days when she used to want him to hold her.

"You're going to scare the horse," Flint cautioned softly. Beneath the sequins, the dress felt like liquid silk. Flint had all he could do to stop his hands from caressing Francis instead of merely holding her firm so he could lift her off the horse.

"Where'd you get the horse, anyway?" Francis forced her mind to start working. *Everything has a place,* she reminded herself. If she could only find the place of everything, this whole nightmare would come aright. She could make sense and order out of this whole madness if she worked at solving one piece of the puzzle and then went on to the next piece. She'd start with the horse.

"A small farm outside of Billings," Flint answered. His hands spanned Francis's rib cage. He could feel her heart pounding. "They rent horses."

"Why would you rent a horse?" Francis persisted. One question at a time. It helped her focus and forget about the hands around her. "You don't live around here. They must usually rent to ranchers."

Flint stopped. He could hardly say he needed a horse to rescue her. She'd never believe that. Then he remembered he didn't need an answer. "That's classified information. Government." Flint had her circled, and there was no reason to stall. "Move with me on the count of three."

All thought of the horse—and its order—fled Francis's mind.

"One. Two." Flint braced himself. "Three."

When Flint pulled, his hands slid from the middle of Francis's rib cage to the top. He almost stopped. But Honey was beginning to tap-dance around again, and he had to follow through.

Francis gasped. The man's hands were moving upward from her rib cage. There was nothing for it but to put her arms around his neck and swing forward.

"Atta girl," Flint murmured. Even he didn't know if he was talking to Francis or the horse. And it didn't matter. He had Francis once again in his arms. Well, maybe not in his arms, but she was swinging from his neck. That had to count for something.

Francis winced. Her leg was swinging off the horse along with the rest of her body, and her leg was protesting. But she gritted her teeth. "Let me down."

Flint went from ice to fire in a heartbeat. He'd been without a jacket after he gave it to Francis, and his chest was cold. But the minute Francis swung against him, his whole insides flamed. His jacket had only been draped over her, and now it fell back to her shoulders. He felt the cool smoothness of her bare arms wrapped around his neck and the swell of her breasts pressed against his shirt.

"I can't let you down." Flint ground the words out. "You can't walk through a snowdrift in those heels."

"I can walk barefoot."

"Not with that leg," Flint shifted Francis's weight so his neck didn't carry her. Instead, he had his arms around her properly this time. There were no bad guys here. He could carry her like a gentleman. "Besides, you'd get frostbite."

Francis didn't argue. She simply couldn't think of anything

to say. She had been swiveled, swept up in his arms and now rested on Flint's shoulder with a view of his chin. This was not the way anything was supposed to go. She was supposed to be forgetting him. "You nicked your chin the night of the prom, too."

"Huh?"

"When you shaved—the night of the prom, you nicked your chin. Almost in the same place."

"I was nervous."

"Me, too."

"You didn't look nervous," Flint said softly. He had tied Honey to a branch and was carrying Francis out of the pine grove. "You were cool as a cucumber."

"I hadn't been able to eat all day."

"You were perfect," Flint said simply. He was walking toward the small wood frame house. "Everybody is hungry at those things, anyway. You think there'll be food and it turns out to be pickled mushrooms or something with toothpicks in it."

Flint stopped. He was halfway to the house, and he knew someone had been here recently besides himself and Honey. A faint smell was coming from the house—the smell of cigars. He'd only known one man to ever smoke that particular brand.

"I'm going to set you down and check out the house," Flint whispered. It could be a trap. The cigars weren't a secret. "Be quiet."

Francis shivered, and not from the cold. Even in a whisper, Flint's voice sounded deadly serious. For the first time, she was truly afraid. And, for the first time, it occurred to her that if it were known by now that she was kidnapped—and it surely would be known once Jess checked around the barn—then someone would be out to rescue her. And if they intended to rescue her, they would also be out to hurt—maybe even kill—Flint.

The very thought of it turned her to ice. She could cheerfully strangle Flint herself. But seeing him hurt—really hurt—was something else again.

Think, Francis, think, she told herself as Flint slid her out of his arms to a dry space near a pine tree. The shade of the tree made the night darker here than anywhere. Even the light of the moon did not reflect off her sequins when she was sitting here. She could no longer see his face. He was a black shadow who crouched beside her.

"Be careful," she whispered at his back as he turned to leave. The words sounded futile to her ears. And then she saw his black silhouette as he drew a gun from somewhere. He must have had a gun in the saddlebag. Or maybe he had a shoulder holster.

Francis didn't want to be responsible for Flint being hurt. But anyone who was here to rescue her would think nothing of shooting Flint. *Think, Francis, think.* There had to be a solution. She couldn't just sit here and wait for the gunfire to begin.

That's it, she thought victoriously. She knew she could think of a solution. It just needed an orderly mind. If there were no kidnapping, there would be no need for any shooting.

Francis forced herself to stand. Her one leg wobbled, but it would have to do. She took a step forward, praying whoever was inside that wooden house would have sense enough to recognize her voice.

"Flint, darling," she called in what she hoped was a gay and flirtatious voice. She was out of practice, but even if her voice wasn't seductive she knew it was loud enough to be heard through the thickest walls. "I thought you said there was a bed inside this old house for us to use."

There, she thought in satisfaction, *that should quell any questions about a kidnapping.* It would, of course, raise all sorts of other questions, but she could deal with that later. She wondered who of the many Dry Creek men had come to her rescue.

Flint froze. Only years of training stopped him from turning around to stare at Francis. The deep easy chuckle that rumbled through the walls of the house confirmed his suspicions about who had smoked the cigars. The cigars could be duplicated. The chuckle never. It was safe to turn around.

Flint could only see the silhouette of Francis, but it was enough. He walked toward her and said the only thing he could think to say. "I told you to keep quiet. That could have been anyone inside."

"I didn't want you to be shot on my account," Francis whispered airily as she limped toward him. "If you just let me go now, there'll be no kidnapping."

"There never was a kidnapping. This was a rescue."

"A rescue?" Francis turned the word over in her mouth and spoke low enough so that whoever was inside the house could not hear. "Don't you think that's going a bit far? I don't think anyone would believe it's a rescue— I think we better stick with the seduction story."

Flint shook his head. No wonder being a hero was so difficult these days.

"Not that they'll believe the seduction story, either." Francis continued to whisper. Her leg was painful, but she found it easier to limp than to stand. "I must look a sight by now."

The deep darkness of the night that had gathered around the pine trees lifted as Francis moved toward him. "I wonder which of the men from Dry Creek knew enough to drive out here and wait for us. Pretty quick thinking."

Flint held his breath. In the night, he could look at Francis and not worry about the naked desire she would see in his eyes any other time. His jacket had fallen off her shoulders under the tree, and her arms and neck gleamed white even in the midnight darkness. The sequins of that red dress glittered as she moved, showing every curve in her slender body. She was beautiful.

"It's not one of the men from Dry Creek," Flint said softly. "It's my boss."

Francis stopped. She'd never thought—never even considered. And she should have—there's an order to everything, she reminded herself blindly. One needed to know the place of everything. And a kidnapping, she noted dully, required a motive and, in this case, a boss.

Francis stared unmoving at the weatherbeaten deserted house that used to belong to Flint's grandmother. The white paint had peeled off the frame years ago, leaving a chipped grayness that blended into the darkness. Gaping black holes marked where the glass had broken out of the windows.

"He must think I'm a fool," Francis whispered stiffly.

Francis looked so fragile, Flint moved slowly toward her. She looked like a bird, perched for flight even with her sprained leg muscle.

"No, I'm sure he doesn't think that at all," he said softly.

When he reached Francis, Flint picked her up again. This time he cradled her in his arms properly, as he had wanted to each time he'd picked her up tonight. For the first time, she didn't resist him. That should thrill his heart, Flint thought. But it didn't. He knew Francis wasn't warming toward him. She'd just given up.

"And that bit about the bed." Francis continued to fret. "I'm a middle-aged woman. He must think I'm a featherbrain—especially because he knows why you have me out here."

"He does, does he?" Flint asked quietly. It came as somewhat of a surprise to him that he'd rather have Francis kicking his shin with her pointed high heels than to have her lying still in his arms feeling foolish after having done something so brave.

The angle wasn't perfect for what he needed to do, but Flint found that if he bent his knee and slowly lowered Francis until she was securely perched on the knee, he could crane his neck and do what he needed to do.

He bent his head down and kissed her. He knew his lips were cold and chapped by now. He knew that the quick indrawn breath he heard from Francis was shock rather than passion. But he also knew that they both needed this kiss more than they needed the air they were breathing.

Flint took his time. He'd waited twenty years for this kiss and, planned or not, he needed to take his time. He felt the stiffness leave Francis's lips and he felt them move against him like they used to. He and his Francis were home again.

"Thank you." Francis was the first one to breathe after the kiss ended. Her pulse was beating fast, but she willed it to slow. "At least now your boss won't think I'm delusional—he'll think you at least tried to seduce me. Middle-aged or not." Francis stopped speaking to peer into the darkness of the broken windows. "He is watching, isn't he?"

For the first time since he'd bent down on one knee, Flint felt the bone-chilling cold of the snow beneath him. He might be home again, but Francis wasn't. "You think the kiss was for my boss's benefit?"

"Of course. And I appreciate it. I really do."

Flint only grunted. He must be losing his touch. He went back and picked up his jacket to wrap around Francis.

Chapter Three

"There's trouble in Dry Creek." The words came out of the other man's mouth the moment Flint kicked open the door to the abandoned house and, still holding Francis, stepped inside. "Kidnapping."

"I know," Francis said stiffly. She was glad she'd have the chance to show she wasn't a ninny. "That's me."

"Not unless you got here in the back of a cattle truck, it's not," the other man said mildly, a lit cigar in his mouth and a cell phone in his hand. The only light in the room was a small flashlight the man must have laid on the table recently. The flashlight gave a glow to the rather large room and showed some bookcases and a few wooden chairs scattered around the table.

"Well, surely there's no point in kidnapping more than me."

"It appears they have some woman named Sylvia Bannister and then Garth Elkton."

"Oh, no." Francis half twisted herself out of Flint's arms. "I'll need to go help them."

"You can't go." Flint finished carrying her over to one of the chairs and gently sat her down.

"That's right. I'm a prisoner."

"You're not a prisoner," Flint said impatiently and then turned to the older man. "It better be me that goes. I've gotten a little acquainted with the guys responsible for this. Might have picked up a tip or two."

While Flint was talking, he was rummaging through a backpack resting on another chair. He pulled out an ammunitions cartridge and put it in the pocket of a dry jacket that was wrapped around the back of the chair. Then he pulled out a pair of leather gloves.

"Mrs. B called it in." The older man gestured to his cell phone. "Said to hurry. Some kids are chasing the truck in a bus as we speak. You can use my Jeep. Parked it behind the trees over there." The older man jerked his head in the opposite direction they had ridden in from. "It'll get you there faster."

"Not faster than Honey," Flint said with a smile as he walked toward the door. "She can beat a Jeep any day. She makes her own roads."

Flint opened the door and was gone in a little less than five seconds. Francis knew it was five seconds because she was counting to ten and had only reached five when the door creaked shut. Her teeth were chattering and she didn't know if it was because she was near frozen or because she was scared to death. She hoped counting would force her to focus and make it all better. It didn't.

"I've got one of those emergency blankets in here someplace," the older man said as he turned to a backpack of his own leaning in the corner of the room. "Prevents heat loss, that sort of thing."

"I'm okay." Francis shivered through the words. She felt helpless to be sitting here when someone had kidnapped Sylvia and Garth.

"Not much to that dress," the older man said as he walked over to her and wrapped what looked like a huge foil paper around her. "Especially in ten below weather."

The paper crinkled when she moved, but Francis noticed a pocket of warmth was forming around her legs. It would spread. "I didn't plan to be out in it for so long without my coat."

"I expect you didn't." The man went back to his pack and pulled out a small hand-cranked lantern. He twisted the handle a few times and set the lantern on the table. A soft glow lit up the whole room. "Something must have gone wrong."

"Flint kidnapped me."

That fact seemed to amuse the older man. "Yes, I forgot. You mentioned that earlier. Sorry to spoil your plans."

"They were hardly my plans. You're the boss. They were your plans." Francis knew it wasn't always wise to confront criminals. But the old man seemed fairly harmless, and she did like to keep things clear.

"Sounded more like a lover's tryst to me." The man sat on one of the chairs.

"Humph." Francis didn't want to go into that.

"Not that it's any of my business," the man continued and looked around the room. "Although I can assure you that if Flint told you there was a bed, he lied."

"Humph." Francis was feeling the warmth steel up her whole body. She could almost feel cozy. "We don't really need a bed."

"Good."

The man sat for a few minutes in silence and then got up and went to his pack and drew out a can. "Peaches?"

"I'd like that."

The man opened the peaches with the can-opening edge of a Swiss knife.

"Handy thing," he said as he flipped the blades into the knife and put it in his pocket. "Flint gave me this one almost fifteen years ago now."

"You've known him for that long?"

The man nodded. "Almost as long as you have if you're who I think you are."

Francis wondered if this were a trick to find out who she was. But then, she reasoned, it hardly mattered. Flint certainly knew who she was, and he would be back soon to tell his boss anyway.

"I'm Francis Elkton."

The man nodded again. "Thought you must be. But I guess I'll share my peaches with you anyway. Figure you must have had your reasons for what you did."

"Reasons for what?"

The man shrugged. "It's old history. Flint went on and so did you. I wouldn't even have remembered your full name if I hadn't seen that."

There it was. The man was pointing to a faded family Bible.

One of those with the black leather cover stamped, Our Family With God.

"I'm in there?" Francis moved outside the warmth of the foil blanket to stand up and walk to the bookcase. The Bible was closed, but she saw that a ribbon marker had been left through the center of the book. Curious, she opened it.

The man was right. There was her name. Francis Elkton.

The words read, "United in Holy Matrimony Flint L. Harris and Francis Elkton on the day of our Lord, April 17—"

"Who wrote that there?" Even the temperature outside could not match the ice inside her. She'd never seen the words like that, so black and white.

The man shrugged. "It was either Flint or his grandmother."

"His grandmother didn't know we—" Francis gulped. She could hardly say they had gotten married when the most they had done was perform a mock ceremony.

"Then it must have been Flint."

"He must have stopped here before he left that day."

The man nodded. "I expect so. A man like Flint takes his marriage vows serious. He'd want to at least write them down in a family Bible."

"There were no marriage vows," Francis corrected the man bitterly. "We said them before a fake justice of the peace."

The man looked startled. "There was nothing fake about your vows."

Francis felt a headache start in the back of her neck. "I'm afraid there was. The justice of the peace was a phony."

"I checked him out. He was pure gold."

"You can't have checked him out. He didn't even exist. Phony name and everything."

Francis still remembered the smug look on her father's face when he got off the phone with a city official in Las Vegas and informed her there was no such justice of the peace.

The peaches were forgotten. The older man looked cautiously at Francis and said softly, "I did a thorough check on Flint myself before he came into the Bureau. I knew he had potential and would go far. I wanted to be sure we did a complete check. I talked to the justice of the peace personally. And the county sheriff who arrested Flint on that speeding ticket."

Francis felt her headache worsen. "What speeding ticket?"

The old man looked at Francis silently for a moment. "The day after you were married, Flint was arrested on a speeding ticket just inside the Miles City limits. Thirty-eight in a thirty-five-mile-an-hour zone."

"No one gets a ticket for that."

"Flint did. And because he didn't have the hundred thousand dollars cash to post bail, he did ninety days in jail."

Francis put her hand to her head. "That can't be. No one does that kind of time on a traffic ticket—and they certainly don't have that kind of bail."

The man kept looking at Francis like he was measuring her. Then he continued slowly. "I talked to the sheriff who made the arrest. He was doing a favor for someone. The arrest. The high bail. The ninety days. It was all a personal favor."

"Flint never hurt anyone. Who would do that?"

The silence was longer this time. Finally, the man spoke. "The sheriff said it was you. Said you'd changed your mind about the marriage and didn't have the nerve to tell Flint to his face."

"Me?" The squeak that came out of Francis's throat was one she scarcely recognized as her own.

The man looked away to give her privacy. "Not that it's really any of my business."

Francis needed to breathe. *Reason this out,* she said to herself. *Reason it out. Put the pieces in their places. It will make sense. There's an order to it all. You just need to find it.*

"But I hadn't changed my mind." Francis grabbed hold of that one fact and hung on to it. The whole story revolved around that one piece, and that one piece was false. That must make the whole story false. "I wanted to be married to Flint."

The man lifted his eyes to look at her. With the soft light of the lantern on the table, Francis could see the pity in the man's eyes. "I'm beginning to think that might possibly be true."

Francis was numb. She'd fallen into a gaping hole and she didn't know how to get out of it. She couldn't talk. She could barely think. "But who would do such a thing?"

Francis knew it was her father. Knew it in her heart before

she had reasoned it out with her head. He was the only one who could have done it.

Her father had been upset when she and Flint had driven up and announced their marriage. She hadn't expected her father to be glad about the marriage, but she thought he'd adjust in time. She'd been relieved when Flint had suggested he drive into Miles City to buy roses for her. If she had some time alone with her father, Francis had thought, she could change his mind.

She and her father had talked for a while and then she went in to pack. There wasn't much she needed to take. Some tea towels she'd made years ago when her mother was alive to help her. The clothes she'd been wearing to school. A few pieces of costume jewelry. The letters Garth had written her when he was overseas.

She'd filled up two suitcases when her father came in to say he'd called Las Vegas and found out that the justice of the peace was a fake.

At that moment, Francis had not worried about her father's words. If the justice of the peace was a fake, she'd calmly reasoned, she and Flint would only find someone else to marry them again. Flint had made a mistake in locating the proper official, but they would take care of it. They'd marry again. That's what people in love did. She started to fold the aprons her mother had given her.

When she finished packing, Francis went down to the kitchen to prepare supper for her father. It was the last meal she'd make for him for awhile, and she was happy to do it. She decided to make beef stew because it could simmer for hours with little tending after she left.

Four hours later her father invited her to sit down and eat the stew with him. She knew Flint could have driven into Miles City and back several times in the hours that had passed. Francis refused the stew and went to her room. He must have had car trouble, she thought. That was it. He'd call any minute. She stayed awake all night waiting for the phone to ring. It was a week before she even made any attempt to sleep at nights.

''It was my father,'' Francis said calmly as she looked Flint's boss in the eyes. ''He must have arranged it all.''

''I'm sorry.'' The man said his words quickly.

The inside of the cold house was silent. Francis sat with the open Bible on her lap, staring at the page where her marriage vows had been recorded and a scripture reference from Solomon had been added. As she looked at it closely, she could see that the faded handwriting was Flint's. She wished she could have stood with him when he recorded the date in this Bible. It must have had meaning for him or he wouldn't have stopped on his way into Miles City to write it down.

"Surely Flint—" she looked at the man.

He was twisting the handle that gave energy to the emergency lantern on the table. He didn't look up from the lantern. "He didn't want to tell me about you. Didn't even mention your name. But he had to tell me the basics. I was only checking out his story. Part of the job. We needed to find out about the arrest. It was on his record."

"So he thinks it was me who got him arrested."

The temperature of the night seemed to go even lower.

The man nodded.

Francis felt numb. She had never imagined anything like this. She had assumed Flint had been the one to have second thoughts. Or that he had never intended to really marry her anyway. He wasn't from around here. She never should have trusted him as much as she did. She repeated all the words she had said to herself over the years. None of them gave her any comfort.

"He should have come back to talk to me."

"Maybe he tried," the man said. He'd stopped cranking the lantern and sat at the table.

The silence stretched between them.

"Mind if I smoke?" the man finally asked.

"Go ahead," Francis said automatically. She felt like her whole life was shifting gears and the gears were rusty. She'd spent too much of the past twenty years resenting Flint. Letting her anger burn toward him in the hopes that someday her memories would be light, airy ashes that could be blown away. But instead of producing ashes that were light, her anger had produced a heavy, molten chunk of resentment that wouldn't budge in a whirlwind.

There had been no blowing away of old, forgotten memories.

These past weeks in Dry Creek had already proven that to her. She was beginning to believe she would be forever shackled by her memories. But now it turned out that the whole basis for her anger was untrue. Flint had not left her. She had, apparently, somehow left him.

A rumbling growl came from the man's coat pocket.

"Excuse me," he said as he reached into his pocket and pulled out a cell phone. "That'll be Mrs. B."

The conversation was short, and all Francis heard were several satisfied grunts.

"Flint's got them in custody," the man said when he put his phone back in his pocket. "He's holding them in something he called the dance barn in Dry Creek. Said you'd know where it was. Told me to bring you with me and come over."

"So I'm free to go?" Francis asked blankly as she looked up. She'd been so distressed about everything the man had told her she hadn't realized her first impressions of him must not be true.

"Of course," the man said as he stood and put his backpack on his shoulders.

"But who are you?"

"Inspector Kahn—FBI," the man said as he fumbled through another pocket in his coat and pulled out an identification badge.

"But—"

"The cattle business," the man explained as he showed the badge to Francis. "It's interstate. Makes it a federal crime."

"So the FBI sent someone in." Francis took a moment to look at the badge so she could scramble to get on track. She had heard the FBI was working on the case. They had asked Garth to help. "So you really didn't need Garth, after all."

Inspector Kahn grunted. "Not when I have a hothead like Flint working for me."

"Flint works for you?"

Inspector Kahn grunted again and started walking toward the door. "Sometimes I think it's me working for him. I'd place money that the reason he's so keen for me to get there is because he wants me to do the paperwork. Flint always hated the paper side of things." He looked over his shoulder at her. "You coming?"

"Yes." Francis certainly didn't want to stay in this cold house any longer than she needed to. She pulled the jacket Flint had given her earlier over her shoulders and picked up the Bible.

The inspector looked at the Bible. "I expect you'll need to talk to Flint about this marriage business."

"I intend to try."

The inspector smiled at that. "Flint isn't always an easy man to reason with. Stubborn as he is brave. But you know that—you're married to him."

"I guess I am, at that." The ashes inside of Francis might not be blowing away, but she could feel them shifting all over the place. It appeared she, Francis K. Elkton, had actually been married to Flint L. Harris some twenty years ago.

For the umpteenth time that night, Flint wondered at the value of being a hero. He had saved Garth Elkton's hide—not to mention the even more tender hide of the attractive woman with him, Sylvia Bannister—and they were both giving him a shoulder colder than the storm front that was fast moving into town.

In his jeans and wool jacket, Flint was out of place inside the barn. Not that any of the men there hadn't quickly helped him hog-tie the three men who had kidnapped Garth and Sylvia and attempted to take them away in the back of an old cattle truck.

But the music was still playing a slow tune and the pink crepe paper still hung from the rafters of that old barn. And Flint felt about as welcome as a stray wet dog at a fancy church picnic.

"There, that should do it." Flint checked the knots in the rope for the third time. He'd asked someone to call the local sheriff and was told the man was picking up something in Billings but would be back at the dance soon. He hoped the sheriff would get there before the inspector. Maybe then some of the paperwork would be local.

"Who'd you say you were again?" Garth Elkton asked the question, quiet-like, as he squatted to check the ropes with Flint.

"Flint Harris."

"The guy who called me the other night about the kidnapping?" Garth sounded suspicious.

"Yes."

"Still don't know how you knew about it."

"Because I've been freezing my toes off the past few nights following these guys around." Flint jerked his head at the men on the floor. Flint could see the direction Garth was going with his questions and he didn't appreciate it. "If I was one of them, don't you think they'd at least recognize me?"

Flint looked at the three men on the floor. They looked quarrelsome and pathetic. He didn't appreciate being lumped in with them. But at least it was clear that none of them claimed to have ever seen him before now.

"They didn't seem too clear about who their boss was," Garth continued mildly. "Could be they wouldn't recognize the man."

"I can't tell you who their boss is, but he's using a local informant," Flint said in exasperation. "We've got that much figured out. And I'm not local."

"You were local enough for my sister."

Ah, so it's come to that, Flint thought. It seemed he'd never get a square break from an Elkton. "Let's leave your sister out of it."

The mention of his sister made Garth scan the room. "Where is she, anyway? Thought she'd be back inside by now. I heard Jess was looking for her."

"She was with me." Flint resigned himself to his fate.

"With you? What was she doing with you?"

"Don't worry. She'll be back here any minute now."

"She better be or—" Garth seemed unaware that his voice was rising.

"Now, now, boys."

Flint looked up. He'd recognize that voice anywhere. He grinned as he looked at the woman who had been his grandmother's staunch friend in her final days. "Mrs. Hargrove! How are you?"

Mrs. Hargrove had aged a little in the years since he'd seen her last. And she was wearing a long velvet maroon dress tonight instead of her usual cotton gingham housedress. But she held herself with the same innate dignity he always expected from her. "Doing just fine, thank you."

"You know him?" Garth asked Mrs. Hargrove skeptically.

"Of course," the woman replied warmly. "He was in my Sunday school class for six months when he was here, and if he doesn't get up off that floor and give me a hug pretty soon, I'm going to be mighty disappointed."

Flint felt less like an unwelcome dog just looking at the woman. He stood up and enfolded her in his arms.

"I still miss that grandmother of yours," Mrs. Hargrove whispered as she held him.

"So do I," he whispered back.

"It comforts me to know she's with our Lord," she added and then leaned back to look Flint in the eye. "And I'm still working on her final request of me."

"Oh?" This was something Flint had not heard about.

"I pray for you every day, son," Mrs. Hargrove said with satisfaction. "Just like she would be doing if she were alive."

Flint had faced bullets. But nothing had made him feel as vulnerable as those words did. In his astonishment, he mumbled the only thing he could think of. "Well, thank you." To his further amazement, he meant it.

"And here you've come back to us a hero." Mrs. Hargrove stepped out of his arms and spoke loudly so that everyone could hear. "This is Essie Harris's grandson, folks. Let's give him a good welcome home."

With those words, Flint was transformed from the unwelcome stray into the prize guest. A murmur of approval ran through the folks of Dry Creek, and he heard more than one person mutter that it was about time.

"Here, let me introduce you around," Mrs. Hargrove said as she took Flint's arm. "You probably don't remember everyone. Here, this is Doris June—you might have met her, she went to school with Francis."

Flint found himself shaking hands with an attractive blond woman about his age. "You were a cheerleader, weren't you?"

The woman nodded. ''The coach was always hoping to find a way to get you to try out for the basketball team.''

''I was busy helping my grandmother.''

''I know.'' The blonde smiled.

''And this is Margaret Ann.'' Mrs. Hargrove moved him on to another pleasant woman.

Flint noticed Mrs. Hargrove introduced him to the women first. The men hung back. They didn't seem as willing to shake his hand as the women were. In fact, some of them still looked at him with suspicion thick on their faces.

''Francis should be here soon,'' he said to no one in particular. He knew why the men didn't trust him. ''She really is fine.''

Flint had no sooner finished his words of reassurance than the barn door opened and his words came true. Francis was back.

The men of Dry Creek looked at Francis in disbelief and then looked at Flint, the suspicion hardening on their faces.

Flint would have cursed if Mrs. Hargrove wasn't standing, speechless, at his elbow.

Francis stood inside the doorway. She must have had dropped the jacket on her way inside, because she wasn't wearing it, and her neck and arms were pearl white. Her hair tumbled around her head in a mass of black silk that was sprinkled with dry pine needles. She had a bruise on her arm that was deepening into a ripe purple.

Flint could have tried to explain away the bruise and the needles. But he knew he'd have a more difficult time talking his way past the ragged tear in Francis's dress that went from her ankles to a few inches short of her waist. Even now Francis had to hold her dress shut around her with one hand while she carried something behind her back in the other hand.

''It was the horse,'' Flint stammered into the silence. He'd been called to testify in federal drug investigations, but he'd never felt the pressure of his testimony like now.

''She was with you.'' The quiet steel in Garth's voice came from behind him and prodded. ''What happened?''

''Now, boys.'' Mrs. Hargrove found her breath and interrupted again. "Can't you see Francis is frozen to the bone? There'll be time for sorting this all out later."

Flint met the metal in Garth's eyes and smiled inside. He might not like the steel at his back, but he was warmed to know that Francis had such a loyal protector.

"Nothing," Flint assured the other man quietly. "Francis is fine."

Chapter Four

Francis blinked. Her eyes had become accustomed to the black night, and when she stepped into the golden light inside the barn, she felt like a spotlight was on her. She blinked again before she realized that every single person in the barn, even those three men tied in a muddle at Garth's feet, were staring at her.

"What happened to the music?" Francis took an uncertain step forward. The audio system that someone had set up was attached to an old record player, and the scratchy music it had been playing was reminiscent of the fifties. Before she'd gone to look for the Big Dipper an hour or so ago, however, the record hadn't skipped like the one that was on in the background now. "Why isn't anyone dancing?"

"Are you all right, dear?" Mrs. Hargrove was the first to move, and she stepped toward Francis.

"I'm fine—fine," Francis stammered. She looked at her dress, and for the first time realized how she must look. The fabric on her ill-fated red dress was thin in the best of circumstances, but the section she held in her hand was nothing more than fly away threads held together by sequins. "It was the horse."

"The horse did that to your dress?" Garth asked, disbelieving, as he, too, stepped forward.

"Well, no, I ripped the dress when I tried to get off the horse." Francis realized as she said the words that they didn't sound very plausible. The polite eyes of her neighbors told her they didn't believe her. She tried again, a little defensively. "Well, I wasn't just getting off—I was going to ride Honey so I needed to swing my leg around."

"It doesn't matter, dear," Mrs. Hargrove said soothingly as she patted Francis on the shoulder, and then exclaimed, "Why you're ice cold! Come over by the heaters."

Tall electric heaters stood at the far side of the barn. Garth had them installed when the barn was used several months ago for the Christmas pageant. Francis let Mrs. Hargrove start leading her over to them.

"Here, let me carry that for you," Mrs. Hargrove offered as she held out her hand.

"Oh, it's nothing," Francis said quickly. She let go of the threads of her dress so she could slip Flint's family Bible under her arm more securely. She didn't know how Flint would feel about her taking the Bible, even though he'd left it in his grandmother's deserted house years ago and any stranger traveling through could have picked it up and taken it. That fact had bothered her the whole ride in. How could he leave something like that—something that spoke of their wedding—for strangers to take? Or for the wind to blow away?

Sequins fell from her dress as she hobbled closer to the heat. She felt a long shaft of cold on her leg where her dress was torn and a small circle of even colder metal where her garter fastened to her nylons.

A ripple of slow, approving murmurs moved through the group of men—most of them single ranch hands—already standing near the heaters.

Flint felt every muscle in his body tense. He didn't know which of those men around the heaters was Francis's boyfriend, but Flint didn't think much of him. What kind of man would let other men see that much leg of his girlfriend? Especially when the girlfriend looked like Francis. He doubted there was an unmarried man here tonight who wouldn't go to bed with the image of those red threads trailing across Francis's leg.

"Doesn't anybody use tablecloths anymore?" Flint took a dozen long strides to get to the food table and looked around impatiently. The tables were wrapped in a pink bridal paper with pink streamers placed every few inches twisting from the table to the floor.

"You're hungry?" Francis stopped to stare at Flint.

Flint only grunted as he tore several of the streamers from the back of the table. "These will have to do."

The streamers were wide, and Flint had his hand full of them when he kneeled by Francis. "Hold still."

Flint began wrapping the streamers around Francis, starting at her waist and moving on to her hips. The crepe paper wasn't any heavier than the material in that red sequin dress, but it held the pieces of Francis's dress together. Flint knotted the first strip around her waist as an anchor and then began to wrap her like a mummy from her waist to her knees.

"I can do it," Francis said as she shifted awkwardly to keep the book behind her back.

If Francis hadn't acted so uncomfortable, Flint would have taken at least another minute before he focused on the book she was obviously trying to hide from him.

"That's Grandma's," Flint said, tight-lipped. He supposed Francis had read what he wrote that day. Well, there was nothing for it. He had been a fool, but he wouldn't apologize.

He remembered the day he'd arrived at his grandmother's house after leaving Francis at her father's to pack. His grandmother had been at a church meeting in Dry Creek and wasn't home. On impulse Flint had pulled his grandmother's family Bible off the shelf and recorded his marriage. Then he put the Bible back.

The book wasn't his grandmother's reading Bible, but it was important to her nonetheless. Her wedding and the wedding of Flint's parents had been recorded on its center pages. He planned to pull the Bible out and surprise his grandmother when he came back from Miles City that day.

But it was three months before he came back from Miles City, and by then the ink would have been fully dried on the divorce papers he'd signed in jail. He had no calm words to explain what had happened, so he left the Bible on the shelf. As angry as he was with Francis, he didn't want the good people of Dry Creek to force her into accepting a marriage she didn't want. He didn't even tell his grandmother what had happened. If she ever saw the words, she never asked about them in their weekly phone conversations.

Even after all these years, Flint still didn't want Francis to be publicly blamed. He doubted the good people of Dry Creek would think much of a woman who abandoned her marriage vows within hours of saying them. They might not be as forgiving as he had learned to be.

"Don't worry. Your secret's safe," Flint murmured as he impatiently knotted one of the crepe streamers just above Francis's knee. He wished there was more noise in this old barn, but it seemed like everyone would rather watch him wrap Francis in crepe paper than dance with each other. "You were just a kid. I'm the one who should have had sense enough to stop it before it went as far as it did."

"I was no more a kid than you were. I was certainly old enough to know my own mind," Francis snapped back in a low whisper. She hadn't counted on having this conversation in front of a hundred curious witnesses with Flint kneeling in front of her and angrily wrapping crepe paper around her legs. But if that was the only way to have it, she'd do it. "You should have realized that instead of—"

"Me?" Flint reared back when he finally heard the mild tone of reproof in Francis's voice. It was one thing to forgive her. But it was asking a bit much of him to let her take that tone with him. "I should have realized something? The only thing I should have realized was that you were too young for the responsibilities involved in getting mar—"

Flint suddenly heard the silence. The bride and groom who were celebrating their wedding tonight were standing still as statues. Even the men tied together into a pile at Garth's feet had stopped scraping their feet along the wood floor. A hundred people were watching, and no one was crumpling a paper cup or moving in their chair. Someone had shut off the record player, so even that empty scratching had stilled. This old barn had never been so quiet.

Flint willed his voice to a mild whisper. "You were a bit young, is all. That's not a crime."

"It would have been a crime if I hadn't been so caught up in my career," Francis replied as the reality of the situation became a little clearer. Bigamy. What if she had married, never knowing that she was already married? She wondered if the law forgave such silliness. "You at least knew we were married."

"Married?" The word was picked up by someone standing near them and passed around the barn quicker than a fake dollar bill at a carnival.

Flint looked up as a new group of men slowly gathered from around the barn and moved over by the heaters. These men had a look about them he'd seen in combat. He'd wager the lot of them worked for Francis's brother. They all had calluses on their hands and scuffed boots on their feet. He expected he could take any of them in a fair fight. By the hardening looks on their faces, he figured he'd have to do that very thing before the night was over.

"Maybe we better discuss this outside," Flint said calmly as he stood up, twisted the last piece of crepe paper into a tidy roll and set it on the corner of the refreshment table.

Flint didn't want to call Francis a liar in front of her family and friends, but if she thought he'd buy some story about her being drunk or confused that night in Vegas, she was going to be disappointed. He knew she hadn't had a drop of liquor to drink. They hadn't even opened the complimentary champagne that came with the wedding ceremony. And, while she had been wonderfully starry-eyed, she had not been confused.

Francis nodded. The warmth from the heaters was uneven, and she shivered. "Let me look for my jacket."

Francis ran her eyes over the people in the barn, looking for Sylvia Bannister. The last time she'd seen Sylvia she had been wearing Francis's black lion jacket, a remembrance from long-ago high school years. As Francis looked over the small clusters of her friends and neighbors, they began to shuffle in sudden embarrassment and start to move.

"You're welcome to borrow my jacket." Mrs. Hargrove stepped forward efficiently with a wool jacket in her hands. "I won't be needing it since I'll be dancing—if someone will put the music back on."

The crowd took the hint. Someone flipped a switch, and an old Beatles song started to play. A few of the women walked to the refreshment table and poured more punch in the bowl. The kidnappers, tied in a heap to one side of the barn, started to twist their rope-bound feet and complain that there wasn't even a local law official there to see to their comfort.

"We got our rights, too," the stocky brother started to protest. "Ain't right we're kept tied up like this just so he—" the man jerked his head at Flint "—can play Romeo in some snowdrift with his Juliet."

"Yeah." One of the other brothers took his lead. "We ain't even had supper."

"I'm not feeding you supper," Flint said in clipped exasperation, although he almost welcomed the excuse to turn from Francis and focus on business for a minute. "Give me a break, you've only been arrested for fifteen minutes. And it's almost midnight—you should have eaten supper hours ago."

"Well, we didn't get a chance to eat before." The brother whined.

"You should always take time for a proper meal," Francis said automatically as she slipped her arms into the jacket Mrs. Hargrove held out for her. "Good nutrition makes for a more productive worker."

Flint snorted as he nodded his head toward the kidnappers. "Trust me, they don't need to be more productive."

"I think there's some of those little quiche appetizers left," Mrs. Hargrove said as she headed for the refreshment table. "The Good Book says we need to look out for our enemies."

"The Good Book says a lot of things," Flint said as his eyes skimmed over Francis. Yes, she still had it in her hand. His grandmother's Bible. "Not all of the things written in its pages are true."

Flint heard Mrs. Hargrove gasp, and he hurried to explain. "I mean some of the things that are hand-written—by a person in their own Bible—aren't necessarily true."

"Essie stood by everything she wrote in that Bible of hers." Mrs. Hargrove defended her friend. "And I'd stand by them, too."

"It wasn't something Grandma wrote," Flint said softly. He suddenly had a picture of his grandmother sitting down in the evening at her old wooden table and reading her Bible. She'd have her apron on and the radio humming in the background as she'd mouth the words. She read silently, but occasionally—when the words seemed either too wonderful or too horrible to be held in—she'd speak them aloud to whomever stood by.

Flint had never seen anyone else read a book like it was a letter that had come in the morning mail. He had secretly envied her the faith she had even though he knew it wasn't for the likes of him. Even then he didn't feel like he'd ever clean up good enough to merit much faith. But his grandmother was a different story. He didn't want anyone to question his grandmother's faith. "It wasn't something she wrote down. It was something I wrote. By mistake."

Mrs. Hargrove looked Flint full in the eyes before she smiled. "I can't think of a better place to write something—whether it's a mistake or not, only God knows."

Flint snorted. "Well, God isn't the only one who knows on this one. Wish He was. At least He can keep a secret."

"I can keep a secret." Francis was stung.

"I'm not worried about you, sweetheart," Flint said wryly as he smiled at her. "It's my boss I'm worried about. I know you can keep this secret—you've kept it for the past twenty years."

"Sometimes a secret needs a good airing out," Mrs. Hargrove offered breezily as she finished stacking some petite quiches on a small paper plate and started toward the tangle of men on the floor. "Especially those old ones."

By now several couples were dancing, and those who weren't dancing had politely turned their attention to other things.

"We do need to talk about it," Francis said firmly as she pulled the wool jacket closer around her. She searched in the pocket and found a hairpin. Just what she needed. She swept her hair up and gave it a couple of twists. Organizing her hair into a neat bun made her feel more in control. "There are things you don't know."

Flint stood by helplessly and watched the transformation of Francis. She'd gone from being a bewitching damsel in distress with handfuls of silken hair to a very competent-looking executive who wouldn't tolerate a hair out of place or a thought that wasn't useful.

"You don't need to make it right with me, if that's what you're thinking." Flint didn't want to have this final conversation with Francis. He was quite sure the executive Francis didn't approve of that long-ago Francis who had run off to be married. "Whatever happened on that day to make you change your mind, it is okay. I've made my peace with it."

"But that's not the way it was at all," Francis protested.

Francis buttoned the wool jacket around her. Mrs. Hargrove was several sizes larger than she was, and Francis liked the secure feeling the too-large jacket gave her. She must look a sight with the green plaid jacket on top of her skirt of pink crepe paper and red sequins.

"Speaking of the inspector, where is he?" Flint knelt to test the knots on the three men sitting patiently on the floor. He looked at Francis briefly. "Thought he was coming with you."

"He was. He got a call from the sheriff saying he had a flat tire down the road a piece. The inspector went to help him."

Flint grunted as he finished checking the knots. "He just wants to avoid the paperwork with these guys."

The door opened, and a square of cold midnight was visible for a moment before the inspector stepped inside the old barn and brushed a few stray snowflakes off his coat. "Did I hear you say paperwork? Don't worry about that. I'll do it."

Flint had never heard the inspector volunteer to do the paperwork.

"You'll maybe want to…" The inspector had walked over to where Flint knelt and inclined his head slightly in the direction of Francis.

So much for privacy, Flint thought. But if he talked to Francis here, the inspector wouldn't be the only one listening. "I'll talk to her later."

"That's too late." The inspector leaned down and whispered, "You better do it now before—"

The door to the barn opened again, and the inspector groaned. "Too late. He's here."

Flint looked at the open doorway but didn't see what the problem was. It was only the sheriff. The man looked decidedly uncomfortable, with patches of snow stuck to his jeans and his parka pulled close around his head. Tonight wasn't the best night for getting a flat tire.

Then the sheriff stepped all the way inside, and Flint noticed two other people crowding in the door behind him.

They both had big city stamped all over them. The woman was tall, lean and platinum. Her face was pinched with cold, but that didn't take away the look of expensive makeup. Definitely uptown.

The man was more downtown. Flint would peg him as a banker. Maybe vice president or loans officer. He had the look of a bean counter, but not the look of command. He was wearing a brown business suit and lined leather gloves. Expensive gloves, Flint thought a little jealously, wondering what snowdrift his own gloves had ended up in tonight.

"Robert!" the woman exclaimed loudly and started walking to the man Flint knew to be Robert Buckwalter.

So that was it, Flint thought as he stood up quickly. The inspector must be worried that the woman would interfere with Mrs. Buckwalter's secret cover.

No one knew that Mrs. Buckwalter was working with the FBI on this rustling business, not even her son. Until they found out the identity of the person serving as the informant for the rustling outfit, they couldn't be too careful about strangers. Especially strangers who wanted to cozy up to FBI operatives and their families.

Ordinarily Flint wouldn't seriously suspect the woman. Not because she looked flimsy, but because he was pretty sure the informant had to be someone local. Only a local would have a cover good enough to have escaped everyone's notice and still have access to the information the rustlers would need.

Flint intercepted the blonde's path just before she reached Robert. "I'll need to see some identification."

The woman momentarily flushed guiltily, and Flint looked at her more closely. She was up to something.

"Identification?" She stopped and schooled her face into blankness. "I don't need identification. I'm with him." She pointed to Robert.

Flint couldn't help noticing Robert flinching as the other man protested. "Now, Laurel, you know that's not—"

Flint almost felt sorry for the man. He'd seen Robert earlier, working as a kitchen helper to the young woman chef his mother had sent out here with a planeload of lobsters for the party tonight. Flint had seen Robert land his small plane near Garth's ranch a few days ago in the early morning hours. A man as rich as Robert—with the whole Buckwalter fortune at his feet—would have to be besotted to slice radishes for two hours. "She's with you?"

"I wouldn't say with." Robert stumbled. He glanced at the young woman standing next to him in apology. "I know Laurel—of course I know her—our families are—well, my mother knows her better, so, no—I wouldn't say with."

"It was with enough for you on Christmas!" Laurel staged a pout that would do justice to a Hollywood starlet.

"Well." Flint backed away. He would have liked to help Robert out—he seemed like a decent man—but the FBI couldn't arrest a woman for flirting.

It wasn't until Flint turned that he realized his tactical mistake. The inspector wasn't worried about the woman. He was worried about that man who was walking to Francis with a determined look in his eyes that demanded she welcome him.

"You must be the boyfriend," Flint said as he walked to Francis. It was inevitable. The evening had been doomed from the start.

"I hope I'm more than a boyfriend," the man said, a little smugly, Flint thought, as he reached Francis and leaned over to peck her on her lips. "Now that she's had time away to think about things."

"Sam." Francis marveled that her voice sounded calm. She felt a growing urge to scream. "What are you doing here?"

"Well, I got to thinking. It's time you came back—how much thinking can a woman do?" The man laughed a little too heartily. "So I flew up to get you."

"Now's not a good time."

"Oh, I know. The inspector was telling me there's been lots of excitement here tonight. Seemed to think I'd be better off going back to Billings for the night, but I told him it was nonsense. It would take more than a few bad guys to rattle my Francis. She's the most sensible woman I've ever known."

Flint thought the man must be blind to think "sensible" summed up a woman like Francis. Didn't he see the shy warmth in her eyes when she first met someone? Hadn't he felt the slight tremble of her lips when she was kissed?

"Known a lot of women, have you?" Flint asked the man. He refused to think of the man as Sam. As far as Flint was concerned, the man had no name. And no future.

"Huh?"

Flint admitted the man didn't look like he could have known many women, but that didn't stop Flint from resenting him. "Just checking up on your background."

"Flint's with the FBI," Francis said, tight-lipped with annoyance. "He checks up on everybody."

"Oh, well, that's okay then." The man smiled at Flint and held out his hand. "Always nice to meet one of our nation's security men. Men like you keep us all safe."

Flint grunted. The man made it sound like Flint was a school crossing guard. Important enough for someone who did that sort of thing. Flint wondered if Francis actually loved the guy. He glared at the man until the man dropped his hand.

"You own a house?" Flint knew women loved big houses.

"A bedroom loft condo in downtown Denver," the man said with pride. "The Executive Manor complex."

Flint grunted. Close enough. The only house he could claim as his own was sitting just north of here on five desolate acres only chickens could love.

"Francis would want a tree or two."

The man looked startled. "I told her we could get a few ficus plants. They'd do."

Flint nodded. Francis just might settle for them, after all. Suddenly, Flint felt old. He had lived too hard and fast. At least the man standing before him looked stable. Maybe that was enough.

"You ever kill a man?"

"I beg your pardon?" The man was looking at Flint in alarm.

"It's a simple question—ever been in the military?"

The man shook his head. "Bad feet."

"Ever been arrested?"

"Of course not." The man was indignant. "And I certainly

don't see the point of these questions—if I'm under suspicion for something I have a right to know. And if you're planning to arrest me, I demand a chance to call my attorney.''

Flint smiled wryly. He almost wished he could arrest the man. ''No, I'm just checking up on you.''

''Well, I'll let it go this time,'' the man said pompously. ''Mostly because the inspector here said you'd rescued Francis from those hoodlums. I should be thanking you for helping my fiancée, not sitting here arguing.''

''Fiancée.'' Flint felt a cold draft down his neck. It appeared the ficus had won.

''I never agreed to marry you.'' Francis felt the need to sit down and start counting. Everything was unraveling. ''Actually, I can't marry you.''

''Nonsense. Of course you can. I've thought about it, too, you know. Granted, we don't have some fairy-tale romance, but a woman your age doesn't expect that. We have more important reasons to get married. Stability. Companionship. There's no good reason for either of us to stay single.''

''There's him.'' Francis pointed at Flint. The air inside the barn had cooled until it had an icy edge to it, and someone had dimmed the lights for slow dancing. A song of love betrayed was filling the barn with a quiet sadness, and more than one couple moved closer together.

''Him?'' Sam looked at Flint like he suspected him of being part of a police lineup. ''What's the FBI got to do with anything?''

''It's not the FBI. It's him. He's my husband,'' Francis whispered.

''You're joking.'' Sam looked at Flint again and then dismissed him. ''You don't even know him.''

''I used to know him. We were married twenty years ago.''

''Oh, well, then,'' The man visibly relaxed. ''He's your exhusband.''

Flint didn't like the direction the conversation was taking. ''If Francis doesn't want to marry you, she shouldn't. And there's no reason she should ever settle for companionship.''

''If you're her ex, you have no say in this at all.'' Sam looked Flint over like he had been pulled out of that police lineup and pronounced guilty. "Besides, I'm sure she's realized by now that I'm the kind of husband that she should have. Solid. Steady. A man like you is okay for a woman when she's young— What we don't do when we're young." The man gave a bark of a laugh. "Why, I was in a protest march myself once— But that was then and surely by now Francis knows your kind doesn't hold up too well over the years."

"My kind? What do you know about my kind?" Flint forced the words out over his clenched teeth.

"I know you left her," Sam said calmly. The brown-suited man looked smug and confident. He glanced at Francis indulgently. "I know Francis and she'd stick by her word. So I know it's you who left."

"She was young. And scared. And me— I must have seemed like some wild guy back then. I can't blame her for having second thoughts." Flint gave a ragged laugh. "I would have left me if I'd had a choice. I was mad at the world for letting my parents die. Mad at school. Mad at friends. Mad at God. The only good thing about me was Francis. I can't blame her for leaving me."

"But I didn't," Francis said softly. "I didn't leave."

Flint snorted. "That's not what the sheriff said."

"I wasn't the one who had you arrested." Francis said the words carefully. She felt like she was walking some very important, invisible line. She tried to take a deep breath, but failed. "It was my father."

"But the sheriff said—"

"My father may have lied to him." Francis was almost whispering. They seemed to burn their way up through her throat. "I waited for you to come back that day."

Flint heard the words and stared at Francis. He shook his head like he was clearing his ears. What was she saying?

"But—" Flint took one more stab at understanding. He could see in her eyes that she was telling him the truth. "But there were papers—divorce papers—"

"Had I signed them?"

Flint shook his head slowly. "I thought you'd sign them when they were given to you."

Flint still remembered the pain of seeing those papers. At

first, he'd refused to sign them, pushing them away when the sheriff brought them to his cell. But on the third day, he'd decided to give in. The sheriff said Francis was pleading with her father to get the papers signed, that she was not eating she was so upset. He couldn't bear for her to be upset. He'd bruised his fist by hitting the wall of that cell after he'd finally shoved the signed papers through the bars to the sheriff.

"You were begging me to sign them."

Francis shook her head. "No."

Sometimes the world tips on its axis. Sometimes it rolls completely over. Flint's world rolled over so many times he didn't know which side was up. "I don't understand. Are you saying that you never signed those papers?"

"I never even knew they existed," Francis said softly. "I suppose my father meant to give them to me. But I left before long and—no, I never saw the papers."

"But then—"

Francis nodded. "We're still married."

Somehow the music had stopped again, and everyone was listening.

"Well," Mrs. Hargrove finally said softly. "Well, if that don't beat all."

At the edge of the crowd...

The old man slipped into the barn unnoticed. He knew he shouldn't be here. Knew one of those knuckleheads the boss had hired to do the job tonight might recognize his voice or the angle of his chin. The disguise he'd worn when the boss talked to them out at the deserted Redfern place might not hold.

But he'd tired of watching the horse, waiting for that FBI agent to return. The old man had spotted the agent snooping around Dry Creek several days ago, but he hadn't wanted to risk making himself known by trying to get rid of the man.

He hadn't even told the boss about the agent. He was scared of the boss and was afraid the boss would want him to do something to the agent. Something dangerous. When the boss had come to town a year or so ago, he'd been friendly. The boss had seemed to understand that the town of Dry Creek owed him. But now the old man wasn't so sure. The boss wasn't friendly anymore when he called. He kept asking the old man for more and more information.

And it was dangerous.

The old man hadn't figured on the FBI getting involved. The FBI made him nervous. The old man had always figured that the only lawman he'd have to outsmart was Sheriff Wall.

But this agent was a lot brighter than Sheriff Wall. The old man was afraid the agent already suspected something.

The old man couldn't afford to be caught. Couldn't afford to go to jail or have a trial. He didn't think he could bear to speak in front of that many strangers. Why, they put a dozen people on a jury. He didn't talk to a dozen people in a year. And he never gave anything like a speech. No one would ever understand that the town of Dry Creek owed him. No, he couldn't risk getting caught.

The old man knew he couldn't stay in this town. But he didn't know how to leave, either. He didn't drive his old pickup anymore. The tires had long since flattened into pancakes, and he just let them sit. Sometimes, when the mood took him, he'd sit in the battered pickup and listen to the news on the radio. But he didn't drive.

Mrs. Hargrove did his weekly grocery shopping for him, and she'd always been willing to do an extra errand or two for him. But he could hardly ask her to drive him to Mexico.

Chapter Five

Flint sat on the edge of the steps going into the barn. The moon was still high in the night sky. A slight wind was blowing. He'd give odds that a blizzard would roll off the Big Sheep Mountains before dawn. He could hear the sounds of the townspeople inside cleaning up after the party. He'd just sent the three would-be kidnappers off with the sheriff. He wished he had a cigarette, even though he hadn't smoked in ten years.

The door opened, and Mrs. Hargrove stepped out. "There's a cup of coffee left." She had a jacket draped over her shoulders and a mug in her hand. "Thought you might want it. It's from the bottom of the pot so it'll be strong."

"Thanks." Flint smiled at the woman as he reached up for the cup. "The stronger the better. I don't expect to sleep tonight anyway."

"I wouldn't suppose so," Mrs. Hargrove agreed as she sat down beside him. "It isn't every day you discover you're married." She smiled at him kindly. "You should be sitting here with your wife, not me."

Flint snorted. "My wife took off in a puff of exhaust fumes. Back to her brother's place with her fancy fiancé."

"Well, I expect it will take some getting used to—the whole idea."

Flint looked at her in astonishment. "She's not getting used to the idea. Didn't you hear her? She's practically engaged to what's-his-name."

"Engaged isn't married," Mrs. Hargrove replied calmly. She

pulled her jacket around her more firmly, and Flint was reminded of a general preparing for battle. "It's you she's married to in the eyes of the Lord."

Flint bit back his retort. Even a general didn't always know which battles could be won. "Can't imagine the eyes of the Lord will stop her from divorcing me quick as she can. He seems to have been content to look the other way for twenty years. Why break His record now?"

"Why, Flint Harris, what a thing to say—if your grandmother heard you, she'd—she'd..." Mrs. Hargrove appeared at a loss for what his grandmother would do.

Flint helped her out. He smiled. "She'd make me sit in that straight-back chair by the window while she prayed out loud asking the Lord to help me count my blessings and forgive my faults. I used to hate that more than anything. Used to ask her to just take away the keys to my pickup like normal kids."

"That would be Essie," Mrs. Hargrove said fondly. "She prayed over everything."

"She once prayed over a chicken that was sick—fool bird ate a marble." Flint could still picture his grandmother. She had unruly gray hair that she wore pushed back with an elastic headband and strong lines in her face that even wrinkles couldn't unsettle. "I'm glad she's not here to see me now."

"Oh, well, she would understand—you didn't know Francis's dad would set you up that way."

"It's not just that. It's who I am. She'd be brokenhearted if she saw me now."

"Essie was tougher than you think. Her heart didn't break easy. Besides, she always said it was never too late to repent. If you don't like who you've become or what you've done, it's not too late to ask God for forgiveness and start anew."

"She was wrong," Flint said as he took the last gulp of hot coffee and stood. "Sometimes it is definitely too late."

"Flint L. Harris, that's utter nonsense you're talking." Mrs. Hargrove stared up at Flint from her perch on the steps. "Just because you've had a few troubles in life—"

"Troubles?" Flint gave a wry laugh. "Troubles were the good times."

"Essie always worried so over you, child," Mrs. Hargrove

said softly as she stood. "Said you took all the bad times to heart. Like they were all your fault. Your parents dying. Even the weather—you used to fret if there wasn't enough rain to suit you."

"Grandma needed rain for that garden of hers."

"Your grandma got by just fine with what the Lord provided—she didn't need you to fret for her."

Flint remembered the lines on his grandmother's face. "I couldn't stand by helpless."

"Ah, child." Mrs. Hargrove reached out a hand and laid it on Flint's arm. "We're all helpless when it comes right down to it. We're dependent on Him for the air we breathe, the food we eat. So don't go thinking you need to do His job. The world is a mighty big weight for anyone to be carrying around—even a grown man like you."

The touch on his arm almost undid Flint until he wondered what Mrs. Hargrove would do if he confessed what troubles had crossed his path in life. He'd seen corruption. Hatred. Evil at its finest. A man couldn't see what he'd seen in life and remain untouched.

Flint winced inwardly. He sure didn't stack up pretty when you stood him next to a choirboy like Sam. He'd wager the man didn't even have a parking ticket to haunt his dreams.

Flint felt like an old man. He'd seen too much bad to truly believe in good anymore. He wasn't fit for a woman like Francis.

"Oh, don't let me forget to give you this." Mrs. Hargrove reached into the large pocket of the jacket and pulled out his grandmother's Bible. "She'd want you to have it."

Flint grimaced as he reached for the book. "I always regretted just leaving it there after she died. Seemed disrespectful somehow. I should have come back for it years ago."

"The important thing is that you came back now," Mrs. Hargrove said softly. "Even if it was just to do your job."

"Speaking of my job—" Flint had left the inspector inside with the last of the paperwork "I better get back to it."

The barn was almost empty. The folding chairs were neatly stacked against the wall. The crepe paper streamers were being swept into a jumble in the middle of the floor by two aging cowboys. The refreshment table was stripped bare, and that was where the inspector was sitting and filling out the last of the forms.

"I always wonder if it's worth it to arrest them," Flint said softly as he walked over and sat down in a folding chair near the inspector.

The inspector looked up and chuckled. "The bean counters would just add another form asking us to explain why we let them go."

"I suppose so."

"Besides, I'm almost finished. I told the sheriff I'd come by in the morning around six and we'd set up the interrogation. Should really do it tonight, but there's a storm moving in."

"Oh, I can meet with the sheriff—"

The inspector looked up from the papers and assessed him. "You haven't had a good night's sleep in days now—I can meet with the sheriff."

The heaters had been turned off in the barn an hour ago when the guests left. The air, both inside and outside, had gradually grown heavy with the promise of snow. The windows had another layer of frost gathering on them.

"Besides," the inspector continued softly. His breath clouded around his face. "You couldn't bring Francis to the interrogation."

Flint grimaced. "Trust me. I doubt she'd go anywhere with me."

The inspector nodded. "It'll be a challenge to guard her."

Flint wasn't surprised the inspector had followed his line of thinking. They'd worked together for so long they knew the routine. "She's not safe here. Not until we arrest the man who hired those goons to do the kidnapping."

The inspector nodded again. "She doesn't know she's still in danger?"

Flint snorted. "Francis? She didn't believe she was in danger the first time."

"Too bad. If she was scared, we could get her to agree to spend some time in the jailhouse in Miles City. Protective custody. Or to at least have a twenty-four-hour guard on her. I don't like the thought of you having to guard her."

"Me? I've guarded hundreds of folks."

"But never your ex-wife," the inspector said as he laid down the pen and folded the last of the forms. "Besides, it's not her that I'm worried about. It's you. If we weren't out in the middle of nowhere I'd ask one of the other boys to come over and guard her."

"I can handle it."

The inspector grunted and looked square at Flint. The older man's eyes darkened with concern. "Just how come is it that you've never married?"

"Lots of guys in this business are single."

The inspector grunted again. "That's because they marry and divorce and marry and divorce. Not many never marry." The older man paused a minute and then shrugged. "Well, it's your business, I guess."

"I won't even need to see Francis when I guard her," Flint said defensively. "I thought I'd just do a stakeout. Nobody needs to know I'm there."

The inspector looked up at this sharply. "There's a blizzard coming in. Folks around here say it might fall to ten below before morning. You can't play the Lone Ranger on that horse of yours tonight."

The inspector was right. Flint knew it. He just hadn't faced the truth yet. "I'm not sure Francis would let me stay in the house with them."

"That brother of hers won't be too happy, either, but he'd do anything to protect her."

Flint snorted. "Trouble is—it's me he's protecting her from."

"I'll call and give him the order," the inspector said as though that settled it. "If one of my men has to go out there on a night like this, the least Elkton can do is to let you inside the house."

The chair in the Elkton kitchen was comfortable enough for sitting, but not comfortable enough for sleeping. Flint wondered if that was why Garth had pulled it out of his den begrudgingly when Flint had shown up at one o'clock in the morning. The inspector had made the arrangements and Flint only had to tap lightly on the kitchen door to have it opened by Garth.

"Thanks for coming." Garth ground the words out reluctantly. "It wasn't necessary, though. The boys and I can keep Francis safe."

"Like you did tonight?"

Garth grunted. "If you hadn't taken off with her like a wild man, she would have been all right."

"She would have been kidnapped. Maybe worse, with those goons."

The two men measured each other for a moment with their eyes. Garth was the first to look away. "Like I said—thanks for coming."

"You're welcome."

Garth reached behind him and pulled a floor lamp closer to the chair. He snapped the light on. "I've turned the heat down a little, but you should be warm enough. I've brought a few blankets down."

"Thanks."

Garth smiled. "If you get hungry, there's some cold lobster in the refrigerator."

"Thanks. I'll be fine."

Garth turned to leave the kitchen. "We've got a double lock on all the doors now, and the windows are frozen shut. I don't expect trouble."

"Good."

Garth looked at him and nodded before he started up the stairs.

Flint settled into the chair. He'd spent more hours lately than he wanted to count on Honey's round back, so a chair, even an uncomfortable one, was welcome. The sounds of the kitchen lulled him—the steady hum of the refrigerator, the soft meter of the clock, the low whistle of the blizzard as it started to blow into the area.

Only a fool would be out on a night like tonight, Flint thought as he relaxed. The boss of the rustling outfit wouldn't be able to get replacement men into Dry Creek until at least tomorrow. Tonight they were safe.

Flint half woke while the light was so new it was more black fog than anything. Sometime in the night, he'd left the discomfort of the chair and slept, wrapped in several wool blankets, on the kitchen floor. He'd unstrapped his holster gun and laid it beside his head. He'd used his boots for a pillow, even though, with his six-foot-three frame, that meant his toes were sticking out the end of the blankets. He wondered if he wouldn't have been better to have left the boots on his feet for the night. His dreams hadn't merited a pillow, anyway. He'd tossed and turned, chasing faceless phantoms across a barren landscape until, somehow, the face of Francis appeared and his whole body rested.

The air snapped with cold. Frost edged its way up the windowpane nearest him. But, cold and miserable as it was, Flint woke with one thought drumming through his head—he, Flint L. Harris, miserable man that he was, was married to Francis Elkton. Legally married to her. That had to count for something.

He had a sudden urge to get up and go pick her some flowers like he'd done in that long-ago time. Yellow roses were her favorite. He could almost picture her smelling a bouquet of roses. He decided to close his eyes and let his mind go back to dreaming for a few sweet minutes to see if the face of Francis would return.

Francis hadn't slept. The moonlight filtered in through the small frosted windows in her bedroom. She had lain in her bed and counted the stripes on the faded wallpaper of her old bedroom until she thought she'd go crazy. In the past, counting had always calmed her so she could sleep.

When the counting didn't work, she'd mentally made a list. List making was good. She made a list of the groceries they would need to buy to make lasagna for everyone some day this week. With Sylvia, the kids from her youth center and the ranch hands, they were feeding forty-some people at each meal. Planning ingredients required arithmetic and list making. Francis spent fifteen minutes figuring out how much mozzarella cheese they would need. It didn't help.

Thinking of cheese reminded her of Sam. She didn't question why. She grimaced just remembering him. She supposed he was peacefully sleeping downstairs on the living room sofa. What was she supposed to do with the man? He couldn't have shown up in her life at a worse moment. With luck, he'd see reason in the morning and catch a flight back to Denver.

And Flint—she was still reeling from the knowledge that she had actually been married to him for the past twenty years.

When they'd gotten back to the ranch last night, Garth had gone into the den and pulled out an old business envelope. Francis's name was handwritten on the outside of the sealed envelope, and Garth explained that before he died their father had given it to him to give to Francis when she became engaged. Garth had always assumed it was a sentimental father-to-daughter letter. It wasn't.

Francis had left the whole envelope on the kitchen table. She'd opened it enough to know the contents were the old divorce papers.

No wonder she was unable to sleep, Francis finally decided around four o'clock. Her whole life had turned upside down in the past twelve hours. She'd seen Flint again. She'd found out he was her husband. She'd thoroughly embarrassed herself to the point that he felt he had to kiss her to save her pride. She'd felt both sixteen and sixty at the same time. It stung that the only reason he was even here in Dry Creek was that he had a job to do. At least she'd had the decency to come back here to mourn their lost love. He hadn't even come back to pick up his family's Bible.

Finally, the darkness of the night started to soften. The hands on her bedside clock told Francis it was almost five o'clock. She'd given up on sleep, and she got out of bed and wrapped a warm robe around her. She might as well set out some sausage to thaw for breakfast.

She had checked last night, and there was a case of sausages in the freezer downstairs. There were one hundred and sixty links in a case.

If Francis hadn't been dividing the number of sausages by the number of breakfast guests, she would have noticed there was something a little too lumpy about the pile of blankets that someone had left on the kitchen floor. But she hadn't wanted to turn on any lights in case they would wake Sam in the living room. She was used to the half-light of early Montana mornings.

Her first clue that something was peculiar about the pile of blankets was the whispered endearment, "Rose." She recognized the voice even as she was tripping on a blanket corner— or was it a boot—and was falling square into the pile of—

Umph! Chest. Francis felt the breath slam out of her body and then felt her chin solidly resting on a man's chest. She groaned inside. Even if she didn't know the hoarse voice, she'd recognize that smell anywhere—half horse and half aftershave. She moved slightly, and then realized her dilemma. Her elbows were braced one on each side of Flint's chest, and her fuzzy chenille bathrobe was so loosely tied that, if she raised herself up more than an inch or two, any man from Flint's perspective, if he opened his eyes, would see her navel by way of her chin and all of the territory between the two.

Not that—she lifted her eyes slightly to confirm that his eyes were closed—not that he was looking.

Francis studied his eyelids for any betraying twitch that said he was really awake and just sparing them both the embarrassment of the situation. There was none.

Francis let out her breath in relief. A miracle had happened. He hadn't woken up when she fell on him, and if she moved lightly, she would be up and off of him without him even knowing she'd fallen.

The congratulatory thought had no sooner raced through Francis's mind than she had another one—only a dead man wouldn't feel someone falling right on top of him! Francis moved just slightly and cocked her head to the side. She laid her ear down where Flint's heart should be, and the solid pounding reassured her that he was alive.

Francis dismissed the suspicion that he was drunk—she would smell alcohol if that were the case. He must just be so worn out that he'd sleep through anything. She'd heard of that happening.

Flint lay very still. He was afraid if he opened his eyes Francis would stop the delightful wiggling she was doing on his chest. He'd felt the smooth warmth of her cheek as she laid it over his heart. It was sweet and arousing all at the same time. He almost couldn't keep his pulse normal. He sure couldn't keep his eyes completely closed. His eyelids shifted ever so slightly and his eyes opened a slit so that he could see the ivory warmth of Francis—he looked and almost sighed. She could pose for drawings of the goddess Venus rising from her bath.

And then everything changed. Flint could almost see the moment when the warmth of Francis turned to stone.

Francis had managed to locate the belt on her robe and cinch it tighter before she realized what she had interrupted. Flint was dreaming. A floating half-awake dream that kept him in bed even though the only pillows he had were his own boots and his mattress was nothing but hard-as-nails floorboards. A dream that sweet wasn't about some distant movie star or unknown woman. No, Flint was lying there with that silly dream smile on his face because of a woman named Rose. Rose! Suddenly, Francis didn't care if she did wake Flint up.

With the flat of her hands fully open on the floor on either side of Flint, Francis lifted herself up and none-too-carefully rolled off Flint.

"It's you." Flint finally opened his eyes and smiled.

Francis was sitting beside him, a peach-colored fuzzy robe tied around her tighter than a nun's belt. Her hair wasn't combed, and a frown had settled on her forehead.

Francis grunted. "Yeah, it's me. I suppose you were expecting this Rose woman."

"Huh?"

"Not that you aren't entitled to dream about whoever you want to dream about—"

Francis stood up.

Flint lay there. He'd never noticed Francis's toes before—never seen them from this angle before. But right across from him, sitting as they did at eye level to him since he was flat on the floor, he marveled at them. How had he never noticed what dainty little toes she had?

"What are you doing here, anyway?" Francis demanded in

a low voice. She didn't want to wake the whole household. "Who let you in?"

"Garth."

Her brother was the densest man on the face of the earth. "I guess Garth would take in anyone on a night like last night."

Flint didn't answer. He suspected Garth might draw the line at letting him in under ordinary circumstances. But he didn't want Francis to know that. "Blistering cold last night."

"Well, now that you're here you might as well stay for breakfast—I just came down to get it started."

Flint deliberately winced as he lifted his head a few inches off the floor and then fell back into the pile of blankets.

Francis took the bait and knelt beside him. "You're hurt? I'm so sorry about falling on you. I tripped and, well—" Francis had reached out and was running her hands lightly over Flint's sides. "Do your ribs feel all right?"

His ribs felt like a hammer was pounding against them, but he knew it was only his heart. Francis was bending over him and her hair was trailing against his chest. It was like being brushed with feathers. Black, glossy feathers. "It's more the sides of my back."

Francis didn't hesitate. To reach his back without him moving, she had to straddle him again and run both hands along his side.

Flint sighed. There'd been little luxury in his life. Francis's hands felt like silk—or satin—maybe even rose petals.

The sigh was a mistake. Flint knew it the moment Francis's hands stopped.

"You're not hurt at all," she announced abruptly.

Flint grinned. "Can't blame a man for trying."

"You're incorrigible," Francis scolded. She should move. She knew that. But she rather liked staring down at Flint like that. His grin made him look younger than he had since he was nineteen. Only he wasn't nineteen any longer. His early morning whiskers were brushed with gray toward his sideburns. He had a scar on his face that hadn't come from falling out of a tree. And his eyes—his eyes lived in shadows.

Francis didn't realize a tear had fallen from her eye until Flint reached up with a warm hand and wiped it away.

"It's okay," Flint said simply. He didn't move the hand that had found the tear. Instead, he lifted the other hand to cup Francis's face.

Francis heard a grumble behind her, slow and insistent. She didn't want to move. But someone else was up in the sleeping household.

"What's going on here?"

Francis's heart sank. Of all the people sleeping in the house tonight, this was the last person she wanted to have to deal with right now. "Sam."

Francis turned her head slightly, and Flint dropped his hands from her face. She felt the morning cold keenly after their warmth. Sam had plaid flannel pajamas on, and still he had two blankets wrapped around his shoulders.

"There's no need for you to be up." Francis hoped he would take the hint. "Let the house warm up a little first."

Sam grunted. If he heard the hint, he didn't heed it. "What's going on?"

Francis sighed and moved so that she no longer straddled Flint. "I tripped and fell."

Only a blockhead would buy that explanation, Flint thought in bitter satisfaction. He and Francis had been seconds away from a kiss. Surely, it had been obvious.

"Oh." Sam seemed uncertain. He didn't sound convinced, but he apparently didn't want to challenge Francis. "Well, I need to talk to you."

"Can't it wait?" Francis asked as she adjusted all of the chenille in her robe until she looked more respectable than a grandmother. Once she was adjusted, she glanced at Flint again a little shyly.

Flint noticed the pink in her cheeks even if the blockhead Sam didn't.

"Francis is busy now," Flint offered. "You can talk to her later."

Flint had a problem in life—he didn't know when to quit fighting a battle. Sometimes, like today, it cost him. He saw it right away in the way Francis's chin went up and her eyebrow raised.

"No one answers for me. I can talk now."

Flint knew he needed to backtrack. Francis wasn't a woman who liked being told what to do. He rolled his blankets around him closer like he was contemplating going back to sleep. "Yeah, I won't be in the way."

Sam started to puff up. "I want to speak to Francis alone. I am, after all, her fiancé."

"Well, that's a problem," Flint said lazily. "Because technically I'm still her husband."

Sam puffed up in earnest. "I doubt that marriage is even valid anymore."

"Don't count on it," Flint said as he stood.

"Please—" Francis started to scold the two men. She fully intended to. She just hadn't counted on Flint standing up right at that moment. Sam was wrapped in plaid flannel and gray wool blankets. He looked like an overgrown boy. But Flint— Flint looked every inch a man. His shirt was unbuttoned and half off his shoulder. Francis had seen his chest muscles when she'd fallen on top of him, but nothing prepared her for the majesty of him standing there. The sight of him made her mouth grow dry. It also made her cranky. "I can talk to whomever I want to talk to."

Flint nodded and smiled. He wasn't going to lose the war on this one just because he couldn't give in on a battle or two. "Of course you can."

Chapter Six

Flint took his time walking down the stairs. There were creaks in steps fourteen and nine. He'd have to remember that. He had taken Francis's hint and left her alone with Sam so that the two of them could talk. For precisely seven minutes. In his opinion, they'd had twenty years to do their talking, and seven minutes was long enough for whatever Sam had to say.

"Where's Francis?" Flint could see into the kitchen from the bottom of the stairs. Someone had finally turned a small light on over the sink, and it outlined the kitchen appliances. The clock over the refrigerator was illuminated, and the hands shone at half past five o'clock. Early morning still in most places, he thought.

"You and I need to talk." Sam ignored the question. He had wrapped the blankets around him more closely and smoothed back his hair. He cleared his throat like he was ready to give a speech, and Flint's heart sank. "We need to settle some things—"

"You and I don't have anything we need to settle," Flint said mildly as he turned so he could see into the living room. Maybe Francis had gone in there. She certainly hadn't gone up the stairs.

"Francis and I think—" Sam persisted.

"Francis asked you to talk to me?" Flint turned.

The words sliced through the air one syllable at a time. Flint didn't raise his voice. In fact Sam had to lean forward to hear the words clearly. But even in their quietness, the words made Sam Goodman stumble and step back.

"Well, we—"

"You didn't answer my question. Did Francis ask you to talk to me?"

"Well, we—"

"And just where is Francis, anyway?" Flint had finally looked completely around.

"She went out to gather the eggs for breakfast."

"Outside! You let her go outside alone!"

Flint didn't breathe again until he stood in the open door of the chicken coop beside Garth's working barn. There was Francis. She was all right. Well, as all right as one could be in a chenille bathrobe and men's boots in the freezing morning after a blizzard.

"Don't do that again." Flint strapped on the gun holster he'd grabbed on his way out the door. He'd run to the chicken coop, following the footprints in the snow. He'd known the footprints could be a decoy—that a clever kidnapper could have set up an ambush for him. But he ran anyway. The air was so cold his breath puffed out white smoke.

Francis looked up. This wasn't her morning. Every time she turned around there was a man looking at her like she was doing something wrong. "I'm only getting the eggs."

Francis slipped her hand under another laying hen and found a warm egg. The chickens weren't used to being visited this early, but they'd behaved with remarkable poise. Maybe it was so cold they weren't interested in protesting. "Sixteen so far."

She wished she'd stopped to do more than comb her hair this morning. The cold would have added pink to her cheeks, but it was an uneven redness and she wished she'd put on some foundation. Or some eyeliner. Her eyes tended to disappear without eyeliner.

She knew she didn't look as good when she first woke up as Flint did. His rough whiskers and tousled brown hair made him look rugged, especially with the morning light starting to shine behind him.

"You are not to go out by yourself." Flint leaned against

the doorjamb and said the words clearly. "If you want to go get eggs, I'll take you."

Francis slid her hand under another warm hen. There were several dozen laying boxes in the chicken coop, each stacked on top of another. Every hen had her own nest lined with straw. Francis had looked around earlier to see where the rooster was, but she hadn't seen him. He had been unusually aggressive lately, and she always tried to check on him when she entered the coop.

"You're not still worried about me! You caught the kidnappers."

"We caught the goon guys," Flint explained patiently. Why would the sight of a woman plucking eggs from beneath those sleeping chickens affect him like this? "We still don't know who the local contact person is—and we're a long way from catching the boss of the whole operation."

"Well, certainly they won't want me. I'd think by now they'd give up."

"We're not dealing with juvenile delinquents here. They aren't likely to be distracted just because some little guys in the operation get taken in. No, they'll stay with it. They're in this deep already."

"But what am I supposed to do?" Francis laid the basket of eggs on a shelf and turned to face Flint completely. "I can't live my life in a bubble and you can't guard me forever."

Want to bet? Flint thought. "You can take reasonable precautions."

"I do take reasonable precautions. I've been trained by the City of Denver in hostage survival. And how to deal with a terrorist. I'm as prepared as any average citizen could be."

Flint didn't want to tell her how many average citizens were dead today. "Humor me. Until we find the local informant, I intend to guard you."

"But—"

"No argument. That's the way it's going to be."

"But what about—"

"Don't even ask about Lover Boy inside there. He can wait to be alone with you."

"He's not—"

Flint held up his hand. "And another thing. You're going to have to tell me you want that divorce. If you're so set on getting divorced from me, I'd at least like the courtesy of hearing it from your own lips this time."

"Who said—"

"The envelope's on the kitchen table. Still has the coffee stain from twenty years ago—"

In the shadows of the chicken coop Flint could see that Francis looked tired and worried. All of the vinegar went out of his anger.

"I just think you should ask me this time. Tell it to me straight."

Francis watched Flint turn polite. The brief hope that she'd felt when Flint stormed into the coop died. He didn't intend to fight their fate. "I see."

"It was mostly my fault anyway. I had no business asking you to marry me. I figure your dad knew that."

Francis felt every one of her thirty-eight years.

"You'd be better off with someone like Sam anyway," Flint rambled on. *You can stop me anytime.* "He'll give you a stable home and—and—ficus. He seems like a decent enough person. Steady."

"Yes, he's steady all right." Francis didn't like the direction this conversation was going. Flint might be totally indifferent to her, but she didn't want him to encourage her to marry another man. She didn't know why he even needed to pretend to care about who she married. And then it hit her. He had his Rose. He probably wanted that divorce. "You don't need to worry about me. I don't intend to press you on anything. You're completely free."

Completely free. The words echoed in Flint's ears. Why did they have to sound like a prison sentence? "I'm not worried."

"Well, you don't need to be," Francis repeated as she gathered herself together. It had been twenty years, for pity's sake. She searched in the pocket of her robe for a hair clip and found one. She was a middle-aged woman and needed to start acting her age.

Francis reached up, twisted her hair into a tidy bun and then clipped it into place. "I'll finish getting these eggs in and fix you some breakfast."

Flint's throat was dry. "Don't bother just for me, unless the others are getting up."

Francis picked up her basket again and returned to her task. "They'll be up soon enough. I may as well get all the eggs."

Francis knew her eyes were blurry. She told herself firmly it was because of the dust in the chicken coop. All that grain and straw made for dust. Dust led to allergies and red eyes. It certainly wasn't tears that made it hard for her to see.

Francis slipped her hand under another feathery body.

Flint had turned to look outside the coop door. A white expanse of smooth snow covered the area around the ranch outbuildings. The only footprints were the ones he and Francis had made. The thick snow made the silence even more pronounced, and it blanketed the low foothills that led up to the Big Sheep Mountains.

Flint was too relaxed. That's what he told himself later.

The indignant screech of the rooster awakened his instincts. Animals were often the first to notice danger. He turned as the feathered black bird half-flew out of the box it had been occupying.

Francis screamed.

After looking at the snow, it was hard for Flint to see clearly when he turned to look inside the coop. White dots swam in front of dark shadows. He couldn't swear there wasn't something in some corner. Something that black rooster had just noticed. He didn't have time to even look closely.

Years of training kicked in, and Flint took four giant steps toward Francis and wrapped his arms around her before rolling with her to the floor of the coop. Once they hit bottom, he turned so that his bulk would take any bullet that might come from any corner.

Francis couldn't breathe. She forgot all about being a middle-aged woman in a fuzzy bathrobe. Her heart was beating so fast she could be inside the pages of a French spy novel. She could only see the bottom half of Flint's face, but any doubts she had about the danger she was in faded. Flint was stone-faced serious. Deadly, almost. He truly believed someone might still be after her. He'd pulled the gun out of his shoulder holster.

Dear, Lord, someone could really be after me! The realization rose like a prayer to a God she rarely thought of anymore. She wished she had stayed closer to Him. Maybe then this panic wouldn't send her emotions skittering around.

Francis wasn't prepared for the panic she felt. The training sessions she'd had about hostage situations didn't come close to preparing her. "They can have my money."

Flint looked down. Francis was lying on her back beneath him. The clip had fallen out, and her hair spread around her face like black silk. He hadn't realized he'd scared her. "Where's that fool rooster going to spend your money?"

"It's just the rooster?" Francis started to breathe again.

"Looks like." Flint choked back the rest of the reassuring words. He'd spoken too soon. He heard a sound. Outside. The soft crunch of a foot on snow. Very soft. But there. Definitely there. He shouldn't have given in to the urge to reassure Francis. Unless that rooster wore boots, they were not alone out here.

"Shh." Flint mouthed the warning silently.

Francis felt the coil of Flint's body. Every muscle was alert even though he hadn't moved. Francis willed her body to shrink. She'd heard the footstep, too. It didn't seem fair that Flint was obviously using himself as a shield between her and whoever was outside the chicken coop.

There was no other footstep. Someone outside was listening.

Flint almost swore. That meant whoever was on the other side of that knotted wood wall was military trained. Not that that was necessarily a bad thing, he reminded himself. Amateurs were always more dangerous to deal with than professionals, because amateurs sometimes missed and got the wrong target.

Flint slowly moved so that he was no longer sprawled across Francis.

"Move to the corner," he mouthed silently as he jerked his head in the direction of the right corner.

If Francis went to the right, he'd stay in the middle. That

way, just in case there were any bullets, she wouldn't be close enough to him to draw fire. He hoped.

Francis mutely shook her head. She didn't want to cower in some corner while Flint faced the danger alone. She mouthed, ''I can help.''

Flint didn't have any more time to argue with her. He knew whoever was outside would be making a move soon.

''Francis?'' The low whisper came from outside the chicken coop, and Francis recognized it immediately.

''Garth?''

Flint didn't move his hand from his gun holster until he saw the dark silhouette of Garth Elkton in the open doorway of the chicken coop.

''What in blazes is going on in here?'' Garth demanded.

The ground beneath her back was ice cold, but Francis didn't want to move. Her older brother had always scolded her when she'd misbehaved as a child, and she recognized the same sound in his voice today. ''Nothing.''

''Nothing?'' Garth asked incredulously.

''I was guarding Francis,'' Flint explained, in his best government-business, don't-bother-me voice. It usually backed people off. It didn't even faze Garth.

''I can see what you are doing,'' Garth snorted. Francis's brother had obviously rushed out here in a hurry. He'd pulled on a pair of jeans, but he wore nothing over the thermal underwear that covered his chest. ''There's not a square inch of light between the two of you. I don't even want to know what you are doing out here rolling around on the ground.''

''You think I'd pick a place like this to seduce a woman? At five in the morning? In freezing weather?''

''I think you'd pick any place you could, Romeo. Any place. Any time. It's just that when it's my sister, you go through me first.''

Francis looked at the two men and sighed. That's all she needed. A few macho games. ''Garth, I'm not a child. I can take care of myself.''

Garth looked at her and shook his head. ''But the chicken coop?''

''I was gathering the eggs.''

"At this hour of the morning?" Garth finally looked around and saw both the basket of eggs and the rooster, strutting aggressively in the corner. Garth seemed to visibly relax. "Well, no wonder you're flat on the ground. Big Ben here doesn't like to get up before the sun. I'm surprised he didn't chase you out of here."

"I think you interrupted him," Flint said. The black rooster was watching the three humans with a growing annoyance in its beady eyes. "He doesn't want to take on all three of us— at least not yet."

"Don't worry, big fella," Garth cooed to the rooster. "We can take a hint. We'll leave you to your beauty sleep."

It took Francis fifteen minutes to pick all of the straw out of her hair. She sat on a straight-backed chair in the kitchen and willed the full light of morning to arrive.

"Well, I didn't know everything was all right," Sam protested for the tenth time. "I thought I should call the sheriff. What am I to think when I hear a scream and Garth tears out of here like the place is on fire?"

Francis tried to be fair. The fact that Flint had wrapped his body around hers when he thought she was in danger and Sam had merely put a call in to the sheriff did not make Sam a coward. Cautious maybe, but not a coward.

"I can't reach either one of them. That means they're both coming." Flint paced the kitchen with his cellular phone in his hand. "I hate to have the sheriff and Inspector Kahn drive all the way out here when we've got it under control."

"But I didn't know," Sam repeated. "I would never have raised the alarm if I hadn't thought you were both in trouble."

Flint grunted. They were in trouble, all right. Not that Lover Boy had to know about it. "The rooster did make enough noise to raise the dead."

Sam nodded and pulled his blankets closer around his shoulders. "I did what I thought best."

"Of course you did," Francis reassured him. Each time she ran a comb through her hair more straw appeared. She knew what she was doing wrong. She'd given in to vanity and was using a tiny silver comb instead of the working woman's brush she would normally use. And all because Flint insisted on watching her. Well, he wasn't so much watching as guarding. But she wanted him to know she was classy. That she didn't ordinarily lounge around in a fuzzy old robe and pick straw from her hair. She hoped he noticed that the comb was real silver—it was one of her few truly elegant, feminine possessions.

"Well, I expect they'll be here any minute now." Flint nodded toward the basket of eggs on the table. "I think it's only fair that they get some breakfast when they do arrive." He looked at Sam. "You want to scramble the eggs or tackle the pancake batter?"

"Me?" The man looked like Flint had asked him to skin a snake.

"You cook, don't you?" Flint said as he looked around the kitchen. He opened a drawer and pulled out a spatula. Then he reached down and got a glass bowl off a bottom shelf.

"Well, I guess…" Sam stuttered.

"Good," Flint said as he put the bowl on the kitchen table. He hadn't cooked an egg in over a decade, but Lover Boy didn't need to know that. "The inspector likes a little cheese in his scrambled eggs. It's not good for him, but it'll put him in a better mood." Flint opened a canister of flour on the counter. "On second thought, put a lot of cheese in those eggs. It's a long trip out here and the roads are probably packed with snow. He might have had to use a shovel."

"Okay," Sam agreed and then looked at Francis sheepishly. "You'll help me?"

"She can't," Flint said emphatically. He walked toward the refrigerator to get the carton of milk. He hadn't cooked recently, but how hard could it be? He'd read the recipe on the flour sack already. "She needs to go get dressed."

That robe that Francis wore could cover a monk, and Flint would still find it attractive just because he could remember what the soft ridges of the chenille felt like under his hands. And he didn't like her to wear the robe in front of Lover Boy. Sam was slow, but he just might figure out how soft and cuddly Francis was in that robe. Then they'd really have trouble. Flint didn't think he could endure guarding Francis if Lover Boy started hugging her.

"I can put the coffee on first," Francis offered.

"Just show me where the can is and I'll get it going," Flint said.

Flint already knew where the coffee was, but he didn't mind having Francis come over and stand next to him while she reached up on tiptoes to bring the can down from its tall shelf. He could smell her perfume. It was fainter than last night and it was unmistakably mixed with the smell of chicken, but he found that he thoroughly liked it.

"Two scoops," Francis instructed as she handed the gold can over to Flint. "It says three in the directions, but it's too much."

Flint nodded. "Don't worry. We'll have breakfast ready in no time."

The smell of coffee was rich when there was a knock on the kitchen door fifteen minutes later.

"That'll be them," Flint said as he wiped his hands on the towel he'd wrapped around his waist. "Put the eggs in the skillet."

The inspector liked the extra cheese in his eggs and he didn't fuss too much about being called out on a cold winter morning. Sheriff Wall didn't complain at all.

"Glad to be away from them," the sheriff muttered when Flint apologized for the false alarm. Sheriff Wall had left his snow boots by the door and his parka on a nearby chair.

"I suppose they're rattled by the arrest." Flint sympathized. He'd grown to know the three men better than he wanted when he had them staked out. "First time for them, I'd bet."

Sheriff Wall snorted. "They ain't rattled. They keep going on about their rights."

"We read them their rights."

"Oh, those rights they have down pat. It's the other rights they're adding to the list. Some legal mumbo jumbo about humane treatment of prisoners. To them, that means a right to clean sheets. And softer pillows. And doughnuts!" Sheriff Wall stopped as though he still couldn't believe it. "Doughnuts! I asked them if they saw any all-night doughnut shop in these parts. I'd be out getting doughnuts for myself if there were any to be had within thirty miles. Told them they could have their bowl of oatmeal and be grateful for it. We don't run no four-star restaurant here.''

''Doughnuts would be nice,'' Sam said a little wistfully. His banker look had worn off, and he looked disheveled now that he had a little flour on his pajamas and his hair was uncombed. ''Don't even have to cook them.''

''You're doing fine, Lover Boy. Just grate a little more cheese.'' Flint turned his attention to the pancake he was frying. He had poured a perfect circle of dough on the hottest place on the griddle. He'd even slipped a pat of butter underneath it. He'd done everything he could to make this pancake melt-in-the-mouth perfect. He'd timed it to the opening of the door upstairs. He smiled. He was right on target.

''Something smells good,'' Francis said as she walked into the kitchen.

''Good morning.'' Inspector Kahn smiled at Francis.

Francis had showered and washed her hair in a peach shampoo Sylvia had given her. The smell lingered, and she put on some peach hand lotion, as well. She'd scrubbed her face until her cheeks were pink and then put on a light lip gloss. She thought about putting eyeliner and eye shadow on but she didn't want anyone to think she was making a fuss. It was enough that she pulled out the ivory cashmere sweater she'd gotten for Christmas last year and put on her gold earrings.

''Sorry about the mix-up,'' Francis said to the inspector as she sat down at the kitchen table. She studiously avoided looking at Flint over by the stove. ''I should have considered the consequences before I went out to get the eggs. I usually do, you know. I'm in planning—for cities. I know that one thing leads to another and to another.''

''I know your job history.''

''You do?''

''Of course,'' the inspector said as he raised his coffee cup to his lips. ''We made brief profiles on everyone in Dry Creek when this rustling started.''

''You mean I was a *suspect?*''

''Not really.'' The inspector gave a quick smile and looked

toward Flint. "We—even Flint—figured you weren't too likely."

"Well, I certainly wouldn't steal cattle from my own brother."

"Oh, no, that wasn't the reason we ruled you out. Actually, Garth being your brother made you more likely. Maybe you had a grudge. Maybe you figure you should have inherited more when your father passed away."

"I never gave it a thought."

The inspector shrugged. "People do. In the best of families. Whether it's cattle or stocks and bonds."

"Well, Flint would know that I'd never—" Francis started to protest again and stopped. She had no idea what Flint thought of her or had thought of her for the past twenty years.

"Pancake?" Flint interrupted as he set a plate on the table that held a perfectly round, perfectly browned pancake.

"Thank you."

"Would you like some coffee, too?"

"I can get her coffee if she wants it," Sam said. The other man had left his assigned duties of chopping onions for the next breakfast shift and walked over to the table.

Flint noticed Francis wince as she got a whiff of Sam's hands. Flint hadn't spent twenty years fighting crime for nothing. He could set someone up with the best of them.

"I've already got the pot," Flint said as he reached back and pulled the pot off the stove. "I'll take care of Francis."

"You don't need to—I've known her longer than you have," Sam said, tight-lipped. He didn't move back to the counter where he had been chopping onions. "You can't just waltz in here and take over."

"I'm not taking over," Flint said mildly. "Just doing my job. Pouring her some coffee, that's all."

"She's wearing my sweater," Sam said triumphantly as he finally turned.

"You bought her that cashmere?"

Sam nodded. "For Christmas."

Flint didn't like that. A man didn't buy a woman something as soft as cashmere without running his hands all over it, usually with the woman inside it. Flint found he didn't like the thought of Sam touching Francis. He didn't like the idea of Francis wearing that sweater, either.

"We're going to have to be going," the inspector said as he pushed his chair away from the table.

"Yeah," Sheriff Wall agreed. "Roads have been closed to everything but four-wheel drives. I should get back to the office unless anyone needs me."

"I didn't know the snow was that bad." Flint cheered up. "You think it's high enough to keep the bad guys out for a while?"

The sheriff shrugged. "The Billings airport has been closed since last night. Even if they could fly anyone in from the west coast, they'd be stuck in Helena. And most of the rental cars would never make it to Dry Creek."

"That means I'm not in danger?" Francis asked in relief. "Flint doesn't need to keep guarding me?"

The thought of Flint leaving didn't please Francis. But she would like to know if he would stay with her even if he didn't need to guard her because it was his job.

"Now, I wouldn't say you're out of danger," the inspector said slowly as he looked at the scowl on Flint's face and then at Francis. "The odds of trouble have gone down, but they haven't disappeared. I'd say you're in danger until we figure out who the informant around here is. Until then, you'll need to be guarded."

"You mean someone who's already here is the informant?"

The inspector nodded. "Someone who has been here all along. The rustlers are getting a local tip-off."

"I don't suppose you could be wrong?"

"Not much chance."

Francis squared her shoulders and looked at the inspector. "Then we have work to do. I'm happy to help figure out who the informant is—and see if it is someone local. I'm pretty good at setting up a cross-tabbed table—if you want to look at who has been around at different times."

"You'd be working with Flint," the inspector said. "Might be good for you both."

"Oh."

Flint grunted. It didn't escape his notice that Francis was in a mighty hurry to get away from him. You'd think a woman would like a man who was spending so much effort working to keep her alive.

"Why don't you set up shop at the hardware store in Dry Creek," the inspector suggested. "I think it might be good for people around here to see that the FBI is doing something— their taxes at work, that sort of thing."

"That'd be a good place." Francis ate the last piece of her pancake. "It's more businesslike there. We won't be distracted."

And I won't be distracted, Francis vowed. There was a step-by-step path in every relationship, and she fully realized that she and Flint could not take the next step in getting to know each other again until this rustling business was settled.

"We could try the café instead," Flint offered.

"You're hungry?" Francis stood up from the table. "Of course, you probably don't like eggs and pancakes—I can fix—"

"I like pancakes just fine," Flint protested as he waved her back to her chair. "I just made batter for another dozen more."

"Well, then, why go to the café?"

"A café has candles," Flint explained wearily. "I thought we'd like a candle on the table."

Now she understood, Francis thought. Flint wanted to burn any paper they wrote on right at the table. Her face blanched. He was right, of course. There could be an informant around any corner. A dangerous informant.

Flint sighed. He hadn't made that many romantic suggestions to women in the past few years, but he couldn't believe it was a promising sign when the woman's face went ten shades whiter. Times couldn't have changed so much that a candlelit dinner—or lunch—wasn't considered romantic.

Chapter Seven

The café wasn't open yet so Flint had to content himself with taking Francis to the hardware store. It was nearly impossible to date someone in a place like Dry Creek. Especially when the woman you were dating didn't know you were courting her. All this talk of crime didn't set a very romantic mood. And a hardware store! There wasn't even a dim light anywhere. At least not one that wasn't attached to a fire alarm.

Flint was tempted to ask the clerk behind the counter if he could borrow the small radio he had plugged in by his stool. They might get lucky and hear a country-and-western love song. But the clerk was Matthew Curtis, a minister who had recently gotten married and was probably in some romantic haze of his own.

Matthew had married Glory Becker, the woman who had become famous locally as the flying angel in Dry Creek's Christmas pageant. Flint hadn't been in Dry Creek then, but he'd read reports. He'd even heard the gossip about how the angel had brought the minister back to God. A man like Matthew wasn't likely to let folks listen to anything but hymns, and that sure wouldn't help a man's courting.

But that wasn't the only reason Flint hesitated. Flint was reluctant to ask a minister for anything, even a minister who was now a clerk in a hardware store. Flint half expected the man to question him about the Bible Flint still carried with him. Flint knew he could have left the book in the pickup he had borrowed from the inspector, but he didn't. He liked having his grandmother close by—wished she were here now with her brusque no-nonsense approach to life.

"It couldn't be number twenty-six," Francis announced as she consulted the notebook she'd been writing in all morning. She'd given each person in Dry Creek over the age of sixteen a number so that she could be more objective about them. Flint had cautioned her that children under the age of sixteen were also capable of crime, but she wouldn't listen. She insisted no child in Dry Creek could be involved. "Number twenty-four is sweet. And he wouldn't know a Hereford from a Guernsey. I can't see how he'd ever set up an operation like that. I think maybe I should delete people who don't know the cattle business, too."

Francis wished she could delete all the suspects in Dry Creek. It made her feel old to realize that someone she had known all her life could be stealing from the ranchers around here. Anyone from Dry Creek would know the thin line that separated some of the ranchers from success and failure. A rustling hit could mean some of them would need to sell out. Who would do that?

They were both sitting on the hard-back chairs that formed a half-circle around the Franklin stove that was the centerpiece of the store. Flint was relieved to find out that this part of Dry Creek at least was the way he remembered it. Usually, an assortment of men would be sitting around this stove sharing worries about the weather or information about crop prices. But the snow had kept them home today.

"I remember you raised a Hereford calf for 4-H that year," Flint mused leisurely. The snow outside would keep even the most determined villians away. The FBI had already analyzed all the people in Dry Creek. Flint knew Francis wouldn't come up with anything new. The inspector had assigned her the task so she'd have something to worry about while she was with Flint. It wouldn't have taken a tenth of the inspector's powers of observation to see that Francis was all nerves around him, Flint thought. It'd take more than a fancy flowchart to make her happy with him guarding her. "You even named him— what was it?"

"Cat."

Flint chuckled. "Yeah, I remember now. You had wanted to have a kitten instead, but your dad said you were in cattle country and—if you were that set on having a pet—it was a calf or nothing."

"It could be number sixteen." Francis looked up from her list and frowned slightly. "I hope not, though. He has two little kids and his wife has been sick a lot. He needs the money, I'm sure, but—"

"You loved that Cat of yours," Flint continued staunchly. It was real hard to strike a light note when Francis insisted on worrying over the guilt of her neighbors. "Bet there never was a calf like him."

"Her." Francis finally looked up from her list. "I picked a her so that she could go on to be a mother and have calves of her own."

Something about the tightness of Francis's voice warned him. Francis had always wanted children. Should have had children. That was the one dream she'd shared with him back then. "I hadn't thought about that—"

"It's not important."

"Of course, it's important," Flint protested. Until now, he'd just thought of those wasted twenty years as a trick being played on him. He hadn't had time to adjust and realize what they had meant for Francis. "You were meant to be a mother. That's all you ever wanted to be."

Francis blinked and looked at her list. "We don't always get what we want in life."

"I know, but—" Flint had a sudden flash of a little girl who would have looked like Francis. He'd never realized the sum total of his own loss until that minute. He could have had a daughter. Or a son. His life could have meant something to someone besides the FBI. "How could this all have happened?"

Francis looked at Flint. She'd been nervous all morning around him-wondering what he thought of her hair, of her clothes, of the words she spoke. All of those things suddenly didn't seem so important now as she looked at him, the defeat plain on his face.

"It certainly wasn't your fault," Francis comforted him softly.

"Well, it wasn't yours, either."

"I could have had more faith in you."

Flint snorted. "You were a kid. What did we know?"

"It was just one of those things."

"Like fate?" Flint challenged. He had fought many enemies in his life, but he'd never tackled fate before. It was like boxing with a shadow. There was no way to win. "You're saying it was our fate?"

"Well, maybe not fate, but—" Francis glanced over at Matthew and lowered her voice. She'd given this a lot of thought in the hours she'd lain awake last night. She'd remembered snatches of what she had learned in Sunday school as a child when her mother used to take her. "But it must have been God's will."

"Well, I don't think much of God then if He's got nothing better to do than mess up the lives of two young kids so crazy in love they couldn't see straight." Flint knew he was speaking too loudly for Francis's comfort. She kept looking at Matthew. "And I don't care who hears me on that one. It wasn't fair."

Francis looked at Matthew. She remembered pictures of God in his long white robes. She had never considered the possibility that God was unkind until last night. He had always seemed distant, like her father. But never unkind. "I'm sorry."

Matthew stopped polishing the old lantern that was sitting on the counter. "Don't be. I happen to agree with Flint there."

"You do?" Flint was as surprised as Francis.

Matthew nodded. "It's what drove me out of the ministry."

"So you agree with me?" Flint asked for clarification. He thought ministers always defended God. That was their job. "You're not taking God's side in this?"

Matthew laughed. "I don't know about there being sides to this issue. I know it's not fair—" he assessed Flint "—and you—you're probably sitting there wishing there was some guy you could arrest and make pay for all of this."

Flint gave a short, clipped laugh. "There's something about an arrest that levels the field again."

"Only there's no one to arrest," Matthew continued. He

walked around the counter and stepped over to the small table that had been set up next to the window. A coffeepot sat on the table, and the flavor of good coffee had been drifting through the air for some time now. Matthew turned to Flint and Francis. "Coffee?"

"Yes, thanks," Flint said as Francis nodded.

"The most frustrating thing about injustice is that usually we can't do anything about it," Matthew said as he poured coffee into three thick, white mugs.

"You're saying there's nothing we can do about bad things?" Francis asked.

"Now, I didn't say that." Matthew turned to look at them again. "Sugar or cream? Or maybe a flavor? I've got some orange flavor. Or raspberry."

"Plain for me," Francis said.

"Me, too." Flint watched as Matthew balanced the three cups on a small tray and brought them over to where he and Francis were sitting.

"We need to get some TV trays around here," Matthew apologized as he pulled up a wooden box with his foot. "The regular clientele never was one for fussing, but lately—"

"Since Glory's been around," Francis finished for him in a teasing tone.

"Well, you have to admit she does bring a whole new brand of people into the store here." Matthew laughed and then sobered. "I'm blessed to have her in my life."

Matthew carefully set the coffee cups on the box within easy reach of both of them. "And it's a blessing I almost let get away just because I was stuck on the same problem that is plaguing you two."

"And that would be?" Flint prodded. He didn't know the ex-minister well, but he'd watched him at the wedding reception the other night. Matthew had had kind words for everyone present.

"Being so preoccupied with my anger toward God for what had happened in the past that I was totally unable to accept any blessings in the here and now."

"But you still hold God responsible?" The conversation was

getting under his skin, and Flint realized he really wanted to know what the minister thought.

"Of course," Matthew agreed as he pulled up another straight-back chair and joined them in front of the Franklin stove. "But it's not always that easy. Like for you two—you can sit there and be mad at God for letting you be pulled apart twenty years ago or you can sit there and thank Him for bringing you back together now."

"But we lost so much," Flint said.

"Maybe," Matthew said as he took a sip of hot coffee. "But I'd guess there's things you gained along the way, too. Who would you be today if you hadn't parted back them?"

"We'd be chicken farmers," Flint said, and smiled. "Living on my grandmother's old place. But at least the windows would be fixed."

"And I would have had a child," Francis added shyly and cupped her hands around her mug as though she had a sudden chill.

"Maybe," Matthew said. "But then maybe something would have happened and that child would be nothing but a heartache to you—maybe there'd be a sickness or who knows what. The point I'm making is that when God takes us down a path all He asks is that we're willing to go. He doesn't guarantee that there won't be troubles on that path. All He guarantees is that He'll walk it with us."

"That sounds so easy," Flint said.

"Doesn't it?" Matthew agreed as he set his coffee cup down. He grinned at Flint. "Trust me, it's not as easy as it sounds."

Flint reached down beside his chair and picked up the Bible he'd lain there earlier. "My grandmother tried to pray that kind of faith into me when I was here with her."

"Well, she must have succeeded," Francis said.

Flint looked at her in surprise.

"You wrote a verse next to our marriage lines," Francis explained softly. "It must have meant something to you at the time."

"I didn't write any verse," Flint said as he flipped the Bible open to the center pages where the family record was kept. He looked down and saw the writing. "It must have been my grandmother. She must have written something down. And here I thought I'd covered my tracks and that she didn't know—''

"Song of Solomon," Francis said as she stood and looked over Flint's shoulder. "Verses six and seven—chapter eight. Let's read it."

"Now?" Flint looked at the Bible.

"Why not? If your grandmother had something to say about our marriage, I'd like to hear it."

Flint shrugged and started to page through the early part of the Bible. "I guess you're right."

Flint skimmed the verses his grandmother had selected before he cleared his throat and read them aloud. "Set me as a seal upon thine heart, as a seal upon thine arm: for love is strong as death... Many waters cannot quench love, neither can the floods drown it—" Flint's voice broke and he couldn't continue.

"Those are sweet words," Francis said softly. "I thought she might have picked something about the folly of youth or trusting strange women."

Flint smiled. "My grandmother liked you."

"She must have thought I left you, as well."

Flint looked at Francis. "We were all a-tangle, weren't we? So many if onlys—"

"It just wasn't right."

"No, no, it wasn't." Flint looked at Matthew. "You know, you seem like a good person. But I just don't see how God could let this happen."

Matthew nodded, rather cheerfully, Flint thought. "So you think He could have stopped you?"

"Stopped me?"

"Yeah, when you decided to run off to Vegas that night— you must think God could have stopped you."

"Not unless He sent in a tornado."

The door to the hardware store opened, and a blast of snowy wind blew in with the well-wrapped figure of an older woman. She had to remove two head scarves before Flint recognized Mrs. Hargrove.

"A tornado," she gasped when she could speak. "Don't tell me we're getting a tornado on top of this?"

"Of course not," Matthew assured her. "This is Montana, not Kansas."

"Well, nothing would surprise me anymore," Mrs. Hargrove muttered as she removed her gloves and set them on the counter. "Everything in Dry Creek has gone topsy-turvy these days."

"Something must be happening to bring you out in this kind of weather," Matthew agreed calmly as he walked over and helped Mrs. Hargrove struggle out of her coat. Flecks of snow still clung to the plaid wool. "Why don't you sit by the fire and tell us all about it while I get you a cup of that cocoa you like."

"Oh, it's just old man Gossett." Mrs. Hargrove started to mutter as she walked to an empty chair and sat down with a sigh. "I swear I don't know what that man is thinking."

"Mr. Gossett?" Matthew said in surprise as he turned from the coat hook behind the counter. "I've never heard anyone complain about him before—I mean except for the usual—his drinking and his cats."

"That man—I swear he's stretched my Christian patience until there's only a thin thread left," Mrs. Hargrove continued and then looked at Flint. "Oh, I'm sorry—you probably don't know him. I wouldn't want you to think he's typical of the folks hereabouts."

Flint had never seen Mrs. Hargrove so flustered. He turned to Francis. "What number is he?"

"Old man Gossett?"

"Yes."

"Why, I—" Francis was scanning her paper. "I think I forgot to put him on the list."

"Forget anyone else?"

Francis was running her finger down the column. "Let me do a quick count—no, I'm only one short."

"He's an easy one to forget," Mrs. Hargrove said with irritation still fresh in her voice. "Forgets himself often enough—as long as he has a bottle he's never seemed to care about anything or anyone."

"What's his name?"

Mrs. Hargrove looked at him blankly. "Why, Gossett. Mr. Gossett."

"His first name."

"Well, I don't know." Mrs. Hargrove frowned in thought. "He's always called old man Gossett. I try to call him Mr. Gossett myself because it reminds me he's one of God's creatures, but I don't think I've ever heard him called anything else. Just old man Gossett or sometimes Mr. Gossett."

"Didn't his father settle Dry Creek?"

"Back in the big drought in the twenties," Mrs. Hargrove said as she nodded. "Folks here talk about it sometimes—our parents and grandparents all pretty much had settled around these parts after the Homestead Act of 1902. But they wouldn't have stayed if it hadn't have been for the Gossett who was alive then. He started this town and named it Dry Creek to remind folks that they could survive hard times. Made us a community."

"So Dry Creek owes the Gossett family a lot?"

Mrs. Hargrove shrugged. "In a way. Of course, it would be different if it was the first Gossett. I was a little girl way back then, but I remember him still. Quite an impressive man. Never could figure out why his son didn't measure up."

"You must remember," Francis interrupted. She was chewing on the tip of a pencil. "If you knew old man Gossett when he was a boy, you must have known his name."

"Why, you're right," Mrs. Hargrove said. "It's just he's been old man Gossett for so many years—but you're right, back then he wouldn't have been—" She closed her eyes and then smiled. "Harold. It's Harold. Little Harry, they called him. Little Harry Gossett."

Mrs. Hargrove was clearly pleased with herself as Francis added the man's full name to her list.

"Now he's eighty-three," Francis declared.

"Eighty-three in what, dear?" Mrs. Hargrove leaned over to see Francis's list more clearly.

"You didn't tell us your news." Flint interrupted the older woman quickly before she could ask any more questions. He didn't relish telling her that all her friends and neighbors were suspects in aiding the rustlers. So far, most of the people in

Dry Creek all believed the rustlers were outsiders, from the west coast, they figured. They would never look at their own ranks.

"Why, bless me, you're right," Mrs. Hargrove said as she straightened in her chair. "And after I hurried all the way over here."

"It's not the boys, is it?" Matthew asked in alarm.

Mrs. Hargrove smiled. "Your boys are fine. They're with Glory. It's just that Mr. Gossett—Harold—has been trying to talk Glory into driving him into Miles City, and I was afraid she'd weaken and say yes." Mrs. Hargrove looked around sternly. "I told them both no one had any business driving anywhere in weather like this and that if all he wanted was a bottle of something to keep him warm until the roads cleared he'd be welcome to my vanilla."

"I don't think a bottle of vanilla would keep him happy enough." Flint almost smiled.

"I read in the newspaper that vanilla is ninety-nine percent alcohol and alcoholics sometimes tip back the bottle," Mrs. Hargrove announced.

"Unless you have a gallon of it, though, it's not going to be enough."

"Well, Glory might give him hers, too."

Flint had a mental picture of all the ladies of Dry Creek emptying their cupboards to keep Mr. Gossett happy during the blizzard. It was neighborliness at work.

"Do you think we should be giving him anything?" Francis worried. "Maybe now's a good time for him to quit."

"He doesn't want to quit." Mrs. Hargrove grunted in disapproval. "He wants to talk someone into braving this weather just to take him to a store. Or a bar, more like it."

"I could go talk to him," Flint offered. He would like to get reacquainted with the man Dry Creek had forgotten even while he lived in their midst. "I'll tell him there's a fine for endangering lives or something like that."

"Scare him?" Mrs. Hargrove asked, but Flint couldn't tell whether or not she liked the idea.

Flint shrugged. "Just slow him down. If he can wait until tomorrow, the roads will be better."

"The wind might stop, too," Matthew offered. "The forecast says this storm will blow through tonight."

"It really is too bad he can't quit," Mrs. Hargrove said softly. "That little boy wasn't so bad, now that I remember him from all those years ago. Wonder whatever happened?"

Flint kept his hands in his gloves while he knocked on Harold Gossett's front door. Flint had convinced Francis to wait outside in the pickup for him while he spoke with Mr. Gossett. It was probably nothing, but Flint had a feeling about this man. If anyone had a grudge against Dry Creek, he'd bet it was this Gossett fellow. He knocked again.

A shadow crossed the peephole in Gossett's front door. Funny, Flint thought, no one else in Dry Creek felt the need for a peephole. Even if they locked their doors, they just called out and asked who was outside. But you couldn't arrest someone for having a peephole in their door. If you could, all of California would be in jail. Maybe Gossett just wanted to avoid his neighbors as much as they wanted to avoid him.

The door opened a crack. The inside of the house was dark. A subdued light came in through the blinds that were drawn at each of the windows. There wasn't much furniture. An old vinyl recliner. A television that was blinking. A wooden table pushed against one wall with rows of beer bottles stacked up underneath it. The house smelled of cats, although it wasn't an unpleasant smell.

"Hi," Flint said as he took his glove off and offered his hand to the man inside the house. "My name's Flint Harris."

"Essie's grandson." The older man nodded. The man was heavyset with a looseness to his face that came from drinking too much. He was wearing a pair of farmer overalls over thermal underwear that had holes in both of the elbows. If the man was planning to go to Miles City today, he certainly wasn't worried about making a good impression once he got there.

"I wanted to introduce myself," Flint said. He was beginning to doubt his suspicions about the man. He certainly didn't look like he'd come into any money lately. Not with the way he lived. "I've tied my horse out back on the other side of your yard a few times of late."

"Ain't my property."

"I know," Flint continued. "I checked it out first. Still, I thought you might have been curious."

"Nope."

The older man started to close the door. Flint moved his foot to block it.

"Just wanted to talk to you about your conversation with Glory Becker—I mean, Glory Curtis."

Gossett's eyes jumped slightly in guilt. "I wasn't talking to her."

"That's good, because it would be foolish to try to drive into Miles City today. I was worried when I heard that's what you were planning."

The older man swallowed. "I wasn't going nowhere."

"That's good," Flint repeated. He was beginning to see why Mrs. Hargrove found the man exasperating. "See that you don't. At least not until the blizzard breaks. Nothing's that important."

The old man nodded vacantly. Flint had seen that kiss-off-to-the-feds face enough times to know that it didn't mean the man was agreeing to anything. Still, there wasn't much else Flint could do. He moved his foot so the door could close.

Francis opened the door on the driver's side so Flint could slip into the pickup.

"What do you know of Gossett's drinking style?" he asked as he turned the key to start the motor.

"He drinks lots."

"But lots of what? He's got enough beer in there to keep an army happy, but he might be out of something else. Maybe he uses beer as a chaser for hard liquor and he's out of hard liquor?"

Francis shrugged. "Must be. Why else would he be so set on going into Miles City?"

"Maybe he's out of cat food. I understand he's got lots of cats."

"Yes, but he could borrow cat food from anyone in Dry Creek. Folks often borrow back and forth in the winter months instead of making a special trip to Billings or Miles City."

"Maybe he's got a lady friend he visits?"

"Old man Gossett?" Francis asked in genuine surprise.

"Well, you never know," Flint said as he backed away from the Gossett house. At least he had Francis thinking about romance again.

"Old man Gossett," she repeated.

Well, maybe not romance, Flint thought wryly as he started driving down the short road that was Dry Creek. She sounded more like she was thinking of a circus act.

"Oh, look," Flint said as he drove level with the café. "It's open"

A black Open sign was hanging in the window of the café under another more permanent sign that read Jazz and Pasta.

"We could stop for coffee," Flint offered.

The interior of the café smelled of baking bread and spicy tomato sauce. Black and white linoleum covered the floor, and several square tables were set up for dining.

Ah, here we go, Flint thought as he saw a small candle in the middle of each table.

"Allow me." Flint held the chair for Francis.

Now they were getting somewhere, Flint thought.

His heart sank when Francis pulled out her checklist.

"I think we need to consider thirty-four, too," she said. "He got his hair cut."

"His hair cut?"

"Yeah, and it wasn't anyone around here who did it," Francis said. "You can't get a cut like that in Miles City even— I'd say he's been to Spokane or Boise."

Flint sighed. Francis would have been a terror on the force. "You want to talk about some guy's haircut?"

"It could be important," Francis persisted. *Besides, I don't know what to say to you. I'm afraid of saying anything that's going to rock this boat we're on.*

Our lives could be important, too, Flint felt like saying. But he didn't. Maybe Francis was right. Maybe it was too late for them to go back to what they once were.

The minister, Matthew, had seemed hopeful, saying they should thank God for bringing them together now instead of being angry for being separated earlier. But even if God was bringing them together now, why was He bothering? It seemed more like a cosmic joke than anything—bring the two young lovers back together so they could realize what they had missed during all those years.

Flint let his hand drop to the Bible that sat on the seat next to him. He felt comforted just touching the thing—maybe more of his grandmother's faith had gotten under his skin than he ever realized. He had a sudden urge to pray and wished he knew how. Wished that words would form on his lips to express the confusion inside his heart. But his lips were silent.

Chapter Eight

A teenager walked out of the back of the restaurant. She was wearing a white chef's apron over faded jeans, and her shaggy hair was dyed a bright copper red. As she walked she pulled an ordering pad out of the apron pocket. She snapped her chewing gum. "Can I get something for you folks?"

"Hi, Linda," Francis greeted the teen. "How's business?"

"Not bad," Linda said and smiled. "We've decided to open for the breakfast crowd now—so far so good—we got seven breakfast orders from Sheriff Wall already this morning. We didn't have doughnuts, but Jazz makes a mean biscuit served with honey. The sheriff bought a dozen extra biscuits. Asked me to cut little holes in them so they looked like doughnuts," Linda shrugged and smiled again. "And folks around here think I'm weird because I got my nose pierced."

The teenager tilted her face so Flint and Francis could see the sparkling stud in the side of her nose.

"Nice," Flint said with a smile. Linda's face was scrubbed clean and fresh-looking.

"Just the right touch," Francis agreed. She was glad Linda had forgotten about the black lipstick she sometimes wore.

The teen took their order for coffee and biscuits and called out, "Two for a combo—make it sticky!" to someone in the back before walking over to the coffee urn that rested on the counter at the side of the large room.

"What number is she?" Flint whispered to Francis.

"Linda?" Francis seemed surprised. "Well, she's number twenty-seven, but I don't really think—"

"She's in a public place," Flint reminded her. He enjoyed watching Francis's eyes. Their gray depths had lost all semblance of calm. "Good place to get information. Overhear talk about cattle. Maybe know when a rancher is sick and not making his usual rounds."

"But the ranchers don't hang out here," Francis protested firmly. "Besides, their café has only been open since Christmas Eve. Most of the rustling happened before that."

"True." Flint liked the way Francis's eyes got passionate in their defense of the young woman. He tried a different tactic. "How old do you think she is?"

"Eighteen, I think."

"And this Jazz guy that works the restaurant with her?"

"Duane? A year or two older."

"Just like us," Flint said softly. "That was the age we were when we got married."

The old man looked in the back window of the café. He knew that this window beside the black cookstove wouldn't be frosted up and would still be hidden from the people inside the café. He had to stand in a snowbank to get a good view through the window, but that didn't bother him. He'd be a lot colder if he didn't find a way to get to that bus in Miles City.

What were they talking about? The FBI man and Francis. She was a smart one, she was. He'd known her mother. She had been the same way. Never did understand why she had married Elkton when she could have married him. He'd been somebody back then before the drinking.

The FBI man thought he was so clever, coming to his door with some nonsense about the roads. But the old man wasn't fooled. Since when did the federal government care about cars driving in snow?

Besides, he had seen the agent look in his trash barrel the other day and take out an empty jelly jar that had broken. The jelly was crab apple, left over from a summer when Mrs. Hargrove had canned some jelly for him from his tree. The agent put the jar back, but the old man wasn't sure if he'd taken a fingerprint off of it somehow. The agent must have. What did the government care about empty jelly jars?

It all made the old man nervous. He had to get out of town. That Glory Becker wasn't much of an angel as far as he was concerned. Wouldn't even drive him to Miles City in that Jeep of hers. And she had good tires. He'd checked them out. He'd half considered stealing them to put on his pickup, but he couldn't use a tire iron anymore. Couldn't drive his pickup even if it had tires on it, when it came right down to it. He hadn't driven anything for a good twenty years now—he'd be surprised if he'd know how, especially if he was behind the wheel of a newfangled car.

He was an old man, plain and simple. He was surprised the Becker woman hadn't agreed to help him. What kind of Christian charity was she showing—she just said no and kept talking about the twins. You'd think she was their real mother the way the woman went on about them. Little Joshua and little Joey. It made the old man want to gag. He knew it wouldn't hurt the little creatures to stay home alone for a day. Might even do them some good. Take some of the happy shine off their infernal faces.

Disgusting. And no help at all.

He'd have to try something else. And soon. Before any more snow got dumped on the roads and the bus got canceled.

Francis felt her nerves stretch tighter than a new drum. The day had stiffened her like a board. She was grateful Garth had convinced Sam to spend the day with some of the ranch hands in the bunkhouse. She suspected they were teaching him to play poker. If they were, he'd be there until supper trying to win his money back.

She wished she had something like that to worry over. She'd tried to keep her mind organized, but she hadn't succeeded. Her thoughts kept straying—kept going back to the wistful look on Flint's face when he realized that Linda and her fiancé, the Jazz Man, were the same age she and Flint had been when they eloped to Las Vegas.

Linda and the Jazz Man were working toward their dream. The two teenagers had sat with her and Flint after they had their biscuits and talked about the farm they planned to buy when they'd saved enough money. Their faces shone with their dream. They were halfway to their goal already. Every dollar helped. They had looked happy when Flint offered to pay them fifty dollars if they would go out to his grandmother's old place and bring Honey back to the small building behind the café so they could feed and water her for a day or two.

Francis sighed. She wished her own dreams were as simple to fulfill.

"You okay? Flint asked me to check."

Francis glanced up and saw her brother standing in the doorway and looking at her in concern. She had told Flint she was going into the den and didn't want to be disturbed. It was taxing to be guarded—especially by Flint. They'd spent the whole day together. It was almost time for supper, and Francis needed some time alone before she offered to help the others prepare the meal.

"Yeah, sure," Francis answered. "Tell Flint I'm fine."

She was sitting in the old rocker in the den. The room was growing darker as the last of the day's light seeped in through the frost-covered windows. The furniture in Garth's house had been replaced in the past few years, but the rocker was one thing that would never leave. This was the chair their mother used to sit in when she read to them when they were each small. Garth kept it in the corner of the den that couldn't be seen from the door. Francis suspected he used it as an escape place, too.

"Want to talk about it?" Garth offered as he pulled over a straight-backed office chair and sat down. "I suppose you're still mad at Dad."

Francis grimaced. "He could have told me. I spent so much time being angry with Flint. Even if Flint had gone on with his life by then, Dad should have told me."

"Probably meant to." Garth mused. "Dad was never much good at talking, and I'd guess it got harder to tell you as the years went on."

Francis hesitated and then took the plunge. "And I've been thinking about Mom, too."

Garth sat still. "Oh."

"Do you remember her taking us to church? I always remember her getting you and me ready and taking us to Sunday school and then church.''

''Yeah.'' Garth was noncommittal.

''Why did she?''

Garth seemed surprised. ''Why? I never thought about it. She just did. That was part of her being Mom.''

''Do you think it meant something to her? You were older than me when she died, and I can't remember.'' Francis could tell it was painful for Garth to talk about their mother, but she pressed on. ''I can remember her sitting in this chair about this time late every afternoon—just before she started getting supper ready and before Dad came in from the fields. She'd sit a bit and read her Bible and then pray. I know she prayed with us later, when we went to bed, but this was just her time. I haven't thought about that for years. I wonder—did she really believe it all?''

''Yeah,'' Garth said softly. ''I think she did.''

They were both silent for a minute.

''I wish she were with us now,'' Francis whispered. Maybe her mother would know how to untangle the feelings Francis was feeling. Maybe she'd even know how to help Francis pray to the God she herself had known so well.

''So do I, Sis. So do I.''

Francis looked at her brother. She hadn't noticed how weary he was looking, either. ''Troubles?''

Garth shrugged.

Francis took a shot. She'd noticed how her brother looked at the woman from Seattle. ''How's Sylvia doing?''

Garth grunted.

''She likes you, you know,'' Francis offered softly.

Garth's wince told her she had hit the sore spot.

''She's got better things to do with her life than liking me,'' Garth said harshly as he stood up and pushed his chair to the desk. ''She deserves someone better.''

''Maybe you should let her decide that,'' Francis said as Garth walked toward the door.

''It's already decided. If you need me, I'll be out back chopping some more wood for winter,'' Garth said as he opened the door.

Francis had seen the huge stack of wood Garth had already chopped in the last two days. "Don't we have enough wood?"

"Not enough to suit me."

Francis nodded. It looked like she wasn't the only one in the family with troubles in love.

Flint was in the kitchen pacing. The hands on the clock over the refrigerator seemed to crawl. What was Francis doing, locked in the den like that? He knew she had looked more and more strained as the day wore on, but he wished she would talk to him. The fact was, if she didn't come out soon, he was going to go right in and demand that she talk to him. Yes, he said to himself, that's what he'd do. It was his duty, after all. He was guarding her. On official government business. He had a right to know how she was.

Flint looked at the clock in exasperation. Two minutes down. He was beginning to understand why the inspector didn't want him to serve as guard to Francis. Being around her all day was doing things to him that he wasn't able to control. Before he knew it, he was going to make ten kinds of fool of himself doing something like demanding she talk to him. He'd never demanded that someone in protective custody talk to him be-fore—at least not about their feelings. The FBI didn't care about feelings. It worried about the who, where and when questions.

Flint looked at the clock. One more minute. Ah, there she comes. Flint heard the faint click of the doorknob and turned to face the small hall that led to the den.

"Relax. It's just me," Garth said as he walked through the open door.

"Oh."

"She'll come out soon," Garth offered gruffly as he walked over to the rack of coats that hung near the kitchen door and pulled a jacket off a peg. He turned back and looked at Flint squarely. "Don't leave her this time."

"I never left her the first time," Flint protested and then smiled. This was as close to a blessing as someone like Garth would give him. "You don't have to worry. Francis isn't that interested in me these days. I'm only her guard."

Garth grunted as he pulled on the jacket. "I've officially turned down the FBI's request, you know. There's no reason to kidnap her."

"The bid has already been put out," Flint explained. He'd gone over that in his mind, too. "If it's put out with a crime syndicate, it's probably too late to pull back the orders. There might have been a backup in place before we even arrested those other goons."

"I'll tell the boys to keep their eyes open."

"I'd appreciate that."

A rush of cold air entered the kitchen as Garth opened and then quickly closed the outside door. The clock crawled two more minutes before Francis opened the door from the den. Flint tried to pretend he wasn't waiting for her and turned to face the wall. Ah, good, there was a calendar tacked to the kitchen wall about level with his eyes.

"Tomorrow's Sunday, isn't it?" Francis asked as she walked down the hall.

Flint scrambled to look at the calendar more clearly. "Yes, I guess it is, at that. Why?"

"No reason," Francis said as she walked over to the kitchen sink and turned the water on. "I just thought if it was Sunday tomorrow I might go to church."

"Church?"

"I mean, if that's all right with the FBI." Francis reached into a cupboard and pulled out a teakettle. "I know I'm being guarded, but it's only church. The FBI couldn't object to that."

Flint groaned. He knew the FBI would object. He'd be placing the person he was protecting square in the middle of every suspect in Dry Creek. Everyone would be rounded up under one roof with no weapons check and predictable times when everyone from the minister on down would stand for long minutes with their eyes closed. A lot could happen with all those closed eyes. A smart kidnapper could nab their victim and hustle them out the door before the prayer finished.

"I'd really like to go," Francis continued as she put the kettle under the faucet and began to fill it with water. "And you'll be there, so there's really no danger."

The easy confidence with which Francis said the latter was

Flint's undoing. She trusted him. "We'd have to sit in the back row."

"That'd be fine." Francis looked at him and smiled. "I'm sort of a back row kind of person anyway—I haven't been in church for years."

"And I won't be closing my eyes when I pray," Flint assured her.

"Oh, well, surely, there's nothing to worry about at church," Francis said indignantly.

Flint didn't remind her that the hit man that had come after Glory Beckett had chosen the Christmas pageant as the place to make his attempt on her life. The way Flint heard it, it was only the quick thinking of Matthew that had saved the woman's life.

"I'll call Mrs. Hargrove and tell her to be on the lookout tomorrow for someone who is in church but doesn't usually attend," Flint said as he walked toward the telephone. That should pinpoint any problems. "I wonder if it's too late to get some kind of metal detector set up in the entrance hall."

"I don't remember that the church has an entrance hall," Francis offered. She hadn't been in the church for years, but her memories were of a large square room that opened directly onto the street. Concrete steps led up to the double doors that opened into the main room of the church. Two rows of old, well-polished pews faced the front of the church, and tall narrow windows lined the walls. A dark linoleum covered the floor, and a strip of carpet was laid over that to cover the aisle between the pews.

"I should alert Matthew, too," Flint muttered as he picked up the telephone to dial. "Maybe he could shake everyone's hands before the service instead of after. He can do a visual check for weapons that way. Of course, we're probably okay as long as the roads stay closed." He turned to Francis. "Don't suppose you've heard the weather lately?"

"I heard Robert Buckwalter ask Garth earlier. I think that he was hoping to fly his plane out of Dry Creek." Francis grimaced at Flint. "Either that or I hear he's thinking of having more supplies flown in somehow. Tricky business. Garth said the latest forecast was for wind and continuing cold. Unless the county snowplow can get through on the roads, I don't think cars will make it through.''

"And none of the rental places rent anything but cars?"

"No, Sheriff Wall checked on that—also told the places at the Billings airport to let him know if any strange men were making a fuss about not being able to rent a four-wheel drive.''

"What about women?"

Francis looked at him blankly.

"They might hire a woman," Flint said softly. "In a place that doesn't expect a woman, that could be a key element of surprise. And my guess is that they'll go for a professional this time—someone who is supposed to get in and take the hostage out without attracting any attention.''

"But a woman would stick out more than a man," Francis protested. "More men travel through these parts, looking for ranch jobs or following the rodeo circuit.''

"Like Sam," Flint offered.

"Sam would never," Francis protested. "I can't believe you'd even think he'd be a kidnapper.''

Flint shrugged. "It's probably not him. But it could be the woman that came looking for Robert Buckwalter.''

Flint had already had the bureau run a check on the woman, and she sounded like she was little threat to anyone but Robert. The report he had gotten back suggested the woman was there to try and convince Robert to marry her.

Any man who could fly in a load of lobsters on his private plane to feed a bunch of inner city kids, as Robert had done, had money to spare. That meant the woman's motive was simple. She had sighted her prey.

The blonde was having problems paying back some gambling debts and she needed to raise lots of cash fast. She'd already slipped the information to her creditors that she was on the verge of getting engaged to Robert. Flint had taken a close look at that plane Robert landed several nights ago on the snowy pasture by Garth's barn. The plane was so new it still held the smell of the mocha leather seats that turned the cockpit into a relaxation center. No doubt about it. That plane belonged to a rich man.

Marriage to Robert would certainly get the blonde out of

hock. But then so would doing a little favor like kidnapping someone for a crime syndicate.

"We can't be too careful," Flint said.

"Well, I can't live in a bubble," Francis said as she sat down at the kitchen table. "We can take reasonable precautions, but that's all we can do."

Flint started to dial the number for Matthew Curtis. He wondered if the minister would be willing to rope off the last two rows on one side of the church. That way Flint could keep a neutral empty zone around Francis. She probably wouldn't like it, but he would rest easier with that arrangement.

"Besides—" Francis gave a little smile "—if another kidnapper is around here they will have noticed that the woman to kidnap, if they really want to rattle Garth, is Sylvia Bannister."

Flint looked at her in question.

"I think my brother's in love," she said softly.

"Garth?"

Francis nodded. "He might not know it yet, but, yes, Garth."

Francis was even more convinced that her brother was in love when he ate supper in the bunkhouse with a few of the men instead of joining the rest of them in the house. She wondered if all men got as grumpy as Garth when they fell in love. If that was the case, she didn't have to worry about Flint. He'd been smooth and polite to her ever since he'd agreed to attend church with her in the morning. He didn't look like he had a care in the world. He certainly didn't look like a man in love.

"Pass the salt?" she asked Flint as they sat in the middle of the table, surrounded by boisterous teenagers. The beef stew she had helped make for supper didn't really need more salt, but it was the only conversational opener that came to her mind.

"Sure," Flint said as he lifted the little glass bottle and passed it to her. "Want pepper?"

"No, thank you." Francis smiled stiffly. Well, that wasn't much of a conversation starter. At this rate, they'd never get the important conversations going. Not that the supper table was a good place to have such a conversation, anyway. Maybe they should wait until they drove to church tomorrow. Flint had already made it clear the two of them were going alone in the four-wheel-drive pickup he was driving.

Chapter Nine

The supper dishes were done, the cows were fed, and the house was dark. But Francis couldn't sleep. She lay in the single bed in the small bedroom that had been hers for her entire girlhood. When she lay there, the years evaporated and she felt just as young and insecure as she had thirty years ago. She missed her mother.

Strange, she thought, she hadn't missed her mother for years. She thought about her on holidays and sometimes when she saw a woman who had that same shiny black hair, but she never really missed her deeply. Francis had been ten when her mother died, and it seemed like such a long time ago. She had long ago firmly closed the door on those young memories of her mother.

But tonight, Francis missed her. She wished she could ask her mother what she felt about love and happiness. And faith. Had her mother found comfort in her faith or had it been a mere duty to her?

Francis remembered their home had known laughter as long as her mother was alive. After her mother died, no one laughed anymore.

Francis felt a moment's envy of Flint because he had his grandmother's Bible and had something to hold that had been precious to her. Then she remembered that her own mother's Bible was on a shelf in the den. Like the rocking chair, Garth had never moved it even after all those years.

Francis pulled her chenille robe off the peg behind the door and slipped her arms into its sleeves. The night air inside the house was chilled, so she moved fast. She tucked her feet into fuzzy peach slippers and tightened the belt on her robe.

Once covered, she turned on the small lamp beside her bed. If she left her door open, the lamp should give enough light so that she could sneak down the stairs and pull the Bible off the shelf without waking anyone.

Sam was sleeping on the living room sofa again tonight, and she supposed Flint was in the kitchen. She had no desire to wake either one of them.

Shadows filled all the corners of the house as Francis stepped into the upstairs hallway. She always liked the house at night. Everything was peaceful and stone quiet. When she was in Denver, she missed the absolute still of a Montana night.

Francis stepped lightly down the wooden hallway. The light from her room filtered softly into the darkness of the stairway.

Creak! Flint woke from a restless sleep and stiffened. Someone was slowly walking on the stairs. He'd tested the stairs already and found creaks on steps fourteen and nine. With only one creak, he couldn't tell if the person on the stairs was going up or down. Either way, he needed to check it out.

Flint stood silently and shrugged the blankets off his shoulders. He quickly moved along the wall that led to the stairs. He heard another creak, this one closer. Good, that meant someone was coming down the stairs instead of going up. It was less likely to be an intruder.

Flint stood beside the stairs as a shape came into view. He recognized Francis as much by the smell of the peach lotion she wore as by the shape she made in her bathrobe.

He wouldn't have guessed that the sight of Francis in her bathrobe would affect him so deeply. It wasn't even that he'd like to cuddle her up to bed—and he would like to do that—it was more that he was suddenly aware of the nights of lying together in front of the fireplace and talking he had missed.

That bathrobe got to him. It certainly wasn't the sexiest robe in the world. He'd seen his share of see-through black robes and sleek silk numbers. They were all sexier than that old robe. But the robe reminded him of the comfortable love he'd missed.

The kind of love one saw on the faces of couples who were celebrating their fiftieth anniversaries. The kind of love that was for better and for worse. He'd missed it all.

"It's me," he whispered. He didn't want to frighten Francis, and she was sure to see him before she came much closer. He thought a whisper would be soft enough.

Francis yelped all the same as she turned around. "What are you doing there?"

"I heard someone on the stairs," Flint explained softly. "I didn't know if they were going up or going down."

Francis nodded. "I'm just going into the den to get a book."

"Anything I can get for you?" Flint realized he'd never spent an evening with Francis reading. He didn't even know what kind of books she liked. "A mystery? No, not for this time of night. Maybe a romance."

Francis shook her head. "The only reading books my brother keeps around are his collection of Zane Grey novels."

"We could sit a bit and read them."

Flint liked that idea. It was comfortable—the kind of thing old married couples did.

Francis shook her head. "I don't want to wake anyone." She rolled her eyes in the direction of the living room where Sam was sleeping.

"Oh." Old married couples certainly didn't have to worry about unwanted fiancés sleeping in the living room, Flint thought.

"I'll just be a minute."

Flint walked with her into the den and stood by the door while Francis reached up and pulled a large book off the shelf.

"Thanks," Francis said as she left the den. "I remembered this belonged to my mother."

"I don't remember you talking about your mother."

"I didn't."

Francis still couldn't sleep a half hour later. She lay in her bed with her mother's Bible propped up before her. She wished she'd taken the time to look at her mother's Bible earlier. Her mother had written notes throughout the book.

Next to Psalm 100, verse five—"For the Lord is good; His

mercy is everlasting, and His truth endures to all genera-
tions''—her mother had written a note. ''Yesterday my baby
girl was born! I'm so very happy!''

Next to Matthew 5:4—''Blessed are those who mourn, For
they shall be comforted''—her mother had written in a slower
hand, ''What will my babies do without me?''

Her mother's life was bound up in the pages of the Bible
Francis had pulled off the shelf. Her worries were all there in
black and white. Her dreams were noted. Her joys. Francis
hugged the Bible to her after reading it for a time. She'd never
expected to know her mother like this.

The sun strained to rise, and the old man sat in his kitchen
and urged it on. He'd been impatiently waiting for morning as
he sat next to his west window and polished his old hunting
rifle. He'd found a box of ammunition in a dresser drawer last
night, and it was sitting on the table ready to be loaded.

If the sun rose hot enough, maybe some of this blasted snow
would melt and someone would be willing to drive him to Miles
City today, the old man thought. But then he remembered—it
was Sunday. The only folks in Dry Creek he could count on to
do him a favor all insisted on attending church on Sunday
mornings.

He looked around his house. It was like he'd never really
seen it for years. When had the walls gotten so stained? And
those curtains. They were little more than threads hanging from
curtain rods. He should pack some things for his trip, but he
couldn't settle on what. Finally, he pulled out the old photo
album that had belonged to his parents and put it in a plastic
grocery bag. That and the rifle were really the only things he
needed to take.

He was halfway to the door when he remembered the cats.
What would he do about the cats? He put down the rifle and
bag and opened the cupboard door. He pulled all the tins of cat
food out of the cupboard and stacked them on the counter. They
were all gourmet tins—chopped chicken livers and tuna. He
always bought expensive cat food. Then, one by one, he ran
his manual can opener around their lids. As soon as a can was
opened, he sat it on the floor.

By the time he finished, he had twenty-nine open cans on the floor. He didn't pet any of the cats that gathered at his feet, and they didn't expect it. He never petted the cats. He'd been content to simply feed them.

The old man comforted himself about the cats. When people realized he was gone, they'd come and take care of the cats, he told himself. The cats would all find good homes. Surely, the people of Dry Creek would take them in.

The old man fretted until finally the sun had softened the darkness enough so that he could put on his coat, pick up his bag and gun and walk across the street to the pay phone beside the café. He'd never put a telephone in his house—couldn't abide the demanding ringing of one. But today he needed to call the bus depot in Miles City and find out if the Greyhound bus was able to get through on the roads.

The bus wasn't coming. The short phone call let him know that the bus service was canceled for Sunday because the interstate was closed until the snowplows could get through. The next bus was scheduled for Monday.

The old man swore. Monday could be too late. The more he had thought about that cocky FBI agent—coming right to his door and forcing the old man to talk to him—the more nervous he became.

He couldn't stay in Dry Creek until Monday.

The old man had a brief vision of himself driving his old pickup in the other direction, to North Dakota, without tires. The roads were covered with snow. Maybe the tire rims would get him there. He knew it was hopeless as he thought about it. Even if he got to the North Dakota border, he'd still be stranded.

He saw a cream-colored business card slipped into the door of the café, and he pulled it out of the crack. That hotshot Robert guy and someone—the man hadn't written the name clearly—had gone out to the plane. The additional supplies had been parachuted down last night, as ordered. They would be back as soon as possible.

The old man wished he was the one with the plane. That would sure solve his problems. A plane didn't need to wait for any snowplows.

It wasn't fair, the old man decided, when some folks like Robert Buckwalter had fancy planes and a senior citizen like himself didn't have anything but his two aching feet to get himself around in good weather or bad.

And then the old man heard it—the soft whinny of a horse coming from nearby. He listened. It was coming from behind the café. Something about the mournful whinny of the horse told him that she was alone and missing her master.

He rubbed his hands together in triumph. The horse was back! That's what he needed. A horse didn't need tires, and even if the old man couldn't quite remember how to drive, the horse wouldn't care.

Francis let the sunshine filter through the thick frost on her bedroom window. She didn't need full sunshine to feel like this was going to be a good day. She felt more hopeful than she had in years. She'd connected with her mother last night, reading her mother's Bible. Something in her had softened while she read. She was looking forward to going to church this morning more than she had expected when she first announced her desire to Flint. She felt like she'd never really paid attention in church before, and now she wanted to observe everything—to see it through her mother's eyes.

Francis smelled coffee before she started down the stairs later in the morning.

Flint was dressed in slacks and a gray turtleneck and was standing by the sink sipping a cup of coffee. If he'd noticed the creaks she made walking down the stairs, he didn't comment on them.

"You're up early," Francis said as she walked to the cupboard and pulled out a cup.

Flint grinned. "I wanted to be ready in case you wanted to go get eggs again this morning."

Francis groaned. "I think I'll wait until that rooster is awake."

"Suits me." Flint set down his coffee cup and reached over to pick up the leather shoulder holster that was on the counter. The holster was snapped shut, but the butt end of a gun was clearly visible. He hooked it over his shoulder.

Francis heard the hard footsteps on the hallway floor before she saw the outline of Sam entering the kitchen.

"You're wearing a gun to church?" Sam gave a pointed, reproving look in Flint's direction.

Flint felt the joy of the morning harden. Sam looked all starched and pressed. Since when was Sam planning to come to church with them? "I'm on duty."

"Flint's been kind enough to agree to let me attend the services," Francis said stiffly. She had never noticed before just how much of a pain Sam was. Had he always been this self-righteous? "It's been a lot of extra work, especially since he still has his responsibilities."

Sam grunted and adjusted his silk tie. "I doubt there will be many people at the service anyway, the way the snow has covered the roads."

"I've checked with the sheriff," Flint said. "The roads are passable with a four-wheel drive."

Flint had made arrangements for the sheriff and the inspector to both attend the services. One man would sit on each end of the pew where he and Francis sat.

Sheriff Wall had said he didn't usually attend, but he'd wanted to go and check the furnace in the old church, anyway. He was somewhat of a self-taught electrician, and the folks of Dry Creek often called on him for an odd piece of electrical work. He'd told Flint he'd check out the furnace early Sunday morning. That way he'd be there to see if anyone was snooping around the church building before the regular members got there.

"Anyone want some toast?" Flint said as he slipped two slices of bread into the toaster.

"I thought I'd take Francis to breakfast in Dry Creek before church," Sam said smugly as he adjusted his suit jacket. "Give her a break from all of this business."

Flint pushed in the button on the toaster. He studied Sam out of the corner of his eye. The man's face was innocent as a lamb's. But that didn't mean he wasn't capable of betraying someone. Flint wondered if someone could have gotten to Sam. The man certainly seemed intent on getting Francis away from anyone's protection. "You can take her to breakfast when we've caught all the rustlers. Until then, you'll just need to be patient.''

"Of course,'' Sam said smoothly. "I wouldn't want to do anything that would put Francis in danger. Although—'' Sam paused "—she wouldn't be defenseless with me around. I have my cell phone. I could call the sheriff in a heartbeat.''

Flint grunted and bit back his words.

"Anyone like jelly on their toast?'' Francis asked from the corner of the kitchen where she was bending to examine the shelves in a lower cupboard. "The kids have used all of the jelly Garth had, so Mrs. Hargrove brought us some she had canned.'' Francis pulled up a jar. "I think this is apple jelly.''

"Does everyone around here make their own apple jelly?''

"Well, maybe not everyone.'' Francis opened the jar with a pop to the lid. "Some folks make chokecherry jelly instead— or rhubarb jam.''

Flint let himself imagine what it would be like to live in a place where everyone had the time to make jelly. It certainly wasn't anything like the cities he'd lived in over the past ten years, where people didn't even take the time to smear jelly on their toast let alone make the stuff.

"I'll have my toast dry,'' Sam said as he sat down at the breakfast table. "I wouldn't want to get jam on my suit.''

For once Flint was glad he could claim official business. He wouldn't have to offer Sam a ride into church with him and Francis, and in ordinary circumstances there would be little he could do to avoid it.

It was an hour later before it was time to leave for the church service. Garth and all of the kids had had a pancake breakfast while Francis was upstairs taking a shower and getting ready.

Francis lingered in the hot spray of the shower. The air inside the house was cold even though the steam from countless showers upstairs and the cooking downstairs were warming it up. When Francis stepped out of the shower, she wrapped a thick towel around her head and quickly slipped into her robe for the dash to her room.

She might as well not have dashed, Francis thought. Ten minutes later, she was still shivering, standing in front of her closet, wondering what to wear.

Her problem was one of image. She wanted to look competent—to show Flint that he didn't need to worry about her safety—but she also wanted to look appealing. A man like Flint must have dated many women in the years since she'd known him. Probably sophisticated women, too. The kind of woman who finds it exciting to date someone who wears a gun. The kind of woman who, if she wore a robe at all, wore a silk and lace one instead of a fuzzy one.

Francis sighed. Her navy striped suit was the obvious choice for competency, but it seemed a little needlessly drab. Not feminine enough. It was, however, the kind of suit that made up the endless parade of suits she'd worn for years in her job. And it was the kind of suit that filled her closets in Denver, and here, as well.

The only truly feminine dress she owned was the long ruby evening gown she had worn to the dance the other night.

Francis wondered when the last time had been that she cared what a man thought about what she wore. She'd never asked Sam, and she couldn't remember him ever remarking on anything she wore. Except for her old bathrobe, and that was only because it annoyed him.

Thinking of her evening gown reminded her that she did have pieces of that outfit left. If she put on the ivory lingerie she'd gotten to wear with that sequined ruby dress, she'd at least feel desirable. The ruby dress was little more than threads in her closet now, but the accessories were still good.

Finally, she settled on wearing the navy suit skirt and a light blue silk blouse with a pearl necklace.

By the time Francis slipped her feet into the strappy high heels she'd also purchased to wear with the sequined dress and ran a mauve lipstick over her lips, she decided she could at least compete with women like this Rose person who apparently visited Flint in his dreams.

"Coat?" Flint held up a parka jacket for Francis almost as soon as she came into the kitchen.

Something about Francis was different, and Flint didn't like the hungry look he'd surprised in Sam's eyes. The other man might look like he was all starch and collar, but Flint guessed he wasn't as comfortable with Francis as he looked. And who could blame him? Francis had a softness about her face that would make any man want to explore her further.

"So soon?"

Flint nodded. "I want us to be all set in the church before the regulars start to come in."

"I'll see you after the service," Sam said a little grimly to Francis as he looked at Flint.

Flint nodded. Sam hadn't been too happy about the arrangements, but Flint had insisted. There was only a remote possibility of trouble, but he didn't want to have to worry about Sam if anything did happen.

Everything looked white and gray when Francis stepped out of the house. She had accepted the parka from Flint and had wrapped a wool scarf around her neck, as well. It was hard to be a fashion plate in the middle of a Montana winter. The air was so cold her breath made short white puffs, and she pulled her scarf up so that it covered her chin. White snow lay softly over the yard outside the house. A few dog prints and the prints Flint had made when he went out earlier to warm up the pickup were all that disturbed the soft white blanket.

"Garth said we got another four inches last night," Flint noted as he opened Francis's door on the four-wheel-drive pickup. At the same time, he looked in the back of the pickup to check that the usual winter shovel hadn't been taken out to be used on some farm chore. It hadn't. "The roads will be rough."

"Maybe some of it will melt off by the time we come home from church," Francis said as she climbed into the pickup cab. She'd needed to take her high heels off and put snow boots on, but she carried the shoes in her hands. She's slip them on when she got to church just like most of the other women would do. "Might all melt."

"Not likely." Flint had already become accustomed to the Montana cold. When it snowed, the air was heavy. But the rest of the time, the air was light and brittle.

Flint opened and closed his own door quickly. The heater was working, and the air inside the pickup cab was slightly warmer than that outside.

Flint removed his gloves and turned the heater to defrost.

The windows were fogged over, but the defroster was already clearing small circles on them. He breathed in deeply. He could smell the fragrance of peaches coming from Francis. "Nice perfume."

"It's just lotion."

Sylvia had lent her the lotion when she had heard Francis and Flint were going to attend church together.

Francis smiled to remember the other woman standing with the bottle of lotion in her hand.

"But it's not a date," Francis had protested halfheartedly as the other woman flipped open the cap to the lotion and tipped it toward Francis's hands. "It's just church."

Sylvia had smiled and squeezed some lotion into Francis's outstretched hands. "You're going to a church, not a convent. Lots of romances start there."

Francis had smoothed the lotion into her hands and arms and now, talking to Flint, she was glad she had. "Winter is always hard on the skin."

Flint shifted from park into reverse and looked in the rear-view mirror.

"It's the cold moisture in the air," Francis muttered as she watched Flint back the pickup away from the ranch house. He'd shaved since last night. His skin was smooth, and the lines of his face were more pronounced than when he had a little stubble. He'd put a suit jacket over his shoulder holster, and his gun blended into the contours of his chest so that it wasn't noticeable. His head was turned so that he could look back while he steered the pickup past a snowdrift. Francis had never noticed what a strong neck he had. Of course, when she'd known him, he'd been a young man of twenty. His neck had had plenty of years to change since then. They'd both changed in those years.

"And the wind," Francis continued. "It's been windy for the past few months. Must be El Niño or the drought or something,"

Flint had turned the pickup around, and he was heading down the gravel road that ran down Garth's property to the main county road. The road was bumpy. The November rains had filled the road with ruts. Those ruts had frozen solid in December and stayed that way.

"The drought makes it hard for the ranchers around here," Flint said. He had listened to the ranch hands at Garth's place. The men talked about the weather first thing in the morning and the last thing at night. Last summer had been dry, and although the winter had been cold, the snowfall in the mountains had been below normal.

"Some of them are on the verge of selling out," Francis said. "One more dry summer could do them in. The cost of feed gets too high, and they can't afford to run as many cattle."

Flint grunted in sympathy. "They need to diversify. Ranch part time and then do something else."

"Don't think they haven't tried to do that," Francis said. "But there's no business around here. Only three or four jobs—the post office, the job Matthew does at the hardware store, and then the café—but Linda and Duane run that."

"It'd be a pity for anyone to leave," Flint said. The morning sun was fading from red to pink as it inched its way up the sky. When he looked to his right, he saw the foothills of the Big Sheep Mountain Range covered in a thick collar of snow. Snow hadn't collected on the sides of the mountains, and they were a gray-brown. "It's a beautiful, restful place to be."

Flint was surprised at the sentiment he felt. He thought he'd grown more callused than that over the years. A home was only a place to hang one's hat. He would have bet he'd learned that lesson. Any land was the same as any other. Each plot of dirt the same as any other plot.

"Everyone has been thinking of business ideas," Francis said. "From dude ranches to quilting factories. Even jelly making—Mrs. Hargrove said folks might pay for some of the homemade jelly folks around here make."

"I still can't believe everyone around here makes jelly," Flint said incredulously. "What century is this, anyway?"

Francis only smiled. "We've lived through long, hard winters in Dry Creek. Makes us appreciate home-canned jellies and fruit. Nothing tastes better when the snow is deep than something you've grown yourself. Brings back the smell of summer."

For the first time, Flint began to think about those five acres his grandmother had left him in her will. He hadn't given them any attention for years. Maybe now, before he left, he should plant something. He didn't need to plant fruits or vegetables on them, but some kind of plant would be nice. Maybe some rose-bushes would do well down by the trickle of a creek that ran through his grandmother's land during the spring months when the snow ran off the mountains. Wild roses might grow without extra water. Or a tree. A tree would surely grow. He suddenly realized he'd never planted anything anywhere before.

The sun had lost its pink and was a thin bright yellow that hovered over the day.

The pickup cab was warm enough, and Flint turned the defroster off. The steering on the four-wheel drive was stiff and required all of Flint's attention. Still, it was cozy inside the cab as he and Francis bumped along the county road. On each side of the narrow country road were wide ditches that caught the snow. Beside each ditch was a fence running along the road, dividing the grassland. The road rose and then dipped along with the low, rolling countryside.

"Robert moved his plane," Flint noticed. The small plane had been parked beside that far fence for the past three days. Now a thin path made by the plane wheels ran through the snow. "Must be desperate if he's thinking of taking off in this kind of snow."

"I hear the café needed supplies and he was having some airlifted in. I think they're just dropping the supplies by the old plane. That's why he moved it—so the drop would go smooth."

"Must be nice to be rich."

Francis smiled. "I hear he's bringing in crates of frozen asparagus and caviar. His mother is determined to bring the finer foods to Dry Creek for the kids. It's almost a cross-cultural experience for most of them to tackle something like caviar."

"They can live full lives without caviar," Flint said.

Francis shrugged. "It doesn't hurt them to try new things."

Garth's ranch buildings were behind them as they drove, and Flint saw another ranch off to the left in the distance. The house and outbuildings were sheltered by a small grove of trees, their branches leafless and stark on a winter day. Someone had planted those trees in some past hopeful time.

Flint was looking for the low-lying outline of a small plane, but instead he saw something else low on the horizon. He could see a horse and rider from a distance coming down the road.

Now what is some fool doing out with a horse on a morning like this? Flint thought, forgetting that it had not been that many mornings ago when that rider would have been him.

Chapter Ten

The horse grew more familiar as Flint drove closer to it. Finally, he even recognized the man riding the horse.

What had possessed that old man to strike out on horseback with the snow from last night's blizzard still fresh on the ground? If the old man didn't care what happened to himself, he should at least be more considerate of Honey.

The last Flint had seen Honey she'd been cozy in the old chicken coop on his grandmother's place. He'd made arrangements for Duane Edison to bring her back to the café and keep her in the shed behind the place. Flint planned to visit Honey there after church and take her a few of the apples he'd gotten from Mrs. Hargrove. He'd discovered the horse had a fondness for them.

The ruts in the road were deeper, and Flint needed to slow down as he came closer to the old man. The pickup wasn't going more than five miles an hour. The old man crossed the road so that he would be riding past the passenger side of the pickup.

"What's he up to?" Flint asked.

Francis started to roll down her window. "Must be rabbit hunting. He's got his rifle with him. Mr. Gossett," Francis called cheerfully. "Good morning."

The old man was still in front of the pickup when he stopped riding.

A warning prickle ran down Flint's spine. Something about

the determined set of the old man's shoulders made him uneasy. "Don't open the door. And roll that window back up."

Francis turned to him in disbelief. "You're going to leave him here?"

"Yes."

"But he's an old man and it's freezing out there," Francis protested. "Look at him. He might even be senile. Wandering around without a scarf on his head. He'll catch pneumonia."

Flint hesitated. He didn't want Francis to think he was heartless. The old man did look almost senile. Maybe Flint's spine had known too many bad men over the years so that he couldn't tell the bad from the simpleminded. Still. "I didn't tell him to saddle up and play cowboy on a morning like this."

"But he's on Honey," Francis added as though she and the horse were now fast friends. "You know she isn't enjoying this romp through the snow. Look at her. She looks hungry."

"She's had plenty of oats. She just wants one of those apples I have in the back of the pickup."

Francis looked through the cab window to the bed of the pickup. There they were—a dozen apples tied in a red mesh bag.

"Tell him I'll send someone back for him," Flint said to Francis as he pulled closer to the old man. "But then roll up that window. We can't be too careful."

"You suspect Mr. Gossett?" Francis asked in surprise as she eyed the old man through the windshield dubiously. "Surely he's harmless. I wouldn't think he'd be—you know—"

"Bright enough?"

Francis nodded. "And he doesn't know anyone but a few people in Dry Creek. Never has any visitors or anything. No friends. No family."

"A man doesn't need friends to commit a crime. Nor does he need to be particularly intelligent."

Francis began rolling down the pickup window again. The crank was stiff and she bent her head as she moved it. She stopped when the window was a third of the way down and called to the old man who was just a little ahead of the slow-moving pickup. "Don't worry. We'll send someone back for you. And you should have a scarf in weather like this. Is there one in your pockets?''

The old man scowled. The woman in the pickup sounded like his mother. Scolding him for forgetting something like he was a little kid.

He'd show her who was a little kid, the old man thought in satisfaction.

''I don't need a scarf,'' the old man said as he took the barrel of his rifle and slapped it against the rump of the horse so that she nervously jumped into the middle of the road and reared up.

Flint swore as he pushed his foot hard into the brake pedal. Honey was practically on top of the pickup hood when she reared up like that. ''What in blazes?''

The pickup stopped, and Flint instinctively put his right hand out to push Francis down in the seat.

''What—'' Francis resisted the shove, more out of bewilderment than anything else.

But it was enough. The time he'd taken to try to shield her behind the metal of the pickup cost him. He should have gone for his gun first, he told himself later. By the time he brought his hand to his holster the harmless old man had swung his rabbit-hunting rifle around and had drawn a bead on Francis.

''Easy now,'' Flint murmured. Francis was staring at the rifle. ''Don't move.''

''Throw the gun out of there.'' The old man sat on the horse and yelled.

Flint put his hands up in plain view. Next time, he'd trust his spine. ''Let me step out first.''

The first thing Flint needed to do was to put some distance between himself and Francis. Guns went with guns, and he'd bet the old man would swing the barrel of that old rifle around to follow him if he stepped outside the pickup. At least then, if there were any bullets fired, Francis would have a chance. An old rifle like that probably wouldn't hold more than one bullet. If Flint could get the man to fire at him, Francis would be safe.

The old man snorted and steadied his gun. ''I ain't that stupid. You've got to the count of three.''

Francis was frozen. She told herself she should know what to do. She'd taken a hostage negotiation class at work. She was supposed to know what to do. But her mind was blank.

"One." The old man called out the number with a certain amount of satisfaction.

"I'm putting it out now," Flint said as he slowly moved his hand toward the holster. The defroster had been off long enough that the windshield on the pickup had a thin film coating it. In another five minutes, the view would be fuzzy from where the old man sat on the horse. But Flint didn't have five minutes. "I'll need to open the door to throw it."

"Stick it through the window," the old man ordered.

So much for that idea, Flint thought. He'd considered opening the door and swinging down to shoot at the old man from there. He'd be far enough away from Francis that the bullet from the man's rifle wouldn't be coming in her direction.

Francis was cold. She could feel her teeth start to chatter.

Flint could hear her teeth start to chatter. He didn't dare look at Francis, though. He kept his eyes on the old man.

"Two." The old man counted loudly.

Flint touched the butt of his gun as he unsnapped his shoulder holster smoothly. "Take it easy. It's coming."

"Handle first," the old man instructed.

Flint drew the gun out with the fingertips of one hand. "No problem."

Flint squeezed the barrel of his gun as he swung it around to the side of the pickup. The cold made the gun slippery, and he had to hold it tight.

"I need to roll my window down."

The old man shook his head slightly. "Push it through the other window by Francis."

Flint didn't like reaching across Francis with his gun. It would keep the eyes of the old man focused on her. But Flint didn't hesitate. He reached over to the few inches of open space in Francis's window.

The gun slipped over the side and clanked against the side of the pickup on the way down.

The old man lowered his rifle a little. Not much, but enough so that Flint began to breathe again.

"It's not too late to let us go, you know," Flint called out the window to the old man. "Whatever it is that's bothering you—we can talk about it."

"Ain't nothing bothering me," the old man said. "I just need to get out of here."

"Well, why didn't you say so?" Flint forced his voice to relax. The safe period in any hostage situation was the setting of the terms. "I'd be happy to take you someplace. Just put the gun down and we'll see that you get where you need to go."

The old man slid off the back of the horse right next to the pickup. The barrel of his rifle wavered, but Flint didn't make any sudden moves. A gun in the hands of an amateur was always a potentially deadly thing. It was too easy to underestimate someone.

"I'm sure the boys in the bunkhouse have something to drink, as well," Francis offered quietly. "Whiskey, for sure. Maybe some Scotch. I'm sure you'd like a little drink for the road."

"Don't have time for a drink," the old man said as he reached out and opened the door beside Francis. "Move over. I'm coming in."

The old man grabbed the inside back of the cab and started to pull himself in. He must have remembered Flint's gun, and bent down to pick it up from the ground.

"If you want me to drive you somewhere—maybe Miles City—I'd be happy to," Flint said calmly, not commenting on the other gun. He was afraid of this. His own gun made the man's rabbit rifle look as harmless as a water pistol. "But we don't need Francis to come along. Why don't you let her get out and ride the horse back to her brother's ranch."

"I'm not stupid," Mr. Gossett snapped as he shoved himself into the cab and slammed the door behind him.

"No one ever said you were," Flint murmured soothingly.

The heat inside the cab was beginning to warm the old man's clothes, and they were starting to smell.

The old man eyed Flint and Francis. "Nobody's leaving here, and you'll drive me where I tell you—but it won't be Miles City. The road past Dry Creek is closed. I heard Highway 89 is blocked off until the snowplows get through. Don't think a pickup will get through."

"Maybe your best bet is the horse, then," Flint said. *Sorry, Honey,* he thought ruefully. *You take him away, and I'll come get you both—and I'll bring you some of those apples you like. And not just the small bunch I have in the back of the pickup. I'll shake down a whole tree for you.*

The old man snorted. "Couldn't pay me to get back on that animal—she's practically worthless. Stubborn as a mule. Almost had me setting out on foot a time or two."

Flint smiled inside. He could always count on Honey.

"If no one can drive you and the horse won't take you," Francis said, "then you need to decide whether it is really important that you go. If it's groceries you need—or something more substantial to drink than tea—or anything else—"

"What I need is to get out of the state!"

"Then you'll need to wait," Francis said calmly. She had hoped he was just a fool in search of alcohol. The alternatives were not as pleasant. "There's no way to go today."

"There's the plane—the plane that flew in to bring the lobsters for the party," the old man said with satisfaction in his voice. "The plane that that millionaire fellow owns. That's where I want you to take me."

"I don't know where the plane is." Flint stalled. "He might have even flown it out of here."

"Just follow them tracks," the old man said as though that settled the matter. "I was starting to follow them when I spotted you. Decided no point in riding on that old horse. Especially when you've got a warm pickup that'll get us there just as good."

Flint looked over to see the wide tracks of the plane that ran on the other side of the fence. Why couldn't Robert Buckwalter have driven his plane deeper into the pasture instead of along the fence?

The old man nodded. "You can go now."

The roads were frozen, bumpy, and Flint needed both hands to control the steering on the pickup. But he still curved his shoulder slightly away from the seat so that Francis could nestle close to him. Francis sat with her legs on the driver's side of

the stick shift. Flint knew her decision to be so close to him
was made because she wanted to be as far away as possible
from the old man, but he welcomed her presence anyway. It
felt right to have her sandwiched in next to him.

Francis watched Flint's hands on the steering wheel. He'd
taken off his gloves so that he could grip the wheel more securely, and the cold made the skin on his hands whiter than
usual. They were strong hands, the fingers big and agile.

She had a sudden recollection of the last time they'd sat this
close in a pickup.

"Whatever happened to that old pickup of yours?' Francis
asked softly.

The old man hadn't said anything since he climbed into the
pickup. He'd just sat there with one hand holding Flint's gun
and the other steadying the rifle against his leg closest to the
door. Francis tried to pretend he wasn't there.

"My grandmother finally sold it to some other kid." Flint
smiled. Until he'd met Francis, he'd poured his heart into that
old pickup. "Wonder if he ever got our initials off the door."

Francis smiled. She had forgotten about the initials Flint had
painted on the door. Two swirling black *F*s with lots of extra
curlicues.

"He did." The old man surprised them both by speaking.
"Jim Jett bought it—painted it black all over. That took care
of the initials."

"I don't suppose there's much in Dry Creek you don't
know," Flint began tentatively. He wondered how the man
would respond to flattery. "You being a pillar of the community and all."

The old man snorted. "You know I ain't no pillar of nothing."

"Well, your father was," Flint continued the conversation
and prayed the old man had liked his father. "I heard what he
did in the big drought—getting people to stay and make a town.
He was a real hero in these parts."

"He was a fool. He should have left Dry Creek when he had
a chance. The whole town never amounted to anything. And

my father—all he ever had to his name was his few acres in Dry Creek, Montana.''

''He had friends,'' Francis added softly. ''And the respect of his neighbors.''

''It took me two years to save up enough money to buy a decent headstone for his grave,'' the old man muttered bitterly. ''After that, I figured why bother.''

''But you never left the area?'' Flint asked softly.

''Where would I go?''

For a blinding moment Flint envied the old man his certainty about where he belonged in his life. Love it or hate it, Dry Creek was the old man's home. Flint had bounced around for years, never feeling connected to any place.

The old man pointed out the window. ''There's the plane.''

Flint could just make out the dark shape against the white snow ahead. No, wait. There was more than one black shape.

''There's another pickup there,'' Francis said, her voice neutral. Her mind was busy calculating the odds. Another pickup could be a problem or it could be a solution. She wondered which Flint thought it would be.

There was a time when she would have known what he thought. Would have comfortably finished his sentences for him when he talked. At the time, she had thought it was because they were so much in love. Now she wondered. They had been young and foolish. The fact that they had run off to Las Vegas without planning enough to even have luggage with them showed just how foolish.

''You'll stay in the pickup when we get there,'' Flint ordered Francis as he drove closer. He didn't like the fact that the old man was holding Flint's gun closer now. That gun had altogether too many bullets in it waiting to be fired.

''I'll say who stays where,'' the old man protested heatedly.

''She stays in the pickup.'' Flint ignored his words.

The old man grunted.

''Maybe we should all stay—just turn around and go where we need to go in the pickup,'' Francis offered. She didn't like the thought of Flint being alone with the crazy old man. ''The roads might be open. You know those weather people—they're always behind the times. Maybe the roads have been cleared by now. We could drive to the main road and find out.''

Francis's leg had pressed itself against Flint. And her scent— she smelled of summer peaches. He didn't dare turn and look fully at her because he didn't want the old man to get nervous.

Besides, Flint didn't really need to see her to know what she looked like. He had memorized her face over twenty years ago and he could still pull the picture out of his mind. Her eyes were the color of the earth after the first fall frost, full of brown shadows and dark green highlights with shimmer that promised depths unknown. Her eyes were usually somber. He had loved to tease her just to watch that moment when her eyes would turn from serious to playful indignation.

Flint moved his hand to the knob of the gearshift even though he had no further gears left and wouldn't be shifting down. He just wanted to rest his hand closer to her.

Francis had never been more aware of Flint than she was at that moment. Maybe it was because of the danger around them. Maybe it was because of the long years she'd spent missing him.

Whatever it was, she had to slip her hand under her leg so that it wouldn't reach out and caress Flint's wrist. His arm was covered with the sleeve of a bulky winter jacket. His hands had been without gloves long enough now that they would be cold. But his wrist was the meeting place between cold and warm.

The pickup was bumping along closer to the plane. Without the four-wheel drive, the vehicle would have been stuck in at least a dozen different snowdrifts since they'd started following the plane tracks.

Flint had considered letting the pickup accidentally get stuck, but he didn't want to annoy the old man. Especially since staging a delay wasn't the best way to stop Mr. Gossett. Fifty years of progress would take care of that. Flint was confident the old man would take one look at the sophisticated instrument panel on the plane and give up any hope of flying it out of here. Even if the old man had flown a plane once in his youth, he would be bewildered today.

The fact that someone else was at the plane complicated things. Flint suspected it was Robert Buckwalter who had come out to the plane. If it was, the old man had a pilot. That would change the odds on everything.

Francis sensed Flint's worry. Nothing in his face had changed since they spotted that pickup, but she gradually sensed the tension in him. *We're really in danger,* she realized numbly. *Dear God,* The thought came to her almost unbidden. *We need help.*

Francis was tired of worrying about the problems between her and Flint. Just like she instinctively turned to God when she needed help, she also wanted to turn to Flint. They were in trouble, and she didn't want to face it alone. She slipped her hand from under her leg and brought it up to lightly touch Flint's wrist.

Flint's hand responded immediately. It moved off the gearshift and enclosed her hand.

I am home, Francis thought. His hand was cold. Ice cold. But it didn't matter. His hand could rival the temperature of the Arctic Circle and she'd want to hold it. She could face anything if they were together hand in hand.

Chapter Eleven

If a person didn't know better, this could be a view on a post-card, Francis mused.

The morning sun was bright on the snow-covered hills leading up to the Big Sheep Mountain Range. The mountains themselves were low and didn't have any of the peaks that were found in other mountain ranges in Montana.

There were no houses on the horizon and no trees. Usually there were no signs of civilization up here except the thin lines of barbed-wire fence that divided the various sections of land that had belonged to her father and now belonged to her brother, Garth. Some of the land would be planted in wheat this coming spring. Some of it would be left for free-range grazing. Right now, it was empty. All of the cattle had been brought closer to the main house because of the storm.

The only mar in the otherwise peaceful picture was the tracks in the snow. There were now two sets of tracks. One set was partially filled in with drifting snow. The other set of tracks was newer. Both led to the small twin-engine plane that was parked next to one of the barbed-wire fences that followed the country road. Past the plane was a piece of land that had been scraped clean of snow. Either a snowplow had done it or it had been shoveled clean by hand.

"It must be Robert," Flint said softly. There was no one standing outside in the area between the plane and the Jeep, but it must be Robert. Who else would care enough about an air-strip to make one on a day like this?

Flint felt a twist in his stomach. With an airstrip and a pilot, there would be no stopping the old man from flying.

That's what Flint had been afraid of— He didn't want the old man airborne. Not that he knew for sure they would all be safer if old man Gossett had no hope of getting that plane in the air. But gunfire was much more likely if the old man even thought he could get them in the air.

"I'll do the talking," Mr. Gossett announced suddenly. "Don't want you two scaring them off."

Flint stopped the pickup as far away from the plane as he felt he could. Whoever had driven the Jeep in here must be inside the plane. "They haven't got any place to go, anyway."

The old man renewed his grip on the two guns he held. "This won't take long."

"You'll want to be careful with that gun of mine," Flint said softly. "It's federal property. Use it to commit a crime and they'll lock you up and throw away the key."

The old man looked confused.

"You've seen the notices in the post office." Flint kept talking. The old man was of the era that could be intimidated by the government—maybe. "You'd do best to just leave it on the ground. Besides," Flint added for good measure, "that rifle of yours looks like it has seen some action. Don't think you'd need any more persuasion than she can give you."

The old man looked proud as he gripped the gun tighter. "She's a good shooter, all right."

There was a large tarp—no, it was a parachute, Francis realized—as well as ten, maybe twelve boxes sitting next to the plane. The parachute was white, and a dozen ropes swirled around it on the ground. On the other side of the parachute the four-wheel-drive Jeep was parked. Deep boot prints were all around the boxes and led up to the plane.

"That's the Edisons' Jeep," the old man said thoughtfully as he peered out the windshield. "Wonder if it's their boy, Duane, out there."

Flint prayed it would be. He thought the old man might have a harder time hurting someone from Dry Creek than he would a stranger. Sort of a you-never-hurt-the-ones-you-know theory.

"I heard Robert Buckwalter was having some more supplies

flown in for the café—with all the kids around these days they are running low on everything.'' Francis spoke nervously.

Mr. Gossett shook his head in disgust. ''In my day, you wouldn't find anyone flying in supplies. We'd eat bread and beans if that's all that was available. Kids today are too soft.''

Flint believed in diversionary tactics. He agreed heartily. ''You can say that again. Most of them aren't worth their salt.''

Francis felt the faint squeeze Flint gave her fingers. She understood his message.

''They should all be sent to reform school,'' Francis agreed. ''Teach them some manners.''

The old man nodded thoughtfully. ''They wouldn't like it— locked in with everyone else. I know I wouldn't.''

''We could meet with the authorities about this,'' Flint offered. He had his fingers crossed that the old man would take the bait. ''They'll understand how you feel about being locked up. I'll drive you back to the café and we can make a call. If you turn state's evidence on this rustling business, you might get off with probation. I'll see to it that you meet with the right people—maybe even the state governor—or a congressman.''

The old man snorted. ''Worthless politicians. I'd rather deal with them kids any day.''

''The press then.'' Flint continued the bribe. ''Say you don't confess to anything. We could get the press out here and do an article for the Billings paper. You'd be famous.''

The old man paled. Then he raised Flint's gun and jerked it at him. ''Who in blazes wants to be famous? I just want to be left alone.''

Well, that eliminated most of the mental-illness categories, Flint thought in resignation. He didn't know whether it would be easier to deal with someone who was crazy or someone who was stone-cold sane and just mean.

''You call out and let them know we're here.'' The old man jerked his head toward the plane. ''They'll come out at the sound of your voice. Be friendly-like.''

Flint hoped Mr. Gossett was wrong and that whoever was inside the plane would stay right there.

''Anybody home?'' Flint rolled down his window and called

out. "You've got company. Company and trouble—they come together—"

"Hush," the old man hissed.

Francis felt the sweep of frigid air coming in the open window. She wanted to snuggle closer to Flint, but she felt the tension in his body and did not want to be in the way if he needed to move fast.

Flint's heart sank. He saw a figure standing in the open door to the small plane. His hint had gone unheard.

"It's the chef," Flint murmured. Another figure joined the first. "And Robert."

"Let's go meet them," Mr. Gossett ordered Flint as he grabbed the door handle. "I've got plans."

Flint hoped he never heard the words "I've got plans" again. Mr. Gossett kept waving the guns around, and his plans were soon implemented. Robert Buckwalter was able to assess the situation quickly. Flint would wager the other man had had his own share of training in how to deal with hostage situations. Since Robert traveled internationally, he might even have some training on terrorist activities.

It only took a minute for Robert Buckwalter to assure the old man that he would fly him anywhere he could.

"The plane's only got enough fuel to fly to someplace like Fargo, North Dakota—or we could head for Billings if you want to stay in Montana," Robert explained to the older man just like he was a pilot planning a routine flight.

"I'll take Fargo. Let's all get in."

Robert nodded toward the old man and eyed him speculatively. "The fuel will last longer if the plane is lighter. I'd say you're about one hundred seventy pounds?"

The old man nodded.

"I'll go with you to fly this thing, but you don't want to take the others—it's unnecessary weight."

"I'll need a hostage."

Flint stepped forward. "That would be me."

The old man snorted. "I don't think so. I'll take her." He jerked his head at the young woman who was standing by Buckwalter's side. "She's a skinny little thing. Can't weigh much."

"It's not just about weight," Flint said. He kept moving around, hoping to find a moment when the old man was off guard. But Mr. Gossett kept his gun trained on one of the women at all times. "I can talk to the authorities for you."

"You speak English?" He barked the words at the chef.

She nodded.

"She can talk for me," the old man insisted. "Now, you two men get all the boxes out of that plane. I don't want any unnecessary weight holding us back."

Francis shivered. She and Jenny, the chef who worked for Mrs. Buckwalter, were standing together near the door to the plane. Mr. Gossett stood nearby and held Flint's gun loosely in his hand.

"You'll be all right," Francis whispered to the young woman. "Flint will get help."

The young woman nodded mutely.

Francis prayed she was right. Once the plane was airborne she and Flint could drive one of the pickups the ten or so miles back to Dry Creek and get help sent ahead. If they could alert the airports in Fargo and Billings, they should be able to stop the old man without anyone getting hurt.

"Now, everyone out of the plane," the old man ordered.

All the boxes had been thrown to the ground. Flint and Robert jumped to the ground from the open door of the plane.

Flint had his plan. The floor of the plane was about four feet up from the ground. There would be no way the old man could climb into the plane and hold onto both guns at the same time. That would be when Flint would tackle him.

"Now—you two—get down on the ground." The old man jerked his gun at Francis and Flint.

"What?" Flint bit back a further protest. This was a twist he hadn't counted on.

"But it's cold." Robert stepped in. "Let them at least go sit in the pickup—or even the Jeep."

"The ground. Now," the old man ordered, his voice rising in agitation. "I don't have all day, I gotta get out of here."

Francis lowered herself to the ground. The snow was not yet packed, and it was like sinking into a down pillow. An icy cold down pillow. She sat down with her legs crossed in front of her.

"You, too," the old man said curtly as he glanced over at Flint. "I want you with your back to her—" the old man shifted his gaze to Jenny "—and you get some rope from those boxes to tie them up."

"You're not going to leave them like that?" Jenny protested. "It's freezing out here. They'll—" Jenny swallowed and didn't finish her sentence.

Francis could finish it for her. If she and Flint were tied and left in a snowdrift like this, they could die.

"What does it matter to me if they get cold?" the old man demanded. "That'll teach them to come snooping around, asking questions. Butting into a man's private life."

Flint watched the old man and didn't like what he saw. Maybe it wasn't a choice of whether the old man was crazy or a criminal—maybe he was both.

"It's a federal offense to kill an FBI agent," Flint said softly as he moved to step between Francis and the old man.

"Not if it's an act of God," the old man said with a humorless chuckle as he shifted to adjust for Flint's move.

Unless Flint wanted to anger the old man, he knew he shouldn't move again right away. Once step could be casual. Two would be a threat.

"But surely you're not planning—" Robert Buckwalter protested in disbelief from where he stood beside the plane.

"I'm not debating this," the old man said firmly, still keeping his gun bead steady on Francis at all times. "I suggest everyone just do what they're told."

Francis had kept her head down for this entire conversation. Flint wondered if she were praying and then decided he hoped she was. Maybe God would listen to someone like Francis. She sure didn't deserve to be out here in the middle of a snowdrift with a crazy man threatening to shoot her.

"Why should we do anything you say?" Francis looked up, and her chin came up defiantly. "You're going to leave us tied up here no matter what we do. You can't bring yourself to shoot us. But you'll let us freeze to death. From where I sit, there's not much else you can do to us."

Flint cringed when he heard what Francis said. The old man was unstable at best. Defiance wasn't a good choice.

For the next ten minutes, Francis tried to take her words back. She kept saying "I'm sorry" like it was a mantra. It hadn't mattered. The old man hadn't been listening.

She kept apologizing until the small plane moved down the makeshift airstrip and took off.

"It's okay, it'll be okay," Flint said behind her back, and Francis realized he had been saying the words softly for some time now.

Francis stopped apologizing to the old man who wasn't even there any longer. She was so numb she no longer shivered. The old man had shown what else he could do. First he'd taken Flint's jacket, then hers. He'd thrown the coats in the back of the plane. Then he'd forced her to remove her dress and Flint to remove his suit. Those, too, had gone into the back of the plane.

"Just to show you what a good guy I am, I'm leaving you your underwear." Mr. Gossett grinned. "Wouldn't want the proper ladies of Dry Creek to get in a tizzy when someone finds the bodies."

The old man laughed then instructed Jenny, "Tie 'em tight. Don't want either of them wandering around out here and getting lost."

Flint wanted to shout at the old man, to call him names. The strength of the desire shook him. He was losing his edge. It was unprofessional. He knew that. It wasn't by the book. It wasn't smart. *But it's Francis,* his mind screamed.

Flint forced himself to focus. He needed all of his energy just to keep himself and Francis alive.

Before the old man climbed into the plane, he took Jenny with him and walked to both vehicles. The Jeep's hood was stiff, but he had made Jenny open it and then he had reached in and pulled out a handful of spark plugs and stuffed them in his pocket. He had done the same with the pickup that Flint and Francis had driven.

It was at that point that Francis had broken down and started apologizing more loudly. She was still whimpering, the words coming softly from her lips.

Flint tried to move his arms so that he could turn around and hold Francis. He was terrified. The freezing cold was a worse enemy than any he had faced. At least, with a kidnapper or a terrorist, you had the chance of talking them out of their plans. But the cold? What did the weather care for either threats or emotions?

Finally, Flint moved so that his hands could grip Francis's. The plane was growing smaller in the mid-morning sky. It had started east and then slowly turned to head west. The old man must have changed his mind and settled on Billings, after all.

Flint murmured again, "It'll be okay."

Francis hiccuped and then quieted. Her throat was beginning to hurt from the gulps of cold air that she had breathed. Every exposed inch of skin on her body was tingling. She felt like she was being pricked with a thousand daggers. She forced herself to focus. She was facing her death, and only a few things were still important.

"I should say I'm sorry," Francis said calmly. The only warm place on her body was her hand, and that was because Flint held it in his. "I should have waited for you twenty years ago instead of thinking you had deserted me. I should have trusted you."

"I should have trusted you, too," Flint said as he strained against the ropes tying them together so he could move his back closer to hers. Finally, their bare shoulder blades met. Francis leaned into him, and he could feel the elastic ridge of her bra strap. Their skins gradually warmed.

Flint continued to strain at the ropes. The old man had watched Jenny carefully as she knotted the ropes, but Flint believed she would have left them room to escape if there was any way she could.

"I wish we'd gotten to church this morning," Francis continued pensively. "I was thinking of going back, you know— not that I guess I was ever there much as an adult. But still, there's a sense of going back. Looking for the hope I'd lost."

"I know what you mean."

"It would be a comfort to know how to pray to God."

"My grandmother always said you just open your mouth and talk to Him."

"Still, it would have been nice to pray in a church," Francis continued, her voice drifting. "Do you suppose they'll come looking for us when we don't show up this morning?"

"Sure," Flint lied. He'd already thought of that. He and Francis had left early. No one would miss them for a half hour. By then the service would just be starting, and they would think that Francis was taking longer to get dressed or that they had gotten stuck in a snowdrift or changed their minds altogether. It would be a good hour before they would even start to worry.

Flint knew it would be several hours more before anyone would find them. And that would be too long for people left in a snowbank in ten-below-zero weather without even a shirt between them.

"But if they don't come right away we could make some kind of shelter from those boxes," Flint said brightly. He had no idea if a box house would keep them alive long enough. What he did know is that Francis needed hope. He needed it himself.

"And there might be something to start a fire with in those boxes," Francis agreed willingly. "Some cooking utensil or something. Chefs are always flambéing something or another."

Flint felt the ropes at his wrist start to give.

"Twist your hand away from me," Flint instructed. "I think I've got it."

One of Flint's hands scraped through the knot. He pulled his hand up and flexed his fingers. The cold was stiffening them more quickly than he had thought. He needed to act fast.

"If we had a fire, we might be able to find something to burn that would make enough black smoke to make someone curious," Flint said as he twisted his other hand to free it as well.

Finally, both of Flint's hands were free.

He turned and saw Francis's back. Her shoulders were hunched, and the thin line of her spine stood out whiter than the rest of her skin. She had curled her hair for church, and the curls still bounced. Her hands were still behind her back, and with the extra room in the knots since Flint had removed his hands, she was twisting her hands to free them.

The threat of death does strange things to a man, Flint reflected. It certainly made him dare things he wouldn't otherwise.

"Come." Flint turned Francis and drew her to him.

Francis knew that their only victory might be untying their hands. She knew they might not have a way to burn the boxes for heat and that they might freeze to death after all. But she would still be glad that they had freed their hands and could hug one another.

Flint's chest had changed since they used to embrace. He'd been a lanky young man, and his chest used to be wiry. Now his chest was solid. Muscles rippled as his arms tightened around her.

Flint almost couldn't breathe, and he wasn't so sure it was because of the biting cold in his lungs. He had Francis in his arms once again. He wanted to let his words of love spill out and cover them, but he didn't.

"I'll get us out of here," he said gruffly as he pulled away from her. "If it's the last thing I do, I'll get us out of here."

Francis nodded. She was too cold to think.

Dear Lord, she thought, *we might actually die out here.* This time the thought did not terrify her.

"But if not, you'll hold me some more, won't you?" Francis asked quietly. "I mean, if it turns out that there's no hope? I don't want to die alone."

"You're not going to die," Flint promised fiercely as he forced himself to stand. The cold was beginning to slow him, too. "I'm going to look through those boxes that just came in. Then I'm going to see if the cigarette lighter in the Jeep works."

Flint stood and eyed the boxes. It was so cold the snow wasn't melting, and the boxes were not damp at all. He slowly counted ten large boxes. Quite a parachute drop. Nine of them had the red stamped logo of a supermarket on them. Howard's Gourmet Foods.

Flint was walking toward the first of those boxes when he noticed the tenth box in more detail. It was a rectangular box with the imprint of some clothing store on it.

"Bingo!" Flint shouted, and turned to Francis.

She was huddled in the snow where they'd been tied. Her

skin was too white, and her eyes were half-closed. That was a bad sign.

"You need to move around," Flint urged her as he quickly walked to her and held out his hand. "Come over here and let's open the boxes."

"I'm not sure I can," Francis said. But she took Flint's outstretched hand, and he slowly pulled her to her feet. Her body almost creaked as she moved.

"There's a clothing box." Flint led Francis over to where the boxes had been dumped. "Robert must have had them drop off some winter clothing along with the food."

"Maybe a—wool jacket—or thermal long johns," Francis whispered as Flint tore through the tape on the box. Her teeth were chattering in slow motion, and she needed to pause between words. "I do—hope—it's long johns."

"Well, it's—" Flint held up the first piece of clothing he pulled out and announced in disappointment "—a tuxedo."

The black jacket was made of silk. Even packed away as it had been, it was obviously expensive. Expensive and light enough for a summer evening.

Francis hugged herself and rubbed her arms slowly. She couldn't even feel her fingers.

"They must have come late," Francis said hoarsely. "The dance is already over."

Flint noticed that a small receipt was tucked into the box under the tuxedo jacket. He pulled it out. "I don't think it was meant for the dance—these are addressed to Laurel Blackstone."

"The woman who came in—the one who knew Robert Buckwalter?"

Flint nodded as he pulled out a pair of man's slacks. The black slacks had a shiny dark gray stripe down the leg. At least the slacks looked like they'd keep some of the cold away.

"My guess is she knew him rather well," Flint said as he pulled out the final garment in the box—a frothy wedding gown.

"My word," Francis breathed and then realized the implications of the dress. "Poor Jenny."

Francis had seen that the young chef was smitten with Robert

Buckwalter. But it looked like Laurel Blackstone had expectations of her own.

The gown was beautiful. Francis reached out to touch the beaded flounces in the full skirt. Even in the bitter cold, she had to appreciate that gown. The bodice was made of soft ivory satin. A square-cut neckline was lined with satin trim and embedded pearls. Yards of sheer net fell from the waist and formed a train. "I've never seen anything so exquisite."

"Well, it's yours," Flint said as he handed the dress to her.

"But, I can't—"

"I suppose we could reverse them—but I don't think the dress would do nearly as much for me as it would for you," Flint joked.

"But it's Laurel's wedding dress," Francis protested. She might be in an extreme situation, but good manners should still mean something. "I can't just put on someone's dress and then—lie down and die in it."

Flint's heart gladdened at the pink consternation on Francis's face. She always was one to be concerned about the proper time and place of things. It was good to have her back. He'd been worried when she seemed so listless.

"Well, I guess that means I have to get into it then," Flint teased as he lifted the cloud of net over his head.

"Oh, don't be silly," Francis protested like he'd known she would. "Give me that thing."

"Gladly."

Flint couldn't restrain himself. He lifted the cloud of white net high and then, stepping forward, settled it over both Francis and himself. Inside the tangle, his lips found hers.

Francis felt Flint's warm breath seconds before she felt his lips on hers. She didn't bother to hide the purr that vibrated deep within her. A kiss, she decided, was a very nice thing.

Flint was adjusting his violet silk cummerbund and muttering about the fact that only a woman would buy a fancy cummerbund and no shirt when he heard a sound that made him turn and scan the horizon.

"Well, hallelujah! Look at that!"

Francis turned to look in the direction Flint was pointing.

The dress was strangely warm for being so frothy. "What is that?"

Flint didn't need to see more of the distant figure to know in his gut that it was who he thought it was. "Honey!"

The horse neighed in response to Flint's call and started to trot toward them.

"Well, well," Flint said to himself. He was right about that horse. She made a fine partner.

"She came to get us?" Francis asked in gratitude.

"Close enough." Flint grinned as Honey did as he suspected she might and stopped at the back of his pickup to sniff the bag of apples he'd tossed there earlier. "Close enough."

Flint was careful to give Honey only half of the apples before handing the red mesh bag, half empty, to Francis. "Hold these."

Flint put his foot in the stirrup and swung himself into the saddle before reaching down and helping Francis climb up behind him.

Honey fidgeted for a moment, uncertain about the two adults on her back.

"Easy, girl." Flint soothed the horse as he smiled. The fidgeting made Francis lean in closer to him and clutch him fearfully around the middle.

Now this is how a hero is supposed to feel, Flint said to himself in satisfaction as he recalled the last time he and Francis had been riding Honey.

"Let's go to town," Flint said softly to the horse. "We've got a bride to warm up."

Chapter Twelve

Heading down the country road into Dry Creek, Flint held Honey to a fast walk, at least most of the time. Now that he and Francis had some clothes on their backs, their heat loss was much less. He didn't want to risk Honey overexerting and becoming so cold she couldn't go on.

"What time is it?" Francis asked behind Flint's back. She'd recently lain her cheek against his tuxedo jacket for warmth, and he liked her nestling against his shoulder blades.

Flint lifted the back of his jacket so that Francis's arms would be covered as she clutched him. It left a draft on the middle of his back where the cummerbund ended, but it kept her arms warm, and she snuggled even closer to him.

"Ten to eleven," Flint said after looking down at his sports watch. Mr. Gossett had apparently considered watches in the same necessary category as underwear and hadn't demanded that Flint take it off.

"Everyone will be at the church," Francis mumbled.

"That's what we want," Flint said. "We'll be able to mobilize everyone right away. The sheriff should be there still, and he can get in touch with the Billings police and any security they have at the airport."

"Do you think Jenny and Robert are all right?"

"Robert knows what he's doing." Flint comforted her as well as himself. "He won't take any unnecessary chances."

Flint didn't add that he was more worried about Jenny. He searched the skyline as though he might see the small plane.

The young woman was high-spirited. High-spirited people tended to make themselves targets in hostage situations.

The morning seemed to warm a few degrees as the sun rose higher in the sky. It still wasn't warm enough to disturb the snow, however, and soft banks lined both sides of the country road they were riding down.

Honey seemed to sense they were close to Dry Creek and started to move faster as they took the last turn in the road before coming into the small cluster of buildings that made up Dry Creek.

Flint steered the horse toward the church. The white frame building with its steep roof and empty belfry had never looked so good to him. The double doors at the top of the cement steps were closed, so that must mean the service had started. If he remembered rightly, they kept the doors open in the summer during the services, and the hymns spilled out into the area around the church. He had sometimes sat on the last step and listened as a teenager. But in winter, the cold didn't allow open doors so the thick stained pine doors were closed.

"Let's get you inside," Flint said to Francis as Honey stopped at the bottom of the church steps. The sky had grown overcast and dark. There'd be snow soon.

Flint swung his leg around awkwardly so he could dismount before Francis and help her. Once on the ground, Flint lifted his arms. "Just slide down. I've got you."

"My leg's like wood," Francis whispered as she leaned over.

Flint's heart would have stopped if it hadn't already been frozen. Thick rich waves of black hair tumbled from her porcelain face, and the wedding dress was cut to show off her curves.

How much torture can a man stand? Flint asked himself as he clenched his jaw and did his duty. He reached up, grabbed Francis by the waist and pulled her off Honey. Flint almost welcomed the prickles of icy pain that ran along his chest as Francis slid down him.

They were both freezing. Inside the church, the piano had begun to play an introduction to a hymn that sounded vaguely familiar. But outside, where they stood, snowflakes were beginning to fall.

"You just need to get your circulation back," Flint said soothingly, careful not to reveal either the tension that stretched inside him or his ever-increasing worry. At least they'd had snow boots and socks, so with luck they wouldn't have frostbite on their toes. "You'll be fine once we get you inside. Does that retired vet still go to church here?"

Voices inside, some off-key and some too loud, began to sing "Amazing Grace."

"Dr. Norris?" Francis tried to steady herself. A snowflake landed on her cheek. "I think so."

Flint hoped the vet was sitting inside right now. Francis relaxed her grip on his shoulders, and Flint could see she was trying to stand. She winced, and her face got even whiter than he'd thought possible. He needed to get her inside.

"Lean on me," Flint commanded. "Don't try to walk yourself."

"No," Francis protested. "I'll do it." She drew a breath of the frigid air to steady herself. "I take care of myself."

"Not while I'm around."

Flint didn't know where he got the strength. His arms shot daggers of icy pain through him every time he moved them. His feet had gone numb long ago. But he could not bear to see Francis struggle. Flint bent his knees slightly and scooped Francis up in his arms.

"Oh," she breathed in surprise.

Flint shifted Francis so one hand was free to grab the railing that divided the cement steps. Francis hung around his neck as he pulled them both up the five stairs. He could as well have been climbing Mount Everest for the effort those five steps took. His legs were like frozen sausages, and that lace—Flint thought he'd never seen a wedding dress so full of lace. Layers of ivory froth were everywhere. They trailed between Flint's legs. They covered his arm. The bag of apples that Francis still clutched in her hand beat a gentle tap-tap on his back. Snow was falling everywhere.

Flint reached for the doorknob and tried to turn it. It was no good. His hand couldn't grasp it. He couldn't bend his fingers. He tried again. Finally, he gave the bottom of the door a thudding kick.

Please, God, let someone hear me.

The words to the second verse of "Amazing Grace" were filtering through the door. Someone was trilling a soprano harmony.

Flint kicked again.

The door slowly opened, and a young girl looked around it. She must be about seven, Flint thought. She had serious eyes and short blond hair. Her eyes grew wide as she saw Flint and Francis.

"I thought it was Johnnie," she whispered. "He's the kind that'd kick at doors. You're not supposed to kick at doors," she added virtuously.

"I know. Can we come in?" Flint asked softly.

The girl nodded. "It's church. That's where brides are supposed to go."

The girl turned and opened the door wide.

Francis looked inside the church she'd visited often as a child. The walls were painted a light yellow, and thin sunshine streamed into the main room from tall rectangular windows of clear glass. The pews, made of solid oak over a hundred years ago, had an uneven patina because of the years of use. The church should look shabby, but it was too clean for that.

Today, the church was half full. Obviously the snow had kept some people away. But Francis looked and saw Mrs. Hargrove and the Edison family. Glory Beckett Curtis was there with the twin boys. Doris June was sharing a hymnal with a handsome man Francis didn't recognize.

The air inside the church was warm, and the faint hum of the heater could be heard from the doorway. Someone had fashioned a bouquet from pine boughs and holly branches and put it in front of the solid pulpit.

Everyone in the small church was looking at their hymnals, singing in unison.

We'll just slip into a back pew and whisper with the sheriff, Francis thought. *No need to disturb everyone.*

But Francis hadn't reckoned on the little girl.

"It's a wedding," the girl announced loudly as she opened both doors wide for Francis and Flint. "They need to get married."

Everything in the church stopped. Francis swore she heard a gasp, but maybe it was just the last note sung. The pianist stopped with her hands half-raised off the keyboard. Matthew Curtis, the minister who had been leading the singing, lifted his head and looked straight down the aisle at them. Every other head in the church slowly turned and looked at the open doorway.

Flint almost swore. Then he looked at Francis and saw what the citizens of Dry Creek saw at that very minute. Francis was all ivory and pink, with wet snowflakes like dewy sequins scattered over her face and arms. Ivory lace and netting spread out from her in luxuriant waves. The curls in her black hair had softened, and strands of her hair hung down, covering his hands. Flint had never believed in fairy-tale princesses until now. Francis was so beautiful he ached just looking at her. She was a bride.

Francis almost fainted. Then she looked at Flint's face and saw what the citizens of Dry Creek saw. He was fierce and elegant all at the same time. The black silk of his tuxedo jacket fit his broad shoulders like it had been tailored for him. But his bare chest where his shirt had been—ah, Francis thought, she could see why the women looking their way were speechless. He looked more pirate than groom, but he looked every inch a man to be reckoned with.

"We're not—" she whispered.

"We don't—" he murmured.

But no one listened. There was a long, indrawn breath of silence, maybe even of awe, and then an eruption of joy.

"Congratulations!" someone yelled from the front pew.

"Hallelujah!" someone else shouted. "It's about time!"

And then everyone moved at once.

"Oh, your grandmother," Mrs. Hargrove said as she stepped out of her pew and started toward them, dabbing a handkerchief at her eyes. "If she could have only lived to see—" She looked at the ceiling. "Or are you watching, Essie?"

The pianist's hands went to the keyboard, only now they were playing, "Here Comes the Bride."

Francis felt the gentle hands of two young girls touching her dress reverently.

"We're not," Flint tried again.

"We don't," Francis tried, joining him.

"Why doesn't anyone tell me anything?" Sheriff Wall complained as he slipped out of the last pew and walked toward them. "If I'd know you were planning this, I'd have brought my marrying book."

"I've got my book," Matthew Curtis said, smiling widely from the front of the aisle. "What a great way to start a Sunday morning! A surprise wedding!"

Flint felt the twinge in his stomach grow into a knot. He'd been scared when old man Gossett pointed that gun at him. He'd thought he was a goner when the old man left him and Francis to freeze to death. But nothing—absolutely none of it—terrified him like this moment.

He knew now why he'd asked Francis to elope twenty years ago. That was all he had the courage for. Some quick marriage in Vegas had none of the glow that standing in this church in wedding clothes had. The good people of Dry Creek stood around him, and he was almost undone by the expectation he saw on their faces. They expected something from him—something good, something important, something lasting.

He, Flint Harris, did not have the grit to face that kind of responsibility. It was beyond him. He couldn't bear to disappoint everyone, and he was sure to fail.

Francis felt the joy leave her. For a moment, she'd been caught up in the dream. Maybe, just maybe she and Flint would go along with the enthusiasm of those around them. They'd be married—truly, gloriously married—finally.

Then Francis had looked up and seen the change in Flint's face. If she hadn't known him so well, she wouldn't have seen it at all. His jaw had tightened—not much, it was true, but enough. His eyes got a hunted look in them and grew hooded, like he wanted to hide his feelings. He was smiling, but it was only a motion of his lips.

He doesn't want to marry me, Francis thought dully. *He doesn't want to be impolite—to embarrass me in front of all of these people—but he clearly doesn't want to marry me.*

"There's been a misunderstanding," Francis said calmly. Strange how the cold that had nearly frozen her earlier hadn't touched her heart the way the cold in Flint's eyes did now. She nudged Flint, and he opened his arms so that she could slide to the floor and stand alone. She was, after all, alone. No sense pretending otherwise. "The clothes—they're not ours—"

The church went silent once again.

"Old man Gossett has kidnapped Robert and Jenny and is making them fly him into Billings."

"Why, the old coot," Mrs. Hargrove said indignantly. "Doesn't he know that's dangerous? It's already starting to snow again."

"I don't think he cares," Francis continued. "He has two guns and he wanted to meet some bus in Billings."

"Where's he got to go that's so all-fired important?" someone muttered.

Flint met the inspector's eyes. The inspector had been in the last pew, as they had agreed earlier, and the pew had been roped off with a gold cord, waiting for Francis to arrive.

"He's our man?" the inspector asked Flint quietly. "The informant?"

Flint nodded. "We'd better alert the police in Billings to pick him up at the airport. He's running."

"Armed and dangerous?" Sheriff Wall stepped closer to Flint. "I'll put out an APB."

Francis felt soft hands tugging at her dress. She looked into the face of the young girl.

"You're still a bride, aren't you?" the little girl asked, worried. "You're wearing a bride's dress."

"A dress doesn't make a bride," Francis answered softly.

"But the dress is the best part of the wedding," the little girl said, confident in her knowledge. "Except for the cake, maybe. Does this mean there's no cake, either?"

The girl's mother appeared at her side, "Hush, now, don't bother Francis with your questions."

"It's no bother," Francis said woodenly as she made an effort to smile at the girl. "And I wish there was a cake— I love wedding cake, too."

When Francis looked up from the girl, she noticed that Flint had gone to talk with the inspector and the sheriff. They were standing in the back pew muttering, and the inspector had his cell phone in his hand.

Flint had already borrowed a parka from the inspector and had replaced the tuxedo jacket with it. He hadn't wasted any time getting back to normal, Francis thought, as she let Mrs. Hargrove lead her to a pew so she could sit.

"Such a pity," Mrs. Hargrove muttered as she settled Francis in a pew and tucked her coat around Francis's shoulders.

Francis didn't know whether the older woman was talking about Mr. Gossett or the wedding that didn't happen, but she didn't ask.

Chapter Thirteen

Flint spit, then drove another nail into the side boards on his grandmother's house. The air was cold, and he felt a bitter satisfaction with the way the frigid air caught in his throat. The board didn't need that nail. It hadn't needed the other ten he drove in before it, either. But it was hammer or go crazy, and so he kept his hand curled around the tool and his mind focused on the nail. The solid blows of iron on iron suited him.

He sank that nail deep and pulled another one out of his shirt pocket. He had it positioned ready for striking when he heard the sound of a Jeep pulling itself up the slight incline that led to his grandmother's old house.

House, nothing, he said to himself as he looked at the weathered boards. The old thing could hardly be called a house anymore. It was more shack than house at the moment. When the windows had broken out, the snow and rain of twenty-some years had broken down the interior.

It would need to be gutted, he thought. A new roof and gutted.

The driver of the Jeep honked the horn as the vehicle slowed to a stop in front of the house.

Flint didn't want company. He'd already had a dozen congratulatory calls on his cell phone, telling him he was brilliant for figuring out that Mr. Gossett had changed his mind a second time and asked Robert fly him to Fargo, after all. Flint had cut all the calls short.

Flint knew he wasn't brilliant. It didn't take brilliance to know what a cornered animal would do when you felt like you were one yourself.

Flint hit the nail square and grunted. He wondered how many nails he'd have to hit before he felt human again.

"There you are." Mrs. Hargrove's cheery voice came from behind him.

If it had been anyone else, Flint would have asked them to leave. Since it was his grandmother's dearest friend, he only grunted and hit the nail again. He hoped she'd take the hint. She didn't.

"I brought you some oatmeal cookies," she continued. "I remember how you used to like them."

Flint had no choice but to turn and smile at the woman. "Thanks. I appreciate that."

"I thought you might be out here," she mused as she set a small box down and wiped the snow off the top porch step, Then she eased herself down and unwound the wool scarf she wore around her head. "Never can hear with that scarf on."

Flint had a sinking feeling that meant she was going to expect conversation. "I'm fixing the side wall here."

Mrs. Hargrove nodded and was silent.

"Thought I'd put some windows in, too." Flint went on. Her sitting there silent made him nervous. "Maybe fix that leak in the roof."

"Essie would like that," Mrs. Hargrove finally said. "You living here."

"Me? Live here? No, I'm just fixing it up."

Mrs. Hargrove nodded. "You're going to sell it then?"

"Sell it? I couldn't do that—it's Grandmother's house."

Mrs. Hargrove was silent so long that Flint positioned another nail and hit it.

"Essie doesn't need the house anymore, you know," Mrs. Hargrove finally said gently. "You don't have to take care of it for her."

"She wouldn't like it if it was run down."

"She wouldn't blame you for it if it was."

"I wouldn't want to disappoint her," Flint said softly as he gripped the hammer and hit the nail again. "I've disappointed enough folks as it is."

"Essie was never disappointed in you."

"She should have been— I messed up enough times."

"Everybody messes up sometimes," Mrs. Hargrove said softly. "Your grandmother knew that—She was a big believer in grace and forgiveness."

Flint grunted. "My grandmother was a saint."

Mrs. Hargrove chuckled. "Not to hear her tell it. She used to say the vein of guilt that ran through your family was thick enough to make somebody rich if they could only mine it."

Flint looked up for the first time. "But she never failed anyone. She was as close to perfect as anyone could be. What did she ever need forgiveness for?"

"We all need forgiveness," Mrs. Hargrove said softly as she placed a motherly hand on Flint's arm. "We all fall short somewhere or other. But we can't let it stop us or we'd never—" Mrs. Hargrove stopped abruptly. "Why, that's it! That's why you're out here pounding away at those rusty old nails instead of sweet-talking Francis! You're afraid."

Flint winced. "I wouldn't say that."

"And just what would you say, then?"

Flint grimaced. "I'm cautious—based on my knowledge of myself, I'm cautious about promising something and then disappointing someone."

"You don't love her, then?"

Flint squirmed. "No, that's not the problem."

"You intend to marry her and then leave her someday and break her heart?"

"Why, no, of course not, I wouldn't do that."

Flint wondered if it would be too impolite to climb on the roof and take care of those loose shingles while he was thinking about them. Mrs. Hargrove had the tenacity of a bulldog.

"Well, son, what is it that's eating away at you then?"

"I need to fix the roof."

"And that's why you can't get married?" she asked incredulously.

Flint sighed. There was no way out of this one but to go through the scorching fire. "I'm just not good enough, all right? Somewhere, sometime, I'd let her down. I'd forget her birthday. I don't make jelly, you know. Never learned how."

Mrs. Hargrove looked at him blankly.

"Even old man Gossett has a cellar full of crab-apple jelly.

He must be able to make it. Me, I can't even make a company cup of coffee—what kind of a husband would I make?''

Mrs. Hargrove didn't say anything.

''Besides, I've noticed some thinning in my hair. I could go bald someday.''

''Your hair looks fine to me,'' Mrs. Hargrove interrupted skeptically.

''That's not the point,'' Flint said in exasperation. ''It's just an example of what could happen, and anything could happen.''

Mrs. Hargrove eyed him thoughtfully. ''You don't have a clue about grace and forgiveness, do you? And after all those Bible verses I taught you in Sunday school, I would have thought one or two would stick.''

''They did stick,'' Flint said softly. ''It's just that being forgiven by God isn't quite the same as being forgiven by a flesh-and-blood wife you've disappointed.''

Mrs. Hargrove snorted. ''You can't fool me. You don't remember them, after all, do you? Recite me one.''

''Now?''

Mrs. Hargrove nodded.

Flint's mind scrambled. ''I remember one about four times forty—or was it eight times eighty?''

''Seven times seventy.'' Mrs. Hargrove shook her head. ''That's how many times we're to forgive someone.'' She fixed him with a challenging eye. ''Do you figure you'll mess up more times than that? That's almost five hundred times. Francis isn't likely to have nearly that many birthdays.''

''Well, there'd be anniversaries, too. Every year April seventeenth will roll around—''

''Surely you're not planning to forget them all?'' Mrs. Hargrove demanded. ''Give yourself some credit.''

Flint stopped in the middle of a swing with the hammer. He knew he wouldn't forget the anniversaries. He hadn't forgotten one of them yet. ''I might not need to worry about the anniversaries.''

Mrs. Hargrove nodded complacently. ''They've been a sore spot, have they?''

Flint looked at her indignantly. How did she know these things?

The older woman laughed. ''You're a Harris. None of the

folks in your family ever took lightly to love. Essie used to say it gave everyone another reason to suffer.''

Flint grunted and then admitted slowly, ''I've hated April for years. The first five anniversaries I went out and got stinking drunk on April seventeenth, and then sat down and wrote a scathing letter to Francis.'' He smiled. ''I wrote down all my disappointments for the whole year like they were all her fault. Finally, I was able to tell her the good things, too—and how I missed her.''

Flint concentrated on steadying another nail.

''Well, if you remembered your anniversary for years, what makes you think you'd forget it if Francis were with you?''

Flint didn't know. That was what had been gnawing at him for the past two days. He didn't know why he was so nervous about taking a flying leap into matrimony, he just knew that he was.

''You need to sit down with Essie's Bible,'' Mrs. Hargrove declared. ''Maybe then you can make some sense out of yourself.''

''Yes, ma'am.''

The older woman eased herself off the porch and stood. ''Remember, this is lightning country.'' She nodded at the nails in the piece of board. ''Much more of that and this place will catch the next bolt that comes flying through.''

Flint smiled. He wasn't so sure the bolt wasn't already here. ''Thanks for stopping by.''

''Just see to your reading.''

Flint had no intention of reading the Bible, but he felt almost like he'd promised. And so he opened it after Mrs. Hargrove had left and began to read the verses his grandmother had highlighted. The afternoon slipped into dusk and the sun was going down before he realized he'd spent the afternoon looking for the answers to the gnawing inside himself.

When he realized what time it was, he pulled out his cell phone and made a call to the manager of his apartment building.

''Yes, I'd like you to send them overnight express.'' He finished his instructions. ''I'll go into Miles City tomorrow and get them.''

Francis was standing in the small bedroom she used at Garth's house. She was packing. Her old-fashioned suitcase was open on the bed. It was a good-quality suitcase, but it had none of the modern pockets and compartments. Francis always maintained that a neat person didn't need to fear packing and certainly didn't need compartments.

Francis's socks were neatly paired and folded with the toes under. Her bras were folded and laid conveniently close to her panty hose. She had loose tissue to pack around her slacks and two dresses. Organizing her clothes made her feel like there was something in her life she could control just the way she wanted it. She might not be good with men, but she was good with avoiding creases.

Francis had waited around for Flint Harris once before, and she couldn't bear to do it again. Flint's face had been cold when she'd last seen him three days ago, and it had nothing to do with the weather. Sam was getting restless and wanted her to fly back to Denver with him. She'd told him she'd be ready tomorrow. He might be a little dull, but Sam was a good man.

"You're leaving?"

The deep voice came from the doorway to the small bedroom, and Francis whirled.

"Who let you in?" Francis swore she'd fry the culprit in hot oil.

"Garth," Flint said simply. "He told me I have five minutes."

"That's five more than I would have given you."

Flint had his outdoor parka on, and there were flecks of snow melting on his shoulders. He might have had a hat on his head, because his hair was slightly rumpled. He was fresh-shaven, and his hands held a small plastic bag with the name of a Miles City drugstore stamped on it.

Flint nodded seriously. "I figured as much, and you don't even know the half of it." He hesitated and took a deep breath. "I have a drawer full of mismatched socks in my apartment, and baldness runs in my family."

Francis looked at him in astonishment.

Flint nodded glumly. "It's true. One of my mother's brothers. That's the worst odds, they say. And I don't know how to make jelly—or really good coffee—I guess I could maybe manage a cup of tea and dry toast—"

"What in the world are you talking about?"

"I've had to kill two men. They were evil men and I had to do it, but it's there all the same—plus I work too much." Flint staunchly continued his list. "Although I have been thinking about chickens for the last day or so, and maybe it's time to quit my job and take them on. I've made good investments over the years so money's not a problem. It'd work out."

Francis was becoming worried. "Did Dr. Norris check you out when we got back to Dry Creek? I've heard of sunstroke doing this to people, but maybe extreme cold acts in the same way—"

"Of course, if you don't still want to do chickens, we could try our hand at something else." Flint cleared his throat and continued his speech. He didn't want to get derailed. If he did, he might not get back on the track again. "I've decided I like Dry Creek. I like the church here and I think that's going to be important to me. And the air is good. Hard to get good air anymore."

Francis looked at Flint. His eyes looked clear enough to swim in, and he didn't have any strange twitches happening with his mouth. Then she remembered the drugstore bag he carried.

"Is that medicine you have with you?" she asked gently. Maybe that's why she hadn't heard from him for three days. "You poor man."

Francis stepped to Flint and placed her hand on his forehead. "Did Dr. Norris give you something to take?"

Flint's mouth went dry. His voice croaked. "I'm not sick." Flint swore no man in the history of the world had bungled a job like he was doing.

"Of course you are," Francis said softly. "What else could this be?"

Flint took a deep breath and plunged. "It could be a marriage proposal."

Francis stared at him, her hand frozen on his cheek.

"Not a good proposal, I'll admit," Flint continued shakily. "But I thought you should know the problems up front. I've always believed in saying the truth straight out."

"Marriage?" Francis's voice squeaked. "But the medicine?"

"It's not medicine," Flint said softly. "It's cards—for you."

Francis looked around for support and sat on the bed.

Flint opened the bag and held up twenty envelopes. Some of the envelopes were white. Some pink. A few ivory. One even had pale green stripes on it. Each one had the number of a year written on it in black ink.

"They're anniversary cards," Flint said softly as he fanned them out on the bed next to her. "Bought the whole store out. One for each year—and inside is the letter I wrote you in that year."

"You wrote me?" Francis whispered.

Flint nodded. "I had to."

"Oh." Francis brushed a tear from her eye. She tried to focus, to think this new information through, but for once in her life she didn't care about the order of anything. "I thought you'd forgotten me."

"How could I forget the only woman I've ever loved?" Flint said softly. The tears gave him hope. He would carry this through in any event, but the tears did give him hope.

Flint pulled a long-stemmed yellow rose out of an inner pocket in his parka. It was the only yellow rose to be had in Miles City, and it was a little peaked. Then he dropped to one knee and offered the rose to Francis. "Will you marry me again? This time for good?"

"Oh." Francis swallowed.

"Is that an 'oh, yes' or an 'oh, no'?" Flint asked quietly.

"Yes," she stammered. "My, yes. It's an 'oh, yes.'"

Flint reached up and brushed the tears from her eyes before he leaned forward and kissed her. The pure sweetness of it sang inside of him. He didn't deserve someone like Francis.

"I could maybe do something about those socks."

Francis laughed and touched his cheek. Yes, he was real. "I don't care about the socks."

"This time let's get married in the church here in front of everyone in Dry Creek," Flint said. "I want to see my bride walk down that aisle."

Francis smiled dreamily. "Dry Creek does love a bride."

"Not half as much as I do," Flint said, smiling as he bent his head to kiss Francis again. "Not half as much as I do."

*   *   *   *   *

Dear Reader,

I should have my mother write you this note. She, having raised five usually wonderful children (of which I am blessed to be one), knows far more of the hope that goes into love than I do. Actually, most mothers know that kind of hope—the hope that their love will bear fruit, that their love will ease someone's pain and that it will even give that person an anchor in life.

Love laced with hope is a useful kind of love. It sees beyond the romantic parts of love and looks to the future.

That's why, when I chose to tell the story of Francis, I knew it had to be a story of hope. We never know when we love someone what our hopes will bring. Francis did not know. Flint did not know. Only God knew.

May this story of Francis and Flint encourage you to love with hope and to trust God for a happy ending.

Janet Tronstad

Hideaway

E.R. doctor Cheyenne Allison seeks a break from her stressful life, but instead finds a dangerous vandal and terror.

Will trust in her charismatic neighbor and faith in Providence get her through a harrowing ordeal?

HANNAH ALEXANDER

Available October 2003 wherever hardcovers are sold.

Hideaway

E.R. doctor Cheyenne Allison seeks a break from her stressful life, but instead finds a dangerous vandal and terror.

Will trust in her charismatic neighbor and faith in Providence get her through a harrowing ordeal?

HANNAH ALEXANDER

Available October 2003 wherever paperbacks are sold.